MW01489007

The Cursed Mage

A.M. Josephine

Contents

Welcome to Horcath

A guide to the kingdoms & their mage types (alphabetized), with pronunciation guide

BRIGHTLOCK

"bright • lock"

The second largest kingdom within the borders of Horcath.

Mainly supplies and exports ores and metals from the vast mines in the Shattered Mountains.

MAGE TYPE: Erru:

"air • oo"

The ability to manipulate and control the state of light. An erru-mage is rendered powerless when there is an utter absence of all light. Erru requires its mage to maintain clear and focused emotions.

CARLORE

"car • lore"

The third largest kingdom within the borders of Horcath.

Mainly supplies and exports timber, colorful clothing and fruit tree saplings.

MAGE TYPE: Eirioth:

"air • ee • oth"

The ability to conjure fire, manipulate preexisting fire, and summon and control lightning. Some eirioth-mages are capable of all three, but the majority are only capable of the first two. An eirioth-mage is rendered powerless if their body temperature drops too low. Eirioth requires its mage to have enough physical strength to keep it in check.

COLDMON

"cold • mon"

The largest kingdom within the borders of Horcath.

Mainly supplies ships and means of transport for cargo traveling between kingdoms.

MAGE TYPE: Aclure:

"ack • lure"
The ability to manipulate preexisting water, freeze preexisting water, and manipulate preexisting ice. The majority of aclure-mages are capable of all three. An
aclure-mage is rendered powerless when there is no water nearby. Aclure requires
its mage to maintain constant focus on the magic.

FREETALON
"free • talon"
The fourth largest kingdom within the borders of Horcath.
Mainly supplies and exports medicines and healing substances.
MAGE TYPE: Recle:
"reek • le"
The ability to create remedies that heal more than any remedy made without magic,
to create poisons more potent than any poison made without magic, to heal external
wounds with the touch of a hand, to heal internal wounds with the touch of a hand,
and to poison someone with the touch of a hand. The majority of recle-mages are
only capable of the first two, but there are a rare few capable of the third and fourth;
almost no recle-mages are capable of the fifth. A recle-mage is rendered powerless
when they are unable to access the ingredients necessary for their potions, or when
they have no way to physically touch another being. Recle requires its mage to have
access to the tools necessary for their potions, at least a minor knowledge of healing,
and strong focus.

OLD DUSKFALL
"old, dusk • fall"
The sixth largest kingdom within the borders of Horcath.
Since its downfall, the kingdom has remained largely secret, focused on resolving
issues within itself. It occasionally supplies sandcat and Horcathian camel pelts to
other kingdoms.
MAGE TYPE: Andune:
"an • dune"
The ability to manipulate preexisting sand and very fine grains, like salt or loose
dirt, and the ability to host bone reading rituals, which have long been outlawed by
the royals. Any mage found practicing bone reading is sentenced to life in prison
or immediate execution. An andune-mage is rendered powerless when there is no
sand nearby. Andune requires its mage to have a clear mental state and a strong
connection to the earth.

OLD NIGHTFALL
"old, night • fall"
The smallest kingdom within the borders of Horcath.
Old Nightfall is supposedly the Glass City in the sky. Some don't believe it exists at
all.
MAGE TYPE: Whorle:
"whirl"
The ability to manipulate certain aspects of the weather such as fog, wind, and
clouds, and the ability to summon powerful storms. A whorle-mage is rendered
powerless when in extremely dry or hot conditions. Whorle requires its mage to have
a cool body temperature, a hydrated body, and a clear and calm mind.

WISESOL
"wise • sole"
The fifth largest kingdom within the borders of Horcath.
Mainly supplies and exports fish, fishing tools, and stone and slate-wolf pelts from
the Slated Mountains.
MAGE TYPE: Bering:
"bear • ing"
The ability to manipulate the state of and grow preexisting plant life, the ability to
calm and coax animals with their connection to life, the ability to see the 'life glows'
of any living thing, and the ability to deeply connect to an animal through physical
contact. All bering-mages are capable of these things, but some more than others.
A bering-mage is rendered powerless when there are no forms of non-human life
around them. Bering requires its mage to have a clear and positive emotional and
mental state.

The people born without magic are referred to as "underlings".

A guide to the characters and creatures within this story, as well as a pronunciation
guide for them, can be found in the back of the book. Those guides will contain
spoilers for The Cursed Mage.

The only pronunciation guide I fear people will need at the beginning is this:
Ksega's name is pronounced "say - guh", NOT "ka - say - guh".
Get it right.

Prologue

Calysto brandished his melting ice-whip, cringing at the cold drops that splattered onto his bare feet and chilled his toes. His feet were planted firmly in the solid earth, his muscles bunched, prepared for an attack to be launched upon him. Or for him to launch an attack on his opponent. But instead they just stood there, panting at each other, glaring heated daggers through the clammy air, challenging the other to make the next move.

Bodies littered the ground around them, some with melting spears of ice jutting from their chests, others with arrow and crossbow tips poking out their backs. The earth soaked up the blood like a sponge, eagerly sucking it in as the bodies slowly let it free. It was a disgusting sight. He couldn't believe it had come this far. He couldn't believe he had *let it* come this far.

"Make your move, Ice King," spat Therol across from him, blood trickling down his lip. "And I shall make mine."

Calysto gripped the ice-whip tighter, summoning his power. He was weakened from the fight and his cracked collarbone was doing him no favors. The magic seeped slowly into his bones, coiled and, despite its faintness, powerful. It yearned to be set free, and he freed it, allowing it to course through his freezing fingertips and re-solidify the ice-whip.

Sensing the reinforcement of the weapon, Therol gripped his massive battle-axe tighter, his muscles tensing and glistening with sweat. He was breathing raggedly and heavily, his dark eyes sparkling with murder. Behind him, at least a hundred more Brightlock soldiers, all still standing and ready to fight, were scouring the battlefield, hunting down their injured to bring them back for care. They left Calysto be. He was Therol's to take, and Therol's alone.

"Surrender now," the Brightlock king rasped, taking half a step forward. He may have been imagining it, but it seemed that the very earth shook from the impact. "And you may live."

"In what? Your prison cells? A box at the bottom of the lakebed?" Calysto sneered, lifting the coiled whip and preparing to strike. "If those are my options, I'd much rather die."

"Have it your way," Therol shrugged, hefting the battle-axe up again. It was swinging down towards Calysto in seconds.

The Ice King had little time to react, but he was well-trained, and dodged the blow, snapping his ice-whip forward to twirl around the battle-axe's handle. Once it was securely in place, he pulled it taught, yanking with all his might against the icy rope.

Therol gasped as his shoulder was jerked to the side, but his grip on the axe remained firm. He stumbled back to his feet and pulled at the axe, but it was still caught in the ice-whip. He snarled and tossed the axe to the side, his hands reaching for the long daggers at his belt.

Calysto released the whip as well, letting it fall to the blood-stained ground, and conjured up his magic again. It took much of his concentration, and a splitting headache began to form in the back of his head, pulsing as it moved to just behind his eyes. Despite the new painful tingle in his nerves, he was able to draw up the last of his magic from the reserves deep within him, and a dagger of thick ice, identical to the two Therol now held, was forged in his grasp.

"Your frozen water will not save you now," growled Therol, advancing on him. Calysto stumbled backwards, grimacing as he felt his boot heels dig into the wrists of dead bodies and knock against their skulls.

At last he could not stumble away any farther. His head was spinning from the exertion of making the dagger, and he hardly had the strength to lift it and block Therol's oncoming blow when it fell down on him. The steel shrieked horrifyingly against the ice, grating across it until the surface became too slick, and the dagger slid away. Another ring of metal on ice, and another, and on the next blow, a thick white crack sprouted at the edge of Calysto's blade, feathering out towards the handle. A bloodthirsty grin peeled across Therol's face as he raised his daggers again. On the next strike, the ice gave way, leaving Calysto clutching a rod of useless ice.

He cast it to the side and dodged another swipe of the daggers, throwing himself back towards the ice-whip, his best weapon. If he could just get close enough, unravel it from around the axe, he could win. He was sure of it. Finally, his people — or what was left of them, after this battle — would be able to live amongst the others at last, like normal humans.

As his fingers slid around the familiar handle of the whip, embracing its melting chill, he heard a throaty chuckle from somewhere to his left. Seconds later, Therol appeared. Calysto winced, expecting him to bring the daggers down in deadly arcs, ripping his back to shreds and severing his spinal cord. But he didn't.

Instead, the daggers hissed to the ground beside Calysto's hands, working frantically to unwind the whip. He didn't have the strength to make another one. He *had* to retrieve it, or he was going to die. Die, and leave his poor son to lead their people. Would he follow in his father's footsteps, and seek out a better life for their people? Or was he going to succumb to failure, and stay back, hiding like a coward?

It drove Calysto onward, to think of his people deprived of something of which they were worthy. Something they deserved.

He crawled forward desperately, his fingers tugging mercilessly at the ice-whip. He had to free it so that he could be free. So that all of them could be free. He wouldn't let this be taken from him. He wouldn't watch as Therol tore away everything for which he had worked and planned so hard. He would end this, here and now.

As he finally began to unwind the whip, the axe jerked forward suddenly. The blade skidded along Calysto's arm, and he hissed as crimson blood bubbled up from the wound. He looked up, fury blazing in his eyes, to see that Therol had lifted the axe into his hands again.

"You rotten little-"

"Watch your language, Ice King," Therol hissed. "It would be a bad way to go out. Your family would speak for generations of how bad of a sport their famous Grandfather Calysto was."

"You know *nothing* of my family!" Calysto spat, scrambling back into a sitting position and gripping the ice-whip handle tightly.

"You're right, I don't," Therol peeled his lips back in a sneer. "And I don't want to." He snapped the axe back, and with a fuzzy *crack*, the ice-whip broke. Shards of gray-blue ice tumbled to the ground in front of Calysto's hands, and he gawked at them.

"No . . ." Calysto whispered, hardly daring to believe it. He *didn't* believe it. He was going to lose. He was *actually* going to lose, after all he had done to ensure his success.

"Yes," Therol grinned broadly, lifting the axe as Calysto knelt in front of him, staring dumbly at his fractured whip, trapped in denial. "This all ends here, Ice King. It ends here, now, and forever."

And with that, he brought the axe's blade down on the Ice King's neck.

1
SAKURA

Almost 200 Years Later

Sparks flew across my vision, bright orange and streaking by before I even had a chance to register them. Seconds later, another wave of flame battered past me, and I only barely managed to leap backwards. I landed awkwardly on the base of my heel, sliding sideways until my foot knocked against an upturned root, sending me toppling backwards. My hair caught in straggling root fingers and loose rocks, and I felt my back being prodded and poked by every stick it passed, but they were the least of my worries. A snake of bright orange flame was creeping down after me, hovering just over the roots as it prepared to strike.

I was still falling, but the roots had slowed me, and I reached out to grab a thick one on my left. I gasped as the rest of my body was suddenly thrown beneath my head, nearly jerking my shoulder free of its socket. Gasping, I looked down to see nothing below. The King's Scar yawned beneath me, black and merciless, waiting for me to fall into its unforgiving jaws.

A hiss of smoke drew my attention upwards again, and I saw the snake was only a few inches away from my slipping fingers. I groaned, trying to ignore the knot of tension that was forming in my belly as my sweaty palms allowed me to inch ever closer to that deadly drop.

Use your brain, I scolded myself. My right hand was hanging limp at my side, but I should've been using it for something already. The sword strapped to my back would be useless, only cutting the flames away temporarily, not to mention a stray swing could cut the roots I so precariously held onto.

Grimacing, I swung myself sideways, slinging my right arm up to grip another root. My strength — which had already been worn thin before I fell — was almost gone, and I could feel my muscles trembling from my weight.

"Come on," I hissed at myself through gritted teeth, kicking my legs up to catch them in a net of roots in front of me.

The snake was close now, but I wasn't paying any attention to it; I was a little more concerned about the fact that if either of my hands lost their grip, I was falling upside down into the great abyss of the King's Scar.

My power surged to the surface, sensing my struggle, attempting to break free, but I shoved it back down. I couldn't use my eirioth here.

I took a shaky breath, ignoring my shaking arms, attempting to ignore the worm of fire so close that I could already feel its heat on my skin. The tree whose roots I clung to was above, tall and twisting and elegant, and the thickest of its roots were to my left. Those were my best bet for climbing back up to ground level without getting swallowed up by shadows or fire.

Taking a bracing breath, I tried to shove down the feelings in the pit of my stomach and pour as much strength as I could back into my muscles, then I shoved off with my right hand, kicking against the weak roots with my feet, and rolled sideways through the air. My heart felt like it had plummeted down into my stomach, and my head spun as I tumbled over a nest of roots. Then, without warning, there was nothing beneath me.

I shrieked and snapped my eyes open — I hadn't even realized they had closed — clawing desperately at the roots. My fingers snagged in some of the small ones, dangling from the very bottom of the tree. I was as close to the drop of the King's Scar as I could get without actually falling into it, and that was the last place I wanted to be.

Gasping, trembling from the terror that coursed through my body and the thundering of my own heart, I looked back up above me. The fire had paused, as if it had a mind of its own, and was surprised by my sudden movement. But it was moving again, coming steadily closer to me, and I had to make a new decision.

I could see the bottom of the tree now, half jutting out over the bottomless blackness of the King's Scar, and realized there were plenty of handholds there beneath it. The cliff walls were jagged and dangerous, impossible to climb, but if I could get to the center of the tree, I could go sideways and find a new way back up.

Keenly aware of the heat pressing towards me, I knew I had no other choice. Swinging myself forward, I put one hand out in front of the other, grasping the rough roots that would support my weight the best. Dust and dirt peppered down into my hair and onto my face, and I had to blink it out of my eyes, ignoring the sting it caused me. My arms felt like they were on fire, but if I didn't keep going, they really would be, so I pushed past the burning pain and dragged myself onward.

At last I came to what was roughly the middle of the tree, almost to the rock surface of the cliffs. I had looked behind me only once to see the fingers of flame crawling beneath the tree as well, scurrying along it like an upside-down spider. Luckily, it couldn't actually see me, so it was moving slowly and blindly.

With another groan of exertion, I swung again and pulled myself to the left. I was close to the end now, and I redoubled my efforts. My shoulders were screaming at me to stop, my abdomen ached from how much I was kicking my feet about, and I was still half-blinded by the falling dirt, but I had finally found a root thick enough to sit on, and I was determined to find a way to swing myself around and onto it.

My fingers clawed at the rough bark of the tree, but my arms were weakened, and I knew I didn't have the strength in me to drag myself up onto the root. I flailed my feet out behind me and felt them connect with another root. I pushed off as hard as I could and felt myself sliding up onto the bigger root. I gasped, allowing my shaking hands to release the root and raise to my head, brushing dust out of my hair and rubbing it free of my eyes.

As soon as I could see, I looked up. I wasn't far below the ground level, and I was eager to get up there. I scrambled up the maze of roots, blowing hair out of my face as I did so. I glanced behind me once to see the flame spider twisting back into a snake to slither up after me, and I quickened my pace. Finally my hand reached the moss-like grass of the ground, and I bounded up the last root and rolled onto the earth. I breathed a loud sigh of relief, groaning and laying face-down in the dusty ground, slowly letting the knot in my belly unravel.

"You're just giving up?" a voice chided behind me. I felt a prickle of heat against my right side and rolled away from it, glaring at the owner of the voice, who was on the other side of the training glade, leaning against a tall eirioth tree with softly falling blue leaves.

"Next time, throw *yourself* off the cliff," I shouted back, glaring at the tongue of flame that twirled through the air once, then vanished in a puff of light smoke.

"You're losing your stuff, Rura," Finnian said as I walked up to him, sweat dripping down my neck. I glared at the nickname, feeling my nostrils flare, but it was hard to stay mad at my brother, especially when he was wearing that stupid, self-satisfied grin.

"I'm not losing anything," I clarified. "I'm just a bit tired from last night."

He grinned broadly at that, and I knew he was reliving the memory. Personally, I couldn't stand it. He had woken me up in the middle of the night, dragged me out here, and put me through eirioth-mage drills until dawn. I had slept for half the day, and then he had pulled me out again, and here we were.

"And hungry," I added, my stomach rumbling to remind me that I still hadn't eaten since dinner the night before.

"We'll get you some food," he rubbed his hands together and looked at the two lumps of feathers beside him. "And them. Elixir's stomach's been grumbling since we got here."

I rolled my eyes. I could care less about how hungry his eirioth dragon was, but it was true that Sycamore also hadn't eaten, and if I was taking her to get some food, I might as well let Finnian and Elixir tag along.

"Hey pretty girl," I cooed softly as I stroked the soft white feathers on Sycamore's head. She blinked at me tiredly, and I could see the weariness in her blue eyes. "I know," I said as she stood and stretched. "Those boys are a handful, aren't they?"

"We are not," Finnian grumbled from where he was waking his own dragon. "We just know how to have a proper bit of fun every now and then."

"There's no time for fun when the Curse is out there," I growled, and he fell silent, pinching his lips together in a somewhat bashful look. I felt a pang of guilt, but didn't bother to apologize.

"Come on," I told him. "Let's head back to Hazelwood. We'll do Gamma a favor and take Honeysuckle out for some dinner." I ran my hands lovingly along the bridge of Sycamore's ashy beak, but it was more a distraction than anything else. An excuse not to look at Finnian anymore.

"Yeah," he agreed, and I looked over my shoulder briefly to see him swinging up onto the soft orange feathers of Elixir's back. The dragon tossed his head eagerly, a bright light in his shining aquamarine eyes. He stamped his golden talons impatiently, his big feathered tail waggling as he waited to be instructed into the air.

I swung onto Sycamore's back, pressing her smooth white feathers down and hugging my arms around her neck, ignoring how her warmth only made me hotter, and focusing instead on the pleasant softness that shrouded me when I touched her.

"Let's fly, Rura!" Finnian called happily, seemingly over his moment of humility. He whooped, and Elixir shot up into the air. After a moment, I urged Sycamore after them.

The wind felt good and fresh on my face as we soared up through the air. We rose up above the tops of the eirioth trees, and I leaned forward to look down at them. The bright colors of their leaves — blue, green, pink, orange, every color imaginable — swayed and danced in an evening breeze, and I allowed a small smile to tug at my lips. I would never get tired of this view.

We turned south, and I looked over my shoulder at the Fruit Spring, trying to see if I could spot anybody down there. Only the bravest of eirioth-mages would be out there towards dusk, and even then they would be packing up to head home as soon as possible. I caught sight of a single person on the northern shore, but we were too far away for me to be able to identify them.

"Race you home?" Finnian had drawn level with me, leaning over Elixir's neck to try and avoid most of the wind, although it still streamed through his wavy brown hair and stirred it up into the air around his face.

Instead of answering him, I leaned forward and spurred Sycamore forward. Dragon races were a common sport and pastime in Carlore, and although we never competed in any of the official races, I knew Finnian and I were some of the best racers in the kingdom.

As the wind tugged at my hair and streaked past my face, leaving my cheeks flushed and stinging, a laugh bubbled out of me. I could rarely help it when I was up in the air like this. Even with all the darkness clouding my thoughts and creeping into the back of my mind, there was something so freeing about flying like this. Something so exhilarating about defying gravity, yet something so calming about being unable to tame the wind. The first time I had flown, I had felt almost *fragile*, like a dead leaf that could be easily torn. But now I understood that flying was something truly breathtaking; truly magical.

And Finnian being there only made it better.

When he heard me laugh, he glanced over at me, still at his side, and grinned, letting his own laugh get swept away by the wind. Slowly, he and Elixir were creeping ahead of Sycamore and I, and he was going to make sure I knew it, just like he always did. But with my competitive spirit, there was no chance of him winning this race.

As we kept pace with each other, we flew over Walnut, one of the five towns on the western side of the King's Scar, and I saw Finnian looking below and waving. He always did that, no matter what village it was we were passing and no matter how many people he actually knew that lived there. I used to tease him about it when we were younger, but I'd learned it had little effect on him, and gave it up.

While he was distracted, waving at anyone he saw down below, I angled Sycamore to the left just a little, and shot us forward. We swept through the air, over one of the smaller veins of the King's Scar, and sped towards another town, Chestnut, which was a neighbor to the town Finnian and I lived in, Hazelnut. The Scar was named as a part of our kingdom's history. It was said that the earth opened up into great, yawning caverns to sympathize with the wounds the first king of Carlore suffered to conquer it.

As we passed over Chestnut, I could hear Elixir racing through the air behind us, trying to catch up. I had a good four foot lead on them, and if I timed my turns just right, Sycamore and I would slide into the stables seconds before Finnian and Elixir did.

A few more minutes of flying saw us charging through the air over Hazelnut. We rushed past houses and decorated eirioth trees, over Duke Ferin's temple and the community section of the town. Finally we turned sharply to the right and headed for the westernmost side of Hazelnut, swooping down towards the Hazelwood Inn. The dragon stable's door faced to the west, and since we were coming from the east, we would have to turn around to get in.

Finnian was slowing Elixir down, preparing to land on the packed earth in front of the stable and have his dragon run inside. Sycamore and I whooshed on over them, heading almost to the border Hazelnut shared with Cashew.

Suddenly, Sycamore and I made an impossibly steep turn to the left, sweeping around in the blink of an eye and zipping back the way we had come. Sycamore tucked her broad, feathered wings against her side and pulled her legs up beneath her, angling down towards the wide open doors of the stable.

Wind whipped at my hair, making it hard to see clearly, but Sycamore knew what she was doing, so I wasn't concerned. I could see bright flashes of orange where Elixir and Finnian were, already landing on the ground in front of the stable. Even from this distance, I knew Finnian was grinning, confident he'd won, but Sycamore and I were soaring through the air so fast, speeding like an arrow fired from a bow with the most tension Horcath had ever seen, and I knew we would win.

Just as I had predicted, Sycamore and I blurred into the stables, her wings blooming out to slow us down as we skidded down the aisle between the stalls, mere seconds before Elixir and Finnian trotted inside.

"I let you win that time!" Finnian shouted from behind me, chuckling as Elixir tossed his head and squawked loudly, stamping his feet and brushing the dusty ground with his long orange tail.

"Sure you did, Finn," I rolled my eyes as I slid breathlessly from Sycamore's back, ignoring the wobble in my legs. It was always a little strange coming back to solid ground after you'd been swooping magically through the air on a dragon.

"You always win," he said, his voice booming across the stable. When the stablehand, a cranky old man named Walter, glared at him, he lowered his voice and came up to me. "Come on, Rura, tell me your secret. It's Sycamore, isn't it? You've given her some kind of speed potion, or had some andune-mage cast a spell on her." I snorted as I guided Sycamore into her usual corner stall, not bothering to latch it since I knew we'd be coming back to take them for dinner as soon as we got Gamma's permission.

"It has nothing to do with Sycamore," I told him, poking Elixir in the chest. "It's this foolish goat. Look at him. He can't go an hour without chasing a butterfly or trying to play with his own shadow." In fact, Elixir was one of the most distracted, playful dragons I'd ever met, even though he was fully grown.

"Elixir is an excellent racer," Finnian argued as he stuffed the jumpy dragon into a stall and followed me out of the stable. I raised an eyebrow at him as he came up beside me. "Well . . . he has potential."

"Sure," I muttered as we walked up to the Hazelwood Inn. It was a four-story building, built from the dark wood of eirioth trees and currently peppered with the fallen petals of the five tall trees that surrounded it, a mix of orange, blue, violet, red, and deep purple. I'd never get tired of admiring the beauty of our home.

As we stepped inside, I breathed in the hearty smell of rabbit stew, wafting through the inn's bottom floor from the kitchen in the back. I could feel saliva pooling in my mouth, and Finnian must have caught my eager look, because he poked me in the ribs.

"Careful not to start drooling now. That Derek boy is here." He jerked a thumb across the tavern to where a group of boys around our age were sitting around a table playing a game of cards.

"Like I care," I rolled my eyes again. Without waiting to hear whatever taunting thing my brother was going to say next, I pushed through the crowded tables to the counter and the little gate that led back to the kitchen. Instead of opening it, I just lifted one leg over, then the other, and heard Finnian sigh behind me.

"Show-off, are you?" he muttered as he opened the gate, stepped through, and closed it. I shrugged and we went into the kitchen.

"There you are," I couldn't help the grin that spread across my face at the familiar voice. Gamma — whose real name was Gretchen — was standing over an enormous pot of stew, portioning it into little wooden bowls to take out to her waiting customers.

"Hello, Gamma," Finnian greeted her as he went scrounging for bread rolls.

"Out of the pantry, you glutinous boy!" Gamma smacked him on the shoulder with the back of her hand, but she was smiling as she folded me into a tight hug, then did the same to Finnian. "You're just in time for supper. Grab yourselves some bowls."

"Don't have to tell me twice," Finnian said cheerily as he stepped forward. I looped my finger through the chain around his neck and yanked backwards. He coughed and stumbled back a step, frowning at me.

"Actually, Gamma," I said coolly, ignoring Finnian's glare. "We were going to take the dragons to get some dinner first. Has Honeysuckle eaten?"

"Not yet, no," Gamma squinted at me. "But Sakura, dear, you're thin as a twig. Come eat."

"Yes, let's," Finnian agreed.

"Not you, you big galoot," Gamma waved him away in a shooing motion. "You've eaten plenty. Look at all this," she pinched his thick upper arm, which all three of us knew wasn't fat, but muscle. "You'll survive if you have supper a little late. Go take care of the dragons while your sister eats, then she can help me get desserts ready while you eat. Go on now, scram," she waved him out with both hands, allowing him to grab one bread roll before he left.

"But Walter's always so grouchy towards me," he complained under his breath, even as he made his way out of the kitchen.

"Be nice to Sycamore," I called after him. The only reply I heard was a muffled grunt through a mouthful of bread roll.

Gamma made the best food. There was no argument to be had when it came to that, and if anyone tried to pick a fight about it, I'd sooner dig my sword into their gut than admit someone else's cooking was better than Gamma's. The rabbit stew was rich and meaty and delicious, and the broth soaked wonderfully into the cooled bread rolls. Washed down with a tankard of mulberry wine, it was one of the best meals I'd had in a while — although that may have been because I hadn't eaten in an entire day.

When Finnian returned he wolfed down his own helping of the meal while I helped Gamma dole out plates of her famous peach pie to the waiting customers. When he was finished eating, he helped us with the desserts, then we all started washing dishes. I gathered them up and scraped the leftovers into the scraps bin; Gamma washed them in the tub of water and soap; Finnian dried them and put them away. It was an efficient system, a smooth rhythm that flowed between the three of us as smoothly as a stream burbling over the smooth stones of a riverbank.

An hour or so passed, and I looked out the little kitchen window over the scraps bin to see that the sun was setting. Most of the customers would be turning in soon, whether that meant going upstairs to the inn rooms they'd rented or heading out to mount their dragons and fly back to their town or just walk across the street to their own home.

My aching muscles and tired feet cried out for a hot bath, and I had already promised myself one in the back of my mind. But first, I had to make sure Sycamore and Honeysuckle were properly bedded down for the night. I could care less about Elixir's comfort, but I knew I'd check in on him anyway.

The front porch of the Hazelwood Inn was small, but stretched the entire span of the front of the building, with two swinging benches on either side of the door. As I stepped out there, I saw a couple only a few years older than me cuddling and rubbing their noses together on one of the benches. Looking discreetly away and stifling a gag, I went down the steps and crossed quickly across the little yard to the tall dragon stable building. It was massive, tall enough to fit the dragons on the ground floor and plenty of bedding up in the loft. The rows of stalls on either side stretched down for almost two hundred feet, with only five stalls on each side.

There were currently only four dragons in the stable: Sycamore, Elixir, Honeysuckle, and a guest's mint green eirioth dragon that was currently curled up comfortably in the corner of her stall.

Sycamore had plenty of bedding and water, so I pressed a brief kiss against her slate-gray beak and went to check on Honeysuckle, who slept in the stall beside her. The golden eirioth dragon was the oldest I'd ever met, yet she still seemed so young. She had lots of her energy, and none of her personality had left her from when I was just a little girl first meeting her. She sort of reminded me of Gamma in that way, and I thought they made an excellent pair.

Elixir was beside Honeysuckle's stall, watching me with bright, curious eyes as he rested his chin on the stall wall. I stopped and crossed my arms when I stood in front of him, looking bored. He was a beautiful dragon, one of my favorites that I'd seen in terms of color, but I'd never let Finnian know that. Elixir's vibrant orange feathers covered most of his body, but there were spots of yellow on his chest, and the end of his tail was crimson and scarlet. His bright yellow beak and talons kept with the flame-like motif of him, but then there were the sudden flares of sky blue and aquamarine feathers that surrounded his talons and his belly, and there were even some speckles of dark blue on the feathers around his beak. His stunning eyes had always been my favorite, second only to the icy blue of Sycamore's, but again, if Finnian knew that, he'd never let me hear the end of it.

"Good night, dragons," I told all four of them, even the mint green one I didn't know. I looked up at the dark shadows of the bedding loft. "And good night to you too, Walter."

"Good night, Lady Sakura." Came the gruff reply.

I'd never liked him calling me 'Lady', but it was a habit he refused to break. He called Gamma 'Lady Gretchen' as well, and even Finnian was referred to as 'Sir'. It seemed a little silly to me at first, but I had come to respect the old stablehand for keeping such good manners throughout his life, even when he was humbled low enough to be a stablehand.

As I came back up to the inn, I saw that the couple was still there, only now they had changed from flirting with each other to throwing their lips together. It was disgusting, and I should've just walked on past and left them alone, but the part of me that couldn't stand to see people doing that in public won out, so I said loudly,

"If you two want to get a room," I walked up to the door past them. "They're only seven ingots inside." A silence followed that, and I took it that this was a good time to leave. I stepped inside and, after a few moments, heard two sets of footsteps thumping down the porch steps.

There weren't many customers left in the inn now, just the usual stragglers staying up late, guzzling some beer and betting on pointless card games. As I was walking past them towards the kitchen, planning to let Gamma know I was headed upstairs to take a hot bath, I overheard someone speaking at one of the card tables. I realized it was the one Finnian had pointed out to me earlier, the one where Derek Plow was sitting with his friends.

"There's no way," said one of the boys, taking a swig of whatever was in his mug.

"I believe him," said another. "I heard reports of a Cursed fox sighting up near the Fruit Spring a couple days ago. Up until then, I didn't know they came that close to civilization."

A chill slithered down my spine. The Cursed. Those foul creatures, wrought with some sort of terrible disease, the beasts that tore life from homes and laughter from kingdoms. My gut churned to think of them and what they had done.

"They've come closer before," I blinked, wondering where the voice had come from for a moment before I realized it had been me who had spoken. All the boys craned their necks to look at me. Derek's eyes flickered with recognition, and he nodded a greeting.

"Have they?" he said, raising an eyebrow. "Please, tell us about it. Come, sit down." He gestured to the empty seat beside him. It had been occupied earlier, but whoever had been sitting there had clearly gone home earlier than his friends.

I stepped forward and slumped back into the chair. This wasn't the first time I'd settled into a conversation with a customer, but it was the first time I'd been invited to actually join them at the table.

"I was out doing some flying training with Finnian," I said, realizing all of them had been looking at me expectantly. "We were near Column, flying towards the center of the Columns, when we saw it. Them, really. It was a small group of Cursed raccoons. We flew right past them, and I don't think they took much notice of us. We were careful to make sure they weren't following when we came back."

"Woah," one of the boys breathed, a blond-haired fellow who looked a little younger than me.

"That far south?" Derek frowned. "I thought the majority of them stayed in or around the Evershifting Forest."

"So did I," said the boy who had been the first I heard speak. He was dark-haired and making a failing attempt to grow a beard. "All the reports I've ever heard of have said they stay there. Something powerful's in there, some kind of source. That's where they're coming from."

"You don't know that," I grumbled, and he raised his eyebrows at me.

"Like you know anything about it?"

"She'd know more than you, Gideon, so shut your trap," Derek said before I could reply. "She's spent most of her life looking into those wretched creatures. Signed up for one of the night watch rotations, didn't you, Sakura?" he looked over at me for confirmation, and I nodded.

"I started a couple weeks ago." I added, giving him a brief nod of gratitude. Derek wasn't exactly a friend, but he wasn't *not* a friend. We used to hate each other when we were much younger, and it had landed both of us in heaps of trouble often enough. As we'd grown up, though, we'd come to a sort of mutual understanding. We looked out for one another, but never really made it a goal to spend time together. Despite the fact that we still didn't really get along, my older brother had decided to take all the times we had defended each other for flirting, and he was heart-set on getting us together.

"Either way," Gideon said, rolling his eyes. "They stayed there for the most part up until about a week and a half ago. There have been more stories of them coming closer to the Spring and — apparently — the Columns."

"I wonder if Brightlock's having similar problems," the blond boy mused. "I mean, the majority of the Forest *is* in their territory, after all,"

"Who cares if they're having similar problems?" another boy spoke up, a black-haired one that had yet to speak. "They aren't exactly our best pals or anything, are they? Leave that to them. We should be focused more on ourselves if the Cursed really are getting braver and coming closer to the towns."

"Have there been any really dangerous sightings?" I asked. All this Cursed talk was making me feel a little queasy, but I genuinely wanted to know. Anything I could find out about the Curse, anything that could tell me more about what drove them onward — and what their weakness was — was valuable information to me, and I could stand feeling a little sick if it meant learning more.

"Not really," the black-haired boy answered me. "I think the worst of it so far has been a Cursed python, coming close to the point of the Scar."

The point? That was where Finnian and I did most of our eirioth-mage training. I'd never thought of it as too close to the Evershifting Forest, but if there were creatures coming closer . . .

"Interesting." I said, then feigned a yawn and stood up. "Well, nice chat, boys. I'm turning in — long day of training. Good night, Derek," I nodded a good night to the rest of them and started to head towards the kitchen again. Before I was out of earshot, though, I heard the blond boy speak again.

"You really think something in the Evershifting Forest is the source of part of the Curse?"

Then came another sentence from the Gideon boy, one that sent another chill through me.

"Evan, I think something in the Evershifting Forest is the source of it *all*."

2
SAKURA

*D*awn came far sooner than I would have liked, and I was certain that if I went through another night without getting more than three hours of sleep, I wasn't going to make it much longer. Finnian had snuck into my bedroom again last night, shaking me awake to tell me there was a fight going on down in the street. I had shoved him away and told him I wasn't interested until he said he had heard talk about someone stealing one of the dragons from our stable.

That had been enough to drive me from my bedsheets, and I'd slid into my leather boots and a scratchy old wool coat. I'd followed Finnian out of the inn, and sure enough, there were about five drunk men staggering about farther down the street, maybe a hundred feet from the stable.

Two of them were yelling at each other, hurling slurred curses through the air and wobbling around on shaky legs. I heard dragons mentioned briefly — or at least I *thought* it was dragons. It may have been dogs, or even dancing, with how muddled the words were — and decided that was enough. If these idiots wanted to cause a commotion in the middle of the night, they were welcome to do it elsewhere.

"Hey!" I shouted at them, loud enough so they could all hear without me having to come any closer. They swung their heads around to look at me, blinking wide eyes as Finnian and I strode up to them. I had left my sword up in my bedroom, but Finnian had a dagger at his belt, and I doubted any of these men were in any real fighting condition.

"Well hello there, pretty thing," one of the men grinned, his gaze rolling over me. I shook my head at him, already sick of this. The darkness around us had begun to eat away at my nerves, and I was eager to get back inside.

"If you want to scream your heads off and throw punches like little girls, I'd appreciate it if you do it just a little bit louder, that way the Cursed know *exactly* where to find us." I made sure my voice was dripping with sarcasm, and was glad to see that the point had been made, at least to a few of them. Two of them nodded somewhat-soberly, and dragged their friends away down the street. A few more snide and inappropriate comments were tossed my way from the two drunk fighters, but I ignored them. Instead, I turned to Finnian.

"Next time," I told him, gritting my teeth. "Wake Elixir up and have *him* help you."

"Where's the fun in that?" he asked, but didn't argue any further as we trooped back to the inn.

I tried to get back to sleep after that, but it was a futile effort, so I just lay there staring at the boards of my ceiling and trying not to dwell on the shadowy thoughts that lurked in the back of my mind, never truly gone, but always willing to come forward if I even considered them for a brief moment.

My mom, my dad, and Aurora. The awful memories that I had linked to them. All those bright, happy moments with them were gone, replaced with those few flashing, terrible minutes. The snarling of the Cursed animals that charged through the building, the awful sounds of ripping flesh and screaming people flooded my ears. My senses were overrun with the memory: I tasted blood and dust, felt myself being jostled around and thrown about, smelled the sour, almost acidic smell of the Cursed surrounding me. Surrounding *us*.

I gasped, scrambling up into a sitting position before I could fall back into the memory. My breath hitched as I saw sparks scatter around the room, clicking against the walls before falling, harmless and ashen, to the floor. I hadn't even realized I'd called my eirioth, hadn't even realized I'd lain there in some sort of fitful half-awake state for so long. Sweat beaded down the back of my neck, stained my pillow, and clumped in my hair. A hazy light shone into my little room from the single square window in the far wall, barely enough for me to see my surroundings.

Taking a shuddering breath, I crept out of bed and got dressed. I didn't always like wearing the typical Carlorian robes, with their sashes and big sleeves, but sometimes they were the most comfortable option. This morning, they weren't, and I opted for the silk undershirt, a belt, and a sleek pair of pants.

I slid my sword scabbard on and tucked the sword into place on my back. I fastened my belt around my waist and made sure my little iron sword hilt was in its respective pouch before sliding my leather boots on and sneaking out my bedroom door.

It must've been early dawn, because I didn't hear Gamma downstairs cooking breakfast yet. I went silently down the stairs, past the hallways to the rooms where guests slept quietly in their beds, down to the ground floor. I slipped past tables topped with upturned chairs, easing the front door open and stepping out into the cool air.

This end of Hazelnut was relatively quiet, and pretty small. There were some houses, and a few small shops, but most of the town was located farther to the west. Hazelwood Inn was right on the outskirts of the town, and it was surrounded by a big grove of eirioth trees, very thick on the southern side, near one of the little streams that rolled past towards the edge of Horcath.

I crunched down the worn down path to the dragon stable, already itching to be up in the air. As I inched the door open just enough to slip inside, I saw a flicker of yellow light up in the loft, and knew Walter was awake.

"Good morning, Lady Sakura," he said, and the light flared brighter, illuminating his lined and weathered face high above me.

"Good morning, Walter."

"Thinking about them again?"

"Trying not to." I kept my voice thin, but part of it wasn't intentional. It was that strain that appeared in it every time I spoke about my family, and I hated it.

"Want to talk about it?" Walter offered, and I heard whatever book he was reading creak closed. I sighed. On the outside, Walter was very thick-skinned and grumpy, but he did have a soft spot for some people. I was one of those people. Finnian was not. Gamma was.

"Not right now," I told him, and I heard a grunt before the flipping of book pages sounded again. Inwardly, there was always that flicker of doubt, of silent urging to tell *someone* about my nightmares and the war that raged inside my own head. But nobody needed to share that burden; I could hardly stand to bear it myself.

I woke Sycamore and gave her a few strips of jerky before coaxing her out of her stall and towards the door. As I tugged it open farther so that she could fit through, Walter's voice echoed through the stable behind me.

"Have a nice ride, Lady Sakura."

"I will. Thank you, Walter." Then I stepped outside with my dragon, and we flew into the dawn.

Sycamore and I had our own eirioth tree.

We didn't exactly *own* it, but few other people really cared to come and bother us about that. Few people ever even knew we were out there, nestled safely into its dark, twisting branches, cocooned in its net of sticks and twigs and surrounded by its soft rosy petals.

We flew there now, swiftly and, for the most part, silently. It was still dark out, with only the faintest glimmer of pink haze beginning to show in the eastern sky. This was the best time to get out of the Inn, if I could manage it. This was that magical moment between night and sunrise, that eerie cluster of precious minutes where, for a moment, the world seemed to stand still and display all of its beauty, turning its scraggly side away as if it needed to collect itself before facing it again.

We flew south, all the way to the very edge of Horcath, which wasn't too far; the Inn was located in one of the southernmost villages of Carlore anyway.

Our eirioth tree was there, tall and majestic and perfect, waiting for us to come seeking calm in its embrace. It stood near the edge of the cliffs that dropped down to the Endless Sea, but not too close — there were still a few more trees between it and our tree. Right beside the tree was one of the many streams that wound its way through Carlore, running through and down, down, down to the Endless Sea.

We swooped up over the soft green grass, and Sycamore landed deftly on one of the thick branches of the tree. She hopped up between them, squeezing between the tight gaps and curling over the smaller limbs until she found her way almost to the top, where a cluster of branches met, forming a comfortable space for the two of us to huddle together.

As I slid off her back, she tucked her legs beneath her and rested on the tree, her head tilted back to embrace the warmth of the rising sun, eyes closed as she allowed herself to drift steadily towards sleep. I plopped down beside her, leaning back against her soft white feathers and looking at the canopy of pink above us.

I'd never really liked pink. I thought it was too girly, too expressive. Too bright. But my mother had always loved it, and so had Aurora. After they died, the tree — where the three of us used to eat picnics and have tea parties — had become a safe space for me. A place where their memory didn't threaten tears of sadness, but tears of joy. A place where I didn't have to worry about judgy townspeople wondering what the local grump was up to today.

In a way, it was a piece of me, and I had made it a habit to come here with Sycamore in the early mornings and late evenings whenever I got the chance.

I was grateful for that chance now. My heart was still pitter-pattering in my chest, and I had a feeling it wasn't just from the exhilaration of the ride. My mind was still in my bedroom, seeing those scattering sparks of flame and hearing the echoes of my family's screams.

I shut my eyes tight, my fingers absently stroking the feathers on Sycamore's foreleg. I tried to turn my thoughts to the positive, but it was clear my mind didn't want to go there. I started to think about my next turn on the night watch rotation. I thought about my previous watch nights, about the distant flashes of sickly green I'd seen glowing and shaking in the darkness. I thought about what I could do to help my people. Not just other Carlorians, but *my* people. Gamma and Finnian. Walter. Myself. Even the dragons. Maybe even Derek, if I was in a good mood.

The thought made my mind focus on what I had heard last night at the table with him and his friends. They thought the source of the Curse was coming from the Evershifting Forest. In a way, it made sense. That place was dark and deadly and had always reeked of magic, even before the Curse came into existence. That, or it had always been there, hiding in the dark until *something* had driven it forward, searching for things to destroy.

The sound of wings beating made me open my eyes, and I looked up to see a brown eirioth dragon circling the tree, looking for a good way in. When he found one, he ducked in and landed on one of the thick branches sprouting from the clump where Sycamore and I sat.

"Speak of the devil," I muttered, recognizing the burly brown dragon. I raised my voice so the rider could hear. "Surprised to see you up so early."

"Are you?" Derek replied, sliding off his dragon, whose name was Bear. He made his way across the branch to where I sat as Sycamore stood up to greet Bear.

Derek was tall; taller than Finnian, and definitely taller than me. His shaggy hair was black, and his eyes were very dark. His skin was paler than that of most other people in Carlore, but he didn't spend a lot of time outside in the sun anyway.

"Yes," I scooted over to make room for him, and he sat down beside me. Sycamore and Bear started to hop between the branches, climbing and jumping and playing a very hyper game of tag. "It's rare to see you out and about before the sun's up."

"With skin this light?" he raised an eyebrow, lifting his hand, which seemed to glow almost white in the dim light. I shrugged, and he rolled his eyes.

"Why're you here?" I asked. It wasn't the first time he'd come to visit me sitting in the old eirioth tree. In fact, it was a common occurrence, and unless I was particularly aggravated with him, he usually stayed for a chat. It was just about the only time we spent together, outside of chance meetings in town.

"Same reason I always am, I suppose," he mused, tilting his head back to watch the dragons playing together. I nodded silently. It had become a sort of routine for the two of us: one of us asks why the other is there, and they give that as an answer. I don't really remember how it started, or even how he found the tree and knew that I liked to spend time there, but somehow I didn't mind.

It was a personal place, but there were certain people who were welcome there. Gamma never came, and Finnian only did when he wanted me for something. Derek came to either enjoy the silence, or talk about something. Sometimes I was the one that did the talking, and he just sat and listened. It was an odd ritual that we went through often, but it was an enjoyable one nonetheless.

"What's up with you?" I asked finally, looking out into the vast expanse of the Eirioth Wood before us. The soft green ground was littered with brightly colored petals, curved and drifting in a slight wind that rolled across the earth. I could feel it climb the tree and tug gently at my hair, which was a tangled mess from my fitful sleep.

"A lot of things, I guess." He muttered, his voice barely audible. I sat and waited. The sun crept up into the sky, and soft yellow light spilled across the world, sweeping across it and filtering through the leaves of the trees like molten gold being gently poured onto Horcath.

Time passed. I was silent. So was he. I waited for him to gather his thoughts, waited for him to find a way to share what he had come to get off his chest. *This* was that mutual understanding we had. We both knew the other well enough to understand that both of us always had a lot on our mind, and sometimes we needed to release a bit of the tension that clouded our thoughts. We shared with each other and no one else.

"Another Cursed came close last night. Too close." His voice was heavy, tired. I inhaled sharply, my hands clenched into fists. I felt a flicker of power deep within me, but subdued it. Now was not the time to release my rage for the Curse.

"How close?" I asked softly, keeping my gaze trained forward. Though I would never admit it aloud, I used to have a big crush on Derek, and always tried to sneak glances at him, just to see his expression, to see if he was sneaking looks back. But he never did, and I'd eventually grown out of it. Now, we were stuck in the middle-space between friends and enemies, and that somehow made it easier to get along.

"Close enough." He sighed and raked a hand through his dark hair. "It was in Walnut. We lost another night watchman."

My breath hitched. Another death? Already? The last one had only been the previous month. The Cursed were growing bolder, and we weren't ready for it. It was costing us.

"How bad?" I whispered, trying to push away the ache that rose in my chest as I thought about what the family of that poor watchman must be going through. What I *knew* they were going through, and what I had gone through myself.

"It was quick, if that's what you mean," Derek sighed heavily. "They think it was some kind of bird. A big one. Eagle, or maybe even a raptor. They're not sure."

"You mean . . ." I gulped, scolding myself for being almost afraid to talk about it. I'd spoken about the Curse all my life — why was it always so hard when my family came up? I should've been able to push those feelings away just as I could any others.

"No," he said quietly, as if sensing my discomfort. "Nobody saw it."

Good, I thought, a little relieved. Nobody deserved to see something as terrible as that. Finnian and I knew all too well what the Cursed could do, and we'd witnessed it first hand. I would hate to think that some poor townsperson was now traumatized after seeing a night watchman getting his guts ripped out by a Cursed raptor.

"And is that all?" I murmured when I could find my voice again. Above us, the branches trembled, and I looked to see that Bear and Sycamore were tackling each other, batting playfully at each other's faces and flaring their wings. She didn't like to play often, and I was glad to see her in a lighter mood.

"Yeah." He said, but I could tell there was something else, sitting right on the tip of his tongue. Something he wanted to say, but was hesitant about. I used to be offended when I knew he was hiding things from me like this, but I had learned to be patient with him. Some things just weren't ready to be shared.

I called Sycamore down while I waited, and Bear followed her. Dawn had come, and above us all sorts of shades of pink and purple and orange and red merged together into a blanket of sky. They reflected onto Sycamore's feathers, giving her the appearance of a moving rainbow.

"I'm sorry about what Gideon said last night." He said finally, and I raised my eyebrows in surprise. *That* was what he was concerned about?

"In all honesty," I told him. "I've forgotten what he said."

"Have you?" Derek looked at me, doubt in his dark eyes, but I genuinely couldn't remember. It had been something about me not knowing much about the Curse, but why should he have known I'd spent most of my life studying it? I was supposed to be that normal town girl that helped run the local inn. I definitely wasn't supposed to be signing my name on the night watch roster, at least in his mind.

"I have." I assured him, then I looked to the north. I couldn't see the town from here, but I knew that it would be waking up now. Gamma would already be down in the kitchen preparing breakfast, and Finnian was either taking Elixir and

Honeysuckle to get breakfast, or he was headed this way to find me and Sycamore. I didn't want to hear any teasing about Derek and I, so I stood up.

"Time to go, then?" he asked, whistling to get Bear's attention. The burly brown dragon perched himself on one of the nearby branches, waiting for his master to mount.

"Time to go." I confirmed. I looked over at him, and for the first time in all the years we'd done this, I was tempted to give him a time to meet again. We'd always sort of played it by ear, never setting a specific day or time to meet up, just doing it whenever we needed to.

But what if the time when we needed to meet daily was coming? With the Cursed coming closer and closer, I knew he was getting more and more concerned, and I was too. We had both lost people we loved to them, and we didn't want to see that happen again.

"What are we going to do?" I asked finally, and heard him sigh. I wondered if he'd been having similar thoughts.

"I don't know." He looked over his shoulder at me as we prepared to get on our dragons. "But I'll figure it out. Until then, you and Finnian stay out of trouble."

"No promises. Same for you and Violet." He grunted, but said nothing more as we swung onto the backs of our dragons and took to the air.

We flew alongside each other for a short bit, then he swerved away and headed to the west, to where he lived in Cashew. I continued straight, passing over the Hazelwood Inn and heading instead for the center of town, where the big dragon feeders were located.

As I swooped in to land, Sycamore thumping to the earthy ground beside Honeysuckle, I heard Finnian call my name. I looked around for the source of his voice and spotted him standing away from the dragon feeders, out of the crowd. I dismounted and patted Sycamore on the neck, making sure she had a secure position around one of the big stone basins filled to the brim with all sorts of grimly delicious animal parts for them to feast on before I made my way over to my brother.

"What's for breakfast?" I asked, and he grinned.

"Eggs, bacon, and biscuits."

"Ah," I nodded. "A rare treat. What's got Gamma in such a good mood?"

"Walter gave her a vase of flowers this morning," he raised and lowered his eyebrows a couple times, still wearing that broad grin. I smirked.

It was no secret Walter fancied Gamma, but I didn't know if she would ever return the feelings. She had been married before, and after her husband had died, I had been sure she would never search for love again. Still, Walter was a good friend of mine, and I couldn't help but hope a little bit that things might work out between the two of them.

"I suppose word hasn't spread too far, then." I muttered. His grin waved, and he frowned at me.

"Something happened?" he asked, and I nodded, gritting my teeth.

"Another Cursed attack, up in Walnut. A watchman died." I shook my head, pursing my lips together, and saw Finnian reacting similarly beside me. I knew he didn't feel as much emotion about these sorts of things as I did, but he hadn't been *right there* when we had lost our parents, when we had lost Aurora. He hadn't seen what I had, and while I knew that meant he would see things a little differently than I would, I still hated when he was so optimistic about the future.

"That's terrible. Do they know what it was?"

"A bird or a raptor, they think. Nobody saw." I sighed and ran a hand through my hair, grumbling to myself as it caught in the mass of tangles near the base of my neck. "This can't go on forever. Somebody has to find a way to stop them."

"It'll wear itself out eventually, just like any other plague or sickness." Finnian always talked about it like this, with that calm, reassuring tone, and that comforting smile. But it didn't always work, and it definitely didn't work this time.

"It isn't a *sickness*. It's something infectious, yes, but it's not . . . *natural*. You've seen how much it takes to kill one of those things. You've seen how they glow from the *inside-out*. There's something else at work, and we just don't know what it is. *Why* don't we know what it is?!" I clenched my fists in frustration, feeling heat prickle the tips of my fingers, threatening to spew out of them in long tongues of flame. I regained control of my breathing and pushed the eirioth away for the time being.

"Hey, someone will figure it out someday."

"*Someday* isn't good enough, Finn," I hissed, crossing my arms and glaring at where all the gathered eirioth dragons were eating. There were so many different colors, so many feather textures and beak shapes and eye sizes and tail lengths, it was easy to get lost in the maze. But it was never hard to find the three we were in charge of.

"Well what do you want to do?" Finnian demanded, crossing his own arms. It was rare he got agitated with me, but it wasn't unheard of. "Go off on your own in search of a solution? Hope you'll find it all on your own? Is that what you're going to do, Rura? You're going to run off and leave Gamma and I behind so you can satisfy this-this-" he gestured briefly at me. "This need for *revenge* that sits around you like a pool of slime?!"

"*Revenge?*" I echoed, blinking, my jaw tensing. "You think that's what this is about? I don't want *revenge*, Finn, I want *justice*. I want to know that our family was one of the last to be lost. I don't want to see others suffering the way we have!" I could hear my own voice rising in pitch, and I grimaced, realizing if it went any higher, we'd start to draw attention. Finnian noticed this, too, and lowered his own voice.

"Is that true?" he huffed, his eyes shadowed. "Or is that just the speech you practiced over and over, not just trying to convince us it's true, but trying to convince yourself, too?" he shook his head, dragging a hand down over his face, his expression tired. "Rura, I don't want to see you get hurt, and I don't want to see you so . . . so vengeful. I know you hate the Curse because of what happened to us, but you can't just walk out there and lop creatures' heads off willy-nilly hoping that will do something! Nobody knows what's at the core of this, and risking your life to find out isn't worth it."

"How do you know that?" I snapped, turning away from him, already growing tired of the conversation. I could feel a prick of heat behind my eyes, tears trying to push their way forward. I swallowed them back.

"Because I love you," he threw his hands up in the air. "And Gamma loves you, and Walter loves you, and Derek loves you-"

"He doesn't love me."

"-and none of us want to see you get yourself killed." He looked at me sadly then, his face pinched in sorrow. "Don't drive yourself too far, Rura, please. That's all I ask."

I took a sharp breath, ready to argue again, when I paused. I knew he was right. None of them wanted me to get myself killed. But if I wasn't willing to risk my own life to get to the bottom of this Curse, then who was? Everyone was such a coward, standing back and shaking in their boots, hoping somebody else would be brave enough to step forward and claim the challenge. If someone in one of the other kingdoms had taken it upon themselves to do that, we probably would have heard by now. That, or they had all failed.

I wouldn't fail. I wouldn't *let* myself fail. I would find what was at the center of the Curse, and I would destroy it. I would free Horcath from the terrible creatures that ravaged it, and I would come home to Finnian and Gamma and Walter all safe and sound.

"I'm sorry, Finnian," I shook my head, feeling those tears resurface. "I can't just let it go unanswered. I have to find out. I *have* to know."

I expected him to argue. Expected him to order me not to do anything rash, and promise to chain me up in the darkest corner of the cellar in the stables. Expected him to tell me he'd warn Gamma, and neither of them would let me leave. Instead, he did something even worse.

He just stared at me for a long moment, his eyes brimming with sorrow, then he turned and walked away, towards the dragons, to take Elixir and Honeysuckle home. My chest felt like it had been ripped in two, and I nearly fell to the ground as I watched him. The sadness in his eyes made my heart ache, and the way he had so resignedly turned away left me feeling guilty. But what was worse was how he simply took the dragons and flew home. He didn't look back.

Somehow, that was the thing that hurt the most.

3
KSEGA

*T*he ship swayed unsteadily beneath my feet, sending me staggering to the left, then the right as the gentle waves of the Port made it bob back and forth.

I grimaced and forced myself to grip one of the heavy crates resting against one side of the cabin, fastened securely in place with tight straps of rope tied to thick steel bolts in the ship's wood. It was unhelpful, seeing as the surface didn't have anything to hold onto, and in the next lurch of the ship, I fell hard onto my backside.

"Stupid boat," I snarled at the damp air around me, fumbling for something else to hold onto. It was dark, and the only light was a small sliver of it that shone through a crack between boards in the trap door that led into the storage cabin. Eventually, I found one of the cables holding the crates in place, and I clung to it desperately, shaking saltwater from my hair and trying to squeeze it free of my sopping shirt when the ship wasn't jerking around too much. After several more minutes, I felt the ship steadying and slowing down, and hesitantly released the rope. It was a mistake, because a second later the ship bumped up against the docks of the Port, and I fell down again, this time on my front.

"Secured!" a voice boomed from above, slightly muffled through the weathered wooden boards.

Moments later, the thud of many heavy footsteps sounded above me, thundering towards the docks, then coming back to help unload more. There was a heavy catch of fish aboard, all of it on the upper deck, and they would spend the majority of their first few minutes in the Port unloading it. I had to slip out before any of them decided to come unpack the things here in the storage cabin.

I scrambled across the boards, my soaked boots squelching from my weight, and I came up beneath the trap door. The trick was going to be finding the perfect moment to get out. The trap door was located near the main mast of the ship, so it would be in plain view to most anyone. I had to make sure I looked casual, and not draw any attention from the crewmembers themselves. Dripping wet the way I was, that wasn't entirely likely, but I had to at least try.

I waited, until most of the footsteps appeared to have gone to the docks, to lift the trap door up. It gave way easily, but the tired muscles in my arms and back protested against its weight. I scanned the deck briefly, making sure nobody was watching, and shoved it up the rest of the way. I trotted up the steps and shoved my hair out of my eyes, glancing around.

I'd never been able to see a view of the Port clearly, and I had to admit that the water out here had the best view of it. A wide expanse of water, flowing in from the Great Lakes, filled the Port, where ships and boats and skiffs bobbed in the tide, full of fishing and hunting gear, nets and boxes packed with chewy, dried up foods, and scraggly men that reeked of the sea.

The docks were sturdy wooden bridges that zig-zagged in a maze around the edges of the Port, allowing access to floating shop stalls or the stone side streets that led back up into Lourak. These docks were currently crowded with people, bustling to get to their boats or their shops, carrying loads of fish or brightly colored water tunics, made from fabrics specially designed to repel water.

The best part of the view, though, was the scenery of Lourak. The capital of Wisesol, it was sprawling and magnificent, built from strong, pale stone, rising hundreds of feet into the air. It was almost as if the buildings were stacked one on top of the other, with elegant arches in the windows and flower boxes on every balcony. There were floating bridges passing from tall building to tall building, shaded by their canopies and decorated by the extravagant carvings in their support beams.

Dusk was falling, and lanterns flickered to life all around, both on the docks and in the distant windows of the buildings of Lourak. I saw shutters being pulled closed and drapes being drawn. The entire town was awash with soft golden light, flickering and playing on the pale surfaces of the walls as if it had a mind and personality of its own. Bushy little trees and plants dotted the scene, appearing near the ground or up on top of buildings or in pots on porches and balconies. I could see people walking on the floating bridges and sitting, spending a pleasant evening on the balcony of their home and watching the sunset's light cast magical reflections on the rolling waves in the Port.

"Oi, you lad!" a loud voice from my left startled me, and I tore my gaze away from the magnificent view. A burly seaman was approaching me, and I saw with a start that he had a jagged scaling knife clutched in one hand.

"Captain," I nodded politely at him, calling up the most easy-going grin I could muster.

"What're you doin' aboard my ship, son?" he glared at me, his bushy dark eyebrows hanging low over his eyes.

"Helping unload," I lied easily, gesturing towards the nets still full of shiny fish that were waiting to be taken onto the docks.

"I didn't 'ire you," the captain sneered, and I licked my lips, waving a hand vaguely towards the docks.

"'Course not. I was sent from the docks to help unload your ship faster."

"Liar!" he poked me hard in the chest with a finger on his free hand, and I saw the other clench tighter around the scaling knife. "You're a little stowaway, ain't ya?"

"No, no sir!" I shook my head, making my eyes go wide and hoping I looked innocent. My heart began to thud in my chest as I looked around for an escape. The docks were too crowded, and the crew of the ship was there, watching us. Behind me was the pile of fish and the boatrail.

"C'mere, boy-" the captain reached his massive hand for my arm, but I jumped backwards and out of his reach.

My heel landed on a coil of rope, and I stumbled until I fell onto my back again. Whatever bruise had been on my backside before doubled in size now, and I felt my head knock against the rail of the boat. The captain was advancing on me, shiny scaling knife in hand, and I tugged my legs back underneath me, springing up and backwards.

I toppled over the boatrail, yelping as I was suddenly falling upside-down into the salty water of the Port. The world seemed to crash around me as I fell beneath the water, everything suddenly becoming muffled and distant. Fear spiked through me, and I flailed my arms and legs wildly until I righted myself and began to swim upwards towards the surface. A chill rushed through me as I broke through the surface, sputtering seawater and gasping for breath. Above, the captain was yelling unintelligibly at me over the rail.

The water was freezing, and I grimaced as it stung my eyes. I began to back-paddle towards the docks, but the crew was already running over there, glaring down at me. I flashed a grin at them, then pinched my eyes closed and dove underwater.

The seawater burned my eyes and nose, and it made my skin feel sort of scratchy. My shirt billowed in the tide, trying to tug me backwards, but I kicked forward until I was beneath the docks, where I came up again. I gasped, spitting salty water out of my mouth and accidentally hitting my head on the boards above me.

My tired limbs complained as I swam farther into the Port, staying beneath the docks to avoid the crew of the ship I had stowed away on. I could hear — and feel — all the people above me, hurrying back and forth, shouting and babbling and muttering to themselves and each other, but I ignored all of it, putting all my focus into the next push to move my legs.

At last I couldn't keep swimming, so I swerved to the side and reached up to grip the edge of the docks, hoping nobody stepped on my fingers. I could see some of the floating market stalls bobbing next to me, and I smelled something rich and delicious coming from one of them. My stomach grumbled at me, begging for something to eat, but I didn't have any money on me. I'd just have to get back to Willa's place before I passed out from exhaustion.

With a grunt, I kicked my legs and pulled myself up, flopping like a limp fish onto the boards of the dock. I heard a woman cry out in surprise, but I ignored her as I climbed to my feet and wrung my shirt out, combing my hands through my hair and watching as water dripped down the bridge of my nose.

"There he is!" a voice yelled over the crowd, and I jumped as I looked to my right and saw the crewman charging for me from the boat, which wasn't as far away from me as I'd hoped it would be.

I turned and bolted, shoving past people and sliding on my slick boots, shouting apologies over my shoulder as I ran by. Shouts of surprise and condescension chased me down the docks, as well as the heavy boots of the fishermen hurtling through the throng after me.

As I ran my breathing came faster, and my heartbeat quickened. I sucked in a breath and felt drops of seawater catch in my throat. I coughed, feeling it burn my throat, as I skidded and slid around a corner, then regained my balance and tried to run straight again. Just before I could, though, a strong hand grasped me by the wrist.

I cried out in surprise, looking to see that it was one of the crewmen, and one of the bigger ones at that. I gulped, my eyes widening as he grinned and yanked me backwards, towards his companions.

"I wasn't a stowaway, I swear!" I yelped, but my voice was high and squeaky. I tried to pull away, but my feet just slid out from under me, and I felt myself being held up only by my arm and the burly man's strength. I got the feeling that my arm was about to be torn off the rest of my body.

"No?" the man sneered, his voice slightly accented. I couldn't place where he was from, and I really didn't want to. "Looked to me like you was," he leaned close, and I caught a whiff of dead fish and some sort of alcohol. "And you know what the penalty for that is?"

"No," I lied, flexing my arm to test his strength again. There was no way I could tear myself loose from his grip.

"A boy like yourself? You oughta know, surely," he said smugly, and I scowled at him, more annoyed from how much of a kick he was getting out of this than anything else. Well, if he wanted a kick out of something, I could certainly give him one.

"You're right," I growled, my voice lowered back to its usual octave. "I know exactly what it is." Then I lifted my leg and kneed him in the groin. He groaned and doubled over, releasing me, and I took off before one of his companions got the chance to grab me.

I was almost to the end of the docks now, and I let out a small laugh as I rounded the last turn to sprint for the street winding up into Lourak. Those stupid fishermen. They never learn anything unless it's from some curvy woman they managed to talk up at a bar.

My soaked boots stopped thumping on the damp wooden boards of the docks soon enough, now leaving watery footprints on the cobbled street that bent sharply to the left, right out of the Port, taking me up through a small copse of trees, past a pleasant little glade, through the thick walls around Lourak, and right into the heart of Wisesol.

Normally, I'd love to stick to the usual road and see what mischief I could get myself into — and, hopefully, out of — before the day was over, but today I had to get home. It was nearly dark now, and Willa would be starting to fret. I almost *never* missed dinner unless I was in a lot of trouble.

For this reason, I took a shortcut.

I lived with my grandmother, Willa, in a small house in Rulak, the northernmost town in all of Wisesol. It was a pretty long distance from Lourak, or from any of the other towns, for that matter, but that's what the caravan system exists for, and it's what I used to get around for the most part. I used it almost every day.

The caravans were carts drawn by sturdy horses that went back and forth between two designated towns, carrying people and goods who didn't have the means to travel swiftly themselves, and they were in a hurry. My favorite caravan belonged to a girl named Jessie, and I hoped I could find her caravan heading back to Rulak before the system shut down for the night.

The shortcut I was taking intercepted the main road between Lourak and Rulak, but I had to go fast, and that wasn't exactly easy. While Wisesol is, for the most part, just hilly plains, especially the northern end, those hilly plains can be very treacherous. There were holes in the ground, bushes and twigs dotted all over the place, and the worst of it all were the raptors. It was rare you stumbled across one, since they didn't come out of the Veiled Woods often, but they usually did when it was breeding season, and they wanted to make their nests in hollows in the ground of the plains to keep them hidden from other raptors. It was very annoying when you came across an angry mother raptor. It was very annoying when you came across a normal raptor, actually. But especially so if it was an angry mother, and you'd happened a little too close to her nest.

Luckily for me, it was late summer, and most of the raptors would have already returned home to the Veiled Woods, meaning I made quick time across the plains to the main road. And, sure enough, there was a caravan rolling up along it, heading from Lourak to Rulak. The horses drawing it were a mismatched pair: a white one speckled with dark brown spots, and a dark bay. I recognized them immediately as Tooth and Dagger, Jessie's horses.

"Jess!" I shouted, sprinting through the long grass, growing wearier by the second as my soaked clothes sagged around me. The caravan slowed as she heard me, and I saw her head pop around the edge of the driver's seat.

"Hey, there he is! Where've you been, Trouble?"

"Around," I said as I came up beside the halted caravan. I patted Tooth on the rump and launched myself up into the driver's bench beside Jessie. She had her long red hair put up in two braids, like she always did, and wore a broad straw hat.

"Well, I hope you haven't got another bounty on your head," she chuckled as she snapped the reins, and the horses resumed their steady trot down the road. "I'd hate to be caught harboring a fugitive."

"That was *one time*, and it wasn't a real bounty," I lounged back on the bench, glancing back into the caravan to see what she was transporting. There were a couple sacks and a barrel full of something, but nothing noticeably interesting.

"There's no food back there, if that's what you're looking for." Jessie told me without taking her eyes off the road. "You'll have to wait until you get back to Willa's place for supper."

"Unfortunate," I sighed, folding my arms back behind my head and shutting my eyes as we rolled along the bumpy path.

"Hey, watch it! You're getting my skirt wet," Jessie yanked her skirt away from me and scooted farther down the bench, glaring at the growing damp spot on the wood. "Did you go swimming in the Port or something?"

"Yes, actually," I saw her eyebrows raise, any trace of her irritation vanishing.

"I thought you hated swimming."

"I do," I picked absently at a sliver of wood sticking out of the edge of the bench. "But it was necessary. I mean it was that or get gutted with a scaling knife for being a stowaway, and I wasn't particularly fond of that idea." I pursed my lips, feigning a thoughtful expression. "Still not fond of it, come to think of it."

"You were a *stowaway*?" Jessie cried, gaping at me. Dagger tossed his head as she loosened his side of the rein, and she quickly readjusted her grip before she shot me a venomous look. "You're an idiot, Trouble; you know that, right? What would I have told Willa if you'd been caught for that?"

"I wasn't caught."

"But you could've been!" she shook her head, exasperated. "When are you going to learn that being stupid gets people killed?" she looked over at me then, and my grin vanished as I saw the look of fear in her blue eyes. "The world we live in isn't safe, Trouble. I know the Curse is dangerous, but that's not even our biggest threat. All of Wisesol is teeming with thieves and murderers, and if you're not careful, you'll end up on the wrong side of a sword."

"Or a scaling knife." I meant it as a joke, but my voice couldn't quite muster the right tone for it, and she gave me a grim, tight-lipped look. I dropped my gaze.

A long silence stretched between us, the only sound that of Tooth and Daggers' hooves clopping on the road and the caravan rattling behind us.

"Just promise me you'll be more careful in the future, okay?" Jessie said finally, her voice low and thin with worry.

"I promise." I answered solemnly.

"And you might want to climb through the window and change before you walk in," she advised after another moment of tense quiet. I glanced sidelong at her, and a hesitant grin pulled across her features. "Willa would throw a fit if you walked through the house looking like a waterlogged weasel."

I returned the grin, and we fell back into another silence, although this one was much more companionable. I craned my neck to look up at the sky above us, now dark, with stars winking to life across it. A cool breeze rolled in from the Great Lakes, and I turned my head to look to the east. I couldn't see the Great Lakes from here. In fact, you couldn't see them at all unless you were exiting the Port, on the edge of the Veiled Woods, or all the way at the eastern end of my hometown, Rulak. Despite not being able to see them, the knowledge that they were there, just past that dark blotch of trees on the horizon, left me with a sensation of discomfort. I hated swimming and anything to do with water, and the mere sight of it — and the smell — was enough to set me on edge.

"It reeks of salt and fish guts." Jessie had said the first time I'd told her. "Who would want to spend their time there anyway? I feel bad for the people who work around the Port, and even more so for the people who live out there in Coldmon."

Personally, I thought the people in Coldmon were quite happy. Since I lived in Rulak, I didn't see many travelers or traders from the other kingdoms, but during my few visits to the vast markets of Lourak, I'd seen a few of them. They were pleasant, light people, and they liked to make friends. I supposed they had to, since they lived directly in between most of the other kingdoms, but it seemed to suit them all well, and I'd never seen an agitated Coldmoner, much less an angry one.

Maybe that was why I disliked the water so much. It reminded me of those peaceful people who, while they may have had their own inward squabbles with each other, were able to be polite and respectful to people from other places. Solians were never afraid to show their irritation, and they wore it like a heavy cloak, letting it conceal everything else about them and putting everyone else off.

"Whatcha thinkin' about?" Jessie's voice sucked me back into the present, and I realized I'd closed my eyes. I opened them and slid my gaze sideways at her.

"What a waterlogged weasel would look like."

"Take a look in the mirror."

"Don't got one with me," I quirked my lips to the side and looked up at the sky again. After a moment, I spoke again, softly. "You ever think about how different we are from other people?" a silence followed that question, and I wondered for a moment if she'd even heard it over the rustle of wind and the clicking of hooves.

"Sometimes, I guess. There's nothing wrong with being a caravaner, though, and it's not too terrible. I'm not treated awful or anything. I even have some pretty respectable friends, yourself excluded."

"Thanks," I deadpanned, and she smiled radiantly at me. "But I meant just Wisesol as a whole."

"Oh," her smile faded, and she looked thoughtfully at the dark road ahead for a long moment. "I suppose so. Why? You're not thinking of running off, are you?" she gave me a hard look.

"Of course not. I'm far over that idea." I had suggested it to her several years ago, when I was maybe six or seven, and she had immediately shot the idea down. She called it unreasonable and dangerous, and I knew there was sense in that. Still, a part of me couldn't help but want to see what the other kingdoms were like. I'd only ever visited Freetalon for a day many years ago, and I'd hardly seen very much of it.

"Good." She turned her head to look towards the west plains, miles and miles and miles of rolling grasses and soft hills. I knew she was thinking about her younger sister, and I felt a pang of regret for reminding her.

Rulak was one of the furthest Solian towns from the captial, Lourak. If someone was on a horse, going full-speed, they'd probably cross the distance in six or seven hours. At the steady pace of the caravan, it was usually closer to thirteen or fourteen.

I didn't mind the ride, especially if it lasted into the night like this, but I knew Willa minded.

Jessie liked to joke that I'd be home in time for supper on nights like these, when we both knew full well it would be close to dawn by the time I got back into the building.

I sighed and tucked my legs up against my chest, letting my head rest back against the canvas of the caravan, and tried to fall asleep. It was a long ride home, and I might as well try to gain whatever rest I could — just because I missed one night's sleep didn't mean Willa would let me off on chores and deliveries.

Before I knew it, I'd nodded off.

An elbow digging into my ribs woke me without warning, and I was so shocked from the sharp pain that I jumped up and off the caravan bench completely. A sharp cry from behind me reminded me where I was, and as I hit the side of the dusty road I heard Jessie screech my name — my real name, not the nickname she'd given me. That's how I knew she was truly terrified — before the caravan wheels rolled right past me. Tooth and Dagger stopped suddenly, stamping their hoofs and tossing their manes in agitation, and I heard Jessie's boots thump to the ground beside me.

"Trouble!" she yelled, and I winced, holding up a hand.

"I fell off the caravan and bruised my backside. I didn't go *deaf*. Although if you keep screaming, I might," I groaned, my voice groggy. That shut her up for a moment, and she grasped my wrist to help haul me to my feet. Her cheeks were bright red, her eyes wide and startled.

"Sorry," she said sheepishly. "I just panicked. You've never fallen asleep on my caravan before, and I didn't know you'd react that way."

"No worries," I waved the matter away as I dusted off the seat of my pants and rubbed my knuckles against my tired eyes. My clothes were still damp, but at least they weren't heavy with water anymore. I looked up to see that light was just beginning to creep across the sky, and in the distance ahead of us, I could just make out the houses of Rulak.

"We're almost there," she said, even though I could clearly see that. She walked back around, giving the horses a loving pat as she went, and pulled herself back onto the caravan bench. I followed her, rolling my stiff shoulders and working the kinks out of my neck.

"I'm hungry," I complained, feeling my stomach rumble. Jessie sighed beside me, and I gave her an impish grin.

"Willa will feed you when you get home." She told me, and I shrugged. Sometimes, if I was lucky, and Jessie was tired enough, she wouldn't have the energy to argue with me, and she'd simply stop on our way into town and buy us a quick meal.

We arrived within half an hour, rolling across the waking streets of Rulak and calling greetings to the early risers we saw already out and about. Jessie, despite being awake all night, waved and cast more well wishes to the townspeople than I did. I stood there and nodded, and smiled when I could muster one, but for the most part I kept my head and eyes down. The fewer people that recognized me, the better.

Willa and I lived in the northwest corner of Rulak, on the property neighboring Jessie's family's farm. This was part of why Jessie and I were such good friends; after years of growing up right next to each other, we'd learned to get along.

As we pulled up to the narrow, beaten- down path that led up to the front porch of my home, Jessie wished me a good day, and I returned it before she snapped the reins again and drove her caravan towards her farm, leaving me to face Willa's wrath all on my own.

It wouldn't be too terrible, I knew, but I'd still rather not walk in looking like I'd crawled my way out of a mud hole, so I looped around to the back of the house, where our orchard backed right up to the wall, and climbed the pear tree that grew nearest to my window. The latch was undone, just as I'd left it when I headed out of the house the day before, and I opened the window and slid over the sill with ease.

My room was small and messy, but the mess helped to muffle any sounds of my entry. The bed was up against the wall with the window, and it stretched the span of the room, so I had to jump off the sill to avoid getting dirt on my sheets, but it didn't really matter, since my sheets were usually crumpled on the floor somewhere.

The tall wardrobe against the wall to the right of the door was open, and my clothes were strewn about, under the bed and lying in heaps in the corners. I kicked a pair of pants out of my way and looked in the compartment I'd built onto the side of the wardrobe to make sure my longbow was still in place. It was there, as well as the elegantly crafted leather quiver that Willa had made me, stuffed with a full sheaf of thirty sharpened arrows.

I shut the compartment door and quickly changed into dry clothes, leaving the damp ones on the floor of the room as I climbed back out the window and down the pear tree. By the time I got back around to the front door, the sun had appeared in the distant east, steadily rising and chasing away the dark skies of the night.

I ran a hand through my hair to be sure it looked decently unkempt, scooped up a handful of dust and clapped my hands together before rubbing the grime onto my shirt, and, just for good measure, I chewed on the corner of my lip until I felt a trickle of blood in my mouth. Only then did I step up to the door and swing it open.

"*Ksega Copper.*" The voice was high and shrill, and I winced as it echoed through the small house. Almost subconsciously, I began to worry the new cut on my lip with my tongue, and already I could feel it swelling.

"Good morning Willa!" my tone was cheerful, bordering on hysterical, but I managed to keep a laugh down as I stepped through the small living space into the cramped kitchen.

"Just *where* have you been?" Willa was standing with her back to me, hard at work on her latest order of perfumes. My grandmother was shorter than I was by nearly a foot, with curly gray hair and a portly frame.

"Around," I looked at the scattered items on the countertop. Mangos, strawberries, dried lavender, a few fragrant oils in glass bottles, and a number of other flower petals and seeds that had been torn or pressed or folded until they were hardly recognizable.

"Well, that is simply *unacceptable.* You can't be staying out all night doing goodness knows what — pass me those tongs there, dear — and leaving me to worry about you! You wasted a perfectly good bowl of banana porridge, you know. Thank you," she turned briefly to accept the little metal tongs I'd offered to her, and her eyes widened as she saw my face. "Ksega! Your lip-" she started to look around the little kitchen, almost frantically, but I put a hand on her shoulder.

"I'm just fine, Willa. Bad scuffle with a raspberry bush and a crocodile playing a fiddle." I winked at her. "Long story. Look, the point is, I'm home now, and I'm alive — watch it there, your petals are burning — isn't that all that really matters?" I spread my hands out innocently as she cursed and turned back to lift some sunflower petals away from the hot pan, where they were curling and turning black at the ends.

She sighed and gave me an irritated look, then rolled her eyes and turned back to her work. She did things with flowers and oils, clicking her tongs when she was waiting on something, then added drops of water and fruit skin and flower petals to her mortar and pestle and mashed it up into a paste. When she dumped it into her concoction, a puff of strawberry-scented smoke plumed up into the kitchen. Willa sighed, and I coughed as I pushed open the little kitchen window to let some fresh air help clear out the smoke.

"Any deliveries for me today?" I asked as she began to stir the mixture up in her big iron pot.

"A couple, but not many. Nothing I can't handle. I'll need you to get ready for a journey to Famark. You're leaving this evening. Here, wash this," she passed a small porcelain bowl to me, and I began to scrub at it in the sink.

"Alright, shouldn't be a prob-" I stopped, blinking and turning to look at her. "Famark?"

"If you'd been here this morning," Willa turned to me and waggled her eyebrows. "You would've known that a very large order of my perfumes has been purchased by a Coldmonian gentleman on the island. He has some big psychic business over there, and he wanted some of the perfumes to resell in his market. You'll be going on the ship to make sure everything arrives safely." She started to ladle her latest perfume into little glass vials, corking them and scribbling their names onto the top.

"I . . ." I looked over my shoulder, towards the door of the house. "Um . . . alright." I went back to washing the little bowl.

"Something wrong?" Willa asked, and I shook my head.

"Nothing. It just seems a bit soon. He ordered them today?" I didn't look up from my work, but I furrowed my brows at the soap bubbling up around the bowl.

"The message *arrived* today. The order was placed several days ago, and the messenger only came to me this morning. What with loading and unloading everything, it will probably take you two or three days to get everything there, and I want you to stay an extra day to rest before you come back." She hesitated at that, and I felt her frail hand on my back. "You'll be okay alone for a week, won't you?"

I grinned at her. "Of course I will. I'm more concerned about *you* being alone for a week. You can get up to some pretty naughty business. What happened last time I left again? Something with old Mister Hank?" she smacked me on the arm and rolled her eyes skyward.

"He was *sick*, and you know that brother of his is an unreliable drunkard. I couldn't very well leave him to get worse when I had a spare bed available."

"We don't have a spare bed."

"You weren't home. That makes your room free for anyone who needs it."

"I'm just joking, Willa."

"I know." She shook her head and offered me a towel to dry my hands and the bowl as she finished tidying up her perfume crafting kit. "And you won't be completely alone," she added, and I raised my eyebrows at her. "There will be the crew of the ship you're taking, obviously, but I've also asked Jessie if she'll tag along. She said she'd love to. I told her to keep you in line." She took the little bowl from me and went to put it away. I grinned and leaned against the side of the sink.

"Keep *me* in line? Why, I've never set a toe *out* of line." She gave me a nonplussed look, and I shrugged. "Besides, I'd be more concerned about her getting seasick than anything I'd get up to-"

"I wouldn't."

"-because I've heard that caravaners do *awful* on the water. You wouldn't think so, what with the tilting and rocking of the caravan, but no," I shook my head, plastering a mock expression of surprise onto my face. "I've heard some pretty terrible stories of them heaving out their breakfast, right there on the deck."

"Ksega, enough of that," Willa ushered me out of the kitchen and headed towards her little bedroom at the end of a side hallway. She called back to me as she disappeared into her room. "You know Jessie's got a stomach of steel, and an iron will to go with it, so you'd better not do anything stupid."

"Wouldn't dream of it." I called back, crossing my arms and smiling at the empty hallway. A moment later, Willa reappeared with a shawl draped over her shoulders and an awkwardly shaped leather bag clutched in her wrinkled hands.

"Pack up," she said as she started to delicately lift the little glasses of perfume into the leather bag. "I expect you ready to go by this evening, when Jessie's picking you up to leave for the Port."

I frowned. "This evening? It's such a long trip, though. Wouldn't it be smarter to leave earlier?"

Willa sighed and gave me a tight look. "Ksega, I know you like to make things work the best for you, but sometimes we have to make exceptions. Jessie has her own job, and she'll be busy until it's time to come pick you up. You'll probably have to camp somewhere along the road to Lourak, unless she wants to drive all through the night again, which I doubt." She shook her head as she closed up the pack and lifted its strap over her shoulder. "How that poor girl does it, I don't know, but she's a tough one. Alright, I'm headed out," she stopped to pat me on the cheek and rise up on the tips of her toes so she could kiss my forehead — I still had to stoop a little so she could reach — and walked to the door. "I'll be back after you've left. Goodbye for now, Ksega," she opened the door.

"Bye, Willa. I love you."

"Love you too."

And then the door was shut, and I was left all alone.

I stood there for a moment, trying to make sense of my emotions, but that wasn't always the easiest task, especially when strawberry-scented smoke was clogging my nose and agitating my eyes. I would have to get out of the house for a bit before I could fully comprehend everything I had left to do.

I jogged through the side hallway and eased open the closet door, climbing hurriedly up the ladder until I popped my head out of the floor of another closet. I pulled myself up and opened that door, stepping into my little bedroom. The clothes on the floor probably needed to be stuffed into a rucksack, as well as some food and maybe a cloak or two, but at the moment I didn't want to work on that. Despite my sore muscles, I was itching to get in some more archery practice before I left. I'd bring my longbow with me on the journey, of course, but who could tell if I'd get the chance to use it?

I stepped around piles of limp clothing and opened the side compartment of my wardrobe, first pulling the quiver out and fastening it in place at my hip, then pulling my longbow out and stringing it before pulling it over my back. It was a pain to go down the ladder with my longbow equipped, so I opened my window and slid out onto the branches of the pear tree.

It was late dawn, and the air carried a pleasant breeze. I took a deep breath as it ran through my hair, drying whatever strands had managed to retain some amount of seawater. Autumn was coming, and I was eagerly awaiting it.

I climbed quickly down the tree and took off through the orchard. It was pretty big, a giant box of fruit trees two miles wide and two miles long, with random little flower gardens planted here and there. It provided a healthy supply of ingredients for Willa's perfumes, and it made summers bearable with all the shade it provided.

My usual archery targets were a pair of old wooden crates, thoroughly filled with holes where my arrows had penetrated the wood, and covered in plenty more dents besides. I left them near the peach trees, and when I arrived at them I stacked them one on top of the other and backed up about a hundred feet or so away, rolling my shoulders and stretching my arms as I prepared to practice.

When I was ready, I shrugged my bow off and took three deep breaths, my eyes closed. My heart was, as usual, beating fast, but I did my best to calm it, honing all my focus into this one moment, summoning all my concentration.

Then, when I was ready, I opened my eyes.

The arrows went flying. Three of them thudded into the crates in rapid succession, and seconds later two more hit home. A sixth arrow whirred past the targets, burying itself in the ground several yards away, but it hadn't even stopped moving when a seventh and eighth arrow struck the target, embedding themselves in the wood.

I released a total of twelve arrows before I stopped. The crates could only take so many at a time. I walked up to the target to review how well I'd done. I always tried to aim for the same spot, whether that be the center of one of the crates and the corner of the other, or one specific spot in one specific plank that I randomly chose. Either way, it let me see how much my aim was improving.

I'd been getting better, but it still wasn't great. Two arrows had flown just shy of the crates, digging into the ground farther on, and one of them had gone wide and missed completely. The other nine had hit the crates, but two of them had strayed farther from the target than I'd have liked.

As I pulled the arrows free, splinters of wood came free, and I winced as a hole the size of my fist revealed itself where one of the targets had been. I placed the arrows back into my quiver and gripped the sides of the crate, grunting as I shifted it so that another side faced where I'd be shooting from. This was the last unmarked face of this crate. The bottom crate was alright for now, but this one was on its last leg, and I doubted I'd be able to use it again after this practice session.

Once I'd regained the twelve arrows, I went back to my hundred foot mark, rolled my neck and shoulders to try and loosen up my muscles, and closed my eyes again. I knew how to fire the bow, and I knew how to aim, it was all just a matter of not getting too excited. I couldn't rush any of the shots, because that was how my arrows missed their mark.

I took a deep breath, letting the sweet fragrance of the orchard around me seep into my senses, calming my nerves and allowing my heart to slow back down to its normal rate. My fingers brushed over the fletching of my arrows, familiar and comforting. My callused hand gripped the longbow tightly, and I felt my muscles tense. Then I opened my eyes, and within seconds, my arrow was flying towards its target.

4
SAKURA

*T*raining with Finnian was rarely fun. Most of the time it either made me want to pull my hair out, want to pull *his* hair out, or want to throw everything in sight at his smug face. Sometimes it was all three. All of our most recent training sessions had definitely resulted in my wanting to do all three of those things, and this most recent one was just about the last straw, but none of them were really options for me considering he was my brother, and Gamma had actually told us to go and train this time. If Gamma was behind it, I couldn't really find a way to pin the blame on Finnian. Normally I couldn't find a way to pin it on him anyway, since it was my fault for going along, but I never liked to admit that to myself.

Elixir and Sycamore were lying down in the shade on the outside of our training glade, Elixir watching when he wanted to, but getting distracted by every rustle of leaves or flash of color he could find. Sycamore was much more refined, her front talons crossed over each other, eyes bored as she watched Finnian and I practice.

It was two hours past noon, and I was ready for lunch. Gamma had kicked us out when she had started making it, and we'd been annoying her in the kitchen. Finnian refused to let me go back until I beat him in a duel. We both knew I couldn't beat him in a duel — yet.

Sweat rolled in heavy beads down the side of my face, sliding down my neck and making it feel like I had little bugs swarming over me. My silk undershirt clung to my skin, plastered there from perspiration. I was out of breath, and my arms and legs ached. The tips of my hair were singed, and there was a welt forming on the back of my hand from where Finnian's eirioth had glanced across my skin.

"Come on, Rura," he taunted, dancing just a few steps back from me so that, if I could manage to summon enough power to revive my flame-sword, he wouldn't get his head lopped off.

"I'm tired," I whined, readjusting my grip on the iron sword handle in my hand. Despite the calluses that had formed from years of hard training with it, I could still feel blisters forming where the metal had rubbed my skin raw.

"No lunch until I see you win." Finnian clicked his tongue at me, and I groaned.

"I'll never win, not against you. Can't we at least go and get something from the Fruit Spring? Just a drink of water and an apple, that's all I want." I shuffled sideways, edging closer to him, even though I knew it wouldn't do anything. He was too watchful, and he matched my movements, keeping us a safe distance apart.

"With that attitude, no, you won't win. Pick up your feet! Use your brain! You're useless against the Curse if you can't win a fight against me." He twirled his own iron sword handle in his palm, allowing the eirioth flame to shoot out from it. A beam of sharp white fire, hot enough to melt metal and somehow strong enough to chop through solid bone. Bright orange tongues of flame danced around the center of the blade, forging the rest of it and casting a strong red glow on its surroundings.

I lowered my sword handle, running my thumb over my knuckles as I tried to hide the sting his words had caused me. Ever since that night in the inn, I'd been thinking about the Curse. I was on the night watch tonight, and my nerves were all over the place. What if a beast came close? What if I was killed tonight? What would happen to Finnian and Gamma and Sycamore if I was gone?

The emotions had solidified deep in my gut into a sort of stone of spite. I *wouldn't* die, because I had already sworn to myself that I was going to do something to fight against this Curse. I was going to do something to stop it. If that meant finding a way to beat Finnian in a fight, I would do it. I would do whatever it took.

"Okay," I groaned, lifting the sword handle again. "Let's do this." I took a deep breath, in through the nose, out through the mouth, and closed my eyes briefly. Eirioth was always there, beneath the skin. It pulsed and thrummed in my blood, as much a part of me as my arms or my eyes. Except it was more than that. It was something bigger than anything we could imagine, something we couldn't create or replicate, only channel and control.

The fire pressed up to the surface of my skin, burning into my hand. It coursed through my fingers into the iron handle, and immediately a spark ignited into a flame-sword identical to Finnian's. It burned and roared hungrily, but as it flared I could feel my power draining away from me.

Across from me, Finnian was advancing, and by the time I'd opened my eyes again his sword was arcing through the air towards me, leaving a trail of angry fire. I yelped and lifted my flame-sword to block it. The swords clashed together, warping away from each other at the point of impact before remerging into the rest of their respective blades. I grunted as Finnian used his heavier body and stronger muscles to his advantage, pressing down on me and trying to force me back.

I'd learned my lesson during our last training session, and had intentionally positioned myself at the beginning of this practice so that Finnian's back was to the King's Scar, and I was safely backed by the Eirioth Wood. At some point during our practice duels, though, we'd gotten turned around, and I cursed inwardly as I realized my back was now to the Scar. If he pressed me back far enough, I'd find myself climbing up tree roots again.

"Use your brain," he repeated, and I felt my anger flare as I realized there was no strain in his voice.

I unlocked the swords and darted to the left, dropping low and ducking around him just in time to block another blow as he swung his sword backwards. The blades skidded across each other, sending both of us stumbling in opposite directions from the momentum. I regained my balance quicker, lunging for him and bringing my flame-sword up to swing into his knees. He blocked it at the last second, deflecting my blade so that it skimmed across the brittle grass on the ground.

"Faster!" he scolded, but there was amusement in his voice, which only served to redouble my aggravation.

Sweat was pouring down my face now, and I blinked it out of my eyes and wiped it angrily from my forehead as we circled each other. I was careful to keep my steps fast when my back was to the Scar, just in case he decided to strike then. But he didn't, and I realized he wanted me to make the first move. Of course he did. He always won when I did that.

Then again, I never practiced making the first move. Maybe now was the time to start.

As soon as the King's Scar was behind him, I darted forward, my blade snaking through the air towards his chest. He'd caught the attack coming, and parried easily. I twisted the sword and swung it back towards his ribs, but angled it up at the last second. He hadn't been expecting that, and he narrowly avoided losing an ear.

"Nice one!" he grinned at me, his sword whirling through the air towards my head. I ducked and blocked another swing. "Try to add more unexpected moves like that," he deflected another blow from me. "And do it faster."

I let out a guttural noise, something between a groan and a growl, and I could hear Elixir chirping excitedly behind me. I was going to kick the blasted dragon if he kept trying to find ways to distract me. I was convinced Finnian had taught him to do that, just so he could see how I performed when there were other noises around.

I side-stepped to avoid getting my arm shorn off, then hurriedly lifted my sword to catch his as it came bearing down on my head. I grunted in shock at the force of it, and felt my muscles begin to tremble from the effort. This training session had gone on long enough, and I was ready to end it. But what could I *do*?

Use your brain. That's what I had to do. I had to find a way out of this, and it had to be a way Finnian wouldn't expect. I could feel the blades inching closer to my face, feel the heat they sent off hitting my skin in waves.

An idea came to me, a dangerous one that I probably shouldn't attempt, and I hesitated. It cost me, and the flame-swords came another inch closer to my face before I flexed my muscles and pushed against him again. I gasped from the effort, realizing I had to at least try.

I took a shaky breath, then released my eirioth magic. The flame-sword vanished in a wisp of smoke, and I felt that magical cord within me lose some of its tension. I ducked to the side, shaky from the remaining magic that coursed through me.

Finnian's flame-sword swung sharply past my head, barely missing me, and I heard him cry out in surprise. He stumbled forward while I dove to the side, hitting the ground shoulder-first and rolling as I curled myself into a ball.

Ignoring the complaints in my limbs, I bounded back to my feet as fast as I could and, in one final push of strength, I rejuvenated the power in my blade and brought the flame-sword down towards Finnian, stopping it just above his neck, ensuring he could feel its prickle of hungry heat without actually causing any damage to his flesh.

For a long minute, we just stood there, panting and shaking and sweating, until he let out a short laugh.

"You did it! You beat me," he turned his head and grinned, letting his flame-sword extinguish. I did the same, then promptly flopped onto the ground, lying on my back and staring up at the blue sky above.

"Finally!" a lazy grin tugged at the corners of my mouth as he appeared over me, offering me his hand. I accepted it and allowed myself to be pulled back to my feet, even though I didn't want to stand. Every part of me was shaking from exertion, and I was sure that no amount of soaking in a tub would ever free me of the clammy feeling of my sweat, but I couldn't help the feeling of pride that swept over me.

I'd done it. I'd finally beaten my brother in a flame-sword duel, and it had hardly taken ten minutes. Where had that motive been all the other times we'd practiced?

"That was risky, though," Finnian remarked as we tucked the iron sword handles back into place on our belts. Out of the corner of my eye, I caught Elixir hopping around playfully, and Sycamore watching him sharply. He was still making those high-pitched chirping noises.

"I know," I admitted, letting a bit of smugness into my shaky smile. "But I'm glad I attempted it. And look, I didn't die!" I spread my arms out wide and laughed. I knew that it was stupid to retract my power like that, especially when another flame-sword was so close to my face. Few eirioth-mages tried to drop and then summon their power in such quick succession when they were just training, especially if they were drained of their energy. If it were a life or death situation, they might risk it, but it was a trick to be used with caution when in training scenarios.

"That's right," Finnian chuckled, and I noticed his gaze linger briefly on the dragons before returning to me. "And I'm glad you didn't. Gamma would have my head if you came back with more than just bumps and scratches."

I turned my head to peer at the dragons, then glanced back at him, a clear question in my eyes. He swallowed and shook his head, telling me it was nothing to worry about, but I could see a glint of confusion in his emerald eyes.

"What is it?" I looked over at them again, and now I could see it too. Sycamore had stood up when Elixir had begun hopping around playfully, and she was slowly taking steps away from him, her feathers ruffled, wings puffed out, eyes sharp and alert. I'd seen her annoyed with the other dragon, but this was something new. It was almost as if she was *afraid* of him.

Finnian and I started to walk towards them, and as we came closer I noticed something strange about Elixir's movements. They were sharp and jerking, unnatural, sending his head twitching or his feathers flaring. His talons trembled, and he was shaking his head around as if there was something on it that he didn't like.

I could sense Finnian's unease growing as we stopped a short distance away from the struggling dragon. I'd never seen any eirioth dragon behave this way before, and I knew something was wrong when I suddenly heard a quiet, mewling cry spill out of Elixir's golden beak.

"What's wrong with him?" I asked Finnian quietly, swiping a drop of sweat off my chin. I didn't take my eyes off of Elixir.

"I don't know. Elixir?" he said the dragon's name louder, and Elixir stilled. He stilled a little *too* much. His entire body locked up, his muscles stiff, eyes glazed.

Then he snapped out of it and, with a loud squawk, collapsed to the ground.

*F*or the hundredth time, Gamma, *I don't know what happened.*" I ran my hand through my hair again, yanking my fingers through the tangles.

"Well *someone* must know!" Gamma snapped back, creases of worry forming at the corners of her eyes. She was standing across from me, behind the bar, preparing dishes of sandwiches and leftover stew for the few customers coming in and out of the inn.

"I'm telling you, he's not sick. There's no fever, no loss of appetite. He seems fine again, but more distracted than usual." I propped my elbows up on the counter and sighed, drumming my fingers on the black marble.

As soon as Elixir had fallen, Sycamore and I had flown to Walnut for help while Finnian tried to wake him up. A few hours later, Elixir had woken up in one of the dragon stables in Walnut, and he'd eaten so much food we'd expected him to throw it back up. He seemed fine, but wary. He looked a little crazed whenever another dragon came into view, and he got antsy when he was still for too long.

We'd stayed with him for another hour before Finnian decided we should come back to Hazelwood Inn. Elixir had been fine during the flight, but he was now in the stables with Finnian and Walter, and apparently he was unsettling Honeysuckle, Sycamore, and the mint green dragon that was still in there.

"I honestly don't know, Sakura," Gamma set the dishes down in front of me. "Tables four and seven, please. Then go check on your brother, will you?"

I nodded and took the bowls, carrying them to the instructed tables before I slipped out the door of the inn and jogged down the path towards the stable.

As I came closer, I could hear the uneasy grunts of the dragons inside, and it made me slow my pace. I hoped everything was alright. But what was I going to do if it wasn't? What if this was some sort of new sickness that could spread fast between dragons? Would Elixir ever calm down again? Was he going to pass out more often? Would that make it too dangerous to ride him?

The thoughts fell into my mind faster than I had time to register them, and before I knew it I had a headache. I rubbed my temples, standing outside the stable doors, trying to calm myself down before I went inside.

"What's going on?" the familiar voice came from to my right, and I arched my neck to see that Derek was walking up to me. Bear was in tow, his slender ears twitching and his eyes glued to the stable doors.

"Something's going on with Elixir." I answered, trying to keep the tremble out of my voice. "We don't know what it is. Finnian and I were training, and suddenly he just fell down."

Derek's brows furrowed, a line forming between his eyes. His gaze slid to the stable doors, and he started for them. I followed, and as he pulled it open I couldn't help but bite my lip to keep my chin from shaking.

Finnian and Walter were sitting on stools at the end of the aisle, Finnian with his head in his hands, Walter eyeing Elixir's stall warily. As Derek and I walked in, Bear hovered near the doorway, and neither of us beckoned him in after us. Walter looked up and gave us a brief nod before he returned his attention to Elixir's stall. I could just barely see a spot of bright orange feathers over the wall.

"How's Finnian faring?" Derek said softly, and I pursed my lips. My brother had been uncharacteristically quiet ever since Elixir had woken up frantic and panicked. Neither of them had managed to calm down since.

"Not great. He's still hoping it's some sort of sickness." I replied. I felt Derek's gaze on me, but I didn't meet it.

"You don't think it is?" I shook my head, feeling the words on the tip of my tongue, but unable to find the will to speak them. He was silent for a long moment, then said, "You think it's the Curse."

"I don't *think* it's the Curse," I corrected. "I'm *worried* that it *might* be the Curse." I shuddered, lifting my arms to hug myself as we came up beside Elixir's stall door. The dragon was curled up into a tight ball in the corner, his eyes staring wildly around him, never focusing on one thing, always ready to move on to the next.

"That's impossible though," Derek muttered at my side, turning his head to look over at Finnian's hunched form. "Isn't it?"

I looked down at my brother, then at his dragon. Both of them shook just a little bit, hardly noticeable unless you knew something was wrong. It was terrifying and heartbreaking and gut-wrenching all at once, and I felt like my meager lunch might make a second appearance.

"Isn't it." I repeated, pressing my lips together tightly.

We fell silent for a long moment, lost in our own thoughts. I could hear Derek breathing beside me, the slight rustle from inside Elixir's stall. I felt the curious gazes of Honeysuckle, Sycamore, and Bear watching from a safe distance, near the stalls on the other side of the stable. The mint green dragon was nowhere to be seen.

We didn't know a lot about the Curse. In the past nearly-two-hundred years, it had remained much of a mystery to everybody, but there were some things we'd managed to learn about it. One thing was that it was highly contagious, and it spread rapidly across Horcath. Every land was plagued by Cursed creatures, although some worse than others. The only thing that linked them together was the fact that all Cursed beasts had little to no will. Rodents, lesser animals, and most types of birds and reptiles were the most common, but young, old, or sick animals could be corrupted as well. I'd never seen these creatures myself, but I'd heard tales of Cursed cats coming out of the Evershifting Forest, and even runeboars falling victim to its deadly snare.

But a dragon was a powerful creature. Even when young, like Elixir, it had a lot of strength. Even when old, like Honeysuckle, it had a lot of vibrancy. Even when a dragon was sick it still managed to fare better than anything else would in its position. So how could a perfectly healthy dragon be corrupted by the Curse? The answer was haunting the back of my mind, but I didn't want to pay it any attention. Not yet. I didn't want to believe it was a real possibility.

"There's no real *proof* that it's anything," I murmured, rubbing my knuckles. "I mean, he might just be tired, right? Or overstimulated?" a grunt from beside me told me Derek heard my words, but obviously didn't believe them. I wasn't sure I did either.

We were silent for another long moment before I finally lost my patience. If nobody was going to tell me what was going on, I was going to find out. I turned to Walter and Finnian to see that the old stablehand was already watching me expectantly, clearly anticipating a question.

"Has *anything* changed since he got here?" I asked, my gaze flickering to Finnian before returning to Walter. "In either of them?"

"Very little." Walter replied, rising to his feet. He wasn't exactly a tall person, but I wouldn't describe him as short either. His thinning gray hair sat in an unruly mop on his freckled head, sticking out in all different directions as he scratched at it thoughtfully with one hand.

"Have they eaten?" Derek asked, leaning back against one of the thick beams that supported the loft and the roof above. He crossed his arms and looked into Elixir's stall, where the dragon was flexing and unflexing his talons over and over.

"The dragon's had some. Finnian won't eat. Or speak, for that matter," Walter grumpily kicked at Finnian's shin, but my brother just gave an irritable grunt in response, his head still hidden behind his hands.

"Lunch is ready," my tone was forcibly light as I stepped closer to Finnian. "You should come eat."

"Not hungry." He sighed between his fingers.

"Doesn't matter. You have to eat something. That was an intense training session, and your legs won't work if you don't get something into your system. Here, let's go get you a bowl, then we can come right back out when you're done, okay?" I placed one hand on his shoulder and gripped his arm with my other, trying to pull him up, but I knew there was no way I could lift his entire body weight.

"She's right," Derek pitched in. "And you'll think better on a full stomach." He grabbed Finnian's other arm, and we hauled him to his feet. He dropped his hands and looked at each of us, and I felt something inside me twist with pity when his gaze met mine.

It seemed like he'd aged far beyond his nineteen years in a matter of hours. The corners of his mouth were turned down, and he seemed more tired than I'd seen him in a long time. It was such a shocking difference I had to force myself to look for the familiar lines of his jaw and set of his nose, just so I could reassure myself that it really was him.

"Alright, you've got options," I kept my voice as positive as I could manage, but it was difficult when Finnian was looking so miserable. "Gamma's got leftover stew, sandwiches, and-"

"You can see it." He cut me off, and I blinked, snapping my mouth shut. Derek and I exchanged a brief glance, then I cleared my throat and asked,

"What was that?"

"You can *see it.*" Finnian repeated, his voice steely. I looked behind us at Walter, but the stablehand only shrugged. I swallowed, returning my attention to Finnian.

"You can see *what*, Finn?"

"Look." He shrugged Derek and I off of him, and we didn't fight it. He turned around and unlatched the door to Elixir's stall. Beside me, Derek stirred uneasily, and my own hands drifted closer to the iron sword handle at my belt. I felt a pang of guilt for doing it. This was *Elixir*. The annoying, stupid little dragon I hated to be around so much. The dragon who would try to play with Sycamore, even on her worst days. He would never hurt Finnian. *Never.* And yet . . .

"What am I looking at, exactly?" I asked gently as Derek and I edged closer to the stall door. Walter came closer, too, frowning deeply, his brows furrowing together.

"This," Finnian answered, stepping into the stall and coming up close to Elixir. The dragon lifted his head, but it didn't look like he could actually see where Finnian was. "Come in. Look." He knelt by Elixir's head, gesturing for me to follow him.

I hesitated, then swallowed my fear, telling myself it was irrational, and stepped inside. I crouched beside Finnian, looking at the elegant curve of Elixir's beak, the familiar speckles of dark blue along his face.

"Here," Finnian pointed down at Elixir's front claws, which were folded in front of him. I looked, and at first I didn't understand. They were yellow and black. They looked exactly like the talons of hundreds of other eirioth dragons.

Then I remembered. Elixir didn't *have* black on his talons. They were pure yellow. I sucked in a shallow breath, dropping onto my knees to peer closer. The scales were smooth on gold parts, but the blotches of black were cracked and shriveling. One of his toes was completely black, and it remained still while the rest of his foot flexed and twisted from his agitated movements.

"What is it?" Derek asked, stepping into the stall after us. I felt him kneel next to me, heard him say something to Walter when he saw the black spots, but I couldn't understand what they were saying.

A part of me had been worried it was the Curse, but it had seemed so unlikely. The chances of a dragon becoming Cursed were ridiculously small, almost nonexistent. I shouldn't have even had the thought in the first place, because it was *impossible*.

But what if it wasn't? What if the Curse was *growing*? What if, instead of wearing itself out, like Finnian thought it would, it was only getting stronger? What if sick cougars and old runeboars had only been the beginning?

The questions made my head spin. If the Curse could corrupt eirioth dragons, could it corrupt other fully sentient beings? Could it corrupt a healthy smith? Could it corrupt the adult monstrous sandcats of Old Duskfall? Could it corrupt a human?

I lifted a hand and placed it over my eyes, my fingers massaging my forehead. My headache had returned, and I was getting tired of all these unanswered questions. A hand on my arm made me drop it, and I looked up to see Finnian watching me.

"It can't be." I whispered, as if keeping my voice small would keep the problem small, too. As if it would make it a sickness, or some sort of infection on Elixir's talons that we'd never seen before. But that was too much to hope for, and from the heartbroken expression on Finnian's face, we all knew it.

The black spots became a well-kept secret between the four of us.

After we'd all seen them, we took turns watching him closely for the rest of the day. The spots didn't change. They didn't grow, which was good, but they didn't shrink, and I don't think any of us expected them to.

Elixir didn't seem to change much either. Over the course of the next six hours, he moved around more. We got him to stand up and take a short flight around outside, but we didn't let him go to the feeding stations in town.

Derek hadn't gone back to his home in Cashew, instead having Bear settled into one of the other stalls in the stable so he could stay and help us monitor Elixir.

"We can't keep it a secret forever," he told us that evening as we all hunched over our bowls of strawberry oatmeal. "If it is what we think it is, we've got to try and do something about it, and if we can't figure out a solution on our own, somebody else has to be brought in."

"He responds well to warm things," Walter said, poking at a chunk of strawberry at the bottom of his bowl. "Freshly killed weasels and the like. He won't drink his water if it's cold, either. He hardly drinks it at all, matter of fact. It's like it scares him."

"Are Cursed things afraid of water?" I asked, trying to ignore how Finnian winced at the word *Cursed*. None of us liked to use it, but it had become almost the equivalent of a swear ever since we'd seen the black spots.

"Can't be," Derek said around a mouthful of oatmeal. "There are all sorts of Cursed animals in the Great Lakes."

"Well there's got to be *something* we can do, right?" I looked around at the three of them. I'd never been one for optimism, but things changed when someone you loved was involved. Now, I felt like I was the only one clinging on to this idea of hope that Elixir would be just fine.

"Not on our own, that's for sure." Derek said grimly, wolfing down the remainder of his oatmeal. "We've waited long enough. Someone else has to know. If this is the Curse, people have to be warned, or dragons will start turning on their masters before we can do anything."

"How can you say it like that?" Finnian spat, clenching his fist around his spoon.

"Guys, can we not right now?" I whined, my shoulders slumping. Finnian had been snippy all day, and I didn't want him getting into an argument when all of us were so stressed.

"Say it like what?" Derek ignored me, his tone even as he held Finnian's gaze.

"Like it doesn't bother you! You're saying that any of our dragons could get infected with the Curse any second now, and we'd just have to live with that. You're saying people could die or lose a bond with an animal they've had since childhood.

You're saying it like it doesn't affect you at all!" Finnian set his spoon down and splayed his hands out on the table, clearly trying to rope in his anger.

"It *does* affect me," Derek leaned forward, keeping his voice low enough so that only our table could hear. "And that's why I'm trying to do something about it. You think I don't want to keep Bear safe?"

"Enough." Walter huffed, pushing his empty wooden bowl away from him. The three of us looked at him curiously. "Plow's right. We can't keep this a secret forever. But we can keep it a secret for a little while longer. Let's let him rest and see what the morning brings, eh?" he stood up, looking between us to make sure we were all okay with it. One by one we nodded, and he grunted. Without a goodbye, he returned his dishes to Gamma and left the inn, trooping back towards the stable.

"Should someone help him keep a watch on Elixir through the night?" Derek asked after the long silence had grown unbearable.

"No, he'll manage it just fine." Finnian sighed, waving a hand in dismissal. "Although I'll probably end up going there sometime in the night, just to check on them."

"I've got watch tonight," I said wearily, nudging the few remaining bites of my oatmeal around my bowl and finding I didn't have the appetite to finish it.

"Sure you'll be able to stay up?" Finnian looked at me apologetically. "I know I haven't exactly let you get a lot of sleep the past few nights."

"You never let me get a lot of sleep, what with all that snoring you do." I muttered.

"Want some company?" Derek asked, and I raised an eyebrow at him. He shrugged. "I haven't got watch back in Cashew until later this week, and I might as well stay here until we help Elixir. I can help keep you awake."

"Oh, can you?" Finnian wiggled his eyebrows. "What'd you have in mind?"

"Idle conversation." Derek told him, a muscle in his jaw twitching. I could tell he wanted to punch my brother, and I didn't blame him. I did too.

"That's all?" Finnian teased, and even though it annoyed me, I was glad to see he at least had the energy to make jokes.

"Not sure," Derek said through gritted teeth. "Maybe I'll perform an interpretive dance, and throw in a song about river toads while I'm at it."

Finnian snorted and stood up. I did as well, and Derek followed. He frowned at my bowl, giving me a questioning look. I shook my head and offered the bowl to him. He traded with me and finished whatever oatmeal had remained in my bowl as we came up to the counter.

"Let me guess," Gamma said as we stopped in front of it, setting the bowls down on the countertop. "A bat, a bear, and a mouse walk into a bar." She leaned forward and peered at us. "What's up with all of you? You don't appreciate a good joke?"

"I don't get it." Derek was frowning, and I rolled my eyes.

"We're just tired, Gamma. Long day, lots of training. I'm heading out to go to the watch post. Do you need anything from me before I go?" she looked between me and Finnian, then glanced at Derek.

"No. You're sure everything's alright?"

"Peachy. I'll see you tomorrow." I gave her and Finnian a quick hug and headed for the door. Derek hovered by the counter another moment before I heard his footsteps following me.

As we left the inn and headed for the watch house just west of Hazelwood Inn, Derek came up beside me. The watch house rested in a nest of tall tree branches a little ways into the Eirioth Wood, safely away from the ground, and equipped with plenty of defense and warning systems. The problem was, one rarely noticed the Cursed nearby until it was too late.

There was no clear path to the watch house, since most people on the watch roster for Hazelnut didn't live this far to the south, and they usually flew to the house on their dragons. It wasn't too bad, though. The Eirioth Wood was a very pleasant place, with few bushes and tall grasses. It was all tall eirioth trees, with dark, twisting branches and colorful, petal-like leaves. The grass was always bright green, even in winter, and it was almost as soft as fur.

"Why does he do that?" Derek asked as we stepped into the trembling shadows of the trees. They rose like giant curving figures, frozen in the darkness as the wind ruffled through their leaves.

"Do what?" I asked, my eyes searching the ground in front of me for any exposed tree roots. The darkening sky made my stomach turn, but I tried to conceal it.

"Make all those comments like that. Like he thinks you and I *do stuff* when we're alone." I could hear the anger in his voice, and I understood it well. It was the same anger that was reflected in me whenever Finnian started teasing like that.

"He's worried I'll never find love," I admitted sheepishly, shrugging to myself. "He says I'm too prickly, and since you're my only friend outside of the family, I should be trying to get you to marry me." I gave him an apologetic look, but he was watching the ground in front of us. "I would've told you sooner, except it seemed a bit weird. I still don't see why I'd have to find someone at all."

"I can sort of understand," a wry smile pulled at his lips. "You *are* prickly. But I see what he's trying to do. I don't want Violet to grow up all alone. I mean, one day

I'm not gonna be here for her anymore, and who will take care of her after that?" the smile faded into a tight-lipped expression. "Not only that, but I sort of feel the same way about you." He eased a low-hanging tree branch out of our way as we filed into a narrow path between a wonky line the trees had formed.

"Do you?" I chuckled, hopping over a bundle of roots. "Funny."

"I'm serious," he took the lead, disappearing for a moment around a tree before reappearing on the other side. "You're like a sister to me, and I don't want you to end up alone if anything happens to Finnian and Gamma."

I stopped in my tracks. Derek kept going for a little way until he realized I wasn't following, when he paused to look back. His pale face was clearly visible in the moonlight that found its way past the tree leaves, and I could see the confused expression he wore.

"Sakura?" he asked, his voice hesitant and guarded, eyes looking at the dim forest around us for any sign of danger.

"Sorry," I shook my head, wetting my lips nervously. I rolled my shoulders and forced myself to catch up to him. "Sorry," I said again. "I just . . . I've never thought of that."

He frowned. "Of me thinking of you as a sister?"

"No, of . . ." I swallowed. "Of something happening to Finnian and Gamma."

"Oh." I could hear the guilt in his voice, but I didn't want him to feel guilty. He was only being reasonable. Probably without meaning to, he had helped me to realize why Finnian *really* dragged me out for midnight training sessions and teased me about boys and tried to get me to try all these different new things.

I licked my lips again, trying to ignore the sting I felt as I remembered all the times I'd insulted and threatened and hit him out of annoyance. Of course I never really meant any of them, but the fact that I'd said them at all was enough to make me feel a little sick.

He just wanted me to be ready in case something happened. But 'in case' wasn't a possibility with the Curse. No, he wanted me to be ready for when something *did* happen.

"Come on," Derek's voice pulled me out of my thoughts, and I blinked as I realized tears had tried to break free. I gulped and nodded, letting him lead the way as we hurried along through the dusk, trying to make it to the watch house before anything lurking nearby got brave enough to come out and try to eat us.

The watch house was a great, hulking shadow above us, stretched across four golden eirioth trees. There was no ladder, no set of stairs. The trees themselves were practically impossible to climb unless you knew where to go. Cursed creatures wouldn't. Derek and I did.

We climbed a nearby blue tree and carefully walked across its branches, using another eirioth tree, this one a vibrant green, as a bridge to get to the branches of one of the yellow trees. From there we hefted ourselves over the thick wooden wall and landed lightly on the planks of the balcony.

The watch house was a one-story, square building with a three-foot-wide balcony wrapping around it. All of it was crafted from the dark wood of the eirioth trees, and at night it was almost invisible until you were right up on it. The roof was low and slanting, so that rain would run off of it and over the walls of the balcony. The interior of the watch house was unadorned and, to put it simply, dead. Not in the sense that it was dilapidated or abandoned, but it had a sort of haunting air about it. There was something dark that clung to the air, thick tendrils of unease that wove through the space and encircled everything it could find. It gave me chills every time I entered.

There were three windows, a small one in each wall, and a thick door in the last. There was a single grubby cot in one corner, but the rest of the room held no furniture. There were racks of swords, crossbows, and longbows. Sharpening tools, bowstrings, quivers of arrows, spare cloaks and thick wooly socks, small packets of non-perishable foods, and canisters of water were strewn about it what looked like an unceremonious jumble, but as I'd come to the watch house more frequently, I'd learned there was a sort of unorthodox system to it all.

We entered the watch house without any light. Slivers of moonlight danced on the floor and some of the walls, but it was very little. We didn't bother to light any eirioth flames. The whole point of the night watch was to stay invisible, watching things that couldn't watch you, keeping the sleeping towns of Carlore safe. The sooner our eyes adjusted to the darkness, the better, because we would need to be fully alert all night long.

With that said, though, I still couldn't help the urge to set a flame ablaze over the palm of my hand. The shadows in the corners of the room seeped down towards the floorboards, creeping towards my feet like spindly claws. It made me feel sick to see them.

Some of the pressure was eased off my shoulders now that Derek was here to help. Normally there was only one person on watch per night, since the roster was so short, but with Derek's help, I was confident that tonight would be an easy watch. In the past I'd seen distant flashes of green, and occasionally a Cursed beast had come close enough for me to shoot it, but I'd never encountered anything too dangerous. With

Derek here as an extra pair of eyes and ears, I knew we wouldn't have a hard time keeping anything the Curse threw at us at bay.

"Bow?" Derek asked as he poked through the rack of longbows, searching for one that fit his height best.

"I'm better with the crossbow, actually." I told him, and he nodded as he selected a bow and a quiver of arrows. I hefted a large crossbow into my hands and located my own quiver of bolts, then checked to make sure my sword was in place strapped to my back, and my iron sword handle was still in my belt.

We stepped out into the cooling night, taking up positions side by side at the northeastern corner of the balcony. We stood there, staring out into the darkness, for ten minutes, then we turned and walked to the southeastern corner. When another ten minutes had passed, we moved on to the southwestern corner. Up until that point, we'd both been silent, but now Derek spoke.

"What was the joke Gretchen was trying to make?"

For a long moment I didn't answer, partly because, at first, I didn't realize who he was talking about, and partly because I was pulled back into memories of my early childhood to find the answer.

"A bear and a mouse walk into a bar." I answered, my voice small. I spoke a little louder as I went on to explain it to him. "It was always her joke that Finnian was a bear, growing fast and strong, while I was a mouse." I shuffled my feet uncomfortably. How had Derek and I known each other for so long, and yet, somehow, we still knew so little about each other?

"And the bat?" Derek asked.

"Oh, she just throws that in. Her late husband, Eric, always joked that she ran a bar, so he sort of invented that part of the joke when we were old enough to come eat dinner with them. If we're ever with anybody, she calls them whatever animal she sees fit." I smirked. "Walter is an angry badger."

"I could see that," Derek mused. "I could see that very easily."

We fell into another silence, but this one was a little more awkward. The question he'd asked had made me realize just how much the Curse affected our lives. If it hadn't taken away people we loved, would we even be friends? I knew for a fact we wouldn't be meeting up in my eirioth tree to talk about things we're confused about.

But would we know these things? Would he know all my family's little inside jokes, and all the dreams I'd had as a little girl? If the Curse didn't exist, and it didn't force us to grow up fast and learn to fight faster, would we see each other differently?

I'm going to end it. I pursed my lips. I was done watching children learning how to wield a sword, how to summon their eirioth before they could even pronounce the word. Why should they be learning to fight in a war that nobody will ever win? Everyone was too cowardly to try and make a stand, and that left generation after generation of people to suffer.

I refused to see people continue to grow up the way I had. To suffer the way my family had. I was going to find a way to end this Curse. I was sure I was. But how could I? How could I be so sure I had that kind of power? How could I be so sure I could leave my brother behind like that?

Don't drive yourself too far, Rura, please. That's all I ask.

"Over there." Derek's voice made me jump, and he threw me a panicked glance as he knocked an arrow to his bowstring.

"Sorry," I mumbled, lifting a bolt to my crossbow. "Lost in thought. Where?" I looked up and followed his pointing finger, squinting into the darkness. For a long moment, I saw nothing except the pale glow of moonlight on the forest floor and the gently swaying shadows of the trees. Then, I caught a flash of green.

When a Cursed animal is involved, you never quite feel safe. You could have the best armor, the best weapons, the best fort, even the best army lined up right behind you, and your heart would still jump into your throat. Your muscles would still lock up and your gaze would still spin wildly around you until you had a clear sight of the creature. With the darkness surrounding us, I felt even less safe.

This one wasn't very big. It was still a good way off, but I already had a few guesses as to what it could be. A raccoon, a fox, a young wolf, a badger of some kind, possibly even a bird or a small raptor, but it was rare you saw them this far south. Still, there had been that attack in Walnut . . .

I adjusted the position of my crossbow and forced the thoughts from my mind. The last thing you needed while on the night watch was a jumble of distracting thoughts, and you *definitely* didn't want any distracting thoughts while a Cursed animal was approaching.

"Can you still see it?" I whispered as I lifted my crossbow and aligned my sights. Whatever the animal was, it had disappeared from my view.

"Yes. It's coming closer. I'll have a clear shot in a minute. Back up a bit." Derek lifted his bow and pulled the arrow back to full draw, aimed carefully at the darkness ahead.

I took a step back and, as I did, the animal came back into view. It was shuffling along, almost lurching, and I realized it only had three limbs. It was definitely badger-like, possibly a raccoon. It was black and shriveled, but there were messy patches of vibrant green showing on its mangy legs and tail. One of the eyes was missing, but the remaining one glowed bright green, casting eerie shadows in front of it as it scooted along.

Almost as soon as I caught sight of it, I heard Derek's arrow hiss free of the bow. I couldn't see it as it arced through the forest, but I knew when it struck the animal. A high-pitched shriek split the night air, abruptly cut off as the animal's life ended.

"Good sh-" I began, but stopped when Derek lifted a hand.

"Do you hear that?" he whispered.

"The ringing in my ears?" I raised an eyebrow. "Yeah, I do. I forgot how loud Cursed can-" I stopped speaking with a gasp as he whirled around and gripped my wrist, his jaw clenched.

"Quiet. Listen." His gaze lifted above mine, scanning the forest behind me.

I pressed my lips together and listened. I heard the soft rustling of the limbs around us, I heard Derek breathing, I heard my heart thumping in my chest, its beat irregular from the new spark of fear that was threading through me.

"Do you hear it?" he asked, and I shook my head. His brow twitched, and he opened his mouth to say something when a loud crash sounded in the distance.

"I heard *that*."

"It came from the town," he was already hurrying towards the edge of the balcony, to one of the branches he could swing down from. "Stay here. Keep watching."

"No way!" I set my crossbow and quiver down and followed him as he slung his longbow over his back and started to climb down. He scowled at me, but didn't argue as we both descended to the forest floor and took off at a run, heading back towards Hazelwood Inn so we could retrieve our dragons.

As we came closer, though, I realized it wouldn't matter, because the commotion was coming *from* Hazelwood Inn. My heart leapt into my throat as we ran, and I could feel my pulse beginning to race beneath my skin, alive with eirioth awakened by my rising panic.

We sprinted out of the trees and down the road, rounding a wide bend as the Inn came into view. Derek and I both stopped suddenly, but mine was more of a stumble, and he caught me against him as I gasped.

The entire dragon stable was on fire, pieces of timber cracking and falling into the blaze. Pieces had been torn off and strewn about, and some of the windows of the inn itself were broken. Ash and embers hovered in the smoke-filled air, and standing in the middle of it all were two figures, one old and stooped, the other young and tall.

"Finnian," I whispered as I caught a bright flash of light from the flames reflecting off the silver chain he wore around his neck. My eyes flew to the burning stable. "No."

"How did the fire start?" Derek was trying to walk forward, but I was gripping his arm so tightly, and my legs refused to move, so he didn't manage more than a few sluggish steps.

"*Finnian*!" I shouted, and his head lifted, spinning in our direction. I couldn't see his eyes from this distance, but I know he saw us. He yelled something, but I couldn't make out his words over the roar of the fire.

"Let's go, we can get to them." Derek gripped my wrist and pulled me along. I stumbled after him, my free hand clenching into a fist as we ran.

There was a small wedge of rock that stuck out the side of the road, and there was a gap between the fire there. It was unbearably hot, and I could feel drops of sweat forming and sliding down the back of my neck as Derek dragged me past the walls of fire. We wound through it like a maze, trying to keep below the smoke and away from the hungry flames.

"Rura!" we came up on Finnian and Walter so fast I didn't realize we'd found them until Finnian's arms crushed me in a hug.

"Hi," I squeaked, wriggling out of his grasp. I looked up and saw that his hair was in complete disarray, there were smudges of soot and ash all over his face, and his eyes were shining with unshed tears. I knew without asking what that meant, and I gave him another quick hug before I turned back to Derek.

"Where is he?" was the first question from his lips, and I watched Finnian expectantly.

"Still in the stable," he replied, his voice strained. I could see his lower lip trembling slightly.

"How did the fire start?" I asked, trying to keep my voice steady. I knew Finnian was upset, and that upset me. I knew why he was upset, and that upset me. But despite that, I was sure what I was most upset about was the fact I still hadn't seen Sycamore or Gamma, and Sycamore had been inside the stable when Derek and I had left for the night watch. Was she still in there?

"Elixir started getting antsy, so I got up to see what he wanted," Walter shouted over the fire. I could see him flicking his wrist every now and then, and the flames would warp and bend away from us.

"And?" Derek prompted.

"He's not Elixir anymore." Walter's gaze flicked apologetically to Finnian, but he was looking away. I felt my gut knot with fear. "He knocked my lantern out of my hand and it broke. That's what started the fire. I got out of there fast with Honeysuckle, and Sycamore got out on her own. Gamma's taken them into town to find more help for the fire, but it's still not safe . . ." he looked back at the burning stable, and now I could see why.

Inside, thrashing behind the flames, a great black figure was screeching and clawing and flailing about, trying to find its way out of the fire. There was a good chance it was blind, or it didn't have any eyes at all. That was an advantage for us. A disadvantage was the fact that this was a dragon, and it was much, much larger than any other Cursed beast anyone had ever faced.

A quiet sob escaped me as I caught a brief flash of the familiar silhouette of Elixir. The angles of his beak, the curve of his neck, the flare of his broad wings. For a moment, it was him, bright and orange and as daft as ever. And then the illusion was gone; the flames died down, and I saw a sickly green glowing vibrantly beyond the red.

"Is he . . . is it-" I felt like my heart was going to leap out of my chest. I could hardly hear anyone speak over its thundering beat and the roaring fire.

"Completely." Walter shook his head and squinted at the flaming building. "It worked so fast . . . it had hardly been a couple hours since I'd last checked in on him."

"Why is there no *water*?" Derek yelled, glaring at the fire around us as if that would diminish it.

"It's coming," Walter snapped at him, flexing his hand and shoving it towards the fire. The nearest flames hissed and pressed into the dirt, vanishing in a wisp of smoke, but they were quickly replaced by more. Walter cursed.

"From the townspeople?" I gasped, looking back at the stable. "But . . . it's too dangerous, with him . . . with-" I sucked in a sharp breath. "It's not safe for them here."

"We'll take care of him first, then," Finnian had regained control of his features, but even though his jaw no longer quivered and his brows were set, I could still see the pain in his eyes.

"We need to get him out here," Derek looked around us. The fire wasn't spreading very fast, since the grass here was thin, with hard dirt and stone beneath, but it was tall and strong, and it took a lot of work from our fire-manipulation to bend it into the ground and extinguish it. By the time we managed it, new flames had sprung to life in its place.

"How do we do that? I don't think he can see." I shoved my palm out towards a reaching tongue of fire. The fire was like a part of me, except it wasn't. It was connected to the eirioth within my blood, and I felt that connection grow tight. I reached out and seized control of the fire, and as soon as I clenched my fist I felt the spark of the fire let go, and the flame curled away into the air.

"We'll get his attention," Derek lifted his bow and knocked an arrow. "Clear the smoke for a second. I need a clear shot."

Walter and I stepped forward, and I took a deep breath, ignoring the tickle in the back of my throat from the smoke. I reached out for that invisible tether of the fire, gripping it tightly. The fire was big and it was growing. It was alive and moving, fighting to get away from me, but never quite succeeding. Controlling and vanquishing small parts of it was different from moving larger amounts, but with Walter's help I could do it. I felt his power working alongside mine as I pushed the fire to the right. Walter pushed it to the left. Sweat broke out along my arms, but I didn't let my focus waver. Fire-manipulation was easier than fire-conjuring, but it still sapped up your energy. It pulled it away slower, bit by bit, and in some ways that was even more exhausting than the consistent drain from fire-conjuring.

As soon as the fire had been moved enough, I heard the *twang* of Derek's bow being fired. I saw a glimpse of the arrow as it rushed through the smoke, leaving a trail of cleared air behind it, then it vanished into the stable. I don't know where it struck him, but I heard Elixir's roar of fury, then the crashing and snapping of wood as he whirled around and charged towards us.

When he jumped out of the wreckage of the stable, I couldn't contain a muffled sob. My concentration broke and the fire flared back to life, but it didn't matter, because seconds later Elixir pommeled through the flames, stamping most of it down to ashes as he stumbled onto the road in front of us.

He was hardly recognizable. The aquamarine eyes were gone completely, replaced with hollow sockets. His once colorful feathers were black and ashen, frail and falling from him with every step. Patches of bare skin were revealed in places like his shoulder and haunches, glowing bright green and flecked with silver. Black and green sludge oozed from his flesh, falling onto the ground and unveiling bones and tendons.

It was a sickening sight, made a hundred times worse by the fact that I knew him. Or, I had known him once. He wasn't the same dragon anymore. He wasn't Elixir. He wouldn't recognize me or Finnian, or even Sycamore or Honeysuckle. He was too far gone. He was Cursed.

I pulled my sword free of its sheath on my back as Derek knocked another arrow to his bowstring. I could see where his previous one had struck, lodging into Elixir's left shoulder.

My weapon was comfortable in my hand, familiar and easy to manage. The problem wasn't with the blade, but me. I could feel the hesitation in my hand, in the way I gripped the handle. I wasn't sure I could bring myself to harm my brother's eirioth dragon, much less kill him. Could Finnian do that? Could Walter? I wondered if even Derek had the strength to kill a dragon.

"Watch out!" I felt a hand grip my arm and tug me sideways just before Elixir's black claws raked through the air where I'd stood. I yelped as I knocked into Finnian, who quickly twisted my arm to avoid getting impaled on my sword.

"What should-" I shrieked and ducked as I saw another claw swipe coming at us, and Finnian did the same. "What should we do?" I finished as we stood up again. Elixir couldn't see, but his ears were swiveling all around, following our shouting voices and shuffling feet.

"Kill him," Derek yelled in reply, firing another arrow. It hit Elixir in the chest, but not near his heart. "But don't get yourself killed." He grunted as he dove to the side, avoiding a screeching Elixir's beak as it snapped shut dangerously close to him.

"I don't-" I panted, looking sidelong at my brother. "Can . . . can we? Can you?" I could feel my hands shaking, feel my legs begin to tremble. In the distance, I heard loud voices coming our way, and the faint sound of beating wings. The townspeople were coming. Elixir had to be down before they arrived.

"I have to, Rura." Finnian drew a dagger from his belt, ignoring the sword on his back. His gaze was set forward, locked on the thrashing dragon. Flecks of black and green flesh and feathers splattered and drifted down around us, and I shuddered as a spot of it landed on my boot toe.

"What can I do to help?" I asked, fully aware of the quake in my voice. At this point, I was sure there was nothing either of us could do to avoid the emotions warring inside of us. I could still see the tears glistening in his eyes, and I wondered how he kept them at bay. Mine flowed freely down my cheeks; I couldn't even remember when I'd started crying.

"Distract him. You and Derek — watch out — get him down," we ducked to the side again. "Have Walter keep the other people back until then. I'll handle the rest. Go!" he shoved me roughly in the direction of Derek, and I stumbled over to him. He caught my shoulder and hefted me up to my feet, pulling me out of the way just as Elixir's claw smashed down onto the ground.

"What's the plan?" he asked, and for a moment I was furious with him. Here I was, crying and shaking and trying not to lose my mind as my brother and his dragon tried to kill each other, and Derek was speaking as if this was an everyday occurrence.

Like he had no emotion. But that wasn't why I was furious. I was furious because I envied him.

In all the time I'd known him, we had shared a similar grief. We'd shared the same pain, the same memory of watching someone we loved being torn apart by something Cursed. I was still scarred, still afraid, still hurt. But Derek was different. He could separate his emotions from the rest of his mind for certain periods of time, only coming back to them when it was safe, when he was alone and could go unguarded. I wanted that power. I yearned for that separation.

"Get him down," I cried, tightening my grip on the sword. "Get him down, and let Finnian finish him."

"I can do that. Distract him." Derek rolled to the side and bounded back to his feet while drawing the bowstring back as Elixir turned again, hearing the sound of our voices.

For a moment, I didn't move. I couldn't. Then my instincts kicked in. All that training with Finnian rushed into my mind, and I started to look at Elixir in a new light. He wasn't Elixir anymore. He was an enemy, and he was a threat to my home and my family. He was a threat to me.

I slid to the side, jogging around until I was near his wounded shoulder. Green slime slid from the wound the arrow had created, pooling on the ground and smearing across the dragon's talons. It wasn't exactly a slick substance, thicker than blood, but it wasn't sticky, and with the right force, one could easily slip on it.

Darting up close, I swung my sword. Elixir was still tracking Derek's movements, turning his head in time with his steps, so he didn't notice me until my blade struck him in the wing. The metal sliced through feathers and bit into bone, tearing away an entire chunk of his wing. Elixir screamed in pain, lashing out with his talon, but I yanked my sword free and leapt away.

At the same time, another of Derek's arrows found its mark in the dragon's neck. Tossing his head, Elixir stumbled into the ground, rolling furiously and lashing out with his claws. The next few moments were a blur.

I vaguely remember Finnian darting forward, dagger in hand, tears flowing down his face. I closed my eyes, refusing to watch, but I could still hear it. The strangled crying of the dragon, the beating of his wounded wings, and then, finally, silence.

5
SAKURA

*T*his settled it. I had been fighting with myself over what I would do for the past few days, but the battle with Elixir had been what won.

After the townspeople had put out the fire, everyone had gathered in a circle around the limp form of the eirioth dragon. Only five came close: Finnian, curled over the dragon's head, crying softly; me, crouched at his shoulder, my own body shaking with tears; Derek, standing just behind us with his bow at the ready; and Walter and Gamma standing uncertainly beside us, looking down at the dragon sadly.

With the fire gone and smoke slowly curling from the damp remains of the dragon stable, it was dark again. Dawn was still several hours away, and the only light came from the dancing flames in lanterns or cupped over the palms of other eirioth-mages. That, and the still faintly glowing green ooze that coated Elixir's onyx feathers.

"Let's go," I whispered to Finnian, my fingers tightening on his shoulder. His only response was a weak shake of his head. I tried not to look at the wound in Elixir's neck, the long black gash drawn by Finnian's dagger. It was hard, though, because out of the entire monstrous body the Curse had given him, that wound was the most eye-catching, pouring thick black and green blood, pulsing and undulating with a life of its own. It made me sick to the stomach.

That was what had won me over. That sick feeling, that urge to turn away and heave up the contents of my belly. It had driven the point home: something had to be done to stop the Curse, and I was the one to do that something. I stood up and wiped the awful grime from my hands, lifting my gaze to look first at Derek, then at Gamma and Walter. There was a light of recognition in Derek's eyes, one of understanding in Walter's, and one of horror in Gamma's. I knew all of them knew what I was going to do, and I wouldn't let any of them stop me.

Turning on my heel I marched back towards the Inn, untouched by the flames, but still marked in other ways. Windows had been blown inwards, and there were four pale stripes on the wood of the front porch railing, showing where Elixir's angry claws had struck it. The windows could be repaired, but the entire porch would have to be torn down and rebuilt to remove the claw marks.

As I stepped up and into the inn, I heard someone following me. Without turning back, I knew who it was, but I didn't stop. I went up the stairs, all the way to the top floor, and made my way into my bedroom. I had few belongings: a few spare changes of clothes, tools to care for my sword, and my bedroll for travel. It wouldn't take me long to pack everything up.

"Sakura," Gamma stepped into the room after me, but I didn't look up as I grabbed my rucksack and began to throw things in.

"You can't stop me." I swiped my drying tears off my cheeks with the back of my hand, stuffing my pillow into the sack. "I'm going to do this. I have to."

"It's too dangerous," I felt her hand on my back, but I shook my head and pulled away, reaching for a pair of pants.

"*This* is too dangerous, Gamma," I looked up at her then, ignoring the pinch in my chest as I saw the tears brimming in her eyes. "You saw what just happened. Finnian *killed* Elixir. He killed him, because if he didn't Elixir would have killed us all. What if Elixir isn't the first? What if there will be others?" my voice hitched, and I clenched my jaw. "I can't watch my home torn apart by the Curse. I've seen it tear apart families and animals and relationships, but I will not let it destroy everything. I'm done hiding and pretending like I'm doing something by shooting little things that sneak up during the night!" I cinched the rucksack closed and paused, letting out a heavy sigh. "I can't, Gamma. Don't you see? I have to do something, or nothing will change."

"People are out there trying to stop this *every day*, Sakura. People have been studying the Curse for years, hunting and searching and hoping for a breakthrough, but they have made no progress. Why do you believe-"

"Maybe it won't make a difference." I cut her off, my jaw clenching. "Maybe anything I do won't help, but I have to *try*. I'm not doing enough here. I'm standing by and letting my world be torn apart, and I can't stand to see it. I need to feel like I'm *doing* something."

We were both silent after that. I sniffled, gripping the strap of my rucksack, unwilling to meet her eyes. She stood there, shivering, more quiet than I'd ever heard her. Outside, I could hear raised voices and the loud *crack* of breaking timber. At last, I heard her voice, regretful but firm.

"I know, Sakura. I don't like seeing it either. But you can't *leave*. Where will you go? What will you do that nobody else already has?"

"I'll do what has to be done!" I looked up at her, hearing the desperation in my voice. "I'll do whatever it takes to get rid of the Curse. I'll find a way. I'll start . . . I'll start in . . ." I paused, racking my mind. Where *would* I go? The memories of the conversation I'd sat it on between Derek and his friends returned to my mind. "The Evershifting Forest." I finished. "I'll start there. I'll find out where to go next."

"The Forest?" Gamma shook her head, her fists clenching at her sides. "No. I won't let you go there. You'll be killed! The Cursed aren't the only thing you'll have to worry about in there — there are smiths and raptors and runeboars and who knows what else!" she reached out and grasped my hand. "You can't go in there, Sakura, or you'll be killed."

"What other choice do I have?" I pulled my hand free, taking a shaky breath as I lifted my rucksack up over my shoulder. "I have to give it a shot." I waited a breath to make sure she understood, then stepped forward and wrapped her in a tight hug. "I love you, Gamma."

"I love you too, Sakura." Her frail shoulders trembled as I held her, and I bit my lip, trying not to cry again.

"Tell Finnian I love him, too."

"You won't tell him yourself?" she pulled back, holding me at arm's length. I shook my head.

"He'd only try to keep me back. Please, Gamma, promise me you'll look after him?" I swallowed, my head spinning. Was I really doing this? Was I really going to leave Finnian in this state? It would only hurt him more, but the pain wouldn't last. When I came back, everything would be better, and there would be less hurt overall. For everybody. I was doing the right thing.

"Of course," she placed her hand on my cheek, searching my eyes. I tried to put on a brave face, but I wasn't sure that I was successful. "Be careful, my love."

"Always." I leaned forward and kissed her cheek, then ran out of my room, down the stairs, and out of the inn, stopping only to grab a pack with food. I had to run, because if I walked, I was afraid I might break down and start sobbing, crawling my way back to her and curling into her arms. I couldn't do that. Now was not a time for weakness.

Outside, a crowd had gathered. I recognized several of the merchants from farther inland, and I was mildly surprised to see that Duke Ferin was there as well. The dukes were the mayors of their respective towns, and Ferin was rarely seen outside his temple. Apparently, the news of a Cursed dragon was exciting enough to draw even the most secluded out of their hiding places.

There were eirioth dragons around as well. Some of them wore expensive saddles, others were bedraggled and scruffy. All of them looked frightened, including three familiar ones standing near the edge of the throng.

I hurried over to them, shouldering my way past anxious townspeople, all of them muttering things under their breath. I heard curses, worried mumblings, and worst of all, comments about Finnian. They said he was a foolish boy, or that he shouldn't be sitting so close to that "wretched creature". Couldn't they see what it was? Were they so daft they couldn't recognize the form of an eirioth dragon? Had their fear of the Curse torn away any scrap of their compassion for other living things?

I resisted the urge to yell at them, staying quiet and hiding beneath my rucksack until I came up beside Sycamore, Honeysuckle, and Bear. All three of them were stamping their feet and throwing anxious looks towards Elixir's body and the scorched ground. I could still feel a connection to the places where the fire had burned the longest, still trying to reach up and set the world ablaze.

"And just where are you going?" I grimaced at the voice. Two sets of footsteps sounded in my ears, and I looked up to see Derek and Walter watching me.

"The Evershifting Forest." I knew there was no point in lying. If Derek hadn't already guessed where I'd been headed, he would have soon enough.

"Absolutely not," Walter reached forward to keep me from mounting Sycamore. Somewhat to my surprise, she willingly stepped behind him.

"I have to." I shot back.

"Not alone," Derek growled, looking up at Bear. I shook my head.

"You're not coming with me."

"Why not?"

"I need you here. You have to stay and take care of Finnian and Gamma."

"Walter can help with that."

"Don't sign me up for things without my consent, boy," Walter spat, but I knew he wouldn't mind. Not when it came to this. He would always help take care of Gamma, and with Finnian in such a state, I knew he'd help with him, too.

"Please, don't fight with me on this," I turned my head to look at Finnian, barely visible through the crowd. He was still huddled over Elixir, only now he was huddled there alone, surrounded by the gawking crowd. "I have to know you'll take care of them. I can't leave them behind with nobody to keep them safe."

"Finnian is here," Derek pressed. "And who will go with you to keep *you* safe?"

"Finnian can do nothing, not like that," my breath hitched as I gestured feebly in my brother's direction. Derek didn't bother to look, only stared into my eyes and waited for me to answer his question. "I can take care of myself. And Sycamore will be with me."

"No, she won't," Walter jabbed a finger at the limp form of Elixir's body. "While you were inside planning on running off, the Duke started talking with some of his officials. I've heard muttering of using the War Cells to keep the dragons contained." He glared in the direction of the wiry Duke, and I followed the look, unease roiling in my stomach. "The Curse being able to corrupt them makes them too dangerous to keep-"

"Elixir wasn't like the others." I cut him off. "He was . . . younger. More distracted. Maybe he was just weaker than them. Maybe he wasn't in his right mind. There's no proof the Curse can really corrupt any of the other dragons. I mean, none of the others have black spots sprouting on them, do they?" I knew I was speaking out of pure hope at this point. There was no proof the other dragons could fall victim to the Curse, but it was too dangerous to leave them out in the open like this if there was even the smallest chance it could happen.

"The War Cells are our best bet at keeping Carlore safe," Walter went on, as if I hadn't spoken. "Besides, if the Curse really is contagious, it's most likely spread through the air. If the dragons are locked up in the Cells, there's a better chance it won't reach them. Not only will we be safer, but they will be too." He pressed his lips together and gave me a sorrowful look. "I know you want to help, Lady Sakura, but the most you can do to help right now is by setting a good example and letting the Duke do his job. He will help keep us safe, and he will send word to the rest of Carlore to help keep *everyone* safe. Do your part, and follow along." A long silence stretched between the three of us. My heart squeezed as I looked up at Sycamore.

I knew I had to do this, no matter what. Even without a dragon, I knew I still had the strength within me to find a way to destroy the Curse. The problem was finding a way to leave Sycamore behind. Could I really let them take her down into the War Cells? Would she be chained up down there?

The War Cells were ancient, and they hadn't been used in hundreds of years. Inhabited by prisoners of war during the Havoc Ages, the War Cells were massive, located deep underground and only accessed by a thin staircase that ran along the side of the King's Scar. It used to be heavily guarded, with booby traps and sentry stations hardly ten feet apart, but it had since been abandoned. I had never been down there, but I'd heard enough stories to tell me I didn't want to see it.

"It doesn't matter." I said softly. "It won't change the fact that the Curse is changing. Someone has to do something, or we'll all die."

I didn't wait to see what either of them said after that. I stepped forward and kissed Sycamore on the beak, then adjusted the way my rucksack rested on my shoulder and set off into the Eirioth Wood. It was still dark out, but dawn would come soon, and I knew I could keep myself safe and warm if need be. Eirioth pumped through my veins, invigorated by the heady emotions that coursed through me. I didn't know how long that energy would last, but I was going to take advantage of it and let it take me as far as it could on my journey.

I wasn't surprised to hear someone following close behind me, but I wasn't about to argue with him while we were still in earshot of the townspeople. I waited until we were well away from them before wheeling about to glare into his dark eyes.

"I'm not letting you go alone." His voice was firm, and I knew he expected me to see no point in arguing. I saw plenty of point in arguing, and I was going to make sure he knew it.

"I'm not letting you come with me." I tried to make my voice match his, but I didn't quite succeed. It didn't matter. I came close enough, and I could tell I got the point across. An aggravated scowl flicked across his features.

"You're going to get yourself killed if you go out on your own."

"I'll be fine. I need you to stay here with Finnian and Gamma. Please, Derek, you're the only person I trust with this," I clenched my jaw and tried to put all the emotion I could into my eyes. I had to make him understand. I needed him to stay behind. That, at least, gave him pause, but it only lasted for a moment.

"They can take care of themselves. And Finnian would kill me if he knew I'd let you go off alone." Derek furrowed his brow and crossed his arms, jutting his chin out stubbornly. I rolled my eyes.

"Not like this he wouldn't! He can hardly think straight. He just *killed* Elixir. Can you imagine what would happen to you if you had to drive a knife into Bear's throat?" I shook my head, trying and failing to keep the image of killing Sycamore out of my mind. Hot tears burned behind my eyes as I shoved the thought away. "He's not okay right now, and he needs someone to support him. I can't be there, so you have to. *Please*, Derek, I need you to help them."

He was quiet for a long time, his gaze level with mine, his expression unreadable. I wasn't sure how I felt right then. Angry, devastated, scared, maybe all of them. I couldn't even identify my own emotions, and it worried me. I had to be able to think clearly if I was going to enter the Evershifting Forest.

"Okay." He said finally, and my eyes widened. I hadn't actually expected him to agree to it. Had some part of me wanted him to come along? Maybe, but I knew I could never let that happen. It was more important he stayed behind to keep Gamma and Finnian safe.

"Okay," I breathed, running a thumb over my knuckles. "And . . . and you'll make sure Sycamore's taken care of?" I couldn't help but ask, even though I felt a little selfish in doing so.

"Of course." He took a deep breath, then pursed his lips, his guard temporarily let down. "Be careful, Sakura. Please. Finnian still needs his sister."

"I'll do my best." I promised, and before I could talk myself out of it, I threw my arms around his neck and hugged him. I'd never hugged him before, and it felt almost like a violation to do so now. But it also felt right. We were no longer stuck in that in-between space. He was my friend, and it was about time I started treating him like it.

"Goodbye, Sakura." He hugged me tight and then stepped back. I bit my lip to try and keep from crying.

"Goodbye, Derek." And then he was gone, disappearing into the trees as he ran back towards Hazelwood Inn and the wreckage of the dragon stables.

I didn't know if he looked back. I was already running in the opposite direction.

The Evershifting Forest was farther than I would have liked from the main towns of Carlore.

On any given day I would have explained that the distance was wonderful. It helped keep the towns safe. Most of the Cursed animals stuck to the seclusion of the Forest, rarely wandering farther than the Fruit Spring, and that kept all the humans well out of reach of their slobbering jaws.

Today, though, I wished it was right up next to the edge of Hazelnut. I wished it enveloped the entire Fruit Spring and crawled right up to the brink of the Scar's foreboding drop.

My trail took me north, around the outskirts of the Columns and towards the Fruit Spring. I tried to avoid any thoughts of how close that would bring me to Finnian and I's training glade. While there were plenty of bright memories of that place, the most recent ones stuck to my mind like hot tar, and I did my best to steer away from them if I could.

The gently rolling grass of the Columns appeared as a soft golden gray on my left as the sun rose steadily into the sky. My legs were already growing tired from the miles of ground I'd covered, but I wasn't about to slow down to rest. Early dawn was the time when lots of people started to let their guard down. They assumed that, because night had passed, they were safe from the Curse for another day. They ignored the fact that sunlight didn't affect Cursed beings at all, and there were reports of several hundred daytime attacks. I wasn't as ignorant, and I kept my eyes and ears alert, hands always braced above the handles of my weapons in case danger decided to show itself.

The Columns themselves could be seen in the distance, tall and watchful. They rose like thick, limbless tree trunks, their tops hidden in the early morning clouds. Ash gray and full of strange rivulets, nobody had ever identified the purpose of the Columns, but they had earned the fields tucked into the western corner of Carlore their name, and nobody had dared suggest they be cut down.

I kept a steady pace. I walked for a few hours, then stopped to catch my breath. I only stopped once to eat an apple and drink a bit of water, but it was a small breakfast, and I wasn't sure how long I could go before I needed more. I hoped to reach the Fruit Spring by then. It was a wonderful place, a popular location for romantic couples to spend time and the perfect spot for a mid-summer swim. The best part about it, though, wasn't the waterfalls or the chilly water or the hot ponds — although those were all wonderful — but the fruit trees. They wrapped around the Spring like a protective family, tall and thin and always full to bursting with fresh fruit. I could easily replenish my food supply there, although there was no telling how long the fruit might last.

As I traveled, time began to blur together. I wasn't even out there for very long, but with nobody to converse with, and not a lot to think about — actually there was plenty to think about, but I wasn't exactly in the mood to think about any of it — it was easy to lose track of time.

I walked for an entire day and several hours into the night, only stopping to catch my breath and snack on pieces of dried jerky, before I finally climbed high up into a purple-leafed eirioth tree and settled myself into a dark hollow hidden in its branches. It was a risk going to sleep when I didn't have anybody to watch my back, and the threat of Cursed raptors loomed in the back of my mind as I tried to get comfortable, but if I was being rational, it was important that I got some sleep, so I put the thoughts of Cursed beasts and night watchmen getting ripped apart out of my mind and tried to get some sleep.

Wherever I walked, and wherever I slept during the night, I felt like there were thousands of tiny bugs crawling over my skin. I couldn't escape the sensation that I was being watched or followed, that there was something murderous waiting for me in the darkness. The terror consumed my thoughts so much I nearly threw up. But I didn't. Because I had to try and stop this Curse, and that meant I had to try and get some sleep, despite my fears of the shadows.

In the end, I was successful, and I rose early in the morning to eat a tiny breakfast of shriveled prunes and chewy dried meat. I didn't have a lot left, but I knew I'd reach the Fruit Spring by evening, so I wasn't terribly worried.

On the bright side, I woke up with all my body parts attached and no sign of Cursed disturbance in the area. As long as I kept quiet, I shouldn't draw any unwanted attention to myself.

Starting to walk again that morning was harder than it had been the night before. Then, I'd been fueled by anger and fear and desperation. I'd had the sight of Finnian crying and Elixr's death to motivate me to take action. Now, I only had the memory of those sights. Not that it wasn't enough; of course it was. My throat felt like it was closing up whenever I thought of them, but that wasn't why I struggled to keep moving.

I was tired already. I was scared and alone and I was feeling impossibly helpless. What if everything Finnian had taught me wasn't enough to keep me safe out here? What if it was enough to keep me safe, but it wasn't enough to defeat the Curse? What if the source of the Curse wasn't even located in the Evershifting Forest, and I was just wandering around until I wandered too deep into a smith's den? The thoughts gnawed at my brain as I walked, constantly adjusting the way my rucksack rested on my shoulder as new spots began to ache along my back.

In the end, I managed to keep walking while I worried, and by nightfall I found myself meandering, whole and uneaten, between the wiry trunks of fruit trees. That was when I finally felt a little more at peace with everything. Maybe it was the soft, sweet aroma of peaches and plums, or the promise of juicy pears and crunchy apples that soothed my nerves, but I didn't really care to try and find out. As long as I wasn't shaking from terror, I was happy.

The trees around the Fruit Spring stretched out about half a mile away from the Spring itself, so I still had a good bit of walking to do before I could seek a new sleeping place among the boulders and rocks around the hot ponds, but I didn't mind.

The Eirioth Wood was a dark place at night. It was safe, for the most part, but there was the ever-present threat of Cursed creatures wandering into its boundaries and hiding in the thick cover the eirioth trees provided. Here in the borders of the Fruit Spring, everything seemed lighter, airier. Not many of the fruit trees were very climbable, and there weren't any good hiding places until you arrived at the Spring itself.

The Spring filled you with a sense of surety and confidence to walk through it, and I was grateful for that surety and confidence now as I struggled under the burden of my rucksack. It wasn't very heavy, considering how little was actually in it, but my feet ached and my legs ached and while I was at it I decided to go ahead and complain about the very faint but evident ache flowering between my shoulder blades.

The Fruit Spring came into view a short while later, and despite all the times I'd joyfully leapt from Sycamore's back into the depths of the water, I knew I'd never been happier to see it than I was now. The Fruit Spring was a huge pool of water, very deep and crystal clear. One side of it had large rocks and boulders surrounding it, almost a small mountain, and a waterfall cascaded from the highest point all the way to the Spring itself. Pooled in sizable divots throughout the rest of the boulders were the hot ponds, bubbling collections of water that burned hot enough to relax your muscles but not quite scald your skin off.

I left my rucksack tucked safely away at the base of one of the boulders and ate whatever remained of my food rations. It was dark out, and I was looking forward to getting some sleep. I climbed up the boulders until I found a not-quite-comfortable gap between two huge rocks where I could squeeze in for the night. Anything any bigger than a person wouldn't be able to reach me down there.

It was another dreamless night, but at least it was quiet. There were no signs of any Cursed beasts when I woke up except some fresh animal prints in the mud near the bank of the Spring, but it could've been from an uncorrupted creature just as well as a Cursed one.

I would have liked to stay at the Fruit Spring longer, but I knew I had to keep moving. My heart seemed to ache more with every step farther away from home, but I had no choice. If I was going to make a difference, I couldn't let myself get homesick only two days after leaving. I needed to be stronger than that.

That evening, I came close to the edge of the Fruit Spring. I'd eaten the fruit from my bag and only had a little bit left, but I was still surrounded by fruit trees, and until I left the Spring's borders, I would have no shortage of food. Unfortunately, the very next day I would be going beyond the Fruit Spring into the Evershifting Forest.

I'd only heard stories of the Forest, all of them from varying ages. The most recent ones were unpleasant, filled with grim details of Cursed bears and runeboars and wolves. Some of the ones written in old books had drawings depicting foul beasts with withered fur and taught skin and jagged bones. I knew several of them must have been exaggerated, but that knowledge did little to comfort me as I came up to the edge of the Fruit Spring.

The older stories of the Forest were much better, of course. It was an ancient place of powerful magic. Some said it had a life in and of itself, that it was a breathing being that had strong magical powers. I wasn't sure what I believed, but there were definitely consistent facts I knew were much more likely to be true.

The Forest had earned its name because of the bizarre phenomenon that occurred within its boundaries. It was a dense forest, but what kind of forest it was could never be told. Sometimes it was a splendid summery forest, filled with towering oaks and berry bushes with sunlight streaming through the gaps in the canopy above. Other times, it could be a pleasant autumnal forest of aspen and birch trees, with wild pumpkins and ivy crawling over rocks, gentle breezes rolling through the air and leaves falling delicately to the softened earth below. I'd also heard stories of the entire forest blanketed in snow, the tops of its pine trees invisible in the gusts of snowy wind that blew through the air. The point was that the forest was constantly changing. You could go to sleep in a hot, muggy patch of dry and brittle grass and wake up shivering and covered in frost.

I stopped for the night before I could see the treeline of the Forest. I knew it was going to be a little dangerous sleeping so close to the place I suspected to be riling up the Curse, but I didn't have much of a choice unless I wanted to wander in in the middle of the night, which I most certainly did not. So I found the low branches of a pear tree to nestle into for the night.

It passed without issue, and when I woke up I realized I'd slept in later than I'd intended. My luck with the Cursed had been good so far, but who knew how long that would last. I had to pick up my pace once I was in the Evershifting Forest.

I came up to it hardly thirty minutes after I set off from my sleeping place. It was in a spring-like state, and I felt my jaw drop when I saw it. The trees were tall and spindly, pale grays and browns with bright green leaves that crowned the trees in great flowering caps. Covering the ground was soft grass that rose just above my ankles, and there were wildflowers. *So many* wildflowers. They were all sorts of colors, vibrant blues and yellows and faded purples and pinks. Some were tall, others rounded, several pointy. The sheer variety made me dizzy. I'd never known so many kinds of flowers existed.

The trees weren't clustered too close together, and I could see quite a way into the Forest. Bright sunlight flowed through the space like a golden current, carrying with it pale butterflies and the distant sounds of wildlife: birds chirping merrily, the burbling of a stream, the faint call of an animal. It was truly magical.

My moment of awe was short-lived as I realized any animal I might come across could be Cursed. It was hard to focus on that thought, of course, with so much beauty surrounding me. The more steps I took into the Forest — trying to maintain a somewhat straight course — the harder it was to believe it could be home to such awful things. I'd always imagined the home of the Cursed to be a dark and foreboding place, full of shadow and decay and everything terrible.

This was splendid and happy and bright and exhilarating. Nothing Cursed and evil belonged here. And yet, there was no denying the fact that this was where the majority of the Carlore's Cursed animals came from.

I didn't see any animals for a little while, and when I did, I jumped at the sight of them. I'd seen birds and squirrels and other common animals around Carlore, but for some reason my mind didn't want to believe normal animals existed in the Evershifting Forest. To me, they all had to be Cursed and twisted and murderous. Not these big-eyed, fluffy rabbits that scurried out of my path or the cheerfully chirping birds overhead.

I spent half the day walking before I stopped to sit on a moss-covered log and eat an apple. I was tired already, and now I could feel doubt beginning to creep into the back of my mind.

What was I *doing*? The Evershifting Forest was massive, stretching over large portions of both Carlore and Brightlock. I didn't think anyone would arrest me or charge me with spying if I crossed the border, since I doubted anyone would be roaming through the Forest, but that was exactly the point. Nobody in their right mind would be marching into the Evershifting Forest to look for the Curse. It was insanity.

The Forest was so big, it would take me ages to trek through all of it, and I'd probably get all turned around and confused every other hour or so. By the time I made any real progress, I'd probably have been eaten by runeboars. I pondered this as I sat crunching on my apple, anxiously rubbing my knuckles. I was beginning to wonder if it had been wise to turn down Derek's offer of help. I knew I needed him to stay behind with Finnian and Gamma, but didn't I still need someone here to help *me*?

With a sigh I stood up and shrugged my rucksack higher onto my back. I had chosen this path, and I was going to see it through to the end. This was what needed to be done, and I'd find a way to do it if it took the rest of my life.

I looked up at the clear blue sky above and tried to determine which direction was north. The center of the Evershifting Forest was in Brightlock, and I figured that was as good a place as any to start.

A rustling in the grass to my left made me break my concentration. My head whipped around, but there was nothing between the tall tree trunks. I turned in a slow circle, my eyes scanning everywhere. I could feel my eirioth hovering just beneath the surface of my skin, itching to be set free, but I kept it back. The last thing I needed to do was burn down the Evershifting Forest. That thought made me pause. Maybe if I burned it all down, that would eliminate all the Cursed animals along with it. But despite its gruesome reputation, I didn't think I could bring myself to destroy a place of such beauty and magic.

"Is someone there?" I asked, squinting at the swaying grasses. Part of me sort of hoped it was Derek, or even Finnian, challenging my order to stay behind and following me anyway. The other part of me, the rational part, knew that was unlikely.

A sound from above caught my attention, and I lifted my gaze to see a figure huddled in the thin branches of a tree, splayed awkwardly over the limbs that trembled beneath its weight. I couldn't contain a gasp when I saw it, stumbling half a step away as my hand instinctively lifted to the sword on my back.

It was a raptor, maybe as big as I was, covered in sparkling green scales. Horns sprouted like antlers from its head, but they were made of wood, with little leaves sprouting along them. Moss and grass grew in shaggy patches across its back and shoulders, trailing along until it ended on the raptor's whip-thin tail. It didn't *look* very menacing, but I knew better than to believe the somewhat docile appearance. A few flowers blooming across scales or soft amber eyes weren't going to convince me to let my guard down. I'd heard too many stories of the viciousness of raptors.

As my gaze locked with the raptor's, I drew my sword. I didn't want to summon eirioth yet, since it would burn the grass and the trees faster than I could get away from it, but I could feel it pulsing beneath my skin, scratching at my resolve and trying to get free.

The raptor seemed to sense the uneasiness that spread through me, and it hopped off the tree, letting the air catch beneath its moss-covered wings to slow its descent. It was closer to me than I wanted it to be, but I didn't really have any choice but to be close. I could never outrun it, so the only choice was to kill it.

I'd killed my fair share of Cursed animals on the night watch, but those had all been with a crossbow. It would be different driving my blade into it. It would be harder. Finnian had told me that. Shooting and stabbing were not only different in terms of execution, but they were also different in how they affected people and things. Taking a deep breath, I shuffled sideways, away from the log I'd sat on. The raptor tracked my movements carefully, cocking its head and trilling curiously as I circled it. Once the log was to its back, I lunged.

Raptors couldn't breathe fire. Most raptors didn't even have scales that protected them from much of anything; but they were fast. One moment the tip of my blade was driving forward toward the raptor's heart, and the next I was staring at empty air. The raptor had simply vanished. Except it hadn't, because I could hear it doubling back somewhere behind me to attack my back.

I twirled at the last moment, my sword lifting, and I screamed in surprise at how close the raptor was, mid-flight and heading directly for my head with claws outstretched. My sword sliced into one of its legs, nearly severing the bottom half completely. With a screech of pain, the raptor veered to the side and landed awkwardly on three legs a few feet away.

I moved again, my sword arcing down towards the raptor's wing. It twisted away, and my blade chopped through the end of its tail. Another screech echoed around us as it limped away, hissing at me and baring its yellowed fangs.

I groaned, jabbing my sword at it again. I caught it in the side, opening a wound in its belly. It trailed blood through the clearing now, dragging itself through the grass and watching me with frantic golden eyes.

Just put it out of its misery, I scolded myself. It couldn't do much to me now. I stepped forward again, and the raptor flinched away. For a moment, I paused. It was weak and injured and mewling, and I was going to kill it. I had to kill it, because if I didn't, it would kill me.

But would it? With the injuries I had given it, there was a chance it could recover, but nowhere near fast enough to do any damage to me. My hesitation was all the raptor needed. It pushed itself forward, good claw reaching out, and I felt its talons rake across the surface of my shin. I yelped and rammed my sword into its head. The blade sank through its skull and drove itself into the soft earth beneath the raptor.

"Stupid," I muttered, yanking the blade free and looking down at my legs. The fabric had three clean cuts in it, and I could see blood trickling out of shallow scratches in my skin. None of them were bad, but they stung, and I looked up to see if I could find a stream to clean them.

When I located one, I sat on the bank and gently treated the wound, trying to figure out where I was. I knew it was hopeless, though. With the Forest being able to not only change its season, but also its structure and layout, there were no landmarks or memorable paths I could use to reorient myself. I would just have to keep walking until I found the other side, then turn around and head for the center again.

With a sigh I started seeking out a place to camp for the night. It was going to be a long journey.

6
KSEGA

Jessie's caravan was packed with all the goods and supplies we'd need for our vacation.

She insisted I stop calling it that, but there wasn't another word for it. We were getting away from home, finding ways to enjoy ourselves, and experiencing completely different cultures. That counted as a vacation to me.

"Seagulls, sea wraiths, and smelly fishermen do not count as a different culture," she had commented as we rolled through the streets of Rulak.

"But Coldmon does."

"The *capital* of Coldmon does, as do the surrounding towns. Famark is almost like a different kingdom in and of itself." Jessie reminded me.

"Still, it's different from Wisesol, and I'll take it." That had ended the discussion, and I leaned back with my arms propped behind my head as Tooth and Dagger pulled us along to the rendezvous spot on the road between Rulak and Lourak.

We were meeting our crew there. The captain had needed some parts for repair, crafted in Rulak. His crewmembers had retrieved those parts and began their journey back to the Port by the time word reached them that we were joining them on their trip to Famark. They had stopped on the road and made camp to wait for us to catch up.

We met them a few hours after night had fallen, and quickly became acquainted. Only ten of them had been sent to retrieve the parts, and the other nineteen members of their crew had stayed behind to keep an eye at the Port.

The first mate was there, a fellow named Chap. None of them gave last names, and Jessie and I didn't give ours. Chap was very tall and well-built, the kind of man you respect before he's even earned it, but the effect was slightly diminished by his wavy red hair. His personality — what I could see of it, anyway — was very different from his outward appearance. He liked to laugh and talk. A lot.

The other nine were lower-ranking members of the ship, all of them looking pretty cut-throat and usually missing some part of their person.

Old Hank was missing an eye and wore a worn down leather patch that left a streak of matted silver hair across his head. Kaden only had one ear, and he wore a bandana to cover the ugly scar. Ritch was missing two of his dark fingers, and didn't bother to elaborate on why, although Chap told us it was because of a previous job they'd done involving some cruel pirates and a chest full of diamonds. From the expression on Ritch's face, I knew better than to believe him.

Bubba — whose name wasn't actually Bubba, but that was what everybody called him because, according to Chap, nobody knew his real name anyway — was an absolute bear of a man with arms the size of watermelons. Or, *an* arm the size of a watermelon; he only had one.

Wendell, whom they all called Wendy, was missing a hand, and there was a shiny curved hook attached to the stump of his wrist. He seemed to be in a jolly mood all the time, his fluffy blond hair bouncing upon his head whenever he moved, a light in his emerald eyes. Tuar and Paul were brothers, both of them peg-legs. Gawain and Laurence were the last two. Gawain didn't have a tongue, and somehow communicated to the other shipmates with his hands. Laurence . . . well we didn't really know what was missing on Laurence. Chap just told us something was missing, and we were probably better off not knowing what it was.

Overall, it wasn't exactly the most welcoming group of people we'd ever met. Luckily, Jessie and I were used to being the odd ones out, so we kept to ourselves and spent most of our time in or around her caravan. The night passed with little excitement, and early the next morning we were rolling along on the road. Chap drove his own caravan, filled with the parts they'd needed, but not all the shipmen rode on it, and our pace was slowed so they could walk with us.

As we traveled, Chap regaled us with exciting tales from the sea. He spoke very fondly of their ship, *The Coventry*, and about the treacherous waters it had been through. Even though the Great Lakes were really the only place one could sail, since the Endless Sea was not only unreachable without falling to your death, but there was also no way to get you back up to safety, Chap made it sound like they had sailed all over the world, even beyond Horcath, although no one had heard of places other than our own continent.

We heard about encounters with dirty-handed pirates, blood-thirsty sea wraiths, vengeful merchants, and runaway kings. As Chap spoke, Wendy had sidled up beside Jessie's caravan and carefully interrupted to point out what actually happened.

"Just before the pirate captain lopped my head off, I kicked his legs out from beneath him, grabbed his sword, and flipped him overboard, where he was devoured by the swarm of sharks!" that would be Chap. Then Wendy would pitch in with,

"The ship was rocking so much that a bucket rolled into the pirate's legs and knocked him over. He hit his head and broke his nose on the ship rail, and the next lurch of the ship sent him over. He sank. We don't know if he was eaten by sharks. Chap was screaming the whole time, and a bit after that, too. Took a whole bottle of whiskey and some badly sung shanties to get him to shut up about it."

"-and right as the sea wraith got its jaws around me, I retrieved the harpoon from where it was wedged in his teeth and drove it into the roof of his mouth! He spat me right out, the bugger did. Sank into the deep blue never to rise again." Chap would continue.

"Peeler threw the harpoon to him, but he didn't catch it and it nearly fell into the water. It got caught in the wraith's teeth, and he was lucky enough to grab it. I'm pretty sure it survived." Wendy scratched the side of his nose with his hook disinterestedly. "Wouldn't surprise me if it didn't, though. Those things aren't too bright. Probably swam into a rock."

Ignoring him, Chap would excitedly go on to his next tale. The merchant one was definitely Jessie's favorite, because Chap went into great detail explaining the valuable dresses he sold. Chap declared they had stolen them and left without getting caught. Wendy explained that they had ended up having to dress up as women with the dresses to sneak past the guards, and they didn't get caught because the merchant selling the dresses was too busy trying to flirt with a wig-wearing Kaden to notice.

I preferred the story of the runaway king, where Chap told me they had sort of adopted an unsuspecting cabin boy without realizing who he was. By the time they figured out he was a king, they were like family, and the boy went on to lead his own transportation crew. Wendy whispered to us that the boy was in fact a forty-year-old grump that hurled insults at all of them, and he wasn't a king, but some duke from Carlore, running away to escape a needy wife. When they discovered who he was, they sailed him back to Carlore and all but chained him to an eirioth tree.

Whichever way it was told, a story was a story, and Jessie and I were happy to nod along and laugh where it was appropriate. Anything to keep our minds off our aching bums and the potential dangers of our journey across the Great Lakes.

We reached Lourak a little later than midday, rolling into the town warily. It was a beautiful place, but one I'd only been to a handful of times. The buildings were tall and white-washed, with colorful planter boxes on windowsills and beautiful designs on elegant windows. The exterior of the entire town was massive and alive and eye-catching, but the insides of the buildings were often of poor structural integrity. Light fixtures were scarce and small, and most furniture was broken in some way or another.

The people were similarly cloaked, being very beautiful outwardly. Most people here were tall or fit, and if they weren't, they made up for it in sheer beauty. I'd never seen someone I would refer to as ugly walking through Lourak, even if some of them had had marring tattoos or misshapen noses or unruly hair. At least, I'd never refer to their *looks* as ugly. On the inside, they were just about equal with a rabid sewer rat.

Cut-throats, thieves, murderers, you name it, there was always something evil lurking inside someone in Lourak. You could see it in the way they smiled, that glint of dark intent behind their eyes, the way their smile stretched just a little *too* wide, the way their gaze stuck to you until you disappeared down another street. It was an unsettling place to be, and I'd never liked spending time there. The sooner we got out and headed towards the Port, the better.

The crew of *The Coventry* seemed to feel differently. They walked along the streets with a sort of sure authority, swaggering and sneering and acting downright arrogant. Chap was in on it too, acting like some sort of escorted king atop the bench of his caravan. Jessie and I just kept our heads down and urged Tooth and Dagger along after them.

We took a small detour to grab some lunch — I wouldn't say the sandwiches made in Lourak made up for the awful crime that goes on around there, but they definitely come close — and we stocked up on rations for the journey at sea before finally steering our caravans towards the road leading to the Port. I could sense the relief in Jessie when we left the immediate borders of the capital town.

Coming back into the Port, I had my own worries. I hadn't been a stowaway on many ships, but I hadn't exactly been the most innocent being ever to walk on the planks of the docks. I must've come close to it, of course, considering the types of people that worked on ships and around the Port, but I had to at least be generous and count the crimeless stray dogs and seagulls.

The caravans couldn't be taken onto the docks themselves, since they were teeming with people and feet to run over. Ships bobbed in the gently lapping waves of the water, tall masts rising into the clear blue sky. My eyes quickly scanned the painted hulls for the *Sea Cloud*, but I didn't see it, and I felt my nerves settle just a little bit.

"That ship you were on isn't here, is it?" Jessie asked me as we started to help Chap and his men unload the caravans.

"Just checked. It's gone." I grunted as I hefted a crate of ship parts into my arms, following after Old Hank and Bubba as we marched towards *The Coventry*. It was impossible to miss among the mass of other ships.

Most of the ships were fishing boats and skiffs and cargo ships, crafted to transport goods from one place to another as fast as possible. They had two decks, and were relatively easy to man, only needing about fifteen to twenty men on board to manage it.

The Coventry was like no ship I'd ever seen before. It was massive, easily having three decks, plus a crow's nest and two separate cabins built on either side of the ship. Instead of the usual one mast, it had three, each with its own complicated rigging. A ferocious slate-wolf figurehead snarled at the ship's bow. It wasn't very hard to guess what it was.

"You sail on a *pirate ship*?!" I gawked at it, wide-eyed, as we followed the branch of the Port that led up to where *The Coventry* was docked. Beside me, I saw the usually grim-faced Ritch crack a grin.

"Just wait until you see the sleeping quarters." I would have asked him to explain, but he had gone ahead of me and boarded the ship already. After a moment of silent wonder, I followed him aboard.

We were loading the ship parts into the cargo hold, where Wendy explained the previous owners of the ship — pirates, by unspoken understanding — had kept all their precious loot with a fond wave of his hook. The space was surprisingly big, even after we'd loaded all the parts into it. As soon as they were all there, Peeler — a wiry man with scruffy gray hair in charge of repairing the ship when needed — began to go through them to find what he needed. Apparently there was some minor damage to the hull of the ship that he needed to tend to before we set sail.

That gave me and Jessie time to familiarize ourselves with *The Coventry* and the remaining nineteen members of the crew. It was a bit overwhelming, meeting so many new people so soon, and I was still struggling to put names to faces, but at least I remembered the names at all.

The first person we met was Peeler, but he didn't seem very interested in either of us, too focused on his work fixing the hull. That was fine by both Jessie and I. He didn't strike either of us as the most companionable person.

After that, Chap had introduced us to the second and third mates, one of whom turned out to be Chap's wife, Molly. She was a pretty woman, somewhere in her twenties with dark skin, raven-like hair and sharp black eyes. She wasn't very interested in us either, but she did give Jessie a warning to stay away from the youngest members of the crew if she knew what was good for her.

The third mate was Chap's younger brother, Thomas, a boy a little younger than me with coiled red hair that matched his brother's in color. He seemed a bit shy, but shared Chap's loud and obnoxious laugh.

The next person we met was the captain himself, a man named Howard. Again, no last names were given, and, again, Jessie and I were careful not to use ours. Captain Howard was a grim-faced man, but he didn't pay us much attention, just told us to stay away from any goods he was transporting and not get too attached to our quarters.

The rest of the crew was harder to tell apart. Molly was easy because she was a woman, and Chap and Thomas were the only red-heads aboard. Howard was tall, broad-shouldered, and intimidating. The rest of them were almost the same person, if you set aside the most obvious differences.

Some of them were easier to recognize. Wendy was the only one on board with a hook for a hand. Old Hank was the only one missing an eye, and he was easy to pick out, because the only other man with a patch, a fellow named James, was missing two. Bubba was the only one missing an arm. A younger boy named Davie was the only crewmate to go shirtless all the time, because, through some brutal incident, part of his back had been torn open, and the tips of two bones could be seen protruding from the since healed flesh, ripping through any shirt he tried to wear.

Everyone else was hard to distinguish. I could remember their names well enough, but I knew it would take me some time to call everyone the right thing.

Luckily I wasn't the only one having this problem, so Jessie and I were able to stand together awkwardly as everything was prepared for our departure. We even made it a game to see who could correctly name more of the crew.

Tooth and Dagger were bedded down in one of the small stables next to the Port, where they would stay for the next few days while Jessie and I were away. I could see Jessie was worried about leaving them there, so I did my best to reassure her that they would be just fine. In truth, I was more than aware of how ruthless and sneaky people around the Port could be, and while I didn't tell her that, I knew I wouldn't be surprised if we came back to see that the stallions were dead or stolen.

"Here we go!" a hand slapping me on the shoulder drew my attention to Chap, who had appeared beside us. Jessie and I were standing near the central mast of the ship, near the trap door that led to the sleeping quarters below.

"We're leaving?" I asked hopefully, and Chap grinned, revealing yellowed teeth.

"We're leaving. Look lively, people, we're off! Hopefully this won't be as bad as when we set sail from the docks of Match."

"What happened when you set sail from the docks of Match?" Jessie's eyes had widened, and I had to keep from rolling mine. I was surprised she had bought into most of Chap's stories until it had become apparent from Wendy's interruptions that they were embellished.

"Aye," Chap gave us a wild grin as the crew did things with ropes and sails. I knew nothing about ships, so I just watched out of mild curiosity. "Thieves tried to harpoon us as we pushed off, and immediately after that, a band of Cursed whales nearly flipped us over!" he laughed heartily, so heartily it bordered on becoming a cackle.

"They weren't thieves," Peeler had silently walked up to us, and he peered through wire-rimmed spectacles at us. "They were a band of starving orphan boys trying to steal some of the jerky we were taking to Brightlock. And there weren't any Cursed whales. Chap was stone-cold drunk and thought a piece of tarp or some other rubbish tossed in from the docks was a giant sea creature." He shook his head.

Jessie and I chuckled, but Chap didn't seem fazed. He only nodded and grinned as the repairmen retreated towards the galley.

"Make yourselves comfortable, lads," his grin wavered as he looked at Jessie. "Or, lad and lass, I suppose I should say. We've got a long trip ahead of us."

"Not too long," I said, but he had already turned and was heading over to where Molly and Thomas were standing near the opposite rail. I looked over at Jessie. "Not too long, right? It's only a day or two, isn't it?"

"That's right," despite how pale her face looked — which was to say paler than usual — Jessie gave me a bright smile. "Now let's head below decks and find some food. I heard Knuckles is making clam chowder."

That was one of the names I *did* remember. I didn't know how Knuckles had earned his nickname, but judging by the violent tattoos and the constant expression of anger on the ship cook's face, I didn't really want to find out.

I followed Jessie down through the sleeping quarters until we came to the galley. Several of the other crewmen were down there already, eating their dinner before they went back up to help man the ship. I recognized Bubba, Tuar, Paul, Gawain, and Laurence. Once Jessie and I had claimed our bowls of clam chowder, we went to sit with them, squeezing in on the end of the table. I sat beside Gawain so Jessie could have the end seat.

"Hello, hello, crewmates," Paul said, his voice not unfriendly, but definitely not welcoming. I wondered if he thought of us as a nuisance. I pushed the thought aside.

"Hello, Paul. Tuar, Gawain," I nodded to each of them in greeting, but only a couple nodded back. I wasn't offended. None of them appeared to be very open people, and while I knew that might unsettle Jessie, I'd had enough dealings with grumpy seamen at the Port to ignore it.

"What all are you bringing to Famark?" Laurence asked, shoveling a mouthful of chowder into his mouth. "That crate seemed awfully heavy."

"Perfumes." I answered. Tuar snorted, and a twisted smile pulled at Gawain's lips, but I only smirked alongside them. "Not the most manly product, is it? My grandmother makes them from scratch. Some of them can be surprisingly effective."

"*Effective*?" Bubba echoed, and my brows shot skyward. He hadn't spoken at all on the journey to the Port, and his voice was like a boom of thunder in the galley. It took me a moment to gather my wits.

"Yes. Perfumes can have different purposes. Some are to mask other scents, some are to give something a new scent, and some," I waggled my eyebrows. "Are to attract the ladies."

"Ladies? What kind of ladies?" Laurence looked up briefly from his meal, his bright green eyes curious. I grinned at him.

"All kinds. Tall, short, slim, flat, curvy, take your pick, there are perfumes to attract them all." My voice jerked awkwardly at the end, thanks to an elbow in my side. It took great restraint to keep my expression one of business-like indifference.

"Are there really?" Tuar raised a black eyebrow, his gray eyes shining with doubt. "I thought perfumes were made so women could clog up your nose when they walk past."

"I-" I blinked, frowned, and blinked again. "*Why* would that be the purpose of perfumes?"

"Why should I know?" he shrugged. "You're the expert here."

"Quite right. I am." I shrugged my shoulders to adjust the way my shirt hung on me. It was a little big, one Jessie's father had given to me when he'd outgrown it.

Gawain tapped his fingers on the table to gain everyone's attention, then twisted his hands a few different ways, keeping steady eye contact with Bubba. After he was finished, the burly man spoke.

"He wants to know why you're taking perfumes to Famark."

"My grandmother doesn't make perfumes for the fun of it," I began, then hesitated. "Well, I'm sure she would, if she didn't need money to keep us fed, but she does, so it's a business. A man on Famark purchased all of the ones I'm taking with me. I must say, I'm already very pleased with the transportation service." I grinned broadly at him. "Who knows how that old merchant will react when I say those perfumes arrived aboard a pirate ship."

"Speaking of which," Jessie spoke up, stirring her chowder around with her spoon. The ship gave a sudden lurch, and she yelped, but it soon settled back into its steady sway, and she cleared her throat to continue. "How did you come into possession of a pirate ship? Aren't they made by pirates specifically *for* pirates or something?"

"Some of them are, yes," Wendy strolled into the galley, pulled up a stool, and sat at the end of the table. Paul offered him his half-eaten chowder, but Wendy waved it away with his remaining hand. "I'm alright, thanks. Yes, little lady, pirates make pirate ships, but it's not always pirates who sail with them." He paused, tilted his head to the side, and shrugged. "Granted, it is *mostly* pirates who sail with them, but *The Coventry* is different. Most pirates pay for their ships in gold or blood." He leaned forward and winked at us. "*The Coventry* was taken the way a pirate ship *should* be taken."

"Stolen?" Jessie gasped.

"No," I told her. "They paid for it in duck feathers and boot leather. Of course they *stole* it, Jess! It's not like normal transport crewmen would ever have enough money to buy a legitimate pirate ship." I lifted the metal mug of water Knuckles had given me and took a long swig. When I lowered it, I realized the crewmen were throwing each other amused glances. "What? Am I wrong? Do you secretly make a ridiculous amount of money but just not tell anyone? Have I been making the wrong career choices my whole life?" I rubbed the back of my neck. "I mean sure selling perfumes doesn't pay *great*, but it's better than nothing. Seriously, do you guys get a lot of money?"

"We have a high-risk job," Paul chugged from his own metal tankard, although I was fairly sure his didn't have water in it. "We get paid enough to take that risk. That's all you need to know. Now," he stood up and clapped his brother on the shoulder. "We'd best be heading up to help."

And with that, all of them stood and left, even Wendy. Jessie and I sat and finished our chowder before we left the galley.

"What now?" she asked, messing with the end of one of her long red braids.

"It's getting late," I looked at the sleeping quarters we were in. "Why not turn in?" I suggested. The sleeping cabin was for most of the crew. Only those of higher ranks were allowed their own cabin. Chap and Molly had their own, as did Captain Howard. The rest slept in here unless they were out manning the ship.

"I call the corner hammock." Jessie made her way into the dark little corner. I took the hammock beside hers. The little blankets were scratchy and irritating, but I'd make do.

As we shuffled around, trying to get comfortable, other members of the crew filed in slowly. I saw Kaden and Peeler, muttering softly to each other, as they went to claim their own hammocks. Before long, and despite the lurching and jerking of the ship, I fell asleep.

*D*awn hadn't even reached us when Jessie and I were woken by Molly and half-dragged into the galley for breakfast. When we got there, I smelled something greasy and salty, and I hoped it was bacon. I loved bacon.

"Sausage and pickled greens," Davie grinned at us as he fell in step beside me, waiting in the line that led up to where Knuckles was dishing out breakfast.

"Pickled?" Jessie wrinkled her nose as the acidic smell.

"I was hoping for bacon," I admitted. "But sausage will do." Davie shrugged.

"Bacon's not the best at sea. Always seems sort of soggy, even if it hasn't been in water." He rolled his shoulders, and I was mildly surprised to see how much muscle was there. He couldn't have been as old as I was, maybe thirteen or fourteen, and yet he'd had more adventure in his life than I'd had in mine. The bones sticking out of his back proved that.

"Couldn't we have apple slices on the side? Or just a salad? Why did the greens have to be *pickled*?" Jessie complained, throwing a disdainful look at the line ahead of us. Five more people, then it would be our turn. I could see brief glimpses of Knuckles' ever-present frown between the bodies.

"*Apple slices*?" Davie snorted. "Fruit's never any good on a ship. Rolls around and gets all bruised and mushy within a couple hours. And salad's too bland!"

"That's a shame," I said. "I always love a good fruit pie."

Davie chuckled and jerked a thumb towards Knuckles. "Don't worry. Uncle Knuckles makes the best pickled greens you'll ever taste. You won't even need a pie to finish the meal off."

"Uncle?" I echoed as we stepped forward. "Knuckles is your uncle?"

"Well, no," Davie scratched behind his ear. "But that's what everybody calls 'im."

Jessie and I shared a look. *We* would never call the grumpy ship's cook "Uncle", but it was sweet that the rest of *The Coventry* did.

"You crew really are like family, huh?" Jessie asked.

"Trauma sort of has a tendency to bring people close together," said Davie with another shrug, then he stiffened. "Just, uh . . . you know, long histories, huh?" he gave us another grin, but this one seemed a little forced. "Anyway, I've got to go up above deck. I'm on crow's nest today." And with that he was gone, not even stopping to get some breakfast.

"What sort of trauma would the crew of a transport ship go through?" Jessie muttered to me as we moved forward again. In front of us was a squat man whose name was either Vex or Zarr, but he didn't seem to be paying us much attention. He was too busy picking at the flakes of dead skin clustered around an ugly patch of burn scars along his forearm.

"No idea," I answered. "Maybe we should ask Chap. He certainly seems to think they've been through a lot."

"It isn't just him though," Jessie pointed out as we moved again. Vex — or Zarr — was now watching as Knuckles portioned out another plate of food for him. "Remember how Wendy kept telling us what actually happened? That means that, even if Chap *didn't* save the day, they still came in contact with a crew of pirates, and they really did steal dresses from a merchant. Why would they do that? Their job is taking things from place to place, not robbing people and getting into skirmishes with sea bandits." We fell quiet as we stepped up to get our own food. Once we had it, we went to sit alone at a table in the corner of the galley.

"We *are* on a pirate ship, Jess." I reminded her, scooping a bite of pickled greens into my mouth. I froze, and so did she. The greens were excellent; Davie hadn't been kidding when he'd said they were the best I'd ever taste. But that wasn't why we stiffened.

"You don't think . . ." Jessie looked warily at the crewmen around us. She looked like she might start crying. She looked terrified. I, on the other hand, was sick to the stomach. Partially because I hadn't figured this out sooner, and partially because I had a sinking feeling my meal was about to make a second appearance.

"Why didn't we think any of this was suspicious to begin with? Half of them are *missing body parts*. Most of them have tattoos. They sail in a pirate ship. Their ship needed repairs to the hull, and I caught a glimpse of the damage. It looked like it had been caused by something big and moving." I grumbled, pushing the meager scraps of my meal away. Bile rose in the back of my throat, and I was sure I was going to throw up.

"A cannonball?" Jessie's eyes widened, and I nodded, my head swimming as I did so. Cannons were a rare sight, a new development in our world. There were rumors people were trying to replicate it into a smaller, hand-held version, but little to no progress had been made there.

The point was, cannons were rare. Only the richest people could get them. People as rich as pirates, and if *The Coventry* had come into a battle with pirates, there must have been more going on than I'd originally thought.

"That's not . . . but . . . well maybe they just transport valuable goods." Jessie suggested. "Maybe pirates were after them for what they had on board." I could hear that she had no conviction in her voice. Even if she had, I wouldn't have believed her anyway.

"It's fine. I think they'll leave us be once we're on Famark. It's pretty obvious they're trying to keep it a secret from us anyway." I looked down at the sausages on my plate. Jessie hadn't touched her food, and judging by the look on her face, she wasn't going to. With the state of my stomach, I wasn't going to touch mine again either.

"Trouble, they're *pirates*. We're on a ship full of *pirates* in the *middle of the sea*. What're we going to do?" she fretted, staring at the galley around us. I could hear the crew laughing loudly behind me, but I didn't bother to look at them. Instead, I answered her.

"Nothing. Let them take us to our destination. I don't think they'll hurt us. We've done nothing to deserve becoming prisoners."

"Have you?" the voice came from the table beside us. Jessie and I looked up to see Ritch, Laurence, and three other crew members watching us with dark expressions. "Finding out our secrets seems like a reason to lock you up to me."

Jessie let out a frightened squeak as the crewmen — *pirates*, I corrected myself — stood up and moved towards us. I leapt up from my seat, backing into the wall. My bow and quiver were with my pack by my cot. I had no way of defending myself as they stepped closer. Ritch reached for me with his three-fingered hand.

"You've gotten yourself into a good bit of trouble, lad," he shook his head and *tsk tsk tsk*ed at me, looking over at Jessie, who was similarly cornered by Laurence. "Now we see what Howie has to say about it."

7
KSEGA

As it happened, Howie — whom we were required to refer to as Captain Howard — was preoccupied with a number of things, all of which were top secret and under no circumstances to be revealed to us, so we were handed off to the three mates.

This was an improvement to the situation, if only a small one. We were thrown into the cargo hold with Chap, Molly, and Thomas, since it was more spacious and a bit cleaner than the cells in the bottom of the ship. I was surprised by their reasoning — Wendy had actually said he didn't want us dirtying ourselves or getting sick down there — and how polite they'd been about it, but I wasn't about to return the kindness. We were still locked in the cargo hold with three pirates.

"What were you thinking?!" Chap demanded, looking a little offended. "Snooping around on a pirate ship is just about the stupidest thing you could have done!"

"Hey!" Jessie glared at him, crossing her arms defensively over her chest. "We've hardly been *snooping around*. We'd only been in the sleeping cabin and the galley today!"

"She's right," I added, making myself comfortable on top of one of the supply crates. It wasn't very easy, considering my stomach was roiling. I was certain I was going to throw up again. "It wasn't very hard to figure it out. You don't do a great job of concealing, what with all the scars and the tattoos and the . . . well," I gestured around us. "The pirate ship."

"Oh," Chap looked around. "Well I suppose you're right." He added after a moment, frowning at the walls of the hold as if it were their fault.

"Doesn't change the fact you snooped," Molly remarked, her voice steely. I quirked an eyebrow at her. I couldn't place where she was from, but I was fairly certain she was from one of the eastern kingdoms. "You poked your nose where it doesn't belong, and now we have to do something about it."

"Why?" I asked, shrugging. "I know we *look* pretty stupid, but we still have brains, otherwise we'd be dead, and like I said, it's sort of obvious. Why would you even agree to take us somewhere if you don't want us to know you're pirates?"

"We're not pirates." Molly snapped.

"Most of the evidence we've found says otherwise-" my voice hitched at the end, and I snapped my mouth closed, grimacing as my stomach tightened.

"Shut your smart mouth, if you know what's good for you," she hissed, placing her hands on her hips. She scowled. "What's wrong with you?"

"Seasick." Jessie shifted her glare to the black-haired woman. "And he's right. You *are* pirates."

"We aren't pirates," Thomas pitched in, crossing his arms and raising an eyebrow at me. I ignored it, shutting my eyes and trying to ignore the swaying of the ship. "This is why we don't tell anybody this stuff. It's very complicated, and I don't think we can make you understand. The bottom line is, we *aren't* pirates, no matter what you might think." I was slightly surprised by how surely he spoke. He'd only ever laughed at a few comments, never said anything until now, and it was shockingly different from his older brother's typically joking tone.

"But why do you have to lock us up for knowing that?" Jessie whined, leaning back against the crates. "It's not like it's a crime or anything."

"We aren't locking you up," Chap adjusted the sleeves of his grubby shirt. "But we definitely can't let you go on around thinking we're pirates." He chewed his lip a moment, then shrugged. "Not really sure why that is, but it's the rules."

"It's because we don't want you seeing us any differently." Molly said, rolling her eyes at her husband. "If we were labeled as pirates, business would go downhill very fast. We can't afford to let that happen, so we make our way as simple traders. Few of us leave the ship, mainly the ones with the nastiest scars, like Davie or James."

"But . . . you *are* pirates." I frowned. "Sort of. I don't understand."

"I don't expect you to." Molly started for the door. "And I don't expect you to try to understand. The point we're trying to make here is: don't go out and call us pirates, because we're not." Her gaze darkened. "If you do, we'll know, and we will come for you."

"Not really to kill you," Chap clarified, and Molly's shoulders slumped. With another eye roll, she left the hold. He shrugged after she'd left. "But really, you should keep it down. Howie especially doesn't like being called a pirate by the common folk. You know, that reminds me of a time when we came across some *real* pirates! It was, oh, maybe four years ago or so, but I remember it clearly!" he rubbed his hands together eagerly, and Jessie and I threw each other weary looks. Hardly a full day into our journey, and already we were growing tired of the company on this ship.

"I'm sure it's very fascinating, but my friend hasn't had breakfast, and we'd like to-" I began, but Chap cut me off, already telling the story.

"We were sailing along, heading towards Sea Serpent Crevice, when they came. Nearly killed us, they did! But we shot them down with our crossbows! Didn't stand a chance, the idiots. The battle took less than twenty minutes. We defeated them, then stripped their ship of its loot and sank it!"

"That isn't what happened," Thomas said as we all headed towards the door. "But I don't want to embarrass my brother by telling the true story, so you'll have to speculate as to what actually happened."

And then both of them strolled out onto the deck, smiling in the creeping light of early dawn, as if nothing had happened.

"You know, I sort of prefer Wendy and Peeler's approach to it," I said as we made our way back down towards the sleeping quarters. Before we got there, I split apart to heave over the side of the rail. I was glad Jessie didn't mention it as we continued down to our hammocks.

I was relieved to see that my pack was still there, and I quickly slid my quiver onto my belt and my bow over my back.

Jessie seemed to feel the same, and I noticed her watching her own pack. I knew she had some types of poison in there, and with her recle they could all be made lethal. Some might even be able to be made into medicines.

"Best leave them in there for now." I told her. "My bow will be enough. Plus, I wouldn't want Davie to try and get into it." She frowned, and I added, "He seems like the type to drink things he sees, whether consumable or otherwise."

"Fair," Jessie agreed as we kicked our packs back into place beneath our low cots. "Want me to give you something? For the seasickness?" she offered, and I nodded.

"Please."

She bent over her pack and did things with vials and water, and after a few moments she offered me a small glass to drink from. The liquid inside it was a horrid green color, but I didn't hesitate to tip it into my mouth. I'd learned from previous sicknesses that as foul as the tinctures may appear, Jessie always made sure they tasted sweet. Sure enough, it was like honey running down my throat, and almost immediately I felt a little better. Having a friend that was a recle-mage must have been on some sort of everyone-needs-one-of-these list — I knew it was on mine.

We had still been winding along the long river between the Port and the Great Lakes when Jessie and I had finally fallen asleep last night, and we were out in open water now. The western lands of Horcath were visible behind us, and I could just make out where the river mouth opened to let ships into the Port. In front of us was nothing but water, but I knew Famark would appear on the horizon before the day was over.

Dawn was just arriving, the sun climbing steadily up into the sky and letting its orange-gold light skim across the surface of the waves. Salty sea air whirled past us in heavy breezes, whipping up our hair and stinging our eyes. I found I preferred it over the flowery, fruity smell that often occupied my home.

The day would pass without much for Jessie and I to do, and not wanting to get on the bad side of the not-quite pirates, we kept to ourselves. Wendy let me climb the rigging to view the sea from the crow's nest at one point, and I learned how to man the giant crossbow mantled up there. It was easy to reload fast, and it swiveled around with surprising ease, allowing an effective attack from above.

When it was lunchtime, we enjoyed a small and dry meal of stale biscuits and dried meat. According to Ritch, this was because they didn't always have enough food to cook into big meals for each meal of the day, so they usually had to settle for something less appetizing for lunch.

After lunch, Knuckles had given both of us damp rags and a bucket of water and ordered us to go scrub down the galley. The *entire* galley. With how much the ship rocked and swayed, food occasionally spilled or fell off the tables, leaving us with plenty of sticky globs and stains to scrub at.

Despite the work we were given, I was thoroughly enjoying myself. There was that constant threat of being jumped by pirates at any moment, but I wasn't very concerned about that. While the few times I caught Captain Howard out of the corner of my eye were mildly terrifying, I didn't think anyone besides him on the ship might try to do us any harm, and if we kept our heads down and mouths shut, I doubted he would either.

Jessie seemed to feel differently about all of it. She looked constantly uncomfortable, standing away from the rest of the crew while I chatted amiably with them. I offered to include her in the conversations, but she never stepped forward to join us. I knew she was nervous about them being pirates, but nothing had really changed. They'd always been the tattooed, scarred, intimidating men they still were. The only thing that had changed was how we perceived them. That was what Molly had been trying to tell us in the cargo hold.

"They don't want to be seen as pirates because, strictly speaking, they aren't. They seem like pirates in a lot of ways, yes, but I don't think they quite meet all the qualifications." I explained to Jessie as we headed down towards the galley for dinner that night.

"It doesn't matter," Jessie had grumbled. "They're close enough to pirates for me."

That had ended the conversation, but I still wasn't convinced any of them were actual pirates. Maybe they looked like it, but then again, they could've been a band of turned-around thugs and thieves from somewhere on Horcath, maybe even Wisesol, where I was from, that had ended up looking for honest work when they got their lives straight. Howard had somehow come into possession of a pirate ship, and he was looking for a crew to help him transport goods from place to place in exchange for money. It was a perfectly reasonable, perfectly legal situation.

Jessie still didn't believe me, even when I'd explained my theory, and that was fine with me. She normally thought my ideas were stupid or far-fetched, and sometimes I agreed with her. Not on this, though. I was sure I was right about these so-called pirates she was convinced were evil. They weren't evil, they were just a little misguided.

Peeler, Ritch, Bubba, and Gawain sat with us when they'd collected their plates of food — tonight was baked lobster with a side of scalloped potatoes, seasoned to perfection — and proceeded to carry out a very polite and casual conversation. Where all of them had been distanced and hesitant before, now they seemed a lot friendlier, at least in my eyes. I assumed it was because they were now aware that we knew they weren't completely normal, innocent tradesmen, and we didn't think any differently of them for that. Or at least, *I* didn't think any differently of them. The same could not be said for Jessie, who was sitting in the corner seat poking at her buttery potatoes with a downcast gaze.

"What's the deal with Chap?" I asked as I dug into my lobster.

"How do you mean?" Bubba asked in that uncomfortably deep voice of his.

"I mean all the stories. He always tells a story, then someone immediately says he's lying. Why does he keep doing it? And why does he look almost *happy* when they point that out?" I frowned at them, as if they were the reason for it. "It doesn't make any sense."

"Oh, that? He's only making stuff up because he thinks it's a pirate thing." Bubba shrugged his one shoulder and returned his attention to his lobster. Jessie and I shared a confused look, but the big man didn't elaborate. After seeing our expressions, Ritch pitched in.

"He and his family are the only ones who came by this profession honest. Like, the transport profession. The rest of us . . ." he scratched behind his ear. "Well, we came into it. How, that's hard to say. Anyway, he thought all the tales we told were made up and whatnot, so now he takes whatever opportunity he sees to make up some crazy story where he's the daring hero." Ritch shrugged. "Little point trying to convince him we ain't never lied about those stories before. He won't listen. Even Molly and Tom know how it is by now. Poor fellow's a little empty between the ears, if you get my meaning." He wolfed down the rest of his meal and started to get up, but I stopped him.

"What do you mean the rest of you? You mean you're *actually* pirates?" I gaped at him. "But I thought . . . but Chap said-" I shook my head. "Or, well, *Molly* said you weren't pirates."

"Them three aren't pirates," said Peeler, blue-gray eyes twinkling behind the lenses of his glasses. "They never said nothin' 'bout the rest of us."

"You mean-" but I never got to finish my sentence. By then, they'd all finished eating and stood up to return their dishes to Knuckles. Only Gawain stayed behind a moment to give us that twisted smile of his, then he waved and followed the others.

Jessie and I were silent for a long moment, staring wide-eyed at each other. For some reason, the possibility that some of these people were *actually* pirates had never seemed real in my mind until now.

"Ksega . . ." Jessie said slowly, and I shook my head at her. If she used my real name, she wasn't happy, but there wasn't a lot I could do about it right now. We were in the middle of the sea with nobody around to help us.

"They all seem friendly enough." I reasoned, swallowing nervously. I didn't want to give her any sense of false hope, but what I said was true. So far, the only hostility we had received was from Howard and Molly. Everyone else may have been a little grim or a little quiet, but they were, for the most part, a friendly lot.

"What if they're kidnapping us?" she gasped, tugging at her braids anxiously. "What if they agreed to take us because they wanted to use us as . . . as . . ." she trailed off, a line forming between her brows as she tried to think of the word she was looking for.

"Leverage?" I guessed, and she snapped her fingers.

"Leverage! Leverage for ransom! What if they bled Willa dry of all her money? What if they bled my pa dry too? We'd be left broke, and even then the pirates might kill us anyway!" she pushed her plate of food away, folded her arms on the table, and buried her face in them. Her shoulders shook, but I didn't think she was crying yet, only close to it. If I didn't want to have a bawling Jessie on my hands, I had to find a way to reassure her fast.

Truth was, I wasn't sure I knew how to do that. My own thoughts were foggy and muddled, bleeding together and not allowing me to form coherent thoughts. I didn't *think* the pirates would kill us, but now I was having my doubts. Technically, Chap, Molly, and Thomas hadn't been lying about not being pirates, not according to Peeler anyway. But what if that was their strategy? What if they had the mates tell that to all the innocent occupants of *The Coventry* to reassure them, while the real pirates plotted their ransom or their untimely demise? I could no longer deny that it was a possibility, but I wasn't about to tell that to Jessie.

"I'm sure everything's fine," I told her, reaching out to pat her hand. She lifted her head and raised a red eyebrow. "I mean think about it. They let us keep our weapons, and if they didn't find your poisons, that means they probably didn't go through our bags. I would think real pirates would do that first thing, wouldn't you?" I flashed her my brightest smile, but I didn't think she was convinced.

"They've probably been in this business for years, Trouble. They probably know all the tricks — they're lulling us into a sense of security, tricking us into thinking they're safe and friendly."

"And why wouldn't they be?" I splayed my hands out on the table in front of us. "There's no reason for pirates to kidnap people to hold for ransom when they could just go and steal a few gold pieces from the nearest town. Think about it."

"I still don't like it." Jessie admitted, but at least she pulled her plate back and poked at the food a little more. If her meager appetite kept up, there'd hardly be any of her left by the time we got back home. And we *would* get back home.

"Just keep your head up and try not to get into trouble," I finished up my own meal and stood up, giving her another grin. "Famark will come into view tonight, and we'll be sailing straight for it. You'll see." I didn't want to be making her any empty promises, but as long as it kept her from having a panic attack, it would do for now.

Knuckles took my plate from me and gave a gruff grunt in acknowledgement of my existence before I made my way back towards the sleeping cabin. As I passed the table where Jessie was sitting, I gave her a small wave, then headed up towards the deck, careful to make sure my bow and arrows were easily accessible.

Wendy and Chap had struck me as the friendliest out of the entire crew of *The Coventry*. While some of the others had seemed a bit willing to talk — Peeler and Laurence were talkative at times, but never seemed up to answering questions — the first mate and the navigator were more willing to share with us, so it was them I was searching for as I stepped out into the evening light.

I found Wendy up in the crow's nest, and I started to work my way up there. Halfway up, I heard him shouting at me, laughing about something, but the salty sea breeze carried his words away, and I wasn't able to make anything out until he was offering me a hand and tugging me up to my feet on the wooden boards.

"Peeler says you and your girl have had quite the revelation over dinner, eh?" he chuckled. "Don't worry, most of us are harmless, as long as you stay on our good side."

"Right," a nervous laugh burbled from my lips. "I wasn't too worried, anyway. Jess is a lot more concerned about it than I am. And for the record, she's not my girl."

"Sure." He winked at me, and I rolled my eyes. "Completely understandable, how she feels. You've seen how many women are aboard this ship. Let me tell you, a bunch of pirates isn't the safest lot for a lass to be around alone, even if they're friendly pirates."

"And that's what you are? Friendly pirates?" I asked, and he only grinned in reply.

"Look over yonder," he jerked a thumb to the east, and I looked up to see a dark smudge along the horizon, nearly blending perfectly with the darkening sky beyond. "Famark. We'll settle into its docks sometime tomorrow, probably around noon, if the weather stays nice." He looked up at the sky, squinting. I followed his gaze, looking between the sparkling stars showing themselves against the blanket of deep purples and blues.

"Can you read the weather?" I asked, and he laughed.

"Pretty well, I'd say. Not as well as anyone from Old Nightfall, of course, but I'm good enough at it to keep us out of any bad storms. What about you?"

"Can I read the weather?" I blinked at him, slightly taken aback. He laughed again.

"Not specifically. Got any talents? Any element that calls to you?" he twirled his fingers through the air, mimicking the motions most types of mages make when using their magic.

"Ah, right. Some, I guess. Not much."

"What can you do?"

"Make some flowers bloom. Move rocks around. If I have enough time, I can make trees grow and move around a lot. Takes a lot of focus, and leaves me famished." I scratched behind my ear, shrugging. "Nothing too impressive."

"Bering-mage, then?" Wendy raised a thin, pale eyebrow. I nodded, and he repeated the movement, but slower, more thoughtful. "Gawain's a bering-mage, too. Not very strong. Spending time at sea and all, he never gets much practice."

He turned his intelligent green eyes to me. "How does being at sea make *you* feel? Queasy? Disconnected?"

"Sort of," I shrugged again. Since we'd boarded *The Coventry* the feeling had slowly faded away, but I could still feel the distant tug of the land we'd left behind. I always forgot it was there until I found myself on the water. "A little . . . hollow, almost. It isn't bad. I've been to sea before. Not without being seasick, of course." Brief flashes of my abrupt journey aboard the *Sea Cloud* came to mind, but they weren't exactly pleasant. Dark, damp, bumpy, and frequented by vomit. Not pleasant at all.

"Suppose that's only to be expected." He laughed. "How about that Jessie girl? She faring well?" Wendy asked, clasping his hands behind his back as he stared out into the softly rolling waves of the black sea.

"She's alright," I answered. "She's traveled enough in her life that she won't get seasick, but I don't think she likes being on the water a lot. Always complaining about the smell of fish and salt and sweaty seaman." I ran a hand through my sandy mop of hair. "She's a recle-mage, from Freetalon. No special connection to the land, like I have, but she definitely feels better with solid ground beneath her feet." I wasn't entirely sure why I'd told him that. Thus far, Jessie and I had been trying to keep a low profile, and we should have been doubling our efforts now that we knew some of them were pirates. And yet there was something so trustable about Wendy. He seemed to sense my apprehension, and he laughed again.

"Don't worry, I'm not gonna track her family down and kill them!" his face went suddenly serious, frozen like stone. "Though I could."

My blood chilled, my eyes widened, and I could feel one of my feet slowly sliding a step away. His features broke into another loud laugh, and I hesitantly chuckled alongside him, although my nerves were still jumbled.

"I'm kidding, lad! Only kidding!" he clapped me on the shoulder and gave me another wink. "Go on and get some sleep now, kid. Big day tomorrow. Business deals overseas! Ever handled something like that before? No? It's a whole different experience, believe me, but you'll enjoy yourself. Goodnight, Ksega."

"Goodnight, Wendy." My voice was crisp and betrayed none of the emotions warring inside of me. I was suddenly terrified that as soon as I turned around, Wendy would drive the end of his shiny, sharp hook into my back or flip me over the rails of the crow's nest. But he didn't, and I climbed down the rigging and hurried down to my hammock before anyone else could stop to chat with me.

I found Jessie already lying in her hammock, curled up beneath the sheets, warily watching Laurence and Davie talking in quiet tones on the opposite side of the cabin.

When she spotted me, her features broke with relief, and I thought she might start crying.

"There you are! I was worried about you. I didn't know where you'd gone." She propped herself up on one elbow, her expression somehow managing to be intimidatingly stern and pityingly fragile at the same time.

"You could've come looking for me," I said, sliding my boots off and tucking my legs beneath the grubby sheets of my hammock.

"And go on the deck? No thank you. I'd prefer *not* to get dragged into a dark room by a bloodthirsty pirate, thanks." She stuck her nose up in the air, making a scowling face. It didn't last long, though, crumpling into a look of relief. "I'm glad you're alright. Where'd you go?"

"Crow's nest," I replied, shrugging my shoulders as I laid down. Somehow, the day had stolen my energy, and I could already feel sleep tugging at the back of my mind, trying to pull me into an abyss of emptiness.

"Why?" Jessie's voice broke through the fog.

"Talk to Wendy." I muttered, my words slurring and hardly distinguishable. Jessie grunted and murmured something, but I was too far gone to figure out what it was, and I found I didn't really care to find out. I let myself fall into that abyss, slipping into another rocking, dreamless sleep.

When I woke up again, Jessie was gone. I wasn't too worried right now, since she was probably hiding in the corner of the galley. Beside me was a small glass vial of green-ish liquid, and a note written in her scrawling handwriting labeling it as more of her medicine for seasickness. I gratefully downed it and rose into a sitting position.

It smelled like grease and salt, and I guessed it was time for breakfast. I slid groggily out of my hammock, and only barely managed to convince myself not to curl up into the warm sheets again before I changed into something that smelled slightly less like salt and sea slime, yanked my boots on, and meandered towards the galley to find her. I checked to make sure my bowstring was taught and all thirty of my arrows were in place in their quiver before I did so. Even though Wendy had told me none of the pirates were going to be a danger to us, I was still wary, and I had to keep my senses alert to keep both myself and Jessie safe.

As I stepped into the galley, I quickly glanced along the queued line, and my pulse hummed in my ears as I didn't catch sight of Jessie's bright red braids. There was Gawain, Bubba, and Davie, chatting amongst themselves as they moved along. Peeler was having a conversation with two other crew members, a lanky fellow named Cape who was little more than skin and bones, and a burly blond man named Earl who was missing a large chunk of his nose.

My worry vanished a moment later as I heard a high laugh ring around me. Looking to my left, I saw that Jessie was sitting at one of the tables with a group of other people. Ritch was the only one out of them I was somewhat familiar with. The other three — Rex, a dark-haired brute missing a hand, Frances, an older man with a thick pink scar through his face, and Lester, a wiry boy with a sixth finger on his right hand — were people I had only been introduced to, but never spoken with. Jessie didn't seem to be having any trouble making conversation with them, and I wasn't able to conceal my evident surprise as I saw them.

"Trouble!" she crowed when she saw me, grinning broadly. There was a gleam in her emerald eyes that I hadn't seen since the day we left the Port. "Stop making a face like a blubbering pufferfish and join us when you've got your food," she laughed, gesturing at the line. I only nodded numbly and gave them a brief smile before stepping into the line behind Peeler.

"Sleep well, did you?" the repairmen asked as I scratched my head. I gave him a tired grin and nodded. It had been a surprisingly peaceful night, and I'd managed to get many more hours of sleep than I had the night before. I guessed it was apparent on my features.

"You?" I asked groggily. He grinned, and I realized some of his teeth were missing, replaced by silver and gold replicas.

"About as good as I ever do." He cackled after that, and I gave a small chuckle. He was much less cranky than usual, but I guessed the prospect of bacon in the morning could do wonders for anyone's mood. I knew it had already improved mine.

I could smell the greasy strips of bacon, hear them popping as they cooked, see them on the plates of people who had already obtained their food. My stomach grumbled loudly as we shuffled forward. Behind me, I heard another one of Jessie's laughs, and I wondered what they were talking about.

When it was my turn, Knuckles handed me a plate packed with thick strips of bacon, steaming scrambled eggs, and crispy hash browns. I almost drooled over it as I went to sit with Jessie and the others, squeezing in on the other side of Ritch.

They were mid-conversation, and only Jessie bothered to give me a wave of greeting. Frances, who was speaking, didn't pause as I joined them, but his blue eyes did hover over me briefly in acknowledgement before he returned his attention to Ritch.

"-nasty piece of work. Barely made it out with my life." He gave a gap-toothed grin. "Not that it'd be the first time, of course."

"Sounds awfully dangerous," Jessie raised her eyebrows, clearly impressed. I suddenly wished I'd been there to hear the rest of the story. After Chap's exaggerated ones, I was interested to hear what some of the actual pirate stories entailed.

"Most things in our past are," Rex said through a mouthful of scrambled eggs. "You know most of us come from a background of piracy, and it's been interesting adapting to the more normal life of work and trading." His vibrant green eyes — almost inhumanly so — turned to me, sparkling with life and mischief. "Sometimes, though, I'll find myself willing to trade anything to go back to some of those good ol' days."

I raised an eyebrow, wondering why anyone would want to go back to times where their life was put at risk. My life had never really been in a lot of danger at any one point in my life, even though I'd had my fair share of skirmishes with angry boat captains or shop owners for the odd stolen item, but I never really feared for my life. Looking back on those encounters, I had no wish to return to any of them. Was it different when you grew up a pirate?

I was about to say as much when a loud voice called out from the deck. It sounded like Wendy, and a hush fell over the entire galley as everyone turned their attention to his booming voice.

"Preparing to dock! I need more hands on deck!" as soon as the sentence was complete, several of the men stood up and ran for the doorway, including Ritch, Frances, Rex, and most of the others already seated. Some, who were still in line, didn't bother leaving their breakfast to help. There were enough crewmembers already rushing to Wendy's aid.

Jessie and I looked over at each other, and I could see the same excitement I felt reflected in her eyes. Even through the thick wooden walls of *The Coventry*, I could feel the tug of the land as we came nearer. It was almost like a drug, making me slightly dizzy, yet full of power and light. I could feel it fizzing through my veins, my fingers twitching with the anticipation of using my bering again.

Jessie didn't have the same connection to the earth that I did, but I knew she was antsy to be back on land. We both stood up after gobbling down a few more bites of our breakfast, eager to get up to the deck and see how close we were to Famark's docks.

The deck was humming with life. Captain Howard was up at the bow of the ship, hands clasped behind his back, long coattails flapping in a slight gust of wind that rolled across the wood. I hadn't seen him much during our journey, and I was sort of glad about that fact. He didn't strike me as the most enjoyable companion, especially not when Chap or Wendy was around to talk to instead.

Men with rippling muscles and shiny black tattoos and flexing scar tissue worked about the deck, pulling ropes and tightening sails and doing things with hooks and barrels and preparing for our arrival at Famark. I caught sight of Davie helping Peeler pull a heavy black tarp into the cargo hold, presumably to conceal some of the parts in there. Somehow, I guessed some of them might be worth stealing if anyone came across them. Even if they were menacing pirates aboard a menacing pirate ship, I was sure there were still thugs brave enough to sneak on and have a look around. There were definitely some brave enough back in Wisesol. Were the people of Famark much different?

The sun was still coming up, casting the sky into all different shades of pink and gold and pale, pale blue. A few of the stars were still visible faintly in the sky, but they were fading more and more with each passing second.

I spotted Wendy near the central mast, and I made my way over to him, Jessie following close on my heels. When he caught sight of us, his grin broadened, and he waved at us with his shiny hook.

"Good morning, mates! Looks like we're a bit ahead of schedule. Even better."

"Why's that?" Jessie asked, frowning slightly. Wendy shrugged and let his grin crook a little.

"Just because we're at home on the sea doesn't mean we pirates don't appreciate a good tavern with some beer and, if we're lucky, a few bar fights." He winked at us, and Laurence grinned as he stepped up beside him.

"And some women," he added. Wendy snorted.

"Like any women would take you, with your little *affliction*." He sneered, and Laurence turned bright red, his lips pressing into a thin white line. Jessie and I stifled a laugh.

"I hope you'll help us find the shop we're making a delivery to before you all go and get drunk," Jessie said. "I don't think either of us have an address."

"Oh, we'll have someone to help you, don't worry. Maybe Laurence will go, since he'll have no luck with the ladies," Wendy offered, placing his hand on his hip and holding his hook up to examine it in the morning light, ignoring Laurence's glare. I wouldn't have thought it was possible for his face and neck to flush a deeper red, except it was happening before my very eyes.

Obviously very offended, with skin as red as the ripest of tomatoes, Laurence strolled off towards the lower decks, eager to get away from Wendy's taunts. I guessed it wasn't the first time he'd been more than a little bullied for the certain unnamed body part he was missing, but I couldn't really blame the rest of the crew. Even if they were nice pirates, they ought to know how to have a little fun, and I was pleased to see that that was the case.

It was only another couple hours before the ship sailed into the harbor, and when we did, Jessie and I both gasped loudly. Beside us, Wendy laughed.

The Port was a magical place, there was no doubt about it, with its alabaster cobbled paths and all the scenery and the floating merchant shops. In fact, the place was renowned for being the most beautiful out of all the docks in Horcath, but somehow, it didn't quite compare to the marvel of Famark's Western Harbor.

The piers were crafted from a smooth, pale wood, bobbing gently in the water. The support posts of the piers, jutting up above the walkways, were carved into leaping dolphins, frothing waves blooming around their tails, the eyes hollowed out and filled with some sort of shiny blue resin.

Beyond the piers and the docked boats, rocking and creaking in the rolling waves, there was a massive stone platform jutting out over the water, bustling with people and life. Just beyond it were high stone walls, decorated with curving iron sconces that brandished ashen torches. Directly in the center of that wall was a set of tall iron gates, wound from twisting and twirling black waves, dotted through with dolphins of all different sizes. At the top of the gates, two dolphins leapt free of the iron, connected only by the ends of their tails, arcing towards each other so their noses almost touched and giving the gate an elegant finish.

"It's stunning," Jessie remarked as *The Coventry* was secured in the harbor. We both stood right up next to the rail, leaning over and trying to see everything. There were even more people here than there were in the Port, which seemed nearly impossible. They wore all sorts of clothes, types of clothes from different cultures and kingdoms, even. I spotted the darker skin of Carlorian people buying goods from the small market stalls on the stone platform, the pale blond or red heads of Freetalon shuffling through the crowd, the proud golden faces and dark hair from Brightlock, strutting past the hardworking sailors. And the *magic.*

Snakes of water hissed out of the sea beneath us, curling around ships or protectively lifting small children into the arms of their caretakers. Someone was altering the size of a flame to get a better look at an object they were inspecting. A tall Talon man was helping to heal the bloody scrape on the knee of a little boy, mending the skin together with a brush of his fingers.

"Just wait until you see the Merchant Corner." Thomas appeared at our side, his expression bright, fiery curls bouncing in a salty breeze. "It's my favorite part on the entire island."

"If we visit it at all," Molly remarked as she came up on Thomas' other side, her wavy black hair bunched into a messy bun on the back of her head, tied in place with a red bandana. Her dark skin shone in the morning light. "Remember, we're only going to be in town for a few days. May not have time to visit Merchant Daynor."

"A few days?" Jessie frowned at her. "I thought we were only staying the night."

"Don't worry about it," Molly answered smoothly. "Peeler says the damage to the hull wasn't quite repaired the way he'd wanted it to be when we set sail before, and the journey worsened it a little. We'll only be staying long enough for him to make the necessary adjustments." Her smile was pleasant enough, but I caught a flicker of something in her eyes. I couldn't place what it was, but it was definitely suspicious, and I knew she was lying.

I would have asked her about it, but two things kept me from doing so. One, I was slightly scared of the hard-faced woman, and two, we were finally beginning to disembark.

8
SAKURA

*D*awn brought with it the scent of decay and a bitterly cold winter breeze.

I had managed to find a huge hollow log and nestle myself inside, rolling heavy boulders into place on either side to deter any Cursed predators who happened to catch my scent. It had been a fitful and uncomfortable sleep, and when I woke I found several fresh bruises had made themselves at home across the entire left side of my body.

That hadn't been the only thing I'd found when I had awoken, though. The most obvious change was the fact that my log bed had disappeared entirely, and I was left sitting on a damp patch of earth with my fingers and toes numb with cold.

There wasn't any snow visible around me, but the promise of it was heavy in the air, and a light dusting of frost coated the tops of the branches of the pine trees around me. The forest was thick with them, and the needles littered the floor all around, spreading as far as I could see and dotted with dark little pinecones.

There was no sign of animal life, but I could smell something rotting not far off. Whether it had been a natural or Cursed beast that had killed the poor creature, I didn't want to know, I was only grateful it hadn't turned me into its next meal.

My scuffle with the raptor had left me more wary, and I hadn't gotten as much sleep as I'd have liked, but I had to keep moving forward. I opened my pack and slid on an extra layer of clothing before I set off, gnawing my way through a half-frozen pear as I went. My limp wasn't very bad, since the scratches the raptor had given me were shallow and already healing fast, but the wound still stung and stretched, protesting against the freezing cold.

My breath plumed white in the air before my face, and whenever I walked through it I winced, wishing I had a pair of gloves and more water-resistant boots. Even if snow hadn't begun to fall yet, I knew it would soon from the smell in the air and the prickle around me. Once it was down, it would mask any sounds of animals approaching me. It might help conceal me from danger as well, but that advantage worked for both sides, and it made me uneasy just thinking about it. Part of me wanted to find a safe place to hunker down and hide for a little while, but the other part of me insisted on moving forward. Who knew how many more dragons could be corrupted in the time I was gone? Who knew how many more lives could be put at risk?

I shook my head, reminding myself to be reasonable. I knew I had enough food to last me another two days at least, and if I could hide out in a cave until the Evershifting Forest decided to change again, I knew I could make a lot more progress, and fast. It hurt my head to think about it, and I didn't like the thought of stopping for any amount of time, but I had to think realistically. Finnian didn't want me rushing any decisions, didn't want me leaping into situations I couldn't handle and that could get me killed. Despite every instinct within me telling me to keep moving forward, I knew that his voice of reason, echoing in the back of my mind, was the one I should follow.

I kept a good pace walking across the frozen ground, the soles of my feet aching with every step onward, my muscles seizing and shaking and trembling from the cold. I blew on my fingers and shook out my arms and rubbed the sides of my face to try and keep warm, but it rarely lasted more than a few seconds, and whatever warmth I managed to create was unsatisfactory. I relied on the heat of my eirioth, smoldering somewhere in the pit of my stomach, to keep me alive.

I was keeping a steady course, ignoring the chilly setback that blew at me, but I wasn't sure how long I could keep it up. I was stiff and tired and ready to curl up under my blankets back at home in Hazelwood Inn. I knew that wasn't an option, and wishing it was probably wasn't helping, but with so much dead silence, it was hard not to.

It didn't start to snow until close to noon. I had been walking for several miles, and my legs ached. The scratches on my shin throbbed, but I ignored it, trying to focus on just taking the next step forward. When the frozen flakes started to drift down from the sky, I grimaced, hugging my hands under my arms in an attempt to keep from getting frostbite. I had called my eirioth once to warm them, but the winds had blown it out, and it was hard to maintain a steady flame when you could hardly feel your fingers. If I could get somewhere out of the wind, it would be much easier to warm myself up.

As I shuffled through the thin layer of snow drifting down onto the ground, I became keenly aware of how everything was slowly becoming muted. The snow muffled the sounds of my footfalls. It quietened the rustling of the pine branches. It dulled all the senses I had so that all I had to rely on in the end were my instincts and whatever I could see. It wasn't a very encouraging feeling.

It was three hours past noon when I first realized I wasn't alone anymore. I had been walking along, safe and relatively unworried, and at some point the atmosphere had changed. Something prickly and dangerous had entered the air, and my senses had been so nullified that I hadn't been able to notice the change until now.

I forced myself to keep up my steady pace, not wanting to startle whatever was watching me, but I could feel my pulse quicken, I could notice the subtle change in how I saw the forest around me, in the way I listened to the sounds of nature, or the lack thereof.

I knew there were no birds to be heard in the wintry wood, but there may have been other, smaller animals. I'd seen a number of snow hares and chipmunks and other small creatures, but none of them had brought on such a strong sense of unease. Something big and dangerous was watching me, and that was part of what confused me so much. If it was so powerful, why hadn't I seen it yet?

A low growl rippled through the air, crackling like a thread of audible lightning, and I froze. I couldn't help it this time. My muscles locked up, my heart gave a jump, I inhaled sharply without even realizing I had. The hairs on the back of my neck stood up as I slowly turned my head to face the trees behind me. How had I missed it? It was so big, so furry, so obviously *there*.

A smith, lurking, crouching right there beneath the snow-laden boughs of a pine tree, orange eyes glowing with a clearly dark intent. It was massive, bigger than an eirioth dragon. The tips of its ears brushed the pine needles of branches nine feet above the ground, huge muscles bunched and rolled beneath its matted black fur, and a broad, flat nose jutted out from its square muzzle.

I stumbled backwards, and the smith took two steps forward, shaking snow loose from the tree branches it passed, revealing the rest of its body. Its head was huge and almost bear-like, but there were the sharp lines of a wolf's face around the edges and the pointed ears. Black lips peeled back to reveal hundreds of fangs dripping with muddied saliva. Most of the creature's fur was thin and varying dark shades of gray, sort of reminding me of a raccoon, but it had thicker, longer black fur around the neck and along the ridge of the back, like a mane. The tail faintly resembled that of a wild cat, but fluffier and less flexible. The thing that terrified me most, though, were the muscles. You could see them flexing and unflexing beneath the fur, shaking and twitching with the beast's restraint. They were *huge*, proving that the animal was much stronger than anything I'd ever encountered before, even anything Cursed. The powerful legs ended in massive claws that scraped and dug into the frozen earth, gouging scars into the ground as it teased the soil, eager to leap forward and sink its strong jaws into my flesh. The thought made my stomach turn.

Instinctively, I called for my eirioth flame, my fingers brushing over the sword handle in my belt. Fear temporarily gave my power a jaunty boost, and fire spewed in an angry red beam from the other end of the metal. That only seemed to anger the smith, and it let out another terror-inducing rumble, eyes gleaming with murder.

The cold and the long hours of walking had sufficiently drained me of most of my energy, and I could feel my eirioth already sucking the rest of my resolve away from my body. It was a hard thing to control, fire was. All magic had a life of its own, but each behaved differently. All of it longed to be set free, to breathe and thrive and have a will of its own. But erru was happy and vibrant and willing to let itself be guided. Recle was focused and purposeful and required a strong mind to help it. Even aclure was open to being molded. Eirioth was hungry and stubborn and demanded a long and powerful life, an endless leash and a steady fountain of power to draw from. In my current state, I was a fountain that could hardly supply that power for even a few minutes.

The smith probably sensed this, because it was edging closer, undeterred by the sputtering flame-sword grasped in my hand, held up towards its face. It couldn't have been more than six or seven feet away from me, barely a few steps' worth of space for the beast. It could leap on me faster than I could blink, and I would be powerless against it.

Running was out of the question. With legs as long and powerful as that, this smith could catch anything. It knew the forest well. I could see the marks of age and time that it bore, the pale white scars across its muzzle, the patches of shorn or seared fur, the cracks in its claws and teeth; this was an old wolf, but it had learned much, and there was still plenty of fight left within it.

The problem was, there wasn't much fight left within me. I didn't know how long I could hold it off, if I could hold it off at all. What I wouldn't have given for Finnian or Derek to be by my side at that moment, if not both of them. They would have been able to form a plan. One of us could distract it. Derek could shoot it with his bow and arrow. Finnian's flame-sword would give us more strength to fight against it.

But they weren't here, and I was trapped in an impossible situation, my mind racing as I tried to calculate a way out in the few seconds before my certain death.

That was when I spotted it.

Out of the corner of my eye, just beyond the smith's rear, I could see a rise of gray stone. It was much wider and much taller than any of the boulders around the rest of the Evershifting Forest. It must have been a mountain, a jumble of rocks, a cave, something that would have nooks and crannies and places for me to squeeze into and hide until the smith lost interest in me. If only I could get past it to find that hiding place.

The smith lunged almost too soon for me to react. I slid to the side and tucked myself into a ball just before it whirled past me in a flash of black and orange. My focus snapped and the connection to my eirioth was severed as my body hit the ground, rolling away from the smith. My flame-sword vanished in a curl of smoke, and I cursed loudly as I scrambled to my feet, trying to bring it back, but I was just too numb from the cold.

The smith was twisting back around to face me in a matter of seconds, snow clinging to its fur, roars echoing out from its throat in waves as it charged again. This time I was a little more prepared, but so was it, and I feinted left before ducking back to the right. The smith almost had me with a quick snap of its jaws, but I rolled out of the way, and its fangs closed on empty air.

I nearly tumbled into the trunk of a pine tree, but I veered to the left at the last second and half-crawled my way beyond it. I heard the aggravated snarling of the smith behind me and knew I only had a few moments before it came at me again. There was no way I could climb into the tree, but the caves were to my right now, only a hundred feet or so away. I could make it if the smith was distracted.

I jammed my hand into my satchel and flung the first thing my fingers found to my left, my feet twisting and shoving off from the ground at the same moment. There was a *thunk* as the frozen apple knocked against another tree. I heard the smith dive for it, but I didn't look at it as I took off, sprinting for the caves. I'd hoped for a few extra seconds to get my pace settled, but the smith wasn't falling for it. I heard it crash through the pine tree I'd hid behind moments ago and knew it would reach me in a matter of strides.

I shot to the left, circled around a tree as it doubled-back, sprinted backwards and then to the right, zig-zagging and trying to make progress towards the rocks, but the smith was too fast. It was confused, I could tell, but I couldn't lose it, and it wove between the tall trunks of the pine trees with more agility and speed than I did.

Gasping for breath, ignoring the hot sting of the frigid air against the back of my throat, I pushed onward. My whole body felt numb, and running was doing me no favors, but I had to at least try. As I raced towards the rocks, I heard the smith thundering after me, I heard its raspy breath and the snap of its jaws as it came closer and closer. I closed my eyes, pumping my arms and legs, trying to just get out of its reach. Then the earth threw me to the side.

I screamed in surprise, sure the smith had caught me and thrown me aside to try and break my legs or crush my skull against a tree, but as I fell to the ground I realized the soil itself was moving. The smith didn't look as surprised, only infuriated, as the soil it stood on was pulled in the opposite direction. The frost and the snow around us began to melt, and I felt drops of water on my head as they fell from the pine needles above.

Then there was more water. Tons of drops raining down from the sky, roaring and crackling with lightning, shaking with thunder and soaking everything around me. The pine trees, fuzzy through the downpour, began to change. They thinned and stretched and twisted around until they took the form of a new tree or vanished entirely. Trees appeared in places that had moments ago been empty. Grass sprung from stone and dirt disappeared to be replaced with pebbles and drooping flowers. The earth sucked itself in and began to fill up, creating a pond between the smith and myself.

The only thing that didn't change was the mass of boulders, only twenty feet farther to my right. With a gasp, I jumped to my feet and ran. The growls of the smith were already coming closer behind me, but I tried to ignore them. The ground still shifted beneath my feet, feeling rubbery and unstable, but I kept my balance and reached the rocks sooner than I'd expected. I nearly slammed right into the rock, throwing my hands up to catch myself on the slick surface. I threw myself to the side, sliding through mud, and heard the crash as the smith slid into the stone.

I was right. It was like a small mountain, tons of boulders piled around a rise of stone that led into the ground. It must've been close to a mile wide, and almost two miles long. There had to be a good place to hide.

I hauled myself up one of the smaller rocks nearby, scrabbling up the wet surface until I was nearly twenty feet off the ground. When I paused to catch my breath and look down, the blurry black form of the smith was leaping up the rocks behind me. With a whimper of exhaustion, I turned again and started to climb. The cold had receded impossibly fast, replaced with the torrential rain and an overpowering humidity. I felt my eirioth reaching for freedom, but when I tried to summon it, the damp air around me suffocated the flames and put them out. I cursed and continued to climb, my muscles screaming at me as I pulled myself higher.

Great. My eirioth was just as useless now as it had been in the snow. At least the rain was giving me a small advantage: it was masking my scent, muddling the senses of the smith. I knew it could still smell me and see me, and probably hear me too, since its senses were so powerful, but the rain must have been doing *something* to mute them, and that meant I had a chance of escaping.

I could hear it snarling through the din, and as soon as I found a patch of somewhat flat ground, I turned around and reached for the sword at my back.

It would make no difference now, considering how unstable my footing was, so I released the handle of the sword and squinted at the blotch of shadow moving towards me.

I had the high ground, but that rarely made much of a difference when it came to animals like this. I'd never seen a smith before, but I'd heard enough stories to know that unless you had people with you, you wouldn't get away alive. Even if you had people with you, your chances of survival were slim.

I wasn't feeling very optimistic right now, but I tried to keep any thoughts of imminent death out of my mind. The smith was snarling and spitting and coming closer with each leap, occasionally losing its footing on the slippery rock. I tried to edge farther away from it, but the stone was becoming too steep to climb safely in the rain. My best chance was to use the high ground to my advantage and hope I didn't slip and fall into the waiting smith's jaws.

The rocks were piled haphazardly around a giant dome of stone, and I was able to maneuver my way along them, creeping slowly backwards around the dome. The smith was scrambling up after me. As soon as it was level with me, it would charge, and I would have no way of escaping it. I had to find a way to fight it and fast.

But there was nowhere else to go. When I rounded the next bend, I looked back to see that I had climbed almost twenty feet into the air, and my pathway was gone. There was a drop all the way to the ground, and a gap of almost eight feet between me and the next stone that wrapped around the pile. I turned back towards the smith, and I could see its ears peeking over the tops of the rocks. It was close.

The giant mound of rock was almost impossible to climb, but I didn't have much of a choice if I wanted to survive. I would be dangling over the drop, supported only by the strength of my limbs, a waiting piece of meat for the smith. But if I went now, I might make it to the other side before the smith made it to me.

I dug my fingers into the stone, hauling myself up and blinking rainwater from my eyes. I shuffled along, my boots struggling to take hold of the slippery rock. I was barely a quarter of the way there when one of my feet lost its hold and my knee scraped painfully along the surface of the stone. I grimaced, but kept going. Out of the corner of my eye, I could see the smith dragging itself up onto the level stone.

I was halfway there now, panting and sweating and shaking from the strain. The cold from the wintery day had seeped deep into my bones, and although the humidity that surrounded me now helped a little, I was still stiff and slow, and it was costing me. I forced myself to move faster, hand over hand, ignoring the new scratches I was earning in my haste.

I was so close now, just a few more struggling shuffles and I would be there. I could climb up over the rocks and keep evading the smith. I could find a place to hide.

A low growl stirred the air around me, and I looked frantically over my shoulder to see that the smith was there, at the edge of the drop, its black fur soaked and matted with rain. A strangled gasp escaped me as the smith's muscles bunched, its hindquarters dropping as it prepared to jump. I knew it could make it. I knew it could catch me in its jaws as it hurdled past. This was it. I hadn't even made it two days in the Evershifting Forest, and I was going to die.

I kept going. The smith leapt. I shoved off the stone and slammed into the edge of the rock. My hands slid on the stone, catching on rough patches. I clung to it miserably, trying not to listen to the snarling of the smith that was racing up behind me.

I shut my eyes tight, trying to focus on the sound of the rain and the smell of the earth and any happy memory I could find. Finnian and Elixir and Gamma and Sycamore and my parents, all of us together, having a good time and laughing and being a big family. I went back to those moments, letting myself drown in them before the smith caught me between its teeth.

A loud yelp drew me out of my thoughts, and my eyes snapped open. I coughed, surprised and dizzy, as I returned to the present. The ache returned to my muscles, the rain and chill soaked back into me, and I got my bearings. With a groan of triumph, I hauled myself up over the edge, rolling onto my back and sputtering as I caught my breath. I frowned, looking up. A big black opening could be seen in the rock above, invisible from the other side of the gap, or even from the ground. You could only see it from a few angles. As I squinted, I thought I caught one of the shadows inside moving.

With another groan I crawled back to the ledge and peered over, and I was unable to contain a gasp at what I saw. The smith was curled up on the forest floor, a pale white object lodged in its chest, driven into its heart. It was completely still.

I gaped down at the beast, rooted to the spot. It was dead. Something had killed it. What *was* that buried in its body? A knife? A tooth?

"You're welcome." A voice rumbled from all around me. I scrambled away from the edge, pressing my back against the stone and looking around me. The tall trees were still but for the leaves bending to the weight of the rain. Besides the obvious pattering of the raindrops, all was quiet.

"Who's there? Where are you?" I demanded, my fingers straying towards the handle of my sword. I wasn't sure how I could fight off an invisible foe, but I hoped

I could at least put on a good show of bravery, even if my nerves were completely shaken from the encounter with the smith. The smith, which was currently oozing blood and quite dead down below.

"How rude. I said *you're welcome*. Are you not going to thank me?" the voice came again, and this time I could tell it came from above me. The trees? The hole in the rocks?

"That was you?" I asked, scowling at the gray sky above. "You killed it? Where are you?" I repeated, dragging myself wearily to my feet as I stepped away from the wall to look up at the cave mouth again.

"Is there really no more decency in this world? Tell you what, you grab me my knife, and I'll tell you where I am so you can throw it to me. How's that sound?" the voice was male, deep and sort of gravelly, like stones being grated together. I still couldn't pinpoint exactly where it was coming from.

I paused for a moment, contemplating his words. I didn't know how I would get back up on the rocks if I went down to retrieve the white blade, but maybe I wouldn't have to. Perhaps this stranger would come down to me once his weapon was returned. Following that line, though, he might try to use the knife on *me* once he had it. In my current state, I wasn't willing to risk it.

"No. Come get it yourself, if you're so eager. Who are you? Why are you out in the middle of nowhere?" I kept myself in the middle of the stone area, not close enough to the edge that I could fall off if I lost my footing, but far enough out that I could see that black opening. I was right. There was someone standing there, shifting around in the darkness, just far enough back that I couldn't see him clearly.

"I'm not in the middle of *anywhere*, actually. I'm somewhere on the eastern side of the Evershifting Forest, and I'm quite comfortable here. The question is who are *you*, and why are *you* out in the eastern side of the Evershifting Forest?" I could see what looked like an arm move briefly into the gray light, but with all the rain, I couldn't see it clearly.

"Doesn't matter to you." I replied sharply.

"Actually, it does. I live here, you don't. You're an invader in my space, and I just saved your life, so I think I've earned a few answers. Come on now, don't make me force them out of you." The voice didn't sound irritated, exactly, just mildly annoyed and, to an extent, somewhat amused. I didn't like that. Only Finnian and Gamma were allowed to have a laugh at my expense.

"I'm from Carlore. I'm looking for the source of the Curse. If you're so knowledgeable about this area, then maybe you can help me." I crossed my arms and waited for some sort of sarcastic answer. Instead, I was met with an empty silence. For a moment, I thought the stranger had gone, but then his voice returned, much more solemn, almost humbled.

"The Curse? Yes. I know a bit about that." He sounded distant, like he was lost in thought. He was silent for another long minute, then he spoke again, and a bit of that taunting amusement was back. "Grab me that knife, and I'll help you. I'd get it myself, but rain isn't exactly the safest weather for me to be out in. I haven't got the best grip on the ground."

I scowled at the opening. "Seriously? You can't just scurry down here and grab it yourself?"

"Please?" the voice asked, not sounding very happy to have to ask again. I sighed and shook my head. "Honestly, are manners not even taught anymore? You should respect your elders more, young lady."

I was already making my way towards a spot that looked safe to climb down, but I stopped and looked up with a confused frown. I still couldn't see anything clearly through the cave mouth, but there was definitely a human-shaped figure hovering in the opening.

"You don't sound very old." Another silence followed that.

"Really?" the voice sounded almost eager, happy. "How old do I sound?"

"Bit of an odd question," I shouted, now making my way down the side of the stone. This was a strange person, and I wasn't sure why I was indulging him, but if I could just keep him talking, and maybe keep him entertained, I might be able to get some answers. He said he could help me with the Curse, and whether he meant it or not, I was willing to take the chance.

"Don't drag me along," the voice shouted back. "Just tell me."

"Alright. You sound thirty something. Maybe forty, but that'd be a stretch. Oh, gross," I wrinkled my nose as I came up to the smith. I'd been around my fair share of dead things, and most of them did smell pretty awful, but the smith was something new entirely. I'd never smelled anything so foul in my entire life.

"You really mean that? Thirty or forty something?" the voice laughed joyfully as I pulled my shirt up over my nose and waded through the muck and rain towards the smith's chest. "Incredible! I'd never have guessed it! Oh . . . oh yes, I forgot how much those things stink. It's really terrible, isn't it? Smells something awful. Sure glad I'm not you. Ah, there you go! Thanks! That thing means a lot to me, it really does. I appreciate it." The voice rambled on as I pulled the knife free of the smith, rolling my eyes and trying not to gag at the smell.

Even covered in the thick crimson blood of the smith, I could tell the dagger was a beautiful one. It was about as long as my forearm, made completely of a hefty bone.

The handle was a thinner part of the bone, sanded down into a comfortable grip and wrapped in coarse rope, and there was a glittering sapphire embedded in the pommel.

"It's quite beautiful," I yelled as I wiped as much blood off on the smith's fur as possible. I tucked it into my belt, careful not to cut myself on the sharp blade, and turned to make the climb back up the rocks.

"You think so? I made it myself. His brother's up here, with me. Didn't think I'd have to use both of them to save you." I could practically hear the grin in the voice, and I scowled at the sound of it. How could he be so cheery with all this rain pouring down around us? Didn't he have other ways to entertain himself than peering out the mouth of a cave and waiting for something exciting to happen?

"Brother, huh?" I shouted, hoping to keep him talking so I could find him. I was nearly back to the ledge where I'd been before.

"Yes. They're made from the canines of a smith. Biggest smith I've ever seen, it was. Quite a challenge to kill, that one, but I managed it. What better mark of such a prize than two fine daggers from its teeth?" his words almost made me lose my grip and fall, but I managed to pull myself up the rest of the way, rising to my feet on the stone and looking up at the cave mouth.

"Smith teeth? Just how many smiths have you killed?" I demanded, resuming my climb a moment later. The route up to the cave mouth seemed well-worn, traversed many times before. I assumed this was where the stranger lived. What didn't make sense was the fact that this giant cave hadn't changed at all when the world around me had. Why couldn't the Evershifting Forest change this part of its environment? Or maybe it could, it just didn't want to.

"Including the one I just saved your hide from? Eighteen." I really did lose my grip from that, staring up at the black opening in complete shock.

"I've never heard of someone surviving *one*, let alone *eighteen*. How did you manage it?" I was close enough now to see the outline a little clearer, but it was like he wasn't all there. Parts of him were missing, like they were bits of smudged charcoal on paper.

"Wouldn't you like to know, little miss nosy. Come on, hurry up, the storm's worsening," I was nearly up, my eyes trained on my next handhold to make sure I didn't slip again. When I looked up, I was startled to realize the form had gone.

"Where are you going?" I yelled, pulling myself up into the shadows of the cave mouth. It was very dark, but now that I was up here, I could see distant slivers of light breaking through from gaps in the ceiling of the tunnel.

"Home. Come on, it isn't far. Just follow the tunnel." His voice bounced back at me along the cave walls. I hesitated, licking my lips nervously, before stepping farther inside. Immediately, I felt like the shadows were swarming around me, grabbing my ankles and twisting my hair. It didn't make any sense; I was standing alone. But I was sure I could sense *something* there, and it made my heart hammer.

One of my hands rested on the metal sword handle in my belt, ready to summon eirioth if I needed it, and the other settled gently on the pommel of the smith tooth dagger, still sticky with the remnants of the smith's blood.

Small stones and bits of dirt and gravel crunched beneath my boots as I limped along. It was almost as if the damp weather made the ache in my leg even worse, and the new cuts I'd earned in my rushed climb weren't helping either. Even so, I pushed past the pain with a grimace and tried to focus on the voice of the stranger, echoing back to me from ahead. Occasionally, I could see him pass through a sliver of light, but it was only a brief glimpse, and he stuck to the shadows as much as possible. Some parts of him seemed to glow faintly, but it may have been a trick of the light. With how much he was talking, my thoughts were too scattered to try and find out where he may have been from. And oh how much he was talking.

"-been ages since I've last had a visitor. A human one, I mean. Plenty of nasty little critters that like to find their way into my caves, you know?" he went on and on, and I tried to tune him out as much as possible. If he wasn't saying anything helpful, I didn't really want to listen to his rambling.

I walked on after him for almost ten minutes before I stopped focusing on trying not to trip in the darkness and shouted up at him.

"Just how far are we going? Don't you want your knife back?" his voice paused at that, and so did the crunching of his footsteps from ahead. A moment later they resumed, and he answered.

"Not much farther. Just a couple bends more." And he was right back to sputtering nonsense. I ignored him again and followed his voice, occasionally lifting my arms in the darker parts of the cave to make sure I wasn't about to walk into a wall.

A total of twenty minutes had passed when I finally spotted an opening ahead. It didn't look very big, and I saw the stooped shadow of the stranger sprint through the rays of drab gray sunlight filtering through an opening in the ceiling.

As I stepped into the small room, I saw that it was somewhat circular, and the jagged crack in the roof of the cave had been filled in with some sort of glass. The rain pounded on it, the drops sliding harmlessly down the sides in rivulets. The room itself was empty but for a small doorway in one corner, tucked away in the misshapen rock. There was a big wooden door there, left open by whoever had passed through a moment ago.

"Hello?" I asked uncertainly, jumping a little at how my voice bounced off the walls around me. Behind me, there was a clatter of pebbles, and I jerked away from the tunnel entrance, my wide eyes scanning every surface. My heart was still racing in my chest.

The stranger must have gone through that doorway, but there were no sounds beyond it. It was completely dark but for the slice of light from the glass, and I was terrified to go any farther without knowing where he was.

"Sorry about that," the voice was closer than it had ever been now, and I took a surprised step back as a shadowed form appeared in the doorway. Again, I had the distinct impression that he wasn't all *there*, but he was still too shrouded in the darkness for me to tell why.

"Come into the light." I ordered, tired of his little game. The way he blended into the shadows so well was unnerving, and I was determined to uncover his secrets.

"Knife first." He retorted.

"No. Come and get it." I pulled the smith tooth dagger from my belt and held it forward on an open palm. I watched the form closely. He had stilled so much it was hard to see him in the shadows. Finally, a sigh echoed around us.

"You're going to regret that." And then he shuffled forward into the silver light flowing through the glass above. I gasped and stumbled backwards, dropping the knife.

The first thing I registered was his size. He was impossibly tall, around seven feet, but that was probably the least abnormal thing about him. At first I thought he might be one of the darker-skinned people from Carlore or even one of the travelers from Coldmon, but then I realized he didn't have skin at all. He was just *bones*.

A living, moving skeleton made from a jumble of black and ashen bones, eerily still in my moment of panic. But it wasn't the black bones or the empty eye sockets or the ever-present grin on the skull's face that made me freeze with terror. It was the little flecks of glowing green that laced the bones of his arms, that bloomed like flowers along his shoulder blades or the rungs of the spinal column.

It was the Curse.

9
SAKURA

I scrambled backwards faster than I had when Finnian accidentally set fire to my bowl of porridge, which was a considerable feat. As I slid along the stone, my hand was already grasping my sword handle, pulling it free of my belt as the flame-sword blazed to life. My heart was pounding, my pulse roaring in my ears, my scattered thoughts slowly coming together as I crouched into a fighting position, my eirioth prickling and eager beneath the surface. My attention was wholly on the black skeleton, but he didn't seem very concerned.

Instead, he bent down and picked up the dagger, sliding it into a leather sheath strapped to the inside of one of his forearms. An identical sheath and dagger pommel could be seen on his other arm. When I twitched at the movement, he half-heartedly raised his hands — his hand *bones*, that is, all of them just hovering in the air — palms out in a show of peace. I wasn't having it. What *was* he? A Cursed *human*? Impossible.

Is it? I hated doubting myself, but ever since Elixir had become corrupted by the Curse, I had been more prone to doing so. I had worried that the Curse might be growing, and one day be strong enough to take a human. Was it possible for the Curse to have evolved so fast?

"Who- what-" I shook my head, my confusion and anger and fear fueling the powerful stalk of fire spewing out the metal handle of my sword. I'd rarely used my eirioth in such a burst of emotion, but the sudden realization of what was standing before me had been enough to jostle my mind back into a state of defense.

"And *this* is why I haven't had a visitor in so many years." The jaw bones moved, naturally and calmly, as the voice echoed out around the room. I gaped at him, eyes wide, jaw slack. A moment later I regained control of my features and shook my head at him.

"You . . . you're Cursed. How-" I pursed my lips, steadying my voice. "How long have you been like this?" I had to know. I had to know if I was in danger, or if Finnian and Gamma were. Could the corruption have spread from Elixir to them?

The thought chilled my blood, and I tried to shake the thought as the skeleton spoke again.

"This?" one of his arms dropped, and he examined the back of the other hand, which was flecked with bright specks of green. "Years." His voice was distant, sad, but I didn't believe it for an instant. If the Curse drove animals to hunt and kill people, it could probably drive humans to do the same.

"That's not . . . it isn't possible." I shook my head, standing up as tall as I could and holding my flame-sword between myself and the skeleton. "Who are you? What's your name?"

"My name doesn't matter to anyone. Neither do I." He tilted his head — skull, I suppose — to the side, and even though he had no eyes, I could feel his gaze on me. It was the feeling of being watched from somewhere in the distance, from somewhere you couldn't see, and somewhere you couldn't find. It unsettled me.

"I'm sure that's not true," I hissed through clenched teeth. "Who are you?"

"Not yet," the skeleton held up one long finger. "I want your name first. Tell me who you are and why you're after the Curse, then I'll spill."

I huffed air out through my cheeks. I didn't like this. Too many things were unnatural about it, too many things were running through my head. It wasn't safe here in this small cave, alone with a seven foot tall dead man. But what choice did I have? I was willing to risk my life to find the source of the Curse and destroy it, and if this pile of bones could help me, shouldn't I at least try to gain his help?

"Sakura Ironlan. I'm an orphan from Carlore. I want to find the source of the Curse and get rid of it for good. I want to rid Horcath of this awful thing that plagues it so that my family and my friends can be safe. Now explain yourself. Who are you, where are you from, and how in the name of all the stars and clouds are you *Cursed*?" I held the flame-sword up again, the tip grazing the skeleton's chest. He didn't move, didn't even flinch. I hadn't expected him to, but I was still a little disappointed that the sword had had no clear effect on him.

"You think you can do that?" he asked skeptically, avoiding my question. I glared at him, but he ignored it. "You think there's a way to get rid of the Curse permanently? Keep everyone safe from it?" he didn't sound doubtful, he sounded . . . hopeful.

"You don't?" I challenged, and for a long moment we were both silent. I hated that I couldn't read him. There were no features to read.

"Of course I do. I just don't have a body capable of pursuing such hopes." He held up one of his arms, flexing the finger bones and curling them into a fist. He was quiet for a long moment, then he dropped his hand and nodded. "Alchemy."

"What?"

"My name. It's Alchemy. Just call me Chem. Now, we've got a lot of work to do," he was suddenly out of his glum mood, jumpy and lively once more. He rubbed the bones of his hands together eagerly before turning around and bounding into the dark corridor he'd come from moments ago.

I blinked, flame-sword flickering and spitting, mind racing. What had just happened? Was this stranger an ally or an enemy?

He's Cursed. Nothing he says can be believed. He's probably trying to lure you back there to kill you. I could practically hear Derek's disdain in my head. I could hear Finnian's gentle chiding, pointing out how stupid it would be to listen to a talkative skeleton.

And yet I had to. Without this Alchemy character, I might never learn more about the Curse. This could be what I needed to finally take the first steps in the right direction, if I was only brave enough and smart enough to navigate my way through them.

With a shaky breath, I released my eirioth. It left begrudgingly, complaining beneath the surface of my skin and waiting for me to call it back, but I didn't. I tucked the handle back into my belt and stepped into the darkness after Alchemy.

It was a cold, narrow passage, and I felt a tingle rushing through me as I walked through it, using my hands to guide me through the blackness. My head spun, stars appeared in my vision, and I lost my footing once or twice. A coldness stole over me that seemed to numb everything, chilling me to the bone and making all sense of being and emotion fade into the background.

When I was through the cramped tunnel, I blinked and gasped as everything came back into sharp focus. The beating of my heart, the ragged rhythm of my breath, the shaky fear lurking in the back of my mind.

I was in another dome-shaped room, but this one was much larger and more well-lit. There were more doors leading off to various other rooms, but they were all closed. The ceiling was whole here, and there were lanterns with flickering flames inside them dotted at regular intervals around the room's curved walls.

There was a tattered old animal skin on the floor, one I presumed was bear or smith, but didn't bother to ask about. A curved desk was set against the wall on my left, scattered with browning papers and worn books and scraggly quills. On the right was a roughly constructed wooden rocking chair, sitting and collecting dust and cobwebs.

"You live here?" I asked, spotting Alchemy hunched over the desk. I squirmed at the sight of him, the bones of his fingers picking through the pages he was looking at. Was he even looking at them? Could he see?

"Yes." He replied, sounding distracted.

"How can you speak? Or see? Or even be alive?" I wasn't prepared to come any closer to him, but I didn't back away when he straightened and looked over at me. The black skull was eerie, and if I hadn't been so spiteful of my own fear, I may have averted my gaze.

"The Curse does many things," he said finally, his jaw moving in time with the words. "One of those things is keeping dead things alive. You've seen the creatures it inhabits. Their skin falls off, their blood seeps out, their eyes roll back in their heads. But they still live."

"Not for long," I pointed out. "They die eventually, and so does the bit of the Curse inside of them." This much I knew from what little research had been done on the bodies of the Cursed.

"Oh?" Alchemy steepled his fingers and tilted his head to the side. "Do you think so?"

Of course I thought so. All the facts pointed to that. But just how many of those facts were there? Not enough to prove anything concrete. There was still so much we didn't know about the Curse, about what it did to animals.

"Tell me something," the skeleton turned around and rested his hip against the table, looking at me with that creepy, blank expression. "What is the Curse?"

"A disease. A sickness."

"Wrong. What does the Curse target?"

"The weak."

"Right. When does the Curse leave it?"

"It doesn't. It dies with it."

"Wrong again, Miss Ironlan." He shoved off the table and began to pace in front of me, the bones of his feet clicking on the stone. "It's a complicated thing. Nobody knows it as well as me, for obvious reasons, but I still don't know everything." He paused in his pacing, staring down at the floor, then resumed. "What I do know is that it is not a disease. It is alive, and it is dangerous. It possesses things, killing them from the inside-out. It hunts down the minds most susceptible to its power and corrupts it, using it for its own evil purposes. When it no longer has a use for that body, it leaves it." He looked up at me again, his hands folded together in a knot of bones. "When the host body dies, the Curse leaves to inhabit another. Do you understand? The Curse cannot die. It only grows."

"Would it be possible for the Curse to become stronger? Strong enough to corrupt a stronger-minded being?" my brows furrowed. "How did it corrupt you? How come you're still here? Doesn't it control you?"

"So many questions, so little time," Alchemy shook his head. "If we want to find a solution to all this, we need to get moving fast, and I know just the place to start." He pointed at the papers on the desk and said, "We'll start in Clawbreak. There are all sorts of back stabbers down there, so they're bound to know something."

"Why's that?"

"The Curse murders people. Who better to utilize it as a weapon than murderers?" he was marching towards me now, and I scrambled backwards into the tunnel, racing back through its stomach-turning passage until I was back in the dim, round room.

"But how will we get there?" I asked, looking over my shoulder. He was right behind me, but he seemed unfazed by my attempts to keep a good distance away from him. "And why Clawbreak? Isn't it dangerous?"

I'd heard of Clawbreak before, a vile place for thieves and thugs. No tourists ever went there, and neither did travelers. Why would they, when its sister island, Famark, was so much more welcoming? The reason behind Clawbreak's cruel reputation was unknown to most people, but it didn't matter to me. If it was a place where I could potentially die, I wanted to know why exactly I was going there. Alchemy said we might learn something about the Curse, but would we learn it and then be able to use that knowledge before we got chucked into the sea with chains around our wrists? I raked a hand through my hair anxiously, yanking my fingers through the tangles they found there. Why was I already thinking through this with Alchemy in mind? I hardly knew him. I shouldn't be putting so much trust in him so early. But what other choice did I have?

"Dangerous to you? Maybe. Dangerous to me?" he was ahead of me now, and we were walking through the first tunnel. He turned around to face me, walking backwards, and in the next patch of fading sunlight gestured to himself. "I don't think I have much to worry about."

I shuddered at that. Could Alchemy be killed? I was sure his bones could be broken, but surely they had been before. Did the Curse heal him? Was it impossible for him to die again?

"How long have you lived in these caves? Maybe Clawbreak has changed." I argued. Alchemy had mentioned being here for a long time during his rambling, but exactly how long *was* a long time? Ten years? Twenty? Fifty?

"From your concerned warbling," Alchemy called from in front of me. "I don't think it has."

I clenched my fists, trying to come up with a clever question, something to slow him down or tell me more about who he really was. Did he have family? What had landed him in the Evershifting Forest? Why didn't the Forest change his cave? How had the Curse taken hold of him? Did he not have a special connection to other Cursed beings, or even the Curse itself?

I wanted to ask him all of these. I wanted to know if it was possible for him to sense the Curse's location, to follow it and find it and destroy it. But there were too many risks. Maybe it would give the Curse a stronger power over him and drive him to kill me. Or maybe it already was. What was I *doing*, following a living skeleton through a cave? He was too human, and that was making me let down my guard. He still belonged to the Curse, and that meant he was a threat and should be treated as such.

"You sure do frown a lot." With a start, I realized he was walking backwards again, facing me. My startled expression was wiped off my face as I scowled at him.

"You sure do talk a lot." I spat back.

"Not normally, I don't. I've never been much of a talker. But being alone for so many years gives you so many stories to tell. Have the kingdoms changed much? Is good ol' King Warin still around?"

"Warin? Warin Dearsol?" I frowned. King Warin, the leader of Freetalon, had died over two hundred years ago. I hardly remembered him from my history lessons. He had been succeeded by his heir, Reginald, whose son Adam took the throne after he'd died. King Adam had died years ago, though, and now *his* son, Allan Dearsol, was the king.

"No? Poor fellow. S'pose he has a grandson or something that runs the kingdom, then? He ever marry that gal of his? Ellie something?" the more Alchemy talked, the more I frowned. How could he know so much, yet know so little?

"A great-grandson, actually. And I don't remember Warin's wife's name. That was from hundreds of years ago. Why do you care so much? Are you from Freetalon?" I felt crazy having this conversation. It hurt my head thinking back through all those old royal bloodlines.

"Great-grandson? Oh my . . ." Alchemy's voice turned distant again. "And yeah. I'm from Freetalon. Has it changed a lot?"

"A lot since when? Just how old are you? How long have you been here?" I was ready to get some answers, but some part of me didn't fully expect them to be given.

"Not long enough to go crazy, not short enough to remember everything. Are there any wars going on?" his voice turned joyful again, but I wasn't finished yet.

"No, there aren't. Not any major ones, anyway. Why? Who are you really?"

"Don't remember. Come on, be careful, these rocks are slippery. You know, this magical forest leaves my home alone, but it won't give me a safe staircase down to the forest floor. Bit rude of it, don't you agree?" we had exited the tunnel, and he was now hopping down the rocks, his bones slipping on all of them. He was right; he had no way to grip the slick surface.

I followed him as quickly as I could, but he was already disappearing into the forest, winding between the tall stalks of the tree trunks. He was so hard to see, blending into the shadows, that I relied on the sound of his footsteps and his voice alone, but even that was hard to tell apart from the pouring rain and the rumbling thunder.

"Hey!" I shouted, stumbling through the mud after him. "Where are you going?" I could hardly even tell up from down, much less the direction we were going. Alchemy seemed to know exactly where he was.

"I told you! Clawbreak!" came the voice from ahead of me, gravelly and rumbling to the point I almost mistook it for the thunder roaring overhead. Cursing, I ran after him, boots sliding in muck, face damp with rainwater.

I didn't want to dwell on what would be waiting for us in Clawbreak. I was still too overwhelmed by everything else to begin comprehending what troubles I might run into crossing kingdom borders with a giant talking skeleton.

Speaking of kingdom borders, was I even in Carlore anymore? There were no dividing walls or markers between Carlore and Brightlock in the Evershifting Forest. It was simply too treacherous a place to try and construct anything, so after a few failed attempts, nobody had bothered to make something concrete. After the Curse started causing problems, the Forest had been abandoned completely, and had remained so for the past couple hundred years.

The thought of no longer being in my home kingdom sent chills ricocheting through my body. I didn't like the thought of already having traveled so far from Finnian and Gamma. Was it even possible for me to have traveled so far in such a short time? I knew the Forest had ways of moving things from one side of its boundaries to the other, but could it do that with living things as well?

I shook the thoughts away. Now was not the time for homesickness.

"Hold still." I yelped as the voice sounded directly beside me, and I realized Alchemy had come back to stand in front of me. He was nearly invisible in the black and gray forest around us.

"Why?" I demanded, trying to make it sound like I hadn't been so startled by him. I shrugged my light packs higher on my shoulders and pushed soaked, dark hair out of my face to stare more intently into those black eye sockets.

"The Forest is shifting. It's best to be as still as possible to avoid falling into the ground. Quiet. I don't want to answer any questions about this place, because that would be a lengthy and tiring answer for both of us." He crossed his arms, creating the sound of clattering bones that I found I didn't much care for, and stood as still as stone. I did my best to mimic him, keeping my mouth clamped firmly shut.

Even though I was ready for the shift this time, it still took me by surprise. One moment, everything was gray and blue and soaked and sad-looking, and the next, it was all smudged together into a whirlwind of color and sound. My head spun, and I thought my eyes had rolled back into my head when sparks started to appear in my vision.

I was about to fall over when the flashing colors disappeared. Alchemy and I found ourselves standing in a forest of tall white and gray trees, thin and spindly, with hundreds of gold and orange and red leaves. The ground was littered with them too, drifting around our feet in gentle gusts of wind. The sun was shining bright over our heads, and I could hear the gurgling of a stream somewhere off to my right. The rainwater that had chilled me moments ago was drying shockingly fast, leaving me warm and cozy.

"Stop gawking like a surprised school child," Alchemy chided, even though he sounded merry. I glared at him as he turned to walk on again. It was even more unsettling seeing him in the clear light like this. His black bones looked like they were chalky, like charcoal, like I might be able to break off a piece of his ribs and scrawl my name onto the side of a boulder.

"How long will it take us to reach Clawbreak?" I asked, my mind turning to the supplies in my pack. I only had enough for another day or two, and that was only for myself. I doubted Alchemy could eat, due to his obvious lack of a stomach, but he might surprise me with an appetite, and I wasn't prepared to share my meager rations.

"Not very long. I think we're much closer to the western borders of the Forest now. A few more miles that way, and we'll be looking down at the Great Lakes from those blasted cliffs." Alchemy replied, and I raised my eyebrows.

Now that he mentioned it, I could smell the distinct sting of salt in the air, rolling towards us on a breeze from the west. The hulking pile of boulders that had been behind us moments ago was also gone, replaced with the sprawling landscape of a forest trapped in the sleeping moments of autumn.

"How can you tell?" I asked as I followed him towards the west. I looked up at the sky, then all around us, but there was no way to tell where we were other than the scent of the sea. Could Alchemy even smell things?

"You pick up a skill or two when you live alone for so many years." Alchemy replied, just as cryptic as he'd been before. I decided to stop trying to wheedle information out of him for the time being, but I would definitely try again later, when we were in a situation where I wasn't relying on him to get me out of a giant magical forest full of dangerous creatures.

But just because I wasn't going to keep trying to get him to tell me about himself didn't mean I couldn't learn more about where I was and what Alchemy knew about the Curse.

"Why haven't I seen any Cursed animals here yet? Isn't the Forest supposed to be where all of them are coming from?" I tried to keep alongside him, but not only did that make me slightly uncomfortable, his legs were so ridiculously long that I had no hope of matching his stride.

"Is that what they've told you? Anyone who says that is an idiot. The reason most of the Cursed animals come from the Evershifting Forest is because the Evershifting Forest is where all the animals *live*. It's a plentiful breeding ground for the Curse, so it likes to play around in here, but it certainly isn't the source. There are probably more Cursed beasts in the Great Lakes than there are in here." Alchemy started to climb a small slope to our left, and I hesitantly followed. The smell of salt was much stronger here, and I knew we must've been getting close to the cliffs.

"What do you mean breeding ground? You mean it spreads? Because it's contagious?" I frowned at him as I crested the hill. My heart beat a little faster in my chest as I saw the dark blue of the Great Lakes beyond the trees. We were almost there.

"How many times will I have to tell you before it gets through your thick skull?" Alchemy looked over his shoulder blade at me, and somehow, even with no features to bear expressions, I could see his contempt.

"I'm a bit confused about all this," I admitted, my tone hard and agitated.

"Obviously," he huffed. "Look, the Curse is not a *disease*, Ironling. It's a living thing. It doesn't make things sick, it *inhabits* them, lives inside them until they've served their purpose, then lets them go." He waggled the bones of his fingers in my face, imitating a butterfly. I scrunched up my nose at him, my brows drawing together.

"Don't call me Ironling. How can it be alive? That makes no sense."

"It's dark magic. Someone's been tampering with things they shouldn't be. Come on now, we've got some docks to get to."

"Hold on," I stopped walking, and he looked back at me again, his shoulders slumping with irritation. I could care less about his impatience. If he'd been hiding out in the woods for 'so many years', as he kept saying, he could spare a few seconds to think straight.

"What now?" he complained.

"How do you expect to get yourself on a boat? You can't very well march on and demand to sail with someone. I mean, no offense, but you aren't the most approachable person." I gestured vaguely at his skeletal frame.

"Aren't I though?" he sounded amused again, and I groaned. Was he always like this? I wasn't sure I could stand traveling with a companion with so many mood changes. I wondered for a moment if he could still talk if I shoved a gag in his mouth, then decided I didn't want to get close enough to put that gag in anyway. The whole living skeleton thing was still an eerie ordeal to me.

"Seriously, how do you plan on getting us to Clawbreak?" I crossed my arms and tried to muster up a commanding expression, similar to the one Finnian always wore in our more difficult training sessions by the King's Scar. Thinking of Finnian made my heart ache, and I was grateful when Alchemy spoke again so I could pull my mind away from thoughts of my brother.

"'Us'? Whoever said you were coming with me?" that sent a jolt of surprise through me. For some reason, it hadn't occurred to me that Alchemy could really be the one to call the shots here. He was taller than me, knew the terrain better, and was, as far as I knew, indestructible.

"You need me." I said simply, not entirely sure if that was true or not. The best I could do for now was hope he was dense enough to believe that my help really would be valuable to . . . to what? "Why do you want to go anyway? If you really had a good reason to go, why wouldn't you have gone sooner?"

"Drat. You're smarter than I give you credit for, Ironling." Alchemy shrugged his broad shoulders and looked back towards the Great Lakes, ignoring my nonplussed glare. "You're right. I do need you. You know more about the current state of Horcath than I do, and I know more about the Curse than you do. I suppose we ought to share what we know with each other, yes?"

"I'm not giving you a history lesson, and it's pretty obvious you don't want to give me more than bits and pieces at a time. Why not focus on what I asked before, and tell me your plan?" I flexed my fingers over the iron sword handle in my belt. I'd never paid much attention to anything relating to bone injuries before. How much damage could fire do to bones?

"Right. We'll be stowaways, of course, and then-" he stopped speaking suddenly, frozen. He didn't move for a long moment, and the only sound was that of the distantly bubbling stream and the rustling of leaves around us in the sea breeze. I raised my eyebrows in a mock question.

"Well?" I asked finally, and he jerked sharply, as if he had forgotten I was standing there. I nearly jumped myself, having thought for a moment that his soul or his consciousness or whatever it was that inhabited this skeleton had simply left it.

"Sorry. I heard something coming this way. It sounded like a . . ." he looked down at me, tilting his head to the side. I squirmed under his scrutiny, unnerved by the fact that I could feel him watching me when he had no eyes to watch with. "Nevermind. Come along now, we've still got a good bit of traveling to do. We'll make camp on the cliff's edge."

What, so you can push me off in my sleep? I didn't dare speak the thought aloud, but it crossed my mind mere seconds after he'd said it. I would have to be careful to make sure he was closer to the cliffside than I was, and even then, I probably wouldn't be sleeping tonight. That beckoned another question: could *he* sleep? If he could, did he have to?

My head was starting to hurt from all the mysteries surrounding Alchemy, so I chose to think about something else as we picked up walking again, marching steadily closer to the sounds of crashing waves and the smell of salty sea spray.

Thinking of other things was dangerous, because all my mind wanted to think about was home or the Curse, or maybe even my family. Not just Finnian, but our parents and our older sister. What would they do if they were still alive now? Would they support my decision to go hunting for the Curse? Would any of them come with me?

Losing them had been the worst pain I had ever experienced, and I would never wish it on anyone else. The sudden, cruel grip of loneliness had seized me in a vice-like claw, dragging me into a horrible reality where Finnian and I were left to our own devices. We had Gamma, of course, but what was she to us when we had just lost our parents? Nothing but a shoulder to cry on, at least until the grief had passed.

The memories were painful, not even whole. I sometimes wondered if I did that subconsciously, afraid I wouldn't be able to handle seeing it all strung together, flowing through my mind like a fully constructed story. Even so, the few flashes I had of that day were enough to bring tears to my eyes and ice to my heart.

It had started out like any other day, beautiful and sunny and clouded by the threat of the Curse. It wasn't as looming as it was now, but it was certainly there, and people were wary of it. My family wasn't too afraid. Hazelnut was well out of harm's way, backed by the King's Scar and the borders of its fellow towns. My family had complete trust in the people set in position to defend us from the Cursed animals, and I shared that trust. I was safe and warm and happy; we all were.

The day had started with Aurora taking Finnian and I to visit Duke Ferin in his temple. It was a weekly tradition of ours, one that wasn't always pleasant, but it kept us from being bored. The Duke of Hazelnut never welcomed us with a smile or a joke or a treat, but his wife, Lady Nala, always did. She was Finnian and I's favorite part of every visit. After the required formalities with Duke Ferin, where we told him about our studies that week and Aurora showed him the newest decorations for his temple our father had crafted for him, we would always go find Lady Nala in the upper floors of the temple to share cookies and spooky stories. Sometimes she would take us to the Duke's dragon stables and introduce us to his many dragons.

"You're only supposed to bond with one dragon," she had explained to us once, as we marveled at one of the Duke's grand feathered beasts. "But the Dukes of the towns have never been fond of that rule. They like to show off just how much money they really have."

"Do you have many dragons?" I'd asked her, but she had laughed that pretty, lilting laugh of hers and shook her head.

"Only one, my dear Sakura. She's the only one I'll ever need. One day, when you have your own dragon, you'll understand that bond." And only a few months later, when I'd met Sycamore, I did, and I cherished it just as much as Lady Nala did.

That particular visit to Duke Ferin's temple was unlike any we'd had before. The Duke was busy with papers concerning something troubling in Walnut, although Finnian and I hadn't known the details. Aurora had seemed nervous about his attitude that day, even though he was just as grumpy and pushy as he usually was. I didn't think much of it until our older sister had ordered us out of the Duke's office, giving us clear instructions to go find Lady Nala and stay with her until we were ready to go home.

When the heavy office doors had swung closed, Finnian had looked at me and told me to go to Lady Nala and hang out with her for a bit. He said he'd catch up, but I said there was no way I would let him have all the fun of eavesdropping on Aurora and the Duke.

After a short argument, he had relented, and we stood out there in the hallway with our ears pressed up against the office door. It was thick wood, but pretty soon Aurora and the Duke were shouting, and it was easy to make out what was being said.

It was eleven years ago, when I was only five years old, so I don't remember all the details, but I do remember Aurora mentioning something about the Curse and how dangerous it was. She had said something about doubling the soldiers we had stationed at the watch posts. Ferin was furious that she suggested he waste money and resources on such a thing. He had said that the Curse was kept sufficiently at bay, and none of its creatures slipped past their defenses.

She had been ordered out of his office after that, and Finnian and I had sprinted down the hallway towards the stairs, hurrying up to find Lady Nala. We said nothing as we crunched down our butter cookies, and we tried to steady our breathing and hide our flushed cheeks by the time Aurora came upstairs to retrieve us.

She looked tired, her usually pristinely-kept ebony hair untidy, a few of the strands hanging down over her face. Despite the obvious lack of energy she had, her green eyes were still bright, and she flashed that dazzling smile at us when she reached the top of the stairs.

"Come here, you two, Moma and Papa will be waiting." She'd held out her hands and Finnian and I had run to grab them. We said goodbye to Lady Nala and let our older sister lead us out of the temple.

Finnian didn't accompany us all the way home. He had been asked to help at one of the local saddle-making shops in Hazelnut, and Aurora and I had dropped him off there with a joyful farewell and a promise to pick him up for suppertime. Once he was inside the building, Aurora had beamed down at me.

"Ready to go home?" she'd asked. With a brilliant, gap-toothed grin, I'd nodded. Those were the last words she'd said to me.

The walk home was short and sweet. We stayed quiet, like we normally did, but it was peaceful, even happy. It stayed that way until our house came into view. A small, shabby building tucked into the Eirioth Wood, a short walk from the Hazelwood Inn, with just enough rooms to squeeze the five of us in. When Aurora and I arrived, half of it was in shambles.

With a horrified scream, Aurora had run inside. I'd stood outside, shaking and gawking at the splintered timbers and the broken glass and those awful smears of something dark along the wood.

I stayed that way until I heard another shriek from inside the remaining half of the house, followed by a guttural snarl. I don't know what drove me to move, but I ran inside, screaming for Moma, yelling Aurora's name at the top of my lungs as I ran with vision blurred by tears.

When I'd reached Moma and Papa's room, I'd stopped in the doorway, screaming and sobbing and screaming some more when I realized what was happening. A Cursed wolf and some sort of Cursed badger had my family cornered. Papa was in the far corner of the room, bleeding profusely from his side and a long gash in his thigh and fending the wolf off with a broken table leg. Moma was lying motionless on the floor, the badger close to her neck, making awful squelching noises as it dug into her flesh.

"Sakura!" my father had yelled when he saw me, horrified. Aurora saw me, too, from her position huddled near Moma and Papa's wardrobe. The attention of the Cursed wolf shifted as it looked up at me.

I'll never forget what it looked like. Foaming at the mouth, missing one eye, a rippling tide of glowing green muscle and mangy black fur and snapping jaws. I don't remember it lunging for me, but I remember Aurora throwing herself out at the last moment.

The memory cuts off there. I'm always glad it does, because I don't think I could bear to see what came after that. I know I witnessed it, but some part of me won't let me see it all again, only moments of splattering blood and flying flesh and the terrible, piercing screams of my sister's agony.

The next thing I remember clearly is waking up in the arms of Gamma at Hazelwood Inn, surrounded by yelling and crying adults, but most importantly by Gamma and Eric and Finnian.

"Ironling?" the sounds splintered and distorted, and before I could stop myself, a hysterical scream tore from my throat. My head spun.

The black wood walls and the yelling people and the sobbing Finnian were gone, replaced by whorls of orange and gold and gray, and a giant, spindly black figure hulking in the corner of my vision.

"Hey, quiet! You're gonna draw attention! Are you alright?" my focus returned, and I realized I was staring into the face of a blackened skull. Reality slowly reasserted itself, and I remembered everything that had happened in the past few days.

"Alchemy." I said bluntly, partially to confirm I was remembering everything correctly and partially because I wanted to hear my own voice and be sure I wasn't dreaming. I still felt a little disoriented, but slowly my senses returned in full force, bringing me the scent of an autumn breeze and the sounds of rustling leaves and distant birdsong.

"Chem." The skeleton before me said, and I blinked, confused for a moment, before I vaguely recalled him telling me to call him Chem.

"Right," I shook my head, cleared my throat, and looked around. How long had I zoned out for? Had I cried? I didn't feel any particularly heady emotions, other than embarrassment and the rumbling anxiety that often accompanied any reflection of that part of my past, but I wanted to be sure. If Alchemy had seen something in my expression, in the way I'd suddenly frozen stiff. Finnian had told me after previous visits into my memory that I always looked lost and sad whenever it happened.

"What just happened?" Alchemy asked, as if reading my mind. I cleared my throat again, pointedly keeping my gaze averted. I was too unsettled to look into those empty eye sockets steadily right now.

"Nothing. I got distracted. Camp on the edge of a cliff? Sounds great. Let's go." I pushed past him, following the sound of sea birds and the gusts of salty air that pushed to us through the trees.

I didn't hear Alchemy following me for a long moment, but I wouldn't look back at him, and eventually I could hear him crunching along through the leaves after me. I didn't like having him at my back, but some part of me wanted to leave him there to see what would happen. There must have been an ulterior motive behind his helping me, and I believed he needed my help to reach his goal, but I had my own motives, and I needed his knowledge on the Curse. I knew it was a risk giving him a chance to get to me like this, but if he didn't want me around him, why offer to help? Why save me from the smith in the first place?

I lifted a low-hanging tree branch out of my way and gasped as I stepped onto a thin stretch of land free of trees. Ahead of me, barely ten feet away, was a jutting cliff face, a craggy drop to the crashing waves below. I inched forward, just enough to peer over the edge and see the frothing white water, the soaked black rocks, and the low-flying gulls seeking food in the nooks and crannies of the cliffside.

"Have you never seen the seas?" the gravelly voice was startlingly close to me, and I leapt to the side, my head snapping up at Alchemy. I stepped away from the edge of the cliff, bringing me to Alchemy's side as I looked up at him.

"No. The biggest body of water I've ever seen is the Fruit Spring. It's like a mini sea in and of itself." I wasn't actually sure if that was true. I didn't know a lot about the Great Lakes, and I certainly didn't know anything about sailing, but I was defensively proud of the Spring and its walls of fruit orchards.

"Curious. Whatever drove you to leave your own kingdom?" Alchemy tilted his ashen skull towards the sky, burning a low orange and red above us. I couldn't see any clouds, so I wouldn't set up a tent. Even if I was slowly finding it within myself to place a small amount of trust in this Cursed man, I wasn't ready to seclude myself behind walls just yet, even if they were walls of tent canvas. I wanted to keep one eye on Alchemy as much as possible, just in case.

"My family was put in danger by the Curse. I'm ready for it to be gone." I clenched my jaw, trying not to let myself be drawn back into the memories of the fight with Elixir.

"You aren't the only one, it seems," Alchemy looked back towards the Forest behind us, and I frowned. Before I could say anything, I heard something coming closer. Rhythmic, powerful, a sound that was all too familiar to someone who had grown up around dragons.

I would have told Alchemy to try and get out of sight, but it was already too late. A burly shadow erupted from an opening in the trees a little to the south of where we stood. The eirioth dragon banked sharply, swooping over the deadly drop down to the Great Lakes and landing with a hefty *thud* on the stone overhang before us. I didn't even have to look up at the rider to tell who it was; the rich brown feathers of the dragon told me all I needed to know.

"I thought I told you to stay with Finnian," I snapped, my gaze lifting to meet Derek's. He scowled at me, sliding down from Bear's back and stepping forward to stand beside me.

"Like I've ever taken orders from you. Who in the world is *this*?" Derek's glare shifted to Alchemy, who stood patiently a safe distance away. Bear was watching him with wide, fearful golden eyes, but Derek only seemed irritated by his presence.

"Alchemy," I replied dryly. "He knows a lot about the Curse. He's helping me." Derek raised a dark eyebrow, unimpressed.

"You sure do make friends fast. Where did you find him?"

"Technically, I found her," Alchemy pitched in. "And really, Ironling, I'd prefer to be called Chem. Who might you be?" he turned his skull to face Derek, and I saw a flicker of hesitation cross Derek's features. No doubt he was having the same mistrustful thoughts I'd been having since I met the skeleton.

"Derek." He said simply, his dark eyes returning to me for a brief moment before recentering on Alchemy. "What are you?"

"He's a Cursed skeleton hermit, what more do you need to know? Derek, what are you doing here? Why is Bear here? What's happening back home?" I knew I hadn't been gone very long yet, but the Curse moved fast, and I was desperate to know how my brother was. Had he and Gamma known Derek would come after me? How long had he been hunting for me? "How did you even find me?" I added.

"You screamed." He said bluntly, and I pursed my lips. Before I could say anything, he went on. "Everyone's fine back home. They're locking all the dragons up in the War Cells; there was no way I was letting you come out here alone, and there's no way I'm letting them trap Bear down there." He hesitated, an apologetic look crossing his features. "I tried to get Sycamore out, too, but I wasn't able to. She'll be safe, though. The Curse shouldn't be able to reach her down there."

The War Cells. I'd nearly forgotten what Walter told me, that Duke Ferin had spoken of using them to contain the dragons, keeping them and us safe. In all the mess since then, I hadn't had the time to worry about it. How much was I going to worry about it now? Sycamore was locked up down there in those awful, dark cells. They'd been made for prisoners of war, the powerful mages from the Havoc Ages, not the peaceful dragons the people of my kingdom loved so much. How could the Curse take a bond so special and put bars between it? Would it keep growing, keep finding ways to split people away from the things they loved?

"It's okay. She'll be fine." I told him thickly, trying to conceal my unease at the thought of Sycamore in those rank stone cells. "And Finnian? Gamma?"

"They're okay. Finnian is getting a bit better, and he, Gamma, and Walter are already helping to redouble the defenses against the Curse. They reassured me that they had it under control. Now I need you to reassure me that *you* have things under control, because from where I'm standing, it doesn't look like you do." His glower returned full-force, any sign of the compassionate boy facing me a moment ago erased. I felt that familiar stab of envy at how well he could conceal emotions.

"I've got it under control. We're going to Clawbreak to see what we can find out about where the Curse might be originating from," I told him, trying to put all the surety I could into my voice.

"I thought he knew everything," Derek argued, gesturing at where Alchemy stood, bone-arms crossed, looking out at the Great Lakes.

"Not everything, just some stuff. Look, I'm hungry, and it's been a long day, and I'm sore and scratched, so can we please set up a camp before we get to the tough conversations?" I shrugged my pack off my shoulder, already reaching inside to pull free some of the dry kindling I'd stocked up on my first night.

Derek huffed, cast Alchemy another glare, then reached towards Bear's back to help. The leather armor strapped around the dragon fell away as he undid straps and buckles, pulling free the large bags that hung from the back of the saddle. He produced a thick slab of rabbit meat to cook and started to assemble a fire pit while I set the kindling inside and summoned my eirioth.

Eager as ever, it erupted from my skin in a dozen tiny pinpricks, making sure I understood how much power I held at my command. As freeing as it might have felt to let all that power free, I knew it would leave me more exhausted than I already was, and besides, I only needed a small spark. I sent a sliver of flame into the pile of kindling, urging it to catch, and a moment later a bonfire was blazing in the pit Derek had built, fueled by the logs Alchemy had somehow obtained while Derek and I had hunched over the pit.

When the rabbit was cooking and we were all sitting cross-legged around the fire, Bear flopped on the stubbly grass behind Derek and I as we looked over the flames at Alchemy, an expectant silence fell. The crackling of the fire, the chirping of crickets, and the sounds of the seas were the only ones to ride on the gentle winds until Derek finally lost his patience.

"Someone had better explain to me what's going on before I knock down a tree." I knew he wasn't angry, because there was no real reason for him to be angry, at least not that I knew of. He was just trying to make sure I understood that there was a definite possibility of him *becoming* angry if I didn't start providing answers soon.

"You can't knock down a tree," I rolled my eyes at him, and there was a light chuckle from across the fire.

In reply, Derek elbowed me in the ribs and held his hand up. A line appeared between his brows, concentration sparking in his dark eyes, and I fell silent. A hum seemed to curl in the air around us, and a moment later there was a jagged beacon of light streaking across the sky. It struck the base of a nearby tree, blackening the trunk and sending limbs crashing to the ground. A moment later, a loud *boom* rumbled through the air. I gaped at the smoking tree.

"You can conjure *lightning*?" I whirled on him, my hand already flying out to smack him hard in the chest. A *whoof* escaped him, and he rubbed where I'd hit him, although it couldn't have done more than knock the wind out of him.

"I've been working on it. I didn't know I could do it until recently. But it's not important right now, other than the fact that it means I can turn you and your friend here into a pile of ash if I want to." The corner of his mouth quirked into a smug half-smile.

"You're not threatening me," I told him, and he shrugged. I shook my head in disbelief. The strength of someone's eirioth magic would have to be incredible to allow them to summon lightning like that. I'd never seen it done before, even though I had heard of it. It wasn't too rare to be able to summon lightning, but it was impossibly rare for someone to have the ability to summon lightning *and* fire.

"Maybe not, but the point still stands. Now answer me." The smile disappeared and I sighed.

"Where to begin?"

Derek wasn't thrilled to hear about my journey thus far. There wasn't a whole lot to tell, but he seemed to be increasingly agitated at how long it had taken me just to get this far.

"You make it sound like I haven't gone very far. We're in *Brightlock*, Derek. We aren't even in our home kingdom. Technically, we're being illegal right now." I had told him, but he'd only shrugged again and told me that that was only because the Evershifting Forest had helped me out.

"I've been flying since the day you left, and it's taken me that long to catch up to you. Using the Forest's magic is cheating." Had been his argument.

"Do you plan to accompany us to Clawbreak?" Alchemy asked him, reaching one of his spindly arms towards the fire, then retracting it as the flames singed the tips of his fingers. It wasn't a pained or even a startled movement, and when he held his hand up to contemplate the damage, I could see no difference.

"Maybe. That wholly depends on why you're going. You haven't told me anything about yourself yet," Derek's gaze was daggers, and I pressed my lips tightly together. Somehow, even though I had hardly known Alchemy for a few hours, I felt some obligation to try and defend him from Derek's accusing glares. I knew that if I did, though, Derek would scoff and say that's exactly why someone so emotional shouldn't be allowed to run off into a magical forest on their own, so I kept my mouth shut.

"Like I should have any reason to?" Alchemy countered, his voice even. "I'll tell you what's important. If what I've heard is true, the Curse is finding a way to adapt and enter into stronger-minded beings, and it needs to be stopped. Due to obvious blights, such as my blinding charm and swindling charisma, I'm not able to go out and seek such things on my own, not if I hope to collect the vital information needed to solve this problem, that is. All of us want the same thing, right? Curse gone, everyone happy. Why not work together to make it happen?"

"Who are you?" Derek asked, ignoring the question. Alchemy scoffed.

"You really don't need to mess with all the formalities," he muttered.

"How did you become Cursed?"

"Story for another time," Alchemy pushed himself up onto his feet. "I won't be interrogated any further. It's been a long time since I've socialized, and I'm afraid I've gone too long without practice. I'll tell you more when I'm ready, and I won't be ready until I'm sure we've got your help. Will you lend us the aid of your dragon to get us to Clawbreak?"

"'*We*'?" Derek echoed, his angry eyes swooping back to me. "You can't be serious. You've teamed up with this thing? He's not even human! He's Cursed! You can't trust anything he says!"

"I know that," I said, shrugging. "But if he can help to stop this Curse . . ." my gaze flicked to Alchemy, then back to Derek, and I lowered my voice. "You know what it's done to us. To everyone." Taking the hint, Alchemy stood and walked away, muttering something about getting more firewood. I lifted my voice, but only barely, so I was no longer whispering. "Nothing is going to bring our families back, and nothing is going to bring Elixir back either. But if we don't stop this Curse, it will keep taking and taking and taking until there's nothing left to take. Please, Derek, help us. I know he's not the ideal travel companion, and I know he's probably dangerous, but we outnumber him, and we could probably get away before he did any real damage, right?" I knew I was saying nonsense now, and it was probably a vain hope to think Derek would accept any of this. That was why I was so surprised when he nodded in resignation.

"Alright. I'll help. But I'm doing this for you and for everyone back home." His sharp eyes flew to the place where Alchemy had disappeared into the forest. "Whatever it is he wants, I could care less about. What are you gawking at?" he frowned at me, and I blinked, surprised to find I'd been smiling at him.

"You're taking this better than I thought you would," I said with a nervous chuckle. He glared at me, but said nothing as he went to climb onto Bear's back. I hesitated, looking at my pack. I could set up my tent and my bedroll, but I was awfully tired, and didn't really feel like it. I glanced over at Derek, already sinking into Bear's feathers, then at the grassy earth.

"We may want to take turns sleeping," his voice was lowered now, just loud enough for me to hear. "Just in case. I still don't trust him."

"I don't either," I agreed, rubbing my hands together and reclaiming my seat by the fire to wait for Alchemy to return. "I'll stay up first."

10
SAKURA

Derek and I each took two turns sitting up and keeping the fire alive while the other one slept on Bear's back. Alchemy had laughed when I'd first woken Derek up to switch, and as far as I knew he hadn't slept at all, but he at least helped to keep me awake when it was my turn.

He never said much about himself, but he was willing to talk plenty about the Evershifting Forest. He explained that it had a life of its own, and its mood determined what sort of environment it shifted into from time to time. He had spent several years learning the ways of the Forest, and it had never torn down or shifted the structure of his caves. On my second turn, he asked about my sword, and I'd reluctantly unsheathed it to show him. When he'd returned it, he'd drawn the twin smith tooth daggers strapped to the insides of his forearms, gently handing them to me. They were surprisingly light, and sharpened to a deadly point. When I handed them back, he slid them easily into their sheathes with a swift movement that crossed his wrists and sent the blades hissing into the leather; he'd done it so fast, I'd nearly missed it.

When dawn came, I was reluctant to wake up. I woke to Derek poking me with the end of his longbow, and as I slid down from Bear's back, I was presented with a rather unappetizing breakfast of slightly bruised apple. Still, I didn't have a lot of room to complain, so I crunched it down and forced myself to pay attention when Derek and Alchemy started to talk about our plan.

A part of me was glad to let them take the lead with this. I wasn't sure how much stress I could handle, especially after my rushed decision and everything that had happened back at home with Elixir. But at the same time, another part of me was irritated that I was no longer given much control. If Derek hadn't shown up, I would be the one discussing strategy and tactics and whatever else they were rambling about. I would be the one negotiating and trying to get Alchemy to understand he wasn't entirely in charge here.

I knew Derek was more likely to make an efficient plan with Alchemy than I would be, but I still wanted to feel like I was doing something more than sit and offer suggestions that probably wouldn't help at all. It had been decided we would ride Bear to the island. I had been doubtful of the dragon's ability to carry that much weight, but Derek had reassured me that he could handle it. His argument was that I didn't weigh as much as he did, and Alchemy probably didn't weigh as much as either of us. I hadn't been sure if that was an insult or a compliment, so I'd settled for replying with a cold glare.

"Why are we going to the island, exactly?" I asked as I tossed my apple core over the side of the cliff. It was a chilly morning, and the sea's salty breeze wasn't helping. I knew we were going in hopes of learning more about the Curse, but I didn't understand why Alchemy was so sure we *would* learn more there.

"The people there are likely to have used the Curse to their advantage," Alchemy answered. "They probably have some sort of Cursed animal fights or . . . I dunno, something like that."

"They seem like the sort of people to do that," Derek mused, tapping his fingers together as he stared into the flickering embers of the dying fire. He seemed to be deep in thought, and I was sure I saw a scheming light in his eyes.

"I'm almost afraid to ask what you're thinking." I muttered, frowning at him. His gaze flicked up to mine, and immediately I knew I wouldn't like the next words out of his mouth.

"Thugs and thieves seem like the type of people stupid enough to try something like that. What if they succeeded? What if there's a way to contain Cursed animals? Do you know what sort of progress could be made in research of the Curse if we could do that?" the excitement hinted in his voice made my stomach turn.

"You can't be serious," I shook my head, feeling slightly sick. "How could that ever be a good thing?"

"We could learn more about it and what it does to creatures. Besides, isn't that why we're going to Clawbreak? To see what they've learned about it?" he leaned forward eagerly, the tapping of his fingers speeding up with his energy.

"If you want to study something Cursed, Alchemy's right here." I waved a hand at the black skeleton, who lifted his head at the sound of his name. He didn't seem to be very interested in the argument Derek and I were having, and I took that as a sign that it was pointless. Now that I acknowledged it, I felt a little foolish, but it still seemed too cruel, almost inhuman to think about locking a creature up like that. If it was Cursed, it was already as good as dead, bleeding and missing limbs and body parts; why not go ahead and put it out of its misery instead of shutting it up in a cage?

"I never offered myself up for scientific examination," Alchemy protested, although he didn't sound particularly concerned about it. From what I'd already learned about him, he had probably already combed every inch of himself and his thoughts to learn what he could.

"What does the Curse do to you?" I asked, the question springing from my lips the moment I had the thought. "I thought it controlled the animals somehow. Doesn't it try to do the same to you? Do you resist it somehow?"

"I wish I understood all the inner workings of the Curse and what it does, really, I do," Alchemy stood and rolled his shoulder blades, flexing his fingers and stretching his arms out, even though there wasn't anything there to stretch. I assumed it was just a habit from when he had been a normal human.

"Surely you can tell us what it does to you, though," Derek pointed out, also rising. I mirrored the action, helping Derek collect our things and strap them to Bear's saddle.

"I can try to explain it," Alchemy conceded, his fingers folding together into a jumbled knot of bones. "But there's really no good way to go about it. To begin with, what it does is decompose a body from the inside-out. The vitals of the body simply give out, but the Curse somehow sustains a sort of half-life within it," he stepped up to Bear's side as Derek and I climbed on, then started to haul himself up behind me. "The Curse normally doesn't find a permanent home in any one host, mainly because the animals it controls don't have the will to live after being in that much misery. Humans, however, have a lot of will to live," he sighed, the sound like rough bark grating against stone. "After the Curse shed the rest of my body, I expected it to leave me, but it never did. I guess I'm the ideal host for it."

"And does it control you?" I asked, shifting my sitting position. Eirioth dragon saddles weren't made for more than two people, and Alchemy was awkwardly perched on the lip of the back. I circled my arms around Derek's waist, and half expected Alchemy to do the same to me, but he didn't, instead holding onto the sides of the saddle. I didn't doubt that he could hold on that way the whole ride, and I wasn't about to encourage him to grab onto me instead.

"It used to," Alchemy admitted as Derek soothed Bear, who had begun to shuffle uneasily when Alchemy mounted him. "But the longer I lived with it, I learned how to come to a sort of understanding with it. I can still feel it calling me, tugging at the back of my mind, but I'm strong enough to ignore it. It only gets hard when the Curse is trying to work towards something, when all of it is called to one purpose.

It doesn't happen very often, but it's almost impossible to ignore the call when it does." A long silence followed that, and I could feel how tense Derek was. "Don't worry," Alchemy added after a moment. "It only happened a couple days ago. I've got at least another two or three days before it happens again, and even then, it's very rare that it's able to overcome me."

That did little to settle my nerves, and I was beginning to wonder what I'd gotten us into, but Derek seemed to accept that as an answer for now, and a moment later he was urging Bear towards the cliff's edge at a run. Seconds after that, I knew we were flying even before I looked down to see the churning waves far below. There was a sense of freedom and power that surged through you when you took to the air, and no matter how many times you took off, it would always hit you just the same each time.

"How did the Curse corrupt you, anyway?" I shouted over the roar of the wind. Without the reins or neck to hold onto, I felt a little more unsteady than I did when I usually flew, and the endless abyss of blue water beneath us didn't help to ease my anxiety. I was hugging myself tight against Derek, hoping Bear would be able to carry all three of us all the way to Clawbreak. Already I could feel him wavering beneath the weight. That, or his flying style was just a lot shakier than Sycamore's.

"It targets the weak-minded," Alchemy replied, his gravelly voice even and seemingly just as loud as it had been before, even though he must have been shouting to be heard over the winds. "Things that are sick or small are easy targets, but older beings and distracted ones can be taken too. I've always been more of a hermit than anyone else I've ever known, and, well, the easiest way to put this is I made myself far too vulnerable, and the Curse took advantage." He went quiet after that, and it took me a second to realize he wasn't going to speak again.

Derek didn't seem to want to keep talking either, so I kept my mouth closed. The wind rushed past us, whistling through Alchemy's bones and thundering in my ears. Below us, the ocean was like a softly rippling panel of blue glass, never-ending and vast. The longer I looked down at it, though, the more I could see. Little silver flashes of light revealed schools of fish just below the surface; white blurs racing above the waves were gulls hunting for breakfast; I even spotted a large gray beast, bigger than an eirioth dragon, lurking deeper in the water. I hugged closer to Derek, my stomach squirming at the thought of falling down, down, down into waters with *that* thing.

At one point we flew past two great pillars of stone, rising from the depths of the Great Lakes like some formidable beast's claws. Just below them, a small island was nestled in their shadows, bustling with life.

I wasn't sure if Bear was going to last the entire flight, but within a couple hours, Clawbreak came into view. I rarely underestimated an eirioth dragon, but I had done so this time, and I was pleasantly surprised at how fast and strong Bear was.

Clawbreak was an awkwardly shaped island. I didn't know a lot about it other than its ruthless reputation, but I knew enough to know we wanted to land somewhere nobody would think to go looking. I didn't think a town full of killers and thieves would be particularly friendly to newcomers, especially not newcomers with a dragon.

We approached from the south side, where the Waste Ponds were. Before we'd left, I'd learned a little bit more about the layout of Clawbreak from Derek and Alchemy. According to Derek, the Waste Ponds covered several miles of ground on the southern side of Clawbreak, a smelly, swampy place where the people of Clawbreak dumped all their waste and even dead bodies.

I wrinkled my nose as the sour smell that announced itself when we drew nearer, flying lower as we came close. We had been lucky enough not to fly over any ships while we traveled above the Great Lakes, but there was no telling if we'd been spotted swooping into Clawbreak.

Bear was hesitant to land, but finally he did, his claws squelching inches deep into the grayish-green muck that coated this part of the island like a blanket of sticky snow. Alchemy, Derek and I didn't want to get down, but we knew we had to. Derek was the first one to slide down, groaning as he sank knee-deep into the sludge. His nose curled at the smell, and he glared at the drooping trees around us. They were gray-barked and wispy, with floppy branches and sad-looking leaves. I didn't blame them; if I had grown up surrounded by waste and decay, I'd probably look pretty miserable too.

Alchemy dismounted next, but he seemed relatively unfazed by everything. He didn't sink as far into the mud as Derek did, or as I did when I finally slid out of the saddle. As soon as I did, I regretted doing so.

The mud was cold, seeping down into my boots and caking around my legs. I felt myself sinking farther and farther into it until finally I stopped, feeling solid ground somewhere beneath my feet. The muck was halfway up my thighs.

"Why did we land right next to the cliffs, again?" I spat, bunching my fists. If what Derek had said was true, we had a while to walk before we arrived at the town.

"Bear couldn't carry us much farther, especially not navigating through these trees," Derek replied, although he didn't sound any happier about the arrangement than I was.

"Look on the bright side!" Alchemy chortled, sounding merrier than ever. He couldn't feel the cold of the slime. He probably couldn't even smell its awful stench, either. It was just enough to make me want to hurl a glob of it onto his grinning skull.

"I doubt there *is* a bright side to a situation like this." I bit out, my mind flooding with memories of everything that had gone wrong in the past week.

"Enough squabbling." Derek ordered, grabbing his longbow from its place strapped to Bear's saddle and slinging it over his shoulder. He brushed his fingers against the fletching of each of his arrows, counting how many there were, then nodded, satisfied, and turned to begin wading through the muck.

With a huff, I followed him.

I nearly fell over with my first step. I'd been sure it would be difficult to walk through the thick mud, but it was surprisingly soft, and I walked only a bit slower than I would if I was on normal ground. I marched after Derek and heard the *shuck shuck shuck* of Alchemy and Bear behind me.

Derek seemed to know where he was going, and I was content to let him lead the way. We passed under more of those droopy, sad trees, and past big, oblong ponds filled with murky gray water. I saw a few shapes slithering into them when we passed, and couldn't help but feel a chill run down my spine. I'd seen plenty of snakes in the Eirioth Wood, but none of them had seemed very menacing. Now that I was here, in this dreary place shrouded in fog, my legs going numb from the cold mud clinging to me, they seemed a lot more dangerous, and I kept my eyes open for any of them in the tree branches above me or the mud around me.

After a little while, I lost track of time. The heavy gray mist that clung to the Waste Ponds smelled cloyingly sweet, only adding to the sour reek of the gray muck around us, and it blocked any clear view of the sky, making it impossible to pinpoint where the sun was. I tried not to dwell on everything this muck could consist of, but without much else to distract my thoughts, it was hard not to.

My legs began to ache, or at least what I could feel of them. My toes were completely numb now, and I was losing feeling in my feet. Every inch of my body felt clammy and slick, and I was sure I'd fall over at any moment.

Derek didn't falter, though, and neither did Alchemy. He'd come up beside me at some point, and now we were wading through the sludge together. He seemed to move with less ease than I did.

"I don't have as much mass to use to push through it," he'd said as when he came up alongside me.

"At least you don't have to worry about losing your toes," I'd grumbled back, grimacing at a spike of pain that rushed up my leg. I had forgotten about the scratch the raptor had left on me. It had almost healed up completely, but it still stung when I stretched my leg out too far. All I could do right now was focus on taking one more step, then another, then another.

Finally, after what seemed like ages, Derek stopped and turned back to face us. He didn't seem cold, at least not from the waist up, but I could see how his legs shook. My own were trembling from the chill.

"Bear stays here," he said, walking back through to his dragon and patting him on the beak. Bear snorted in disapproval, but Derek only shrugged. "We can't really bring a dragon into this place. They'll be on him in seconds."

"You want to leave him in here?" I asked, my eyes widening. I couldn't begin to think of leaving Sycamore in a place like this, cold and all alone with those snakes. What if someone came in to dispose of a body or something? What if she was spotted? I couldn't begin to fathom the thought of losing Sycamore like that.

"I don't have many choices right now, Sakura," Derek snapped. He paused, took a deep breath, and shook his head. "I don't *want* to, but I have to. It won't be for too long, so he should be fine. C'mon, boy, up here," he stepped backwards until he was level with the base of a tree, then tapped his palm against the wood. Bear huffed, a growl rumbling in the back of his throat. Derek didn't waver, only tapped the tree again.

Resigned, Bear inched forward and jumped up into the low branches of the tree. They groaned and bowed beneath his weight, but he soon found a spot at the base of the cluster of branches to curl into, resting his head against one of the limbs.

"Not as cozy as the ones back home, but it'll do." Derek mused, his eyes darting to me briefly. I knew he was thinking about my big pink eirioth tree, and I felt a pinch in my chest as my own thoughts turned there too. This place was so dead and desolate compared to the beauty of the Eirioth Wood, and it only drove me to want to get out of here even more.

"Let's go." I said, unable to handle it anymore. Derek nodded, and moments later, he, Alchemy and I were back to wading through the muck, marching to the north one step at a time.

It couldn't have been more than twenty minutes before we found ourselves on a slight incline, pulling us up and out of the mud. When we were free, I gave the land before us a quick glance. The Waste Ponds wrapped around to the east, but just ahead and stretching to the west was a sprawling but dilapidated, town. It looked glum and barren and abandoned, but I knew there were people somewhere in there.

I looked down at my legs, grimacing. They were caked nearly up to my waist in clumps of quickly-drying gray-green mud. Alchemy and Derek weren't looking much better, already swiping at their legs to break the worst of the chunks away. I mirrored the action, trying not to gag as a strong whiff of the mud's sour tang wafted out from the cracking slime.

"What now?" I grumbled once we'd shed the crust of mud. Flakes of it still clung to my pants, and I didn't think I'd ever be rid of the smell, but at least I could move easier once it was off and I'd scraped what I could from both the inside and the outside of my boots.

"Now, we go in," Alchemy started forward, but before he could get very far, Derek stopped him with his longbow.

"Not you. You're far too noticeable. We'll find someplace for you to lie low for a bit while Sakura and I go in." Derek shrugged his longbow into place over his shoulder alongside his quiver of arrows. Alchemy stared in his direction for a long moment before he spoke again.

"You've got to be joking."

"Afraid not," Derek said, walking towards the town. I followed, and Alchemy fell in step beside me. We were headed for the back of a two-story building, but half of the top story was caved in on itself. As far as I could tell, there was nobody inside.

"We'll split up," I suggested, although I tried to make it sound more decisive. "Derek can go searching for some answers. His skin's a bit lighter than mine, so he'll probably be less noticeable. I'll go and see if I can't find some sort of giant cloak or something and some big boots so you can walk around with us." I directed the last bit towards Alchemy, which earned me a frown from Derek, but he didn't argue. It didn't do much, but it helped me feel less useless in the moment.

"Fine." Alchemy huffed after a long silence. I nodded, and we all fell silent.

We came up to the back of the building, the sickly sweet fog still curling in creeping tendrils around our feet. There were small windows placed at regular intervals in the building's rough wooden walls, but they were all too smudged to see through. Derek kept us away from them, guiding us around to the side of the building with the caved-in second floor.

"We'll get up there and leave him in the wreckage while we snoop around," he explained as he started to climb. The walls seemed unstable, but there were plenty of holes and nooks to use as hand and footholds, and he scaled it easily.

"You talk about me like I'm some sort of animal," Alchemy whined as I began to follow Derek. The wood was brittle and splintered beneath my hands, and I winced as it dug into my palms. I didn't think it had broken the skin, but it still gave me the impression that a thousand tiny needles were being pressed into my flesh.

"Well you definitely aren't human," I pointed out as I joined Derek amid the debris of the second floor. The wood creaked, and a board snapped as Alchemy followed us up, dragging himself to his full height beside us.

There had once been two big rooms, split in the middle, on this level of the structure, but one of them had fallen in. Wood and bits of stone lay in heaps on the floor, all of them coated in dust and mold. It looked like it had been this way for a while, some of the boards rotted and water-stained. I wrinkled my nose at the musty smell.

"Home sweet home," said Alchemy, stepping around the boards and into the room that was still intact. Derek and I trailed after him, and I was pleased to see that this room was in much better shape. It was empty, except for the dust, and the only window in the back wall was shattered, but it provided a shelter and a hiding place. There was no obvious way down to the ground level, so I assumed any ladder or staircase must have been accessed from the fallen room.

"This will be a good place for you to hide out until I can find something for you to wear," I told the skeleton as he inspected the window frame, lined with fragments of sharp, jutting glass. He poked at one aggressively, and it fell to the floorboards with a *clink*. I rolled my eyes. "Stop messing with things. Just stay put and don't cause any trouble. Can you manage that?"

"I should think so," he answered, stepping away from the window and looking back the way we had come. Part of the divider wall had been destroyed, but most of it was still securely in place, leaving only a few little holes and the big gap we had entered through. "Just be quick. I know it won't be easy to find anything in my size," that amused tone returned. "But I don't do well being kept up like this."

"Didn't you live 'kept up' for several years in the Evershifting Forest?" Derek sniped, shrugging his quiver and longbow off his back and tucking them into the corner of the room before carefully covering them with some of the fallen boards. He still had the handle of his flame-sword at his belt, but I could see him concealing it inside his shirt now. Alchemy didn't answer him.

I mirrored his actions, taking off my own sword sheath and laying it beside his bow. I didn't like parting with the blade, and I definitely didn't like leaving it here with Alchemy, but I knew it wasn't safe to walk around with obvious weapons like that in a place like Clawbreak. Besides, I would have my own flame-sword and eirioth to defend myself if I needed it.

"We're heading out now," Derek said, directing his words at Alchemy. "Don't leave." Alchemy crossed his arms and groaned.

"For all the stars, I'm not *five*. I won't leave. Go on now, go find me some new clothes." He made a shooing motion with his hands, and I shook my head as I followed Derek back out into the wreckage of the other room. We didn't look back as we stepped around the debris and scaled back down the side of the building.

"He sure acts five sometimes, doesn't he?" I muttered as we walked down the narrow alley that we ended up in at the bottom of the wall. It was littered with trash and pieces of wood, and even an overturned barrel.

"You talk as if you've known him forever. It's hardly been a few days," Derek accused, frowning at me again. I was beginning to grow a little tired of that particular expression from him, but I knew if I complained about it nothing would happen, so I clenched my jaw and frowned back.

"I was only saying that's how it seems." We stepped out of the alley into a broad central street. The mist was still thick here, so much so that I couldn't tell what the road was made of other than the feel of it beneath my feet. It must have been packed dirt, but it could have been some sort of stone as well.

Now that we were out in the open, I felt a lot more exposed as I looked at the town around us. The central road was very wide and ran the length of it, but I could see where it branched off into smaller streets farther to the east. All of the buildings seemed dusty and abandoned, but every now and then I would catch a shifting, torn curtain or a darting shadow. It was all eerie and empty. There wasn't another person in sight, other than hovering figures in doorways or beyond the smeared glass of windows.

"Bit creepy, isn't it?" I murmured, aware of how close I'd leaned to Derek. I would have moved away if it wasn't for the grasping fear that overcame me. My entire body felt sluggish, and while it may have been a side effect of breathing in the mucky air, I was sure it was just my apprehension at going off on my own.

"You'll be fine. Finnian's helped you train for this." Derek's voice was monotone and unimpressed, and instantly my fears felt childish and dramatic. My tense shoulders slumped and I gave him a blank look, putting all my contempt for him into my eyes.

"Not for *this*. For battling Cursed animals and trained soldiers."

"I hear it's much the same thing." Derek shrugged and took a step away from me, nodding towards buildings farther to the east that looked slightly more occupied. "You'll probably have more luck starting over there. Good luck. Meet back with Alchemy by nightfall." Before I had a chance to reply, he was gone, jogging lightly across the street into a large cluster of buildings that looked less like residential housing and more like old tourist attractions. The decorations were faded, and the signs were virtually impossible to read, but there was something obviously themed about it. Beyond the haze, I could make out figures moving through the fog.

I forced myself to take a deep breath, although it was very shaky and not very effective. I forced my feet to move, but it was just a small shuffle. I rolled my shoulders, let my fingers brush over the reassuring metal of my flame-sword hilt, and looked towards the buildings Derek had suggested I start at. There were more signs of life that way, but they were small. A few trimmed plants here, a clean window there. Some of the signs seemed to be painted clearer, but I was still too far away to read any of them.

"Go on! You've got this!" a voice cheered from behind me. I nearly jumped out of my skin, whirling around and flicking my sword hilt into my hand. I saw nothing but the sad face of a building staring back at me, empty and dark. "Psst. Up here." The voice said, and I looked up to see a skeletal black hand waving at me from around the corner of a broken wall.

"Get back inside!" I hissed, afraid to speak any louder than absolutely necessary. My gaze darted around to see if anyone was nearby, but the closest living thing was a drooping weed by the gaping doorway of the building.

"Fine. But go quickly. I'm tired of being naked." The hand disappeared, and I rolled my eyes before turning back to face the buildings I planned to go to.

When I did, I almost screamed. Roughly twenty feet away from me stood a man, dressed in grubby rags and wearing a broad-brimmed hat. He had his head tilted down so that I could only see his pale, pointy chin. He didn't even look alive. His hands were bony and long-fingered, twitching around his waist as if searching for something they wouldn't find. He was swaying very gently back and forth.

I became aware of a lump that had appeared in my throat, and realized I was on the verge of tears. I'd never signed up for anything like this. All I'd wanted was to find a source in the center of the Evershifting Forest and destroy it. How had that turned into illegally crossing kingdom borders and trying to steal clothes for a living skeleton?

I watched the man warily, rooted to the spot and desperately hoping he would just turn and walk away. It was sort of mesmerizing about the way he was swaying, back and forth, back and forth. There was some sort of pattern on his shirt, something swirly. I'd thought it was dirt before, but now I was second-guessing myself. Back and forth. Back and forth. I was a lot more tired than I'd thought I was. How much sleep had I gotten the night before? Or the night before that, for that matter? Back. And forth. Back. And forth. Back . . .

"*Ironling.*" The voice was chilly, jarring, *right in my ear*. It rang around my head like echoing bells, cold and unwelcome. I jerked my head to the side, seeking the source of it, and everything snapped into sharp focus.

The man was right in front of me now, grinning and revealing the fact that he was missing several teeth. His hat was tilted sideways, and there was a curved dagger gripped tightly in his hand. It was drawn back, prepared to be driven down into my chest.

With a yelp I slammed my palm into the center of his chest, summoning my eirioth as I did so. I only allowed a fraction of it to seep through my fingers, singing my handprint into the front of that swirly shirt. He cried out, a strangled, raspy sound, and stumbled backwards, surprised. I moved on instinct, darting forward and sweeping his legs out from beneath him. He hit the ground hard, and before he had a chance to react, I pivoted and rammed the back of my foot into the side of his head. He slumped to the ground, eyes half open.

My heart was racing, an irregular beat in my chest, and I pushed loose strands of dark brown hair out of my face, turning to look up at the broken building. Alchemy's skull was only visible if you were actively looking for it, peering through a hole in the crumbling wall.

"Thanks. I don't know what just happened . . ." I told him, my gaze automatically flicking back to the road and then the unconscious man at my feet, paranoid that there might be more of him.

"Hypnotism. It's pretty rare. I'm not surprised one of these thugs knew about it. Just try not to wait too long when you see someone. Scurry along now, you're a weed waiting to be plucked just standing around in the middle of the street." Alchemy's skull vanished, and I nodded to myself.

Hypnotism. I'd never heard of it before. How did Alchemy know about it? He'd been stuck up in that forest for so long, or at least that's what he was leading me to believe. Was hypnotism something older, or something so rare it had really remained such a big secret for so long? Either way, I didn't want to stick around and find out who knew it.

Shaking the rest of that drowsy feeling from my body, I started to walk swiftly towards the more lively side of the town. I kept to the side, in the shadows of the buildings, even though it unsettled me to be so close to the places that might be teeming with more of those creepy criminals. It was still better than walking directly in the center of the road and announcing myself to everyone with access to view it.

It was late afternoon by the time I'd crossed all the way to the market side of the town, and the buildings were cast in a bright golden glow. There were several narrow alleys I could venture into, but I stuck to the branches of the central street and tried to find a good place from there. None of the buildings looked like they would have anything I would find helpful, but some of them had racks of old clothing in them.

The first building I entered had a big sign out front that read '*Adda Jawle*'. It must have been in Old Coldmonian, a language rarely spoken anymore. I knew that many places in Coldmon still bore names in the language, and some common phrases were still spoken, but for the most part the language had died, and only studious scribes were able to translate it.

When I pushed the door open, a rain of dust fell down on my head. Coughing, I waved it away and stepped inside. There was no source of light in there, casting the entire back half of the store into shadow. The front half was easier to see in the dying light, and I could make out several old coats and dresses, hanging from racks or folded neatly on tables. Everything was coated in a healthy layer of dust.

"Can I help you, miss?" a rattly voice echoed from somewhere farther in the shop, and a moment later a hunched figure hobbled out from behind a rack of clothes. He was stooped over, with a big nose and a wrinkled face. One of his eyes was white, and the other was a muddy brown color. When he smiled, I saw that he only had a few yellowed teeth.

"I'm looking for a cloak," I told him, trying to keep my tone even. The person shuffled forward, and I realized the shaggy dress that hung around his frame was made of some sort of matted fur. No, not *him*. It was a *woman*.

"Of course!" she croaked, smiling again. It was an unsettling expression, made even more so by the knitted hat that sat slightly askew atop her scraggly gray hair. It gave the impression of a bedraggled, malnourished bear.

"A big one," I added as she hobbled away, disappearing behind another rack. I took a deep breath, nearly coughing again at the dust I inhaled, and forced myself to follow her. "One that might fit someone around . . . I dunno, seven feet?" it was a peculiar ask, I knew, and it was confirmed when the woman looked over her shoulder, her gaze scanning me up and down briefly. Few people were that tall, at least not in Carlore. The people of Wisesol and Coldmon weren't very tall, either, and although most Lockers and Talons could be of exceptional height, I'd never heard of anyone breaching seven feet.

That reminded me of the conversation Alchemy and I had had before, when he'd told me he was from Freetalon originally. He had asked after Warin Dearsol, the king of Freetalon from nearly two hundred years ago. The way he had spoken had made it sound like he'd known him personally. How old *was* Alchemy? Could the Curse have kept him alive for so long? But the Curse hadn't even been around for that long, had it?

"Here we are." The scratchy voice sucked me out of my thoughts, and I blinked. The sun was setting fast, and the shadows in the shop were growing. The woman before me was hardly more than a blob of darkness.

"Thank you." I said curtly, and the woman cackled, as if manners were some sort of joke in this town. Considering what I'd seen of it so far, maybe they were.

"Hope you find what you're looking for. You'd best hurry and be off with what you need, too. This place gets rough after dark, 'specially for little ladies like ourselves, eh?" she laughed again, the sound like cracking glass, and wandered off into the shop, seeming to melt into the shadows.

I almost called after her to ask if I needed to pay, but a moment later the sound of her shuffling footsteps vanished, and her presence seemed to leave the room. I was frozen there for a moment, keenly aware of how fast darkness was falling, before I leaned forward and rifled through the stack of cloaks before me. All the clothes here were in a larger size than I'd ever seen before. I selected a big shirt, a cloak, a pair of gloves, a pair of pants, and a set of tall leather boots. It was almost too much for me to carry at once.

I folded the shirt, cloak, and pants over one arm and stuffed the gloves into the boots so I could hold them in my other hand, then I hurried out of *Adda Jawle* before its creepy owner could return. When I stepped out onto the fog-shrouded road, I saw other people out as well. Some of them were down the road to the south, clustered together and forming some sort of circle. I didn't want to stick around and find out what they were up to, so I hurried back towards the broad central street that ran east to west and began making my way to the building where Alchemy was hidden.

When I reached the street, I could still see the slumped form of the man I'd knocked unconscious in the center of the road. I kept to the side of the street, desperately hoping he wasn't awake and scolding myself for not taking that curved dagger when I'd had the chance.

As I walked, more figures appeared in alleys and at the other side of the street. A big group of people was visible at one point, lurking in an alleyway as I passed. None of them seemed to take any notice of me, and I was grateful for that fact, because most of them looked to be missing body parts.

I picked up my pace, and in doing so lost my grip on the boots. One of them slid out of my hand, and then the other. The wadded up gloves bounced from inside them, and I cursed as I stopped to retrieve them. There were people everywhere now, and it may have been my imagination, but I was sure they were converging on me. I snatched up the boots and the gloves and started to run, sprinting as fast as my full arms would allow until I was tucked into the alley beside my destination.

"Alchemy!" I hissed, frantically looking up and down the alley. The only person in sight was a huddled figure across the central road. "Derek?" I tried, attempting to keep any sign of panic out of my voice.

"I'm here," Derek's head appeared over the side of the wall.

"I can't climb up with these clothes," I explained, holding them out so he could see, even though I doubted he could make them out clearly in the shadows of the alley. "I'm going to throw them to you."

"Okay." Derek held his hands up.

On my first try, the boots fell back down, but I stuffed the gloves all the way into the toes and tried again, and this time he caught them. I wadded up the pants, cloak, and shirt and hurled them up next. He snatched the cloak and the pants, but the shirt fell back down. Cursing, I scrambled to grab it from the dusty ground, missing in my haste, and grabbing at it again. I tossed it over my shoulder and began to climb the wall, faintly aware of the sound of shuffling footsteps from around the corner of a building.

"Hurry," Derek whispered as we made our way around the debris of the fallen room. I was too panicked to think clearly, and while Derek avoided stepping on any of the wood easily, I knocked my shin against one of the boards, sending it banging loudly against the floor. I winced, ignoring Derek's glare, and followed him through the gap in the divider wall.

"Finally!" Alchemy's gravelly voice bounced around the room, and I looked up to see him sitting in the corner beneath the broken window, his position portraying his obvious boredom. "Took you long enough."

"Stop whining. Try these on. They should fit." I tossed the shirt at him, and a second later the boots thunked down beside it, followed by the pants and cloak from Derek. I looked over at him to see he was retrieving his longbow. I hurriedly returned my sword and its sheath to their rightful place on my back, instantly feeling more at ease with its familiar weight.

When I turned around again, Alchemy had already shrugged into the shirt and the pants. They hung loosely around his bony frame, but did a good job at concealing what he really was. When he put the boots and gloves on, the only thing left exposed was his skull and the beginning of his spinal column.

"What did you learn, Derek?" I asked, poking through the small packs we'd brought with us when we'd left Bear in the Waste Ponds to make sure we still had everything.

"Not much," he admitted, sounding agitated. "I found someone who was talking about the Curse in some sort of old tavern, but they didn't talk much about what causes it or where it's coming from. There was mention of Old Duskfall, though."

"Old Duskfall? Yes, that makes sense," Alchemy was fidgeting with the gloves. "Their magic is very closely linked with the dead. Perhaps we could learn something there." I pressed my lips together, lifting the cloak up to offer it to the skeleton.

"Put the cloak on. Let's see how hidden you look," I instructed, but Alchemy had frozen solid, his skull angled towards the gap in the divider wall.

"One moment," he said, holding up a finger — with the gloves, it was very convincing — and nodding at the hole. "We've got company."

11
KSEGA

*U*nloading *The Coventry* would come later, once we were all certain we were allowed passage beyond the Western Harbor.

When Jessie and I walked down the ramp onto the docks, we were instantly transported into a new world. The people around us were from all sorts of different cultures and kingdoms. A dark-skinned Carlorian woman was standing around selling brightly colored fruits to passersby; a tall, red-haired Talon was helping to direct the traffic of so many people, and I could even see people of different races boarding and unloading ships together, using their magic to help each other.

It wasn't uncommon to see the people of the kingdoms mingling like this, especially not since the Curse had taken hold in Horcath, but it was still a pleasant surprise. Everyone knew that certain kingdoms still had high tensions between each other. But these people were all smiling and laughing and working alongside each other, oblivious to their countries' squabbles.

Loud music swam through the air, happy and boisterous. Small children danced to its melodies, earning them scolding looks from nearby parents.

"This way," Thomas said, walking beside us. He seemed to be in a better mood than when I'd first seen him, and he led the way confidently along the docks, towards those magnificent iron gates.

Jessie and I followed him through the throng of people, marveling at everything we saw. The sights weren't the only thing that amazed me; there were all sorts of smells, rich or sour or sweet, wafting through the air and luring me towards the markets near the iron gates. Thomas was unfazed by the merchants holding out their goods and shouting for attention, continuing until we were right up next to the gate.

Even from the elevated position of *The Coventry*'s deck, it had been impossible to see everything through the crowd of people, and now that we were closer, I could see that there were several guards lined up in front of and around the gates. They were all dressed in the official garments of the Coldmonian army. I racked my brain for the name of the armor. *Adda*. It literally translated to 'armor' from Old Coldmonian.

I couldn't help but gawk at the *adda*, crafted from a modified version of the cheap waterproof fabrics used to make the water tunics sold from the floating merchant stalls back in the Port. They were a deep blue, reinforced with pieces of black leather and plated with sewn-on silver scales around the chest and the waist. The gloves were made with thick webbing between the fingers, and the helmets were specially designed to allow breathing underwater. The helmets were silver and gold, molded into the shape of a fish's head. When it was brought down over the face, there was a filter in front of the mouth that provided its wearer with oxygen.

"Peeler is obsessed with them, too," said Thomas, following my gaze. "He's been trying to get his hands on an *adda* for ages, but they're surprisingly well-hidden. I've never seen one outside of being worn by a Coldmonian soldier."

"I don't blame them for keeping them hidden," I muttered as we came closer. There was a line queueing up to be let in, and we filed in behind it. The rest of *The Coventry*'s crew joined us. "With technology like that, I'm sure *adda* are very expensive."

"Of course they are." Captain Howard had come up behind us, his face just as grim and expressionless as it had been every other time I'd seen him. Jessie took an involuntary step back, surprised at his voice. She hadn't known he'd been standing there.

"Helpful for traveling underwater," Ritch said,. "bBut useless against a sword."

"*Near* useless." Peeler had appeared beside him. He pushed his wired spectacles higher up the bridge of his nose. "Those scales are made from real silver, and they're sewn in at strategic angles. Unless the blade slides in from beneath, they're impenetrable."

"Yes, but you do realize those scales only cover the top portion of their chest and back, and those skirts of scales only go to their knees. You could gut one of them as easy as that." Ritch argued.

"Their defense training is impeccable," Peeler retorted, a line forming between his blue-gray eyes. "They're trained for combat on land, ship, and underwater. Few people have managed to best them."

"Only in the last twenty years," Captain Howard grumbled beneath his breath. "It's a new routine issued by the latest Ice King. The people on that throne have been incompetent and lazy through the years of the Curse, and that Matthias boy has decided that needs to change." He nodded, the gesture one of approval. "When this Curse is finally banished from this world, kingdoms will be weakened, and kings will want to take action. Coldmon is the most exposed of any of the kingdoms, and Matthias is wise to prepare them for the inevitable."

I nodded in agreement, even though I didn't fully believe him. When the Curse was gone — if it could ever be removed — the kingdoms *would* be left in varying states of ruin, and while some kings may be ambitious to move against their enemies, each would have to take some time to rest and strengthen themselves before they made such a drastic move.

"Do you think the Curse will be gone before King Matthias dies?" I asked, careful to keep my voice low. I wasn't entirely sure if talk of the king's death in his own kingdom was considered treason, but I wasn't keen on finding out.

"Possibly." Captain Howard tilted his head to the side thoughtfully, steadily holding my gaze. "But I wouldn't hope for it, boy. The Curse is a vile thing. I would only hope Matthias' descendants are wise enough to keep up the tradition of these training routines."

"You don't want to see Coldmon defeated in a war?" Jessie asked, frowning. Howard didn't strike us as the type of person to care about the wellbeing of any one kingdom.

"I don't want to see my seas claimed by unfriendly kings." Captain Howard clarified, his voice like sharply cut glass. Jessie swallowed and dropped her gaze, reminded of the worrisome fact that he was a pirate captain. I'd forgotten it myself, and now that the thought had returned to me, I felt my skin crawl with unease.

Why would a shipful of pirates agree to bring us to Famark? Although we'd been reassured that the whole crew was past their pirating ways, I didn't fully believe them. A transportation ship captain wouldn't refer to the seas as his, at least not that I knew. Then again, what did I really know about transportation ships? Or pirates, for that matter?

Maybe I was dabbling in things that didn't concern me, but I wasn't exactly known for keeping my nose in my own business. Still, for the time being, I wasn't willing to poke around into Captain Howard's motives behind agreeing to take Jessie and I here. I wasn't looking to get locked in the cargo hold again.

The line moved very slowly. Famark was Coldmon's most popular tourist location, and people from all the kingdoms commonly traveled to and from it. The guards in charge of directing the traffic and controlling who was allowed to pass through the gates were very meticulous about their system.

Out of all the times I'd run off to explore somewhere while traveling around Wisesol or boarded ships in the Port, I'd never crossed a border between kingdoms. Obviously, I had now, since I was in Coldmon, but I'd never been through any of the Gates. I knew the basic protocol each of them had to follow — some form of payment was required, as well as proof of a peaceable reason for passage — but each kingdom was allowed to add whatever they wanted to those as long as they were within reason. Willa had explained to me the requirements for crossing into Freetalon before, since she had traveled there on several occasions, but I had no idea what to expect from Coldmon.

Every so often, the big gates would open to allow a person or small group of people through, then they would close again as the process started over. Two Coldmonian guards stood at the head of the line, asking questions, accepting payments, clearing cards and slips and luggage, while four others supervised the activity of the rest of the line. If anyone was noticed trying to hide something on their person, or toss something away, they would be pulled aside and interrogated further.

It took almost two hours for us to reach the front of the line, and all thirty-one of us were getting a bit bored. The most exciting thing that happened was an outburst of angry voices from down one of the piers. When we craned our heads to look, we saw a crew being roughly forced back onto their ship with their cargo. They yelled and rebelled against the Coldmonian soldiers pushing them, but as I squinted, I could see that the Coldmoners had their hands coated in ice, which had spread to the wrists of those they'd grabbed, freezing them together. I shuddered to think of how awful that must have felt for the crew members.

When they were all back on the ship, the soldiers released them and stepped back onto the pier. Before anyone had a chance to get back down, the ramp was drawn away, and the anchor began to weigh itself. The waves sloshed around the ship, and I realized the group of Coldmonian soldiers were bending the water, guiding the ship out of the docks.

The captain of the ship yelled a string of curses down at them, refusing to leave. The Coldmoners continued to ease the ship away, but once it was beyond the edge of the pier, they redoubled their efforts. The water swelled into a great hand, gripping the prow of the vessel and pushing it away into the sea and leaving great wakes of white churning in the water. Within minutes, it had shrunk to a small speck in the distance.

"Always fun to see," Peeler muttered as everyone slowly lost interest. We all perked up when the two guards stepped forward, demanding we hold still while they pat us down. Jessie and I were beckoned forward first, and I tried not to flinch as they examined me. Both of us had left all the belongings we'd brought besides the clothes we wore back on *The Coventry*, but I was still terrified they might find something on me.

They didn't, though, and Jessie and I were instructed to stand to the side while the rest of the crew was patted down. That took almost another hour, and by the time the guards started going through asking for payment and validation papers, it was past lunchtime.

Jessie and I both paid the small fee required for entry, and I answered the questions I was asked. Did I have any weapons with me? Yes, a bow and a quiver of arrows. Did I have papers confirming I was authorized to carry that weapon? No. I wasn't allowed to bring it with me into the city. What business did I have on Famark? I was delivering perfumes for my grandmother's business. They would have to go through the crate of perfumes before it was allowed into the city, but other than that, it would be permitted.

And that was it. They just had to go through and do it for each and every one of us, and by the time they were done, I was starving, and Jessie looked like she might be about to fall asleep standing up.

But we got through, and it was all worth it.

You couldn't see much through the iron gate, just the ridiculously wide main road — Thomas had pointed to it once he'd been pat down and joined us, explaining that it was called Ark Road, and it was so wide because of the Merchant Run — and the fronts of a few buildings. None of the details were clear, though, because the guards didn't allow us within ten feet of the gate.

After we'd all been cleared, the gates were unlocked, and the oiled hinges allowed it to swing open just wide enough for us to walk through two or three at a time. When Jessie and I passed through after Thomas and Molly, I heard her gasp, and my jaw dropped.

The Ark Road was teeming with life, but it was broad enough that there was still more than enough space for all the entering travelers to pass through. There were people wearing all sorts of clothes, bearing all sorts of bags and crates and miscellaneous items, smiling and chatting and weaving their way through the crowds. Musicians stood on the sides of the street, playing their instruments and belting merry songs.

The Merchant Run was on either side of the Ark Road. On the southern side, the Merchant Run went all the way from east to west, a long row of tall buildings, all of them at least two stories tall, and all of them vibrantly painted and decorated. There were all sorts of items displayed beyond glass windows, from stunning dresses to wooden carved items to food shops, and Jessie and I marveled at them as we walked.

The Merchant Run on the north side bent, following a thick branch of the Ark Road that led to the northern end of Famark. As we came up beside that branch, Thomas guided us up it, explaining that the best inns were on North Ark Road.

"It's also close to the Merchant Stores and the Merchant Corner, so we might be able to stop by and say hello to Merchant Daynor." He'd added when Molly was turned away, enthralled by a golden dress in one of the store windows.

"Who is he?" I asked, shrugging around a man in a puffy trench coat that was pushing along a little wooden cart.

"Merchant Daynor? A wonderful man," Thomas answered, pressing his lips tightly together. "I've known him since I was little. Chap doesn't like him as much as I do, and his neighbor . . ." he cringed, the expression unnatural on his freckled face.

"Are you wanting us to meet him?" Jessie asked, tugging nervously at her long red braid. Her vibrant blue eyes were darting every which way, resting longer whenever she spotted a sparkly dress or a shiny piece of jewelry in one of the windows.

"Maybe," Thomas shrugged. "I think you'd like him. He's the friendliest Merchant I've ever met."

"The only Merchant you've ever met," Molly added, raising an eyebrow at him. He frowned at her.

"I've met others. They're never very memorable is all it is. They sit around all day chugging tea and counting their coins. Where's the action? Where's the *life*?" he gestured with his hands at the streets around them. "They run this place. They're second only to the guards and the king, but they act like they're over them, too. It's stupid. *They're* stupid. Daynor is the only one with an ounce of sense in him."

Molly didn't look convinced, but she kept her lips sealed, and moved her dark gaze back to the street in front of us. Neither Jessie nor I said anything, not wanting to get involved in what seemed to be a recurring argument between the siblings-in-law.

We reached the end of North Ark Road, which halted abruptly in a tall stone wall. Thomas was right. There were a few inns located in the eastern Merchant Run, and we entered one painted bright teal with white moldings. The windows had little designs etched into them, depicting ships at sea surrounded by spitting sea wraiths, or a forest of snow-capped trees, or even one of a mountain. I recognized a little image of a slate-wolf on one of the peaks, and I felt a smile tug at the corner of my mouth. The slate-wolf here looked sort of fluffy, almost dog-like, while in reality the creatures resembled big, blind, wolfish rats.

As we entered, I looked up at the gently swinging sign over the door. It read '*King's Pearl Inn*', and I blinked in mild confusion as I stepped over the threshold. Despite being a king over the Great Lakes of Horcath, there had never been any special connection to the Ice King and pearls, at least not that I knew of.

"Most people aren't familiar with the history of the Coldmonian royal family, or any royal family, for that matter," Wendy had appeared beside me, golden hair swept back on his head, eyes bright and alert. "The people here use it to their advantage. What's this I'm selling? Well it's a green crisp apple. Did you know it's the king's favorite?" he mimicked an enthusiastic merchant trying to sell his goods. He rolled his eyes and chuckled. "If anyone had spent two minutes learning about the Coldmonian royal family, they'd know fruits are very uncommon for them. They've always preferred seafood over anything else, and there aren't many good ways to get fresh fruit to *Dagabid*." I chuckled with him, following him farther into the inn.

We had entered into a long hallway, decorated with vibrant orange and gold paints and dramatic copper sconces, and we reached the end of it now, coming to a small reception desk. It was notably simple compared to the flourishing decorations we'd seen so far, but the candelabra that sat atop it and the massive ledger that sat open before its occupant held enough flair to make up for it.

"Big group this time!" the receptionist cheered, eyes lighting up. He was a young boy, scarcely older than thirteen, and dressed in a bright red outfit excessively adorned with golden buttons and chains that winked at us in the firelight.

"We'll need rooms for thirty-one people," Wendy declared proudly, smiling broadly at the youth. The boy's delight seemed to double as he looked at our group, oblivious to the menacing point of Wendy's hook or any of the other obvious mechanics on the bodies of over half the men.

"Absolutely, sir! Let me see . . ." he looked down to consult his ledger, picking up a quill and scribbling on the paper. "Could I get a name to cover those rooms, sir?" he asked politely, tilting his head up and looking at us through his mop of unruly copper hair.

"Howard Smith." Wendy answered smoothly. I glanced over my shoulder, seeking Captain Howard's close-cropped blond hair in our little crowd. He was no longer dressed in the nice coat he'd worn aboard *The Coventry*, but instead adorned in simpler clothes like the rest of us wore.

"Howard Smith. Wonderful." The boy bent over his work again, scribbling down the name, which I was more than certain was fake, then beamed up at Wendy again. "You'll get twelve rooms. I should think it'll be enough. Will you be needing dinner or baths or anything?"

"No, thank you."

"Okay then. That'll be a hundred and seventy-four rupees, sir."

Jessie and I shared a glance. Rupees were the traditional form of currency in Coldmon, and I'd never seen them myself. Wisesol, Freetalon, and Brightlock typically dealt in the common nameless silver and gold coins. I wasn't sure what currency was used in Old Nightfall, but I knew copper pieces referred to as shins were used in Old Duskfall, and Carlore used coins called ingots. I'd never seen any of the foreign currencies, and I wasn't sure how Wendy would be able to pay this boy in rupees.

"Here you are," Wendy didn't miss a beat, producing a small velvet drawstring bag, holding it out to the boy with the string looped over his hook, and the boy snatched it up and peered inside. His eyes widened.

"Th-that's more than enough, sir," he stammered. Wendy winked at him.

"A little extra for you, my boy. Now, where are those room keys?"

I ended up splitting a room with Wendy and Peeler, and I considered myself lucky for that company. There were definitely worse men to share a bunk with.

Jessie and Molly got a room to themselves at the other end of the inn, but there wasn't much anyone could do about that. The inn only had so many open rooms, and we wouldn't all be together, but for only a night or two, it would work just fine.

The room I was sharing with *The Coventry*'s navigator and repairman was surprisingly spacious, painted a striking shade of pink and furnished with dark oak bedside tables and shockingly clean cots. The blankets were completely white, and there were towels folded up on them, should we change our minds about the baths. The carpet was thin, but unstained and printed with a swirling orange and white pattern.

"It's a very . . . colorful place, isn't it?" I asked as I pulled back the lace curtains to the one window at the back of our room, peering out into a sizable backyard of the inn. There was a small green space back there, and I could see a donkey and two horses grazing.

"All of Famark is," Peeler explained, experimentally tapping his bedpost. "It attracts more tourists."

"And you can tell it works. Here we go," Wendy grinned at us and opened the door, revealing the yellow-orange walls of the hallway. He gestured to it with his hook, which gleamed dully in the light from the window. "We've got to go back and unload the ship. Come along, Ksega, and we'll get those perfumes dropped off for you while we're at it."

I nodded and followed him out. We ran into Thomas and Chap in the hallway, and the two of them fell in step beside us as we made our way along the hall, down the spiraling white stairs, through the dizzyingly patterned sitting room, and down the entry hallway to the front door. As we passed, the cheery receptionist wished us well on our tourist shopping. Wendy only grinned and winked at him in reply.

"Smells like the sea here, doesn't it?" Chap asked as we stepped outside, taking a deep breath.

"Smells like a tourist trap." Peeler muttered, looking through the lenses of his glasses with obvious disdain.

"Smells like *profit*." Wendy pitched in, rubbing his hand eagerly against the spine of his hook. I blinked at him, and Thomas threw me a brief glance, but none of them elaborated, so I stayed silent as we walked back towards the Western Harbor.

"Will we have to go through that whole ordeal at the gates again?" I asked, reminded of what time it had been when we'd arrived in Famark and what time it was now. My stomach growled to remind me I hadn't yet eaten lunch, and it was almost dinner time.

"Don't worry about that, lad," Chap laughed and ran a hand through his unruly red hair. "We'll be allowed to come in and out as we please until *The Coventry* sets sail again. Speaking of setting sail, do you know what happened the last time we set sail from this port?" he looked down at me with such an eager intensity I had to indulge him, smiling as I answered,

"I don't believe I do."

He proceeded to tell me all about how, the last time he had been in Famark, he'd set off from the Eastern Harbor with half the crew left back in the Merchant Run, caught up by a band of thieves. His excuse was that he'd been forced to go on without them, but he'd valiantly promised to return for them. After he was finished, Wendy leaned towards me and said Chap had been drunk again, hallucinated about the thieves, and ordered them to set sail while Peeler was still in the harbor working on the hull of their ship. They hadn't gone anywhere, and half an hour later, Chap was out cold in his quarters.

By the time we finally made our way back to *The Coventry*, several other crew members had reunited with us, including Old Hank, Bubba, Gawain, and a dark-haired man named Han who was missing both of his thumbs. We all worked together to unload the perfumes and whatever other supplies we would need for our stay. It was a minimal load, the heaviest thing being the big crate of glass perfume vials carried between Bubba's one arm, Wendy's hand and hook, Thomas, and Chap.

As we walked back towards the King's Pearl, I helped to guide them and their load through the crowded Ark Road. The shop I was delivering the perfumes to was called *Erique's Otherworld*, a squat purple building with spiky black trim around its tinted windows and a door that creaked loudly as it swung open.

"Welcome, welcome!" a portly man wearing dramatic silver and purple robes whom I assumed to be Erique waddled out from behind a broad black desk, his thinning hair plastered onto his head with some sort of shiny gel. His eyes lit up at the sight of the wooden crate. "My perfumes, I assume?"

"That's right," I told him, trying to keep my tone as friendly as possible. The shop was full of peculiar items, and some of the decoration choices made me slightly queasy. A black cat's head was mounted on the wall behind the desk, and there were snakeskins and animal teeth and glass eyes adorning the rest of the shelves along the wall. Even more disturbing things were lined up on racks and hanging from poles across the little shop, but I didn't look too closely at any of them.

"Where would you like them, good sir?" Wendy was much more successful at mustering a pleasant tone than I had been.

"Right this way, please," Erique led the way farther into the store. There were candles lit on some of the shelves, but they were intentionally sparse, leaving the shop cast in ominous shadows.

Erique unlocked a black door concealed behind a thick velvet drape, letting us into a small room filled with trinkets and old crates and sacks of various items. A single lantern lit the space, hanging and flickering in the corner.

"Just set it anywhere," the shopkeeper said, waving a hand. "It's a bit of a mess, but most everything is fragile, so make sure it doesn't crush anything. I'll go get your payment." He left the room with one final look at the heavy crate they held.

"What do you suppose he'll market them as?" I asked when he'd gone, helping to clear a space on the floor for the crate. "I somehow doubt he'll want to be selling anything called *mango cloud* in a psychics shop."

"Who knows?" Wendy grunted as they set the crate down. He brushed his hand off on his pant leg, then did the same with his hook, and shrugged.

"Here you are! Dealt in silver coins." The shopkeeper returned and handed me a hefty sack that jingled merrily as I took it from him.

"Thank you very much." I smiled politely at him. He returned it and ushered us out of the store room. We left the shop as discreetly as possible, then stood there in the cooling night air.

North Ark Road was much quieter now that the sun had set. Locals and tourists alike would be preparing for bed or staying out late drinking and gambling around the island. As for me, I planned to find a nice dinner and tuck in for the night.

"Ksega," Chap drew my attention. I glanced at him questioningly. "We're all going to visit Merchant Daynor." His eyes darted up the street worriedly, towards the King's Pearl Inn. "When you get back, do you think you could cover for us if Molly asks? She's really not fond of the fellow."

I raised my eyebrows at that. Thomas had said earlier that Chap wasn't very fond of Merchant Daynor either. But Thomas was younger than the rest of us, and Chap probably didn't want his brother going off alone, even if Famark was a relatively safe place. I did wonder why Bubba and Wendy and the rest would be joining them, though.

"We're all fans of his," Wendy said, as if reading my mind. He smiled warmly at me. "We'd love to stop by and say hello. We should be back within a few hours, but don't wait up for us. Visits with Daynor can sometimes be too entertaining to leave early."

"You'll need to be regaining your strength for the journey home, anyway," Peeler added.

I looked between all of them. Bubba was glowering at me, but that wasn't anything new. Gawain and Han wore similar expressions, and Old Hank wasn't even paying attention to the conversation, his eye trained on a group of staggering drunk men farther down the road.

"Of course." I returned Wendy's smile, and I hoped they couldn't tell that it was forced. "I'm fairly good at lying, but I'm not used to lying to pirates. Will any old story keep Molly from being suspicious?" I kept my voice slightly disinterested.

"Yeah," Chap nodded. "She may not even be awake. Just, you know, if you do happen to bump into her." He clapped me on the back and gave my shoulder a squeeze. "Thanks, mate. We'll see you tomorrow, if not later tonight."

And then they were gone, walking back down towards the central strip of the Ark Road.

I wasn't sure where Merchant Daynor lived, but something told me it wouldn't be in the Merchant Run. Thomas had mentioned something about a Merchant Corner, hadn't he? Where was that?

I looked up and down the street briefly, pleased to find a big board with a map of the island just across the road. I'd seen them around as we'd walked, placed there for the benefit of travelers who weren't familiar with the layout of Famark. I walked up to it and squinted at the writing.

Just as I'd thought, the Merchant Corner — which was apparently off-limits to normal tourists — was in the northwestern corner of the island, behind the Merchant Run on North Ark Road. Chap, Wendy, and the rest of them had gone south. The only thing other than the Merchant Run in that direction was a big space simply labeled '*Peasant Homeland*'. There were smaller labeled things, too, like a big block marked as the supply houses, and another patch of the island called the Saddened Fields. There were the Arkane Peaks on the eastern side of the Peasant Homeland, depicted as crude points. Lastly, there was a thick black strip that wound through the Peasant Homeland, labeled '*South Ark Road*'.

There would be nothing down there for the pirates, and I somehow doubted a Merchant would be down there. That only left the Merchant Run and the Eastern and Western Harbors. I somehow doubted that Wendy was going hunting for a souvenir.

I stood there for a long moment, contemplating the map. I knew I was wasting precious time, and if I was going to do what I wanted to do, I had to move now. I knew Thomas had lied about Merchant Daynor. He probably existed, but there was a good chance the pirates didn't even know him personally. It was just an excuse to get out.

I didn't want to leave Jessie behind, but there was no time to go back and get her. I would just have to trust that she would be alright with her own wits and recle for the time being.

Making up my mind, I pivoted on my heel and took off at a sprint down the road, making my way towards the Western Harbor.

12
KSEGA

I got past the guards and the intricate iron gates just in time.

Bobbing gently in the waves, *The Coventry* was being prepared to shove off. I could see someone climbing the rigging, and the glint of firelight against metal told me it was Wendy. Once he was up in the crow's nest, he might see me, so I moved fast down the docks.

When I came up alongside the pirate ship, the ramp had already been lifted away, but that was alright. I wouldn't have used it anyway.

In all my sixteen years in Wisesol, I'd only been a stowaway a meager five times. Out of them, only one had ever left the confines of the Port's canal, and that had been the *Sea Cloud*. I remember it vividly, getting tossed around the cargo hold and bruising myself profusely as I scrambled to hold onto something. The other four ships had been smaller fishing boats sailing into the canal to retrieve their fishnets. The only reason I had ever been a stowaway was to get away with some sort of thievery, and the *Sea Cloud* and a fishboat called *Raptor's Knife* were the only two I'd ever been caught on.

The Coventry had a lot more people on board, but not all twenty-nine crew members were there right now. Some of them had to have stayed behind to keep up the pretense that nothing suspicious was going on. Molly and some of the others would be keeping Jessie occupied, and were supposed to be doing the same with me.

There were several thick coils of rope draped over the shiprail, and I knew one of them was connected to the anchor. I reached up and grabbed one of the coils just as *The Coventry* cast off, and seconds later I found myself dangling over the lapping black waters, holding on by the one hand I had clasped around the rope. My breath hitched in panic, but I forced myself to keep quiet.

Swinging my other hand around, I looked back towards the docks. Several Cold-monian guards were stationed around, and a few of them were making rounds. Some were watching *The Coventry* sail off, stoic and stone-faced. The rest of the harbor was eerily still and quiet.

I was hidden in shadows at the moment, but when the ship was backed out of the harbor completely, the moonlight would expose me.

I scrambled up the ropes, my heart launching into my throat when the coil shifted unexpectedly, and peered over the top of the shiprail moments later. There was only one lantern lit on the entire deck of the ship, and it hung from a hook beside the door to the upper cargo hold, above a crate where Peeler was sitting, hunched over some sort of small metal contraption. Up on the crow's nest, I could just make out Wendy, perched behind the massive crossbow. Old Hank and Han stood near the prow, and Gawain was a short way behind them, fiddling with his cloak. Chap was up by the steering wheel and Thomas was sprawled nonchalantly over a stack of barrels near Peeler, a broad-brimmed black hat tipped over his eyes, arms crossed, and a toothpick wedged between his teeth.

I couldn't see anyone else immediately, but I was sure there were more people aboard. I didn't plan to go below decks, since there weren't any good places to hide safely down there. I wasn't sure where we were going, but I knew we would be back by the next day. Peeler had already patched *The Coventry* up, but Molly had said he wasn't satisfied with it. That was all a cover to keep us on Famark for an extra day so the pirates could . . . what?

I had a growing feeling of unease forming in my gut, and hundreds of thoughts were running through my head, too fast for me to identify any of them. I knew I'd risked both Jessie and I sneaking on board, but I didn't have many options now.

I pulled myself up and over the shiprail, setting my feet lightly on the bundled ropes on the deck. Since there was only one lantern, I was safely tucked into the shadows, and would remain so until I came closer to the cargo hold.

Cargo holds were always the safest places for stowaways. There were usually plenty of crates or barrels or tarps to hide inside or underneath, and in a ship like *The Coventry*, it would be extra secure. As far as I knew, the cargo hold wouldn't be used for anything tonight.

Unless they're stealing something. I realized, my gaze flitting briefly around the visible crew members. Was that what this was? Some sort of pirate heist? Where were they going? What had I gotten myself into?

I crept slowly along the wall of the ship, debating if I should assume a more purposeful demeanor or stick to sneaking. Would I be able to trick the pirates into thinking I was supposed to be on the ship? As long as I didn't run directly into anybody, it might work, but there was still a thread of doubt in the back of my mind. These were pirates, master swindlers and thieves. Some of them had probably pulled that trick before, so wouldn't they be able to spot someone else doing it?

I continued to argue with myself as I made my way along, and by the time I'd come to the conclusion not to stand up and walk across the deck, I'd reached the barrels behind Peeler and Thomas. I paused here, unsure what to do next. I couldn't get past Peeler and Thomas into the cargo hold without alerting one of them to my presence, but I didn't have many options in the way of distraction. As I pondered what to do, a flash of light caught my attention, drawing my gaze towards Peeler and the item in his hands.

Now that I was closer, I saw that it was a device of wood and iron. It fit snugly in the pirate's hand, and there was a place for his finger to rest on some sort of small lever, but aside from that, I couldn't make out many details. It was something like a thick iron pipe secured to a handle of wood, with various bands and levers dotted throughout.

I'd never seen anything like it before, and I had no idea what it would be used for. Peeler was currently fiddling with little metal bolts securing the iron bands to the wood, leaning unnecessarily close to his work. I was somehow fascinated by the way his hands moved deftly over the surface of the tool adjusting the way the metal sat or the tightness of the leather. How was he able to do it with such ease?

"Bering-mage." A voice, clear and smug, sounded in my ear. I jumped to the side, knocking my knee loudly against one of the barrels, and looked up to see Thomas standing beside me.

"I-" I looked back at Peeler, who had glanced up from his work and flashed me that gold-and-silver smile. "What?" I asked, turning back to Thomas. I cleared my throat, trying to ignore the buzz of pain in my knee.

"Bering-mage. Peeler's a bering-mage. That's how he manipulates the wood." Thomas gestured back at the little machine, where Peeler was adjusting the thickness of the wooden handle. "I hear you're one, too. Have you never done that?"

"That wood is dead," I said bluntly, swallowing nervously as I looked up towards the prow, then at the crow's nest. Wendy waved at me from above. I scowled. "How long have you known I was here?"

"The whole time." Peeler said, refocused on his work.

"You did good. I lost sight of you a couple times in the shadows, but," Thomas shrugged and made a *tsk*ing sound. "Can't best a pirate there, mate."

"Right." I nodded, letting my gaze return to Peeler for a moment. Thomas' statement had puzzled me. Bering-mages were more connected to the earth than any other type of mage, but that earth always had to have some sort of substance to it. Rocks and boulders had substance, soil had substance, plants and animals had substance, but all of them were capable of losing it when they died or were destroyed.

"Come closer," Peeler mumbled without looking up, beckoning me to him with his hand. I hesitated, glancing at Thomas, but the third mate only nodded encouragement.

Shuffling forward, I sat on a barrel beside Peeler and bent to examine his work further. He ran a hand along the wood, then settled his fingers atop it, beginning to pull a long thorn from the timber. When it was pulled into a jutting point, he pressed the tip of his finger to it and gently coaxed the thorn back into the body of the wood. I gaped at it.

"How?" I asked. The wood here had no life, no substance. It was dead, nothing but a husk of the malleable clay it might once have been to me. Peeler's eyes were alight with joy.

"Bering, my boy. You know how to bend the living, but can you bend the dead?" he lifted the device towards my face, and I blinked down my nose at it. An unsettling chill crept up my spine.

Humans couldn't be controlled by any mage. It was just the way it worked. Animals couldn't really be controlled, either, but they could be convinced into doing things on occasion, if you were a strong enough bering-mage. If an animal was dead, though, there was obviously nothing one could do about it, and nothing one could do to convince it of anything. It worked the same with plant life.

"How do you think *The Coventry* recovers from her wounds so quickly?" Thomas had somehow obtained an apple, and he crunched into it as he leaned against the door to the cargo hold, his hat casting his face into shadow.

"You're saying you can close gaps in the wood like *that*?" I gasped, gesturing at where the thorn had been drawn. I'd never heard of anything like this before. It shouldn't have been possible.

"Not close completely," Peeler conceded. "Dead wood doesn't have as much flexibility as living wood, but if I can obtain a few small pieces of living wood — even twigs from trees can work — I can make short work of any breaks in *The Coventry's* body."

"Incredible," I marveled, looking at the wood all around me. I could feel no connection to it. If I really reached, I could sense the earth from Famark, rich and deep and comforting. Other than that, I was lost in this big empty space of the sea. It was freeing, but also terrifying.

"You don't practice a lot with your mage skills, do you?" Thomas asked through a mouthful of apple. I shook my head. I rarely had much of a chance to practice at home, always running around helping Willa or Jessie or trying to get myself out of trouble.

"You should." Peeler muttered distractedly as his hands delicately worked the handle of the machine into a smooth finish. "Bering-mages hold a lot more power than most people know."

"I'll keep that in mind." I looked between the two of them, waiting for something else to happen. Thomas spat his toothpick out onto the deck and started to head for the rigging. He waved me along behind him, and I followed.

We climbed up to join Wendy in the crow's nest, and I realized we were sailing around the southern side of Famark.

"Where are we going?"

"Clawbreak." Wendy answered smoothly, looking up into the sky. The stars weren't visible, hidden behind a veil of heavy autumn clouds. "We've got some business to attend to there."

"You, however, do not," Thomas chimed in, peering at me from beneath his hat. "Why'd you come aboard?"

"Curiosity?" I guessed, a little unsure myself.

"Sure." Thomas didn't sound the least bit convinced, but I didn't have a better answer, so I stayed silent. Wendy had an amused light in his eyes, but said nothing, keeping his gaze trained on the sky above and around us, and occasionally looking down at the black seas below us.

"Have you ever seen a sea wraith?" I asked, struck by the thought that there might be some giant snake-like beasts lurking beneath the waves. I'd heard plenty about sea wraiths around the Port, and I'd even seen some of the tadpoles myself, although they had been dead and sold in the markets. They were of a surprising size, as long as my arm, and in all sorts of colors.

"I have," Wendy replied, leaning back against the rail of the crow's nest. He tapped his hook against the crossbow in front of us. "Shot one down with this very bow, actually. I saw another one in my first few years at sea, but it never came close to us. The one I killed was attacking *The Coventry*, and it nearly took her down."

Thomas nodded along, although I got the feeling this was the first time he was hearing this story as well. As far as I could tell, he didn't have any scars or missing body parts like most of the other men aboard the ship. Neither did Chap or Molly, for that matter, and I wondered briefly if that meant the family was good at staying out of trouble, or it was just more proof of how different they were from the rest of the crew. They were the only ones who weren't actual pirates, after all.

Or were they all pirates? This seemed like awfully pirate-like business, and Thomas was disconcertingly at ease about it. I had no doubt he'd done something like this before, and he had grouped himself in with the pirates in previous statements. Maybe they weren't so different, when it came down to it, but I didn't want to look close enough to find out.

"What's waiting for you in Clawbreak?" I asked, unwilling to let *myself* be grouped in with the pirates. I had gotten myself into a fair amount of trouble back in Wisesol, and while the title might seem roguish and have a slightly rugged appeal to it, becoming known as Ksega, Scourge of the Seas, wasn't something I wanted to add to my list of achievements.

"Good stuff, gold stuff," Wendy shrugged, grinning at me. "Almost anything can be found in that pig hole. Except pretty women."

"The real question is, what's waiting for *you* in Clawbreak?" Thomas poked me hard in the chest, and I winced, even as the pain receded almost immediately. He tilted his head to the side, and without the flickering light of the lantern, he looked older and more ominous than before, and the hat hiding the top of his face didn't help.

"Not entirely sure," I admitted, hoping my voice sounded as nonchalant as I wanted it to. What did pirates do with stowaways? I'd heard stories about walking the plank, or being beheaded, but for some reason, that didn't strike me as *The Coventry*'s style. It would probably be something with a little more flair, like an arrow fired through my chest, or a dramatic tossing of me, bound at wrists and ankles, into the depths of the sea.

"I know what awaits you," Wendy held his hook up and jammed it at me, and I jerked my head back instinctively. He laughed, retracting his arm. From the light below, I could see an excited sparkle in his eyes. "Your very first pirate heist."

Wendy bid Thomas and I a temporary farewell as we descended back to deck level, where we ran into Laurence and Paul, who both greeted me with an unsettling grin. I walked with them and Thomas down to the galley to see who else was a part of the mission crew.

In total, there were twelve of us. Me, Thomas, Chap, Peeler, Gawain, Laurence, Bubba, Paul, Old Hank, Wendy, Davie, and Han. Each of us were equipped with some sort of weapon, and I had been given my bow and quiver of arrows. Everyone had a task for the job except for me, but Thomas patted me on the back and guided me to one of the tables to explain that I was definitely going to have one.

The target was a building in the northeastern corner of Carove Town, the scheming, deceptive little place inhabited by whatever scum lived on that wretched island. The building had no official name, but it was known to be a place guarded heavily by a band of thugs who stored their treasures there. The treasures varied from currencies of all kinds to valuable dishes and adornments to priceless artifacts and heirlooms passed down through families, all of them acquired in some illegal way or another.

We would be splitting up into groups of three. Chap, Gawain, and Laurence were going to be the primary attack force, rushing in to get rid of any remaining thieves after Bubba, Paul, and Wendy provided a distraction. Anyone that was left after that would be taken care of by the second rush, Peeler, Han, and Thomas. Old Hank, Davie and I were in charge of getting in and locating the treasure, then alerting the others so we could load up and get away.

The plan was straightforward, almost concerningly so. There was nothing complicated or strategic about it. The pirates were relying completely on surprise and brute force to obtain this treasure. They didn't even have a layout of the building itself.

I would have pointed this out, except we were already being split up into our respective trios to find a way to work well together. Old Hank didn't seem like one to appreciate complaints, and Davie probably wasn't interested in the logical risks of just about anything.

Old Hank, Davie and I were sitting in the sleeping quarters, all of us seated in a separate hammock in one corner of the room. Old Hank was rattling on about something, but I wasn't really listening, and Davie didn't appear to be either. I was still a little shaken up by everything that had happened since I'd snuck on board — although I wasn't sure if it counted as sneaking, since Thomas had obviously known I was there to begin with — and I was trying to think of a way out of this whole pirate heist deal.

I could handle being a well-known piece of scum in my own hometown, because crime was relatively normal in Wisesol, and there were too many criminals for the authorities to pay attention to every pesky teenage boy. It was slightly different when you were stealing something in a different kingdom where the law system was entirely different and crime rates were much lower.

My head was starting to hurt from all the problems and possible solutions running through my head, and my stomach wasn't very happy with the swaying movements of the ship — Jessie wasn't here to give me her seasickness remedy — so I sought an escape from my own mind. The first thing my gaze landed on were the bones jutting out of Davie's back, surrounded at the base by mounds of gnarly pink scar tissue.

"How did you hurt your back?" I asked, and he looked up from what he was doing, messing with a loose thread in his trousers. For a moment, I thought he might get offended, or maybe emotional, if he was shy or self-conscious about the bones, but then he grinned.

"A sea wraith tore my back out." He said simply, that pleasant smile still plastered to his face. There was something almost expectant in his eyes, and I guessed he was awaiting my shocked reaction. I'm sure I didn't disappoint.

I was sure my eyes were bulging out of my skull, and I could feel my jaw go slack. This boy was hardly twelve years old, nothing more than skin and bones, and he had been attacked by a sea wraith? Based on how well he moved and how healed the flesh was, it must have happened when he was very, very young. As if he could read my mind, he told me,

"I was almost five. My mum tossed me into the Great Lakes, right beside the Gates of Brightlock, actually. The guards saw her and went to arrest her, but they never got to her. A sea wraith came up and bit right through the docks, taking her with it. One of its teeth caught me in the back and nearly went straight through me," he was grinning broadly as he told the story, and I was sure I only looked increasingly horrified as he went on. "The guards drove the wraith away and pulled me out of the water just in time. They got me to a very skilled Talon before I died, but some of the damage was irreversible." He pulled his arm behind his back and poked the ends of the ribs. His grin turned slightly mischievous. "Wanna touch them? It's like a giant tooth. But in my back."

"I'm good, thanks," I recoiled from him, curling back into my hammock. He shrugged and went back to tugging at the thread on his trousers, as if he hadn't just shared the most traumatizing story I'd ever heard. Not even Chap could make up something as scarring as that, surely.

"Much more exciting than my story," Old Hank rasped from my other side. He grinned crookedly at me when I looked at him in question. "Got it gouged out by a rival pirate." He blinked his green eye, tapping a finger against the black leather patch that covered the socket of the other. "Used his bare hands, he did." He cackled loudly, tossing his head back. "What about you, bering boy? Any scars about you?"

"Not that I know of," I replied, inching myself farther into the depths of my little hammock. Why couldn't I have been stuck with Wendy or Chap? Even judgemental Bubba or condescending Thomas would be better than these loons.

Luckily, the distance between Famark and Clawbreak was relatively small, and we were soon called up to the main deck. All lanterns and torches were extinguished, cloaking us in darkness. I peered towards the dark waves lapping at the hull, unsettled by Davie's tale of a hungry sea wraith. Had that actually happened? Was he only making things up, like Chap had?

There aren't many other explanations for a wound like that, I reminded myself, glancing at the pale bones again. A shiver ran through me, but I tried to conceal it as we came closer to the dark blot of Clawbreak. I didn't want any of these pirates thinking I was afraid of a little action. Of course I wasn't afraid of action; I was Ksega Copper, brat of Rulak, ruffian of Wisesol. The problem here was I wasn't Ksega Copper the pirate.

Clawbreak didn't have any docks or harbors. The only way onto the island was to brave the cliffs around the island, or crawl through the sludge-covered beaches of the eastern Waste Ponds. The pirates were taking the cliff route, and that meant I had no choice but to go along with it.

The Coventry was brought around to the southern cliffs of the island, and Peeler and Wendy let down the anchor. We weren't too close to the cliffs here, far enough away to be safe from the frothing waves that churned against the black stone. We would go closer by rowboat, locating a cave tunnel that Chap said led right up into the heart of Carove Town.

From what I could see of the roaring waves by the cliffs, I didn't want to go any closer than I was now, but I didn't have many other options. If I said I didn't want to do this, Thomas would probably call me a coward and have me thrown overboard to be eaten by a sea wraith or dragged onto the rowboat anyway. Best to save myself the extra embarrassment and save my childish screaming for when I was being tossed against the jagged cliff rocks.

"Off we go!" Chap cheered as the first rowboat was sent into the water. His trio and mine would be in that one, and the rest of the crew would be in the other rowboat. The smaller boats had come from a compartment in the hull of *The Coventry*, and left me wondering what other secrets this pirate ship held, most likely implemented by Peeler and his peculiar bering-mage talents.

I hadn't expected to do very well in the little rowboat, but it was even worse than I'd expected. The few times I'd been in a smaller vessel in the Port hadn't gone too well for me. They rocked and jolted a lot more than the larger ships, and I was usually quite sick when I disembarked. They were also much closer to the surface of the water, and when it was sitting on a very deep body of water — especially one that was like shifting black glass — I felt more disconnected from my bering than I ever was.

I gripped the boat tightly, unable to help row, and I kept my eyes shut tight. I'd always loved the water, always been fascinated by its creatures and entertained by the way light danced on its surface. I could put on a good show of loving it, too, and I was always fine when I wasn't alone on the sea. The problem was I was also terrified of the ocean.

As soon as we hit the churning waves, I tried not to scream. I could hear the pirates shouting at each other over the din, but I wasn't able to make out their words. The little boat lurched to the side, and icy spray showered down on us. We were tipped up and backwards, and I felt myself falling upside-down out of my seat. We crashed back into the water, somehow right-side-up again, and a small wave sloshed over the side of the boat, soaking all of us. I was losing feeling in my fingers, and all sense of direction was gone. I could only hold on and hope Chap knew where this blasted tunnel was. My stomach roiled in protest, but there was nothing in it for me to retch up, so I was left with a piercing ache in my belly and a sour taste in the back of my throat as we rocked and shifted on the tameless waves.

"There it is!" Chap's voice was loud in my ears, and I pried my eyes open. I regretted it immediately.

White waves slammed against the black rocks of the cliffs right beside us, showering us with broken shards of water. We were sucked away from them, then sent careening towards them again, coming so close I pressed my eyes closed again. I didn't see the tunnel entrance, and I wasn't sure how Chap was able to spot it through the chaos, but I hoped he knew how to get us there fast and preferably without dying.

"Hold on!" someone shouted, and a moment later a jarring impact rattled our little craft. I grunted, and I may have let out a small yelp, and opened my eyes to see that we had landed ourselves between two large rocks, wedged in place and tilted awkwardly. Water rushed over the back end of the boat, pommeling poor Gawain.

"Come on, up!" Laurence said, offering me a hand, and I realized he had climbed off onto the rocks. I accepted his help and allowed myself to be pulled up and onto the slick stone. He gestured for me to walk along the rock, and I saw that there was indeed a tunnel opening ahead. Davie and Chap were already waiting for us by the entrance.

Spitting seawater, I stumbled over to them and allowed myself to be ushered into the cave. It was completely black, and it was a tight fit, but I didn't mind. I knew Jessie was claustrophobic, and the little opening reminded me of her. I hoped she was okay, and that the pirates wouldn't do anything to her once they realized I was gone. If Thomas had been able to guess I would follow them, wouldn't the others? Jessie knew nothing about this, and surely they would have the good sense to know that.

Shortly after I started walking into the cramped tunnel, it grew even smaller, and I had to lower myself onto my hands and knees to crawl on. Sharp rocks poked and prodded at my skin, tearing holes in my shirt and attempting to tug my boots right off my feet. Every now and then, a wave would crash into the mountain and make the tunnel rattle, pebbles falling down onto us as the excess water rushed through the cave with us. It came up halfway, making the little tunnel seem even tighter, but then it would recede and leave us shuffling along on slick rock.

"Keep going, Ksega," I heard Chap's voice say from behind me. "The cave will keep going, but you'll want to be feeling for an opening on the left. That will lead us up to the town. If you miss it, you'll slide down into . . . well I'm not sure, actually. I just know nobody has been able to get back up."

I swallowed nervously, unsure if that was him exaggerating again, and lifted my hand to start feeling along the left side of the tunnel, letting my fingers explore every dip and crevice to ensure I wasn't missing something. It took a long time to find it, and by the time I did, I was shivering and soaked. My clothes were heavy with frigid seawater, and I had lost feeling in my fingers and toes.

I dragged myself up into the new tunnel entrance, squinting at the faint gray lines appearing in my vision. Was there some sort of light source up above? Was it already daytime? Had we crawled through the whole night? My stomach growled loudly, begging for some breakfast. Or maybe dinner. As I climbed, I wasn't sure if the light came from the sun or the moon.

Behind me, I heard someone grunt as they began the climb. This tunnel was much steeper, but there were lots of good handholds. I could feel the bow slung across my back scrape the other side of the tunnel occasionally, and tried to press myself closer to the rock to prevent damaging it. My muscles ached and I was sure they would give out just before my head hit something sort of soft. I paused, lifting one hand with a grunt to press my fingers against it. Dirt?

"Chap?" I asked uncertainly, my voice thin and strained.

"It's a trap door. Go ahead and push it open." Came his reply.

I took a bracing breath, then shoved with all my might on the dirt above. I felt resistance, but a moment later, the hinges gave, and a round door creaked open above my head, thumping back onto a field of short, brittle grass. I climbed up and crawled onto the grass before I flopped onto my side, letting my eyes slide closed. I was so tired and hungry. Why did I always have to go poke my nose into other peoples' business?

The others hoisted themselves out after me, grunting and panting from the exertion of going through the tunnel. Most of them were very fit though, and had a lot more muscle than me, so they didn't fall over as I had. I felt a twinge of jealousy at how easily Davie and Chap jumped up to their feet and started to reestablish their teams of three.

Dragging myself onto my feet, I groaned. It was still dark out, and there were no signs of dawn. We couldn't have been crawling and climbing for more than two hours, although at the moment it had felt like days.

We were standing in an oblong rectangle-shaped field that stretched across the island. To the north, I could see a sort of cluster of crumbling structures and unstable-looking buildings. To the east, in the distance, was some sort of forest, and to the south there was a sad-looking town. It was dark and shadowy and foreboding, and I didn't want to go any closer to it than I already was, but I knew I didn't have much of a choice at this point.

"Here we go!" Old Hank grinned at me, his green eye glimmering in the moonlight. Davie stood beside us, cracking his knuckles and rolling his shoulders. All of us were dripping water, and I marveled at how Davie didn't shake from the cold. We stayed there for another few minutes until the other boat-full of pirates joined us, then we got ready to set off, wringing out our shirts and trying to restore feeling to our limbs.

As we all started to jog towards the town — my muscles protested against it, but it was warming me up — I tried to think back to my team's part of the plan. It seemed like so long ago that we'd gone over it, but it was such a simple plan I should've been able to remember it more easily. As we came closer to the town, it came back to me slowly. We were supposed to go in and find the treasure after the other teams had provided a distraction. That was it. It was easy. It was *safe*.

We entered the town on the north side, slinking around through some sort of tourist attraction section. There were crumbling stone buildings and broken toys everywhere, and a sort of depressed air all around. I shuddered as I stepped around the rubble after the pirates. They were unfazed by the torn canvases and the chipping paint on the big wooden signs that lay splintered on the ground.

There was hardly any life here. My bering was stretched taught seeking something strong and breathing, but I could sense nothing. There were hundreds of bugs all around us, and a few measly plants, but there were no trees, no growing grasses. Everything was dead or withering.

It was almost a sickening feeling. I'd grown almost used to having my bering drained of any source of power on the sea, but here on land? There was something so wrong about it. Land was supposed to mean life. I tried to reach out to the dead wood around us, seeing if I could manipulate it as Peeler had the handle of his device, but I felt nothing. The wood was just a shell of what it had once been, as useful to me as a stone.

I didn't practice with my bering much, but I had to use it every now and then to keep myself sane. Every mage had to put their skills to use at some point, otherwise the power was so weak it was practically nonexistent. I knew I wasn't a very strong bering-mage, but I liked to try and use it when I could.

I reached out now, wrapping the invisible threads of my power around a small patch of gray-green moss that had sprouted on the ground before us. As soon as my bering touched it, color flooded into it, make it easily visible against the drab ochre of the earth around it. Seconds later, as I allowed power to flow into it, little flowers bloomed along it, bright pinks and purples. It was small work, but it made me feel a little better to know there was at least *some* life here.

The main road of Carove Town was even worse. There were hunched figures in every shadowed corner, and almost no sound. It was an unnerving sight, made even more so by the fact that almost every human-shaped shadow was so still they appeared to be dead.

We crossed the main road and entered the alleyways on the other side, trying to keep to the shadows, even though it was a futile effort to try and keep a group this big hidden in a place with so many people around. None of them seemed very interested in us, but I knew they saw us, because some of them would turn their heads to track our progress. The alleys were dark and dusty and filled with rubble. I was glad to see that the pirates were stumbling and knocking their shins just as much as I was, because that meant I wasn't the inexperienced idiot here.

We said nothing as we looped around the buildings, weaving through the alleys and avoiding contact with anything living. My eyes adjusted to the darkness as we moved, but it didn't help much. Even when I could see what was on the ground before me, it was practically impossible to identify what it was.

As we jogged lightly through the alleys, I looked around for any signs of people approaching. This place made me uneasy, and I didn't want to be here any longer than I had to. I didn't feel very safe running with the pirates, but it was better than going off alone.

We paused only once to catch our breath, then resumed our steady pace. I was beginning to grow certain nothing exciting would happen until we reached our destination, but then I saw something move swiftly out of the corner of my eye. I was at the back of the group, so when I slowed to a stop, none of them noticed. I looked down the alley and saw someone bending over to grab something they'd dropped. I was about to keep running when I realized it was a girl. I couldn't make out any details of her face or clothing, but there was an obvious sense of control about her that put her out of place in this town.

I glanced towards the pirates, already disappearing around another bend. I had to go now if I wanted to catch up, but something about this girl intrigued me. She didn't look to be much older than me, and she was walking away now. No, not walking, running. Her pace picked up until she was out of my sight. Nobody else had run, at least not that I'd seen.

The last time I'd let my curiosity get the best of me, I'd landed in the middle of a pirate heist. If I let it get the best of me now, the results couldn't be any better. At the same time, they could be a lot better, and they could get me out of risking my neck for some pirate treasure.

Making up my mind, I pulled my bow off my back and an arrow from the quiver at my hip, knocking it as I set off after the girl. She had been in the main road, and I felt vulnerable when I came out into it, but I saw her disappear into another alleyway a short way down. I ran after her, my heart pounding in my chest, senses alert.

When I reached the alley she'd gone into, I saw no sign of her. There was a man curled up farther down the alley, but he seemed to be in his own little world. The girl was gone.

Panic began to rise in me. What had I been *thinking*? Willa would kill me if I ever got home. I should have just stayed with the pirates. I had no idea where they were now. No, I shouldn't have snuck onto *The Coventry* after them in the first place. If I'd had any common sense, I would've gone back to the King's Pearl Inn and stayed with Jessie until it was time to go home.

A sound above me brought me back into the present. I snapped my head up. The building beside me used to have two complete levels, but half of the top floor had caved in, exposing sharp spikes of wood. There were soft sounds coming from inside the other half of the top level.

I glanced around me, spotting a few figures ambling my way, some of them taking a more indirect path. My stomach squirmed, aching from hunger and fear. I threw my bow back over my back and began to climb the side of the building. It creaked and groaned beneath my weight, but I tried to keep it out of my mind as I pulled myself up and over onto the top. I instantly unslung my bow and knocked the arrow again, looking up at the still intact dividing wall. There was definitely someone in there, shuffling around.

I took a deep breath, stepping carefully around the fallen timbers around me. One helpful thing about bering was that it gave you a sense of life around you. Even if it wasn't life you could manipulate, like that of a human, you could at least sense its presence. It was hard to determine how many people there might be in one place if there were a lot of them, but if there were a few, it could sometimes be done.

I could feel the life of someone beyond the wall. There might have been two of them, but they must have been standing close together. There was something else, too, a sort of buzzing sensation beside them. I'd only felt that a few times before, and only when I was facing something Cursed.

I hesitated. My bering wasn't very strong, and I knew I wasn't the most reliable when it came to detecting how many life forms there might be around me. It wasn't very likely something Cursed would be in the same room as a human without someone dying.

You can't exactly go find the pirates now, I scolded myself. Why did I have to follow this girl? Why couldn't I stop and think about the consequences of my actions for once in my life?

I stepped forward again. There was a dark gap in the wall, just big enough for someone to slip through. As I came closer to it, I heard muffled voices. My pulse was thrumming so loudly in my ears I couldn't make out what was being said, but I could make out a pair of boots in the corner, shifting around on the dusty boards.

The voices stopped suddenly, and I held my breath. Did they know I was here? They must have. I thought I was good at sneaking around, but the past few hours had proven me to be very wrong about that. Rolling my shoulders, I stepped forward through the gap, bow at the ready.

As soon as I saw who — or *what* — was in the room, my bow came up, and I pulled the arrow to full draw. Across from me, almost too fast for me to see it, another boy flicked an arrow from a quiver on his back and drew his own bow.

"Who are you?" the girl demanded. She stood slightly behind the boy with his bow trained on me, a silver sword handle clasped in her hand. Her skin was several shades darker than mine, and I recognized the item she held as the hilt of a Carlorian flame-sword. The boy also had skin darker than mine, but only just.

"Who are *you*?" I asked, furrowing my brows. My heart was hammering in my chest as I tried to keep my gaze trained on the two humans. I was attempting to ignore the looming figure behind them, where that awful humming was coming from. I knew what it was, or at least I *thought* I knew what it was. But how could it be? How was that possible?

"Answer me, or he'll put an arrow into you." The girl spat. Her eyes were hidden in the shadows, but I could sense the intensity in them. Her dark hair fell around her face, concealing most of the details. The boy also had dark hair, and his eyes looked black in the night.

"I could put an arrow into him just as easily." I tilted the tip of the arrow down so it was pointed at the boy's heart.

"You're outnumbered," a gravelly voice rumbled around us, and without looking, I knew it had come from the thin figure behind them. It was wearing clothes, and if you only saw it from the shoulders down, it could probably pass as a very tall man. But the blackened bones and the grinning skull told me what it really was. The faint green glow emanating from beneath the shirt told me everything I needed to know.

"Why are you here?" the boy asked, his eyes narrowed.

"Why are *you* here?" I repeated his question, less because I actually wanted to know and more because I didn't have a good answer for him. What *was* I doing on Clawbreak? Should I tell them I was helping a crew of pirates to rob the people here?

"Stop stalling and give us some real answers, or you're dead," the girl spat, and her flame-sword sputtered to life. The fire lit the room in a deep orange glow, and I could finally see who I was standing with clearly.

I squinted my eyes against the new light, my stomach tightening as the skeletal figure behind them was illuminated clearly. The firelight set eerie shadows dancing in the empty eye sockets. The girl was clearly irritated, her brows set low, hand bunched tightly around the handle of the burning flame-sword. I didn't know much about eirioth-mages, but I knew their powers were sustained by their energy, whereas bering was fueled more by emotion and state of mind.

"I'm Ksega. I'm here with some friends. We're here for some goods. Now tell me who you are." It was always easier to tell the truth where you could, even if it wasn't the whole truth, but none of them seemed to believe me.

"Ksega who?" the boy demanded. I shrugged.

"Nobody. I'm not important in my home, I'm not important here. Who are you?" I didn't know how much practice this boy had had with a bow and arrow, but he was definitely stronger than me. He held his arrow steady, but I could feel my arms beginning to tremble from the strain of keeping my bow at full draw for so long.

"We're from Carlore." The girl replied. "We've kept out of everyone else's business so far. Why did you follow me here?"

"To be honest, I wasn't too keen on staying with my current company," I let my gaze flick briefly to the small window in the corner of the room, the glass busted out of it. It was still dark out, but dawn couldn't have been too far away. "A girl running all alone through a place like this seemed like a promising adventure."

"Did it?" the boy's voice dropped into a sort of threatening rumble, and I raised an eyebrow at him.

"Not *that* kind of adventure. I'm just bored. Why are you people here, and what in the name of the Endless Sea is *that*?" I lifted my shaking bow to point the arrow at the skeleton standing behind them.

"Doesn't concern you. Get out of here and tell no one what you saw." The boy snapped, lowering his bow. I hesitated only a brief moment before doing the same, my muscles relaxing as I relieved the tension. I didn't like putting my bow away, or the arrow, but I did so anyway. I didn't want these people to see me as a threat.

The boy put his own arrow away in its quiver, and slung his bow over his back the way I had. The girl's flame-sword remained flickering and spitting, crackling angrily and matching her overall demeanor. She was glaring at me, but she also looked thoughtful. She didn't want me to leave like the boy did. There was something about that skeleton behind them that she didn't want shared.

"Or else what?" I shoved my hands casually into the pockets of my trousers. The boy's scowl deepend, and his tense posture hadn't relaxed at all, but he at least looked a little less hostile.

The boy didn't seem to have an answer for that, and he glanced sidelong at the girl. She didn't look at him, keeping her intense gaze trained on me. It sort of reminded me of Jessie's eyes, but this girl's eyes were darker and sharper than Jessie's; they held none of my friend's lighthearted promise.

"He has to stay." The skeleton spoke, and I tensed. I didn't want to break my nonchalant stance, hoping I could convince them I was perfectly at ease here, but just the thought of a speaking skeleton made me shudder. It was so empty of emotion, so empty of any sort of life. My bering was repulsed by its trembling hollowness, and because of that, so was I.

"Why?" the boy snarled, turning to look at the skeleton. "I'm already stuck with you. I don't want anything else to babysit."

"He's right." The girl's voice was like ice, chilly and unrelenting. She was just as happy about it as the boy, but she seemed to be reasoning with herself. Her expression was pensive, and I held her gaze coolly as I waited for her to make up her mind.

Inwardly, I was on the verge of panicking. I hadn't really wanted to get grouped in with this girl and her strange companions. I had expected . . . what *had* I expected?

Stupid, I scolded myself, watching the expressions of the people before me with wide, expectant eyes. The pirates would have noticed my absence by now, but I wasn't sure what they would do about it. Would they search for me? Would any of them even care to try? I hoped Wendy would, but that may have been me desperately searching for any excuse to call one of the pirates my friend.

"We could just kill him." The boy suggested, his dark eyes looking me up and down. My fingers twitched over the fletching of my arrows.

"I'd really prefer you didn't." I chuckled nervously, looking at the girl, hoping she'd stand against it. My heart sank to see that she appeared to be considering it.

"I agree with him." To my surprise, I saw that it was the skeleton that had spoken. He crossed his arms, tilting his skull to the side to examine me. I swallowed nervously, suddenly very uncomfortable.

"You . . . do?" I mumbled, unsure what else to say. The boy and the girl didn't seem very surprised by his statement, but they didn't look happy about it.

"Sure I do," the shoulder blades lifted in a shrug. "These two are awful company. It'd be nice to have someone with a sense of humor added to the group."

"We do not have a *group*, and we certainly are not adding *him* to it." The boy spat, dragging a hand down his face with a groan.

"Besides, Bear couldn't fly with four of us," the girl finally tore her gaze away from me to look at the skeleton. With a flick of her wrist, the flame-sword was extinguished, and we were cast in darkness. I blinked furiously, trying to keep track of where they were in the room, but none of them seemed to be moving.

"We can't very well let him go back to the thieves he came with, can we?" the skeleton's gravelly voice grated in my ears.

"What makes you think they're thieves?" I asked. Was it possible they knew about the pirates?

"Why else would a group of people sneak onto an island like Clawbreak in the dead of night?" the skeleton countered, and I fell silent, unable to find a response to that.

"We can still kill him," the boy argued.

"I'd hate to do that. I like him." The skeleton was full of surprises.

There was a sigh from the girl. "What do you propose we do with him, then?"

"I say you let him go back to his friends." I pitched in, keeping my tone as light as I could manage. Then, in a slightly more serious tone, I added, "You're right about them being thieves. They're a cutthroat band of pirates, but they do have one of my friends with them. Not here on this island, but back on Famark. She doesn't know I'm here, and I should really get back to her before she loses her head. Please, just let me go back to them," I had no idea how I might find the pirates on this island, but the town wasn't very big, and I had to at least try. This was all seeming like some sort of bad dream. A bad dream where my usual stupidity was multiplied seven times over.

"I'm sorry, but we can't let that happen. You don't seem like the type to keep your mouth shut, and we really don't need anyone trying to hunt us down." The girl stepped toward the window and poked her head outside, looking up and down the narrow alleyway. "We aren't going to learn much here, so we should be leaving anyway. You're coming with us."

"I can't!" I protested, my voice rising in pitch. I should have stayed with Jessie. I knew this. Why had I been so stupid? If it had been just me, maybe it would be alright, but now I'd left Jessie alone, and these strangers were going to kidnap me, and she knew nothing about it.

"You have to," the boy snapped, picking up the few packs that had been resting in the corner. It seemed this group liked to travel light.

"Please," I looked at the skeleton. I wasn't sure why I did, but he seemed like the friendliest out of the three, and I hoped he would help convince them to let me go. But he stayed silent, and the girl turned back to me.

"It's your fault for following me."

"You don't understand. My friend doesn't know I'm out here, and if the pirates go back and I'm not with them, she'll go crazy. Really, she will. She's supposed to be keeping me safe." How could I make them understand? Why would they care if Jessie was going crazy or if she was drinking tea and knitting stockings?

"She's not doing a very good job then, is she?" the boy asked, pushing past me towards the opening in the wall. I looked after them, then at the girl, exasperated.

"Someone has to tell her. I have to at least tell the pirates where I'm going."

"I'm not telling you where we're going until we're off this island," the girl stepped forward, and I took an involuntary step back. "And I don't have any proof that you won't just run off as soon as I let you out of my sights."

"So come with me." I knew I was jeopardizing the entire heist by doing this, but what other choice did I have? If I couldn't find a way to get away from these three on my own, someone had to tell Jessie. I couldn't just leave her in the dark, not when it was my fault for getting myself into this mess.

The girl walked past me and went through the opening after the boy. I followed, and then the skeleton did, shrugging on a massive cloak and lifting the cowl up over his skull. It did an effective job of concealing the eerie reality of his body.

"If I let you go to them," the girl looked back at me, her eyes narrowed. "You must tell them nothing about what you've seen, only that you have to go. Do you understand?"

"She can't be left alone," I pleaded. "We don't know the pirates. She's not safe with them."

"What sort of net have you managed to get tangled in?" the skeleton rumbled behind me as the boy started to climb down the side of the building.

"Enough." The girl said sharply. "We're going to find these pirates, but you're not going to get a chance to talk to any of them until I get an explanation. Otherwise, we're leaving right away, and your friend doesn't get a message. Deal?"

I looked off the side of the building. I couldn't see the sea from where we were, but I knew *The Coventry* was bobbing in the waves only a few hundred meters away. I suddenly wished I was home, and that I'd never set foot on that blasted pirate ship in the first place.

But I had, and now I was here. I had to think of Jessie. I had to think of Willa. I could worry about myself later, but those two would always come first.

With a nod, I turned back to the girl, taking her extended hand. "Deal."

13
SAKURA

*I*didn't like Alchemy in most cases.

I hadn't liked him when we'd met, I hadn't liked him when Derek had found us, and I hadn't liked him at just about any point since then. There were definitely moments when I saw him almost as a normal person with a normal life, but then I actually *saw* him, and I was reminded how terribly inhuman he actually was. The moment when he had declared he liked this stranger, though, was undoubtedly the moment where I liked Alchemy the least.

This Ksega character was obviously not to be trusted. He had come into our little hideout with a bow drawn and aimed at Derek's heart, and ever since that moment he'd been completely and utterly confused about everything. He didn't even seem to know his own intentions behind following me in the first place, and it only served to make me want to punch him in the face.

He didn't have a very memorable look about him. As we walked through the alleys of Carove Town, searching for the building he had said the pirates planned to raid, I would look at him often to make sure he wasn't trying to get away. We were in the shadows, for the most part, but every now and then the moonlight would catch his face, and I could see his features more clearly. His hair was ruffled and blond, and it didn't look to have been combed in some time. He wasn't very muscular, and he walked stiffly between Alchemy and Derek. He stumbled over pieces of rubble lying in the path, and was muttering something to himself as we walked. Overall, he gave off a very peasant-like air. The most memorable thing about him was his height. He was nearly a foot taller than me, so I guessed he came from Freetalon or Wisesol. The people on the western side of Horcath had always been prone to exceptional height.

The only thing I thought was fascinating about him were his eyes. They were such a clear, bright blue that they could have replaced the Great Lakes themselves. I'd never seen eyes that color, and I was surprised at how often my own gaze was drawn to them as we walked.

Every instinct within me told me not to trust him. A bit odd, since I'd completely ignored those instincts upon meeting Alchemy, the Cursed man, yet here I was glaring at a boy who had hardly done anything suspicious other than follow me because . . . because what? He still hadn't been very clear with that.

"There it is," Derek's voice drew me out of my thoughts as we stopped in the shadows.

The building was across from us, a big place located behind the shops where I'd acquired the clothing for Alchemy. It was completely dark, and also completely silent. According to Ksega, the pirates' invasion should already have been underway. I glanced at him questioningly, but he only shrugged, looking as confused as I was, although lacking the suspicion that I was sure was displayed on my face.

"We should split up," Derek said softly. "Alchemy, you're with me." I raised my eyebrows at him.

"You're actually volunteering to do something with him?" I whispered as Alchemy sidled up to Derek, his gloved hands flexing towards the inside of his shirt sleeves, where I knew his smith tooth daggers were concealed.

"Those two can't go off alone together, and I'm not going to get stuck with the new kid," Derek grumbled, unslinging his bow. "We'll go low, you two go high. When you find them, get them to meet back here in this alley."

"Two problems with that," Ksega whispered, glancing up at the building across from us. "One, there are eleven of them, and they're split up into small groups, and two, they won't be giving up on their treasure. If you want them to talk to you, you'll have to negotiate somehow, and that probably means helping them finish the heist." He gave us an apologetic look, and I was surprised to find it looked sincere. If Alchemy had said something like that so shortly after I'd met him, I would never have believed him, but Ksega seemed too oblivious to trick us about this, and too stupid to concoct any convincing lie.

"Fine. We can do that," I looked up at the building. It was three stories tall, and most of the windows were missing their glass panes, but I was used to that by now. I was more worried about the people inside. On our walk here, Ksega had explained the brief details of the pirates' mission: distract the band of angry people that guarded the treasure, find the treasure, steal the treasure. He hadn't spared much time to explain how dangerous these angry people might be, so I could only hope we could pluck them off if they became trouble.

"Go fast." Derek started across the street, and Alchemy rose to follow. From the back, you couldn't even tell he wasn't human. Derek called back to us, "Follow us after a few minutes. Keep quiet, try to be out before dawn."

And then they were gone, disappearing into an alley across the street.

"Start talking," I hissed. "While we're waiting, you may as well explain yourself."

Ksega looked at me, his expression startled. He had his bow in his hands again, and an arrow was already knocked to the string in case of trouble. At first I had been worried he might accidentally shoot himself in the foot, but I was reassured to see that he seemed to know what he was doing with the weapon.

"Well . . . it's sort of a long story. My grandmother and I live together in Wisesol, and she makes perfumes. A man from Famark bought some, and my friend Jess and I boarded a pirate ship to get there. I delivered the perfumes, and should have gone back to where Jess was, but the pirates were going somewhere, and I got curious, so I stowed away, and . . ." he shrugged, giving me a nervous look. "I know I'm pretty stupid, and I've had a lot of regrets over the past couple days, but I'm not always like this."

I raised an eyebrow at him, my thumb running over my knuckles as I thought over his words. His story didn't seem very likely, but revisiting my previous thought, I doubted he could come up with a story like that on his own. There were some parts of it that didn't line up, though.

"Why would you board a pirate ship and then expect it to be a normal trip?" I asked, looking back towards the building. There was still no sound from inside.

"Well we didn't exactly know the crew were pirates at first."

"But you knew the ship was a pirate ship?"

"Yes."

"And that didn't make you the teeniest bit suspicious?"

"No . . . I thought it was sort of cool."

I stared at him for a long moment, unable to form a response to that. He kept his expression blank and open, looking behind us occasionally when he heard something. There was a sort of scrabbling noise coming from back there, but I wasn't too concerned about it.

"Let's go." I said finally, rising and jogging lightly across the street. Ksega followed me on nearly silent feet, bow at the ready, eyes alert. We stayed alongside each other, scanning our surroundings with slow turns of our heads as we moved.

Despite his clumsiness on our walk to our original vantage point, Ksega moved deftly around the planks of wood and other unnamable objects littering the alleyways, making no noise besides the soft scuffling of his boots on the packed earth.

My flame-sword handle was clutched in my hand, and I could feel my eirioth pulsing through my body, ready to leap to my aid if I called for it. The anticipation that crackled around us had excited my power, and it was eager to be set free. I was tired, though, and I wasn't sure how long I could maintain a steady flame, so it was best to save my strength for when danger showed itself.

This building seemed to be in better condition structurally than almost every other building I'd seen so far on the island, and when Ksega and I finally found a side to climb, I was satisfied with how sturdy the available hand and footholds were.

"Ladies first," he said, looking up. He had put his bow back in place over his shoulder, but I could see how tense his arms were, and his fingers still brushed over the fletching of the arrows at his hip. My own muscles were bunched and ready for action.

"After you." I jerked my flame-sword's handle at the wall. "Third window up. Try to get it open without breaking it." Ksega held my gaze for a long moment, then shrugged and began to scale the wall.

I was surprised at how easily he pulled himself up to the third window. What I knew of Wisesol was limited, but there weren't any good places to climb aside from the Slated Mountains, and those were riddled with dangerous creatures. As someone who had grown up climbing the eirioth trees and hills and caves of the Eirioth Wood, I had always prided myself in my climbing skills. I felt a surge of anger at the knowledge that he was just as good, if not better than I was.

Within a few minutes, he had opened the window and slipped inside, leaving me staring up from the alley floor. A moment later, his head reappeared, and he waved me up.

The wood was rough and splintered in places, but it held securely beneath my weight, a fact I was extremely grateful for as I maneuvered around the windows on the way to the top floor. I hadn't seen any sign of people inside yet, but I didn't want to risk being seen when I wasn't ready to be.

When I reached the open window, Ksega was waiting to help me inside. The room was very dark, but for the most part, empty. There was a stack of old crates in the corner, but they were so coated in dust and cobwebs that I knew whatever they contained hadn't been touched in a long time.

"Let's go," I whispered, walking softly towards the dark doorway. The door itself was half broken off its hinges, hanging at an eerie angle and obscuring half the hallway.

We were on the top floor, and it was, as far as I could tell, entirely abandoned. As much as I hated letting Ksega out of my sight, we agreed to split up to poke through the few rooms and hallways to be sure there was nothing of interest on that level. When we regrouped at the top of a steep, rickety staircase, he had cobwebs in his hair and a bright look in his eyes.

I hadn't trusted him when we'd first met, and I didn't trust him now, but there was something so friendly about him that made it hard not to be equally friendly back. I kept having to remind myself that he knew things that could potentially put us in danger. If he got away from us and started blabbing about Alchemy, we could have bounty hunters and pirates and all sorts of low-life scum hunting us down in hopes of gaining some sort of reward.

As we began to creep down the stairs, they creaked and groaned loudly, a sour sound that echoed through the hollow building. I grimaced as we continued down them, wishing the staircase wasn't so long. Ksega was reacting in a similar way, flinching each time one of our boots scraped against the wood. His bow was back in his hands, and an arrow was knocked loosely against the string. My palm was growing sweaty around my flame-sword's handle, and I wiped it quickly on my trousers, ignoring the urge to call my eirioth and illuminate the room around us.

The second floor looked empty of people as well, and as we slid into the shadowed corner at the base of the stairs, I could see no one. There were obvious signs of human activity here, though, so I knew we had to be more careful. The darkness was thicker here, and everything was tighter. Big crates and barrels hogged the space along the walls, and I could see rolled up carpets and lengths of fabric resting against a far door.

I paused for a long moment, listening intently. I could hear only the loud beating of my heart, and the breathing of Ksega and I. Satisfied we were alone, I began to step forward, testing the floorboards carefully with my toes before I put my full weight onto them. The planks on the upper floor had been nearly as loud as the stairs, but these ones seemed to be in better condition, and they were silent.

Before I could take two steps to see more clearly around a tall stack of crates, someone grabbed me around the wrist. I jerked my hand away instinctively, turning my head back sharply. My eirioth surged to the surface, ready to flare out, when I realized it was only Ksega. I took a slow breath, forcing my eirioth to calm into a low simmer. It fought against me, eager for action, but I knew better than to give us away now.

"What?" I whispered as quietly as I could manage. He was combing a hand through his hair, dragging away tendrils of cobweb and shaking them away. He leaned closer to me and replied, in the same low tone I had used,

"There's someone on the other side of the crates."

As if whoever it was could hear him, there was a scuffling sound beyond the stack. I stiffened, carefully leaning around the crates to take a peek. Sure enough, there was the definite outline of a man lurking near the corner of a hallway. He wasn't facing in our direction, but he was obviously alert, a heavy-looking club gripped tightly in his hand.

"How did you know that?" I whispered to Ksega, frowning at him. He'd said he was from Wisesol, which meant he could be a bering-mage. I didn't know a lot about the other mage types, but I was fairly certain none of them were able to sense life forms like that. Bering-mages had a stronger connection to life than anyone else, but only animal and plant life. It was only another mystery about this boy I intended to solve before we even left Clawbreak.

Instead of answering, Ksega lifted a finger to his lips and made a waving motion with his hand in the general direction of the man with the club, then pointed to himself. I watched with a frown as he stepped around me and gestured towards the flame-sword handle I held. He reached for it, and I hesitantly passed it to him. My eirioth tingled at the tips of my fingers as I watched him step forward.

I was shocked at how silent Ksega's footsteps were, and within seconds he was beside the man. A moment later, the handle was thrust down onto the man's head, just behind his ear, and Ksega was lowering him to the floor.

"Nice," I muttered as I took my flame-sword handle back. He flashed me a brief smile, but it didn't quite reach his eyes. I knew the feeling. In all the time I'd trained with Finnian, I'd never dealt a true injury to him. I wondered briefly if this was the first time this boy had ever knocked someone out. Or worse, maybe he had done it so many times he no longer felt anything.

I swallowed and followed him farther into the hallway, trying to ignore the buzz of nervous butterflies in the pit of my stomach. As uncomfortable as I felt, I always wanted to feel this sick when I was in a situation like this. At least it reminded me that I was human.

We were in the back corner of this level, and it didn't take long for us to find out there were a lot more people here with us. The rooms were fairly big, and all of them seemed identical in dimension, connected by thin hallways that wrapped around the outside of the building. The rooms themselves had no windows, and the ones the hallways had were smeared with grime or missing panes. The whole place was cast in a shifting darkness, and it reminded me somewhat of the Cursed animals I'd seen in my life.

Ksega seemed to know where he was going, leading the way through the shadowed hallways. I was more than happy to let him stay in the front. If we ran into any trouble, he was dispensable to me.

The entire place reeked of alcohol and dust, and I saw more than a few rat carcasses as we walked. I hadn't seen any other people yet, but Ksega appeared to sense where they were, motioning for me to stop or go whenever we came to a doorway. Most of the doors were closed, and every now and then I could hear a muffled voice beyond them, but for the most part it was silent.

"How do you know where they are?" I whispered as Ksega eased open a door that had already been left slightly ajar. He took one brief look, then shook his head and continued. He didn't answer me, and I didn't try again. Alchemy had done the same thing, and I knew there was no point in asking him anything after he'd made it obvious he wasn't going to give me answers. Perhaps Ksega was the same way, and besides, it wasn't exactly like he had any reason to trust me.

We had almost cleared the entire second level when Ksega suddenly stopped. I didn't see him halt at first, and I nearly walked directly into his back. I opened my mouth to ask what it was, when a resounding *crack* echoed through the hallways. The entire building seemed to shift to the side, as if a wall on the lower level had been taken out. We were both thrown violently against the wall, the barrels beside us crashing to the ground and rolling towards us.

"Move!" Ksega's voice was hoarse and almost inaudible over the sudden ruckus around us. He gripped my arm and pulled me to the side just as a heavy barrel slammed into the wall where my legs had been moments ago, the timbers giving way and letting the barrel roll and disappear into a black gap.

Shouting voices began to filter in through all the crashing and the breaking wood, and none of them sounded very happy. I heard the clash of blades somewhere in the distance, and a man screaming in pain, but I couldn't pinpoint the direction it was coming from.

"Where are the pirates?" I demanded, carefully righting myself and side-stepping along the angled walls. Ksega was just behind me, eyeing the other crates and sacks as they slid down towards us.

"Downstairs?" was his uncertain reply. "But the treasure will be up here. It's in that room." He lifted an arm and pointed down the final hallway, the one we hadn't cleared yet. I turned my glare on him.

"Have you known that this whole time?"

"No. But there's some sort of plant in there. Whatever treasure is here, it's going to be in that room. Come on, we'll climb the debris," he slung his bow over his shoulder and jumped forward onto the slanted floor, climbing up the fallen barrels and boxes. They shifted and crunched beneath his weight, and some of them started to roll out from beneath his feet, but he was moving fast, and was nearly to the door.

There was nothing remotely special about the door, and I could see no sign of a guard posted outside it, but I didn't have many other choices right now, so I stuffed my flame-sword back into place in my belt and started to climb after him.

My heart was in my throat, and I couldn't tell the rumbling of the falling supplies apart from the drumming of my own pulse in my ears. Everything was trembling beneath my feet, and I heard another cracking sound somewhere down below. It was a deafening, almost distant sound, but it was unmistakable where it came from and what it meant. The entire building was coming down.

"What are those pirates *doing*?" I yelled, throwing myself up the falling barrels. Some of them were bursting open, sandwiched between heavier objects, and I could see sand and grains and valuable metals tumbling down the stack. When the bars of metal hit the wooden planks of the wall, they opened new gaps into the wood. At first they looked like black holes, but soon I could make out a gray haze beyond them, the early dawn light spilling into the alleyway.

"You're sure it's not your skeleton friend?" Ksega had reached the door, and he was struggling to open it from the awkward angle. There was a *click*, and he forced it open, hauling himself up and into a dark room. I was almost to it now, and I waited a moment to see if anything happened.

"All clear?" I asked when I reached it, curling my fingers around the doorframe.

"All clear," came his reply, followed by the sound of metal coins, then, "Could you get some light in here?"

I pulled myself up into the room, but it was at a terrible angle, and I lost my balance. Toppling forward, I fell into somebody else — I assumed it was Ksega — and we tumbled all the way to the far wall, landing in a pile of something hard and cold.

"Ow." Ksega muttered, his voice right in my ear. "There's something poking me. Get off me, will you?" he wriggled out from beneath me, climbing up something. There was a sound of jingling coins, and seconds later, when I righted myself, I summoned my eirioth.

It answered my call immediately, and a flickering tongue of flame erupted over my palm, hovering mere inches from my flesh. It was a bright orange, and it illuminated the small room completely, revealing the treasure we'd uncovered.

"That's a lot of gold," I said wonderingly, my eyes wide. I'd never seen so much of it in my life. They would all be useless in Carlorian stores, unless they were used solely for trade, since it was obvious they were diamond-shaped, signifying that they were Coldmonian rupees.

"Look at this," Ksega had wound his way to the other side of the room, and he held up a handful of jeweled necklaces, silver rings, and a goblet made from solid gold and inlaid with rubies.

"Where did they get this stuff?" I marveled, dragging myself shakily to my feet. Seconds later, the room lurched sideways, and I was back on the wall. Rupees and jewelry and golden dishes crashed down around me, bruising my skin and half burying me, extinguishing my eirioth flame.

"Pirating," a voice called from the doorway. I tried to shift my position to see who it was, but I could hardly move beneath the weight of all the gold. "But not the respectable kind."

"Is there really a *respectable* way to be a pirate?" Ksega asked, apparently unsurprised by this person's appearance.

"Hey!" I shouted. "Help me get out of here." I squirmed beneath the rupees, freeing one hand and rekindling the flame.

"Aye, that would be a good idea," a boy hopped into the room, landing at an angle on the coins above me and sliding down a few feet so that he was nearly level with me. He had tightly coiled red hair, and sparkling green eyes. A broad-brimmed hat sat slightly askew on his head, casting half his freckled face in shadow. "The place is burning down. Get us a rope out the roof there, Ksega, will you? Wendy! Get in here! We've found it!"

Without question, I could see Ksega already reaching for something in the room. Had he found a rope? There was also someone else coming towards the doorway, and moments later, I heard a lot of people rushing towards the room.

Another loud *crack* echoed through the building, and now I could smell smoke. I hadn't really understood what the strange boy had said a moment ago, but now it was sinking in, and I realized that Derek must have had a part in the fall of the building.

"Peeler, go give Ksega a hand," the boy beside me instructed as more people piled into the room. A man with spiky gray hair and wired spectacles clambered across the rupees to assist Ksega, followed by a tall man with golden hair tied into a small bob at the nape of his neck. As he moved with his arms out for balance, I realized one of his hands was replaced with a silver curved hook.

"Who's that?" one of the men who had entered the room was broad-shouldered and brutish, with close-shaven brown hair and angry eyes. He was missing an arm, and was intently glaring at me, then looking over at Ksega, who was wholly concentrated on something in front of him.

"Help me get her out," the red-haired boy beside me was already working at shoveling the rupees off of me with his hands.

"She could be one of *them*, you stupid boy," the man snarled. More people were pouring into the room, filling satchels and cloth sacks with all the treasure they could get their hands on. Or hand. Most of them seemed to be missing some part of their body, and I realized that I'd seen this group before, snooping in one of the alleys.

"She's a Carlorian, Bubba, and she went in with Ksega. Hurry up. Chap, come give me a hand," the boy argued, not looking up. Another man slid down on the rupees to join us, reaching for my arm to help pull me from beneath the coins.

I would have argued, except he was shockingly strong, and he managed to pull me free in a matter of seconds. Smoke was also seeping into the room, thick and black, and the timbers around us were breaking by the second.

A deafening crash sounded around us, and I looked up through the smoke, my eyes watering, to see that the far wall, which was now above us, was peeling itself backwards. I'd never seen anything like that before in my life, and I looked around to see who was responsible for it. I knew the work of a mage when I saw it.

"Get out! Climb the vine!" the one-armed man bellowed over the cacophony. "Leave the rest, climb!" everyone started to move beneath the opening in the roof.

Much of the treasure was gone now, loaded into the pirates' sacks and bags, but a great deal of it still remained, sliding back to the wall I had been pinned to moments ago and causing the boards to creak and groan and bend dangerously.

"Go on," someone poked me in the back, and I realized it was the curly-haired boy, urging me towards the opening.

I scrambled over the rupees, letting myself skid to a stop beside Ksega. He was sweating profusely, and he seemed unnaturally calm, almost in a trance. His blue eyes were distant and unfocused, but they looked so happy and at home; I'd never seen anything like it. He was staring forward, and I followed his gaze. There was some sort of small plant in the boards. Or, it *had* been small, before Ksega had used his bering on it. It was writhing and expanding and reaching up, up, up towards the hole in the roof. The man with the spectacles seemed to be helping, making the fibers of the vines twist into ladder-like rungs. The pirates began to climb up and towards the orange sky of dawn.

"Ksega," I snapped my fingers in front of his face, and he blinked, jerking his head back. The peacefulness left his eyes, replaced with the anxiety and confusion of the moment. "Where are the others?" I asked, gesturing at the pirates climbing out of the hole in the roof. There had been no sign of Derek and Alchemy.

"They'll get out on their own," he reassured me. "Now let's go, before we die of smoke inhalation." He moved forward and joined the row of pirates climbing up and out of the room. I cast one final glance around at the glittering rupees and the precious gemstones before I followed, shaking the eirioth flame out of my hand and climbing away from the dark.

As we reached the roof and began to jump to the next roof over, the morning sun crested the rooftops to the east, sending a golden glow over the island. Smoke billowed from the lopsided building, and tall walls of fire were hungrily consuming it. The sounds of shattering glass and breaking timber rose to our ears, but to me, the loudest sound was that of all the rupees and golden goblets and intricate bracelets, tinkling and falling as the wall finally gave way and let the treasures collapse into the flames.

*K*sega wanted to speak with the pirates alone. While I didn't want to be left on my own when surrounded by these scarred thugs, I knew he was only going to be negotiating how he would find a way to come with us.

By now, I was confident that he knew I wasn't letting him return with the pirates. Even if they had been the way he'd arrived on Clawbreak, and even if they were his only way back to his friend, I couldn't let him go with them. If word got out about Alchemy's existence, the consequences could be dire for us.

I was left standing on the corner of a roof, my flame-sword clutched in my hand, looking at the crumbling wreckage of the structure we had left. It had fallen in on itself now, and the wood was black and ashen. There was still no sign of Derek or Alchemy yet, and I hoped they were alright. I could live with Alchemy being gone, even if he could be a key link to the secrets of the Curse, but I wasn't going to lose Derek. Even if I'd never admit it out loud, I was glad he had followed me, and I wasn't prepared to have him taken away from me unless it was on my own terms. He and Bear were the only living connection I had to Carlore right now, and while I hated to concede the fact, I was a little homesick. Him being there, while aggravating, helped a little.

Ksega returned after a brief conversation with a small group of the pirates. The one with a hook for a hand walked with him over to me, closely followed by the two red-haired men. One of them was hardly more than a boy, really. He was the curly-haired one who had started to help me out from beneath the rupees, and looked to be a few years younger than I was.

"You're good to go." Ksega said simply, gesturing at the ground far below us. The building we stood on now was also three stories tall, and I had no intentions of climbing down the side of it with my legs as shaky as they were.

"Just me?" I questioned, raising an eyebrow. I looked up at the blond-haired man. His short ponytail had come out, and his long golden hair hung around his face. If he was a friend of Ksega's, and Ksega had convinced him that I was attempting to kidnap him or something of that sort, I had no doubts he could deal some serious damage with that gleaming hook.

"Just you." Ksega's blue eyes were pleading. There was soot smeared across his face, and I could tell he was weary. The dawn light revealed how tired he really was, but I couldn't let him leave with what he knew.

As if reading my thoughts, the curly-haired boy added, "He's got a friend who needs looking after. We won't be responsible for her when we get her back to Wisesol."

"He's coming with me." I argued, looking sharply at Ksega. "I'm sure you could explain it to her when you get back." His expression was unreadable, but I could sense his irritation.

"The girl in question is a bit . . ." the taller red-haired man, whom I assumed to be the brother of the curly-haired boy, given their obvious physical similarities, rubbed the back of his neck uncertainly. "Weepy, if you catch my meaning. She and this boy are very connected. Whatever reasons you have for taking him with you, I'm sure his own motives for going home with her outweigh them."

"I can assure you, they don't." I wasn't actually sure if that was true. Perhaps Ksega really could keep his mouth shut about Alchemy. Maybe he would go home and forget any of this ever happened. Then again, there was a chance he wouldn't do that, and it was too much of a risk. Besides, he was the sort of boy to get himself into heists with pirates; I doubted he could be very trustworthy.

"I trust the pirates more than she does," Ksega said, pressing his lips together in frustration. "If they return and their word is all she has to go on, she may assume they've killed me and tried to cover it up. The story in and of itself does sound a little far-fetched. If she tells that to my grandmother, it could be very bad news for *The*

Coventry." He leaned closer, lowering his voice so that only I could hear. "Please, I'm begging you. She needs to know I'm okay."

I looked at him for a long moment, contemplating. I couldn't let him go back. There was the slim chance he wouldn't tell anyone, and the slim chance that if he did, nobody would believe him, but I didn't want to take the risk. We had already illegally crossed kingdom borders, and we were heading into Old Duskfall next. The last thing we needed was a bunch of bounty hunters on our tails.

There was another possibility, I knew, but I wasn't sure about it yet. It would mean losing a valuable member of our team, and possibly the most sensible one out of us at that. But it might give Ksega's friend — and Ksega himself — peace of mind, and it might give us the opportunity to learn more about the Curse through a different route of research.

"What if Derek went with the pirates instead?" I asked, keeping my voice in the same low tone he had used. A line formed between his brows, and I elaborated. "Derek could go with the pirates to see your friend. You can tell him something only you would know, or give him something, find some way of telling her that he's a friend. If they could look into the Curse, too-"

"That's all you care about?" he interrupted. "You *just* want to learn about the Curse? That's what this is all about? Do you even care if she thinks I'm alive or not?"

"You don't understand. If we can understand the Curse, or if we can find the source of it, we can destroy it. Horcath could be a safer place. Lives have been lost, Ksega, *hundreds* of lives. People have lost their families. *I've* lost my family. We have a chance to stop all that." I glanced over at the pirates. They had turned away and were muttering quietly amongst themselves. Ksega's voice returned my attention to him.

"A chance? You don't have a *chance*. You have a hope that you have a chance, and that's next to nothing. This friend? She's like family to me. I'm like family to her. Besides my grandmother, she's all I've got. If you don't let me see her, you're no better than the Curse."

A silence fell between us, tense and thick. I didn't know what to say. I didn't even know what to think, because despite all the arguments I'd formed in my own mind, I knew he was right.

Ksega licked his lips, looking away. He leaned back so we weren't so close, staring out towards where the dark sea met the orange sky. For one who towered over me, he looked meek. The soft orange light of dawn glowed on his face, revealing a tired light in his brilliant blue eyes.

I looked down at the roofing beneath my boots, grimacing at my selfishness, at how inhuman I must have just sounded. I knew what I should say, but I wasn't sure I could convince myself to say it.

Gamma would say it. Finnian would say it. I wasn't sure if my subconscious was actively *trying* to make me feel guiltier than I already was, but it was doing a very good job of it. I sighed and kept my gaze downcast as I tried to muster my thoughts.

"I'm sorry." I said finally, my voice barely a whisper. I saw Ksega lift his head in my peripheral vision, but I didn't look at him. "It was unfair of me. I just . . ." I paused, then finished with another sigh. "I don't know who to trust. Alchemy being . . . well, Alchemy *existing* is making it harder."

"I understand." Ksega shifted his feet, and I finally lifted my eyes to look at his face. His expression was solemn, but there was a grateful light in his eyes. "You have a purpose. I don't fully understand that purpose, but I respect the passion you have for it."

I took a slow breath, my mind turning. I knew all the risks of letting him go. I knew some of them might seem a little unrealistic, but the *what ifs* were nagging at the back of my mind constantly. I knew that if I made this offer to him, I could end up regretting it. But somehow, even though I had known him for less than a few hours, I felt confident that I knew his answer.

"I'll let you go back with the pirates. We'll go with you. But Ksega . . ." I swallowed, forcing myself to hold his gaze. "After you reassure her you're okay, would you consider coming with us?" he opened his mouth to speak, but I held up a hand. "I know you're worried about her safety, and I understand that. But you're smart, and it's obvious you have some talents that could prove useful on a hunt for information about the Curse. Don't give me an answer now. Think on it, and let me know when we're ready to leave Famark." I looked over his shoulder at the pirates. "You can go with them. We'll meet you in Famark. Where are you staying?"

"The King's Pearl Inn, but how-" he was confused, I could tell, and there were things he wanted to ask me, but I'd stood up on this rooftop long enough. I needed to get down and find out where Derek and Alchemy had gone.

"We'll find you. Think about it." I walked past him and towards the other end of the roof. The building on that side was half a story shorter, but the drop wasn't terrible. I could hop down to it and climb down from there. I was still shaky from the fire, and I coughed from the smoke I had inhaled, but I was still thinking clearly, and I could manage getting down just fine.

When I turned back to make sure none of the pirates were approaching me for a threatening word, or anything along those lines, I nodded to Ksega, turned, and jumped off the roof.

14
KSEGA

*T*hat's a stubborn one, eh?" Chap had come to join me near the corner of the rooftop when Sakura had jumped down to the neighboring building.

"How could you tell?" I muttered, crossing my arms. The offer she had made me was a curious one, and I was struggling to understand why she had made it. She had been so keen on making sure I stayed with her, to ensure the secret of Alchemy's bizarre state wasn't spread across Horcath. Had something I'd said changed her mind?

Perhaps comparing her to the Curse had been a bit much. I had seen the hurt and the panic on her face when I'd said it, but I was a little hurt myself, and I hadn't been thinking clearly. I had been thinking about Jessie and Willa and what in the name of the Endless Sea they would do if they thought something had happened to me. Despite how fierce she was, surely Sakura could understand what a friendship meant to someone. The grumpy Derek boy seemed like a good comparison to me, and while the thought to use him as an example had crossed my mind, I knew it wouldn't be a wise choice. There was definitely something deeper behind Sakura's actions. I could sense it hovering around her like a dense fog, something she couldn't swat away and couldn't see clearly through.

I would keep my mouth shut about it for now, and maybe forever. She hadn't been very clear, but it seemed to me that she was willing to let me go home with Jessie. She didn't want me to, that much was obvious, but I was fairly certain she would if that was what I wanted.

Was it what I wanted? I knew I wanted Jessie to know that I was safe, but what about after that? Did I want to go home, back to delivering bottles of perfume for Willa? Sakura had offered me an adventure. She had offered me more than that; she had offered me an opportunity to help stop the Curse. If we could accomplish that, we'd be heroes. Nobody could look at me and call me Port scum anymore. Nobody could say I was a worthless shrimp who would never find a real job.

That was a good offer. It was an offer any sensible person striving for something better would take. It was an offer a pirate would take. An offer a thief like me would take. But should I take it, when I had Jessie and Willa to worry about?

Sakura had suggested Derek could stay with Jessie. If she could somehow get him to agree to it, would I trust him to stay and keep them safe? It didn't matter right now. She was giving me time to think about it, and I would, but for now I had to stick with the pirates and somehow convince them to let Sakura, Derek, and Alchemy come aboard *The Coventry*. Would Sakura even dare to try and sneak Alchemy aboard? She wouldn't risk telling the pirates about him, surely, if she was already so worried about me.

"You coming, Ksega?" Peeler's voice sounded to my left, and I looked up to see that the pirates were working their way down to the ground. I nodded and went to join them.

"What happened? I was upstairs with her the whole time." I stepped between Peeler and Wendy as we all filed into a line to climb down the side of the building. I wasn't sure how Wendy would get down with only one hand, but I knew he was more than capable of finding a way.

"We hadn't been in there more than three minutes before this tall fellow and a grumpy boy came in. They alerted our presence to the scum already inside, but it was an easy fight. The boy got pinned by a few of them, and to get out, he burned through the wall behind him. I've never seen an eirioth-mage in person, you know. They don't seem like people to get on the wrong side of." Wendy answered. I nodded silently.

I didn't know if Derek and Alchemy had escaped the building, but I assumed they had. Alchemy didn't seem like he was very easy to get rid of, and Derek was clever. I was a bit surprised the pirates weren't angrier than they were. Only a few of them seemed very irritated by the fact that the heist hadn't gone according to plan.

"Why does Thomas look so down?" I asked as I began the climb down. I'd seen the third mate climb down early, and he didn't look very happy. "They got all that treasure, didn't they? What's he got to be mad about?"

"Oh, he always looks like that," Peeler replied as we melted away into the shadows of the alleyway. We were headed back to the north, presumably for the tunnels that we had entered the island through. I wasn't sure how Sakura planned to find us again. She had told me to go with the pirates, and that she would find me at the King's Pearl Inn, but how would she get to Famark? As far as I knew, she didn't have a boat.

We weren't as careful returning to the big, open field as we had been when we approached Carove Town. We had left enough destruction behind that, if anyone had seen us leaving the wreckage of the building, they wouldn't be curious enough to risk their necks and follow us.

The grass in the field — which I had overheard Davie calling No Man's Land — was short and brittle, but at least it was still alive. It didn't compare to the small stalk I had sensed in the room full of treasure, which had been young and strong and easy to manipulate, but at least it was something. I reached out to it, reveling in the earthiness and the freedom and the promise of potential it harbored. It wasn't much, but it never failed to lift my spirits when I was able to reach out to some form of quiet plant life. It was so different from the busy life source of people.

Sakura had asked me how I had known where the thugs in the building were before either of us could see them, and I hadn't given her an answer. I guessed she had a hunch as to how I knew, but I didn't want to share my secret yet. Most people weren't aware of the extent of bering, and it was sort of an unspoken rule between bering-mages to keep it that way.

Chap was leading the way, and when he stopped, so did everyone else. He reached down and tugged on something. I could sense the roughly circle-shaped gap in the grass there, and knew it was the trap door I had pushed open when we'd first arrived. I wasn't looking forward to the climb down. From our first trip through, I knew it was far too tight in those tunnels to turn yourself around until you were at the very end, which meant we would either be shuffling backwards, or going down the steep slope head-first. Neither idea appealed to me very much, but I was determined to stay with the pirates now.

As the pirates began to climb down, disappearing into the hole, I threw my gaze around the broad patch of No Man's Land. There was no sign of anyone besides us, and I wondered how Sakura planned to find us. A part of me wondered if she would lose sight of us, and by the time she managed to find her way to Famark and the King's Pearl Inn, Jessie and I would have already gone home.

"Ksega." Old Hank's voice drew me back to the present, and I grimaced as I slid my body down into the tunnel, careful to avoid the sharp rocks as I searched for a handhold.

As I lowered myself farther down, I felt a cold draft rush up towards me from the depths of the tunnels, and I couldn't contain a shudder. I already knew it was going to be a cold and wet trip back to Famark.

At what I assumed to be about halfway through the excruciating crawl back to where we had left our little rowboats, I guessed that Sakura probably wouldn't find us. Unless she had immediately left to board a boat of some kind, I doubted she would reach the King's Pearl Inn by the time Jessie and I were on our way back to Rulak. In a way, this was a relief to me, but I was also worried about it. Would she try to hunt me down and drag me back into this mess?

She had offered to let me stay with Jessie, so maybe she wouldn't. But what if I wanted to go with her? The slow journey into the tunnels, dragging my way through rough stone paths and sputtering the seawater that rushed into us from time to time, had given me plenty of time to think about what she had offered me.

I wanted Jessie and Willa to know I was alright, but what about after that? The freedom an adventure promised was a temptation. I knew Jessie could take care of herself when she was back in Rulak, because she'd done exactly that for years. It was the same with Willa. What did I really add to either of their lives besides companionship? I knew they enjoyed that companionship, of course, but what was in it for me?

This was an opportunity to get out into the world and learn something new, while fighting against one of Horcath's worst enemies in the process. Granted, Sakura and Alchemy didn't seem like ideal company, but it would be better if I could get Derek to stay behind with Jessie and Willa. I knew he wasn't likely to agree to it, but if Sakura could convince him, it would put my mind to rest about the matter, and I would feel much safer knowing he was with them.

Another wave of seawater pummeled into me, and I shut my eyes tight. The familiar sense of panic had risen in my chest when the first wave had hit us, but I was slowly getting used to it now. It wasn't easy to ignore it, though, in a cramped space like this. My limbs were pressed close to the rest of my body, and there was nowhere to swim or run. I couldn't stand up, and I could hardly pull myself along after Thomas as it was. The thought that a wave might come crashing into us and take just a little too long to recede hummed in the back of my mind, despite my efforts to push it away.

It became close to unbearable, and I found myself biting into my lip so hard it bled. The crawling was the most terrifying part. With each little push forward, I could feel myself being drawn just a little bit farther away from anything my bering had a connection to. I was pulling myself closer and closer to a deep black abyss of nothing. No feeling, no sensation, nothing but endless water.

There was another reason as to why I hated the ocean. While I could connect to all animal life forms, and even sense forms like humans, it was different on the water. I felt nothing when a fish slipped to the surface to snatch the bread crumbs I'd tossed out for it, and that meant I could feel nothing when something as great and terrible as a sea wraith slid silently just beneath the belly of *The Coventry*.

It took all my strength to keep moving. I kept my eyes squeezed shut, and tried to direct my thoughts to Jessie and Willa. I had to keep fighting for them. Even if I drowned down here, at least I would die fighting for them. As soon as I could unfold myself and rise to my feet, albeit unsteadily, I breathed a sigh of relief. Thomas took note of it and raised a curious eyebrow, but I pretended to overlook it as we piled back into the little rowboats.

The trip back to *The Coventry* seemed shorter than the one from it, but we were also being carried away from the island on the receding waves, and we no longer had to worry about rowing towards the jagged cliffside. I didn't let myself breathe normally again until we had been hauled back up over the rail of the pirate ship and I had made my way on wobbly legs to the central mast, pressing my back up against it as I stared out at the island we had just left.

Thomas ambled up to join me, his black outfit sodden, his broad hat drooping from the weight of the water. He removed it from his head and attempted to squeeze as much of it out as he could, although it appeared to be a futile effort. Without replacing the hat on his head, he leaned against the mast beside me and looked towards Clawbreak. Drops of seawater dripped from the tight red coils of his hair, and his shoulders were slumped with the weight of his soaking coat.

I waited for a long moment, expecting him to mock me or comment on the way I'd run off on the group. I didn't regret it, but I didn't want the pirates to think that it had been a cowardly move. Was there any way to convince Thomas of that?

"Afraid of the sea?" he asked, to my mild surprise. I looked at him, pushing my mop of blond hair away from my face. He wasn't facing me, but there was a slight smile on his lips. "I know what it's like. I didn't enjoy being on the water for a few years after Chap and I joined *The Coventry*."

I didn't say anything, turning my head back towards Clawbreak. The ship lurched to the side as the anchor was drawn up and we began to sail away. I wasn't sure how

I felt about what Thomas was telling me. He didn't seem like the sort to be daunted by anything to do with the sea. Since I'd met him, he'd always looked so at home swaggering around on the deck or lounging on the barrels.

"I don't like deep water." I told him, uncomfortable by the silence he had let drag on. "Shallows are fine, or anywhere I can see the bottom. But when it's so vast and deep, and you know there's *something* down there, something that could eat you or drag you down and drown you?" I shook my head, suppressing a shudder. "You can count me out."

"Sea wraiths are no joke," Thomas conceded, and I nodded in agreement. "Neither are sharks, or rays. A lot of people underestimate the creatures of the Great Lakes, you know, because most of them have never seen any of them," he finally turned his head to look at me, his blue-green eyes unnaturally intelligent for a boy his age. I was reminded not for the first time since meeting *The Coventry*'s crew that some of these people had seen more adventure in their lives than I had. It was only another reason I wanted to accept Sakura's offer.

"I haven't seen many myself," I admitted. "A few dead ones in the markets, but nothing of any remarkable size." I hesitated, looking back towards Clawbreak. It was already growing smaller in the distance, and to the west, I could make out the dark line of Famark on the horizon. "Why did you join *The Coventry*, if you were afraid?"

"Chap." Thomas answered immediately. I had expected him to think about it for a moment, or maybe give me a faux look of offense, like Davie had when I'd asked about his back. But that was another thing I was slowly learning about Thomas. He rarely did what you expected him to.

"Because they wanted him to join?" I guessed.

"Because he wanted to join more than anything." Thomas smirked at his brother, who was across the deck helping Peeler with his bizarre metal-and-wood contraption. "He's always loved the sea and pirates and the thought of finding forbidden treasure. It's his dream to be a pirate captain one day, leading a group of swashbuckling heathens across the waves in search of trouble." He looked back at me then, a mischievous glint in his eyes. "He's rarely been able to find it without my help."

"Then that's one thing we have in common," I grinned at him. "Attracting trouble."

"Tom!" Chap's voice rang across the deck, and Thomas and I both looked up to see him beckoning his brother towards him as he walked towards the prow.

"That'll be me," Thomas pushed off the mast, wrung out his hat again, and set it back in place on his curly hair. He nodded at me and walked off to join his brother.

I wasn't sure why, but I got the sudden, heart-dampening feeling that I wouldn't speak to him again for a long time.

I had already begun to concoct a believable story to give to Jessie when I saw her again.

Wendy had already informed me that he would be arriving back at the King's Pearl closer to noon, and that would only be his group. He told me that when we reached the Western Harbor, we would be splitting off into small groups and returning to the inn at different times. He explained that they did this after every heist to prevent suspicion among any hotel staff.

I wouldn't be going with a group, and I decided that was alright. I would head off into the Merchant Run and poke through a few of the stores. By the time I returned to the inn, I would have dried off and found some food. All the exciting events had made me forget about my hunger, but it had been a full day since I'd eaten anything, and my stomach was making sure I knew it.

When we docked in the Harbor, I followed the pirates' lead and allowed the Coldmonian guards to do a brief pat-down before entering the Merchant Run. I had once again left my longbow aboard *The Coventry*, since I didn't have the money or the time to get permission to bring it onto the island.

The Merchant Run was a magnificent place. It seemed even more colorful than before after our visit to Clawbreak, and I found myself appreciating the cheery yellows and the vibrant teals and loud magentas that coated the storefronts, decorated with white molding curved into the shapes of waves.

A sweet smell carried my way on a soft breeze, and my stomach growled loudly as I made my way towards the source. It was a market stall selling fresh carrot biscuits, miniature honey cakes, and fruit tarts.

I had swiped a couple handfuls of the rupees from the burning building — I was a thief, after all — and used them to pay for a few biscuits and a honey cake before wandering into some of the tourist shops. They were mainly clothes and souvenirs. There were figurines of the Coldmonian soldiers in their *adda*, and even small replicas of their fish-like helmets for children.

I spent an hour or so meandering through them before I finally started back towards the King's Pearl Inn. I was prepared to tell Jessie I'd just been doing a bit of perusing all day, hunting down some food and seeing if there was anything interesting to buy. I doubted she would believe me, since she knew me too well not to suspect I'd been up to something, but she probably wouldn't pressure me to say more.

The King's Pearl Inn was just as vibrant and cheerful as I'd remembered. When I stepped inside, I saw that Davie, Bubba, and Gawain were just returning, too, and I nodded to them as the bright receptionist waved them along.

"Hello!" the receptionist greeted me as I stepped up to his desk. "You're with that group, right?"

"That's right," I nodded, and he waved me along, marking something in his ledger.

When I pushed through the heavy wooden doors to the left, I was immediately hit with a wave of noise. The sitting room at the bottom of the stairs was packed to the brim with the pirates. There were almost enough of us to entirely hide the hideously patterned wallpaper.

"Trouble!" almost before I'd registered the voice over the thrum of conversation buzzing around the room, someone had thrown their arms around me and tugged me harshly into an embrace.

"Hey, Jess, did you sleep we- ow!" I flinched away from her as her fist connected with my ribs. "What was that for?!"

"You bootless beef-witted clotpole!" she cuffed me over the back of the head, and I winced, taking another step back as the door thumped shut behind me. Most of the pirates carried on their conversations, but a few of them cast amused glances in our direction.

"That's a bit harsh, don't you think?" I rubbed the back of my head, frowning at her. "I should be lucky you haven't got a scaling knife."

"Don't be a clever-clogs, you clay-brained coxcomb." She hissed, her cheeks flushed with color. I'd rarely seen Jessie mad, and when I had, I'd been careful to keep my distance. Her hair was in its usual pair of braids, but a few strands had come loose and given her a slightly frazzled look.

"Okay, that one really was too far. What's gotten into you? Have you had breakfast?" I reached into my pocket to retrieve the carefully wrapped half of a honey cake I'd been saving, but she punched me in the shoulder instead of acknowledging it.

"It's *lunch time*, you lumpish oaf!" she glanced down and snatched the wrapped cake from my hands, unfolding the paper to see what it was.

"Enjoy." I said simply as she broke off a part of the honey cake and nibbled on it. She shot me a glare, but said nothing as she devoured the remainder of the cake.

"How did you pay for it?" she asked.

"Whoever said I paid?" I waggled my eyebrows at her knowingly, and she rolled her eyes as I slipped farther into the room, heading for the stairs. I could have told her that I'd somehow acquired rupees, or even that the tourist side of the island accepted other currencies from travelers, but that wouldn't do a very good job of supporting my thieving reputation, so I didn't.

"Where are you sneaking off to now?" she complained as she trailed after me.

"My room. I'm tired."

"We're leaving for home in a few hours. We already packed up. We're going to load everything back onto the ship after lunch." She followed me as I began to climb the white staircase.

"Wake me then," I could tell my voice was slightly slurred. The excitement of the night had kept me lively and alert, and I'd been alright for the first few hours of the day, but I was exhausted and still a little hungry, and actually quite thirsty, now that I thought about it. But all I really wanted was to sleep. I could worry about sustenance after that.

Jessie didn't follow me all the way to the small room I shared with Wendy and Peeler, turning back at some point and muttering something about Molly needing help finding food for all the pirates. Peeler was in the room already, snoring loudly and splayed out awkwardly on his bed. I hadn't seen Wendy since returning, but I knew he'd turn up.

I hardly remember kicking my boots off and pulling myself under the covers. I knew I was a mess, smeared with dirt and ashes and grime, and my clothes were still a little damp, but I didn't care. It wasn't like it was my bed I was ruining, anyway.

Before I knew it, I was soundly asleep.

It was Davie who woke me, violently shaking me by the shoulder until I smacked him in the chest hard enough to push him back against the wall.

"Your lady friend's here," he declared, rubbing his chest as he poked at my head again. I groaned and swatted his hand away, prying my eyes open to glare at him.

"Don't call her my lady friend."

"I don't know her name," Davie reached out and snatched the corner of my sheets, tugging them away. "Come now, up and at 'em. She's being quite demanding."

"You don't know Jessie's name?" I mumbled, rolling over towards the wall and burying my face in my pillows.

"Not the red-haired girl. The angry one from Clawbreak."

My head snapped up, and I rubbed the sleepiness from my eyes, propping myself up on my elbows as I peered at him. He grinned, an expression that had a particularly creepy effect when coupled with the bones jutting from his back.

"Right," I cleared my throat, licking my dry lips. "Do me a favor and grab me some water real fast, would you, Davie? I'll be out soon, but I expect there to be some food."

He nodded and disappeared from the room, leaving me to drag myself upright.

Peeler had woken and left the room at some point while I slept — somehow managing to make up his bed properly before he'd left — and I was grateful for that. The last thing I'd need was him waking up to me looking like a horrified tree worm.

Sakura had found me. I wasn't sure if I should be scared or impressed, or some odd mix of both. She'd said she would, and she didn't seem like the sort of person to make empty promises, but how she had achieved it I couldn't begin to guess. Had she had a boat hidden somewhere all along?

I knew Carlorians were often accompanied by dragons, but there had been no sign of a dragon since I'd met her, and there had been rumors floating around Horcath about the Curse being able to corrupt the Carlorian dragons. I wasn't sure if they held any truth, since most of them sounded like exaggerated whisperings, but after seeing Alchemy, I wouldn't be surprised if they were accurate.

I forced myself onto my feet and pulled on my boots, wondering if only Sakura had entered the inn. Some of the pirates had seen Derek and Alchemy, although from what I'd heard none of them got a good look at either of them.

The King's Pearl Inn had harbored little sign of other visitors, but I wasn't very surprised by that. It was autumn, and that meant it was getting colder. The popular sights and beaches of Coldmon wouldn't be as pleasant to experience this time of the year, so most people would have already come in the summer. This time of year, most people who liked to travel would be making their way to a touristy location in one of the mainland kingdoms. If I had to guess, Old Duskfall would be getting a lot of attention as the days became cooler and their desert heat became more sought after. It would be the same for Freetalon, as their winter festivals would already have preparations being made.

It was for this reason that I knew the raucous noise echoing through the hallway from the sitting room came from our group. The problem was that, with the pirates, it was difficult to tell if they were happy or angry. All their shouting was roughly the same for both.

As I made my way groggily down the spiraling white staircase, the hubbub of voices gradually died down as people took notice of me. Most of them had confused or accusing looks on their faces, while others looked borderline furious, namely Captain Howard, Bubba, Knuckles, and Ritch, although most of them seemed to be suffering from a permanent frown anyway.

Just as I'd expected, Sakura was standing gloomily in front of the doors, arms crossed, flame-sword hilt clutched tightly in one hand. Her hair was put up now, falling down her shoulder in a thick, dark braid. In the light of day, her green eyes were surprisingly dark, and they held all the irritation and malice they had when I'd first seen her.

"What time is it?" I asked, reaching the bottom of the stairs and accepting a fish sandwich and a mug of water from Davie.

"Two hours past noon," Molly answered from where she was sitting in Chap's lap on the sofa, idly munching on shrimp. Her thick eyebrows were lowered in suspicion. "Who's your friend?"

"Yeah," Jessie's voice cut through the silent room. "Who *is* your friend?"

A few entertained glances were shared around the room, but I ignored them. Jessie had always been overprotective of me as a friend, mainly because I was the only one she had, other than Willa and her father.

"She isn't my friend." I answered coolly, taking a swig of my water. It was blissfully cold. "But she is here to talk to me. So, if you'll all give me a minute," I nodded politely at them and started to walk across the room. I stopped in front of Sakura. Her expression hadn't changed since I'd entered the room.

"In the hallway?" she asked doubtfully. I shrugged.

"It's about as quiet as any place around here," I told her, and she pursed her lips. I took a bite of the sandwich, and any thought that had been going through my head suddenly stopped. I turned slowly to face Davie. "This is *delicious*. What is it, and where can I get more?"

"I'm pretty sure it's sea slug," Davie scratched his head. "I just found it in the receptionist's lunchbox."

"Oh well," I shrugged again and took another bite of the sandwich, motioning towards the door. Sakura gripped the handle and opened it, but before we could step out of the room, Jessie's voice echoed behind us.

"You're not going to explain?"

"Of course I am. Get out here," I said around a mouthful of sandwich. Jessie opened her mouth to say something else, then stopped, closed it, and sighed as she followed me out of the sitting room.

As soon as the door clicked shut, Jessie wheeled on me.

"Where have you *been*? It's time for some answers, Ksega."

"It isn't that simple," I began, glancing towards the receptionist desk. I was glad to see it was empty, and I wondered if he had gone in search of the lunch I currently held.

"I think it is." Sakura deadpanned. Jessie turned her glare on her, but the Carlorian girl merely raised an unimpressed eyebrow and continued, "He wanted to play pirate, and it's landed him in some trouble."

"Big surprise," Jessie muttered.

"He's managed to wiggle his way out of that trouble," Sakura went on as if she hadn't heard. "But I want his help with something." Her gaze turned to me, and now that I was closer, I could see that there were flecks of gold in her eyes when the sun hit them just right. "I'm not sure of his answer yet, but I knew there was no chance he'd say yes if I didn't allow him to see you again."

"If you didn't *allow* him to?" Jessie scoffed, looking wide-eyed between the two of us. "What *happened*?"

"I was an idiot, okay?" I pinched the bridge of my nose between two fingers, shutting my eyes tight. "But I think . . . I think maybe, for once, I don't regret making a stupid choice." Her silence was all I needed to confirm that she had a look of utter bewilderment on her face. Before she could say anything, I went on. "Sakura's made me an offer. I want to accept it. I want to go help her."

"You can't leave me alone." Jessie argued instantly, and I opened my eyes. All traces of her anger had gone. She never could stay mad at me for very long. But worse than anger was the sadness and the panic that now enwrapped her features.

"I don't have to," I looked questioningly at Sakura. She held my gaze for a few seconds, then allowed the briefest nod. Returning my attention to Jessie, I explained, "Sakura has another friend that's willing to stay with you. If you're up to it, both of you can help us, too."

"Just in a much less dangerous way," Sakura pitched in. I looked at her, trying to mask how uncertain I was. I knew adventure wasn't a very safe thing to begin with, and nothing involving the Curse could ever come close to being qualified as such, but it was still a little unsettling to hear someone speak about it so coldly.

Jessie was looking at Sakura, then at me, a look of surprise and fear on her face. I knew she wanted to try to talk me out of it. I knew she wanted to ask what she should do about Willa. But I also knew that she knew that this would be best for me. I'd never really fit in anywhere in Wisesol, and I was always too energetic for the simple life I had with Willa. This was the perfect opportunity for me to actually go out and do something with all that energy, and we both knew it.

"Okay," she said finally, her voice shaking. We held each other's gaze for a long moment, an understanding passing between us. I could tell she was afraid. Ever since we'd boarded *The Coventry*, she'd been on edge, and I hadn't been the good friend I should have been by sticking by her side. Maybe I was making the wrong call now, too, but it didn't feel wrong. It felt exactly right, even if I had made a few wrong decisions leading up to it.

"Okay?" I repeated, just to make sure she was certain. She clenched her jaw and nodded.

"Yeah. We'll do it." She looked over at Sakura. "What am I helping with?"

15
SAKURA

*I*f I was being entirely honest, I hadn't expected Ksega to be able to convince his friend to help us, or even to let him come with me, and I definitely hadn't expected him to be able to do it in such a short time.

As soon as I'd entered the King's Pearl Inn and told the babbling receptionist who I was looking for, he ushered me into the sitting room where I was faced with a great number of deeply suspicious-looking people. I recognized a few of them from the pirate heist, and knew I'd come to the right place. The only problem was I couldn't spot Ksega among them.

Luckily, the pirates recognized me, too, and one glare from me sent one of them scurrying up the white staircase in the corner of the room, presumably to fetch him. The other pirates, the ones who hadn't seen me before, interrogated me on who I was. I only gave them what I had to: my name, and who I was here for. As soon as I spoke Ksega's name, the red-haired girl leaning against the wall stood up a little straighter and started glaring at me. Up until her haunted expression in the hallway, the glare had remained in place.

Now, I was briefing the girl — Jessie, as Ksega had introduced her — on what we were doing. Some of it was new to Ksega, too, but I hadn't had a lot of time to explain things to him back on Clawbreak, and besides, I hadn't known if he was actually going to stay with us until just now. I left Alchemy out of the picture, but she would know about him eventually.

As soon as I had climbed down from the roof with the pirates, I'd gone back to the building where Alchemy had hidden while Derek and I went out to gather clothes and information. As I'd suspected, both of them were there waiting for me, covered in ashes and dust. We'd hurried back to the Waste Ponds to retrieve Bear, giving him whatever food and clean water we could before mounting and flying for Famark.

The flight had given us time to go over what we were planning. I explained everything that had happened since I'd entered the building with Ksega, including his strange ability to sense where people were before either of us could see them. I also told them about the deal I'd struck with him on the roof. Derek had said it was a risk, and I agreed, but I'd had a hunch, and it had turned out to be right.

After that, I got to tell Derek that I expected him to be willing to stay with Ksega's friend if that was what Ksega wished. As I'd expected, it hadn't gone over well, but I'd eventually convinced him to do it. He was still sour with me, of course, and I suspected he would be for a while, but none of us could deny the benefits it might have. Him returning with Ksega's friend to Wisesol might give us a whole new avenue of research on the Curse, and that was an opportunity none of us could afford to pass up if we planned to succeed.

We'd also decided that if he did end up going with Ksega's friend, and they did end up finding ways to research the Curse, he would be allowed to tell her about Alchemy when he saw it was fit. Until then, anything to do with the skeleton was to be kept quiet.

When we arrived at Famark, we managed to fly low enough to land Bear on the pirate ship. It didn't take very long to find a place to hide him in the cargo hold, but it *did* take a good while for us to get down and into the town without attracting suspicion. Finding the King's Pearl Inn had also been a fairly simple task, and once Alchemy was hidden in an alley and Derek had found a good place to lounge in the shadows and wait for me, I'd gone inside.

Once I had explained everything I could to Ksega and Jessie, I was bombarded with questions from both of them. As much as the questions irritated me, I knew it would be worth it to answer them, so I did, and by the time everyone was on the same page, it was getting late. The sky was beginning to turn yellow, and my stomach was loudly asking for food.

"The pirates are antsy to get going," Jessie reported when we finally returned to the sitting room. Most of the pirates clearly weren't happy with my presence, but they wouldn't have to deal with it for much longer. Besides, I'd be more worried about Derek. However glum I appeared to them, he was ten times worse, if not more.

"Derek is just outside. I'll go get him." I looked between the two of them. "You guys get to work out how he's going to go with you and the pirates."

Before either could argue, I had retreated back into the hallway, making my way towards the front doors of the inn. That had gone better than I had expected it to, and I was pleasantly surprised. Finnian had always told me I went into things looking for the worst, and that I'd never really be able to enjoy anything if I always viewed the world in that light. I supposed that, in a few ways, he was right.

Derek saw when I exited the inn, and he ambled across the street to meet me. He was wearing a cloak he had somehow acquired while I'd been inside, and his black hair hung over his eyes.

"Well?" he asked.

"You're going with the pirates." His scowl deepend. "Don't worry, they didn't look too bad. The girl you're stuck with, though?" I shrugged and gave him an apologetic look. "She seems a bit weepy to me, but I think she'll be alright." He groaned and dragged a hand over his face, shaking his head.

"How did you manage to talk me into this?" he looked up at me, his dark eyes unreadable. "Finnian would kill me if he knew we were splitting up like this."

"Because he thinks we're in love, or because he thinks I need you to take care of me?" I raised an eyebrow at him, and he huffed.

"Fair enough. Shall I go inside, then?"

"Yes." I hesitated. Was this it, then? For now, at least, was this goodbye? We hadn't talked about if we would ever meet up again. I hadn't thought about what this moment might be like for either of us. What must he have been feeling at that moment? I knew I wasn't the only one to have left a sibling behind in Carlore. His younger sister, Violet, was there too, and surely he would be thinking about her.

"Until next time, then." Derek reached out and squeezed my shoulder. For the first time since he'd found Alchemy and I, he smiled, and it was a genuine smile. I returned it, nodding at him. I was tempted to give him a hug, but I was afraid that if I did that, I wouldn't have the strength to send him off with the pirates.

"Until next time." I hardly even recognized my voice, it was so thick with emotion and unspoken thoughts. I wasn't even sure what I wanted to say. I wanted to apologize for getting him into this mess, even though he had been the one to follow me. I wanted to tell *him* to apologize for letting me get *myself* into this mess, but I knew he had already tried to talk me out of it before.

He nodded once and walked past me into the inn. I watched until the door shut softly behind him, then released a low breath. Not even a minute later, Ksega stepped out the doors and came to stand beside me. We didn't look at each other, just stared across the street at the colorful buildings.

Famark was a shockingly beautiful place, and it reminded me painfully of home. Carlore's colors were more earthy and muted, and of course our architecture was much more refined and detailed than anything here, but the overall liveliness of it was reminiscent of home, and my heart ached to see it. I couldn't wait for us to be sailing towards Old Duskfall.

"Where do we begin?" Ksega's voice was different than when I'd heard it before. I knew he'd also just said goodbye to a friend, with no way of knowing when they would meet again. I'd known what I was asking of him when I'd offered to let him come with us, but I hadn't really *understood* what I was asking until I'd said goodbye to Derek.

"Old Duskfall." I replied, my voice thick. "We'll have to use normal means of transportation to get there, though. I haven't got a pirate ship handy."

"How did you get here, anyway?" he asked as I began to walk towards the alley where we had left Alchemy. I could only hope he was still there.

"Derek's dragon." I replied. I heard him take a breath to ask another question, but I cut him off. "Don't ask. If you have any questions, save them for a time when I've put some food in my belly and gotten a proper night's sleep."

He pursed his lips and nodded, trailing after me silently. I was still a little baffled that he had decided to come with us, even if I had suspected he would from the start. This just happened to work out a little better than I'd anticipated.

The alley where we'd left Alchemy before I had gone into the inn was narrow and dark, set apart from the Merchant Run and well out of the way. It was near the Merchant Corner, backed right up against the colorful brick wall that separated it from the tourist portion of the island. When we reached it, it took a fair amount of wading through various rubbish cast aside by locals and tourists alike, and weaving around tall stacks of empty crates set against the walls of buildings by the respective owners of the wares that had once been inside them.

"Alchemy?" I asked when we reached the bright pink wall. It was decorated with thick swirls of white paint and little blue flowers.

"Chem." A tall shadow moved from the corner of the alley, and Alchemy appeared seemingly from nothing in front of us. He was wearing the clothes I'd stolen for him, and with his skull hidden in the shadow of the cowl, it was almost impossible to tell he wasn't human.

"Right. Sorry." I wasn't sure Alchemy had earned the nickname he insisted I use yet, and I wasn't sure if I'd ever get used to it, but I would try for the sake of escaping his agitation. "We need to get a boat to Old Duskfall."

"You mean to Brightlock," Ksega corrected me, and I scowled at him. He shrugged. "We'll have to find a way to get through Brightlock if we hope to reach Old Duskfall. Unless you wanted to go through Carlore?" he finished the question hesitantly, watching me closely when he asked it.

I didn't look at either of them. I was tempted to say yes. Carlore was home. It was safe and it was secure and it was where Gamma and Finnian and Walter were. I could go there and I could see them and I could see Sycamore. I could enjoy a bowl of soup at the Hazelwood Inn, curl up under my own blankets in my own bed.

But was that really what I wanted? None of it was the same now. The dragons weren't safe from the Curse. Sycamore would be locked up in the War Cells deep underground, heavily guarded along the only entrance that wound down the side of the King's Scar. Walter would have no dragons to tend to at the Inn, but there would be plenty of work helping Gamma with guests. Without dragons to fly around with, people would be stopping by frequently.

And what about Finnian? He wouldn't be the same after Elixir's death. Would he even want me to go back? Would he want me to give up on what I had set out to do?

Then there was Derek. He was expecting me to go to Old Duskfall and learn more about the Curse. He was expecting me to keep to my word and stop the terrible blight that was raging across Horcath, growing stronger by the day. If I went through Carlore, there was a chance I would buckle and fail them all, crawling back into my room and hiding and hoping someone else picked up the quest instead.

"Brightlock is faster." I said firmly, looking down at the ground. "Without a dragon, it takes far too long to travel across Carlore. Come on, we need to hurry. We haven't got any time to spare." I turned sharply and started to walk back out of the alley. I heard Ksega and Alchemy muttering something behind me, but I ignored it.

Maybe Alchemy didn't know what it was to have a home and a family to go back to, but Ksega must have. I had to hope he could understand what this mission meant to me, and what it could mean to all of Horcath. I hoped both of them understood that what we had set out to do could determine the future of our entire homeland.

When it came to travel across Horcath, prices for different modes of transport varied, but the typical fees for the Gates could always be expected to be about the same. The only differences were minor ones, and they all depended on which kingdom you were entering and exiting.

All types of payment were accepted at the Gates, which was very helpful for us, considering we only happened to be rich in rupees, and rich was putting it generously. Ksega had swiped a fair amount of the coins, as I'd assumed he would, but I had also taken my fair share of them, which left the three of us with a few hundred rupees and the small pouch of Carlorian ingots I had brought with me from home. I could only hope it would be enough to get us passage to Brightlock's docks, and then through the Gates into the kingdom itself.

We were planning to find a vessel to take us from the Eastern Harbor, and preferably one that was cheaper. I'd never crossed through a Gate in my life, and from what I'd heard it could be mighty expensive if you didn't have express orders from a figure of power or higher status to be crossing.

We stopped only twice on our way. First to retrieve Ksega's longbow and quiver of arrows — it had proved easier than we'd thought, but it was mainly luck, considering a group of thugs had decided at the very moment we were sneaking the weapon away to try and raid one of the market stalls — and second to grab a quick snack — nothing for Alchemy, of course — and found ourselves walking through the beautiful iron gates of the Eastern Harbor just as the sky was pinkening with evening.

I hadn't seen the Western Harbor very well when we'd arrived there, but I was surprised to find that it was more extravagant than the Eastern Harbor. Ksega seemed similarly shocked, looking around in wonder. The docks here were even more polished than the ones on the opposite side of the island, and the carvings of dolphins seemed to have doubled in number and intricacy. The market stalls, though they were closing now, were more substantial and well-built than those set up to temporarily sell goods on the Western Harbor.

Conflicting with the obvious upgrade of the docks, the ships docked here were considerably less decorated than the ones in the Western Harbor. They were small fishing vessels or trading and transport ships, rarely carrying any people or goods of much value. We saw some Coldmonian guards patrolling around, inspecting ships or cargo, but for the most part the occupants of the docks were seafaring men, most of them very round and unfriendly-looking.

"What are the odds we'll find one sailing to Brightlock?" Ksega asked, grunting as Alchemy bumped into him as we stopped. It hadn't been easy to get the skeleton through the iron gates of the Harbor, but we'd discovered that he was surprisingly light, and had managed to pass him off as a sack of timber until we were safe to let him stand up again. Now, of course, he was walking with his head tilted down just far enough for the cowl of his cloak to conceal his skull, rendering him blind but for the small oval of sight that provided him a wonderful view of his boots.

"I wouldn't think they're too low," I replied. "Brightlock supplies a lot of metals, and Coldmon doesn't have a lot of access to those. Most of the merchants here would be buying their supplies from Locker ships, and if we're lucky, we'll find one getting ready to set sail for home."

Finding one preparing to set off was easier said than done. Since it was already so late in the day, most of the captains were mooring their boats and heading into the Merchant Run to find places to stay for the night. The few captains we could catch the attention of all waved us aside and told us to ask again tomorrow, but there wasn't any time to waste, and we needed to set sail tonight.

"Maybe bargaining Derek off wasn't the best of your options," Ksega mused as we walked down the docks, which were slowly draining of people. There were several shop stalls still open, but they were being packed up and closed down, and nothing they were selling seemed very useful anyway.

"Bargaining Derek off didn't hurt anybody," I said smoothly. "It was his dragon I shouldn't have let go of." There was a grunting noise from Ksega, but he said nothing more. I guessed he could sense my agitation, and I wished I could find a way to conceal it better. Finnian was always getting onto me for scowling so often. I could hear his voice in my head now.

Keep that frown on your face, and you'll never find a suitable husband.

Maybe I don't want a husband.

Don't lie to me, Rura. I've never met a girl that hasn't been itching to get married.

He had, in fact, met a girl that wasn't itching to get married. Me. And of course he knew that, he only liked to tease me about it.

What I wouldn't give to hear that teasing now. Normally, it annoyed me to the point of contemplating snapping his fingers in half, but right now, in this moment, standing on a dock in the dark with two strangers and staring out at a black glass sea of nothing, I ached to to hear him mocking me for not trying to find love. Mocking me for anything, really; holding my flame-sword wrong, or not eating the crust on my sandwiches, or spending all my time with a brooding oaf like Derek, *anything*, so long as it was from Finnian.

I suddenly wanted nothing more than to let go of this journey and go home. I had felt it before, but now it was bordering on overwhelming. I wanted to go home to Gamma's hot stew and the clammy warmth of the Hazelwood Inn. I wanted to slurp loudly on a tankard of cider and listen in on whatever boring farmer drama was floating around the room. I wanted to go racing on Sycamore with Finnian and Elixir and go train in our training glade by the King's Scar and pretend that none of this had ever happened.

But Elixir wasn't alive anymore, and that was how I knew it *had* happened. That was how I knew I had to do this. I had to find a way to keep other people safe from the misery I had been put through. I had to keep them from the awful decisions Finnian had been put through, from that terrible moment of driving a blade through the heart of something you held most dear.

"We could steal a boat," I suggested.

"Unless you know how to sail, I think that would land us in a worse situation than we're in now." Ksega replied dryly.

"We could kidnap someone with aclure and force them to sail us to Brightlock," Alchemy pitched in.

"That wouldn't leave us in a very favorable place with the Coldmonian and Locker guards at the Gates," I shook my head, looking at the docked ships around us. With the sailless masts and the blank sky beyond, it looked like a forest of dead, ashen trees.

"We don't have many choices. Almost all of the captains are gone now," Ksega turned in a small circle, observing the other docks. He was taller than me by quite a bit, nearly a whole foot, so he could see our surroundings better than I could. Alchemy dwarfed both of us, but his range of view was still limited by his cloak.

"Even if the captains are here, I'm afraid the crews won't be." Alchemy pitched in, lifting his head for a moment to cast a look around. "Unless we can find a small vessel. If we get a little boat manned by one or two people, we may be able to get a ride tonight, but it'll be more time at sea."

"No." Ksega said immediately, and I raised an eyebrow at him. He cleared his throat and avoided my gaze. "The sooner we get there, the better. We should find one that will take the least amount of time, even if that means leaving tomorrow."

I frowned at him, wondering for a moment if he was afraid of the Great Lakes. I had felt my fair share of fear flying over the deep waters, sure, but I hadn't been genuinely scared of them. It was only water, after all, and I knew how to swim.

"We could always take a play out of your book," I said slowly. It was Ksega's turn to raise an eyebrow. "If we could find out the schedules for these ships leaving, and we can find one that's leaving tonight or tomorrow morning for Brightlock, we could stow away on one. It would save us some money and some socializing."

"You think we could pull that off?" Ksega asked skeptically, looking up at Alchemy and then back at me. "It's easy when it's just me, but add two new inexperienced people into the equation? That adds a whole new level of difficulty to it."

I groaned in frustration, grimacing at him.

"Well unless you've got any better ideas, I don't see that we've got much of a choice," I snapped, pushing my fingers through my hair. I hadn't had a chance to put it up, and it was a mess of tangles.

"Any records of who's leaving and when will be somewhere inaccessible to tourists like us. There's no way to-"

"Quiet." Ksega lifted a hand to cut Alchemy's gravelly voice off. Both of us turned to face him, caught off guard by the sudden seriousness of his tone. His face was pinched in concentration, staring out towards the northern side of the harbor.

"What is it?"

"You didn't hear it?" he glanced questioningly at me. His attention flicked back to the bobbing boats. "There it was again. Can't you hear it?"

"You're a strange person," I commented. "First you can sense people you can't see, and now you can hear things no one else can." He gave me a nonplussed look, then made an impatient gesture.

"Look, I know I heard something. You probably just missed it because you're . . . I dunno, because you're a girl or something." He waved a hand and started to walk in the direction he'd been looking. I scoffed and followed him.

"Al-" I paused and corrected myself as Alchemy's head lifted. "*Chem* didn't hear anything either, and *he* isn't a girl."

"Well he hasn't got any ears," Ksega retorted, craning his neck to look over the boats. "Now be quiet, I'm trying to listen."

I pressed my lips together, trotting up so that I was alongside him, and spoke in a low voice. Alchemy shuffled up behind us as we stepped into the shadows, going past the flickering rings of light the few torches — lifted high in their bronze dolphin sconces — provided.

"Do you think there's someone out here? Can't you just *sense* them or something, like you did in Clawbreak? You don't have to listen." I hissed. He threw me an irritated look, but at least he answered.

"I *can* sense him. Or her. Whoever it is, they're over there, but something's not right. There's some sort of animal with them, and I think . . ." he paused and shook his head. "That makes no sense. It can't be what I think it is."

"What do you think it is?" Alchemy's whisper was husky and, frankly, not much of a whisper at all, but I doubted he'd had much practice with whispering in the Evershifting Forest. Either way, I threw him a sharp glare and hoped he understood the need for quiet right now.

"Well, it *looks* like a raptor, but surely that's imposs-"

"What do you mean 'looks'? I thought you couldn't see it." I interrupted. He took a sharp breath, biting his lip for a moment before continuing.

"I *can't* see it. I'll explain it to you later, but right now . . . I think this person's up to something illegal." He lowered to a crouch, looking over his shoulder at the Coldmonian guards by the gates. There were sixteen of them total on the harbor night watch, and I counted all of them gathered around the bright flame burning in the grate beside the gate. Some of them stood stoically watching the sea, but they all appeared relatively relaxed.

"Why are we going towards that person, then?" I questioned, lowering myself into a crouch and scooching up beside him where he was peering around a boat hull. Alchemy mirrored the movement.

"I want to get closer, obviously," Ksega answered. "Whoever they are, they're getting onto a boat with this raptor-like creature. I think they're getting ready to set sail. Hurry, follow me," he slunk forward, hugging the shadows and starting to move, still in his crouch, down one of the docks. After an exasperated sigh, Alchemy and I followed him.

It didn't take long for me to see who it was we were looking for. It was definitely a man, relatively tall and awkwardly broad-shouldered. He walked with a sort of hunched posture, and one of his hands seemed to gleam in the moonlight. He was loading some sort of sack onto a small sailboat, one that would normally need three or four men to sail, but this one appeared to have modifications of some sort, the most obvious of which being a thick black strap laying in a heap on the prow.

Beside the man, skulking at his ankles, was some sort of creature, lying on the cool boards and tapping its tail idly. I couldn't see many details in the dark, but it had a very reptilian appearance, and I could've sworn I saw wings folded over its sides.

"What exactly is your plan here?" I whispered in Ksega's ear, my fingers twitching over the handle of my flame-sword. There was a gentle breeze blowing southward, so there was little chance the reptilian beast could smell us, but if Ksega was right, and it was a raptor, it might sense us if we came any closer.

"If he's up to anything sketchy, he's probably going to be sailing that ship alone. This might be our best bet at getting to Brightlock." He replied.

"Assuming he's going there," I corrected. He shrugged.

"We could always blackmail him for whatever illegal business he's up to."

"Unless he and his pet there kill us." I argued.

"Or unless he isn't actually up to anything illegal." Alchemy added.

"Plus, he's bound to know *we're* not up to anything good either, so he could blackmail us right back." I finished, glancing up at the man again. He was nearly done loading the lumpy sacks beside his animal onto the boat. The creature had lifted its head and was tracking the movements of the man closely. Now that I could see a more defined outline, it definitely looked like a raptor. The dragonesque figure of it made me ache for Sycamore, but I tried to shove the feeling away.

"We outnumber him. We'll be fine. Do you want to get out of here tonight or not?" Ksega cast me a sharp look. I looked between him and Alchemy, then back to the man with the shiny hand. "He's almost ready to go. Hurry. Do we go or not?"

"Yes. Fine. Yes, let's go." I waved a hand, slipping my flame-sword from its place in my belt and following as Ksega crept forward, fingers twitching over the arrows at his hip. Even though I couldn't see him, I knew Alchemy had drawn his smith tooth daggers from the soft hiss of metal on leather behind me.

We'd hardly taken ten paces when the raptor — I'd decided that was definitely what it was — lifted its head and let out a low rumble of warning. Instinctively, all three of us slowed to an awkward halt, and the man hunched over the mound of cargo looked up sharply. He was still hidden in the shadows, but now that we were closer, I could tell that he had very short hair, so short it almost wasn't there, and one of his hands was covered by a metal glove. Somehow, he'd managed to draw a knife into that hand, a long, curving dagger that gleamed menacingly in the moonlight.

"Who are you?" his voice was rough, but nowhere near as gravelly as Alchemy's. It carried clearly through the night air, even over the lull of the lapping waves and the distant din of nighttime activities in the bars and entertainment facilities of Famark.

"Could ask the same of you," Ksega replied easily, casually unslinging his bow. Sensing the obvious threat there, the raptor rose to its feet. At its full height, the top of its head came up almost to my shoulder, maybe a little over four and a half feet tall, and it was easily twice that long. I couldn't see it very clearly in the dark, but it had a large, fanning tail, and gradually curling horns protruding from the back of its head.

"Get out of here. You shouldn't be out on these docks at night." The man ordered, stepping off his boat and brandishing the dagger in front of him. The raptor sidled up to him, eyes narrowed into glittering slits. His scales were a pale grayish green, making it easy for him to slip in and out of the shadows.

"Neither should you," I sensed more than saw Alchemy moving, and I kicked at him as surreptitiously as I could, hoping he knew to keep his head down. I glared at the man, clutching my flame-sword tightly. "What are you doing?"

"Why should it matter to you? You ain't a guard. I don't have to answer to you." The man spat.

"We don't really care if you're actually doing anything wrong or not. We're looking for a ride to Brightlock." Ksega looked over at the raptor. "We were hoping that might be where you were headed."

The man squinted at us for a long moment, slowly turning the dagger over in his hands. I looked briefly over at Ksega, but his gaze was trained on the stranger, and he had silently knocked and half-drawn an arrow to his bow.

"So what if I am? This ain't a ferry service. Get lost." He spoke finally, waving the dagger at us.

"We can pay you." I offered, tapping my flame-sword against the pocket of my pants, where my pouch of ingots was hidden. A barely audible jingle sounded from them.

"I'm not lookin' for trouble," the man snarled. "What business do you have in Brightlock?"

"Unless you tell us what your business is, I don't see why we should tell you ours." Ksega coolly straightened his shoulders and tilted his head at the man. He was quiet for a long moment, then said, "You wouldn't happen to be a pirate, would you?"

The man started, taken aback by his comment. "'Course not, you loons. That's a risky line of work. It's all fun and games till you lose somethin', ain't it? And I'm not looking to lose any more than I already have." He lifted the metal-gloved hand and waggled the fingers, and that was when I realized it wasn't a glove at all. The entire appendage was made from a number of cords and metal plates.

"Just checking." Ksega glanced over at me. Our gazes only met for a moment, but I knew what he was thinking. The thought had crossed my mind too: what if the pirates had sent someone to spy on us?

Considering the reputation of pirates, it wouldn't have surprised me, even though what little Ksega had told me about this particular crew had led me to believe they didn't quite fit into the usual pirate guidelines.

"Alright, let's say I take you to Brightlock. What are you, fugitives or somethin'? I don't want to get into no trouble with the guards at the Gates, mind." He slowly lowered the dagger, then tucked it into his belt. The raptor stayed still as stone beside him, a low growl echoing from its throat. The man paid it no attention.

"We aren't fugitives. We're on a mission, and we want to keep it as quiet as possible. Boarding a ship by using more conventional methods might give us more people to avoid than we care to deal with. I'm sure a man like you could relate," Ksega replied, making an almost imperceptible gesture with his hand towards the raptor. I wasn't entirely sure how comfortable I was letting him do all the talking, but he was more used to getting wrapped up in these schemes than I was, so I supposed it would have to do for now.

"What do you take me for?!" the man barked, and Ksega's eyebrows shot up. I saw the string of his bow go taught again; I hadn't even noticed he had loosened the tension. "A common thug?" the man went on, his fingers drumming the hilt of his dagger.

I shared a look with Ksega, uncertain. It wasn't that I wouldn't say this man could be a perfectly reasonable citizen of Coldmon, but his attitude, and the fact that he was out here in the middle of the night packing up a boat with a raptor, wasn't exactly helping his case.

"Well you'd be right," the man laughed throatily. "That's exactly what I am, and if you want to sail with me, there are going to be some ground rules. One, don't touch anything I don't say you can. *Orvyn* is sensitive, and I don't want you messing anything up. Two, steer clear of Wynchell. Even if I tell him to leave you be, there's a chance he might snap; he doesn't like strangers. And three," he leaned forward, even though we were still several feet away from him. "Breathe a word about any of the three of us, and I'll slit your throats. Understood?"

I looked up at Ksega again, then behind me at Alchemy. Obviously, whoever this man was, he couldn't slit Alchemy's throat, since he clearly lacked one, but he didn't know that. We could run along with his threats if it got us where we needed to go.

"Understood." I said. "Two things. Who are *Orvyn* and Wynchell? And who are you?"

"Wynchell," the man made a sweeping gesture towards the raptor beside him, who had finally stopped growling. "*Orvyn*," he gestured at the ship beside him. "And Theomand." He pressed his palm flat against his chest.

"Ah, right, the boat. Should've expected it would've been one of them," I muttered as we hesitantly began to walk forward.

"What was that?!" Theomand snapped. "'*It*'? *Orvyn* is no 'it'! You will show her the respect she deserves, or you're not going anywhere, are we clear?" he jutted a finger at me, and I instinctively paused my step. I looked over my shoulder, worried at his raised voice.

"Yes, we're clear. Perfectly clear. My apologies." I said hastily, turning my flame-sword over in my sweating palm.

"Don't listen to her," Theomand cooed softly, and it took me a moment to realize he was speaking to the *boat*. His fingers reached out and affectionately brushed across the wood. "She doesn't know what we've been through at sea, does she? No, that's right, she doesn't."

As we came closer, we stopped barely two feet from Theomand and Wynchell. I leaned close to Ksega, speaking softly enough that I knew only he could hear.

"Great job, Ksega. You've got us a ride with Captain Theomand. The man who has a metal hand, tamed a raptor, and talks to boats."

16
KSEGA

Sakura's words could have been what sent a shiver down my spine. It could have been the knowledge that we were indeed about to board a boat with a crazy man. Unfortunately, I knew myself too well, and nothing like that would make me so jittery. I had an uneasy feeling the shiver had been caused by the feeling of her breath on my neck.

Don't be stupid, Ksega, I grimaced, trying to dispel the tingly feeling on my skin. I hardly knew this girl, and besides, she wasn't even that pretty. Nearly a foot shorter than me, rather unkempt, and far too snarky for my liking. A prod in my ribs reminded me that we were supposed to be following Theomand aboard *Orvyn*, and I cleared my throat, stepping onto the craft after Sakura. It wasn't a small vessel, but it was not by any means the most noticeable boat in the harbor.

Wynchell slithered up after us, taking a position near the thick bands laying on the prow. Theomand pulled on ropes and tightened straps and did other sailor-y things in preparation to set off. Alchemy, Sakura and I stood to the side, careful not to touch anything.

It was a one-deck ship, but there were cargo compartments accessible through doors in the deck floor, presumably where the sacks Theomand had been loading were. The sail was in fair condition, but it didn't look like it was used very often. I still wasn't sure what the thick straps were for, but they were fastened securely to metal loops embedded in the ship, and there were a number of buckles and switches along the bands.

"You haven't told me your names," Theomand said as he worked, already pushing the boat away from the dock. He moved towards the bands, tapping his thigh with his metal hand to coax Wynchell to his side.

"I'm Ksega," I began. I looked over at Sakura briefly. She was impassive. I was glad she'd let me do most of the talking; I didn't know how much experience she had with criminals, but I was fairly certain it was less than I had, and I was grateful that she seemed to understand that.

"Sakura." She looked over at Alchemy's looming figure. "This is Chem. He's mute."

Theomand looked up and twisted his face into a suspicious sneer, but he didn't question it. I saw Alchemy jab at Sakura with his elbow out of the corner of my eye, but I didn't blame her. Alchemy's voice was like cold stone rubbing against brittle shards of glass, and that was bound to draw attention whenever he spoke. It was for the best that we kept up the pretense of him being unable to speak.

Theomand stooped over and lifted the thick straps, pulling them over and around Wynchell's head and wings and forelegs. It wasn't until then that I realized what they were.

"It's a harness," I whispered to Sakura, noticing that she was watching as well. I frowned at the raptor. He wasn't built for swimming, that was for sure, but the harness must have been there for a reason.

"Hold tight," Theomand cackled, releasing the raptor and stepping away from the lengths of harness still bundled on the boards. Wynchell spread his wings and leapt forward, over the prow and into the air. With a sudden lurch, *Orvyn* swung forward and began to drift over the waves.

The Eastern Harbor of Famark began to grow smaller behind us as we were pulled through the water by the surprisingly strong raptor. As more and more distance grew between us and the docks, Theomand began to hunt down a lantern to light. When a small flame was burning, he hung it from a messily made hook on the mast, and we finally got a good look at our captain.

He had very short hair, shaved even closer to his head than Captain Howard's. His eyes were dark, but his facial features were uniquely shaped: high cheekbones, a well-defined jawline, heavy-set brows. Aside from the unavoidably sharp features, the only thing memorable about him was his metal hand and his unnaturally broad shoulders, complete with biceps so big I wondered if he stood a chance at beating Bubba in an arm wrestling match.

Flying ahead of us over the water, I could now see that Wynchell was a pale green color, and his wide wings somewhat resembled leaves. His long tail waved in the wind behind him, occasionally twisting to help him alter his balance.

I wasn't sure what Theomand thought of us at that moment. It wasn't dreadfully obvious where each of us were from. All of us wore clothing with muted colors, and none of us had any sort of jewelry or adornment that could be traced back to a specific kingdom. Sakura's darker skin signified that she was most likely from Carlore, but mixed skin colors were common in places like Coldmon and Old Duskfall as well, so there was no way he could track any of us to our homes.

I glanced back at Alchemy to make sure he had his head down and his gloves and boots on. He stood eerily still, hardly swaying with the movements of the ship, and I considered telling him to act a little more life-like, but I wasn't sure I could accomplish it without Theomand noticing, so I stayed quiet.

"Odd group, ain't ya?" Theomand said finally, chuckling softly to himself and leaning heavily against the mast. His dark eyes looked all three of us up and down, his gaze lingering longer on the eerily still and silent form of Alchemy, and I hoped he couldn't see anything beneath the cowl of the cloak. Seconds later, his gaze returned to me, and released a small sigh of relief.

"You could say that." I shrugged and looked behind us again. Famark was fading into a heavy fog, and I couldn't see very far in front of us. Wynchell, at the other end of the harness, was only just visible through the dense mist.

Theomand grunted and turned to look towards the raptor. He scratched his chin, which was lightly coated in stubble, and then tilted his head back to look up at the sky. It was a futile effort, since the sudden fog had wrapped *Orvyn* in its cloying arms.

"We'll reach the Gate sometime tomorrow," he said finally. My eyebrows raised in mild surprise, but Sakura didn't seem very moved. Theomand saw my expression and grinned. "You underestimate a raptor's stamina, Sicka, or whatever you said your name was."

"Ksega."

"Whatever." He shrugged his bear-like shoulders and looked out at the waves. They were like rounded shadows rolling past us, nearly silent.

I didn't like *Orvyn*. I wouldn't let Theomand know that, of course, but I couldn't help feeling squirmy. Without a lower deck, I was forced to stay up here and watch the water as we were pulled onward. We were much closer to the surface of the water than I had been on *The Coventry* as well, and it unsettled me. Anything could be lurking in those black waters, waiting to leap out and drag us down.

What made it worse, Theomand seemed to be more on his guard now. His mood had shifted when the fog rose up around us, turning almost suspicious. I had thought it was just him being hostile towards us, but now I could sense something else. It wasn't coming from Theomand, but from Wynchell.

The raptor's demeanor had changed. I could sense him in front of the ship, see a sort of dull green outline of him through the fog. Not his green scales, but the soft green glow of the energy that pulsed through him, the life that allowed me to sense him.

The way he was flying had changed suddenly. It was no longer worryless and confident. It had gone to something slightly more panicked, urgent and afraid. His wings beat faster, the boat's steady rhythm changed to one a little more hectic, and I found myself constantly looking down into the water to my right, over and over again.

What was in there? Being this close to the water made me feel sick. I knew something was down there. I had never been able to sense the life form of any sort of sea creature before, but I knew now. *Something* was down there, close to our boat, and I knew it.

"Theomand," I hardly knew I had spoken until the burly man gave me a sharp look. It wasn't one that showed I had his attention. It was one that told me to be quiet.

He was also watching the water closely, his eyes flicking over the surface of the waves, searching for something. I wasn't sure when I noticed it, but at some point there was a change in his expression, one that went from unsure to grim. Instantly it put me on edge, and my senses heightened. When a soldier got serious, you knew it was something troublesome. When a thief got serious, you knew it was something dangerous.

"What is it?" Sakura asked, looking between me and the captain of the ship. I pressed a finger to my lips to signal for silence. She closed her mouth, her lips becoming a thin white line, but there was a persistent question in her eyes.

"There's something in the water," I whispered, leaning close to her. Her eyes narrowed the slightest bit, and I saw her hand move to her flame-sword instinctively. I shook my head, tapping her knuckles with my finger. "It won't be of any use here. You'd do better with a real sword." I nodded at the sword hilt protruding from over her shoulder. She nodded, pulling her hand away from mine and crossing her arms.

Swallowing the awkward lump that had appeared in my throat, I leaned away from her again and looked down at the water. I was itching to get my bow and prepare an arrow, but Theomand hadn't made a defensive move yet, so I stayed still. I was hoping that whatever it was would decide to leave us alone, but I doubted we would get so lucky.

My thoughts were confirmed seconds later as a wave rocked the boat violently to the side. It hadn't come from the same direction the other waves had, and it set my stomach roiling. My fingers curled around the shaft of one of my arrows, anxiously rubbing the fletching.

"Hold onto something, all of you." Theomand ordered, his metal hand gripping the mast.

I went to reach for the rail, then saw a flash of silver beneath the black water, and jerked my hand away. I stepped backwards until I found myself pressed against the door of a small cabin. I gripped the frame of the door until my knuckles turned white, and saw that Sakura was doing the same on the other side of the door. Alchemy moved and took my place at the rail, his gloved hand bones tightening on the wood.

"What's down there?" Sakura asked as another wave sent *Orvyn* lurching forward. I sensed a spike of fear from Wynchell, and the raptor suddenly dipped to the side, the glow around him distorting as water cascaded around his body. Moments later, a roaring crash echoed around us, and another wave spilled up over the prow of the boat, washing around our feet.

"Sea wraith!" Theomand shouted over the din as the back end of the ship lifted sharply, causing me to tighten my hold on the door to keep from rolling down towards the prow.

I felt like my heart had dropped down into my stomach. My vision swam, and my fingers lost their grip on the grainy wood.

Sea wraith.

I'd heard so many stories of the terrible beasts. Giant, snake-like fish that could be miles long with jutting fangs. Some of them were venomous, others had spikes in their throats to shred you to pieces as you were swallowed. The older ones were impossibly vicious, attacking anything in their sight, including coral and rocks.

There were tales of men being torn limb from limb, stories of boats dragged into the depths of the Great Lakes. There was Davie's story, about being thrown into the harbor by his own mother and left at the mercy of a sea wraith.

That could be me. Us. All of us. We could be eaten by a sea wraith. It could be long enough to wrap around *Orvyn* and crush her completely. It could have the strength to tear a hole in her hull. It could leap up and drag Wynchell down into the darkness, pulling us along with it. A sharp pain in my arm caused me to snap back into focus. I yelped and jerked away, but it was only Sakura, her hand impossibly tight on my arm and her eyes brimming with obvious concern.

"You alright?" she asked over another roar of water. Again, a wave crashed over the rail of *Orvyn*, swelling up to my knees before it spilled up and over the other side.

"Fine." I replied through gritted teeth, flexing my muscles beneath her grip. The tumult around us was increasing, and it was hard to identify which way was up and which was down. I was sure the meager contents of my stomach were going to make a second appearance sometime soon.

"There it is!" Theomand roared over the water, and I squinted through the frothy spray to see him jutting a finger towards the water on the starboard side. When I dared to look in that direction, I saw a silver scaled cylinder sliding across the surface of the water, disappearing back into the depths. I could hardly breathe as the long gray spikes along the ridge of the spine descended into the water, leaving white bubbles in their wake.

It was even bigger than I'd thought it would be. It must have been almost six feet in diameter, coated in winking silver scales dotted through with streaks of gray. The spines that rose from its back were nearly three feet tall, ending in sharp points. I hardly dared to picture what the head might look like.

Sakura was still clutching my arm in one hand, the other firmly grasping the doorframe. My own grip on the frame was shaky, and my strength was depleting fast. Alchemy was still hunched over the rail, splinters protruding from the wood as his bones dug into it.

Theomand was no longer visible through the fog and the dense torrent of water, but I could sense him near the prow, moving quickly and surely while pulling something. Wynchell's faint green glow was growing larger, drawn towards us, and growing more panicked by the minute.

How many sea wraiths had Theomand faced in his life? Was a sea wraith responsible for the loss of his hand? How many true stories could he tell that would out-do any embellished tale Chap had shared?

"Get closer," Sakura's voice was strained as she dragged me towards the door. "We're going in the cabin."

"But we can't see what's happening in there-" I argued, although I didn't have the strength to resist as she muscled the door open and dragged me inside. Almost immediately, my trembling legs gave out, and I fell hard to the slick floor. Sakura's grip was lost, and as *Orvyn* tumbled over another wave, I rolled sideways into a barrel.

"Get up! What's wrong with you?" Sakura demanded, water dripping from her hair as she fumbled to reach for a brace in the wall, barely managing to hold herself upright. There was a small lantern in here, hanging from an iron hook on the other side of the cabin and swinging violently. Everything in here was equally as soaked as everything out on the deck.

"Money?" I grunted, squinting at the golden light of the lantern. The ship lurched again, and I rocked away from the barrel, then was thrown right back into it, smacking my head on the wood and grimacing as pain spurred down my spine.

"*What?*" Sakura snapped, groaning as a smaller barrel, one barely as high as her knee, toppled over and rolled into her leg.

"Money. The barrel-" I coughed, sputtering salty seawater. My eyes itched, my skin itched, *everything* was crawling with a sandy texture. I wanted to curl up into a ball and slip into unconsciousness so that I didn't know what happened next.

"The barrels?" Sakura shouted. Another crash echoed from beyond the door, and water flooded in from beneath the door. It swelled around me, stinging my skin.

I'm gonna drown.

"Money-" I scrabbled at the barrel, coughing more and trying to pull myself to my feet, but it was no use. I slumped into the water and jabbed my elbow into the wood. A buzzing pain coiled up to my shoulder, and a jingling sound came from inside the barrel. "Money." I said again, coughing and letting myself flop to the floor. My throat burned, but whether it was from saltwater or pure fear, I wasn't sure. It was nearly over my shoulders now.

I'm gonna drown.

"Ksega . . . Ksega?" Sakura's voice was gradually growing more distant, even as she began to slide down the shining boards towards me. Her form grew blurry before my eyes. "Ksega. Ksega! Get up! Ksega, what's wrong with you? Ksega?"

My vision blanked, turning into shifting shades of gray and black. I felt her slide down to me, her hands gripping my shoulders. I felt her slap my face, but there was no sting. There wasn't anything. The burn in my throat was gone. The cold that had seeped into my bones was fading away.

Before I knew it, *everything* had faded away with it.

Warmth was the first sensation that returned to me.

It grew from near my chest, flowering through the rest of my body and slowly bringing feeling and life back to me.

The cold was the second sensation that returned to me, numbing my fingers and reminding me of the soaked clothes that clung to my skin. I could feel drops of water running down my face and along my neck, falling from my hair, but there was no longer a swell of water around my body. Even though my pulse was still thundering in my ears, I could feel my breathing slowing to a steady rhythm.

"Ksega?" a hand squeezed my arm, and my eyebrow twitched. I forced my eyes open and saw a blurry form in front of me: dark skin, darker hair, a bright orange glow hovering near my chest.

"Sakura." I croaked, my throat raw from saltwater. My eyelids drooped closed again, and I groaned, an ache sprouting along my shoulders. "What happened?"

"I was about to ask you the same thing. Stay awake. Open your eyes." Her hand moved up from my arm to gently push the hair from my forehead. I opened my eyes, and she drew her hand away, pulling the other one closer to my chest. Hovering over her palm, steady and bright, was a ball of fire, sending off waves of heat.

"Wraith-" I coughed, my throat burning. "Sea wraith?"

"Still here, but I think it's losing interest. Theomand is still out there. I don't think we're supposed to be in here." She leaned back and looked at the stacks of crates and barrels around us. "Ksega, these barrels are full of rupees, and not just normal rupees. Look," she reached her free hand towards something out of my vision, then brought it back to show me a small diamond-shaped piece of gold. It had the customary ridge of coppery-gold around it, but instead of the empty center, the royal Coldmonian sigil was molded into the gold.

"The king's?" I rasped, pulling my elbow up beneath me. As I propped myself up, my vision whirled, and I closed my eyes, grimacing. My shoulder was throbbing, and I felt myself beginning to shiver, instinctively leaning closer to the flame over Sakura's hand.

"Thousands of royal rupees. Whoever this guy is, he's a master thief. There's no way he's transporting them on the king's behalf." Sakura sat back and looked towards the door, which was shaking in the wind. Water still slid along the floor, but the waves seemed to have lessened. Once the sea wraith was gone, Theomand would wonder where we were, and if he found us with the barrels of money he'd stolen, we would be in big trouble.

"We need to get back out there. Whoever he is, he's not working alone." I grunted and forced myself up into a sitting position. The room tilted, but it was getting better. My pulse was racing, but feeling was returning to the rest of my body, and I was able to drag myself to my feet.

"You think there are others on the boat?" Sakura rose to her feet as well, letting the flame in her hand disperse. Immediately, the warmth filtered out of the room, leaving me feeling chilled again.

"No," I grimaced as *Orvyn* lurched again, and grasped at the door handle. "But there's a chance he's meeting somebody at the docks at Brightlock."

"Do you think they're pirates?" Sakura asked as she joined me at the door.

"I don't know, but if they are, I don't think they'll be half as friendly as the pirates of *The Coventry*." I pulled the door open and prepared to take a step out, then stopped dead.

In front of me, barely keeping a grip on the soaked wood, Wynchell stood with wings braced open and eyes slitted. Behind him, at the mast, Theomand was holding a long cloak, and there, sitting on the rail and tapping his fingers, Alchemy had his skull bared and visible, the green cracks in the back of it seeming to glow brighter than they ever had before.

"Looks like you lot have a bit of explaining to do, eh?" Theomand said, his voice carrying easily to us.

I glanced back at Sakura, who was looking between me and Theomand, then over at Alchemy. I couldn't read her expression, but I knew she must have been irritated, if not angry. If we managed to get out of this alive, I knew Alchemy would be getting thoroughly scolded.

Sakura was looking at the sea around us, her gaze calculating, but what plan could she possibly have when we were in the middle of the Great Lakes?

The sea wraith seemed to have gone, and we were swaying gently in the waves, still surrounded by a heavy mist. The mist had taken on a bright orange-gold color, so even though I couldn't see any of the sky, I knew it was dawn. How long had we been at sea? How long had I been unconscious?

I looked sidelong at Sakura. Did she know what had happened? Did she know why I'd passed out? I didn't think she did, but she was bound to ask about it eventually. Was there a believable lie I could give her, or would I be forced to tell the truth?

"Go on," Theomand shouted, shattering my thoughts. "Start talking."

"We're going to destroy the Curse." Sakura stepped forward, her foot twisting away as Wynchell snapped at her, baring long yellowed fangs. Her hand twitched over the handle of her flame-sword. "I wouldn't try to stop us if I were you."

Theomand scoffed, rubbing his arm. I squinted, noticing that a long gash had been torn into the metal, rendering the iron hand useless.

"You can't destroy the Curse. It's destined to end Horcath. There is no way to fight it, no way to be rid of it. It spreads and spreads and spreads, and one day it will have spread so far that there is no going back." Theomand looked towards the harnesses where Wynchell had been bound before. There were pale lines through the leather from where teeth had scraped along the surface.

"Part of what you say is true," Alchemy's graveled voice echoed across the deck, startling Theomand. "The Curse cannot be permanently destroyed from individual entities. But all branches of the Curse are fueled by the source, and if the source can be found and destroyed, all of the Curse will be banished from Horcath."

"Lies!" Theomand roared, slamming his limp metal hand against the mast. Wynchell's tail thrashed on the deck, spraying water from side to side. "How can you know all of this?!" he demanded.

"Because it commands the Curse. The source is being guided by something, and when that guide commands the source, the source commands us. I am able to refuse its commands only because I was once a human with a strong will, and my will lives on in my spirit." Alchemy pushed off the rail and stepped forward. Theomand visibly flinched away from him, and I felt a small spark of satisfaction. If this did come to a fight, even with a raptor on his side, I somehow doubted Theomand could win.

"Don't you want the Curse gone?" I asked, my voice scratchy and almost too quiet to carry to the ship's captain. "Don't you want to sail seas free of Cursed sea animals?" I looked at the open cabin door behind me. "Without the Curse, people wouldn't spend so much on defenses against it. That could mean good business for a thief like you." My gaze cut back to him, and his face pinched in rage.

"You snoop! You had no right to look in those barrels, you underling scum!" he jabbed the finger of his real hand at me, sneering. "I should run you through where you stand just for that." He reached to his belt and withdrew the snaking dagger, brandishing it in front of him and looking nervously at Alchemy.

"But do you?" Sakura asked, her fingers closing around the metal of her flame-sword. Theomand looked up at her, his eyes sparking with anger. "Do you want the Curse gone?"

"Of course I want it gone, you harpy! Everyone does!" he spat, stepping towards us. Sakura lifted the flame-sword from her belt, but Theomand only glanced at it and kept advancing.

"Then let us go! Take us to Brightlock, and let us find a way to get rid of it for good."

"What about-"

"Forget the rupees. The three of us don't exactly have clean slates, and we aren't looking to cause trouble for you. We just want to get to Brightlock, and then we will leave you to your business." Sakura snapped, and a beam of fire erupted from her flame-sword. Wynchell snarled and leapt backwards, his wings flaring.

Theomand looked between the three of us, weighing his options. Alchemy looked relaxed, even though it wasn't very easy to tell if he was relaxed or not considering he was only bones. Sakura was grim-faced and held Theomand's gaze levelly. I could only hope I didn't look too much like a waterlogged weasel. I really needed to stop ending up soaking wet every time I boarded a boat.

"The Curse can't be destroyed." Theomand tucked his knife back into his belt and narrowed his eyes at us. "You can try, but you're going to end up dead. And if you spread word about that," he jerked a thumb at the cabin behind Sakura and I. "You'll also end up dead."

"Got it." Sakura shook her flame-sword and looked down at Wynchell, who was snuffling at the extinguished weapon with suspicion. "Now let's get sailing before any more sea wraiths decide it's time for breakfast."

17
SAKURA

The royal families of each kingdom had their own special version of their respective kingdom's currency, emblazoned with that family's crest. For the Carlorian ingot, it was the set of feathered wings. For the Duskan shin, it was a giant cat tooth, representative of the ferocious sandcats that lived in Old Duskfall. For the Solian silver and gold coins, it was a ship. For Freetalon it was an eagle, and for Brightlock a rearing horse. The Coldmonian royal rupees bore the symbol of the Coldmonian royal family, the leaping dolphin.

It was those rupees that filled the barrels in *Orvyn*'s sole cabin to the brim, and those rupees that presented a new mystery for me to turn over in my mind. Theomand was obviously a thief, and Ksega suspected he didn't work alone. Being a thief himself, I guessed he would be the one to know about that. The question was, why did Theomand need thousands of the king's rupees? Were they for someone? And how would he ever get them through the Gate at Brightlock?

"Don't worry about it," Alchemy had told me when Ksega and I had informed him of Theomand's illegally obtained riches. He had regained his cloak, and it was around him now, but the hood was down. "Whatever it is he's up to, it's his own business, and we're too busy with our own quest to worry about what he's doing. Besides, we aren't the authority figures in this kingdom or in any other. It's none of our concern."

I knew he was right, but it didn't make me feel any better about being aboard *Orvyn*. Theomand wasn't up to anything good, and while most of what I had done on my quest thus far hadn't exactly been legal either, I knew our intentions were both very different.

As soon as all the weapons were put away and we all promised not to stick our noses in each other's business anymore, Theomand had affixed the harness to Wynchell, and then we were on our way again, staying in an awkward, tense silence the whole time. Theomand spent most of his time sitting on a crate near the cabin door, simultaneously guarding the door from us and making meticulous repairs to his torn metal hand.

Alchemy was fascinated with Wynchell, and the way Theomand had managed to tame him, at least somewhat, so he spent the majority of his time near the harnesses, careful not to touch them, but inspecting them very closely.

Ksega had stood close to the mast the whole time, fiddling with his bow or his arrows. He would make minor adjustments to the fletching, or spend unnecessary time straightening the wrinkles out of his shirt. He seemed to be taking great care to avoid looking at anyone. I was standing leaning against the rail, studying him closely.

I wasn't entirely sure what had happened in the cabin, but I knew Ksega had passed out. Why he had, I didn't have a clue, but I planned to find out. The problem was finding a way to ask him. I knew he wanted to be here, going on this quest, helping Alchemy and I to achieve our goal, so that couldn't have been the problem. He hadn't seemed anxious or worried at all until the idea of going to sea had come up.

As if he could sense me watching him, Ksega paused and looked up, his brilliant blue eyes meeting mine for a moment before he hurriedly looked back down at his hands, which were running gently over the wood of one of his arrows. I wasn't sure what he was trying to do, but he had seemed to be fascinated by the wooden shafts of the arrows ever since we'd resumed our journey across the Great Lakes.

Pushing off the rail, I went to join him, leaning against the mast and staring out towards the sea. I hadn't seen any other sea creatures yet, but being someone who had never been on a boat before, I wasn't sure if that was a sign of anything or not.

"Why did you pass out?" I asked finally. He sighed, and I knew he had been expecting me to ask the question. What I didn't know was why he hadn't already told me. Could he be sick? Had it just been the sleepless nights catching up to him?

"I was sort of . . ." out of the corner of my eye, I saw him rub the back of his neck, tucking the arrow he had been holding back into the quiver at his hip, but still tapping his fingers on the fletching. "I had a bit of a panic attack, I guess."

"From the sea wraith?" I guessed. Admittedly, the whole sea wraith encounter *had* been very terrifying, but I wasn't sure I could ever pass out while under attack, whether from a beast or another human. It was in my blood to fight back. It was instinct, after all the hours of training with Finnian.

"You could put it that way." Ksega answered crisply, worrying his lower lip. "But . . . the real reason is a little different." His gaze lifted briefly, lingering on the reflection of the sun dancing on the soft waves of the water, then dropping back down to the boards of the deck.

"The water?" I asked, my eyebrows raising. I'd had the thought before, but I hadn't actually believed it. How could he be afraid of the water? "But you've been on boats before."

"I never said I liked it," he said quickly, pressing his lips together tightly. "I was okay on *The Coventry* because I could avoid being near and seeing the water, but here . . ." he looked towards the waves, grimacing. "I'd much rather be on land. It's better for a bering-mage, anyway. Isn't it better for an eirioth-mage to be on land, too?" he glanced down at my hands, then my flame-sword.

"Maybe," I folded my hands together, tucking them against my chest. His gaze followed, then lifted to meet mine. "I'm not sure. I don't . . . I don't think there's much of a difference. Why? Does the water affect your bering? Is that why you're afraid of it?"

"I'm not *afraid* of it." He said quickly, his tone sharpening in defense. "And yes, it does. The farther I am from the land, the more disconnected I am from it. It's not a pleasant feeling. It's not the same with eirioth?"

"No. It isn't. I'm able to summon it just as easily here as I am anywhere else, but-" I paused, looking towards Theomand, then back to Ksega. "But there's something special about bering, isn't there? Something you've kept a secret?"

I'd known it almost from the moment he'd sensed a person he couldn't see, but I hadn't been entirely sure it had come from his bering until I'd seen him use it on the plant in the room with the treasure. If he could hone his power so strongly on one source of life, maybe he could sense other life, even if he wasn't able to manipulate it the way he could plant life.

"Maybe. But there's probably something special about all the mage types, right? Maybe it's something you haven't discovered yet, but I'm sure there's something eirioth mages can do differently." Ksega dropped his gaze and looked out towards the Great Lakes again, his eyes uncertain as they scanned the waves.

"Some of us can summon lightning, but it's rare." My thoughts reflected back to Derek, and the ability he had shown Alchemy and I when we had camped on the cliff edge.

"But everyone else knows about that, don't they? Isn't there anything nobody else knows? Something you discovered about your power?" Ksega frowned at me, his eyebrows drawn close together. I didn't understand why this was such a mystery to him.

"I don't understand what you're trying to say, Ksega," I told him, running my thumb over my knuckles as I returned his frown. "I've always understood my power to the fullest. There's nothing new for me to discover about it. There hasn't been since I was a little kid." This only seemed to confuse him further, and he angled his head closer to mine, as if he was hearing me wrong.

"Nothing has ever developed over time? You've never had someone else teach you a new skill?"

"Never." I tilted my head to the side, trying to read his expression. "Maybe it's just different for the varying types of mages. Isn't bering more emotion-focused than anything else?"

"Yes."

"I know that eirioth draws power from physical strength rather than emotional strength. Maybe the strength of the powers grows at different speeds for different mages." I looked over towards Alchemy, who was now looking over the iron loops that kept the harnesses securely in place on the boat's rail. "Maybe he knows something about it. He seems old enough to know."

"How old *is* he?" Ksega muttered, following my gaze.

"I've asked myself the same question several times," I admitted, frowning at the skeleton.

Ksega opened his mouth to ask something else when Theomand suddenly rose from his position and made his way towards the prow. Alchemy hurriedly backed away from the metal loops, coming to join Ksega and I, but Theomand only gave him a wary glance before heading to the very front of *Orvyn*, peering on through the thinning mist.

"We're almost there." He announced, looking back over his shoulder at us.

Squinting over the prow, I saw a dark shadow appearing beyond the mist, tall and dark and stretching to the north and the south.

"What will you do at the Gates? Won't they search your ship?" Alchemy rumbled, looking over his shoulder at the cabin. I hadn't realized he had been listening when we were talking about the stolen rupees.

"Won't they search your person?" Theomand retorted, looking Alchemy up and down doubtfully. "What will *you* do at the Gates?"

I looked up at the skeleton. I hadn't had the time to give that any thought. We couldn't carry him through like we had at Famark's gates, because they were bound to look at him anyway, and his height alone was far too conspicuous.

"Surely you have a way of getting the rupees to wherever it is you're going," Ksega looked sidelong at me, and I nodded, realizing where he was going with this. "Could you get Chem through that way, too?"

"Why should I?" Theomand snarled, giving a sharp tug on the leather harness. *Orvyn* lulled to a slower pace as Wynchell returned to her deck, allowing Theomand to unbuckle the harness straps.

"Surely you want the Curse gone just as much as any of us," I crossed my arms, gripping my sides tightly to try and hide my anxiety. "Your help could prove to be valuable. Please, help us through."

"I'm not going with you, if that's what you're wanting," he snapped, throwing a glance at Alchemy. "I won't tell anyone about your friend, if you're worried about that. I've got too many of my own secrets to worry about." Again, Ksega looked over at me, but I wouldn't meet his gaze.

Theomand knowing about Alchemy was a definite risk, just as it had been with Ksega, but at the time, Ksega hadn't been interested in helping us. Theomand was at least curious about us, otherwise he would have heaved us overboard and left us to the sea wraiths. It had been a gamble asking Ksega to join us, but I was confident that Theomand would help us if I could only convince him.

"Then don't come with us. But at least consider helping. We aren't the only ones trying to learn more about the Curse. There's a group back in Wisesol-" I glanced over at Ksega, whose eyes had widened slightly, his brows twitching closer together. "-that we need to stay in contact with. Wynchell might be helpful there."

"He is not a messenger bird." Theomand growled, throwing the harness straps down and ushering Wynchell into a corner of the deck. When he looked up again, I could see the silhouette of the Gates' docks appearing through the haze. "Besides, what's in it for us?"

"You'd be helping to get rid of the Curse. Safer sailing, more riches to steal," Alchemy shrugged, lifting the cowl of his cloak back over his skull. "Not to mention, Wisesol is rife with opportunity for a thief."

"You think I don't know that?" Theomand sneered at us, looking towards the Gates. The mist had thinned enough now that I could make them out.

They were set in a broad gap in the cliffs, where a massive ramp was carved into the stone. It must have spread at least three miles wide, decorated with a set of massive black iron gates, golden leaves curling up their spokes. There was a massive gold circle in the center, split in half from the place where the gates separated, and I suspected it bore the crest of the royal family of Calderon, the rulers of Brightlock.

"You could find more work there. I hear it's a good place for pirates to skulk around." Ksega suggested, his gaze pointedly avoiding mine. What was he trying to do?

"I don't meddle with pirate folk. They ain't trustworthy, that lot." Theomand spat on the deck, and I raised an eyebrow. It was true that the typical pirate wasn't to be trusted with anything, but the crew of *The Coventry* was obviously different. The problem was, Theomand didn't know that, and I doubted Ksega would be able to convince him of it by the time we reached the Gates.

"Alright, if you're sure." Ksega tucked his hands into his pockets, shrugging his shoulders to adjust the way his longbow sat across his back. His posture was relaxed, nonchalant. Looking back at Theomand, I saw his gaze casting nervously around the ship, hovering longer on the door to the cabin and on Alchemy.

"Fine. I'll help you get him through to Brightlock. But that's all. If you hear any more word from me . . ." he looked down at Wynchell, then squinted his eyes at Ksega and I. "Well, you probably won't, so it doesn't matter. Now you, get over here with Wynny," he waved a hand at Alchemy, careful to stay away from the blackened skeleton as he went to crouch beside the raptor, who growled and shimmied away from him.

"Thank you. It won't be forgotten." I told Theomand sincerely, and he grunted. I glanced at Ksega, wondering what that meant in thug language, but he only shrugged and nodded at me.

We were much closer to the Gates now, and I looked anxiously over at where Alchemy was crouched. Even with his legs bent as far as they could go, his head and shoulders were above the shiprail, and even though his cowl was up, someone was bound to see what he really was once we were docked.

"Now whatever you do," Theomand spoke loudly and calmly, adjusting the ship's unused sails and pretending to prepare it for docking. "Don't say nothing, especially you," he jabbed a finger at Alchemy. "And don't look towards any suspicious sounds. It'll only draw more attention. Got it?" he didn't wait for an answer, flicking his wrist towards Wynchell and Alchemy in a twirling motion.

Faster than I could blink, both of them disappeared in a thick fog.

I gasped, and beside me, Ksega straightened, suddenly alert. Near the mast, Theomand cackled, twisting little metal bits of his artificial hand.

Though the haze was thick, I could just make out the dark outline of the shiprail. There was no sign of Alchemy or Wynchell.

"They're still there. You just can't see them. Now be quiet, and whatever you do, don't ask me anything." He made a pinched face at us. "It's hard enough to keep this cover on them as it is."

I looked between him and the spot where Alchemy and the raptor had been moments ago. If I peered close enough, I saw that the lower shadows were irregular, bent in unnatural ways and appearing in places they shouldn't have.

The mist that had hovered around us, only receding as we neared the dock, suddenly swelled again, charging forward towards the Gates. It enveloped the ships and the people, concealing the magnificent gates and everything beyond them.

"You're a Nightfaller." Ksega said, moments before I would have. I looked up at Theomand, reassessing his dark hair, his unnaturally symmetrical features. I had known there was something oddly beautiful about him, something almost glassy, but the close-shaven hair and the metal hand and hunched posture had made it difficult to pinpoint it. Now that Ksega had said it, it was unmistakable.

"So what if I am?" Theomand pulled his lips back to reveal pristine teeth. His dark eyes glittered angrily, and I glanced over at Ksega. With a flick of his wrist, the wall of fog rippled, darkening so that the uncertain shadows beneath Alchemy and Wynchell blended even more into the ground.

I'd never met a Nightfaller before. I'd rarely had an encounter with someone from another kingdom throughout my entire life. From what I knew, the people of Old Nightfall were mysterious and dark-hearted, thinking themselves infinitely higher than all others. Some people believed they weren't people at all. Others believed that not only did the Nightfallers not exist, neither did their supposed Kingdom of the Sky.

Out of the rumors that existed, it was said that they were all beautiful. There was nothing imperfect about their physical appearance, nothing wrong in the way they moved or walked or stood. They were model people, flawless in every way. Theomand was clearly flawed, with his stooped figure and his metal hand. Was he a Nightfaller at all, or were the rumors simply untrue?

Ksega didn't appear to share in my mild confusion, instead peering at the captain of our vessel with an open curiosity in his eyes. Theomand definitely noticed it, but I knew he would be offering no explanations, turning back to face the docks as we slid closer to the harbor.

"Do you really think he's from Old Nightfall?" I whispered to Ksega as we gathered our light packs and adjusted our weapons. He shrugged, eyeing Theomand.

"Only Nightfallers can be whorle-mages." He looked wonderingly at the cloud that had descended around the boat, making it nearly impossible to see the water on either side of it. "And if he's powerful enough to do *this*, surely he must be a Nightfaller." He reached out and waved his hand through the air. The fog twisted and twirled around his arm, clinging to his hand like the pale fingers of ghosts.

I nodded silently, feeling my nails dig half-moons into my palms as the vague shadows of ships and docks and stumbling people filtered in through the undulating fog. Despite all the power I'd felt whenever I'd controlled my eirioth, and despite all the power I had seen eirioth-mages wield, like Derek's lightning summoning, I was so overwhelmed by the sheer immensity of Theomand's power, the way he could control something so big and yet so light, something that could change what people saw and when they saw it with the flick of his fingers.

"Get ready," Theomand said as we pulled into the docks. "And be quiet."

The security at the Gates was better than anywhere else on Horcath aside from the castles of the kingdoms themselves. As soon as Theomand's fog had crept over the docks, bright orange lights began to flicker on throughout the harbor, revealing Lockers in their gold and bronze armor and Coldmonians in their *adda*.

Immediately I looked towards where Wynchell and Alchemy had been. Would the soldiers' lanterns penetrate the fog around them, too? How many times had Theomand performed this trick successfully? Looking sidelong at Ksega, whose face was difficult to see through the thickening mist, I saw that he was skeptical as well, although if it was for the same reasons I was, I couldn't tell.

"Steady, *Oyster*, steady into the harbor!" a voice called from nearby, and I realized we had slipped silently and smoothly between the sturdy wooden docks, and there were ropes with stones tied on the ends being tossed over the shiprail to draw us level with them.

"*Oyster*?" I echoed, frowning towards Theomand, who was steadying the ship and trying to kick Wynchell's harness towards the shadows.

"*Orvyn*'s official name," he waved his metal hand in dismissal. "She finds it offensive, so I wouldn't use it often if I were you. Now shut up."

I gave Ksega a concerned look, but he didn't return it, squinting at the awkward shadows in the mist that told us where Alchemy must have stood. I would have looked there, too, and possibly swung my arm out experimentally to see if he was there, but at that moment there were soldiers boarding the ship, and they immediately had my full attention.

"How many aboard?" one of them was undoubtedly raised in Old Duskfall, despite his Locker livery and his pale skin. The lilting accent was a clear giveaway, although to look at him, you wouldn't know it. He had the obvious broad build and strong features of someone born from a Locker family.

"Three." Theomand grunted, his voice more hoarse than I'd heard it before. How many times had he forced himself to scratch up his throat like that before it had become normal? How long had he stooped to falter his posture? How could someone with a free claim to a home in a place like Old Nightfall wind up as a no-good criminal on the seas?

The thought of having a home to go to made my chest squeeze. Maybe Theomand no longer had a home to go to, like Alchemy. But I knew Ksega did. I knew I did. And I desperately wished I could return there.

It wasn't far. Now that we were about to cross the Gates between Brightlock and Coldmon, the only thing separating me from Gamma and Finnian was the Evershifting Forest. Could I travel safely through it without the help of Alchemy? If it wasn't for him, I would have been eaten by a smith days ago.

Focus. I scolded myself, swallowing the homesickness that had clutched my heart. *You came out here on a quest. You will not give up now.* Besides, there was a good chance we weren't going to make it through the Gates at all. Theomand's plan was sketchy at best, and already the dense fog around us seemed to be wavering, breaking apart as the light from the lanterns forced it away.

"Any cargo? Weapons we should know about?" another soldier said. There were four of them in total, giving *Orvyn*'s deck a cursory survey. One of them came across the harness and nudged it with the toe of his boot, but moved on after only a curious tilt of his head.

"On our persons, a longbow, some arrows, a sword, a flame-sword, and a dagger. None hidden aboard the ship. Only some sacks of grain in this hold here," Theomand's burly shadow moved through the fog to open the hatch in the ship's deck. One of the soldiers bent down to examine the contents of it, then nodded, satisfied, and gave a signal to the one who appeared to be doing most of the speaking.

"Here for repairs, cargo, or entry into Brightlock?" the man squinted at us, making a flicking motion with his fingers in our direction. The Locker with the Duskan accent approached us and did a once-over of our outfits and weapons, setting his lantern down by the mast to poke through our belts. His expression was unreadable, both because his features were grimly set, and because the mist was still thick enough to conceal his face even though it was hardly a foot in front of us.

As his hands skimmed over my belt, I stiffened, eyeing his fingers as they curled around the handle of my flame-sword, drawing it from its sheath. He lifted it towards the light, squinting at the intricate eirioth dragon and feather etchings in the metal, peered into the hollow hole where the flame-sword would appear, and shook it experimentally. Satisfied that it was nothing more than a standard

Carlorian flame-sword, he returned it to my belt and proceeded to review the sword on my back. Ksega stood silently by my side, frowning when it was his turn as the soldier gestured for him to hand over the longbow. Personally, I'd never formed any attachment to projectile weapons, but I assumed he felt just as exposed as I did when I left either of my swords behind.

"Entry to Brightlock," Theomand stated, lightening his tone. "We're traveling to Old Duskfall for my sister's wedding."

Ksega looked over at me, his eyebrow twitching. While Theomand was good at lying, the lies themselves could sometimes be a little strange, and sometimes a little unbelievable. The next words out of the lead soldier's mouth confirmed this.

"A wedding, eh? Aren't those risky affairs in these times?" he looked us all up and down once again as Ksega was given back his bow. I knew we didn't look much like wedding guests, and there were no signs of gifts or spare clothing aside from our satchels.

"Risky, but special. It will be a small matter, anyway, just a few relatives. And the capital of Duskfall will be a safe enough space!" Theomand laughed heartily, but the soldier only grunted in reply, eyeing Ksega and I again. None of us looked similar enough to be relatives of Theomand. We didn't even look similar enough to be related to *each other*, but the guard didn't appear to be very concerned about it.

"Very well then." The man said gruffly, nodding once. "Anything of interest in that cabin?" he gestured with an arm towards the cabin, and the accented soldier started for it, opening the door to reveal a foggy, empty room.

"Nothing." Theomand lied easily when I looked back at him, seeing a warning light in his eyes. I molded my features into an expression devoid of surprise, although my heart was pounding and my mind racing. How could he manipulate the mist to make the room appear entirely empty?

"Very good." The man nodded again as the cabin door was closed. "You may proceed to the Gates. I trust you'll all have the necessary means of payment?" he raised his eyebrows expectantly at us. We all nodded. "Off you go then." He turned on his heel and disembarked *Orvyn*, closely followed by his companions and the three of us. I could only hope Alchemy and Wynchell were right alongside us, but with how thick the fog was, it was impossible to tell. I supposed that was the point, but it still made me uneasy.

"How much money do you have?" the whisper startled me, and I jumped, angling my head to look at Ksega, who had leaned in close to me. I wasn't sure why he kept doing that. It seemed every single thing he said was a secret of the utmost importance.

"I have a few ingots, and some rupees left. What about you?" I looked down at the satchel that was slung over his shoulder. It jingled faintly, like the pouch at my own belt, but there was no way to tell how much money it contained.

"Some rupees. We'll need to combine what we have to get us into Brightlock. Something tells me our captain won't be willing to pay us through." He looked ahead of us at Theomand, who was leading the way across the docks.

The docks themselves were teeming with people, coming in or out of Brightlock, loading boats or repairing hulls or transporting carloads of goods from place to place. There were goats being tugged around on leads and horses anxiously stamping their feet in their ship stalls. The whole place was buzzing with life, yet somehow it was rigid with order. Everyone walked with a purpose, and there were guards posted at almost every corner. Each one we passed paid us little attention, but I felt like their eyes were on me constantly, just waiting for me to make a slip.

I waited for someone to yell or scream or draw a weapon, having spotted Alchemy or Wynchell, but nothing happened. We stepped off the docks onto thick natural slabs of stone and began to push our way through the throng to the magnificent gates, whose tops were no longer visible due to the fog. The great circular emblem in the middle of the Gates was visible once we had come closer and found a place in the line. It bore the proud rearing horse emblem of the Calderon royal family.

"How much will it cost us to get through?" I asked, shrugging my shoulders and edging closer to Theomand and Ksega as a wiry family bustled into the line just behind us. It was packed so tightly, it was a wonder nobody had bumped into Alchemy or Wynchell. That, or Alchemy and Wynchell had lost us, and were wandering around somewhere on the docks.

"Hopefully no more than we have. I've never been to Brightlock before, but I've heard it isn't a terrible cost. What I'm worried about is the extra fees we'll have to pay for our weapons. It's three gold coins per weapon, I'm pretty sure." Ksega replied, his fingers drumming against his satchel as we waited, inching slowly forward as the line moved.

"What's that in rupees? Or ingots?" I asked, clenching my fists as we took another step closer to the guards who stood ahead, surrounded by posts with lanterns hanging from them, scribbling on pieces of paper, accepting and exchanging money with the people in line.

"How am I supposed to know?" Ksega hissed back, pressing his lips together. "I wish I'd paid more attention to Willa's lessons."

"Who's Willa?"

"Forget it. Just get your money out, quickly. I think we'll need . . ." he opened his satchel and peered into it. "All of it."

"*All* of it?" I echoed, shuffling forward as I pulled my money pouch from my hip. "Okay, fine, *most* of it."

"Will you two shut it?" Theomand looked over his shoulder and dug his elbow into Ksega's ribs. "It'll be ninety rupees to get you two idiots through." He squinted his eyes at me. "That's like twenty-something ingots. Now shut up." He turned back, and I shared a worried look with Ksega.

Ninety rupees? I wasn't sure how much I had, but I knew it was only about thirty. Combining it with what Ksega had in his satchel, it might just be enough. If it wasn't, I had to hope I had enough ingots to chuck in along with it.

By the time both of us had our money ready, it was Theomand's turn. He spoke in muted tones to the soldier at the podium, who scrawled something onto his parchment, took Theomand's money, and waved him away with muttered instructions.

"Names?" the man drawled as Ksega and I stepped up to the podium, awkwardly holding our money pouches. He had a thin, nasally voice, and a very bored expression on his narrow face.

"Sakura Ironlan." I replied, trying to keep my voice steady. Ksega's gaze hovered over me for a moment before returning to the soldier.

"Ksega Copper." He said finally, clenching his jaw. He hadn't told me his last name before. Had he given a false name? Did he think I had given a false one?

"Reason for entry?" the man asked, not looking up from his paper.

"Traveling." Ksega looked sidelong at me, then over towards where Theomand had gone, standing with a crowd of other people who were nothing more than a shadowy blob in the mist.

"For a wedding." I added as the man squinted down at his paper. He raised his olive eyes to mine and lifted a pencil-thin eyebrow.

"With thousands of people crossing through these Gates every day, do you really think I *care* why you're traveling?" he sniffed and waved a knobbly hand at us. "Your total fee for entry, including the additional fees of weapons, is ninety rupees, ninety silver coins, eighteen gold coins, forty-five shins, or twenty-three ingots. The form of payment is up to you." He folded his hands neatly together and watched us expectantly.

"Oh, right, um-" I fumbled to lift my money pouch. Ksega offered his to the man, who took it and began to count through the rupees. I waited anxiously with mine, tapping the pad of my finger against the cool metal of the coins inside.

"This is only fifty-six rupees." The man curled his nose and looked at the pouch in my hand.

"Here," I began to pick out the rupees, already sure I wouldn't have enough. As I'd expected, I only pulled out sixteen rupees, and I added seven ingots into the little pile of coins that had accumulated on the podium.

The man thumbed through the currency briefly, even though I knew he had been counting along with me, then took the money and handed us two thin slips of paper painted gold with the Locker royal family's crest displayed across it.

"These are your passes. Hold onto them until you're through. We'll let this next group through the Gates in about ten minutes. Don't try any funny business, or you *will* be arrested." The man folded his hands together again after tucking our money away below the podium. He nodded towards the crowd of people surrounding Theomand. "Run along, now. And remember: just because all this fog is here doesn't mean we're blind. I'll warn you again: do *not* try anything."

We nodded mutely and walked towards the crowd, Ksega relatching his satchel. He looked sidelong at me as we walked.

"He makes it sound like there's something particularly suspicious about us." He mused.

"Makes me wonder if Theomand put in a good word about us." I grumbled, shrugging my shoulders and letting my fingers rest on my flame-sword hilt. I didn't plan on drawing it, but with so many strangers around, I wasn't sure exactly what to expect.

Out in the harbor, waves hummed and crashed against the docks, splashing up over the wood and seeping through the gaps in the railing. With each boom of the water, Ksega flinched, almost imperceptibly, his gaze flying towards the Great Lakes, even though we couldn't see them through the fog. Maybe that was part of the reason for his unease.

"You're jumpy." I spoke casually, hoping he didn't think I'd read too far into the observation. In truth, I was wondering about his fear of the oceans. He had passed out on *Orvyn*, and even if it had only been for a few minutes, there was no way to tell if it would happen again the next time we were at sea. *If* we were ever out at sea together again.

"Am I? Hadn't noticed." He licked his lips nervously, his eyes tracking the source of every minuscule sound he detected.

"Right. It's hardly noticeable anyway." I pressed my lips together and dropped the matter, although I fully intended to ask him about it later, once we were safely through to Brightlock. There was a lot we needed to discuss, not only about our plans for Old Duskfall, but also about Ksega. I didn't know half as much about him as I'd have liked, and I had plans to remedy that as soon as possible.

As we came into the crowd, we saw Theomand, identifying him from the glint of his metal hand in the lantern-light. When he spotted us, he showed no sign of recognition, but we waltzed up to him anyway. His sour expression grew more glum as we approached, but I didn't give him the chance to say anything snide.

"What's your genius plan for getting all those rupees through?" I asked, careful to keep my voice low, although there was little point. It was so loud and chaotic around the docks, I doubted anyone was listening very closely.

"Oi, quiet it down, lassie!" Theomand hissed, throwing his gaze around and seeking out the nearest soldiers to make sure they weren't within earshot. I would have pointed out that that action alone made him easily the most suspicious person in the crowd, but I didn't think he was worth it.

"It's a reasonable question. Besides, we all know you're going to disappear the moment we're beyond those Gates. We want some reassurance that your plans work." Ksega slid his hands into his pockets and assumed a very nonchalant position, shoulders back, head tilted to the side. Any sign of his previous uncertainty had vanished entirely, but I knew he still felt the tugging fear of the nearby sea.

I felt another pang of jealousy at his ability to switch the way he appeared so easily. Derek had always been able to hide his emotions, but Ksega's talent was entirely different. He could pretend to be something he wasn't, and he could pretend to be it *so well.* Even after all the time I'd had to practice hiding my emotions, I still wasn't strong enough to conceal them.

"Fine, but stop your yacking," Theomand glowered at the people around us, leaning in closer and lowering his voice. Somehow, his whisper was less hoarse than his normal voice, and I was able to detect the smoother notes of what may have once been a melodic voice before he had conditioned it to be so rough.

"I've got my own means of getting my stash through. It's of no concern to you how I manage it, but I know it will work. I've done this for years. As for your pal?" Theomand's bushy eyebrows rose, and he looked sidelong at an opening in the crowd, a space just large enough for two people. "He's right here with us."

"Chem?" I questioned uncertainly. If we hadn't been surrounded by people that might overhear his peculiar name, I wouldn't have used the nickname at all, but I wasn't willing to risk getting asked about it.

"I'm here." The voice was gravelly and deep, so unexpected and inhuman that I felt the hairs on the back of my neck stand up. Even though I'd spent the last several days with him, it was as if I'd never heard his voice before, and I couldn't help a shudder. Ksega was also unsettled by it, but, of course, he did a better job of hiding his discomfort than I did.

"Happy? Good. Now zip it. It's time." Theomand took a few paces away from us, lifting his chin up and shrugging his heavy coat higher on his shoulders. His gaze scanned the throng of people, lifting over Ksega and I with the same lack of recognition he had before.

"Uncanny how he can do that." Ksega murmured. "Pretending not to know anybody. Wish I could do that."

I raised an eyebrow at him, but he wasn't looking at me, his attention returned to the distant noises of the sea. I had no doubts Ksega could replicate Theomand's behavior exactly if he really wanted to, but I couldn't tell if he'd said that to be humble or because he underestimated his own abilities.

I would have told him as much if a man with an impossibly loud voice didn't begin shouting at that very moment, his words carrying easily over the gathered crowd.

"Anyone with a pass may now begin to enter Brightlock!" as he was yelling, the massive Gates slowly began to swing open, the well-oiled hinges making no sound as access was allowed to the fog-covered ramp. "Hold your pass in a visible manner and enter five abreast at the most! Guards are positioned to confirm that everyone entering has paid their way through. If you are caught without a pass, you will be brought into custody and questioned further when the Gates close again!"

By the time he was finished with his announcement, the people in our crowd had begun to shift forward, forming rough ranks of five to march through the widening Gates. They surged forward at a pace that was almost animalistic, and it was a wonder any of the soldiers were able to see the passes in their hands, if they had any at all.

We were somewhere in the middle of the pack, shuffling along and trying not to step on anybody. As we came closer and closer to the gates, which seemed to grow hundreds of feet with each step we took, people were forcefully dragged out of the ranks to be held at the sidelines, obviously lacking a pass. Ksega and I were careful to hold ours out on full display, clearly visible to the soldiers whose gazes were raking through the rows of people.

My nerves were buzzing, my pulse humming in my head, my instincts on high alert as I waited for one of the soldiers to reach forward and grip me by the arm to drag me to the side. But we walked through without any problems, and before I knew it, we were past the Gates. I had no idea where Alchemy was, and even if I could see him, there would be no features to use to read his expression. But I could read Ksega's.

It was early dawn, and the golden light of the sun shone brightly through the fog, surrounding us in a cloud of shimmering yellow and burning orange. We were walking, one sluggish step at a time, up the great man-made ramp into Brightlock. It was a long trek, but with the sunlight pouring into the canyon, shining bright on the ground and on every person excitedly pushing forward, packs slung over their shoulders or pack ponies dragged along on leads, I somehow didn't mind it.

Beside me, Ksega was drinking it in as well. He looked better than he had since I'd met him, and I guessed that had something to do with the prospect of no more days at sea. His skin glowed under the light of the sun, and his eyes shone with a light of excitement that was entirely new. Even though I couldn't see him, I knew Alchemy was close beside me, somewhere in the golden fog around us. I may have been imagining it, but I was certain I heard his scuffling footsteps nearby.

The gold reminded me of Honeysuckle's shimmering feathers, which caused my heart to ache for home. My mind forced my feet to move, one in front of the other, even while it turned back to the Hazelwood Inn.

Just find some answers. I told myself, rubbing my thumb along my knuckles. Once I found some answers, and we got rid of the Curse, I could go home. Until then, I would take a deep breath, and keep on moving. One foot in front of the other.

18
KSEGA

*A*s soon as we began to walk beyond the Gates, up into the golden haze that covered the ramp, I felt my life and energy returning to me. I could feel my bering expanding inside me, reaching out eagerly to find any sort of life it could. They appeared like stars across my vision, faintly glowing specks that showed me a budding flower or a sprouting blade of grass. I saw vines creeping down the walls of the ramp, and the roots of trees burrowing through the earth. The power that rattled through me made me feel ten times stronger, and I couldn't help but let a little of my power seep into the world around me. A nearby flower sprouted, almost invisible through the mist, but vibrant and pink and happy. Above, I saw the glowing silhouette of the vines creeping farther down the canyon wall, rejuvenated by my own energy.

The excitement and anticipation radiating off of the people around me helped, too. There were all kinds of people walking with us, twiddling with the dust or wind or light around them, using their magic to entertain themselves as they waited. It was incredible seeing so many mage types working at once. I knew Sakura wasn't very happy to be thrust into a crowd like this, and she seemed more focused on detecting Alchemy's whereabouts than paying attention to the people around us. It wasn't very hard to tell where he was, at least for me, since I heard that faint, unnatural buzz that surrounded him, reminding me that he wasn't dead, but he wasn't quite alive.

As we forged on through the mist, something in the air around me seemed to change. It had been heavy and cold and dreary the entire time I'd been at sea. It was the same sensation that hung around the Port, even on a bright and cheery day. It was fading rapidly now, replaced with a sense of warmth and light, punctuated by the sound of happy birdsong and distant farm animals.

Beside me, Sakura looked unmoved, but there was something about the way the soft yellow light hit her face, making her green eyes appear a dazzling gold. The light shone amber on her dark hair, and altogether it created the picture of a girl of gold and fire.

"What are you gawking at?" her voice bounced through my head, and I blinked, realizing she was looking at me, her face pinched in an unpleasant frown.

"Nothing. Sorry. Lost in my thoughts." I shook my head and returned my attention forward. From somewhere to Sakura's right, I heard a throaty chuckle. Nobody else seemed to notice.

The fog was clearing much more now, and I wasn't sure if that was Theomand releasing his control on it, or if he had finally run out of energy. I wasn't sure what powered whorle, if it sucked its strength from the physical abilities of its user, or if it was more emotion-sourced, like bering, but I did know that it had some effect on Theomand, and there was no way he could have held it for much longer than he already had.

The ramp wasn't drastically long, but it was fairly steep. It was a man-made path, carved into the cliffs that jutted over the edge of the Great Lakes, running back up to the mainland of Brightlock. I didn't know much about the kingdom's geography, or much about it at all, really, other than that it was one of the wealthiest of the seven kingdoms. It was rich not only in money, having the most plentiful ore mines in the Shattered Mountains, and miles and miles of good farmland, but also in status and reputation. The entire kingdom was known for being very diverse and welcoming to all its travelers, despite the fact that the majority of the Evershifting Forest claimed parts of its territory.

"Do you suppose we'll see any of the traveling entertainments?" I asked, not entirely sure Sakura would have an answer for that. Another thing Brightlock was famous for was its variety of entertainment forms for tourists and locals alike. I'd heard all sorts of stories about them, and although their popularity had severely lessened throughout the duration of the Curse and its effects on Horcath, they still sounded like immense fun.

"We don't have time to see some idiot juggle some fruit and then set a pole on fire with his breath." Sakura said crisply, her scowl deepening. I didn't understand why she was so determined to get to the heart of the Curse. I wanted it gone, obviously, of course I did. But there was something different about her drive to destroy it that confused me.

While I would have loved to argue with her, saying there was always time to watch some idiot juggle some fruit, and wholly prepared to demonstrate myself with one of the oranges in my pack, the words died on my tongue as a shadow appeared beside

Sakura. In the withering mist, it was difficult to tell what it was, but by the height and human-like form alone, I knew who it was.

"Sakura," I whispered, trying to nod towards Alchemy as inconspicuously as possible. She glanced in his direction, and her eyes widened. She made a brief waving motion, but the skeleton must not have been looking in our direction, because he marched forward without a waver in pace.

"Provide a distraction," Sakura hissed, her fingers twitching over her flame-sword. "Whatever you do, don't look in my direction."

"Wait- what are you going to do?" I fumbled as I reached for her sleeve, tugging her back into the line just before she could leap out towards Alchemy. "What am *I* going to do?"

"Anything. Do anything, as long as it gets peoples' attention. Fast!" she jerked her sleeve out of my grip and slipped into the fog, shoving Alchemy's shadowy form farther into the mist none too gently. A few of the people in the line behind us frowned, and a few paused in their steps, looking questioningly at the fog where the girl had disappeared.

Quietly, I cursed under my breath and reached out with my bering. While I could sense the people around me — there were so many, it was pointless trying to count them. When I focused my bering on them, they all appeared as one giant green blob — it was pointless trying to bend them to my will. Sometimes it was possible with animals, if you were a talented enough bering-mage and the animal wasn't too stubborn, but with other humans, it was impossible.

I could see the outlines of birds perched in trees above us, up at the top of the ramp, or flying overhead. Somewhere farther to the left, something was skulking, low to the ground and almost slithering, and I assumed it was Wynchell. He was a raptor, and while I was familiar with the smaller raptors that dotted the Veiled Woods or the fields around them, he was new and considerably bigger than those, and I wasn't about to try and convince him to provide a distraction for me.

I didn't know what else I could do. I urged the plants around me to grow, almost without realizing it. Moss bloomed beneath the shuffling feet of the moving people, vines curled down to the floor of the ramp, colorful flowers sprouted in the cracks of the walls. Anyone with bering may have noticed, but nobody else was paying much attention. They were all too focused on moving forward or wondering where Sakura had gone to notice.

One of them kept glancing at me, obviously noticing my anxiety-riddled posture. I stiffly walked forward, purposefully avoiding her gaze as she muttered something to the person beside her. If it had been me that wandered off into the mist, I may have been able to make it look a little less suspicious, but there was no way to go back. As the unsurety rippled back through the crowd, the lines slowing as the suspicious onlookers peered farther into the fog where Sakura had gone, I clenched my fists.

A shriek sounded somewhere farther back in the ranks, a woman, by the sound of it, and it was quickly followed by several more cries of alarm. A wave of surprise passed through the crowd, and I noticed that most people were looking down towards their feet, surprise on their faces. Glancing down, I felt the breath leave my body.

Hundreds of little flowers, blooming over sprawling moss, were expanding over the ramp. There were little bushes sprouting, bright red berries appearing against the dark green leaves. A young sapling began to rise from the ground in the middle of the crowd, breaking the roughly evened ranks.

The gathered people slowly stopped, marveling at the nature that was creeping around them. I felt my bering encouraging the growth of the plants, but could it all have come from me? Experimentally, I honed my focus in on the sapling, just barely giving it a nudge with my own source of energy, and it shot up, branches sprawling from its trunk and sprouting fresh leaves within a matter of seconds. I felt myself gaping at it in just as much wonder as the strangers around me.

The entire gathering of people shifted around, stopping up the steady flow of people traveling up the ramp. A gentle wave of voices floated around the canyon, echoing against the ramp's walls. Only minutes later, the entire throng had pressed themselves against the walls of the ramp to stare in amazement at the growing plant life, which was still expanding, if now only minimally.

"What's going on?!" a voice boomed over the bustling crowd, coming from back towards the Gates. Several heads snapped up, and eyes widened as a Locker soldier plowed his way into the giant oval. Through the slits of his bronze helmet, I could see a lined face and very angry eyes. He let out a noise of frustration at the sight of all the moss and blooming flowers.

"Who did this?" he demanded, his voice bouncing around the silent circle. Everyone looked at the person beside them, then across the ring and all around. I doubted they cared very much who it was that had caused this, and were more concerned about whether whoever it was could be blamed and punished for delaying their arrival into Brightlock.

"*Who did this*?!" the soldier bellowed, turning in a slow circle. When his back was turned towards me, I looked sidelong at the woman who had been giving me suspicious looks before. Her eyes were wide and panicked as they met mine, and I pressed my lips together, barely shaking my head at her.

"If I don't get some answers soon, I will drag all of you back down to those docks and interrogate *each and every person*! Now who-" the man was yelling again, but before he could finish, he was cut off by a piercing scream.

Every head whipped around to face the southern end of the oval, and I felt my heart begin to race in my chest. If someone had seen Alchemy, and Sakura was with him, she would be taken into custody, and possibly even killed. I wasn't sure. Nobody had ever dealt with a Cursed human before. Would they try to kill him? Would he try to fight back?

"Raptor!" a voice shrieked, and panic swept through the crowd. People scrambled away from the cry, tripping over one another and trampling the beauty that had grown, crushing and destroying it within minutes in their haste to escape the reptile.

I couldn't see Wynchell myself, and as far as I knew, nobody else could, either, but he must have come too close through the thin fog, causing a panic. Either way, it was a cover to get out of here.

I began to move away, keeping pace with the panicked crowd and trying to shove my way through to the front, hoping Sakura and Alchemy had the sense to get away, too. My pulse was still pounding in my ears, and my terror only redoubled as I realized I was leaving a trail behind me. The growing moss was chasing me, sprouting from the ground where my boots touched.

Cursing, I tried to release it, letting it go back to its own natural pace of growth, but it resisted, keeping close to my heels as I pushed through the crowd. A few people saw it, but it wasn't clear yet that it was me it was following; I hoped.

"*Enough!*" the Locker soldier roared above the terror of the crowd, his voice bouncing off the walls. There was the sound of his hands clapping together, and then the entire world went black.

My breath hitched in panic as I angled my head all around, trying to find something I could see. What had happened? Had the soldier taken the light away? I knew erru-mages were capable of doing such a thing, but not that they could perform the trick on such a large scale. It wasn't much different from my shock at Theomand's power, or even Peeler's. How much power could one man wield?

I reached out with my bering, trying to see the familiar green glowing of any life form, but there was none. I could feel bodies jostling around me, but I couldn't see them. An icy hand closed around my chest as I realized I was completely blind.

Around me, the screams rose in pitch, ringing in my ears. Without the aid of my sight, I walked directly into someone else, both of us stumbling. I fell to my hands and knees, grimacing as someone stepped on my hand. I pushed myself up, grunting as someone's elbow rammed into my shoulder, and pitching to the side as I lost my balance, all sense of direction lost.

"Everyone *hold still*. There's no sense in moving if you can't see!" the soldier's voice echoed through the ramp, but it was hardly audible over the din. There were still people screaming and feet pounding; if anything, the absence of light had done nothing to improve the situation.

He was right that there was little hope in moving, though. The neatly formed lines we had been marching in were long gone now, and I was sandwiched between two people. Moving was nearly impossible, and even if I could push through the crowd, there was no way to tell if I was running farther into Brightlock or back towards the docks.

As I stood trying to keep my feet, grimacing as hands clawed at my arms and legs knocked into me, I tried to shoved my way towards the wall. I hadn't been standing very far away from it, and that was the direction Sakura had gone with Alchemy.

I shoved against someone nearby, trying to get past them, but whoever it was was much larger than I was, and whenever they shoved back, I was sent reeling into the person behind me. Someone yelled, cursing as they threw me off their back and sending me back onto my knees. I grunted, although the thick moss that had grown cushioned my fall. Even though I couldn't see it, I felt the ground shifting beneath me, the structure of the moss changing as I touched it.

I was about to try and use the plants to my advantage when someone grabbed me by the arm. Instinctively, I pulled away, but their grip was strong, and I felt myself being dragged towards them. Their fingers were thin and bony, digging into my arm so tightly the tips of my fingers began to turn numb.

Someone yelled in my year as I was yanked past them, and I felt a knee dig into my ribs. Whoever was dragging me along behind them was pushing through the crowd as easily as a sea wraith slid through water, nearly tearing my arm off whenever I got snagged between two people.

"Hey!" I shouted, but I could hardly even hear myself over the screaming of the others around me. "Slow down! Wait! Ow-" I yelped as whoever was dragging me jerked their arm, pulling me forward and sending a sharp pain shooting through my shoulder and down my back.

Despite the rough movements, whoever it was had pulled me out of the crowd, and we were now stumbling up the ramp again, moving blindly through the dark. As my foot slipped, I felt my shoulder brush against the rough wall of the canyon, tearing through the thin fabric of my shirt sleeve.

"How do you know where you're going?" I asked, gasping as another jerk of their arm nearly sent me face-first into the ground.

"Mages don't have any effect on me." The voice that replied was low and gravelly, like glass raking against stone. It ground at my ears, and I realized there was another sound, a faint buzzing. I'd grown so used to it hovering in the back of my mind that I almost forgot it was there.

"I should've known," I grumbled, tugging at Alchemy's grip just to see if I could pull free, but there was little hope of that. His bony fingers were closed too tightly around my arm, and I was losing feeling in my entire hand.

"Ironling?" Alchemy asked, and I frowned.

"I'm here," Sakura's voice appeared beside us, sounding breathless and shaky.

"Hey, let go of me, Chem," I complained, trying to twist my arm. "I can't feel my fingers."

"Quit whining. Someone will hear you." Sakura snapped, but Alchemy's grip loosened, and his hand dropped down around my wrist, guiding me up alongside him and keeping me from wandering away in the darkness.

How wide did the blot of shadow spread? Had the Locker soldier made the entire ramp completely devoid of any light?

It was beginning to unsettle me, how little I could see. I could still sense life around me, but without the benefit of my sight, I couldn't pinpoint anything's location. It was an odd feeling, being able to seek out the different plants and even the people around me. It may have been the absence of light, but I could've sworn I felt more connected to the elements around me than I had before.

"Ksega, cut that out." Alchemy's voice had a note of irritation in it, which made my stomach squirm. I very much preferred his cheerful moods.

"Cut *what* out? I'm not doing anything." I whispered back, aware of the sound of shuffling feet behind us. Were there other people trying to escape as well? How many people would the Lockers take into custody to interrogate? Would anyone be falsely accused of what I had done? This was all Alchemy's fault. If he had just found a way to get out of sight, none of this mess would have happened, and we wouldn't be walking blind. At least, most of us wouldn't be walking blind.

What had Alchemy said? That mages didn't affect him? What did *that* mean?

"Your bering. You're leaving a trail."

"I'm not *trying* to," I argued, trying to force my bering down. It was like another emotion that existed inside me, something like joy and laughter, but softer. It was life.

"Well get rid of it." Alchemy hissed, and I grumbled, trying to control my breathing and coax the plants back away from me. I couldn't be sure if it worked, but Alchemy stopped complaining, and I decided to take that as a good thing.

We plowed on through the darkness, and after we had jogged a short while, I noticed it getting lighter. It was very faint, and the ground was only a gray haze before me, but I started to see the green glows of life around me again, and I felt myself relaxing just a little bit. The vein-like cracks that laced the back of Alchemy's skull were also visible, and I realized his hood had flipped down.

"Pull that cowl up, Chem," I said. "We don't know who could be waiting at the end of this ramp." He made no move to fix it, but I assumed he had his other hand clasped around Sakura's wrist.

I was trying to squint through the blackness, attempting to identify any recognizable sort of landmark ahead, when, before any of us could fully register it, the light returned.

Sakura and I both let out sharp cries of alarm, and instinctively shut my eyes tight, feeling them tear up from the sudden brightness. Even though my lids attempted to block it, the bright orange light still burned at my eyes, and I held up my free arm to cast a shadow over them.

Seconds later, I felt the pressure of Alchemy's thin bones release from my arm, and I pried my eyes open, blinking rapidly to try and help my eyes adjust faster. Between blinks, I saw that Sakura was reacting in a similar way.

"Once you two are done acting like you've got sand in your eyes, you'll have to take a moment to admire the view. But only a moment, because we've really got to get moving." Alchemy's voice rumbled in my ears, and I squinted at his back, a shaky blob of shadow in front of me.

"By all the stars and clouds," Sakura's voice was full of wonder, and I grimaced as I forced my eyes open all the way, barely managing to keep them there before the light burned too badly. "That's incredible." There was a pause, then, "Don't be such a baby, Ksega. Open your eyes. *Look.*"

"I'm not-" I started to argue, but then I felt her hand push my arm away, and I blinked furiously, looking out at the land in front of us. Whatever I had been about to say was forgotten entirely as I saw, for the first time, Brightlock.

In front of us was a low, gradual slope, leading to rolling fields of bright green grass and swaying golden wheat. To the north were miles and miles of gentle hills coated entirely in long, soft grasses. To the east, I could see where the road led, winding past the farmland and between quaint little cottages and farmhouses that dotted the plan. To the south stood the Evershifting Forest, currently formed of tall trees, coated in leaves turning bright red and orange for the change of autumn and, despite the looming danger that announced itself in the woods' reputation, looking wonderfully inviting.

Thin puffs of smoke rose from the chimneys of the neat little homes, and horses and cows could be seen grazing in their pens. Way off in the distance, ahead of us, the dark shadows of the Shattered Mountains stood stoically behind the pale stone forms of Brightlock's distant capital.

The great royal castle was hardly as tall as my pinkie finger from this distance, but the capital couldn't have been more than a week or so away, if we traveled hard each day. As for getting all the way to the Gates to Old Duskfall, I wasn't sure.

"Come on, quickly," Alchemy started forward, his hood now back in place, adjusting his gloves. "Those guards won't be much longer down there, and then they'll send out riders to find any stragglers." He began to march down the well-worn road, turning back to look at me with his eerie stare. "You, especially, have made evading them more difficult." His voice was thin and agitated, and I felt myself turning red.

"Sorry." I mumbled, looking behind us. There was a swirling wall of black, like the curve of a massive orb, and nothing could be seen beyond it. Leading out of the shadowy abyss, there was a trail of gradually growing grass.

The trail led almost all the way to us, stopping just a few feet away from our boots. I grimaced at Sakura's disapproving glare. There was no point in telling them I hadn't meant to do it; she wouldn't believe me. The way she saw it, it seemed every mage knew exactly what they were doing at all times.

I'd never struggled to stop using my power, although there had definitely been times where I strained to focus on my bering. Since I'd departed *Orvyn*, though, I felt oddly stronger. At first I'd thought I was only getting over my seasickness, but now I knew it was something different, something to do with my bering. It was much more vigorous for freedom than it had been before, coursing to my aid at the slightest thought.

"Where are we going?" I asked as she and I started after Alchemy, leaving small puffs of dust in our wake. He took us off the main road, leading us to the south, and I had a sinking feeling grow in the pit of my stomach.

"The safest place we can possibly go until tomorrow, when they're done searching," Alchemy replied coolly, making a vague gesture towards the sprawling woods we were approaching, and his next words caused Sakura and I to share an uneasy glance. "The Evershifting Forest."

19
SAKURA

*K*sega and I lacked Alchemy's enthusiasm for entering the Evershifting Forest, but then again, we weren't the ones who had lived there, nor were we the ones who were capable of killing a smith all on our own. At this moment, though, I found I lacked much enthusiasm for anything. Alchemy was in an irritable mood, solely because I tried to drag him ahead through the fog before anyone spotted him, and Ksega was having some sort of miniature crisis with his bering. The way he was acting, it was almost as if he was losing control of it.

The beauty of the Evershifting Forest — and all of Brightlock, for that matter — did help a little bit, but there was still so much pressure on us to completely enjoy the wonder of it all. We stepped into the autumnal forest mere moments before we heard the clatter of hooves along the road. Sneaking farther into the Evershifting Forest, we turned and crouched down behind the trees to watch as a small fleet of riders, clad in Locker armor, galloped down the road, heads turning to scan the land around the path as they passed.

"Let's go farther in," Alchemy suggested, rising back to his full height and turning around to march farther into the woodland. I got up to follow him, and Ksega slowly trailed after me, his eyes searching the trees around us.

"What's going on with you?" I asked, my voice sharper than I'd intended for it to be. I adjusted the strap of my pack on my shoulder and waited for him to fall in step beside me as we followed Alchemy's forged path.

"Nothing. I'm just tired." Ksega replied, his gaze lingering on the canopy of orange-gold leaves above us. The forest floor was just as bright and red as the leaves on the trees. The tall, thin white trunks of the trees rose like ominous bones around us, shining gold in the streams of morning sunlight that fell through the leaves.

"It's more than that. Something happened with your bering back there. What was it?" I tried to make my tone demanding, tried to make it sound like Finnian when he was teaching me a new fighting technique, something he knew in its entirety and was confident in his abilities to share. I wasn't sure if it came across that way, but Ksega's nervousness seemed to increase, so I assumed it had.

"I don't know."

"Yes, you do."

"No, I don't." His tone hardened, and he met my gaze. "I swear, I don't know what happened. But whatever it was, it won't happen again." There was something he was holding back, but I wasn't going to pressure him about it more. Besides, Alchemy was slowing down, looking up at the sky above.

"We should look for a place to make camp. Preferably someplace farther to the east, where we'll be closer to the Gates to Old Duskfall." He turned back to look at us, his ashen skull misplaced in the light of the morning sun. "And preferably someplace a smith won't find us for lunch."

We didn't run into any smiths, and it was late in the evening when we found a good place to set up camp. We had stopped only once to have a quick lunch of dried fruit and chewy jerky, and to let Ksega and I regain some of our energy. I hadn't realized how tired I had become until I'd stopped to lean against a tree and close my eyes for a moment. Ksega also looked exhausted, and now that I was looking for it, I saw that there were bags forming beneath his eyes. How long had it been since either of us had had a full night's sleep?

Alchemy, of course, was unfazed by our journey, and I couldn't help but be jealous of his lack of a need for food and sleep. Ksega had apparently been having similar thoughts, because he'd mentioned it while he chewed on a sliver of dried mango.

"I don't see why you can't help us carry our packs. Just because you don't need the fruit or the bedrolls doesn't mean you can't help with the burden."

"Without me, Ironling here wouldn't have had a starting point for her quest," Alchemy had replied. "And that would leave you without this fun little adventure. If anything, you should be thanking me for the work I've already done."

"You haven't done *any* work. You're just using your old man knowledge to tell us where to go," Ksega had argued, although there had been little conviction behind it. Alchemy must have sensed the same thing, because he said nothing.

By the time Ksega and I had each set up our bedrolls — neither of us had a tent — and we had formed a fire pit, the sun was beginning its descent into the west. The forest appeared even more orange and gold in the dying light of day, and I felt my eyelids beginning to droop as Ksega and Alchemy wandered off to collect some firewood.

When they returned, Alchemy arranged the pieces in a way that would be best for a campfire, and Ksega sorted the rest of it into a neat little pile to one side, making minor adjustments to the way the ring of stones sat around Alchemy's stack.

"Would you do the honors, flame-fingers?" Ksega dramatically flourished his hand towards the pit, raising an eyebrow at me, and I scowled, resisting the urge to curl my hand into a fist and throw it into his smirking face.

"Don't give me a nickname." I snarled as I leaned forward, crouching beside the fire pit and rubbing my hands together as I drew my eirioth up from within me.

"Chem has one for you," he grumbled, although I didn't really hear him, focusing on my own power.

The eirioth was alive and ready to be used. I hadn't summoned it since I'd been with the pirates, and it was eager to be unleashed. If I wasn't careful, it would find a way to eat up all the crinkling leaves that littered the forest floor around us.

Gently, I cupped my hands together and held them towards the kindling. Alchemy and Ksega stilled on either side of me, as if they were afraid any movement might send the fire off course. I ignored them, focusing on the small tongue of flame that flickered to life over my palms, dancing before my eyes and blending with the orange light of sunset. Leaning forward, I blew gently on the fire, coaxing it forward into the timber. As soon as the flame found the wood, it caught, erupting into a mighty plume of fire, and causing the three of us to jerk suddenly back.

Ksega lost his balance, tripping over his own foot, and landed on his backside on his bedroll, his eyes wide as he looked at the fire. On my other side, Alchemy pulled his massive cloak off and bundled it up to set beside my pillow, along with his gloves, before he sat down beside the fire, closer than I would have dared to get for fear of breaking out in a sweat. Of course, he didn't have to worry about sweating.

Ksega straightened into an upright sitting position, and I settled myself onto my own bedroll, tugging at my boots to loosen them up. My feet were achy and sore after being on them for so long, and I desperately wished I could soak them in a hot bath.

"So," Alchemy began after a long silence. "I suppose it's about time we all got to know each other a little better." He leaned forward, setting his elbows on his knees, and angling his head towards Ksega and I. "Which one of you would like to start?"

"Why don't *you* start?" I asked, raising an eyebrow at him. There was still so much I didn't know about either of them, but of the two, Alchemy was more of a mystery. "We'll start with something simple. Why do you want us to call you Chem?"

"It's a good nickname for 'Alchemy'," he shrugged his shoulder blades, turning his skull back to face the fire. "And I don't really like 'Alchemy' . . . it's a little too similar to my dead name."

"Dead name?" Ksega echoed before I had the chance to. I looked sidelong at him, but his attention was wholly trained on Alchemy, who was still looking into the flame, tapping his thin black finger bones against the soil.

"The name I had before . . . *this*." He lifted his hand and turned it around, as if examining it. Thin rivets of bright green ran along them, like threads connecting all the bones together since there was no muscle and tissue there to do the job. Alchemy curled the hand into a fist, a jumble of small black and green bones.

"What *was* the name you had before . . ." I looked up at his skull, the dark, empty eye sockets, the ever-present grin. "Your corruption?" I finished, unsure if that was the right way to phrase it.

"It doesn't matter." He answered after a painfully silent moment. "That was a long time ago, and that name belonged to another man. A man who wasn't weak enough to be taken by the Curse." He lifted his head, facing me again. "Now let's talk about you. Where are you really from? Somewhere in Carlore, obviously, but what did you leave behind? *Who* did you leave behind? Why did you leave?" he leaned forward, expectant, and even though he didn't say anything, I noticed the open curiosity in Ksega's eyes.

I sighed, averting my gaze from both of them to look down into the flames I had created. I felt them tugging at me, playfully, wanting more freedom. They wanted to be set loose so they could devour the entire forest, and a part of me wanted to let them have their fun. If the Evershifting Forest was destroyed, every Cursed animal within it would be destroyed, too, and who knew how many lives that could save.

But what had Alchemy said when we'd first met? The Curse wasn't a disease. It was a living, thriving thing. It was magic. It would only seek out a new host to corrupt, and a new victim to take. There was no way to save *anyone* until the Curse itself was gone.

"The Curse has destroyed too many lives." I said finally, letting my gaze shift away from the flames and towards the dark forest around us. It was terrifyingly dark, and I was certain there was something lurking in the distance, its beady eyes just watching and waiting for us to fall asleep.

"People you knew?" Alchemy prodded, and I realized I had gone silent for a long moment. I looked over at him, feeling my fingers curl into fists.

"Yes." I risked a glance at Ksega, my nerves fizzing when I saw how intently he was watching me. "My parents. And older sister." I took a shaky breath. "That was a long time ago. What really encouraged me to get out here and do this is when my brother had to kill his dragon." I licked my lips, rubbing my thumb roughly over my knuckles. Even though I kept my eyes open, I could see Elixir, the hollow sockets where his beautiful aquamarine eyes had once sat, the silvery blood-like substance seeping from the blackened skin of his hide, the ashy feathers falling from his muscled body in ragged clumps.

The image shifted sharply, still shaggy and black and splattered with glowing green, but it was no longer the body of a dragon. It was the body of a badger, vicious and snarling, and then the body of a wolf, fangs dripping fresh blood and vibrant green eyes hungry for more. I was back in the small, frail body of a frightened five-year-old girl, powerless to help her family. Powerless to help *herself.*

"Ironling?" the raucous voice sounded right in my ear, and I gasped as my world suddenly spun, jerking away from the sound.

"Careful!" Ksega's voice cautioned, and I felt his hand gripping my shoulder to pull me away from the leaping flames, which had roared into the air in my panic.

As I scooted away from the ring of rocks, shaking Ksega's hand off and throwing a look around the darkening forest, the flames gently died back down to a reasonable size. I could feel how shaky my breaths were, and I bit down on my lip, trying to force my voice not to quiver.

"Sorry. It isn't an easy thing to think about." I shrugged uncomfortably, playing with the strap on my boot to avoid looking at either of them. The silence was heavy and awkward, so I cleared my throat and looked at Ksega. "So what about you? Where are you from? What's your family like?" I adjusted the way I sat so I could face him. I didn't want to look at Alchemy right now. With his empty eye sockets and the shifting shadows behind him, it made me far too afraid of what else could be waiting in the hollows around us.

"I'm from Wisesol, where I live with my grandmother," Ksega shrugged, sitting cross-legged and looking into the fire. "That's it, really. I help her with her small business and . . . yeah. That's all. My friend Jessie lives nearby, and I'll help her out sometimes, but there's nothing aside from that." He looked up and offered me a small smile, one that was almost apologetic. "I don't know anything about my parents. Willa — my grandmother — won't talk about them."

I nodded silently. Gamma rarely ever spoke of my parents, either, and I didn't blame her. I remembered enough about them, and I understood the pain it brought to mention them. Finnian wasn't as familiar with the feeling, and would occasionally talk about them, and even Aurora, but it wasn't often around me. He knew how much it hurt me.

"What about your bering?" I asked, hoping to move the topic away from relatives. Thinking about Finnian and Gamma was beginning to make my stomach swirl.

"What about it?" Ksega moved his gaze away from mine again, his fingers drumming against the forest floor beneath his legs.

"You know." I tilted my head to the side, squinting at him. "Or maybe you don't. What happened earlier? And what were you talking about when you were asking about my eirioth back on *Orvyn*?" as if sensing the mention of it, my eirioth pulled at me from our fire, twirling and dancing and reaching, hoping I would take notice of it and give it more freedom. I ignored its taunts.

"I don't practice with my bering very often," Ksega began, licking his lips. "There's still a lot I don't understand about it. But . . ." his hand moved forward so that his whole palm pressed against the earth. "Since I've been back on land, after so much time at sea," he furrowed his brow, focusing on his hand. "It feels stronger. A lot stronger." Around his fingers, bright green blades of grass pushed through the soil, followed by the blossoming of a bundle of purple tulips and a sprout of rosemary. The growth continued until the flowers were fully developed, when he pulled his hand away to reveal a hand-shaped imprint of soft earth in the center of the little ring of new life.

"Fascinating." Alchemy rasped from behind me.

"If I'd been able to grow things this easily back at home, Willa wouldn't have to bother half as much with her flower garden in the yard." Ksega said, his finger lifting one of the little tulips.

"Knowing how to manage without the assistance of magic is a useful skill, you know," Alchemy pointed out, and Ksega and I both looked up at him. He waited a long moment, then his skull tilted to the side. "What, you think I'm not a mage?"

"You've never shown any sign of being one." I admitted after a hesitant pause, squinting at him. He'd said he was from Freetalon. As far as I could tell, he wasn't a recle-mage.

"Not anymore, I don't." A husky sound rattled out from him, what I suspected was the closest thing to a sigh he could manage.

"You were a mage before the Curse took you?" Ksega guessed, his eyebrows rising. "What kind?"

"Oh, a recle-mage." Alchemy's tone was wistful, locked in the past. "I haven't felt that power in several years, though." The blades of his shoulders lifted in a careless shrug. "It can be a blessing and a curse to live like this. I've learnt a lot. Seen a lot. Slept very little." He angled his skull towards us again, and I knew that, if he wasn't constantly doing it already, he would be grinning.

"Speaking of sleeping, since you don't need to do it, and we do," Ksega patted the pillow at the head of his bedroll, lowering himself onto it. "You get to keep watch. Don't let me get eaten by a smith, please." He sighed and shrugged his body until he was in a comfortable position, then grunted. "Good night, Chem. Good night, Sakura."

I watched him for a moment, then faced the fire again. After a long minute, during which I felt my panic swell and subside with each minute noise in the forest around us, I settled down onto my own bedroll. I'd forgotten to remove my sword from my back, and it prodded me now. I sat up again, sliding its straps over my shoulders.

I'd had the sword for many years. It was the first non-wood weapon I'd learned to fight with. Finnian and Derek had been my first teachers, and Finnian had gifted the sword to me on my seventh birthday. I'd cherished it every moment since.

But now it was extra weight. It was a reminder of Finnian and Derek. It was a reminder of home, and every reminder of home was a pointless reminder of all my pain. I hated to leave it behind, and my eyes swam with tears at the thought of it, but it was an item that was precious to me. So precious that it hurt. I didn't want to bring it along, but I didn't want to leave it behind, here, in this awful place where I might never see it again. But I had my flame-sword. I had all those years of training with Finnian and Derek to help me. I didn't need this sword. I didn't need this distraction. I needed to *let go*.

"Chem," I whispered, looking up at him. I knew there were tears in my eyes, but I kept myself turned away from the fire, hoping he wouldn't notice. "Will you get rid of this?" I held the sword out to him. He didn't move for a long moment. "I want you to, Chem. Take it. It doesn't need to stay with me."

"Are you sure?"

"Yes." I had to let go of it. I hadn't had any good use for it since this journey had started. I doubted I would really ever need it — with my eirioth beside me, there was little use for the steel blade other than training with Finnian.

"Very well." The skeleton stepped forward and took the sword from me. I kept my face angled away.

"Good night, Ironling," Alchemy said softly, walking away into the dim Forest.

"Good night," I mumbled, shrugging farther into my bedroll and trying to bury my face in my pillow, forcing away all the haunting thoughts that picked at the back of my mind.

Dawn brought with it a breathtaking change of scenery, and the pleasant aroma of crisping bacon.

The autumnal forest had gone, replaced with tall, thick pine trees and brightly colored berry bushes. Through my blurry morning vision, I could see some sort of creature moving in the distance, probably a small deer or a coyote — whatever it was, it wasn't Cursed, so I wasn't very concerned.

"G'morning," Alchemy's voice rumbled from near the fire pit, where he was baking something in strips on the stones. Looking up, he said, "I found a little boar earlier. Figured I'd make you breakfast."

"Thanks," I rubbed my eyes, yawning and stretching the stiffness out of my back muscles. The fire that was burning in the pit was one Alchemy had made, since whatever fire I had created last night had long since died down, and I was less connected to it than any flame made by eirioth. It was relaxing, being able to be so close to a fire without it constantly pulling at me.

"You seem awfully tired." Alchemy observed, but I didn't respond. I knew what he was referring to.

During the night, I had woken up twice, both in a fit of ragged breath, sweat dripping down my face. Each time had been the result of a nightmare, a vicious replay of the awful day my family had been taken away from me. Alchemy had been standing not far off, and I knew he had taken notice of the events, but he'd said nothing.

"Not as tired as Ksega, apparently," I mumbled, looking over at him. He was snoring softly, his hair a mess, lying on his side and facing away from us.

"Can I kick him awake?" Alchemy asked eagerly, tediously flipping the strips of boar with a stick and looking up at Ksega.

"I'm all for it." I waved a hand at him, feeling my stomach rumble from the tantalizing scent of bacon. It looked like it was almost done, and I was going to make sure I got to it before Ksega did.

As Alchemy stood up to go and wake Ksega, I looked up at the sky. It was difficult to see through the thick branches of the pine trees, but it was there, a glimpse of pale blue through the pine needles.

"Ow!" Ksega grunted as Alchemy's boot dug into his back. I looked over at them, rolling my eyes as Ksega swatted an arm at the skeleton's legs and turned over again. Undeterred, Alchemy bent down and lifted Ksega up off the ground, cradling him like a big baby in his arms.

"Throw him in the fire." I suggested, reaching over to lift one of the strips of bacon from the stones.

"No!" Ksega yelped, struggling to get out of Alchemy's grip as the skeleton turned to face the flames. Before he could take a step, Ksega tumbled to the ground, grunting as his arm knocked against one of the stones.

"Unfortunate," I murmured, crunching into the bacon.

"We should leave as soon as possible, so eat quickly," Alchemy said, gesturing at Ksega and I's bedrolls and packs. "If we travel at a good pace, we'll be going through the Shattered Mountains within a few days."

"Is that bacon?" Ksega pushed himself up into a sitting position, leaning over to grab a few strips for himself. My gaze fell to the earth below him, and I realized it was changing. It was very subtle, but the soil below him was shifting. Was he even aware that he was doing it?

"No sign of trouble during the night?" I asked through a mouthful of bacon, directing the question towards Alchemy, who was stomping on the fire to put it out, holding the leg of his pants up so they wouldn't catch in the flames.

"A smith came past over there shortly after you went to sleep," Alchemy pointed out to the west.

"Did you kill it?" I asked, and Ksega looked over at me curiously. He had seen Alchemy's smith tooth daggers, but I didn't think he knew where they'd come from yet.

"No, it didn't come close. I'm not sure it noticed us. I think it was hunting something else." Alchemy reassured us, shrugging as he stepped away from the smoldering remnants of the fire.

"Good. The sooner we get out of this forest, the better. It'll be one less thing to worry about." I started to pack up my bedroll, gesturing for Ksega do to the same. He ignored me, wolfing down his bacon instead.

It wasn't much longer after that we were ready to go, and we wasted no time setting off. Alchemy seemed to have a better sense of where we were than Ksega and I did, so we let him lead the way, supposedly marching east.

As we walked, Ksega looked around somewhat wonderingly, occasionally pointing out this type of plant or that. I stayed quiet, but he didn't seem to mind. He would talk about how he knew what tuberose was because his grandmother, Willa, used them in her perfumes, which would lead him off on a rant about how smelly their house always was. He insisted it wasn't a bad smell. His exact words were 'it always smells like honey and fruit and flowers. It's just a bit overwhelming sometimes', and then he had fallen silent again.

Alchemy occasionally joined in on a conversation with him, and they talked about the Evershifting Forest for a while. It was an interesting topic. Alchemy would talk about the behaviors of the forest, how it seemed to have emotions and life and energy, and depending on how it felt from day to day, it would change its appearance. He talked about how some of the plants that grew, like certain mosses or rare flowers, wouldn't change with the rest of the forest, staying the same so that it could grow and thrive.

Ksega would bounce off of that and talk about his connection to the plants, how he could see them in a different light. He described it as their life force, the sort of pulsing energy that surrounds anything alive. He demonstrated this ability to us by pointing out birds or reptiles or even little bugs before Alchemy or I had come within twenty feet of them.

I asked him how he was connected to it, how it felt when he used his bering. From the way he described it, he felt happy and full and strong, and that strength didn't waver, whereas when I used my eirioth, it was a constant struggle as I strained not to lose all the energy that my eirioth was seeping out of me. We continued in silence for a while, and slightly to my surprise, I was the next to speak as a thought occurred to me.

"Ksega, I've been thinking about how you can sense animals and such. Does that mean you can sense Cursed things? Can you sense Chem?" I looked over at the skeleton, towering over us and only taking a stride every other time Ksega and I took a step.

"I can sort of hear them. It's like a buzzing. My bering doesn't know what to do with it, since they're not alive, but they're not technically dead. With Chem being near me most of the time, I've sort of learned to tune it out, but if there's ever another Cursed animal nearby, I'll be able to tell. But I can't see him the way I can other life forms." Ksega replied, his gaze sweeping around the Forest.

"You'll let us know if there's another, right?" I squinted through the trunks of the pine trees. There were no signs of animal life so far, but we had stayed nearer to the outlying reaches of the Evershifting Forest, so I didn't expect to see any. Then again, Alchemy had said he'd seen a smith while we'd slept. The thought made me cast a wary look around us, just in case. There was nothing that I could see, but what if there was something hiding?

"Of course." Ksega answered, and I looked back at him. His gaze looked mildly hurt. "We're fine right now, if that's what you're wondering."

"Sorry. I get antsy when I can't see most of my surroundings." I grimaced, pushing a low-hanging pine branch out of my way.

"Well, you'll be able to see soon enough," Alchemy grumbled, pulling his hood back up over his face far enough that only the jutting bones of his jaw could be seen, and only if you were peering closely. "We're almost to the edge of the woods. We'll skirt around Oracle Lake, and stop at one of the villages. There are a few of them dotted around the lake itself, and some others around the shore. It will be a good place to get a better bed for you to sleep in and a table for you to eat at, and maybe find some more money to get you through to Old Duskfall."

"You'll stay outside the villages, right?" Ksega fiddled with the fletching of the arrows at his hip. "You're not exactly easy to hide in a populated area. We nearly got caught a few times in Famark, and on the ramp into Brightlock."

"I'll stay outside of the villages," Alchemy reassured him. I felt my stomach turn a little at the thought of being someplace with only Ksega.

Despite the initial untrustworthiness of Alchemy, there was something assuring about him being with me. He couldn't be killed, because he was already dead. I wasn't even sure that he could be wounded, but he could definitely wound others, and he could do it severely. I was confident he wouldn't turn on us, because he seemed honestly dedicated to finding the source of the Curse. It *had* corrupted him, after all. Surely he wanted some sort of revenge for the life that had been stolen from him.

But I didn't know Ksega as well. What I knew about him was rough, and I hadn't been put in any situations yet where I was forced to rely on him. He had chosen to accompany me on this adventure, but I had also made it clear I wanted him to come along, not only because he might prove useful, but because I was too afraid he would share Alchemy's secret.

I was still afraid he might try to do that. There was no good way to read him clearly. Was he afraid of Alchemy? Did he consider him a friend? Did he consider *me* a friend? Would he take one look at a village and break, running to tell the nearest person that there was a seven-foot-tall Cursed skeleton wandering around Brightlock?

Stop worrying, I scolded myself, taking a deep breath as we forged on through the Forest. I could see the edge of it now, not much farther. Beyond the treeline I could barely make out the distant reflection of sunlight on water.

Sunlight.

I was ready to feel the full force of sunlight again. After so many days on the foggy seas, and then under the shade of the trees, I was itching to be out in open, sunny space again. I could sense its warmth, the strength it would restore in me. My eirioth could sense my excitement, leaping to the surface of my skin and trying to break free.

I was ready to set it free. I was ready to be done with this whole quest, to go home and train with Finnian beside the King's Scar, or to sit down and eat a hot bowl of stew with Gamma and Walter.

Just keep going. I told myself, clenching my fists and forcing myself to keep walking after Ksega and Alchemy, even when my weariness told me to stop. *Keep going, and you'll be home soon enough.*

20
KSEGA

Oracle Lake appeared as soon as we stepped outside the Evershifting Forest, like a giant pulsing plate of silver-blue in the distance. It was larger than I'd expected it to be; it must've spanned almost the entire length of my hometown of Rulak. Granted, Rulak wasn't very big, but Oracle Lake was by no means small. It was closer to a small ocean itself.

There were three settlements that I could see on the lake itself, with docks and little boats for fishing bobbing on the water. There were even a few lake houses. There used to be similar shacks floating in the Port, but they didn't have the proper support, and were made of heavy materials, and in the end they had sunk into the water. These ones appeared to be much lighter, and they bobbed and shifted gently in the soft waves of Oracle Lake.

On the outskirts of the lake were seven small towns, roughly formed into little close-knit squares. There were a few thin, worn-down paths that hardly qualified as roads leading between the buildings, as well as one thick cobbled road that connected all the little towns and leading farther off to the main road, which would eventually lead to the capital.

The lake itself was maybe four or five miles away, down a gradual grassy slope and past a small field of wildflowers, all of them withering into dormancy for the winter. It was an odd feeling, whenever autumn and winter came around. I didn't feel any less connected to the earth, but everything felt tired. Even I became sleepy after working with my bering during the fall months, and the only explanation was that the hibernation of the plant life around me was simply tuning my own abilities down.

"We'll be pretty out in the open once we head out there," Sakura observed, scanning the land before us with a frown. The Evershifting Forest was just about the only woodland in all of Brightlock. There were a few orchards and man-made glades to supply what wood was necessary for the kingdom, but most of the wood could be gained through trading Brightlock's numerous ore supplies.

"Will you stay all the way back here?" I asked, looking up at Alchemy. He had his hood up, and his hand bones concealed by the leather gloves, which would fool anyone from a distance, but there would be few options to get him away inconspicuously once we were closer to the towns. His height alone would attract too much attention.

"No. I'll circle around to the south, sticking close to the treeline, but not in the forest itself. You'll be able to find me easily enough." He looked down towards Sakura. "Will you want to stay one or two nights? You look like you might be in need of two."

"We don't have time." Sakura grimaced, shrugging her pack over so that the strap hung on the opposite shoulder. Her face was set in grim lines. I pursed my lips together.

"We shouldn't run ourselves ragged, you know-"

"Every moment, the Curse could be growing. It took a *dragon*. Who knows what could be next? A sea wraith? A bear?" she shook her head, leveling her glare at me. "It's too dangerous. Lives could be lost if we sit around catching our breath."

"Lives will be lost anyway." I tried to keep my tone gentle. I knew she felt very strongly about all of this. I knew there was no way someone like me could understand — our stories were completely different, after all.

"Ksega is right." Alchemy chided, his own tone as soft as I assumed he could make it. Sakura shifted her glower to him. "You can't save them all, Ironling, as much as you'd like to." He reached out and settled a gloved hand on her shoulder. "If you don't slow down and catch your breath now, you'll be empty of it when the time comes to fight. Don't push yourself too far." He let go of her and nodded towards the towns. "Go on, now. Hurry. The sun will be setting faster than you'll expect, so you'll want to get going now. Find me sometime tomorrow, and we'll talk more then." He gave a brief farewell to each of us, then started off into the forest again, this time taking a southern course.

I waited for a moment, letting Sakura gather her thoughts. She was staring off into the distance, her eyes filled with sadness. I didn't know what she must have been thinking at that moment, but the most I could do was stand there and be willing to listen if she had any more to say. Luckily — for both of us, I think — she said nothing, only nodding and starting off towards the little towns. I followed her silently.

For a long time, the only sound was that of the swishing blades of grass against our boots and the distant sounds of animals and townspeople and *life*. It was relaxing, even with the bite of the autumn wind, promising winter in the next few months. I was the first to break the silence, which I knew was a risky thing considering Sakura's irritable mood, but something she had said was bothering me.

"The Curse took a dragon?" I asked.

The silence that followed my question seemed to drag on forever. What she had said as we'd left the Evershifting Forest had puzzled me. I knew very little about what had happened to her, and what had driven her to leave her home. The night before, she had become very emotional when talking about her brother and his dragon, but she'd never said what had happened to him.

"Yes." She said finally. Her voice startled me; I hadn't expected her to give me an answer. I looked sideways at her, hoping she would say more. I was a little surprised when she did. "Only a few weeks ago, my brother and I were training in our usual glade. We noticed Elixir — his eirioth dragon — acting a little strangely. He passed out, and we got him home, and . . ." she paused here, taking a long, deep breath. I wasn't sure, because she was slightly turned away from me, but I thought I saw her eyes glistening with unshed tears.

"And it was the Curse?" I guessed, my voice barely more than a whisper. She nodded mutely, swallowing and keeping her gaze trained forward.

We fell quiet again, each of us lost in our own thoughts. I remembered another detail from what she had told Alchemy and I the night before, and was able to piece things together in my mind, although I wouldn't say it out loud for fear of upsetting her more. She had said her brother had been forced to kill his own dragon. Had the Curse really corrupted the dragon to the point that not even his rider had any choice but to slay him?

I didn't know much about the eirioth dragons. I didn't know much about a lot of things, due to the fact that education was worth next to nothing in Wisesol, but what I did know of Carlore's famous winged dragons was that they bonded with a human for life. There had once been an old Carlorian man in Rulak, who had moved there when he was much younger, and had brought his eirioth dragon with him. I had been very young when that man and his dragon had passed away, but I vaguely remembered them.

"We should stop and eat something soon." Sakura's voice was almost entirely empty of emotion, but I heard a small hitch at the back of her words. I felt a twinge of guilt, blaming myself for her current state of emotions. Willa often said I always spoke before I thought, and for once I found myself agreeing with her.

Looking up at the sky, I realized Sakura was right. We'd been walking for longer than I'd thought, and it was several hours past midday already. Now that I saw the sun's position in the sky, the muscles in my legs seemed to complain endlessly more. I'd never done so much on-foot travel consecutively in my life.

"What have you got in your pack?" I asked, shrugging my shoulders. I was wearing my longbow across my back as well as a satchel across my chest, and they were beginning to dig painfully into my shoulders.

"Some fruit. It's probably old and a little mushy, though," Sakura had a pack on her back, but had left her sword behind. At some point, she must have decided it was extra weight that she didn't want to carry. I had seen her with it when we came through the Gates at Brightlock, but not again since the night before. I didn't know where she'd left it, but knowing how much she cared about her weapons, I guessed it was somewhere nobody would find it.

"I've got some old bread and some sort of jerky," I bit my lip, squinting at the town ahead. "We'll need to find some way of getting more food here."

"You're a thief, aren't you? Why don't you just swipe some for us?" Sakura grumbled, and I raised an eyebrow at her.

"You think I'm that selfish? You think I would ever use those talents for my own personal gain?"

"Yes."

"Well, you'd be right."

We kept walking for another half hour before we stopped to nibble on what provisions we had. None of it was very appetizing, and neither of us were hungry enough to eat more than a few unsatisfying bites. Soon enough, after a few stretches to relieve our tired muscles, we were back to walking. The sun was sinking fast in the sky, but we were very close to the village now, and would reach it within the next hour.

My first impression when we stepped into the village was that it was very secluded. Now that we were here, I could see that there was a sort of uniformity to the layout. Four rows of buildings, with little dusty streets winding their way in between. All of the buildings were in good condition, with clean little yards and even lively garden boxes on the windows. There were people mulling about, carrying nets of fish or baskets of linens or small children with bright eyes and fuzzy little cotton toys clasped in their pudgy fingers.

It was a happy scene. A scene where everyone knew their role in the village, and everyone was at peace with one another. There were welcoming smiles offered to us and waves from the innocent children skipping in little lines down the street. It was a scene that could never be found in Wisesol.

"Keep an eye out for an inn." Sakura mumbled, peering at the buildings around us. Most of them appeared to be large homes, but most of them also appeared to be inhabited by large families. They were all very uniform, and I couldn't single one out to have a different purpose from the others. There were no signs or indications that any of the buildings were businesses.

"I think this is solely a community-run village," I pointed out, looking towards Oracle Lake. In the light of the setting sun, it was a shimmering mirror of the pink and purple sky above. "There might not be an inn."

"Then use your people-charming skills and find us a place to stay for the night, and maybe some food. We'll split up." She turned off onto a separate road, pausing once to look back at me. "Don't get into any trouble." Then she vanished around the back of a house.

I licked my lips, feeling a squeeze in my chest as I realized that sounded like something Jessie would say. Sweet, caring Jessie, who was always so worried about me. How worried would she be right now? I knew she had agreed to this, but still, there was no way she could simply turn off her worry like a tap.

Shaking my head, I took a deep breath and looked around me. There were lots of friendly faces, and a few people waved at me when I met their gaze. I was sure I'd be able to find someone willing to harbor us for a night or two. With any luck, they'd be willing to feed us a real meal as well.

The first person I talked to was a fair-haired woman with prominent features holding the hand of a thin little girl. She explained that the villages surrounding Oracle Lake were referred to by Lockers as the Stargazing Colonies, because of the superstitious nature of the majority of the older generations, who believed the Lake was a portal to the skies.

"This particular village is called Arvos, named after the founder of the first Stargazing Colony," she patted the pale child's hand and ushered her away to play with a group of other young girls. "It's the oldest settlement out of the ten, and most likely to stick to the traditions of the Stargazers." She smiled pleasantly at me. "I don't mean to bore you with a history lesson, but I say all this to inform you that my great-great-great grandfather was the founder of Fanto, another of the villages, and my family is very strict on following those traditions. Welcoming strangers into our home is against said traditions, as much as it pains me to say so." Her smile remained kind, and I knew it was sincere.

"Thank you anyway," I returned the smile, feeling a worm of unease sprout in my gut. Maybe it would be more difficult to find shelter here than we'd thought. Her next words, though, doused those fears.

"You should speak to Jhapato, though. He's a Locker, although he was born a Duskan. He lives on the southern side of the village," the woman pointed in that direction. "He won't be bound by the same family traditions I am. I'm sure he would be more than happy to harbor you and your friend."

"Wonderful. Thank you so much for your help." I grinned at her, fishing into my satchel to retrieve what few rupees remained there. I offered them to her, but she lifted a hand, shaking her head.

"I won't accept your money. I was simply helping a traveler." Her smile resurfaced, wide and resplendent on her pale features. "You are much kinder than some of the others we have encountered traveling in from the seas. I wish you luck on your journey." She curled my fingers back around the coins and patted them. "Take care, boy."

Before I had a chance to thank her again, she walked off after the little girl that had been with her before and her new group of friends, stopping only to give me a brief wave of farewell. Returning the rupees to my satchel, I began to walk to the south, winding between the buildings and keeping my eyes open for Sakura. If she'd succeeded in finding food, I wanted to debate with her whether we should go ahead and eat, or wait and see if Jhapato would be willing to feed us.

Either way, I was going to make sure I got some dinner within the next hour.

Jhapato wasn't very difficult to locate, with the help of the locals of Arvos. They were more than happy to provide directions for weary travelers such as Sakura and me.

Jhapato's house was one that was slightly more run-down than the others. It looked to be about the same age, but the wood on the porch was worn from many years of use, and the windows were tinted with dust. Jhapato himself was seated on that porch, rocking back and forth in a rocking chair and squinting at passersby.

When he spotted us approaching, he smiled in welcome. His skin was darker than anyone else's that I'd seen, but still lighter than Sakura's. The golden hue of his dark eyes reminded me of a Duskan woman that had once purchased perfumes from Willa.

"Are you Jhapato?" Sakura asked as we stopped in front of the steps to the porch. The man nodded, rising slowly to his feet. This was an elderly man, with wrinkled features and kind eyes.

"I am." He offered a hand to first Sakura, then me, and we both shook. "May I help you?"

"We were told you might be able to help us. We need a place to stay for a few nights." I gave him a brief smile, glancing over his house again. It had the same construction as the other buildings, but as I'd noted before it had a much more lived-in appearance to it.

"Of course. You are travelers from the west?" the man looked us up and down, taking in our dirty clothing and tousled hair.

"Yes. From Wisesol." I shrugged my shoulders and glanced at Sakura. "Both of us." Her eyes squinted only just in acknowledgement.

"Right," Jhapato nodded, motioning towards the door of his house. "Come on in. I'd be more than happy to house you. How long are you needing to stay?"

"Only a night or two," Sakura looked up at the darkening sky. It was a deep purple, now, and tinged with a murky indigo, highlighted by a smattering of emerging stars.

"Come, come," the man turned and opened his door, leaving it open for us to follow behind.

"Dinner would be nice, too." I added, and she elbowed me in the ribs. I grimaced, scowling at her, and whispered, "I thought you wanted me to charm people into giving us food."

We followed him inside, trailing along after him until he stopped us in a small dining room. There was a circular table with a few chairs set around it, and a vase of struggling flowers placed upon it as a centerpiece.

"Wait here. I'll bring what I have." Jhapato retreated into the kitchen adjacent to the dining room, and Sakura glowered at me.

"What?" I asked.

"He might not have much food."

"*We* don't have much food. Ow." I winced as she reached over and flicked me on the ear.

"Here we are," Jhapato returned with a large bowl of rice and what appeared to be a half-eaten roasted bird. He set them on the table and gestured to the chairs. "Please, have a seat. I've already eaten my supper. I'll make up the spare cot." He turned to leave, pausing to look back at me. "You'll have to sleep on my sofa."

"What? Why me?" I frowned, sitting at the table. Across from me, Sakura glared. I shrugged at her.

"She's a lady," Jhapato said, shaking his head at me. "You ought to treat her like one." And then he walked away.

"Why do you keep making that face at me?" I returned Sakura's frown, although mine lacked her ferocity.

"Did you ever learn how to use your manners?"

"I don't want to sleep on a sofa."

"I don't care about the sleeping arrangements — although I'm taking that spare cot — I'm talking about Jhapato! This stranger has welcomed us into his home and offered us food and a place to stay without asking us any questions, and you are acting so *rude*." She hissed, careful to keep her voice low.

"Like you have experience with strangers sleeping in your home." I argued. She raised an eyebrow, and I instantly regretted my words.

"I live in an inn with my brother, you dolt. I deal with travelers and strangers almost every day." She paused, looked around the room, and then stared down at her plate. "Or, I did." She pressed her lips together, and I swallowed nervously, suddenly overcome with a feeling of guilt.

"I see." I served myself a small portion of rice and what I assumed was roasted duck. "I'm sorry," I added after a moment, poking at the bird with the fork Jhapato had provided. "I didn't know."

"Yes, well," Sakura's voice was thin, but it was less angry now, and more like that of a patient mother trying to gently scold her child. "You should at least make an effort to be more polite."

I didn't respond, hesitantly taking a bite of the food. Sakura was digging into hers, but now I felt even worse for taking Jhapato's food. Grimacing at my own ignorance, I shoveled another bite into my mouth, painfully aware of how hungry I was, and also painfully aware of how little food was laid out before us.

"It's all set up for when you're ready." Jhapato came back into the little dining room, gesturing towards the hallway. "It's all the way down, through the living room and on the left. The sofa is in the living room." He looked down at the depleting amount of food and smiled heartily, creases forming at the corners of his eyes. "I'm glad to see you enjoy the food. Please, if you need anything else, just ask."

"We will. Thank you." Sakura smiled warmly at him, and I blinked at her. Thus far, I couldn't remember her giving anyone an honest smile. When Jhapato took the empty rice plate — whatever remained of it was on our dishes — she looked across at me, and the smile faded. "What?"

"Nothing. You just . . ." I paused, closed my mouth, and opened it again. "You have a nice smile." I finished lamely, looking back down at my plate and feeling blood rush into my face.

There was a long silence, during which I forced myself to take great interest in the meal before me. When I'd eaten it all, I risked a glance at her. Sakura was also staring at her food, apparently lost in thought, slowly stirring a grain of rice around her plate.

"Whereabouts are you traveling to?" Jhapato's cracked voice bouncing around the walls of the room caused both of us to snap our heads up. He had reentered the dining room, and took one of the empty seats around the table.

I looked across at Sakura. She had let me do most of the talking in previous situations, but that was because those situations usually involved the sort of people I was accustomed to dealing with. Here, she was much more in her element; and besides, I was still a little flustered by her accusation of my bad manners.

"Old Duskfall." She said finally, looking back at Jhapato, who was peering closely at the two of us. "We hope to reach it within the week."

"A good place, back in the day," Jhapato nodded slowly. He gestured towards the kitchen doorway. "I'm brewing a pot of coffee, if either of you are interested." He folded his hands together and watched us expectantly.

"I'd prefer tea, if you have it, but if not, I think I'm alright for now." I said sheepishly, glancing at Sakura. She nodded, almost imperceptibly.

"I'm not a fan of coffee, so I'm okay." She said, leaning forward. "What do you mean Old Duskfall was a good place back in the day?"

"I have tea," the elderly man assured me. He looked at Sakura. "I lived there for the first thirty-four years of my life. After the downfall of the kingdom, of course, but before it fell into the depths of poverty and ruin." He shook his head sadly, venturing into the kitchen and returning shortly with a mug of steaming tea. I lifted it gratefully to my lips as he disappeared once more and returned minutes later with a mug of coffee, which he tenderly sipped at as he sat down again.

Sakura and I shared a brief glance. I'd heard of the downfall of Old Duskfall. It was one of the major historic events of Horcath, alongside the rising of the Curse and the Havoc Ages. Even lowlifes like me who received no education knew of them.

"Do you think we might be able to find valuable information there?" Sakura inquired, gently pushing her nearly empty plate away from her.

"Depends on what sort of information it is you're wanting to find," Jhapato sipped at his coffee again. "Although yes, I suppose you would. There are lots of very knowledgeable people there." His gaze leveled with mine, and I swallowed nervously as I saw how solemn he was. "There are dark things that take place in that kingdom. It has collapsed into an evil and corrupt place. You would be wise to avoid it."

"Evil and corrupt things are sort of what we're interested in." I was grateful for Sakura speaking, because it gave me a reason to break eye contact with Jhapato. Somehow, the happy warmth that had been there when I'd first seen him had spilled out with his last words.

"The Curse." Jhapato raised an eyebrow, although he didn't say it like a question.

"Yes." I slurped at my tea as Sakura answered. "We're hoping to find someone who can help us learn more about it, and maybe direct us to its source. Do you know of someone who might be helpful?"

"The Curse is nothing to be meddled with, young lady." Jhapato cautioned, his voice hardening. Up until this point, he had been gentle, but it was clear he felt strongly about this.

"We know of the dangers." I said, setting my tea mug down on the table. "We've been faced with them for years. Maybe charging at it head-on like this isn't the best approach, but it's a *new* approach, and if it will bring results, we're willing to risk it. Please, if anyone who may be able to help us comes to mind, we'd like to know." I could practically hear Willa's scolding, telling me to respect my elders, rambling on about how this was no way to speak to your host.

Jhapato's now steely gaze held mine for a long moment. He would break eye contact only to take a drink of his coffee, then meet my eyes again. He looked thoughtful, and I could have sworn he seemed to age ten more years in those minutes. Finally, he nodded once, looking down into the dregs of his coffee.

"Very well. There *is* a woman. Her name is Irina. She doesn't live in one place for very long, and she is well known among the Duskans. *If* you manage to find her, tell her I sent you." He stood up and looked at my half-empty tea mug. "Leave it, when you are finished. I'm going to retire now. Good night, young travelers."

"Good night. Thank you, Jhapato. You've been a great help." Sakura thanked him, and I mumbled it along with her. He put out the candles in the kitchen and climbed the stairs to his room, leaving Sakura and I with a single flickering candle on the dining room table.

"It's late," I said finally, setting my tea mug near her plate. "We should be getting to bed. We'll have breakfast and then find Alchemy and tell him what we've learned first thing in the morning." I stood up, stretching my arms out and groaning as I felt my tired muscles pull taught.

"Since when did you make the plans?" Sakura muttered, although she stood up as well, making her way down the hallway. I followed her, not bothering to answer.

The living room was small and tidy. The sofa looked awkwardly short, and I sighed as I realized my feet would be dangling over the side. Sakura's cot was placed over by the far left wall, far more welcoming than the sofa. I wasn't going to complain, though, because Jhapato had provided both of us with a pillow and a blanket, so I climbed onto the sofa cushions, kicked off my boots, and wriggled beneath the covering.

As the candle from the dining room slowly dwindled down into nothing, the room grew dark and still. The sounds of the world going to sleep filtered in through the walls of the home, and I felt my eyes beginning to droop as I sank farther into the sofa cushions. For the first time in several days, I fell asleep without some part of my body aching with bruises.

21
SAKURA

I wasn't sure how long I lay there, trying and failing to fall asleep on the little cot in Jhapato's living room, but it must have been over an hour. There was something all *wrong* about the situation, and it left me sick to my stomach. Or was it just nervousness? Sadness? I didn't know *what* I was feeling, only that it left my eyes burning with tears and my heart aching for me to slip into unconsciousness. My mind was awhirl with anxious thoughts. Worse, there were *emotional* thoughts threaded in between them. I was barely able to sort out which was which, and it was beginning to give me a headache.

Too much had happened in the past day and a half, and it was all catching up to me at once. Telling Alchemy to get rid of my sword in the Evershifting Forest had been where it started, when this little tear had formed in my heart. Then he had said something, right before we parted ways. What had it been?

If you don't slow down and catch your breath now, you'll be empty of it when the time comes to fight. Don't push yourself too far.

Don't push yourself too far.

It triggered a memory. A painful memory; one that worsened that little rift in my heart.

Don't drive yourself too far, Rura, please. That's all I ask.

"Finn," I whispered into the dark room, feeling a tear slide down the side of my face. Across the room, I could hear Ksega snoring on the sofa. "*Finn.*" I squeezed my eyes shut tight, feeling my chest contract, and hot new tears spill down my cheeks.

Why had I left? Why hadn't I listened to him? Where was he now? Why couldn't I have stayed home, sleeping peacefully until he woke me up for one of his midnight training sessions? I would have given *anything* to be with him now, sluggishly dragging myself out to the dragon stables to fly to our training glade.

"Finnian." A small sob tore from my throat, and I clapped a hand over my mouth. "Finn. *Finnian.*" I couldn't stop thinking his name, over and over again. Soon, it was joined by Gamma's, and then Walter's and Sycamore's, and even Derek's.

Eventually, it became a steady chant of *home*, humming through my mind in an endless whirlwind. The dark room around me seemed to shrink, wrapping its shadows around me in a cold, jarring embrace. Home. *Home. I want to go home. Someone take me home.*

"Sakura?"

The voice made me gasp in surprise, although it was a strangled noise, blending with my sobs. My trembling hand remained firmly over my lips, but my eyes flew open, taking in the dark, blurry room before me. Out of the corner of my eye, I caught a shadow moving closer.

"Hey, you okay? Sakura?" Ksega sat hesitantly a little ways away from my cot, then scooted closer and settled a hand on my shoulder. "Are you crying?"

"I'm sorry." I choked out, my voice thick. "I didn't mean to wake you."

"It's okay. I don't get much sleep anyway." His hand fell away, but he didn't move. After a moment, he asked, "Do you want to talk about it?"

"Mhm." I hummed, trying to calm my breathing. Yes, I did want to talk about it. I wanted to scream and cry and tell him everything, all about my family, all about what had happened to Elixir and Finnian, about why I was here, and how all I wanted was to go back home, to where I was happy. To where I was *safe*.

He waited.

I couldn't say anything. I wanted to. I so badly wanted to tell him, but I couldn't. Instead I lay there, miserable and shaking, small whines and sobs escaping me as I trembled, trying to quiet it by keeping my hand in place. Tears streamed down my face, hot and stinging. They dampened the pillow beneath my head, and matted my hair together, and left sticky trails along my skin.

Still, he waited, silent and motionless. He didn't try to offer comfort, but somehow he didn't need to. He was here, and he was willing to listen. That alone was enough to keep me from slipping too far into the darkness of my own sorrow.

I don't know how long he sat like that, and how long I lay there shaking and crying, but eventually I managed to regain control of my breathing again. I was still shaking, and my throat felt like it was closed up. I wasn't able to find my voice. Shakily, I reached my arm over the side of the cot, my fingers gripping Ksega's sleeve. Almost instantly, his hand lifted to take mine. It was warm and sure.

"I'm still here."

I know. I'm glad. Thank you. I still wasn't able to force myself to speak.

"You know, I miss home, too. There's something about this place that reminds me of it. Quiet nights. Safe nights. Nights with a long, deep sleep after you've had a warm meal and a long day." He spoke softly, his tone gentle. It helped. "It isn't easy, being away for so long. It's fun, when every day brings a new adventure, but it's scary, too." His fingers squeezed mine. "But it's going to be okay. No matter what happens, it will all turn out okay."

More silence, broken only by my whimpering.

Several more minutes passed, our hands clasped together, the sound of a gentle breeze rolling past the house. My breathing slowed to a more normal rhythm, penetrated by high-pitched hiccups. I held my breath, trying to dispel them, but failed each time a new sob rose from my throat. But it was easing away, slowly but surely, and soon enough, I felt my eyelids beginning to droop. I felt my voice return.

"Thank you." I whispered, my eyes already closed.

"Anytime." Ksega squeezed my hand again, then let it go and slowly rose to his feet. "Good night, Sakura."

Before he had finished speaking, I was already asleep.

I woke up to thick, warm sunbeams streaming through the living room window, basking the room in a soft golden glow. Groaning, I slid an elbow beneath my body and pushed myself up into a half-sitting position, squinting and blinking away the grogginess of my sleep. I ran a hand over my face, grimacing as I dragged my fingers through the matted tangles of my hair. I looked around blearily, trying to remember what all I'd done the previous day. I remembered searching for food in the little town by Oracle Lake, failing in my search and then coming into Jhapato's house, and getting onto Ksega for being disrespectful.

Ksega.

I could hear him snoring from across the room, and looking up, I could see him curled up on the sofa, the blanket bunched around his waist, blond hair a disaster. His pillow had fallen to the floor sometime during the night.

My gut twisted as I remembered what had happened between him and me. I had always hated crying in front of others, but in front of people I hardly knew? That was much worse. And to rub salt in the wound, I knew I was going to be stuck facing

Ksega every day until this stupid little quest was over with. Would he think of me any differently now? How had he thought of me to begin with?

I remembered him saying I had a nice smile the night before. It had been unexpected, considering I'd always thought he was too daft to notice anything. But once he'd said it, I remembered other things, small moments where I'd caught him staring, like on the ramp into Brightlock. I remembered not being able to place the way he had looked at me. I was drawn out of my thoughts as I heard the sound of footsteps on the stairs.

"Ksega," I croaked, my throat hoarse. I hadn't had a drink of water for a while. "Ksega, wake up." His only response was another snore.

"Don't worry," the voice came from the hallway entry, and I looked over to see Jhapato standing in the doorway. "He can sleep in. I'll go ahead and start preparing your breakfast." He disappeared again.

Grunting, I dragged myself to my feet, pulling my boots on. I had to go and find Alchemy as soon as I'd eaten, and I intended to bring Ksega with me. Even if I hadn't known him very long, it was already obvious he had a habit of getting himself into trouble.

"Ksega," I crossed the room in a few short strides and shook his shoulder. "Come on, get up." He grunted and pulled the blanket up over his head. "Don't do this right now. You're not a *child*, Ksega," it was my turn to grunt as I tried to yank the blanket away again.

"I'm tired." He grumbled, turning over and pulling the blanket free of my hand.

"So am I. Get *up*." I punched him in the back. He groaned, pulling the blanket down and glaring at me through his flop of hair.

"Why must you be so mean to me?" he grimaced.

"Toughen up. Hurry, we need to eat and then go meet Chem." I used his distraction to pull the blanket away, tossing it onto the floor. "I'll meet you in the dining room. Be quick."

His only response was another grunt, but as I walked away I heard him rising to his feet.

As I stepped into the dining room, pulling my hair up into a messy ponytail as I went, I smelled something sweet coming from the kitchen, and as I took my seat, I saw Jhapato bringing a platter of pancakes out to set on the table.

"That looks delicious," I smiled at him, eyeing the little porcelain jar of hot syrup and the saucer of freshly cut fruit. It reminded me of the Fruit Spring back at home, and I felt another pang of homesickness as I popped one of the blueberries into my mouth.

"Thank you. I've been told they're the best pancakes around." He returned my smile, his eyes lighting up. In more ways than one, he reminded me of Gamma, and it only served to make my heart hurt all the more.

"I'm sure they are." I began to make my own pancake stack on my plate, applying a light portion of syrup and scooping on some fruit pieces.

"I'm going to prepare some tea for your friend, and make some more," Jhapato nodded at the plate. "I doubt it will take long for the two of you to go through them all."

"Thank you." I said as he went back into the kitchen, lifting my fork to cut into my pancake stack.

Ksega walked in, stretching and blinking narrowly at me. He grunted as he relaxed his muscles, running a hand through his disheveled hair. He eyed the pancakes hungrily, then looked up at me and gave me a tired smile.

"Good morning. Feeling better?" instead of taking the seat across from me, like he had the night before, he slid into the chair beside me, helping himself to the remaining pancakes.

"Yeah," I skewered a strawberry and a bite of pancake, stuffing it into my mouth so I didn't have to say anything more to him.

"Here you are," Jhapato returned, placing a glass of water in front of my plate and a mug of tea in front of Ksega's. Looking down at Ksega's plate, I curled my lip in disgust.

"That is *way* too much syrup. Those pancakes are drowning."

"Pancakes are cakes. Cakes are sponges. Sponges soak things up. Therefore, *this*," he gestured at his soggy pancakes. "Is exactly how they're supposed to be eaten. If anything, *yours* are bad. What, do you like eating sand?"

"My pancakes are anything but dry," Jhapato took the seat on the other side of Ksega, serving himself a pile of pancakes. "You'd do well to remember that, boy." His tone was teasing as he took the syrup jug.

There was a long moment of silence as each of us did things with fruit and syrup, then finally Jhapato spoke again.

"You are traveling from Coldmon, but said you are from Wisesol. Have you been on the eastern side of Horcath before?"

"No," Ksega lied, taking another bite of pancake. "We actually came-" he was cut off sharply by a high-pitched scream from outside.

With a panicked look, all three of us jumped to our feet and hurried to look through the blurry window. It was small, and Ksega and I were jostled into each other, shoulders braced together as we tried to get a look at what was happening.

My field of view was minimal, blocked by the smears of grime on the panes and the close proximity of the other houses, but I could see enough to tell that the village was in a panic.

People running, children screaming, doors and window shutters being slammed left and right. In the distance, I could hear something else screeching, something inhuman, accompanied by a faint sound of thunder. I frowned. No, not thunder. Hoofbeats.

"Stay inside," Jhapato ordered, hobbling towards the door. He looked back at us, brow furrowed, eyes stern, then continued out of the house. As soon as we heard the door bang shut, Ksega and I looked at each other.

"We're going out there." I said.

"Absolutely." He agreed. "Let me go grab my bow."

I had to go back into the living room as well to grab my flame-sword, which I had left by my cot while I'd slept. As Ksega fastened his quiver to his belt, I let my eirioth flow up to the surface, twitching and eager to be set free in my flame-sword. From beyond the walls of Jhapato's house, there were more cries of alarm and animalistic noises echoing around the village.

"Hurry," I said as I pushed the door open. Ksega was right behind me as I skipped down the steps and hurried to the middle of the road, looking around to find the source of the commotion.

People were running and shouting, some of them in incomprehensible gibberish, others ordering people about, instructing them to locate weapons or some way of defending themselves. Women and children were ushered inside as men came out of their homes brandishing curved knives and sharpened farming tools.

"What's happening?" I asked the nearest person, a boy hardly our age clutching a long wooden pole sharpened to a point.

"A runeboar attack. You should go back inside." He turned and ran in the direction of the ruckus. I looked up at Ksega, but paused when I saw his expression. His head was tilted to the side, brow pinched in concentration. After a few seconds, I couldn't take it.

"Ksega?"

"They aren't just normal runeboars." He said slowly, squinting at the other end of the road. "There are at least two, probably more." I started to step forward, but he grabbed my arm. "And they're Cursed."

A strand of ice spurred through my veins, chilling me to the bone. That word has always left me in a place of fear, more so after the death of my parents and my sister, but this was something entirely new. At home, I volunteered to help defend my home against the Curse during the night. But that was fighting against Cursed birds and raccoons and the occasional raptor.

Runeboars weren't the most strong-willed of beasts, and there were reports of them being Cursed throughout the history of the Curse's existence, but it was rare. I'd never faced any Cursed beast any larger than a raptor, aside from Elixir, but with the dragon there had been other people there to assist.

"Where-" I began, my voice several notes higher than normal, but I was cut off by the sharp squeal of a runeboar as it barreled around the corner of the road, charging towards us.

Bits of dirt and clay flew out behind it, dug up by its jagged hooves. It was an ugly thing, covered in thick, patchy black hair and oozing green wounds. Sprouting from all over its head were gnarly tusks, curving all around its face and protecting its eyes and muzzle. The eyes themselves were a sickly green, wild and blinded by their craze for destruction.

It was stumbling and lurching and approaching us at an alarming speed. My legs locked up, as if I were knee-deep in mud, like I had been back in the Waste Ponds of Clawbreak. My heart seemed to freeze for a moment, my whole body stiffening in terror.

I distantly heard someone shout my name over the thunder of hoofbeats, and seconds before the runeboar gored me with its tusks, I was jerked to the side, rolling onto the dusty ground and over someone else.

Gasping, I landed with an *oof* on top of Ksega, the tip of his bow digging into my hip. I grimaced, looking over my shoulder. The runeboar crashed into one of the houses, ruthless tusks snapping timber and tearing through the fabric of furniture as it sloppily wheeled around to face us again.

"Thanks," I gasped, looking back down at Ksega. He grinned, although it was pained.

"Anytime. Now get off. You're pushing my bow into my side." He grunted as I rolled off of him.

I lifted my flame-sword as I dragged myself back to my feet, backing farther into the little side road we were on as the Cursed runeboar caught us in its sights again. Ksega staggered to his feet and followed me as I ran to the next central road.

The boar was undeterred by the narrow alley. It was easily twice as wide as the opening, but with one jerk of its head, the buildings on either side gained new holes in their corners. The runeboar was slowed by the debris, but forged on through, sending splinters and slivers of wood flying in all directions in its haste to get to us.

"Come on, this way," Ksega grabbed my hand and tugged me towards another alley, out of sight of the runeboar, but it wouldn't protect us for long. Runeboars had a keen sense of smell, and sharp eyesight, despite the tusks that impeded their vision.

"Can't you shoot it?" I yelled, rubbing my thumb over my flame-sword. I didn't want to call my eirioth now, although it was yearning to be set free. I wasn't going to burn any of these houses down if I could avoid it. There were people that lived there, and these runeboars were causing enough damage to their homes as it was.

"I won't be able to get a clear shot with it on our tail. Can you distract it?" he released my hand and slid around the corner of the house on our right, trying to zig-zag between the buildings. His legs were longer than mine, and I was running out of breath as I struggled to keep up with him.

"If I can, are you sure you can make the shot?" I panted, practically jumping to stay alongside him.

"Pretty sure- *watch out*!" he yelped and jumped backwards as the runeboar appeared in front of us. No, this one was different: it was missing an eye, and silver-green blood ran down its leg. From behind us there was another squeal, and I looked over my shoulder to see the first runeboar shoving its way into the alley.

"Stay back," I yelled, urging my eirioth into my hand. It shot out like an angry whip from my flame-sword, coiling and twisting and searching before solidifying into the trustworthy beam I was accustomed to.

I brought the spitting blade down in an arc towards the boar in front of us. It huffed and dug its hooves into the ground, tossing its head as it prepared to charge. My pulse thundered in my ears, nearly as loud as the hoofbeats of the runeboar behind us. My heart was racing, jumping up and down and all around my ribcage.

"Better do something fast," Ksega said beside me, sounding breathless. "This one's coming up quick."

With a grunt, I stepped close to the boar in front of us and swung. The boar's face was mostly protected by the thick rods of tusk that curled and twisted around its head, but even though they could deflect most blades and even arrows, they provided no defense against the flexible blade of fire I wielded.

As soon as the flames came in contact with the tusks, they warped around them, hungrily seeking the coarse fur and tender flesh beneath.

The boar shrieked and reared back, hooves flailing around so recklessly one of them nearly collided with my chest. It tossed its head, backing away and trying to shove its burned face into the dusty earth to relieve the pain, but its own tusks prevented it.

"Let's go!" now it was my turn to grab Ksega's hand. He had been staring at the boar charging at us from behind, and I pulled him away just as it stumbled through one last wall of debris. It roared past us, slamming into its blinded companion so that both of them tumbled to the ground.

"Shoot fast," I said, feeling my eirioth flame flare again as I spotted a third runeboar rounding the corner at the end of the road. This one was uglier and even more afflicted by the Curse than the first two, with its gnarly tusks turning an ashy black, and the flesh of its haunches peeling away to reveal sticky bone.

Beside me, Ksega tugged his hand free of mine and lifted his bow. He flicked an arrow from his quiver, knocked it, and pulled it back to full draw in one fluid, practiced motion. For a brief moment, his eyes slid shut, then they snapped open and the arrow flew. It was so quick I couldn't track it with my own eyes, but I saw where it hit one of the fallen boars, burrowing through the thick fur and burying itself deep into the flesh.

The boar let out a horrid screech, louder than any I'd heard thus far, and slumped lifeless to the ground, half on top of its brother, which was trying desperately to wriggle free.

"Behind us!" I yelled, my panicked eyes flying between the two remaining boars.

Ksega wheeled around, facing the oncoming boar. It was throwing its head around and running. He drew his bow and fired another arrow, but it ricocheted off the tusks into the dirt. He groaned.

"I can't hit him from head on. Can you draw him to the side?"

"No time. Watch out!" my power surged through me, causing the flame-sword to elongate into a giant whip. I twisted my wrist, letting the fire slither forward to slap the hide of the boar nearest to us, which had almost escaped from beneath its companion. It screamed and leapt away, running to the other end of the road before skidding around to charge us again.

"You take that one. I'll find a way to get this one," Ksega darted towards the first charging boar, the one he had shot at, and disappeared down a side alleyway. The boar squealed and turned sharply after him. Two other men from the village followed them, carrying a pitchfork and a spear.

I was about to argue against his decision, but he was already gone. The boar in front of me was charging full-speed, throwing its head and making all sorts of terrible noises, driven by its fury and pain. I brought my flame-sword — although it was really a flame-whip now — closer, letting it coil like a giant snake around my body, poised to attack at my mildest whim.

I knew my eirioth was draining my strength, and fast. I could already feel my muscles weakening from the effort of keeping the magic alive. But my fear and determination alone were enough to keep it steady, and I braced myself for the approaching boar's arrival. I didn't have a clear plan, but there was one in the works, and it would have to do for now.

As the boar came up to me, I danced to the side and snaked out with my whip, weaving it around the horns and letting it tighten around them. The flame had almost no true substance to it, so it would do little trying to lasso the boar, but the flames were terrifyingly hot, and with a jerk of my hand, it burned clean through the bones, letting the curved points fall to the dusty earth, crumbling with ash.

The boar stumbled, screaming from the pain, and rolled to the ground, what remained of its tusks burrowing into the earth. I ran after it, reeling the flame-sword in before driving it forward into the runeboar's heart, careful to steer clear of its flailing hooves.

As soon as it went limp, lifeless, I dropped my hold on the eirioth. Sweat poured down my face and neck, making my grip on the flame-sword's iron handle loose. The flames vanished in a wisp of smoke. My legs shook like gelatin, and I could feel the tremor in my weakened muscles. My heart was still racing, and the back of my throat burned from a lack of hydration.

I was tempted to stumble my way back to Jhapato's in hopes of seeking some water, but then another crash echoed from the direction Ksega had run in, and it was coming my way. I stood up straight, my muscles tensing, and moments later, all the way down the road, I saw Ksega sprinting full speed out of an alley.

He was making to go across to the next, but there was another roar and a scream from that side, and I felt my heart sink as I realized there was yet another runeboar after him. He tripped over his own feet as he ran in my direction, veering towards one of the alleys. Two runeboars burst from either side of the road, sending debris from the narrow alleyways soaring into the air. They pounded after Ksega, and, for a reason I'm still unsure of, I started to run towards them.

Something was off about Ksega's gait. He was favoring one leg, and as I ran closer — yet still dreadfully far away — my heart jumped to see that there was a trail of blood running down from his thigh.

"Ksega!" I screamed, my voice hoarse. The runeboars would catch him.

I could see the silhouettes of other villagers chasing the boars, trying in vain to catch them before they reached Ksega. It was no use. None of us were close enough to save him. I felt bile rise in my throat as I staggered along the road, trying to revive enough strength to call my eirioth back.

Ksega was losing momentum, and before I knew it, he fell.

It felt like the wind had been knocked out of me as I saw him crash into the dust in front of someone's porch, trying feebly to pull himself farther away from the charging beasts. It would be no use. They were too close. He was as good as dead.

Someone cried out as the first boar reached him, sure its hooves would trample him. I felt my chest burst with panic at the thought of seeing him killed, crushed beneath the runeboar. I waited for a scream from him, one of pain and panic, and the knowledge that this was the end. And a scream came. It was a scream of pain, and a scream of panic. It was a scream that marked the end of a life. But not the end of Ksega's.

With wide eyes, I jolted to a halt, hardly believing what I saw.

Jutting from the porch, sharpened to deadly points, and forming a protective barrier around the slumped body of the boy beneath them, were giant thorns. One of them had gone clean through the runeboar, and the end of it was coated in and dripping silvery-green blood. Beyond the tangle of thorns, I could see Ksega shifting around.

I would have run to his aid, but there was a second runeboar, frightened by the sudden appearance of the thorns, and now targeting its rage at me. I tried to call my eirioth, but all I could manage was a small spark. I was too exhausted to defend myself. The boar barreled towards me, curving tusks ready to run me clean through. I had no way of escape. I was too tired to fight, too tired to run. Too tired to accept anything but the death that was running at me.

Before it hit me, someone darted out of the nearest alleyway. Whoever it was, they hit the boar from the side, and hard enough that the two of them were sent rolling into the closest building. The wall splintered and groaned, giving way to the top level of the house.

As my mysterious savior rose to his feet, I knew who it was immediately. I could tell by the height alone, if not the clothes I recognized as the very ones I'd selected for him. He caught me gaping at him and gave me a brief nod, then gripped the runeboars horns with his gloved hands and twisted. One of the tusks snapped right off. Beyond him, one of the villagers gasped, gawking at the stranger.

The other tusk didn't budge, and the runeboar took its chance, swinging its head violently. Alchemy was sent hurtling across the road, hitting the opposite house with a resounding *crack* before falling to the ground. He landed easily on his feet, racing forward again to take on the aggravated runeboar.

He wasted no time, flicking free one of his smith tooth daggers and driving it directly into the runeboar's skull, just between the eyes. The creature screamed its dismay as he retracted the blade, sprinting away down the alley he'd come from.

Moments later, the whole road was silent. Four dead runeboars and, as far as I could tell, no dead humans. There were close to twenty villagers gathered around, but more were appearing by the second, coming to help those who were injured.

"Ksega," I muttered under my breath, taking shaky steps to the thorny cage. I let myself sag onto my knees to peer through the gaps. I could just make out his face, dirt-stained and paler than usual, eyes and mouth closed.

"Ksega!" I hissed, punching a fist against one of the thorns. It was nearly as thick as the sea wraith that had attacked *Orvyn* on our way to Brightlock.

His eyes opened.

"Hey, you need to take these thorns away," I said, looking for any gaps in the wood that someone could crawl through. "We need to get help to you."

He groaned, looking up at the thorns around him. His blue eyes widened as he took them in, looking them up and down, then craning his neck to peer at the base of all of them: the porch of the house he had fallen next to.

"*I* did that?" he coughed, his voice scratchy and dry.

"Who else?" I rolled my eyes. "Can't you undo it?"

He shook his head weakly. "Can't. No strength." He coughed again, his eyes sliding shut.

"He's hurt," a man appeared by my shoulder, his clothes smeared with Cursed blood. "His leg-"

"I know. I'll get him out. Everyone stand back." I stumbled backwards, lifting my flame-sword once more.

One more time. Just for a few seconds, that's all I need. I closed my eyes, took a deep breath, and felt the last of my strength surge forward into a steady eirioth flame. I opened my eyes, stepping forward and slicing at the thorns. The flames caught and erupted upward, only burning the top halves of the thorns.

Seconds later, my flame-sword fell from my hand, thumping to the ground. I followed it, collapsing in a heap at the base of the thorns. The eirioth flame died instantly, leaving the charred remains of the thorns to be knocked away by the villagers.

"Traveler," a somewhat familiar voice sounded in my ear, and I forced my eyes open. It was Jhapato. "Here. Drink." He lifted a cup to my lips, and I gratefully sipped the cold water. "Who was that man? The one who saved you? Do you know him?" he looked in the direction Alchemy had run. "He must have sustained serious injuries from hitting that house."

I shook my head wearily, looking back towards Ksega. With the thorns crumbling to ashes, the villagers were retrieving him from the center. He was either like me, and very near to unconsciousness, or he was already there.

"No." I croaked. "I don't know who he was." I closed my eyes, feeling myself slowly slipping away into a deep sleep. Jhapato said something else, but whatever it was, I would never know.

22
SAKURA

I woke up on the cot I had slept on the night before, dressed in the same grubby clothes I'd worn during the runeboar fight, but minus my belt and boots. A headache pulsed behind my eyes, making me dizzy as I sat up. I groaned, squinting around the room. It must have been late evening, judging by the angle of the sunlight coming through the window, which meant I had been asleep for several hours. That, or for more than a day. I furrowed my brow as I tried to remember what had happened.

The chaos of the runeboar fight made my head spin, and the throbbing ache worsen. I grimaced as I powered through it, vaguely remembering Ksega's bloodied leg and the sudden appearance of the jutting thorns. I looked across the living room and saw Ksega's bag and his bow and quiver of arrows, but there was no sign of the boy himself. The blanket he'd slept under before was neatly folded and set beside the pillow, which showed no signs of use since that morning.

Grunting, I forced myself up and onto my feet. I couldn't see my belt or boots anywhere, but Jhapato was bound to know where they'd gotten to. For now, I was more concerned about where Ksega was, and what condition he was in. He had undoubtedly lost a lot of blood from that wound, and must have been plenty tired besides from the chase of the runeboars.

As I rose to my full height, I gasped, surprised at how sore I was. Inwardly, I could feel the emptiness, the utter lack of motivation and mental strength, all of it drained by my eirioth. Outwardly, I could feel the strain in my muscles, the burning tension in my shoulders and down my back. It felt like I was on fire from the inside out. This happened often after I overexerted my eirioth, which was rare, and it always left me feeling dehydrated and achy for at least another two days.

Grumbling to myself, I stumbled down the hallway, peering into the dining room and kitchen. They were both empty, but I saw two sets of boots by the door. I recognized one as my own, and while I'd never made it a habit to memorize peoples' shoes, I knew that the second pair were Ksega's, so he was definitely somewhere in the house.

I'd never gone upstairs before, but I could hear noises coming from up there. Just *looking* at the stairs made the muscles in my legs sore, but I forced myself to brace for the pain and started to climb. When I was about halfway up the staircase, Jhapato appeared out of a door on the landing.

"You're awake." He commented. "Your friend is in here," he gestured towards the door he had just come out of. "Try to wake him. I'll make some soup."

I nodded and mumbled my thanks as I reached the top of the stairs, stepping past him and carefully opening the door. Jhapato began to descend the stairs as I clicked the door closed behind me.

The room was relatively small. There was a wash basin in one corner off to the side, a large bed on the far wall with an armchair and a bedside table beside it, and a small wardrobe. Aside from that, the only decoration was the set of drapes on either side of the window.

Lying in the bed and sleeping fitfully was Ksega, his sweat-beaded brow twitching every so often. He wasn't wearing a shirt, and while the bed sheets covered most of his body, I could still see the perspiration glistening on his neck and shoulders. His hair was a dampened mop, plastered to his forehead.

I settled myself into the armchair beside him, reaching forward to gently push the hair back away from his eyes. He grunted, pulling his face away, then angling it towards me as his eyes opened. They seemed a duller shade of blue than normal, which made me more upset than I'd expected. Why was I so worried about the state of his health?

He's all I've got. I pursed my lips, reaching out and taking his hand. His palm was clammy with sweat, but I didn't let go, lacing our fingers together. *At least for now, it's just us and Chem.*

"Jhapato's making soup," I whispered, hardly daring to speak louder, partially because he might have a headache similar to mine, and partially because my throat was so dry I could barely manage any louder. "He'll probably bring it up for you."

He blinked at me, moving his head in an almost imperceptible nod. The movement seemed to cause him pain, and his eyes closed again. I wondered how he was going to force himself up into a sitting position to eat his soup.

I would have spoken to him more, afraid to see him fall asleep again, but his breathing seemed to have eased a little, and I didn't want to disturb any moment of peace he was able to capture. My gaze trailed down to his leg. There was a bulge beneath the sheets, clearly indicating some heavy bandaging. How bad had the wound been? Who had treated them? Did any of these villages have Talons to help with their sick and wounded?

The questions were making my headache worse, so I forced them away, trying to just remain thankful that we were both alive. It only served to remind me of why every moment spent in this village could result in more deaths across the world. Sighing, I leaned forward and rested my head on the bed. I hated when my mind became my own worst enemy.

What we were doing was important. It was going to change lives, and more importantly, it was going to save them. But the only way to succeed was to make sure our lives themselves were safe. Alchemy had been right. I couldn't keep running without taking breaks to catch my breath. But the longer I took to take those breaks, the weaker my muscles became, the thinner my resolve.

A fight without breath is a self-served death sentence, but a fight without determination yields an equally grim result.

A gentle touch on my shoulder made me jolt upright in the chair, but I relaxed as I saw that it was only Jhapato.

"Your soup." He had placed two steaming bowls of delicious-smelling soup on the bedside table. He smiled kindly at me. "Eat what you can. Make sure he eats, too. He needs it." He patted me on the back and then left the room again.

There was a grunt from the bed, and I looked back to see Ksega watching me. His gaze went down to our clasped hands, and I loosened my grip, realizing I had squeezed when Jhapato had woken me. *Woken* me?

I used my free hand to rub my eyes.

"I guess I fell asleep again," I muttered, looking over at the soup, then at Ksega. "You should try to sit up. It'll be easier to eat that way." He looked at me for a long moment, then slowly shook his head. I tried again, my voice sterner. "You need to eat. Trust me, you'll feel better. Come on, up." I let go of his hand and leaned forward, readjusting his pillows so he could sit comfortably. His only movement was that of letting his head flop onto the bed.

I let him lay there for a moment while I shifted my chair around, angling so that I could face him more fully and access my soup easier, then I leaned over and poked him firmly in the chest. He groaned, glaring at me.

"Sit up." I commanded. He sighed, swallowed, and started to shrug his shoulders, shimmying back against the pillows. It took him a minute, and lots of gasps of shock and pain, but eventually he righted himself and slumped into the pillows, looking expectantly at the soup bowl.

I handed him his bowl of soup, and he clumsily accepted it. He struggled to lift the first few bites, but eventually he seemed to have worked out his own system, so my nerves unwound enough for me to stomach my own soup. After a few minutes, Jhapato returned to the room with one of the dining room chairs, setting it beside mine and settling himself into it.

"We lost two men." He began. I closed my eyes. "They were quick deaths, and no others were injured aside from you and a young child. He'll probably lose his arm, but he'll be alright. How do you feel?" he asked Ksega, who was slurping his soup broth.

"Sore. My leg feels like it's on fire." He croaked, then grimaced. "*All of me* feels like it's on fire." He was still sweating a lot.

"The runeboar's tusks were coated in all sorts of grime and bacteria, and it being Cursed undoubtedly did nothing to help the situation. The cut wasn't very bad, but it became infected quickly," Jhapato explained. "There is a Talon who lives in the neighboring Colony, and she came to tend to the wound. She said you would feel sick for a day or so, but would heal up quickly. It may leave you with a limp if you overexert yourself too fast." He turned to me now, his face solemn. "I know you wanted to keep moving quickly, but it would be best if you stayed here a while longer for him to heal up. We've even received word that the traveling performers will be visiting the Stargazing Colonies in a few days. Why don't you stay and see them? It will be a good break for you."

"I'm up for that," Ksega rasped, looking at me hopefully. I pressed my lips into a thin line, debating.

"The Curse is growing." I said softly. "It's growing fast. A month ago, it wouldn't have been able to corrupt so many runeboars at once. The longer we sit around here, the more people there are that die because of it." I set my soup bowl down and put my face in my hands, closing my eyes, trying to think it all through. "If we can destroy the Curse, we'll be saving thousands. Nobody else has to be lost."

"Your friend must heal," Jhapato's hand settled onto my shoulder again, and I looked up at him. "I understand your urgency, and I can see that the Curse has caused you pain." He squeezed my shoulder. "Revenge will not bring you peace. Violence and destruction will never sew the tear within you." He let me go and stood up, leaving the room. I stared at the door for a long moment after he'd left, my mind turning.

I wasn't out for revenge. I didn't want violence and destruction. I wanted justice; for my family, and for all the other families that had been torn apart by the Curse. I wanted it for Elixir and for the two men that had been killed by the runeboars.

"If you really want to," Ksega's voice sucked my attention back to the present. I glanced at him. "I think we can keep moving. But I'll slow us down."

"I'm not leaving you here."

"I wasn't suggesting it." He sighed, groaning and leaning back into his pillows. I took his soup bowl and set it beside mine. He shifted around a couple times, trying to find a position where his breath wasn't an aching rasp. I waited until he found a way to lay comfortably, then leaned forward, elbows on knees, and asked in a soft voice,

"Then what are you suggesting?"

He was quiet for a long moment, but I knew he was awake. He was staring up at the ceiling, his gaze flitting around as if trying to memorize the patterns in the grain of the wood. When he spoke again, his voice was little more than a hoarse whisper.

"Why don't we stay?" he wouldn't look at me, even though I wanted him to. I needed him to see how desperately I needed us to keep going. I needed him to understand that lying around and doing nothing wasn't an option. I needed him to see the fear and the determination that swelled in every word I spoke and every action I took. And maybe that was the very reason he wouldn't look.

"We can rest and heal. I'm not the only one that needs it." He closed his eyes for a brief moment, then opened them again and looked at me. "Last night, when you were crying, you were saying a name. Finn." His gaze softened, concern and compassion flooding into his eyes. I hated to see it.

"My brother." I turned away, unable to hold his gaze. "He's still in Carlore." I sighed and stood up, pinching my eyes closed for a few seconds as I swayed, unsteady on my feet. "I'm going to go find Chem. I'll be back in a couple hours." I started for the door, only stopping to look back at him once, but his eyes had closed again, so I left and went to find the skeleton.

Jhapato stopped me on my way out, but I would only accept a drink of water, and none of his warnings not to venture too far. Whatever concerns he had for my well being, they were nothing compared to the need for answers that coursed through me.

I headed directly south, marching towards the very distant jags of cliffs. I knew the border Brightlock and Old Duskfall shared was a thread of cliffs and sudden drops, all the way to the southeastern corner of Brightlock, which was marked by the tall, dark Shattered Mountains. Alchemy had said he would stay near to that border, far enough out of the way that it was unlikely anyone would find him.

It was a narrow stretch of Brightlock between the Evershifting Forest and the Shattered Mountains, and I doubted Alchemy would try to find a place to hide in either of those locations. I walked for a long while, keeping a relatively straight course of travel, and looking out for any sign of the Cursed skeleton.

My legs complained with every struggling step, but I refused to let it show. I didn't want to believe what Ksega had said. I didn't want to admit that I needed to rest and heal as well, even though I knew in the back of my mind that I did. I had to keep moving. I couldn't be sure why, but I had to keep going, constantly moving forward until this was over. There was no time to rest until the Curse was gone.

In the end, it happened to be Alchemy who found me, seemingly materializing out of thin air by my side. I nearly kicked him when he did, and had I had the strength to call my eirioth, I may have singed his clothes into nothing. What remained of his clothes, that is.

The runeboar's struggle had caused a considerable amount of damage to the shirt. His cloak had some small tears from being thrown against the house, but nothing as severe as the wide rips through his tunic. It wouldn't have been very noticeable, considering his ribs were black, except for the painfully obvious fact that there were veins of glowing green winding their way through the bones.

"There you are," I gasped, a little surprised at how out of breath I was.

"I've been following you for a while." Alchemy's gravelly voice was a familiar sound, although I could still feel the hairs on the back of my neck stand up, and a chill run down my spine as he spoke. "I'm surprised you didn't notice sooner." He leaned closer, examining me. His hood was up, making his grinning skull all the more eerie. "Are you feeling alright?"

"I'm fine." I shoved him away, gulping in a much-needed breath of fresh, wild air. It helped to calm my nerves, although they were still knotted in a panicked jumble.

"If you say so." Alchemy pulled his hood back, looking back the way I'd come. "And how fares our little archer?"

"He'll be fine. The cut got infected, and he's a little sick, but he'll be okay."

"In how long?"

"A couple days."

"So we're staying."

"No." I spoke before I really thought about it. "Yes-" I paused, groaned, and shook my head, anxiously running my thumbs over my knuckles. "I don't know." I looked up at him, considering. He waited patiently. "He says . . . he thinks we both need to take a rest. He thinks we're both hurting, even if it's not in the same way. Physically, that is." I took a breath, as if to say more, then hesitated. What was I even trying to say here?

"And do you?"

"Do I what?"

"Need to rest." Alchemy gestured at me with his gloved hand. "I can see the outward effects the fight with the runeboars has caused you. But more than that, I can see the inward effects." He reached forward and poked me in the shoulder. "The Curse is a personal enemy of yours-"

"It's a personal enemy of everyone's." I grumbled, but he went on as if I'd said nothing.

"-and you are steadfastly determined to do everything you can to put an end to it. The question is why. What are you hoping to accomplish by doing this?"

"Saving people. Stopping all the death." I rolled my eyes as I answered. Wasn't this obvious?

"For who?"

"What do you mean for who?!" I scowled at him. "I knew you would only give me riddles. Why do I even bother?"

"Whose death are you trying to stop? Everyone else's? Or yours?" he leaned closer, towering nearly two feet over me.

"I don't know if you hadn't noticed," I spat. "But I'm not *dying*. If anything, Ksega's closer to death than I am right now!"

"And *that* is the problem!" Alchemy boomed. I flinched away from him, shocked at how loud he was. "The people close to you are always at risk. You know that. You feel it, and you feel it in *here*." He jabbed his finger at me again, poking me directly over my heart. "You no longer care about yourself. Your own safety is nothing when that of your family is at stake. You are risking everything, and you are acting careless, because you're *afraid*. Without them, you are nothing. Without them, you are as good as dead. It isn't your own life you are fighting for, because it is *them* you are fighting for." He crossed his arms, his empty eye sockets seemingly boring through my skull. "*Why?*"

I shook my head, at a loss for words. A lump had risen in my throat, preventing me from speaking. I could feel hot tears pricking at the back of my eyes. I could feel my heartbeat, pulsing in my chest. I could feel my eirioth, squirming deep within the well of my own consciousness, sensing my unease.

"What else?" I finally whispered. "What else is there that's worth fighting for? You're right. Without them, I'm nothing. Why do I have to worry about myself when, without them, there's no self to worry about?" I shook my head again, closing my eyes and dropping my head. "I have to keep going. Don't you see? There's nothing that can stop me."

"Without them, you're nothing." Alchemy's voice had softened. "But have you ever considered that, without you, *they* are nothing?" he reached out and gripped my shoulder, squeezing until I looked up into those dark, endless pits of his eye sockets. "There are people who love you, Ironling. People right in front of you, and you can't see it, because you are so *afraid* to see it. Don't make the same mistakes I did." His voice, for the first time since I'd met him, broke. "Don't turn your back on them because of your fear. Let them *share* your fear." He dropped his arm, rising to his full height again. I kept my gaze down, trained on the yellowing grass beneath our feet. "Go back to the village. Stay the night. Get some sleep. We can leave tomorrow if you're both feeling up to it."

"But-"

"There is no rush. People live, and people die. Not even the absence of the Curse will change that. Now go."

I took another breath, prepared to argue, and then realized all the vigor to do so had left me. With a sigh, I turned and began to trudge back to the village. After hardly twenty paces, I looked back, but Alchemy had vanished once again. I didn't have the energy to be surprised. I barely had the energy to keep walking, to keep thinking. To keep caring. And perhaps that was exactly what he meant.

Almost as soon as I got back to Jhapato's house, I laid down on my cot and fell asleep.

It was late afternoon when I woke up again, and I could hear voices coming from the dining room. One of them was the sandpapery voice of Jhapato, but the other was one I didn't recognize. A woman's.

Sliding my legs off the cot, I rubbed the sleepiness from my eyes and stretched my arms, surprised to feel as refreshed as I did. I stood and crept to the edge of the hallway, close enough that I could hear what was being said, but not near enough for them to see me.

"-is very ambitious. I'm worried about them." That was Jhapato.

"They are on their own journey. You have provided them with the hospitality and kindness they need to keep going." That was the woman. Her voice had the same soft lilt that those of Freetalon possessed. I had heard it only a handful of times before, and some of the Talons I'd met had lost the accent — Ksega's red-haired friend, for example, who had a more country-fairing accent from her time spent in Wisesol — but it was unmistakable where this woman was from.

"And I'm afraid that's exactly what they plan to do. Keep going." I could practically hear Jhapato shaking his head. "There may be nothing I can do to stop them."

"It's alright." The woman spoke gently, almost more so than Jhapato, which was impressive. "I can help the boy heal more, and give him something to help with the pain on the road. The best you can do now is provide them with a more comfortable means of transportation."

I didn't bother to hear any more than that. I slipped back to my cot and gathered my things into a neat pile. I already knew Jhapato would oblige to any requests we made, but I didn't want to bleed him dry of his resources. One of the best ways to do that would be to get out of his hair and keep moving. If the Talon was willing and able to give Ksega better health, maybe he and Alchemy would both be more willing to leave sooner.

As I was gathering my things, Jhapato came into the living room, and I looked up to greet him with a smile. I was a little surprised to find how genuine it was. That nap had done wonders for my mood.

"That Talon that treated your friend is here. She's willing to help the process along as much as possible, if you insist on leaving soon." He spoke in a sad voice, clearly taking note of my packing.

"I think we may leave tomorrow, actually. If that's alright with you." My smile widened just a little. "I've found I have quite a sweet tooth for your pancakes." His own smile was one of warmth.

"Wonderful. You may want to go tell your friend. He's been looking rather pensive all day."

I nodded, already rising to my feet to go see Ksega. I knew he'd been thinking about what I was talking about with Alchemy, and that couldn't have been giving him much time to get the rest he needed.

As I walked past the dining room, I saw a tall, elegant woman with beautiful blond hair with a mug of coffee, sitting with her legs crossed. She smiled kindly at me as I walked past, and I returned it briefly as I took the stairs two at a time.

Ksega was still sitting up when I came into the room, but it was without the aid of the pillows now. He was still shirtless, and I could still see beads of sweat on his neck and forehead, but he no longer looked like he had just come back from a midday swim. The best thing, though, and the thing that made my mood lift even further, was that the vibrancy had returned to his deep blue eyes, and he grinned broadly when I entered.

"You seem in high spirits," I commented as I came to sit beside the bed again.

"As do you." I noticed he was now sitting cross-legged. He must have seen, and said, "That Talon came back. She helped with the infection some more. It's mostly gone, and the only thing that's left is the wound itself." His smile widened to reveal all his teeth, and I couldn't help but snort at how ridiculous it looked. "I'll be as good as new by tomorrow evening."

"Great. That's when we plan to leave."

"Really?" his eyebrows raised. "We're staying another night?"

"Just one." I rolled my shoulders, trying to loosen some of the knots in my muscles. "You were right. We both need some time to rest." *And think.* I could still hear Alchemy's voice echoing in the back of my mind, but I didn't want to dwell on what he'd said until later. Those were after-dinner thoughts. For now, I could smell something rich and delicious coming from downstairs, and my stomach made sure I knew I smelled it, too.

"I'm tired of sitting in this bed doing nothing." Ksega swung his legs around toward me and tossed the sheets aside. The bandaging beneath his pants had thinned, which I took as a good sign. "Do you see my shirt around here anywhere?" he looked around the room, but there were no clothes in sight.

"We'll find you one. Come on, I smell dinner cooking." I stood up and headed for the door, holding it open for Ksega as he limped along behind me. "You'd better be faster than that tomorrow," I said as we started down the stairs.

"I'm sure I will be."

Jhapato and his Talon friend welcomed us into the dining room, and Jhapato fetched Ksega his shirt — which had been thoroughly cleaned — before returning to the kitchen to finish dinner.

"I'm Elana," the Talon introduced herself as Ksega and I took our seats around the table. "I've heard quite a story about you two." Her green gaze rested on me for a long moment. "An eirioth-mage and a . . . bering-mage?" her brows pinched together in confusion as she faced Ksega. He cleared his throat awkwardly and nodded. "Peculiar. I've never heard of a bering-mage being able to bend wood before."

Neither had I, now that I thought about it. I looked sidelong at Ksega, but he had found a sudden fascination in the wood of the table.

"You were both quite heroic, you know," Elana went on, taking the hint that Ksega wasn't willing to speak right now. "Those runeboars were no small matter to deal with."

"Cursed animals rarely are." I pointed out.

"True," she smirked. "And yet the two of you managed to kill four of them all on your own."

I was tempted to point out that we'd only killed three, but there was little point in bringing Alchemy into the conversation. I didn't want her or Jhapato asking any more questions about the mysterious, tall figure that had appeared just in time to save me from being trampled.

"Were there only those four?" Ksega asked, looking up at last, and only because Jhapato had entered with a plate of roast.

"No," he said as he began to carve it, setting a few slices on everyone's plate before retrieving two other dishes from the kitchen: a mash of potatoes and some cobs of corn. "There were five." He smiled at the two of us. "It took three men from the village to kill just one. That proves quite a lot about you two."

Ksega and I said nothing as we dug into the meal. We hadn't eaten anything since the pancakes that morning. This was easily the best meal either of us had had in several days, and we were eager to eat our fill of it.

"Do you plan to move on soon?" Elana asked, eating her own plate of food much slower than us.

Ksega's eyes darted to me, but I ignored it, answering, "Tomorrow, probably. If Ksega is feeling well enough."

"I'll be fine." He mumbled through a mouthful of potato.

"I'm sure he will be," Elana smiled demurely at the two of us. There was something irritably calm about her demeanor. "But just in case, I'll send you with some tonics to help with any pain you may have while traveling."

"And I'll provide you with horses." Jhapato pitched in. "There's no need for the two of you to walk all the way to Old Duskfall."

"It's a generous offer," I said. "But we probably won't be able to get the horses through the desert with us."

"I could go with you," Elana offered. Ksega and I glanced at each other, sharing the same thought.

"We'll be alright on foot." Ksega replied, looking back at the Talon. "Thank you, but you've already done more than enough for us," he directed the last bit at Jhapato.

The Duskan nodded, and nothing more was said for the remainder of the meal. I was grateful for it, because it meant I didn't need to speak, which gave me full permission to stuff my face.

23
KSEGA

I could tell Sakura was distracted with something all throughout dinner, and even more so when it was time for us to go to sleep. I'd learned I was sleeping in Jhapato's bed, and insisted he take it for the night. I would be fine to return to the sofa now that my leg was mostly healed. Before he permitted it, though, he insisted that Elana at least do one more healing session before she left. I allowed it, but only for a short time. I was tired, and was looking forward to a sleep deprived of sweat and pain.

"What did you and Chem talk about?" I asked finally, deciding that must've been what was causing her distraction. Her sigh after my question told me I was right.

"Just . . . stuff. Leaving tomorrow. Your leg. Nothing very exciting." She was lying on her cot, but now she turned over on her side, facing away from me. "You'd better get some sleep. I don't know when we'll leave tomorrow."

"I've been in bed all day," I readjusted the way my pillow sat, grunting as I shifted my leg. "I'm not very tired right now. What did you *really* talk about?"

"Okay, maybe *you've* been in bed all day, but *I* haven't, and I'd like to get some sleep if you don't mind." She snipped, pushing her head farther into her pillow as if that would block me out. I continued to pry.

"Jhapato told me you slept for a long time, too, so don't give me that. Come on, what did Alchemy tell you?"

She sighed again. "I told you."

"Alright, but there's more to it than that." I pulled my blanket up above my shoulders and closed my eyes. I wasn't sure she'd answer me now. It hurt me a little, to think she didn't trust me with her true motives for chasing the Curse, or anything about her personal life, really.

When I'd brought up her brother earlier in the day, she had become instantly defensive, and had left to talk to Alchemy. Had she told him about her family? Why wouldn't she tell me? She hardly knew him any better, and besides, if that fact alone wasn't enough to deter her from sharing her life story with him, he was *Cursed*, and was probably the least trustworthy out of the three of us.

That isn't fair. I scolded myself, furrowing my brow. Alchemy was Cursed, but he was fighting it. He'd told us that he could sometimes feel it calling him, but he resisted. He was stuck like this forever, always fighting this cruel part of himself. It wasn't fair to assume he wasn't worth anyone's attention just because he looked scary.

I sighed, feeling drowsiness slowly seep into my mind. I could worry about Sakura's trust issues another day. For now, I just wanted to focus on getting some sleep. Who knew how long it would be until I got the opportunity to get a full night of sleep again?

*B*reakfast was early and just as good as the previous day's, although it was even better, because it lacked the chaos and panic of an unexpected runeboar attack. Sakura and I wolfed down our pancakes, and after one more visit from Elana, during which she gave me three vials of a pink-ish liquid for my leg, we were on our way.

We found Alchemy in a stretch of plains between the Evershifting Forest and the Shattered Mountains. My leg didn't start bothering me until just before we found him, sitting down in the tall grass — which barely reached his shoulder blades — and paused so that Sakura could address his wardrobe situation.

She had managed to acquire a needle and some thread, and she ordered Alchemy to remove his cloak and shirt for her to mend them before we moved on. During that short break, I uncorked the first vial of Elana's pain remedy and sniffed at it. Sakura raised an eyebrow at me.

"What, do you think she'd poison you, after all she's already done to fix your leg up?" she remarked as she broke the thread between her teeth, tying a knot at the end of the stitch she'd just completed.

"No, I just wanted to see if I could identify any of the ingredients," I replied. I sniffed at it again, tilting my head to the side. There was a sort of sour note, but it was quickly followed up by something sweet and citrusy.

"And what does your magical nose deduct, perfume boy?" Sakura asked as she set Alchemy's shirt to the side, moving on to the smaller holes that needed to be patched in his cloak.

"Aloe vera and eucalyptus." I said simply. I took a small sip of it, squinting my eyes at the sudden film of sugar that coated my tongue. "*Heavily* flavored with honey."

"Very nice." Sakura finished fixing up Alchemy's clothes and handed them back to him. "How long do you think it will take us to reach the Gates?"

"Actually, we're not going through the Gates." Alchemy said as he shrugged back into his shirt. Sakura and I gave each other baffled looks.

"We're not?" she asked.

"No. We simply haven't got the money, and unless either of you have another whorle-mage tucked up your sleeve, I don't see how any of us could sneak past." Alchemy tightened his gloves and gestured at the Shattered Mountains. There was only one road through them. The Shattered Pass. No other travel through them could be deemed safe since the mountains were so notorious for their avalanches and rockslides.

"You want to go around the Gates?" I guessed, but Sakura was already shaking her head.

"Those cliffs are littered with dangers. Not only have the Duskans ensured it, but so have the Lockers. The mutual distrust that existed between the kingdoms before the Curse caused only one safe avenue of travel, and that's the Shattered Pass." Sakura crossed her arms and frowned at Alchemy. "There's no safe way to get through other than going through the Gates."

"There's the Evershifting Forest," I offered, vaguely remembering that the forest crossed through Brightlock and Carlore, and met Old Duskfall in several locations.

"It backs right up to the Oasis," Alchemy said. "That place is heavily guarded. We'll have more luck scaling down the cliffs directly to the south, unless you want to go all the way around and approach from Carlore, which won't give us any more help, considering the King's Scar is there to get in the way." I could see Sakura rubbing her knuckles — a tic of hers I'd noticed whenever she got anxious — as she tried to think of an alternative solution. We all knew she wouldn't find one.

"We can get down the cliffs just fine," Alchemy went on, unfazed by our concern. "The bigger problem will be crossing the desert without getting eaten." He paused, looking up from where he was fiddling with the clasp of his cloak. "Without *you two* getting eaten, that is."

"Eaten by *what*?" I asked, my eyebrows raising. Sakura gave me a look that clearly told me I should already know.

"By sandcats, you idiot." She rose to her feet and stretched, rolling her shoulders and tapping her flame-sword's hilt, as if to reassure herself it was still there. "We should get going and set up camp somewhere farther south. We're still pretty close to the towns here."

Alchemy and I followed her lead, and soon we were keeping a steady pace towards the distant cliffs. I was surprised at how little I slowed us down. The remedy Elana had given me had instantly soothed the throbbing in my leg, and I was able to walk normally for a couple hours. Only once we got closer to our destination, and the sun began to sink in the sky, did the ache slowly begin to return.

I didn't focus much on my leg, though, because I was far more distracted by my bering. Everyone else seemed just as confused as I was about the sudden outburst of thorns from the porch. I didn't even remember doing it. I had been so delirious from blood loss, and so terrified I was about to get trampled by a runeboar, that I hadn't put much thought at all into what I might have done to save myself with my bering. Now that the initial panic was gone, though, I couldn't help but wonder what sort of instincts had caused the sudden appearance of the thorns.

I had known there was a change in my bering after spending so much time at sea. What I hadn't expected was that it seemed *stronger* than whenever I'd used it back in Rulak. I could feel the life pulsing around me more intensely than ever before. At the slightest thought, blades of grass shot up two feet beside me. With a mere twitch of my littlest finger, flowers bloomed across the earth around my feet. Only the smallest ounce of concentration left bushes thick with berries sprouting left and right.

Sakura and Alchemy took notice of it almost immediately, but neither said anything. I could see the wonder in Sakura's eyes as the roots of a bush sprouted out of the ground, reaching up into a spindly hand. It crooked into a curled fist with one finger pointing: the same way I held my own hand. I flipped it and spread my fingers, palm up. The roots mirrored the action. I grinned at Sakura, and she raised her eyebrows in amusement.

"You weren't able to do that before, were you?" she guessed, looking at the flowers around my boots. "It's new. Like the thorns." She squinted up at me, perplexed. "How did you do the thorns? That wood was dead. I thought it was unmalleable for bering-mages."

I shrugged uncomfortably, glancing away. My concentration was broken, and the root-hand ceased its movement, frozen in an open-palmed position. I watched it for a long moment, then blinked, taking a deep breath. I filled my lungs, trying to steady my thoughts into those of peace and beauty. A bright pink blossom formed in the palm of the hand, spinning until it had bloomed fully.

"Lots of mages have secrets about them that few have uncovered." Alchemy rumbled, and we looked up at him. His voice sounded somewhat regretful, and I felt a pang of sympathy for him. I couldn't imagine what it must have felt like, having no magic, but knowing you once did.

Even if I wasn't greatly skilled with my bering, it was always there, coiled deep within me and fueled by every small thing my heart felt. If it ever vanished, it would feel as if a piece of my soul had been torn away from me.

"I've never been taught, anyway," I added, glancing up at Sakura again. "Willa — my grandmother — isn't a mage."

"But you never took the time to practice with it, either," Sakura countered, and I nodded to concede the point.

"I didn't see much point in it. I never thought I was a very strong bering-mage." I looked down at my own hands, barely calloused by the use of my bow. "I don't know where all this power has come from so suddenly, but it's never been here before."

There was a long silence that stretched between the three of us, finally broken by Sakura's sigh as she stretched her arms and rolled her shoulders. She urged us back into our steady trek, bound for the cliffs, and Alchemy and I followed her. My leg complained very little, and after a few steps I was able to push the pain out of my mind.

Brightlock was the flattest Horcathian kingdom after Old Duskfall and Wisesol, and while the landscape was clear all the way to the cliffs, I knew it would take us until nightfall to reach them.

There was little conversation as we walked. I could sense some sort of tension between Sakura and I, although I couldn't put a finger on what it was. It made me uncertain, and caused me to think back to how we'd behaved around each other over the past couple of days, wondering if I'd done something to offend her.

My mind instantly tracked back to all the times we'd held hands. It hadn't seemed to mean anything at the time, but looking back, I realized how fluttery it made me feel. When I had held her hand after she had started crying the first night in Jhapato's house, and when I had taken her hand in the runeboar fight. Both of those moments had been instinctive: I saw her pain, and I did what I could to offer her comfort. I saw the danger, and I did what I could to protect her. But then she had grabbed *my* hand, not only during the runeboar fight, but afterwards as well, when she had insisted I eat some soup. It had made me uncomfortable, but not in a bad way; in a *new* way. A way that maybe I could adjust to if it were to happen again.

I had been uncomfortable around her to begin with, but something about that had shifted subtly at some point. I couldn't name when, but I knew it was around the time we had been on *Orvyn*, perhaps when I'd passed out and woken up to her using her eirioth to help keep me warm. After that, I'd found myself looking at her in a different way. I sort of hated myself for it, but couldn't deny that I kept feeling my gaze tug toward her. I was always aware of where she was, even if I wasn't looking at her, and when I was looking at her, it was only for brief moments, my eyes darting away again before she could catch me watching.

I risked a glance at her now, walking by my side. She and Alchemy had slowed their own pace to stay near me, even though I was hardly limping. I already knew complaining about it would do nothing, so I kept my lips firmly pressed shut.

Sakura stood nearly a foot shorter than me, although with how feisty her personality was, it was often I found myself shrinking away from her. She radiated confidence in every aspect of her body: the way she walked, the way she held her head high, the way she kept her gaze trained forward, even the way one hand rested steadily on her flame-sword hilt, ready for use at any time.

But now that I'd had the chance to spend some more time with her, and now that I'd seen her at her low point, when she had been shaking and crying in Jhapato's house, I could see the breaks in her walls. They were small, and very subtle. Hardly noticeable, unless you had learned where to look.

Every now and then, something in her eyes would change. She was good at hiding what she was thinking, but not at hiding what she was *feeling*. Her emerald eyes spoke volumes more than she ever would with her voice, telling me how deep and fierce the sorrow ran within her.

It rattled through the rest of her body, too. Not all of her demeanor was that of confidence. Her muscles tensed and bunched at every sign of potential danger, poised to attack should the need arise. There was something overly cautious about the way she carried herself, like a high-strung cat that knew it was being hunted.

"The borders are heavily patrolled at night," Alchemy's voice made me jump, buzzing in my ear. The hum that surrounded him was a constant thrum in the back of my mind, and while I had learned to set it to the side, I was careful not to push it away completely. When the runeboars had attacked it had taken me several seconds longer than it should have to realize they were Cursed, and I didn't like that.

"All around the borders?" Sakura asked, her sharp gaze cutting past me to Alchemy. It hadn't gone unnoticed by me that they had taken positions on either side of me, but I didn't like to think it was because I was the injured one out of the three of us. I told myself it was just the way we had started walking, even though I knew the real reason.

"The border Old Duskfall shares with Carlore is constantly under watch. With the aid of dragons, the King's Scar that opens between them could be easily breached. As for the eastern and western borders, they're taken care of by the natural circumstances of Horcath." Alchemy gestured to our right, where the shadows of the Evershifting Forest rose tall in the light of the evening sun. I could see that the trees were wide and sprawling, different from what they had been when we had camped there.

"Is the northern border not as guarded during the day?" I asked, gesturing towards the cliffs we walked towards. The creeping edges of the Shattered Mountains were near to our left, barely two hundred yards off. Beyond the low jags of the mountains lay the Shattered Pass, the only road connecting Brightlock with Old Duskfall.

"The day is when the sandcats hunt." Alchemy looked down at me, the glowing cracks in his skull dimming ominously before flaring brightly again. "They still patrol the borders, but not as much as they do at night. We'll want to move down the cliffs at dawn, and then start across the desert quickly."

"Before we get eaten by sandcats," Sakura added, raising an eyebrow. Alchemy nodded mutely.

I didn't know much about Old Duskfall. The extent of my education had been whatever Willa was able to teach me. Wisesol's education system was practically nonexistent, only showing itself prominent in the noble families, or any rich enough to afford it. That was one of the major reasons the majority of the kingdom consisted of thugs and thieves. Despite that obvious problem, King Richaerd the Fourth and his wife, Queen Sara, refused to address it.

Willa's knowledge of the eastern kingdoms was minimal. Most of what I knew revolved around Wisesol, Freetalon, and Coldmon, although I'd heard plenty about Brightlock as well. The kingdom's riches were broadly known across all of Horcath, after all.

Old Duskfall was the smallest of the seven kingdoms — at least, that's what everyone had been told. Nobody knew how big Old Nightfall might be — and often forgotten, especially by anyone in the western kingdoms; it was penned in by Carlore and Brightlock, anyway, and with the kingdom so small, there was little reason to worry about it rising against either of those kingdoms.

What I did know was Old Duskfall had remained quiet for the last several years. While kingdoms still held council with their nobles and royal families, always reaching out in hopes of forming alliances with other kingdoms, Old Duskfall had melted into the shadows when the Curse had surfaced. I wondered briefly how much Alchemy might know about the desert kingdom.

We stopped to make camp barely twenty yards from the cliff's edge, setting up our bedrolls around a small space I had cleared of plant life for a fire. I had discovered as we'd walked that I could shift the earth very minimally by controlling the roots of the plants around it. When the roots moved, they could drag the earth with them, and I was able to slowly spread a circle of soft dirt in the center of our campground for Sakura to build a fire.

We had predicted that the weather throughout the night would be relatively calm, with only some strong winds, if anything. Spring was the rainy season, and it wouldn't come until autumn and winter were fully past. Until then, the most we had to worry about were heavy winds and the occasional snowstorm.

I could hear a wind picking up as I settled onto my bedroll, tucking my longbow and my belt safely away from the eirioth flame Sakura was slowly summoning in our makeshift fire pit. The wind whistled and thrummed in the distance, coming closer, and I shrugged my shoulders, wishing I'd brought a cloak with me. The only clothes I had were those I wore and two spare changes in my pack. I was tempted to crawl into the warmth of my bedroll to avoid the breeze and skip dinner altogether.

I lifted the small satchel Jhapato had sent with us, noticeably different from the nondescript ones we carried, as it was elegantly crafted from soft leather and the hide of what I assumed was a Horcathian camel. Inside was a stash of provisions, just enough to last Sakura and I the entire journey through the Shattered Pass. Since we were cutting directly down to the cliffs leading to the Duskan Desert, it would last us a few extra days.

I was just about to break into the rations, eager to discover what food he had given us — because I was, quite frankly, sick of dried fruit and jerky — when the wind picked up. It was subtle, but there was one obvious change: it had swapped directions.

That was when I knew something was off. The way the grass around us responded to the wind was odd. It twirled around us, as if being blown in circles. There was something rhythmic about it, and the longer I looked, the more I realized I could *hear* a rhythm, too.

I looked up abruptly, keenly aware of Alchemy's bared skull, and felt my heart lurch into my throat as I saw a shadow hovering above us, wings beating, tail thrashing in the wind.

Sakura and Alchemy were quick to follow my gaze, and Sakura squinted against the gusts of air being blown down at us. She said something, but it was too quiet to be heard over the beating of wings. As I stared up at the raptor, I realized there was something vaguely familiar about it. Then I caught a clearer flash of the tail, and the arch of the wings: they were like big leaves.

"Wynchell?" I squinted as the raptor landed with a thump in front of us, tail still whipping the ground. The rough green scales of the raptor blended with the yellowing grass around us, but it was difficult to miss his practically glowing eyes.

"Theomand's raptor." Alchemy deadpanned, leaning forward to examine the reptile.

"There's something tied to his leg," Sakura observed, and I glanced down towards the raptor's talons, half concealed by his veiny wings. She was right; there was some sort of paper tied securely to him.

"Well, grab it. See what it says." I gestured at the parchment, waiting for her to make a move to retrieve it. She gave me a blank stare, eyes wide. "What?" I asked.

"You must be mad. *You* grab it. I'm not going near that thing." She crossed her arms in defiance.

"But-" I began to argue, then paused, glancing at the raptor again. He was tense and ready to move quickly. His eyes were narrow and slitted, and I instinctively leaned away from him. Swallowing, I turned to Alchemy. "You do it." He made a sound similar to a snort.

"You two are cowards. Getting the *adult* to do all your work for you." He moved forward, reaching for the raptor's leg. He stiffened and snarled, but didn't move.

"It's because you're the one made entirely of bone. Now just give it to me, will you?" Sakura grumbled as Alchemy deftly tugged the paper free of its bindings and offered it to her. She snatched it out of his exposed hand bones — he had shed the gloves for the night — and flipped it open. I scooted closer to read over her shoulder.

Travelers,

I have given some thought to what you said aboard Orvyn. About the pirates. It intrigued me. I often work alone, only partnering when I need to, but the thought of working alongside a crew somewhat appeals to me. You said I might find them in Wisesol, but I wanted confirmation. You three are by no means under my blanket of trust, don't forget that.

But I cannot deny that your presence did help for a smoother transport for those rupees. It hasn't gone forgotten.

Wynchell will bring any message you wish to send me. If I manage to find your
pirate friends, boy, I'll send word, and you can give them a letter. But don't expect
one. I may still change my mind.

Captain Theomand

My eyebrows raised as I read it, my surprise increasing with each passing sentence.
I looked up at Wynchell, but his attention was locked on Alchemy, nostrils and ears
twitching as he watched the skeleton warily.

"He's surprisingly polite, for a thief." Sakura muttered, flipping the paper over.
It was blank, and gestured to the raptor's leg again. "There's a pencil over there. Get
it for me."

Alchemy emitted a sound somewhat like a sigh and pulled the pencil free, tossing
it to her. She held it and the paper up to me, and I frowned. She rolled her eyes and
said,

"You're the one the pirates are all friendly with."

"Fine," I grumbled, taking it and beginning to scribble down a note. I included
brief details about how he might find *The Coventry*, and what to tell them when
he found them. I signed it and handed it back to Sakura, who began to scrawl her
own note on the bottom, her handwriting much neater than mine. Peering over her
shoulder, I saw that she was telling him we were going to be in Old Duskfall for
a time. She finished it and handed it to Alchemy so that he could tie it back onto
Wynchell's leg.

As soon as the letter was secured, the raptor hissed at all of us and flew away. After
the wind had died down, Sakura looked up at me, and I could see a question in her
eyes before she even spoke. I expected something about my horrible handwriting,
and was prepared to give the excuse that someone who sells perfumes doesn't need
to write letters fit to be seen by the kings of Horcath, so I was surprised when all she
said was,

"Your name is spelt with a K?"

I had already opened my mouth to answer her, but now I snapped it shut, taken
aback by her question. All I could manage was a squeaky, "Yes?"

"Wait," Alchemy rumbled, his skull swerving to face me. "It is?"

"Yes." I cleared my throat, frowning at the two of them. "It always has been."

"Then why isn't it pronounced Ka-sega?" Sakura asked, taking the rations satchel
from me to rummage through it herself.

"If it was pronounced Ka-sega, Willa would have called me Ka-sega." I dead-panned, taking the satchel back from her once she'd retrieved a small bread roll to nibble on.

"So why is it spelled with a K?" Alchemy asked. I rolled my eyes, glaring at him.

"I don't know, *Chem*. If you want to interrogate people about their names, why don't you tell us your real one?" I pulled a bright red apple out of the bag and crunched into it, grateful for some fresh fruit after all the dried peaches I'd been eating.

That seemed to be enough to quiet the two of them for the time being, but I had a bad feeling Sakura was going to bring it up again later. The only other person to question the spelling of my name had been Jessie, and she had left it alone quickly after realizing how much the pronunciation "Ka-sega" irritated me. Something told me Sakura would treat that piece of information differently.

After we'd eaten, we each wriggled into our bedrolls, and Sakura let the flame die down a little bit, dwindling until it was just big enough to illuminate a circle around us. She seemed to hesitate before letting it shrink any smaller than it had originally been, but once she was curled up in her bedroll, her anxiety deflated a little, and her eyelids drooped.

My own eyelids were growing heavy, and I sighed as I looked up at the sky above us. It was clear of clouds, but also almost completely devoid of stars. I was staring up into an endless abyss of black, dotted by the smallest specks of light. Sometimes it seemed like that was what Horcath had become, a kingdom riddled with cutthroats and backstabbers, like what I was used to in Wisesol, or what I had seen back on Clawbreak. It was a land corrupted by the Curse, and as I'd learned recently, the Curse was growing.

But there were still places where people were happy. *The Coventry* was a band of pirates, and yet they spent their time laughing and taking care of each other. There were people like Jessie and Willa, pursuing their careers and finding ways to thrive, even in a dying world.

And what did that make me? What did that make Sakura? What did that make Alchemy?

Jhapato believed Sakura was fueled by revenge. He thought she wanted the Curse gone to pay for what had happened to her family. *She* believed it was for justice. And what did I believe? Why was I out here? For the adventure? For the change of pace, for the promise that, maybe, my life was meant to be something more than it always had been?

I'd never wanted to stand out. I never wanted people to *see* me. Even Jessie and Willa didn't fully understand me. I was the underdog. The thief and the rebel that made a living stowing away on boats and swiping food during the night and selling perfumes during the day. I'd never believed there was a role for me to fill even in my own life, least of all everyone else's.

But things had changed. I didn't want to hide anymore. I didn't want to cower. I wanted someone to understand me. I wanted *Sakura* to understand me, to see who I really was, to know that she wasn't the only person who had doubts, who had scars. Who had a history.

Closing my eyes, I let my weariness close in around me. Maybe it was finally time to be different. To step away from what I'd always been and what I'd always known. To look the fears I'd always had of people seeing me for who I was directly in the eye, and blink them away.

Those little specks of light in the blanket of the night sky were stars, and hundreds of people looked up at them, shining fearlessly above them all. For once, maybe, it was time for me to find a way to become a light in a world clouded in darkness.

24
SAKURA

Sleeping out in the open, with nothing but the dark sky above me and no one but Ksega and Alchemy around me left me feeling horribly exposed to the shadows that lurked beneath just about everything. I wouldn't let either of them know it got to me, of course. I already knew both of them could see the uneasiness gnawing away at me, and I didn't need to give them any more reasons to be worried about me. If anything, we should all have been fussing over Ksega to make sure his leg was comfortable as we traveled.

Sleep didn't come easy that first night out of Jhapato's house. I had grown used to the prickly feeling of nervousness that hugged itself around me whenever I slept outside, but after those two nights in the Duskan's house, my mind had forgotten how to find any sense of calm when nightfall came and I was left outside. I knew it was a childish fear, one that had existed since before I could remember, and I ought to have let it go by now. It was even one I'd always had control over: darkness could never entirely consume me, not so long as I was conscious. My eirioth was always at my beck and call, ready to flare as brightly as was necessary to let me see the world around me. So why was I always so terrified of the dark?

I didn't like burrowing so deeply into my own mind. It was a place riddled with painful memories and headache-inducing questions. A muddle of unreadable emotions and inexplicable motives.

Sighing, I turned to lie on my back. The flame beside me was an adequate distraction from the problem, requiring at least some of my constant attention to ensure it didn't spread to the swaying grasses around us. Ksega had done a good job of clearing a space for it, but eirioth was still a strong-willed magic, and it hungered for more freedom.

Alchemy was, as usual, a short way off, close enough that, should Ksega or I need him, he could reach us in a few of his long-legged strides, but still far enough away that it wasn't awkward to fall asleep with him around. As much as his presence had unnerved me to begin with, seeing as he was Cursed and all — not to mention

I hardly knew him and had found him hermitted away in the Evershifting Forest — I had come to have placed some measure of trust in the skeleton, and I was grateful now for him being able to keep watch while we slept. It wasn't the greatest reassurance, but I trusted him enough to know that he wouldn't let harm come to us so long as he was able.

Before I could be consumed further by my haunting memories, I turned my attention to the task at hand, refocusing on why we were going to Old Duskfall.

We had found nothing in Clawbreak; nothing useful, anyway. Old Duskfall was a land rumored to have dabbled in ancient and dark magics. I hadn't looked into it that much, considering there had only been mutterings floating around the Hazelwood Inn, but now that we were hunting for things concerning ancient and dark magics, it seemed as good a place as any to search.

Jhapato had told us to go to a woman named Irina. I wasn't sure if she was trustworthy, but Jhapato had been trustworthy enough. I had confidence in his judgment, and if he said she could help us, I believed him.

Sighing again, I closed my eyes, forcing my mind to continue running through the plan, over and over and over. Again and again until the thoughts became disjointed and confusing, running together as I drifted away into sleep.

Alchemy woke us before dawn's light had begun to spill across the land.

I rubbed my eyes and blinked them open to face a bright pink sky, hued with blue and purple on either side and still speckled with stars that had yet to fade into the sun's light. With the tips of the blades of grass to my left and the flickering light of the fire on my right, only just peeking into the corners of my vision, the sky was framed beautifully between the two elements.

"Up and at 'em, Ironling," Alchemy's voice bounced into my ears, and I let my head flop to the side to look lazily at him. I yawned, stretching my arms out above me, then blinked slowly at where Ksega was laying. He was still asleep.

"Why aren't you yelling at him?" I asked, my voice little more than a croak. I forced myself to sit up, instantly wanting to curl back into the bedroll. I was a little surprised to find that I had slept all through the night, and had woken up well-rested. In fact, I even felt a little *groggy*, which was unnatural for me when I was sleeping anywhere but my own bed at home.

"Oh, he'll wake up soon enough. All you need is a bit of bacon and he's as awake as a squirrel in a thunderstorm." Alchemy waved a bony hand, then gestured towards a stone near my diminished eirioth flame. I hadn't noticed it before, since the wind was blowing the scent away from me, but now I couldn't avoid detecting the smoky, salty scent of cooking bacon.

"Where'd you get that?" I asked, crawling out of my bedroll and beginning to tug my boots on.

"It was in that pack the old Duskan sent with you," Alchemy replied, gesturing to the satchel Jhapato had given us.

I nodded, packing my bedroll up. Even though we talked just beside him, Ksega showed no signs of waking up. He was even snoring a little bit, his hair tousled from sleep, bedroll half folded over itself.

"How soon are we moving for the cliffs?" I asked, and Alchemy, crouching to flip the bacon and scoot the rock closer to the flames, looked up at me. Sometimes I could've sworn he meant that ever-present grin, even if I couldn't see it.

"As soon as possible. You two can eat on the way. Smack him, will you? Poke him in the leg, if you have to, just get him up and get him packing that bedroll. Bacon's almost done."

Tying off the knots to secure my bedroll, I scooted over to where Ksega was and shook him roughly by the shoulder. He groaned and rolled away from me, almost into the grass in a ring around us. I punched him in the back, feeling my knuckles dig into his spine. He yelped and jerked away, glaring at me as he shoved himself up onto an elbow.

"By the Endless Sea, Sakura, you don't have to be so *mean* about it," he groaned and sat up, wiggling out of his bedroll. "A simple 'wakey, wakey' would do next time." He gave me a teasing grin, but I only glowered at him until it dropped and he looked away.

"Bacon for breakfast. We need to move soon. I want to find this Irina person as soon as possible." I told him, gathering all our things together into a neat pile. Ksega was eyeing the bacon, so I started to roll up his bedroll for him.

"If she's as well-known as Jhapato says she is, it shouldn't be difficult. What *will* be difficult is getting me around." Alchemy offered a few strips of the bacon to Ksega, who gratefully crunched down on them. "Duskans are a very superstitious people. Have either of you ever heard of bone reading?" looking up from my work on Ksega's bedroll, I shared a glance with the Solian. He shook his head, and I looked up at Alchemy.

"Nope." I answered for both of us, biting my lip as I struggled to tie Ksega's bedroll in place. He had somehow managed to fill the strings with mud and grime to the point where they were as stiff as dead vines.

"Probably for the best. It's an old, old form of andune. Nobody's really sure how it works, as it was outlawed centuries ago, but . . ." Alchemy shrugged his shoulder blades. "With Old Duskfall in ruin such as it is, I have no doubts there are still those who practice it in secret."

"What exactly is it?" Ksega asked.

"More importantly, how do you know about it? If it was outlawed centuries ago, and you've been hiding in a forest forever, how would you know any of this?" I asked, but Alchemy only tilted his skull at me.

"I wouldn't exactly say that's more important than Ksega's question, but I'll have you know I did have ways of keeping myself informed of the general status of the kingdoms, if not all the details." He turned to face Ksega. "Bone reading is said to be the ability to talk to spirits of the dead. I'm not entirely sure what they do, and I've never seen it in person, but it was deemed far too dangerous for mankind to wield such power. Anyone caught practicing bone reading was to be arrested and sent to a cell where their andune would be rendered useless." He divided the last of the bacon to split between Ksega and I. "I don't know that we'll run into anything like that while we're there, but I wouldn't be surprised if we did. Now, eat up, we'd better get moving."

"Are you sure it's a good idea for you to be going, then?" I asked, standing up and pulling my packs over my back. I let the eirioth flame simmer down into nothing. There wasn't so much as a scorch mark on the earth to show it had been there.

"I'm not staying behind, if that's what you mean," Alchemy insisted. "Yes, if anyone sees me for what I really am, we might be arrested, but . . ." he trailed off, as if thinking, then finished, "If we're found to have crossed the border illegally, we'll be arrested anyway."

"You really shouldn't be so careless," Ksega muttered. "Right now, Theomand is the only person aside from us who knows about your secret, but I really don't think he should have found out to begin with. You need to be more careful."

I nodded in agreement, but didn't say anything. I had been distracted by something Alchemy had said.

If anyone sees me for what I really am.

What he really was, not who. It was as if he wasn't a person anymore. Granted, he was literally nothing more than bones, but he was still *human*. He had a conscience, even if it didn't make much sense that he did. Despite the apparent state of him, I still saw him as a person. It saddened me to think he had given up the hope of seeing himself as a person, too.

"Ironling?" Alchemy's voice drew me out of my thoughts, and I looked up at him, suddenly overcome with the urge to give him a hug. There were no features to read, no way to tell what he really felt in that moment. Even his voice was an unreliable means of looking into his emotions. But something told me his spirits had been dampened, perhaps by the very same thought I'd had.

"I'm fine. Let's go." I took a big bite of bacon to ensure I wouldn't have to speak again, setting off to the south. After a short moment's hesitation, I heard Alchemy and Ksega trooping after me.

Conversation was a small thing on our walk. Mostly it was just the boys talking, and while I didn't say anything, I listened in. It was small talk, really, albeit strange small talk. Ksega recalled tales of all the times he'd stowed away on a ship — six times, total — and Alchemy had pitched in with his own stories of sneaking around after dark in his hometown as a child.

It was hard to imagine Alchemy as a child. He was so wise and so tall and so *ancient*-seeming, even if he didn't sound half as old as his knowledge claimed. How long ago had he been a child? What had his childhood been like? What had led him down a path that eventually brought him to a fate like *this*? It made my heart squeeze to think of it. What was *anyone*'s childhood, if not only a healthy fear of the Curse?

I felt my palm brush against the cool metal of my flame-sword. *That* was what I was fighting for. What I was striving to protect future generations from. Nobody deserved the childhood I had had, one of loss and pain and survival. It was time somebody stepped up to do something to bring this Curse to an end.

The cliff was higher than I'd anticipated. I had a clear head for heights, and was undisturbed by the height. I was a little more concerned by the crumbly edge of the cliff, and was careful to keep away from the loose earth.

Ksega seemed to feel similarly, wary of the edge, but still feeling that tug of curiosity. It was just strong enough to convince him to keep close enough to peer down the cliff face repeatedly, as if he were searching for something. From the calculating look in his sparkling eyes, I was willing to bet he was already mapping out hand and footholds for the climb down, because what else would he be doing? He was a thief, after all.

"We haven't got any rope, and even if we did, I doubt it'd be long enough to get us down there," Alchemy said as he assessed the situation. "So we're going to have to climb." He looked over at Ksega. "You think you'll be alright on that leg?"

Ksega, who was already uncorking a vial of Elana's remedy — he was on the second vial out of the three she had given him — nodded. Once he'd taken a quick swig of the pinkish liquid, he took another peep down the cliffside.

"Definitely." He said, his voice pitched with more excitement than the situation warranted. I raised an eyebrow at him.

"And how often do you climb cliffs back in Wisesol?" I asked, fully aware that the closest thing to a cliff in that kingdom was a stretch of the Slated Mountains, and only a fool would try to climb those peaks for the fun of it.

"Cliffs? None," he grinned at me, and I averted my gaze when I realized how irritatingly charming that grin was. "But I've scaled plenty of building walls. The textures aren't much different. If anything, the walls of the buildings were considerably smoother than this," he gestured at the cliffs. "This will be easy."

"Scaling is going up," I reminded him. "Are you just as good at climbing down?" he scoffed, as if offended.

"*Please*, of course I'm good at climbing down. No thief learns to climb up before he masters climbing down." A grin pulled across his face as he said it. I raised an eyebrow.

"That makes no sense."

"Admittedly, it sounded a lot better in my head." He shrugged. "Either way, this climb will be a breeze for me." He looked up at me, a challenge in his eyes. "How about you?"

I leveled my gaze at him, cocking an eyebrow and not bothering to respond. He shrugged and looked away, refocusing his attention on the cliffside.

I wasn't worried about the climb. After climbing eirioth trees and riding dragons all my life, I was comfortable with the challenge. I hadn't been very surprised that

Ksega was up to it, too, even with the injury to his leg. Out of the three of us, I was most worried about Alchemy's ability to climb down. Not that it really mattered; if he fell, it was only the golden sand of the Duskfall Desert waiting to catch him. I doubted it would do much to his bones, and it wasn't like he could be bruised, anyway.

"Time to get going, then," I said, creeping close to the edge. The loose soil gave way and crumbled towards the sand. I grimaced as it shifted beneath my feet, struggling to keep my balance. The most difficult part of the climb would be finding secure hand and footholds to begin.

Ksega moved to offer me his hand, willing to help lower me down, but I took Alchemy's instead, ignoring the way Ksega's lips tightened as he pulled his hand back. I told myself it was because Alchemy was undoubtedly stronger, and probably able to keep more secure footing than Ksega was, but not even I could fully convince myself it wasn't entirely because I was afraid to hold Ksega's hand again.

As soon as I got a firm hold on the cliff face, I released Alchemy and grunted as I hugged myself against the rough stone. Throughout all the years of climbing eirioth trees and training with Finnian and riding dragons and scrubbing away at all the stains on the floorboards of Hazelwood Inn, I had developed plenty of muscle throughout all of my body. It was easy for me to hold myself there, pressed near to the stone, for as long as I needed to. It was a little more difficult to navigate finding new hand and footholds when I couldn't see clearly beneath me.

Above me, Ksega and Alchemy were tracking my progress, waiting until I had made my way almost halfway down before I heard Ksega coming down after me.

It was a slow process. Parts of the rock were coated in a thin layer of sand, causing my hands and feet to slip off of them before I dusted it off. Other parts were crumbly, and if I wasn't careful, I'd end up with a foot dangling in the air, or one arm dropped to my side.

My back was to the south, and with the sun rising higher and higher to my right, I felt a sweat break out on my temple. It didn't help that my palms had also begun to sweat, making them slick against the stone, and creating mud whenever I gripped a handhold with sand on it.

Every now and then a pebble would fall down, skimming against my hand or bouncing off my head from where Ksega was climbing down after me. I ground my teeth together, trying not to let it interfere with my focus.

I tried not to look down at how far I had left, but the temptation to do so was strong. I still had the strength to climb for longer if necessary, but I was drenched in sweat. I could feel it running in beads down the back of my neck, and it dripped down into my eyes, blurring my vision.

The heat was cloying, making my throat dry. It was as if the sand was in my mouth, soaking up all the moisture. I grimaced and tried to ignore the sensation, telling myself I was nearly to the bottom. But was I?

I blinked the perspiration from my eyes and peered under my shoulder, trying to get a gauge for how far the ground was. As I did so, my concentration was broken, and my left hand slid from its awkward hold in the stone. I cried out as my body swung, curling the fingers of my right hand to try and keep from falling backwards. My heart leapt into my throat as my ankles twisted sharply to the left, scraping my knee along the rock and nearly causing me to lose my footing.

"Sakura?" Ksega's voice came from above me, pinched with worry. I tossed my head back to look up at him. He was several feet above me, and unable to look down. With a grunt, I strained to pull myself back to the wall, frantically stealing a swipe against my pants to free my hand from sweat before I gripped the cliff wall again.

"I'm okay. Just slipped." I called.

"Be careful." He cautioned, and I ground my teeth.

I bit my lip, not giving him a response for fear of my attention breaking again. I hadn't seen how far I was from the ground, but it didn't matter. I'd just take it one handhold at a time until I felt my boot pressing into the sand, making no more attempts to check the distance left to go.

Before I knew it, I felt the grains of sand crunching beneath my boot, and I breathed a heady sigh of relief as I stepped back from the wall, my muscles trembling from the slow strain of the climb. My legs felt like the noodles in Gamma's soup, and I tried not to let it show as I fished for my water skin in my pack.

Ksega wasn't far behind me, and I could see Alchemy above him, moving deftly and much faster than Ksega or I had. I wasn't very surprised, but I was definitely jealous. The skeleton didn't have to worry about the heat of the sun impending his ability to make the climb. I doubted he even had to worry about the glaring light from it.

When we were all on the desert sands, and Ksega and I had taken the time to quench our thirst, I looked out at the desert. I hadn't given it much attention before, being more centered on the climb, but now that I was here, I looked at the sprawling miles and miles of golden sand dunes, occasionally penetrated by a lone tree. There was nothing but sand in sight for miles, except to the west, where I could see the fuzzy silhouette of trees — a forest? — and in the far distant southeast, where I could make out the pale outline of a tall cluster of buildings.

"That would be the capital of Old Duskfall, and the only surviving town." Alchemy said when he caught me looking. "To my knowledge, the only thing left of the other towns are ruins and rubble."

"What happened to this kingdom?" Ksega asked, his brow furrowed deeply. I knew Wisesol was a land riddled with thieves and crime. Was that how it had started for Old Duskfall, slowly leading to the withering destruction of an entire kingdom?

"Nobody's really sure." Alchemy mused, pulling his cloak hood back up over his head. "But whatever it was, I would be willing to bet it has something to do with magic. And if these people know about magic, they must know about the Curse."

I was tempted to say that *everyone* knew about the Curse, but of course, I knew he was speaking about a deeper knowledge of it. After what he had told us about bone reading, I was beginning to think that not only might they know something, but they might have been the cause of the Curse in the first place.

The thought made my pulse hum with excitement. This could be the end. I could find the source of the Curse here in Old Duskfall. Once this was all over, I could finally go *home.*

"Let's go, then." Ksega started forward, pushing his sweat-soaked mop of hair off his forehead. Maybe he'd had a similar thought. Did he often think of home like I did? He had told us before about his grandmother, Willa. The way he spoke of her convinced me they had a strong relationship, like the one that existed between Gamma and I. Surely he found himself missing her.

It felt like an impossible trek, especially for the first hour. No matter how fast we moved across the dunes, our destination didn't seem to get any closer. It was an aggravating situation to be in. There was no shade, and we had very little water. Talking only left us with dry mouths and scratchy throats, so conversation was kept to a minimum, and most of the talking was done by Alchemy.

"Why haven't we seen any patrols?" I asked after a while. There hadn't been any sign of another living thing for hours. I was beginning to think Alchemy had oversold the excitement of sandcats being on the prowl, and soldiers keeping their eyes peeled for intruders.

"The Duskan forces are limited, but determined. Most of their people are working at the Gates, or guarding the edges of the King's Scar between Old Duskfall and Carlore. Several are also stationed in the Oasis, and a few are probably near the Underbrush. The rest of them are scattered across the desert. They patrol the borders at night, and sometimes randomly throughout the day. Just keep your eyes open, though. If you spot a Horcathian camel, let me know."

Ksega and I nodded, even though I was sure neither of us knew what a Horcathian camel looked like. I'd heard of them, obviously, but the closest thing I could get to an image of them in my head was a sandy cat with very long legs and tusks. I didn't know if that was what they looked like, but I found myself searching for something like it anyway.

For the next hour, I kept my senses on high alert, ignoring the sweat that seeped from every pore and constantly checking our surroundings for any signs of life. I watched Ksega, too, aware that he would be able to sense anything living nearby, even if Alchemy and I couldn't see it. But nothing happened, and eventually my nerves settled back into their now-familiar state of buzzing anxiety.

I was beginning to think nothing interesting would happen until we reached the capital, but naturally, as soon as my guard was starting to go down again, I saw Ksega's muscles tense out of the corner of my eye. I snapped my head toward him, waiting as his eyes flicked across the horizon.

"Uh-oh." Was all he said, lifting an arm to point to our left. For a long moment, I could see nothing. There was a rather large dune blocking my view. Then I saw clouds of dust swirling across the top of it, kicked up by . . . *something*.

When the animal crested the hill, I heard two sharp gasps: one from me, and one from Ksega. Alchemy didn't react. Barreling down the dune towards us was the biggest creature I'd ever seen. I had expected something close to the size of an eirioth dragon, maybe a little larger, but compared to this beast, an eirioth dragon may as well have been a pet dog.

It was impossible to tell how tall it was from here, but it must have been close to twenty-five feet tall. It had long legs with knobby knees, and a long, thick neck that ended in the strangest head I'd ever seen, with two big flaps for ears and sharp tusks protruding from its mouth.

As it came closer, I felt myself instinctively taking a step back, even though I knew it would do nothing to stop the approach of the Horcathian camel. It stopped just short of us, barely breathing hard, and blinked down at us with massive, dewy black eyes. There was a harness around its broad chest and neck, and a decorative blanket laid over the hump on its back. Its wide feet gave it a strong stance in the ground as it bent its head down to inspect us.

Drawn by the harness was something akin to a boat, only it was much flatter, and its walls were little more than steps to trip over. It had benches along the sides, and a few sacks and crates stacked near the back, where sturdy poles held up a tent. At the front of the craft was a driving bench not unlike that of a caravan. I'd only seen a few caravans in my lifetime. In a place like Carlore, they weren't seen as a very realistic means of transport.

Sitting on the driving bench was the sole occupant of the entire flat-boat, a woman in a pair of loose-fitting brown breeches with a tight belt adorned with a long, curving blade, and a sleeveless beige shirt. Other than that, she only wore her boots, and her hair up in a messy braid. Her skin was dark, like mine, but that was where our similarities ended. She was definitely shorter than me, if not by much, and had black hair. Her eyes were dark and angry, the suspicion in them enhanced by her thick, low-set eyebrows.

As her vessel slid to a stop, she rose from her seat on the bench and drew the saber at her hip, not holding it in a threatening manner, but holding it in a way that suggested it could be.

"Who are you? Where have you come from?" her voice was lightly accented, tinged with the rural timbre of the Duskans. She narrowed her eyes at us as she hopped off the driving bench. "Travelers are not supposed to be this far west."

"Tell her we got lost." Alchemy hissed.

"We're lost," Ksega said, plastering a smile on his features. I tried to replicate it, but from the way Alchemy's head shook slowly, I knew I wasn't succeeding. Ignoring both of us, Ksega continued, "We're trying to go to the capital of the kingdom. We're looking for someone. Can you help us?"

"Who are you looking for?" the woman had approached us, but stopped several feet away. We were on top of a dune, leaving us at an advantage, should it come to a fight. But I wasn't looking to get into a fight, and I knew that leaving the Horcathian camel out here unattended wasn't something I could bring myself to do.

Ksega paused, glancing over at me with a question in his eyes. I licked my lips, trying to think. My heart was still in my throat from the unexpected appearance of the camel. Now that it was up close, I could see that Alchemy's head barely even came up to its knee.

"A friend of a friend," Ksega said finally.

"Give me a name." The woman said sharply, her gaze glinting like her blade.

"Irina." I said, wishing my voice didn't taper off at the end the way it did. Ksega's gaze flickered to me for a moment before returning to the strange Duskan. Her reaction wasn't what I had expected.

Eyes wide, she had taken what I assumed was an involuntary step back, the hate in her eyes redoubling, and she spat on the sand in front of her.

"*Ista!*" she hissed, her gaze flying between the three of us, lingering the longest on Alchemy, who kept his head bowed to his skull.

"Witch." Alchemy translated, speaking only loud enough for me to hear. I looked from him back to the woman before us.

Witch.

"I'm sorry," I said, squinting against the sunlight and trying to keep my voice as friendly as possible. "Do you know her?" the woman's face pinched in disgust, and I thought she might spit again.

"We do not make dealings with the corrupt." She snarled, her gaze flying around us, as if she was afraid someone might be watching, even though there was no one else in sight.

Ksega and I both looked at Alchemy, but quickly looked away again. It didn't escape the hawk-like gaze of the woman. She pointed at him with her blade.

"Take the hood off, *sagdred*." She ordered. I threw a questioning look into the shadows of Alchemy's cowl, but he provided no translation for the strange word. Instead, he slowly lifted one gloved hand up and pulled the fabric of the cloak back. I gave him a bewildered look.

Hadn't he been the one putting all the emphasis in keeping him a secret?

"*Dasten limga*," the woman gasped, her grip tightening on the sword's handle. Again, Alchemy didn't translate it. I'd heard of the Sandrun language, but never met anyone that could speak it. "I should kill you all where you stand."

"It would be really great if you didn't," Ksega said, stepping towards Alchemy. He had his hands up, palms out, to show he didn't mean any harm. "Look, this man is Cursed. He's living proof the Curse is strong, and growing stronger. We only want to talk to Irina to see if she can help us understand it."

"Fool." The woman scowled at him. "Nobody wants to understand *dasten* magic. They only want to wield it as a weapon!"

Something in me snapped at that. Alchemy had said something similar about the people of Clawbreak. How they would find a way to wield the Curse and use it to their advantage. But how could anyone want something like that?

"The Curse is cruel and evil," I said, before I could think it through. "Anyone who wants to use it as a weapon can't have motives that are any better. We want to learn how to destroy it, and prevent anyone else from using it that way." I squinted up at the Horcathian camel, who mirrored my curiosity. "Now if you and your animal could escort us to Irina, we would be extremely grateful."

"Like I would let you anywhere near Mulligan," she sneered, waving her sword at Alchemy again. "What is that thing? You expect me to believe you are not looking to use the Curse against people when you travel with *that*?"

"I know it looks a bit suspicious," Ksega cut me off before I could speak, giving me a look that clearly said I should stay quiet. He spoke in a much calmer manner than I did. Once he was confident I would keep my mouth closed, he continued, "And that's exactly why he has the hood. He knows more about the Curse than any of us do, but still not enough to lead us to the source of it. That's what we're looking for." He looked up at Alchemy, who nodded once.

"He's right." The skeleton said, and the Duskan woman visibly flinched, her muscles going taught, as if he had attacked her. "If we can locate the source, we can destroy it. We truly want to bring it to an end."

The woman looked between the three of us, brows furrowed, eyes narrowed. I couldn't read her expression. She was almost as good at hiding what she was thinking as Derek.

"Why?" she asked finally. "Why destroy it? You think people haven't tried before?"

"The people who tried before didn't have someone Cursed at their side," Ksega pointed out. I knew that it meant practically nothing, but kept my mouth closed. Alchemy had been of very little use to us when it came to sharing information about the Curse. All we knew was it wasn't a disease, but a living thing; something magical. It tried to control Alchemy from time to time, but he resisted.

"The Curse is growing stronger," I pitched in. The woman's gaze slid to me. "It can corrupt bigger things now. It took my brother's dragon," my voice cracked, and I saw Ksega's hand twitch out of the corner of my eye, but I swallowed, ignored him, and went on. "And just a few days ago it corrupted an entire herd of runeboars. People died because of that." I gestured at the Horcathian camel that was now snuffling at the sand around our feet. "Mulligan is a bit bigger than an eirioth dragon, but if the Curse is changing, how long is it until he could be taken, too? Or a sea wraith?" I pressed my lips in a thin line, unsure where I was going with this. I had had a point, but the mention of Elixir had thrown me off, and my voice died away, carried into the distance by the hot wind.

"Or more people?" Ksega added. "You see him," he waved a hand at Alchemy. "He's the first, but he may not be the last. We can stop it from spreading if we destroy it, and if Irina knows anything, it might make the difference." The woman clenched her jaw, and now I could see it: she was close to caving for our cause. I could see it in the way she cast fearful glances at her camel. Ksega angled his head toward her, his tone calmer again as he said, "Please. Can you take us to her?"

The Duskan was quiet for a long moment, casting anxious glances around her. She looked back at her sand craft, at Mulligan, then at the three of us again. I kept my expression as open as I dared, hoping she could understand the desperation I felt. This couldn't be the end of my journey. Not after I'd sacrificed so much for it.

"By all the saints and souls," the woman shook her head slowly, some of the hardness returning to her eyes. "I can't believe I'm about to say this, but . . . okay. I will help you. But . . ." she paused, staring for a long moment at Alchemy, then at me, then shaking her head and turning away. "Fine. Come on, quickly now, before your skin melts off your bones." She waved us toward the vessel, stepping back and sheathing her weapon before hopping neatly onto the driving wagon.

Ksega and I shared a mildly surprised look before stepping forward. I knew we were getting incredibly lucky. Thus far, everyone who knew about Alchemy seemed willing to keep him a secret. Maybe the sight of him was enough to scare them into helping us defeat the Curse.

"What is this thing?" I asked, climbing over the little rail and hurrying beneath the shade of the tent erected at the back. From her place on the driving bench, the woman looked over her shoulder at me.

"A sand-sled. Haven't you heard of them?" she rolled her eyes. "They're how we get around fast here in the desert. It isn't safe to travel slowly. Hup!" she snapped the reins, and the sand-sled jolted forward as Mulligan tossed his head and started to trot, pulling the sled easily along behind him.

Alchemy and Ksega took positions on either side of me. Sand flew up in clouds behind us as we moved, and I winced as some of the sand slid over the front of the sled and soared towards us.

"What's your name?" Ksega asked. The sand-sled wasn't very wide, but it was long, so he had to shout over the hissing of wood against sand for our driver to hear us. She looked at him, her gaze sharp and suspicious.

"Erabeth." She said finally. "What are yours?"

"I'm Ksega," he said. Grudgingly, I introduced myself as well. Alchemy said nothing, so Ksega added, "And this is Chem."

Erabeth said nothing after that, steering us around so we were riding towards the capital. Mulligan had picked up his pace, but only just. He wasn't galloping like he had been a moment before, and I was grateful for it. I was used to the feeling of moving fast, with my hair swept back and the wind beating my face, but that was on an eirioth dragon. That was when I was a part of the animal I rode, feeling their every movement as they felt mine. This was entirely different. It was rough and slick at the same time. It was bumpy and unstable. It felt *dangerous*.

Ksega looked perfectly at ease, something I was a little surprised to see after how seasick he had appeared on *Orvyn*. It must not have been the turmoil of the waves themselves that had given him an upset stomach, but the sand-sled lurched and turned almost as much as the boat had.

We were traveling swiftly, passing the occasional withered tree or brittle shrub, but still our location didn't seem to get any closer. I wasn't sure if it was a trick of the dunes, or if I had just imagined it was closer than it was, but I was starting to get annoyed with it.

Alchemy and Ksega were quiet at my sides, and Erabeth seemed focused on driving the sand-sled, so none of us bothered her. We knew how risky it was putting more trust in her, but we would have had to ask someone to take us to Irina anyway, and if every other Duskan thought she was a witch, like Erabeth vehemently did, we may have landed ourselves in a worse situation.

I sat on one of the benches and leaned my head back, letting my eyes close as I enjoyed the shade. It wasn't any cooler beneath the tent, but without the blinding glare of the sun, it became a little more bearable. We were moving fast, and I knew it would only be a matter of hours before we arrived at our destination. I planned to try and regain as much strength as possible before we got there.

But as we traveled, something changed. I opened my eyes to see Alchemy still standing, not affected by the same weariness that burdened Ksega and I, and beyond him, the landscape passing by slower and slower. I turned to look towards Erabeth, my view partially obscured by Ksega, who had come to sit beside me at some point. I made sure not to look him in the eye as I looked toward our driver.

"Erabeth? Why are we slowing down? Are we there?" I yelled, causing Ksega to flinch and turn his head away from me. The Duskan tossed her long black ponytail over her shoulder and looked back at me, her face set in tight lines that made my heart plummet into my stomach.

"Mulligan senses something nearby. Keep your eyes peeled. This is popular sandcat territory. They like to hunt here." She loosened her curving sword in its sheath and craned her neck to look around us, even though the dunes blocked most of our vision.

"They do?" Ksega squinted at the sandy landscape. "I haven't seen anything for them to hunt."

"The animals out here are skittish. Now be quiet! Sandcats have impeccable hearing," Erabeth glared him into silence, and we all held as still as we could, breathing as frequently as we dared, wide eyes searching for any sign of a sandcat.

Like with the Horcathian camel, I'd never seen a sandcat, but this one I had at least seen pictures of. Crude sketches in various books from Duke Ferin's vast library. When I'd flipped through them, I had been very young, and couldn't read very well, so I hadn't known what they were at the time. In future lessons with Gamma, though, I had put the pieces together.

The pictures I'd seen were ugly and rough, depicting savage animals with jutting fangs and wild fur. They had long, bristly tails and sharp claws, with jagged stripes running down their shoulders. I shuddered to even think of facing one in person.

I was hoping we would get out of a sandcat fight, but just as I was letting myself believe it might be alright, a high-pitched baying sound echoed from Mulligan's mouth, and he tripped over his own feet, stumbling away from the sand.

No, not the sand. It was a creature the same color as the sand, darting between the camel's legs so fast I couldn't make it out clearly. I glimpsed it every now and then: the end of a tail, the flash of fangs. Nothing to tell me what it was, but I already knew.

Erabeth snapped something on the reins, and the harness disconnected from the sand-sled, allowing Mulligan to gallop away from the sandcat. With his long legs, it was only a number of strides before he had vanished beyond a dune, kicking up sand as he went.

Leaping to our feet, Ksega and I instinctively reached for our weapons. Erabeth already had her blade drawn, glaring at the sandcat that stood before the sand-sled, muscles rippled, tail lashing, ears pinned back.

It was *nothing* like the pictures I'd seen. Sleek and strong, with thick legs and a broad chest. The tail was long and thin, and the head was wide, bearing glowing amber eyes and long whiskers. Smooth black stripes cut through the sandy fur along the shoulders, and a ridge of spiky black hair rode down its back. The only thing the depictions from Duke Ferin's book had right were the teeth: long and yellow and deadly.

I swallowed as I saw the menace in the sandcat's eyes, my muscles tight, waiting for it to attack. My sweaty palm hovered over the handle of my flame-sword, waiting. Waiting. Sweat dripped down my neck, sliding irritatingly beneath my shirt. I ignored it, staring at the sandcat with wide eyes. I could hear my ragged breaths, feel my heart bouncing around inside my ribcage, just waiting for the action.

The sandcat lunged.

25
KSEGA

*T*he sandcat flew through the air, arcing down so that it would land directly on top of Erabeth. She was faster, though, and it landed on bare wood, its claws leaving pale gashes in the timber as it tore after her. She had flipped backwards over the bench, landing smoothly on her feet and lifting her sword. It was a unique weapon, with a broader blade than I'd ever seen, that curved sharply in the middle.

When the sandcat landed, she darted forward, her blade slicing through the air. The sandcat leapt away quickly, but not fast enough, and the sharp tip of her sword left a streak of blood smeared across its foreleg. It wasn't a deep cut, and wouldn't do anything to slow the beast down. The only thing it managed to do was infuriate the cat more.

With a roar that shook the entire sand-sled, it bounded towards the rail, repelling off of it to attack Erabeth again. Her back would have been shredded if someone hadn't leapt in her way, taking the brunt of the sandcat's momentum and crashing to the floor of the sand-sled.

Alchemy and the sandcat rolled across the floor of the sled, grappling at each other. The cat's claws tore through his clothes, clicking against his ribs and scraping along the bones. It let out a furious growl as it clamped its jaws down over his shoulder blade. There was a loud *CRACK*, and Sakura and I both winced.

Grunting, Alchemy dug his heel into the sandcat's belly and flipped it over, punching it in the chest to hurl it into the wall of the sand-sled. It roared as it collided with the wood, the timbers groaning and splintering from the blow.

Erabeth had regained her footing from where she had tumbled to the boards. She lunged at the sandcat, jumping over Alchemy, who was hunched over, one hand hovering over a thick rift that had appeared in his shoulder blade. I gawked as the crack was slowly healed, sewn together with writhing threads of shadow. My stomach turned in disgust, but I couldn't look away until it had healed. Once it was closed, the crack flashed a bright green, matching the other cracks and blooms of green along the rest of his skeleton. I saw Sakura's eyes widen with my own. How many of those brightly glowing seams had been injuries?

Another cry from the sandcat drew our attention back towards it and Erabeth. It had flipped back onto its feet, but Erabeth's blade had slithered forward and pierced it just below the leg, sliding deep between the ribs. It bellowed in pain as blood pooled beneath its foot, but it wouldn't be brought down so easily. With a lashing tail, it whirled around and swiped at the Duskan. I heard her yelp in surprise, even though I never saw the claws make contact. Seconds later, rivulets of blood spilled down from her thigh, slowly running down onto her feet.

It spun toward her, ready to leap, and none of us would have been fast enough to help if Sakura hadn't raced forward and swung her arm toward the sandcat. An arc of flame spurred down and slapped the cat on the hide, singing the sandy fur. It hissed and whirled to face her. She gasped as it lunged, and I felt my heart leap into my throat, but Erabeth struck again, swiping her blade past it and grazing its tail. With a roar it spun once again to approach the Duskan.

I had already unslung my bow — it was the first thing I'd done when the sandcat appeared — and now I flicked an arrow from the quiver at my hip, knocking it to the string and drawing it back within a matter of seconds. I didn't have time to pause and breathe. I didn't have time to close my eyes and center my aim. The sandcat was stalking towards Erabeth, who was retreating towards her driving bench. It was a moving target, something I rarely practiced with.

I angled the bow just slightly, about to fire, when the cat's muscles bunched. I shifted my aim just as it leapt, and the arrow flew with it.

With a yowl of pain, the sandcat's course was altered, falling short as it constricted in pain. Erabeth dove out of the way as it slammed onto the sled, rolling in fury and raking its claws against the boards. As it rolled, the arrow shaft jutting from its side snapped, and the tip was driven farther in.

I had another arrow ready before it leapt to its feet again, but it wouldn't be necessary. Alchemy was still crouched on the boards, closer to the beast than the rest of us. He jumped forward, propelling himself directly into the sandcat's chest. I didn't see the bone dagger gripped in his gloved hand until I saw the blood flooding out of the cat's throat.

It jerked to the side, trying to get away, but that only caused the dagger to rip sideways through its flesh, spurting blood across the sand-sled and all over Alchemy's shredded clothes. I felt my stomach squirm, and bile rose in my throat. A strangled sound of disgust escaped from my lips, earning me a strange look from Sakura, but I ignored it, my gaze still locked on the sandcat.

It was dragging itself away from Alchemy, still kicking at him with its hind legs, but its strength was depleting. Blood flowed in torrents from the gash across its throat, and slid in sticky rivers from the places Erabeth and I had struck it. It mewled pitifully as it slumped to the boards, murder still flashing in its amber eyes until, within seconds, they had glazed over, and the cat went still.

Nobody moved for a long moment, save for the heavy breathing of Erabeth and Sakura. My heart was thumping so loudly I was sure everyone could hear it. The only one that was perfectly still was, unsurprisingly, Alchemy.

"It's going to take *ages* to scrub out all this blood." Erabeth grumbled. I couldn't tell if she was referring to the sand-sled or her pants; probably both.

"That's a pretty nasty cut," Sakura pointed out as she wiped her sweating palms on the thighs of her pants and pushed strands of her sweat-dampened hair out of her face.

"I've got some bandages to take care of it," Erabeth waved off her concern, trooping back to the rear of the sand-sled to root through one of the crates. She hissed as she squatted to open it, slightly widening the slash in her leg.

"Need some help?" Sakura offered, already approaching her. The woman huffed and glared at her, but didn't protest as she knelt beside her to help clean the wound.

"You two can make yourselves useful and get Mulligan re-harnessed." Erabeth told Alchemy and I as she turned and leaned against the crate, hissing in pain as she ripped the tear in her pants open more to look at the wound.

"But he ran-" I began, but she cut me off by pointing towards the nearest dune. Alchemy and I looked up to see Mulligan reappearing, still trailing the straps of his harness.

"He's trained to come back." Erabeth's lips quirked into a smug half-smile. "You think Old Duskfall is in such a state of ruin that we don't even know how to survive in our own desert?" her voice turned condescending at the end, and I pinched my lips, rightfully scolded.

Alchemy and I approached the camel, and I took a deep breath, allowing Mulligan to fade into a green glow before me. I flinched at how bright he was. He must have been young, and in excellent health. Blinking away the life glow, I stopped just in front of him. The one aspect of my bering I'd hardly ever touched was my connection to animals. Some bering-mages were able to connect to an animal, convincing it to do their will; some bering-mages made good money luring animals into their hunting traps and selling the meat later. That fact alone had always disgusted me, and I'd never had much of a reason to use it, anyway.

Now, though, I let my power reach out to the Horcathian camel. I took a slow breath, closing my eyes to focus, and reached out to brush my fingers against him. I could feel my bering inside me, like a living thing within the cavity of my chest, waiting for me to let it expand its reach. So I did.

It was a jolting feeling, at first, as if another arm was physically reaching out of my chest, but when I glanced down, nothing was there. I could feel it twist and bind itself to the camel, and I gasped with the sudden feeling of wonder that came over me.

In an instant, I could hear two heartbeats, one thundering loud over the other. I could feel the hesitation that blossomed in both of us, but also the curiosity and, though it was small, the surety that was growing, strengthening the strands of that invisible arm.

Looking up into Mulligan's eyes, I could read what he felt, even though I wasn't actually reading it, but *feeling* it. The simplicity of his thoughts, the distant feeling of receding panic from the sandcat attack, the adrenaline still racing through him after his run, *everything*.

My mind spun with the effort of it. I'd never felt anything this deeply before. I couldn't separate his emotions from my own. I couldn't tell the difference between one thought and another. I couldn't hear my own thoughts with the pommeling of twin heartbeats in my ears. Panic swelled within me, drowning out everything.

Stumbling backwards with a gasp, the connection was violently broken. I squeezed my eyes shut as the world swirled around me, colors blinking in my vision. I rubbed my palms against my eyes, groaning as my whole chest seemed to turn upside down.

"Ksega," something thin poked me in the back, and I winced away from it, looking up to see Alchemy. His skull was tilted to the side, and I had to admit he looked a little horrifying with his clothes torn and stained with blood.

"Sorry. I was . . . trying something new." I glanced up at Mulligan, but he showed no reaction. Had he felt my emotions the way I had his? Had he felt the same power tethering us together?

"Well, let's not do that for a while. Could be dangerous," he patted me on the shoulder and picked up one of the straps to Mulligan's harness. "Now help me with this. I don't want to get on the bad side of this Erabeth woman."

"Agreed," I muttered, taking one of the other harness straps and stepping towards the driving bench. There were rings embedded in the wood, and clips on the ends of the harnesses. They were all made from thick iron, and I had to use my whole palm to force the clip open and hook it in place. Alchemy didn't struggle with it at all.

When Mulligan was successfully re-harnessed, we climbed back onto the sand-sled, pausing before the body of the sandcat. It was splayed out just behind the driving bench, head lolled to one side. After the way I had used my bering moments ago, it made me feel ill to look down at the cat, its soft pelt stained with scarlet blood.

"What should we do with it?" I asked, looking up to where Erabeth was. She couldn't hear me, I knew, but she was looking at us, and must have seen the question in my eyes. Trying not to move while Sakura tediously bandaged her leg, she cupped her hands around her mouth to yell at us.

"Just throw it off the side. The others will eat it." She said it matter-of-factly, but I felt my stomach drop with unease as I asked the next question.

"The other what?"

"The other sandcats, of course."

I pressed my lips together, trying not to let it show how much that unsettled me. I knew of animals eating each other before, but there was something purely savage about them eating the carcass of their own kind.

Alchemy, unbothered by the work, bent down to grab the sandcat's rear legs, dragging it towards the rail. I wasn't sure how strong Alchemy was, but even without muscles, the Curse left him with impossible power. He hefted it up and rolled it over the top of the rail with apparent ease, dusting his gloved hands off and then looking down at his shirtfront. He pulled his cloak around to examine the damage the sandcat had done, then said, in a voice thick with disappointment,

"I'm afraid these clothes are officially ruined."

From across the sand-sled, Erabeth shrugged and said, "It could be worse. I'm sure we can find something to hide you, Bones."

Alchemy lifted his head to face her, and I knew that if he had expressions, his would be one of utter lack of amusement. She was staring daggers at him, her lips twisted in a frown. I looked between them, desperately searching for a way to defuse the tension.

"Give me the cloak," I said, holding my arm out for it. Alchemy looked down at my extended palm for a long moment before releasing a sigh that rattled through his bones, unclasping the cloak and placing it in my offered hand.

I crouched to begin mopping up what I could of the puddles of blood. It was too late to save the wood from being stained, and too late to spare Erabeth — or whoever cleaned these sand-sleds — hours of painstaking scrubbing, but I needed a distraction, and the slippery puddles of blood provided just that.

By the time I had soaked up whatever blood I could from the place the sandcat had breathed its last and the trail it had left when Alchemy dragged it to the rail, I knew that even if the tears could be sewn closed, the smell alone would prevent the cloak from ever being wearable. I tossed it onto the bundle of clothes Alchemy had half-ripped off his skeleton and left beside the edge of one of the benches, gagging as I looked down to the smears of blood the work had left across my own hands.

"Here," Sakura had appeared at my side, offering me a cloth dampened by the water from her water skin. There were already browning stains near the corners, showing she had used it to wipe away the excess blood on Erabeth's leg. I accepted it and scrubbed away at the blood, glad it came away easily.

"Thanks. Are we going to get moving soon?" I looked up at the sky, and based on the position of the sun, it was a few hours past midday.

"We should be." She replied, looking back towards the Duskan, who was repacking the medical supplies and moving Alchemy's bundle of massacred clothing to the back of the sand-sled. I wasn't really paying attention to Erabeth, though; I was looking at Sakura.

She looked more ragged than usual, with strands of her dark hair loose and curling around her face, some of them plastered against her sweat-slicked skin. Her green eyes had a spark of adventure in them, but I could also see the depth of her weariness. Alchemy had warned her of pushing herself too far, but she had steadfastly refused to listen. I was worried she would continue to push herself as far as she could go until there was no way she could continue.

"Are you alright?" I asked softly, scrutinizing her face. She looked up at me, her eyes for once devoid of their walls. Encouraged by her openness, I reached out, brushing my hand against her knuckles, an obvious question hanging in the action.

She inhaled sharply and tugged her hand away, and trying as I might to conceal it, I couldn't hide the way my jaw clenched as my heart stung. She turned her head, not looking at me, and drew her arms up to hug herself, slowly shaking her head.

"Just tired. I'm fine. I'm going to go see if Erabeth needs any more help. We'd do well to stay on her good side." She started to walk towards the captain of the sand-sled, then paused to look back at me, opening her mouth as if to say something more. Then she glanced away and closed her mouth, pressing her lips into a thin line and walking away to join Erabeth.

"She'll come around." I jumped as the voice sounded beside me, low and grating. I looked up to see Alchemy looming at my side. It was strange seeing him without clothes on, strange seeing the painfully apparent lack of flesh and muscle and *life*. The background buzzing that emanated from him only made it more unsettling to be in his presence. Yet, at the same time, there was something inexplicably comforting about being near him.

"I don't know what you mean." I said simply, trying to keep my voice light. He made a noise akin to a brutal cough, which I took to be his best attempt at a scoff.

"It's more obvious than a naked smith in a flower field." He jabbed at me with one of his slender fingers, the bone digging into my shoulder. I frowned and rubbed the spot where his finger had been, cocking my head to the side.

"You make a lot of weird comparisons," I remarked, and he shrugged.

"Don't change the subject, boy. You know what I mean." He crossed his long arms, creating a knot of bones in front of his ribcage. If he'd had a nose, I knew he would be staring down it.

"Can't say I do." I lied, although the words didn't roll off my tongue as easily as most of my lies did. Of course they didn't. This one was different. This one was about Sakura.

Alchemy released a sigh, waiting to say more until Erabeth and Sakura had walked past us to take seats at the driving bench. They were at least talking, which was a good thing to me. If we were going to stay in Old Duskfall for any amount of time, we'd need at least one person on our side.

Once the girls were past us, Alchemy slid one of his arms over my shoulders and guided me back to the tent. He gestured to the bench, but neither of us sat down. My nerves were jumping around too excitedly to let me hold still for even a moment, and I began to tap my foot anxiously.

"Alright, enough, you don't have to keep it a secret around me." Alchemy removed his arm from around me and chuckled. "Maybe others can't see it as well as I can, but it's so obvious it's almost painful. You like her, don't you?"

I hadn't admitted it to myself, but now that I heard the words out loud, I knew solely from the buzz that bloomed in my belly that he was right.

By all the Great Lakes and the Endless Sea . . . I *liked* her.

It must have shown clearly on my face, because Alchemy's laughter redoubled, and I felt heat crawling up my neck into my face as I looked up at him.

"You can't tell her." I said finally, wishing my voice wasn't pitched so high. "I don't think she feels the same." Once again, as soon as the words were out, I knew how true they were. I sighed after I'd said them. I had felt my hopes go up when we were at Jhapato's house, when we had held hands, but now I cringed to think of it.

Of *course* she had been willing to hold my hand then. She had been thinking of home, and she had been scared and tired. She probably wasn't thinking clearly. She probably regretted it. She must have felt as awkward about it as I did, if not more. Her attitude towards me over the past two days had been proof enough of that, the way she made it a point not to look at me, or to avoid any moment where we touched. While it irked me to no end, I was sort of grateful for it. The last thing I needed was to be getting distracted by her while we were in what was considered to be one of the most dangerous kingdoms.

"Wouldn't dream of it," Alchemy reassured me, and I huffed a small sigh of relief. It did very little to soothe my nerves; they were sufficiently rattled after my most recent revelation.

I lowered myself onto the bench, propping my elbows on my knees and raking a hand through my hair anxiously. The fingers of my free hand fidgeted with the fletching of my arrows, eager for some sort of distraction from the foreign emotions making themselves known inside of me.

The sand-sled was tugged into motion as Erabeth snapped the reins, keeping her eyes forward as she drove, but still keeping a casual conversation with Sakura. I wanted to go up and join them to see what they were talking about, but couldn't bring myself to go close to Sakura again. Not after she'd made it clear she didn't want me close.

Despite the intense heat of the day, I decided I would try to get some sleep. There was no way to tell how long it would take us to reach the capital of Old Duskall, but I planned to nap for as much of it as I could. It was one of the easiest ways to avoid Sakura, the growing ache in my leg, and the anxious thoughts that swarmed through my head.

I leaned back and closed my eyes, trying to blot out the sticky feeling of sweat on my skin and the itch of sand under my clothes and the poke of pebbles digging into my feet. I just wanted to *sleep*. And soon enough, even with sand billowing up around the sand-sled and the whole vessel jolting and jerking and swaying, sleep came.

*K*sega. Ksega, wake up." Someone shaking me by the shoulder caused me to pry my eyes open, blinking blearily at the thin black form in front of me.

"Are we there yet?" I groaned, rubbing the sleep from my eyes and gasping as I stood up, a stiff pain rolling down my leg from the cut I'd received in the runeboar fight.

"Yes," Erabeth was the one to answer. She was near the front of the sand-sled, doing things with Mulligan's harness. "But not quite. We need to get Bones here some new clothes before we head into town." She squinted at Alchemy. "Most people here don't take very kindly to *dasten* magic."

"And you're different from them because . . ?" Sakura prompted. Erabeth cut her a glare.

"I am different because not only have I *seen* the effects of *dasten* magic, but I've *felt it* too." She shook her head sadly, looking up at Alchemy. "I would wish it on no other." Her gaze turned hard again. "Others will not be so understanding. I will take you to Irina, but I will not set foot inside her lair, and I will not help you any further once you are there." She silenced any questions ready on our tongues by snapping her fingers and pointing to the crates in the tent. "I'm supposed to be transporting some cloths and fabrics into the city. There should be some usable materials in there." She looked over at Sakura and pulled a small leather packet from her belt, tucked just behind the sheath of her curved sword. "I hope you're handy with a needle."

Alchemy and I were content to leave the two of them to root through the fabrics, only bothering us when they needed to measure some of the fabrics against the skeleton. Erabeth seemed to know what she was doing, explaining how they would create extra folds in the fabric or use the density of certain materials to their advantages, giving Alchemy a figure he didn't — and couldn't — have.

"What sort of Duskan woman is a warrior, a sand-sled driver, and a seamstress?" I whispered to Alchemy once the girls had begun their sewing, working doubly fast. The sun had already dipped out of sight, and the only light was that of its fading rays across the pink sky, so they had lit a lantern to aid their work.

"This one, apparently." Alchemy muttered in return. I had the feeling he was hiding something, and I knew he could probably get a better read from her than Sakura or I could, but I didn't bother to ask him what it was he'd noticed.

To my mild surprise, it took the two of them only a couple of hours to complete Alchemy's outfit. It was a loose-fitting pair of trousers, tucked into the tall leather boots that had survived the sandcat fight, a baggy shirt with a dramatic yellow vest, a new cloak, this one draping regally across his shoulders and gathering around his ankles, and make-shift wraps to go on his hands.

"We'll get you some new gloves free of blood stains while we're in the town." Sakura had promised when they'd presented the outfit to the skeleton.

"Until then, try not to let your hands in anyone's sight," Erabeth added, then handed him another fold of cloth. "Here, wrap this around the bottom half of your skull." She tilted her head to the side once he'd done so, pantomiming pulling his hood up to encourage him to do so. When he did, the effect was quite startling.

Save for the hardly detectable green glow shining through tiny spots in the shirt or in the depths of the cloak's cowl, he was nothing more than an abnormally tall stranger, perhaps a merchant from Coldmon or a healer from Freetalon.

"We're ready to head into the city, then?" Sakura was rubbing her knuckles again, and I caught her eye, trying desperately to convey all the confidence I had in her with one look. She looked away quickly, but I still saw the flush of color that had appeared in her cheeks.

"Yes. Everyone hold on," Erabeth cracked a crooked grin at us, a mischievous look none of us had yet to see from her. "Mulligan is ready for dinner." She looked up at the swiftly darkening sky. "And so am I. It's going to be a bumpy ride!" she hopped onto the driving bench and flicked the reins, urging Mulligan forward into a heady canter.

I had thought riding aboard *Orvyn* was a rough experience, especially with the sea wraith attack, but this bordered on being as chaotic as riding in the little rowboats with the crew of *The Coventry* as we closed in on Clawbreak for the pirate heist. I clung to one of the tent support poles, and saw Sakura doing the same on the opposite side of the sand-sled. Alchemy had lowered himself into a sort of half crouch, his palm carefully placed on the wooden boards beneath him and somehow managing to keep his balance as the sled rocked and pivoted across the dunes.

It was a very violent journey, but it was a short one. We'd crested no more than four dunes before Mulligan slowed to a trot, pulling us gradually down the slope of a dune towards the capital of the desert kingdom.

"Welcome to *Baske Latel.*" Erabeth said, gesturing broadly at the kingdom before us. "The City of Bones."

I barely even heard her, drinking in the scene before me. The rumors floating across Horcath about Old Duskfall left the kingdom as a place fallen into the depths of ruination in everyone's mind, a land deprived of culture and unique diversity.

The rumors were wrong.

The castle itself rose in the center of the city, a series of tall buildings constructed from pale, sandy stones and designed with elegant arches and tall iron spires. It was surrounded by rings and rings of houses built from the same stone, but the farther out the rings became, the less refined the buildings became. They went from stone to wood to scraps of whatever materials people could find. The city itself was huge;

it must have spread around for hundreds and hundreds of blocks in each direction, flowering out from the central castle.

There were giant stalls outside the city borders, housing tons of Horcathian camels with sand-sleds propped against the side of the stables. At the sight of the familiar location, Mulligan snorted and tossed his head about in excitement.

"Irina lives on the northern side of the city. She changes where she stays every couple of days, so we'll have to track her down." Erabeth steered Mulligan towards the stables, and the camel was more than happy to comply.

"Will that be difficult?" Sakura asked, her eyes wide with wonder as she stared at the City of Bones.

"That depends," Erabeth turned her hawk-like stare to Alchemy. "It *should* prove relatively easy, as long as Taro's been taken good care of."

"Who's Taro?" I asked, but Erabeth only raised an eyebrow at me.

"All in due time, blond one." We pulled to a stop in front of the camel stables, and I was slightly surprised to find that it was unattended.

Erabeth told us to wait on the sand-sled while she retrieved a long wooden pole with a hook on the end, using it to carefully remove the harness and the patterned blanket across Mulligan's neck, chest, and back. The camel held still as she worked, barely even twitching until after the straps and the blanket had tumbled to the ground around his long, thick legs.

I was about to see if I could get closer to see where Mulligan would be going — there weren't many of the large stalls, and the ones that were there were mostly occupied — when I realized Sakura was ushering Alchemy away from the cargo in the tent, because more Duskans were approaching from the town to help unload the crates of fabric.

I joined them off to the side as they began to unload, pulling the crates and sacks onto rings of wood with thick rope woven around them to create a net. The nets were each drawn by a camel. Not a Horcathian camel, though. Just a normal camel. Had I not already seen Mulligan, I may have found their size a little daunting. Now, though, they only seemed like oversized dogs.

"Come this way, and keep your heads down," Erabeth had appeared at our side, and she was waving us away, towards the rickety outskirts of the city. We followed her, and even though I kept anxiously glancing at the men working to unload the sand-sled, none of them objected to our departure.

"What about Mulligan and the sled?" Sakura asked once we were safely out of earshot. I noticed her throwing fretful glances at Alchemy, probably concerned about his height. All the Duskans I'd seen so far weren't exactly *short*, but it was safe to say that not only did Alchemy and I dwarf them, even Sakura appeared taller than average beside them.

"It'll all be taken care of," Erabeth waved her concern away. "These things are arranged for when each sand-sled is set to depart from a station." Her gaze flickered to Alchemy before darting away again. "Not that any of that matters to you three." She sighed, looking pointedly at Sakura. "I don't think it's a good idea for you to go to Irina. She isn't a pleasant lady to deal with."

Sakura's gaze shifted quickly to Alchemy, then to me, but I wasn't able to read her expression by the time she looked back at Erabeth. I already knew what she was going to say, but I didn't bother to try and stop her. Alchemy and I both knew we all would have agreed anyway.

"Thanks for the advice," Sakura told her politely. "But we're going to stick to our course." Erabeth's only response was a tightening of her lips and a tensing of her muscles.

It didn't take us much longer to reach the edge of the City of Bones. I wasn't sure what exactly I'd been expecting, but it hadn't been the rough sort of uniformity that surrounded me as we stepped into what was almost like a whole new world.

The ramshackle homes and buildings had looked unstable and unsafe from a distance, but upon closer inspection, it was obvious that the craftsmanship of each establishment was excellent and well thought out. The buildings had similar structures, and while the majority of them lacked windows or even doors, everything was impeccably clean. The roads were packed sand and slabs of sandstone, except in the roughest areas where the sand was still loose.

There were colors, too. Bright scarves to protect you from the sun hung from lines beside shaded display tables, presenting wares from jewelry to elegant daggers crafted from the bones of Horcathian camels and sandcats to mismatched outfits designed to help hunters and sand-sled drivers blend into their surroundings.

Despite the shadowy little alleys and the rickety homes, the people we walked past were happy and smiling, holding hands with their children or significant other, pointing at the various items for sale around them. People walked in and out of buildings, some empty-handed, others with bits of food or scraps of various materials: fabrics, bits of wood, sheets of warped iron.

"I'd expected this place to be a bit more . . . Clawbreak-y." I muttered in Sakura's ear as we walked, marveling at the city around me. There were flower boxes in front of houses, boasting bright flowers or monotone little cacti.

Sakura eased farther away from me, giving me an irritated frown, but I hardly noticed it, my attention locked on the displays in front of a store, meant to draw curious people like me inside. There were unique arrows I'd never seen before, looking to be crafted from the long bones of an animal, and little necklaces and charms bearing the teeth of those animals.

"Me too, if I'm being honest. Hurry up," Sakura hissed, reaching out to grip me by the arm and tug me along. Erabeth was moving fast through the crowd, and while Alchemy didn't struggle at all to keep up with his long-legged strides, Sakura and I were falling slightly behind, thanks to our bewilderment at the city that surrounded us.

When we came back up alongside Erabeth, she must have seen the way we looked at the people and buildings around us. Nothing about it seemed ruined or falling at all. Nothing about it seemed to hint at the fact that someone in this kingdom might know something vital about the creation of the Curse.

"This is the touristy part of the outermost ring," Erabeth said as she pushed her way past a thickened chunk of the crowd. "We'll be seeing the sneaky criminal activity you're looking for once we reach the northern side."

I wasn't used to the tourist side of Horcath. The Port and Lourak saw the majority of travelers in Wisesol, but it wasn't a place anyone selected for a getaway vacation. Riddled with crime and seafaring men, there wasn't anything very appealing about the kingdom.

Famark had been a new experience for me, with all the shops and colors and people. It had certainly matched the tourist profile. This little section of the City of Bones, though, didn't quite match it. There wasn't the same energy. It was like the happy underbelly.

If all these bone weapons and dark alleys were the happy side, I couldn't imagine what the dark underbelly of Old Duskfall might look like.

The sun had gone down, and lanterns were lit and hanging on either side of the road, spilling happy orange light across the sand. Even though the sun had gone down, people still bustled through the streets, heading in and out of shops, selling their wares, and making loud conversation despite the fact that people might be sleeping.

Erabeth weaved confidently through the crowd, her face grim and muscles taught. She limped only slightly, and kept her hands near her belt, one palm placed on the pommel of her sword. Her gaze swept from side to side, suspicious of everything. She reminded me of Sakura in more ways than one, but there was something much more abrasive about her outwardly than I'd ever seen with Sakura.

The people in the streets used their andune to their advantage, pulling irritating sand out of their hair or shoes, and clearing it out of the road. They used it to lift items into their hands, or catch their hat when it fell, or adjust the straps on their sandals, all these little things that I'd never thought to use my own magic for.

We walked for a little over half an hour before Erabeth entered a building. It was taller than the others, and had windows that revealed a bustling tavern on the bottom floor. As we entered, the strong smell of ale and terrible breath filled my nostrils, and I wrinkled my nose against the smell. Alchemy, dipping his head to enter the room, lifted his head to peer out from beneath the hood of his cloak, assessing the room, and I did the same.

It was broad and loud, filled with round tables and chairs, some of them knocked over. A bar was on the far side, frequently visited by the men that roared with laughter and crowded the room. Most of the occupants were bulky and bearded, dark-skinned and dark-haired, although I saw some people that looked like they may have been visiting from other kingdoms, awkwardly out of place as they avoided the louder customers.

The only women in the room, aside from Erabeth and Sakura, were a small number of Duskan ladies wearing far too little clothing, their hair pulled into tight updos and decorated with jewels and gold chains. One of them looked hardly older than me, and she winked as we walked past, pushing our way deeper into the building. I looked away quickly, glancing at Sakura to see if she'd noticed. She had one hand on her flame-sword hilt, eyes scanning the room as she stuck close behind Erabeth, who was approaching the bartender.

"Ah," he said when we stepped up to the bar. He was taller than most of the other Duskan men we'd seen, coming close to my own height, and he was heavyset with thinning hair. "You again." He deadpanned, his gaze boring into Erabeth. Her face was blank.

"I'm here for my bird." She said simply. Sakura quirked an eyebrow at me, and I shrugged. Lots of establishments that preferred to stay under the radar could often be found through code words or phrases, and I guessed she thought this might be one of those situations.

"Pay up." The bartender demanded, and Erabeth scowled.

"You didn't do a good enough job to get the money." She pulled a pouch from her belt and tossed it onto the bar. "You get half. Now give me my bird."

The bartender sneered at her, but took the pouch and went into the back.

"You have an actual bird?" Sakura asked quietly, and Erabeth nodded.

"Taro. He's helpful." Her frown deepened. "I had to leave him here for this last trip. Part of a business exchange with someone else." She shook her head slowly. "It was something I shouldn't have invested in. Either way," she drummed her fingers impatiently on the wood of the bar. "We should be able to get the information we need soon."

I looked over at Sakura and saw my own look of confusion mirrored on her face. Before either of us could ask, Alchemy voiced the thought all of us had.

"Isn't this a bit . . . backwards?" he asked. Erabeth snorted.

"'Everything's backward in the Bones'. Remember that." She stood up straighter as the bartender returned, this time with a hawk perched on his forearm. He held it across the bar, and the bird hopped to Erabeth's shoulder, eyes sharp and alert. It angled its head down at me, and I instinctively leaned away from its blade-like beak.

"Pleasure doing business with you." The bartender snarled, beginning to turn away, but Erabeth's voice brought him back, a scowl on his face.

"We're not done yet. I need to know where I can find the *ista*." Immediately, the man's face pinched in anger. He opened his mouth to speak, but she cut him off, speaking in a harsh string of words that I didn't recognize. I'd heard about the Sandrun language, but never met anyone who used it until now.

The bartender spat on the wood of the bar in front of Erabeth and said something back. Sakura's brows were furrowed, and I guessed she was trying to translate what they were saying, even though she didn't speak the language. Outside of Old Duskfall, no one did.

The only other word I recognized beside *ista*, which Alchemy had told us was witch, was *sagdred*. He hadn't been able to tell us what that one meant.

After a very heated argument, Erabeth retrieved another pouch of money from her belt and slammed it angrily on the bar. The man stared at it for a long moment before taking it and spitting something else in Sandrun. Again, the word *ista* was mentioned.

Erabeth muttered something offensive under her breath and turned to leave. We all followed, ignoring the few curious stares we earned as we left, most of them direction at Alchemy or at Erabeth's hawk.

Once we were out in the street, I saw that it had cleared out considerably. Only a few stragglers remained to enjoy the night, which was cooling fast now that the sun had gone down.

"Did you get what we needed?" Sakura asked as Erabeth stopped at the corner of the tavern, affectionately stroking the hawk's beak.

"Yes. But there's one more thing. Stay here." She turned to walk down behind the tavern, disappearing from view. Seconds after she had vanished, Sakura turned to Alchemy.

"How likely do you think it is that she won't come back?"

"Not very likely." He tilted his head to the side. "There's something about her. She'll be back."

I would have asked what he meant, but never got the chance as we heard the sound of a door slamming, then people coming to blows. I winced with each grunt, and saw Sakura reacting similarly.

"Should we-" she began, but Alchemy cut her off.

"No. Something tells me she's not on the wrong side of it."

Minutes later, Erabeth's form reappeared down the alley, walking towards us with the outline of her hawk still perched on her shoulder. When she came back into the light of the lanterns, I heard Sakura gasp. A bloody cut on the Duskan's lip had begun to drip down her chin, swelling as it did. Other than that, she looked unhurt, but there was no ignoring the spray of blood across one shoulder. She grinned at us, the look mischievous and a little disconcerting.

"I don't pay people who don't earn it," she explained, holding up not one, but both of the coin pouches she had given the bartender. I saw Sakura's eyes widen, but I wasn't very surprised. I'd seen people do this before.

"How didn't he earn it?" Sakura asked, mouth still agape. Erabeth's eyes twinkled, but her only response was something in Sandrun. Sakura glanced at Alchemy and whispered, "What does that mean?"

He only shrugged.

Erabeth swaggered down the street, something about the lazy walk reminding me of the pirates of *The Coventry*, and how at ease Thomas had always seemed. I wondered for a moment where they were now, and if they had met *Orvyn*. Had they made sure Jessie and Sakura's eirioth-mage friend had reached the Port safely? I'd been so preoccupied, I hadn't had much time to worry about them. I didn't have time to worry about them *now*.

"Keep up, *sagdreds*." Erabeth called to us over her shoulder. She seemed to be in a much merrier mood, and since the only thing that had changed between now and the last time she'd spoken to us was her attacking a man, I felt myself instinctively walking safely apart from her as she continued to speak.

"It's time for you to meet a witch."

26
SAKURA

*E*rabeth had been telling the truth about the northern side of the City of Bones. If you asked me to name the exact moment I could sense the change of the atmosphere, I wouldn't be able to tell you, but at some point I had been aware of the shift in the air, the lack of buzzing conversation and brightly lit lanterns, and the prominent appearance of figures moving in the shadows and darkened buildings.

I couldn't really *see* anything illegal happening, but I could definitely *sense* that it was happening all around us, in back rooms and dark alleys and upstairs attics. It made my skin crawl to think of it. Breaking the law wasn't tolerated in Carlore, and while the sentences weren't terribly strict, they were still enforced. It had given me a healthy fear of the authority in Carlore from a very young age. Even crossing the border Carlore and Brightlock shared when I was first in the Evershifting Forest had bothered me.

Ksega, on the other hand, seemed completely in his element. His gaze was just as curious as mine, roving around the street and every building we passed, but he wasn't as tense as I was, and he made no move to reach for his weapon, even whenever we heard a scuffling coming from one of the porches or a back road.

I was annoyed with how much I kept glancing at him, and somehow even more annoyed when he didn't look back. It was stupid, the way I kept wanting him to look at me, just so I could get a clearer glimpse of those startling blue eyes, or find a way to make him laugh again.

He was a distraction, now. I didn't know when it had happened, but I didn't like it, and I tried everything in my power to ignore it. But by all the stars and clouds, he certainly made it difficult with all that charming grinning of his.

Erabeth led the way confidently, glaring at anyone we saw until they slunk into the shadows, still watching us warily. One of the strangers, a hawk-nosed, hunch-backed fellow, eyed my flame-sword with beady eyes, and I moved closer to Alchemy on instinct, remembering the man with the strange shirt from Clawbreak. Erabeth had noticed, and she chuckled.

"Keep your weapons close. There are a lot of pick-pockets in this kingdom." She warned.

"Duly noted," Ksega murmured, edging closer to Alchemy's other side and letting his fingers graze the fletching of the arrows hanging at his hip.

We traveled deep into the back roads, winding around buildings and avoiding anyone else we saw. I couldn't be sure how long we'd traveled, because the sky was mostly obscured by the fabrics draped between the roofs of houses, casting us in shifting tunnels of shadow, but if I had to guess, it was close to an hour. My body ached from so much travel, and I hoped we were able to find a place to sleep soon.

Just as I was preparing to ask Erabeth how much farther we had to go, she stopped in front of the door to a circular building. It was squat and tucked away behind the others, lacking windows and any outward furnishings.

"Here we are." Erabeth grimaced as she looked at the door. "You can still turn back."

"We can't." I said simply, clenching my fists. "We've come too far to turn away now."

She looked at me for a long moment, her dark eyes searching. I tried not to let it unsettle me, keeping my expression neutral. Finally, she shrugged and turned away, walking off down one of the dark side streets. Before she disappeared, she turned back to address all three of us.

"Take Taro with you," she said, extending her arm. The hawk made a disgruntled noise, but edged out to the end of her arm, waiting for one of us to step forward. "He'll take you to my home, if you need a place to stay." She clarified at our confused expressions.

"Thank you," I said with a nod, stepping forward to take the bird. His talons gripped my arm tightly as he shuffled up to my shoulder. I tried not to flinch as he inspected me, hoping he couldn't sense my hesitation.

"Stay out of trouble, *Faja*." She nodded down at the flame-sword at my belt. "With how dry it is out here, that can do a lot of damage." She squinted over at Ksega and Alchemy. "And still you might not stand a chance against an *ista*. Be careful, and good luck." And with that, she was gone, jogging down the alley and out of sight.

"What does *faja* mean?" Ksega muttered, looking up at Alchemy.

"How should I know? I only know *ista* is witch. Most people do."

"No, Chem, most people don't. Come on, let's go inside." I led them back up to the door of the round house and, before I could talk myself out of it, rapped my knuckles against the wood, ignoring the irritated ruffling of Taro's feathers against my cheek.

I heard a thunking sound coming from inside the building, and my hand settled comfortably on the hilt of my flame-sword. Erabeth's warning echoed in my head, but I wasn't very concerned about heeding it. If I had to use my weapon, I would.

The tension was palpable between the three of us as we waited, holding our breath — with the exception of Alchemy — as the knob of the handle began to rattle as someone unlocked it from the other side. We all braced ourselves; I could see Ksega's shoulders tensing out of the corner of my eye, and even Alchemy looked a little uneasy, swaying impatiently back and forth.

The door swung open, and—

"*Oh.*" Ksega said, and I elbowed him in the ribs. He grunted with surprise and coughed, rubbing the back of his neck. "Right. Sorry."

"May I help you?" the woman who stood before us couldn't have been Irina. She was hardly older than me, maybe close to Erabeth's age, with beautiful bronze skin and long hair that fell in waves nearly to her hips. She wore a tight-fitting dress, but the top was hidden under a thin blanket draped over her arms. Her eyes were wide and dark, and she looked curiously up at Alchemy.

"We're looking for someone named Irina." I said, wondering for a moment if Erabeth had led us to the wrong place, and if she had done it intentionally. But then, why leave Taro behind?

"My mother." The young woman stood up straight, wrapping her blanket tighter around her shoulders. "Why do you want to see her?"

"We need her advice on something." I wasn't sure how vague I needed to be, but I wasn't about to trust this girl. Although Erabeth may have exaggerated about how dangerous Irina was, I still knew there must have been a kernel of truth that her fears were rooted in. "Can you take us to her?"

"She's busy." The woman snapped, easing the door almost closed so that only her face was still visible. "Go away. Find someone else to help you."

"We need *her*," Ksega insisted, reaching out to push against the door as the woman tried to close it. Her face pinched in annoyance.

"*No.* She is too old to be troubled with- with-" she paused, considering, as if looking for the word, then finished, "-with the *antics* of strangers." She made to shut the door, and with her leverage against the floor, I knew Ksega wouldn't be able to hold it, but Alchemy stepped forward and braced his hand against the wood. He reached up and tugged the fabric down from around his skull, revealing it to her. Her eyes widened in horror, and I heard the blanket crumple to the ground as her fingers released it.

She said something that sounded like a name, one hand pressed against her chest as she stared up at Alchemy's bared skull. I felt my stomach writhe with nervousness as I waited for her to scream, to shout, to draw more attention to him. What was he *thinking*, showing her his face?

"Who are you?" she snapped, her gaze turning to me. I noticed the sand at the base of the porch started to swirl with her agitation. "Who brought you here?"

"Easy now," I held up my hands, as much as it pained me to release my flame-sword. "We aren't here to stir up any trouble. We just want to know some things about the Curse."

"My mother doesn't know anything about the Curse." Her eyes slit as she strained against Alchemy, trying to close the door. "She cannot help you. Now leave, before I scream. Believe me, you don't want to find out what some of the people in these alleys are capable of. They'll slit your legs so you can't walk, and whip your back until it's in shreds, then they'll leave you to the vultures!" she kicked at the door, groaning as she tried to shut it, but Alchemy didn't budge. She started to hiss a string of curses at him, some of them in the traditional Horcathian tongue, but others in Sandrun.

"Mariem?" a cracking, withered voice, soft as a hummingbird's wings, drifted from within the house, barely tickling my ears. I couldn't be sure that Ksega heard it, but I knew Alchemy did. The woman holding the door had as well, and her face twisted into a glower.

"Yes, Mother?" the woman, Mariem, peeped over her shoulder, but her gaze darted back to us every other second. Her accented voice was strained with the effort of holding her tongue when speaking to her mother.

"Who's there?" the elderly voice croaked.

"Nobody. Lost travelers." Mariem looked sharply at us. "They were just leaving-" her voice jolted at the end as someone came up behind her and pulled the door open more. Her frown deepened and she crossed her arms as we were scrutinized by her mother.

"Who are you?" the elderly woman asked. She was a little shorter than Mariem, so not much shorter than me, and had salt-and-pepper hair that lay over her shoulder in a braid. Even with the marks of age in her lined face, I could see Mariem's resemblance to her.

"We're looking for a woman named Irina." I said, ignoring the burning hatred in Mariem's eyes. Why did she hate us so much? Was *she* the person Erabeth had been worried about? Surely it couldn't have been the woman before us. She was far too old to pose a threat to anyone.

"That's me." She tilted her head to the side, examining Alchemy. There was no sign of fear in her owlish eyes as she drank in the black skull and the pulsing green glow. "How may I help you?" she turned back to me, and I got the feeling she already knew the answer.

"We want to talk about the Curse." I answered. Mariem took a breath, as if to argue, but Irina held up a wrinkled hand to silence her. She gave her mother a dirty look, but closed her mouth.

"What is there to talk about? It's a terrible thing, and it's a permanent thing." Irina's eyes narrowed, shifting to Alchemy. "Have you been experimenting with things you shouldn't have?"

"No, nothing like that," I began to explain, but Taro stirred on my shoulder. I glanced at him, prepared to ignore it, when I realized there were figures behind us on the streets. They were hiding well, and I was sure there were more out of sight, possibly not even interested in us, but I felt my skin crawl with the knowledge that they were there all the same.

"May we come in?" Alchemy asked, sensing my unease. "It's been a long journey, and my companions need some rest. At least a place for them to sit would be greatly appreciated."

Irina looked between the three of us once more, then nodded, opening the door farther. Mariem made a noise of indignation, but didn't protest as the three of us filed inside, hands once again resting on our weapons, and she slammed the door closed behind us.

The entry room took up the front half of the circular house. The other half was concealed beyond a wall, the only entryway between the two rooms a dark velvet curtain off to one side. This room was lightly furnished, with a dining table and some chairs, a tattered old sofa, and some sort of work station I assumed was the kitchen. It was made very homey by the worn rug on the floor and the warm lantern-light that flooded the room, cast from an old iron oil lamp placed upon the table beside a vase of slowly withering flowers.

"Please, sit," Irina gestured to the sofa, and Ksega sank into it gratefully at once. I was more hesitant to let my guard down, so Alchemy sat next, and to my great annoyance, only left room between himself and Ksega. Concealing a grimace, I took the empty place, keeping as much space between Ksega and I as I could without sitting on top of Alchemy, and ignoring Taro's complaints.

"They shouldn't be here." Mariem grunted, even as she stepped into the little kitchen to prepare a small plate of refreshments. Her mother ignored her, pulling one of the dining table chairs in front of the sofa and sitting in it to face us.

"How did this come to be?" Irina waved a hand in Alchemy's direction, and Ksega and I both twisted our necks to peer at him, waiting for an answer. Neither of us really *knew* how he had become Cursed, only that he had somehow become vulnerable enough for it to capture him, and he didn't like to talk about it much.

"It was a very long time ago," Alchemy began, his gravelly voice lower than usual. "I don't remember a lot about it. It was very painful. It happened at a point in my life where nothing mattered. I was too weak, and it took me." He folded his gloved hands in front of him, clenching them tightly together. "I've fought it every day since it claimed me. There isn't a day that goes by that I wish I had been stronger." He shook his head slowly. "It's a terrible thing, this Curse. It must be destroyed at all costs, and that is why we are here." He looked up at Irina; she didn't so much as flinch at his appearance, but Mariem, who was setting a tray of some sort of crackers and cheese down before us, did, wincing away as she went to retrieve cups of water for us. I thanked her when she handed me one. My mouth felt like it was full of sand.

"What makes you think I can help you?" Irina asked shrewdly, squinting at us. I wondered if she could see us clearly.

"We were told you may be able to help by someone who knew you. A man named Jhapato." I began, and her eyes cut to me, sharp and suspicious. I opened my mouth to say something more, but before I could Mariem cursed again and spat,

"That man has done nothing but bring trouble to our family. How dare you even speak his name in this home!" she peeled her lips back and glared at us. "You should leave before I choke you with sand!" she stepped forward and jabbed a finger at my face, and I jerked back into the cushions of the sofa, shocked.

"Hey, easy!" Ksega leaned over, partially blocking my body with his own, and pushed Mariem's hand away. Taro screeched in annoyance, batting his wings into my head, but I reached up to sooth him by rubbing my finger over his beak the same way I had seen Erabeth do it. That seemed to help him calm down, but his feathers were still ruffled, and he was looking at the people around him with wide eyes, his talons digging into my shoulder.

"We didn't know you had a *bad* history with him, alright? He only told us you might be able to help. We're looking for the source of the Curse, because we want to destroy it." Ksega went on as he turned his gaze to Irina while I tried to wriggle farther away from him, but it was no use. I was sandwiched between his shoulder and Alchemy. "Whatever issues exist between you and Jhapato, they don't concern us. Can you help us or not?"

The silence that hung in the room was long and anxious. I hardly felt myself breathing, waiting for something to happen. I knew we could probably beat them in a fight, if it came down to it, but I didn't really *want* to fight either of them.

"It's okay," I said. "We'll leave." Some of the tension instantly defused, but Ksega turned to face me, his brows knit. I gave him a small nod, then said, "We'll keep going on our own. Thank you for your hospitality. We'll leave now." I gently pushed Ksega out of the way and stood up, and a moment later he and Alchemy followed.

Mariem was still glaring heated daggers at all of us, but Irina looked contemplative. I was tempted to stick around and hear what else she might have to say, but I knew we'd worn out our welcome. It was time to go.

I stepped around them toward the door, and heard the thumping of boots as Ksega and Alchemy followed suit. I had just opened the door a crack when Irina spoke.

"Go to Old Nightfall."

"I'm sorry?" I looked back at her, trying to keep my expression open. She pressed her lips tightly together, as if she didn't want to say it, but forced herself to. Mariem was watching with confused eyes.

"Go to Old Nightfall. There is a well that will take you there. It-" she paused, sighed, and shook her head. "It's in the Oasis. You have only two days to find it, so you must hurry. Now go." She waved her hands at us, ushering us out of her home and shutting the door before I could thank her.

We stood there in silence for a long time, staring at the door. I turned her words over in my mind, trying to make sense of them. I had so many questions, so many things I wanted to ask that I almost opened the door up again to demand answers. But I knew there was no hope in finding them from Irina and Mariem. Now, all I could hope for was Erabeth knowing more, if she'd only be willing to talk of such things.

"Let's go." I said finally, breaking the choking silence and turning to go down the steps. "Lead the way, Taro." I held my arm out, and with a soft cry, the hawk leapt from my arm and flew into the night, leaving us to run after him, blindly stumbling through the sleeping City of Bones.

Taro led us deeper into the town, closer to the buildings that were built from stone rather than wood. We were on the cusp of the rough division of the types of houses when Taro stopped, swooping sharply to the left and landing on the rail of a porch leading up to a shabby two-story house, made from breaking timbers and struggling beams.

"This is Erabeth's house?" Alchemy questioned, looking skeptically up at the hawk, who was preening himself contentedly.

"Shh, come on. I'm ready to get some sleep," I groaned, stepping up to the door and knocking on it softly. I didn't even hear any footsteps, and jumped when the door swung inward, revealing Erabeth holding a little lamp. Taro made a happy clicking noise and leapt to land on her shoulder.

"You're here soon." She remarked, raising an eyebrow. She had changed her clothes, and now wore a thin nightdress with a shawl wrapped around her shoulders. Her hair was in a messy bun at the nape of her neck, although several waving strands framed her face.

"Irina and her daughter weren't exactly the most welcoming people we've ever met." I admitted, and I saw Erabeth take a sharp breath at the mention of them. I tilted my head to the side, curious. "Why do you call Irina a witch?"

"Because that's what she is," Erebeth creaked the door open and waved us inside. "She practices bone reading. It's why she lives way out here. Most people know about her, but the authorities are never able to find her." She scowled. "The people who take advantage of her services offer a protection nobody can get through."

Erabeth's home was small and square. It was mostly cast in shadow, but the lamp provided enough light to see a staircase to our left leading into the dark upper floor, a table to our right with a kitchen just beyond it, and a small living space directly in front of us. Her sword was on the table with her belt and the other items she carried on it, like her small leather pouch of sewing tools. There were clothes and miscellaneous items scattered haphazardly across almost every surface but the floor.

"Do you need a snack before you turn in?" Erabeth asked, and Ksega and I both nodded. She stepped into the kitchen and said, "You can go ahead and take your stuff upstairs. There are only two rooms. You decide how to split them. I'll sleep down here." She ushered us away with a wave of her hand, and I led the way up the stairs into the cramped hallway.

"I'll take this one," I said, stepping into the room on the left. It was small, but neat, with a bed in one corner, a makeshift wardrobe in another, and a small chair set against the wall. I set my packs down beside the bed, sighing in relief. They had begun to get on my nerves.

"Why do I have to share a room with the skeleton?" Ksega complained as he stepped into the other room. It looked like it was mainly used for storage, but there was a small foldable cot against one wall.

"Because you're both boys." I shrugged.

"But he doesn't *sleep*. That's *creepy*." Ksega argued.

"I don't want him in *my* room. Besides, he's always right with us when we camp outside. Stop whining, you'll be fine." Before he could say anything else, I went back down the stairs to see Erabeth clearing some seats at the table, setting down plates of bread and some sort of meat.

I thanked her and took one of the seats. She sat beside me, and Ksega came and took the seat on my other side. I made sure to keep my body angled toward Erabeth, taking a bite of my bread and swallowing it while Ksega asked,

"What do you know about Old Nightfall?"

"Looks like your trip to the *ista* wasn't entirely fruitless," Erabeth huffed. She dragged her finger over the table, making patterns on the wood. She didn't look up as Alchemy came down the stairs to hover behind us. "I don't know much about it. A lot of people don't. My people, especially, like to avoid talking about it." Her eyes narrowed. "Living in the sky? That is powerful magic. It borders on *dasten*." She shrugged and reclined in her chair. "There are people who talk, though. People who aren't afraid of the repercussions of going against the saints." Her finger stopped dragging along the table, instead beginning to tap on the wood. "It's said there's a magical well that takes you from our world to that of the Nightfallers. It's enchanted to move its location every three days. There's a pattern to its movements, but I've never known anyone to memorize it." She tilted her head to the side and looked at me, her eyes piercing. "Did the witch tell you where to find it?"

"The Oasis." I answered with a nod. Her thick eyebrows inched toward her hairline.

"The Oasis." She repeated, testing the words out. "You're lucky it's so close. It could have been anywhere on Horcath." She watched us closely. "How long do you have to find it?"

"Two days." I sighed and stuffed another piece of bread in my mouth.

"Not a lot of time, then. It would take almost that amount of time just to travel there, but there's also all the restrictions, the rules-" she cut herself off with a grunt. "You won't make it there on your own."

"Will you help us?" Ksega asked, and I looked expectantly at Erabeth, hope blooming inside me. We couldn't do this without her, I knew that. We needed a sand-sled to cross the desert fast enough to reach the Oasis before the well vanished.

"Why should I?" Erabeth demanded, a crease forming between her brows. "I told you, my people do not meddle with those things. And what makes you think you will find answers in Old Nightfall? You're so willing to trust the word of a witch?" she leaned forward, glaring at me. "People have fought the Curse for years. What makes you different?"

"Nobody else has gone for the source-" I began, but Erabeth pounded a fist on the table, making the plates shake, and shouted,

"*Everyone* has gone for the source! Everyone has researched it and tracked it. People have crawled all over Horcath in search of the source of this blasted Curse, and *nothing* has ever been found. There is no cure for it, no source, there isn't *anything!*" she stood up, her eyes still burning into mine. "You think you're different, but you're not. You're less capable than half the people who have already gone hunting for a way to destroy it. Compared to them, you are nothing but a hopeful child." She spat, turning to Alchemy. "All of you would do best to go back to your homes. This is a pointless quest. There is nothing more to be found."

"You're wrong." I heard Alchemy's voice, but I didn't really register it as Erabeth's words sank in. "There is more. I know there's a source, because I can *feel* it. It tries to control me. *Us.* It tries to control all of us who are Cursed. I know there is a source, we only have to *find it.*"

Erabeth shouted something at him, but I couldn't hear them anymore. I was drowning in my own swarming thoughts, sinking farther and farther into the depths of the truth.

This is a pointless quest. There is nothing more to be found.

Wasn't there, though? Alchemy was proof there *was* more. There were things we hadn't found, things we hadn't learned. We just had to find out where to look for them.

You're less capable than half the people who have already gone hunting for a way to destroy it.

I wasn't the only one. Of course I wasn't the only one to have gone hunting, but *I* was going to be the only one to make a difference. Nobody else had been successful. Nobody else had had a seven-foot-tall Cursed skeleton to give them information on what the Curse was like. I had something none of the others did, and that meant my journey would have a different outcome.

But then Erabeth's voice faded back in, and I felt my heart plummet.

"You're just going to get yourselves killed! There's no point in hunting something you will never find. Whatever created the Curse, it is beyond our understanding. It is evil and powerful, and it will destroy you all. *None of you* are special! There's nothing different about you! You're just going to die, and people won't see it as heroic, they'll see it as stupid. It's practically suicide!" she jutted a finger at me, similar to what Mariem had done. "Go home to your families, and keep on *surviving*, just like everyone else has done. There's no point in fighting. *Give up.* Go home." She kept glaring as I rose from my seat, stone-faced and empty.

Without saying a word, I turned and went up the stairs, ignoring Alchemy's "Ironling-" and shutting the door to my room firmly. I stood there, leaning against it for a long moment, staring ahead at the far wall, at the grubby little window that sat above my bed. There was a single candle in the room, on top of the wardrobe, and I was tempted to light it, but then all my will drained out of me, and I sank to the floor.

The emptiness that had hollowed me out was gone, replaced with a choking sorrow. I just wanted to go home. I wanted this Curse to be gone. But which did I want more?

Erabeth was right. This was stupid. I had been naive to think that I could do what no one else could. I had roped Alchemy and Ksega into a journey that would lead us nowhere, that would change nothing. It was all hopeless.

I could end it here. I could go home, and tell Ksega to go home, too. He must have missed his grandmother and his red-haired friend, just as I missed Gamma and Finnian and Walter and even Derek.

What would they think of me, if I went home?

I shut my eyes, their voices echoing in my head as I thought of them. Tears burned at the back of my eyes. Derek would say I was a coward for giving up, but he wouldn't argue. He would be happy to go home. Gamma would kiss my forehead and tell me I did my best, and she was glad I'd made it home safely. Walter would welcome me back in his own callous way, and Finnian . . .

What would Finnian do? The Finnian I'd grown up with would have said I should have kept going. He would have told me this was the sort of situation that called for my specific stubbornness. He would clap me on the shoulder and tell me to get back out there, and this time, he would come with me, standing right by my side.

But what about the Finnian he had become? The broken, terrified look on his face when Elixir had died had torn into my heart. I couldn't imagine losing Sycamore. But what if I already had? Anything could have happened when I'd left. I could have left Gamma and Walter vulnerable to the Cursed animals, or to other Cursed dragons.

A soft knock at the door made me gasp, teleported back into the little room in Erabeth's house. My breaths came in shaky rasps, and I realized I'd been crying. I swiped the streaks the tears had left behind off my face and leaned my head back against the door, keeping it closed. Ksega spoke quietly, just loud enough for me to hear.

"Sakura."

"Go away." I croaked, closing my eyes. The last thing I wanted was for Ksega to come in here and coddle me. It had been nice to have him there in Jhapato's house, willing to help, willing to listen. But I didn't need that now. I needed to think this through. I needed to decide if it was finally time to go home.

"Can I come in?" I felt him test the door behind me, but I didn't move.

"Go away." I said again, but it was quieter this time. I was trying to recollect my thoughts, trying to make sense of it all. It was starting to give me a headache.

"I'm not going away, because I'm your friend." I heard him moving around, then felt the door shake as he sat to lean against the other side. "Don't let what she said change anything." His voice was slightly muffled, but the wood of the door was thin enough that I could hear. "You aren't the first one to go looking for the source of the Curse, but you are the first one who's going to make a difference." He echoed my earlier thoughts.

"What can I do that they didn't?" I asked, more to myself than him. "I'm no different than they are. If anything, I'm younger and have less experience. I hardly know what's happening in the kingdoms. I don't know what I'm *doing*. Maybe it is for the best if we go home. Maybe we should leave it for someone else to deal with."

"Maybe that's what everyone else said." Ksega countered. "And maybe that's why nothing has changed yet."

I fell silent, turning his words over in my mind. He had a point. Maybe they did say that. But maybe they didn't. Maybe they went to the very end, wasting every ounce of their life and energy, pouring all their knowledge and will into a quest that ended up doing nothing. Maybe if I kept going, the same thing would happen to me.

"You miss your home. I can tell. But you also want to get rid of the Curse. I mean you *really* want it. I can see how much you want it, and I respect the resolve you have. You haven't been afraid to ignore the words of others before. What changed this time?" Ksega fell silent, and I sighed, burying my face in my hands.

What *had* changed?

I did want this. I wanted it more than anything else, because children deserved to grow up safe and happy, learning how to read and write, and not how to wield a sword and master their magic to become a weapon. I wanted the world to be *free*.

But people didn't see that. Multiple times, I'd been told not to pursue the path of revenge. I told myself it was justice, but was I right? Did I really, desperately want freedom from the Curse, or did I want it gone solely because of what it did to me and my family?

Scooting away from the door, I stood up and turned to open it. Ksega rose to his feet, but I couldn't see him very well. The room and the hallway were both dark. Again, I debated lighting the candle, but decided against it. I didn't want him to see that I'd been crying, even though I was sure he could guess it.

"What if we do die? What if it was all for nothing, and we just leave our families in more pain and loss?" I shook my head slowly. "Finnian has already lost so much to the Curse. I don't want it to be the reason he loses me, too."

"You knew of those dangers when you left," Ksega reminded me, and I pursed my lips, looking down at the floor. "You said yourself that the longer you wait, the more people there are that die. At least you're doing *something*." He stepped inside the room, brushing past my shoulder to find the candle. He held it out to me, and reluctantly, I tapped the wick with my finger, and a small flame bloomed to life, casting a ring of orange light around us.

"But is that something enough?" I asked, looking up to meet his gaze. He shrugged and smiled at me.

"There's only one way to find out."

27
KSEGA

*E*arly the following morning, the three of us gathered around Erabeth's table for a quick breakfast of bread and cheese. It was eerily quiet for the first twenty minutes, at first only broken by Erabeth gifting a new pair of gloves to Alchemy, but after a while, she broke the silence once more, asking,

"Are you still going after the well?"

Alchemy and I both swiveled our heads toward Sakura. When I had talked to her the night before, she had still seemed uncertain, and she had been pacing well into the night. I was willing to leave the decision up to her, even though personally, I wanted nothing more than to keep going. Of course I missed Willa and Jessie and the little house that smelled like strawberries and lavender in Rulak, but I also knew that if I went home now, I would miss *this*. The freedom and the adventure. Not to mention, I would miss the opportunity to make a big change in the world. But this was Sakura's choice, and I was going to leave it up to her.

"Yes." She said, briefly meeting my gaze before she looked back to Erabeth. The woman pinched her lips together, searching Sakura's face, and then mine. I couldn't tell what she was looking for, but after a moment, she found it.

"Very well, then." She crunched into her bread, honing in on her meal and refusing to meet any of our gazes. I gave Sakura a curious look, but she only shrugged. I nodded at Erabeth, hoping she caught on to what I wanted her to ask. She clenched her jaw and shook her head. I nodded again. She shook her head. Sitting between us, Alchemy sighed.

"Will you help us get to the Oasis in time to find it?" he asked, regaining Erabeth's attention. She chewed her bread slowly, meeting each of our gazes before looking down at her plate again.

"No. I won't touch that stuff." I heard Sakura's disappointed sigh, and released one of my own. *"But,"* Erabeth went on, and we all looked up at her again. She wasn't looking at any of us, forcing out each word as if it pained her to say it. "I won't let you go into this without any help. I'll arrange a ride for you. I'll have it ready by noon. Stay here." She stood up without finishing her meal, retrieved Taro from his perch on the back of the final seat, and left without another word.

I looked across the table at Sakura, my eyebrows raising. I hadn't really expected Erabeth to help us herself, but the thought of her finding a way to help anyway hadn't crossed my mind. It must not have crossed Sakura's either, because she stuffed another bite of bread and cheese in her mouth, swallowed, and said,

"We'd better pack up, then." She grabbed the last chunk of her bread and stood up, rushing up the stairs before Alchemy or I had a chance to say anything.

"She's in a better mood than she was last night, at least," Alchemy muttered, rising to his feet slower. I followed suit, grabbing a cheese cube to munch as I followed him up the stairs. "I'm glad she hasn't given up hope just yet. I was afraid she'd come awfully close last night."

"Me too." I agreed, filing after him into the little room we'd shared the night before. I had taken the cot, and, as far as I knew, he had sat on a crate all night long. It was a little unsettling, but I pushed it out of my mind. I had to remind myself there hadn't been a lot of other options.

I gathered my things together and slung my pack and longbow over my shoulder, groaning as my muscles protested against their weight. At least Erabeth was arranging a sand-sled ride for us, so I wouldn't have to carry them all day.

When the three of us returned to the bottom floor, packs and weapons — aside from Sakura's flame-sword — propped against the wall beside the door, we looked at each other expectantly. It was still early, and most of the roads were cast in shadow. With nothing to do, I was tempted to step outside and walk around. After seeing how vastly different the kingdoms could be, I wanted to explore all of them until there was nothing left to learn. But before I could even say I was planning to go look around, Erabeth walked back in the door, looking a little breathless. Her expression was angry, and maybe a little sad. I couldn't be sure, but thought her eyes may have been rimmed with red.

"Alright, it's ready. Now get out." She brushed Taro off her shoulder, and the hawk hopped onto the table. "You'll find him where we left Mulligan yesterday. Go." She shoved my shoulder roughly towards the door, and I stumbled forward, lifting my satchel up over my shoulder.

"Thank you for letting us stay here," Sakura said, but Erabeth was already disappearing up the stairs, her teeth digging into her lower lip. We heard a door slam, then nothing but silence, save for the scritch-scratching of Taro walking across the table.

"What was that all about?" I muttered as Sakura motioned for Alchemy to hide his skull and pick up some of the packs.

"I don't know, and I don't want to ask. Let's just get out of here before she decides to have us arrested." Sakura led the way out the door, clomping down the stairs and kicking up sand as she looked up and down the little street.

Alchemy and I followed her, and the skeleton started to walk to the north. Without questioning him, we trailed along. My limp was all but gone, and while it still ached a little, the wound was almost entirely healed. I was out of the remedy for the pain, but it wasn't bad enough that I needed more anyway.

I had thought the City of Bones was marvelous in the evening, when it was bustling with people and happily swaying lanterns, but it was nothing compared to the morning. Even way out here, in the outermost ring, there were *dozens* of people, carrying hot loaves of bread or homemade scarves or small children or baskets of jewelry and other goods to sell and trade. There were smiles and laughs and swirls of sand as people used their andune to carry something from one side of the road to another. We stopped as a pillar of sand slid across the ground, extending into a hand to snatch up a necklace and lifting it up to meet an identical hand of sand to fasten it around a woman's neck. She inspected herself in the small mirror beside the jewelry stand, then smiled, dropping the sand down to the ground and reaching into a small purse to retrieve the shins needed to buy the necklace.

I was awe-stuck by the abilities of andune-mages. Even when sand was all they had the power to manipulate, they were incredibly powerful, especially out in the desert, where all the sand they could ever need was at their disposal. I could hardly imagine what a fight between two andune-mages might look like.

Alchemy seemed to remember where we were going well enough, so Sakura and I only had to skip to keep up with his ridiculously long strides. Even *I* wasn't tall enough to match his pace when he walked fast.

Some people gave us curious looks as we walked past, especially in the direction of Alchemy, towering over everyone and swathed in his shrouds of fabric. But we ignored them all, offering polite smiles of reassurance to anyone who looked like they might be afraid of him. Nobody seemed to take notice of the fact that he had no eyes, even though he didn't keep his head down.

We weren't the only people who weren't Duskans, and that helped. The majority of the people here had the bronzed skin one would expect from living out in the desert, under the constant heat of the sun. Sakura and I stood out, I being several shades lighter than all of them, and her a couple shades darker. But we weren't alone: I spotted several people with the ghastly white skin of Talons, their hair pale red or sandy blonde. Some of them were taller than me, but still didn't come within three inches of the top of Alchemy's skull. There were also other Carlorians, their ebony skin blending with the shadows as they stepped beneath the shade of the market stalls to inspect the trinkets for sale. I caught Sakura watching them, and I wondered for a moment if she had recognized any of them.

With our quick pace, it didn't take long for us to reach the Horcathian camel stalls. There were only three of them now, two with jutting tusks and one with goat-like horns. I thought one of them may have been Mulligan, but it was impossible to tell them apart aside from the horns.

Standing in front of the stalls with a sand-sled identical to the one Erabeth had driven, except lacking bloodstains, was a tall Duskan man with long, dark hair and a stubbly beard. He wore a tight shirt, and had a scarf tied around his belt. He was adjusting the straps that held crates in place when we walked up to him.

"Excuse us," Sakura said, hand ready on her flame-sword as the man looked up from his work.

"Ah! You must be Beth's friends." The man smiled broadly at us, shaking Sakura's hand and then offering to shake mine. I hesitantly accepted, and he nearly tore my shoulder out of its socket as he shook enthusiastically.

"You could say that." Sakura muttered, looking up at Alchemy. I wasn't sure if Erabeth had told this man about him or not, but we would keep him a secret until we knew for sure.

"Well, come on aboard. I'm about to get Casper saddled up." He waved a hand at the benches on the sand-sled, and we all moved forward as he retrieved the camel with the ram horns from his stall. He skipped around the sand-sled, tossing his head and trying to sniff at the sand whenever the man pulled at his lead.

"What's your name?" I asked as we sat on the bench. I sat beside Sakura, but gave her some space. I had noticed her constantly avoiding getting close to me, but what I couldn't figure out was why. At least she didn't look repulsed that I had sat next to her.

"Kieran." He replied, flashing us a grin. "What are yours?"

Sakura and I both introduced ourselves, and we gestured flatly at Alchemy, introducing him as Chem. Kieran didn't question the skeleton's silence, and started talking.

"I've lived in Old Duskfall all my life. I've thought about becoming a traveler, seeing the world," he paused in his work, as if contemplating then shrugged and started again. "It isn't as appealing as staying here, risking my life doing what I love, with the person I love." He finished harnessing Casper and went to assume his position on the driver's bench. "Hold on, it'll be a bumpy ride, if I'm to get you to the Oasis by tomorrow!" before any of us could respond, he snapped the reins, and Casper charged forward, his large, flat feet kicking sand up into the air in great golden clouds as Sakura and I scrambled for a stronger hold on the sand-sled.

The sled rocked violently to the left as we skirted around a dune, and I yelped as I was nearly thrown from the bench, my arm jerking me painfully back into place. Beside me, Sakura was holding onto the wall of the sled so tightly her knuckles were white. Alchemy was holding it as well, but he showed no sign of struggling to keep himself in place.

By the time I wiped the sand from my eyes, spat it out of my mouth, and looked up, *Baske Latel* was already fading into the distance.

"How far is the Oasis?" I asked, looking at Alchemy. I'd seen maps of Horcath before, but it was always impossible for me to accurately judge distances from them. I'd never had the patience to sit down and learn how to read them.

"Pretty far, if memory serves me right." Alchemy replied, lifting his head to watch the receding City of Bones. It vanished beyond a dune, then reappeared as we went up another tall one, then disappeared again as we dipped down between the dunes. "But at this rate, we'll definitely reach it by tomorrow."

"I'm more concerned about finding the well." Sakura said, half-shouting over the roar of the sand. "We don't even know what it looks like, or where it is in the Oasis."

"Maybe we should have asked Irina more about it," I said, but she was shaking her head before I'd even finished.

"She wouldn't have told us anything more. We'll have to search for it on our own." She grimaced and we all tightened our grip on the wood as the sand-sled veered sharply to the right, skidding around a small lump of fur in the desert. I squinted at it, trying to identify what it was, but it blended in too well with the sand, and by the time I got the chance to look at it, we had already sped past.

There were other animals, too. Some sort of black lizard bathing on a rock in the sun. A fox-like creature, possibly a small coyote, stalking across a dune. There were little rabbits that darted around, and we even saw a few sheep with giant, curving horns hopping on some of the craggy rock formations. Hawks similar to Taro, and even eagles occasionally passed overhead, ignorant of the sun's glaring heat.

There was little to look at, aside from the occasional animal, but with so much sand in my eyes, it was hard to see them anyway, so I just held onto the side of the sand-sled, closed my eyes, and hoped Kieran was a good enough driver to keep us from flipping over.

Nightfall came and went, and while Kieran did slow us down so Sakura and I could snatch a few hours of sleep, he didn't stop driving Casper on. The only time we stopped was early the following morning, when we all had a quick breakfast, and Kieran fed Casper before we all climbed back aboard and held on for dear life as the camel resumed his barreling lope.

We slowed again for lunch, and while Kieran asked if Alchemy needed any food, he didn't argue when we told him no. I took the break in the ruckus of the ride to hone in on my bering. I couldn't feel any plant life directly around me, and while I didn't feel as detached as I did at sea, it was still disorienting.

I tried to reach into the wood of the sand-sled, attempting to replicate the ease with which Peeler had manipulated dead would, but it was no use. I could feel nothing. I tried to sense the same instincts that had dragged the giant thorns out of the porch in Brightlock, but again, I was unsuccessful. With a sigh, I fell back against the bench, sweat pouring down my face and neck, and closed my eyes.

"Beth's given me the money to get you all through," Kieran explained when it was time to get moving again, revealing pouches of shins on his belt. Sakura's look of surprise reflected my own, but neither of us said anything. We owed Erabeth more than we knew.

"So it's almost like going through one of the Gates between kingdoms?" I guessed, having to yell above the hissing of the sand.

"Almost." Kieran yelled back. Any conversation after that was minimal, and mainly between the three of us in the back of the sand-sled.

It wasn't until dusk was just beginning to creep its way across the sky that Casper slowed down, and Sakura and I stepped closer to the front of the sand-sled, trying to get a better view of what was sprawled across the land before us.

The Evershifting Forest had been splendid, magical beyond anyone's imagining. It could have any sort of appearance it wanted, and even then it would find new ways to impress anyone who looked upon it. It had the ability to change the very earth it sat upon, crafting the world around it to be the epitome of happiness and luxury. And yet it was nothing compared to the Oasis.

Even from only the outside, there was no mistaking its beauty. Tall palm trees with trunks as thick as sea wraiths loomed over us, towering hundreds of feet above the ground and boasting coconuts bigger than my head. Grass twice as tall as Alchemy bent and trembled in the wind, dotted with giant flowers that were as broad as the back of a Horcathian camel. The fading sunlight streamed through the canopy of palm tree leaves, landing on a sparkling body of water. I couldn't see the whole thing, seeing as our path was barred by a broad wooden gate, heavily guarded by men in scaled armor and brightly colored turbans, all of them brandishing spears or curved swords, but I knew without seeing all of it that it was magnificent.

Casper slowed and brought us to a stop just in front of the gate, snorting sand from his nose and flapping his ears against his curving horns. Kieran stepped forward to talk to the men, gesturing behind him at us, and I felt my stomach turn with nerves as the soldiers' shrewd eyes turned to us, lingering on Alchemy's hunched figure.

"We won't be able to get him through. They'll want to see his face." I told Sakura, and she nodded along.

"We need some sort of distraction." She started to look around, but there was nothing we could do without it being obvious.

"If only either of us were an andune-mage, so we could summon a sandstorm." I muttered.

"That wouldn't work, because they would just combat it with their own andune." Sakura rolled her eyes. "Idiot."

I brushed the comment aside, still searching for some sort of distraction. There was nothing in any direction for miles, aside from the Oasis, and we couldn't get close enough to it without drawing attention. We were out of options.

"We can't risk them finding out about Alchemy. If they're as superstitious as we've heard, they'll kill us on the spot," Sakura hissed through gritted teeth as one of the soldiers stepped up onto the sand-sled to approach us.

"What do you want me to do?" I asked. I had an idea, but the more I tried, the more I failed. I stretched my bering out to the wood beneath me, trying to find any trace of its connection in the grains of the planks. I searched and felt, but it was all hollow. There was nothing there for my bering to hold onto, and with a gasp, I released it, staggering back a pace. It was no use.

Sakura threw me a confused look, but I shook my head, disregarding her concern. We had bigger problems, namely the Duskan who was walking determinedly towards Alchemy. I wanted to block his path, but that would only draw more suspicion. But what other options did we have?

I had just begun to move, my boot sliding along the sand-covered sled, when everyone cringed down, hands flying up to cover our ears as a roar echoed across the desert around us. It was so loud, I could've sworn it had come from right beside me.

The Duskan soldiers began to shout in Sandrun, and I whipped my head around, searching for the source of the roar. Casper was kicking his feet up, his back hooves slamming into the front of the sled and splintering the wood as he tried to get away. The sand around the Duskan soldiers whipped up around them, coiling like the tentacles of the octopi I had seen sold in the Port and writhing in the air beside them, teasing their turbans and warping to adjust their field of vision.

"There," Alchemy bellowed above the din, pointing a gloved hand to the north. I looked up to see the shaggy ridge of hair along a sandcat's spine shaking in the gusts of wind from the andune-mages as it slunk forward, fangs bared.

"No, there." Sakura pointed in the opposite direction, and my breath hitched to see two more sandcats prowling closer from the south.

The Duskans had noticed them, too, and were shouting even more. Some of them sheathed or dropped their weapons to wield their andune around them instead, while others dropped their hold on the sand to tightly grip their spears or swords.

"Do they normally hunt in packs?" I squeaked, shocked at how high my voice had gone.

"No," Kieran had sidled up to us, avoiding Casper's flailing hooves. "Hurry! Off the sled, before-" he had already gripped both Sakura and I by the wrists and dragged us toward the edge of the sand-sled, and was pulling us along as he spoke. He was cut off as the sand-sled jerked violently forward, sweeping all of us but Alchemy off our feet.

Sakura landed half splayed across my legs, and I cried out in surprise as her shoulder pressed into my thigh, right where the runeboar's tusks had sliced through the flesh mere days ago.

"Sorry!" she gasped as we scrambled to our feet shakily. The sled had stopped moving again, but Casper was dancing uneasily, looking ready to sprint again at any moment.

"It's fine. Come on!" Kieran had let go of us when we'd fallen, and now it was my turn to take Sakura's hand and yank her towards the wall of the sand-sled. We hopped over onto the sand, and Alchemy thumped down beside us seconds before the sled hissed across the sand again, swinging widely towards the gate.

Shouts rang out from the Duskans as the sled crashed into the gate, smashing through the timbers and sending shards of wood flying through the air in every direction. At the same time, the sandcats darted forward, racing across the sand at dangerous speeds and leaping through the air. The one to the north snarled and landed on one of the Duskan soldiers, who screamed and tried to punch it away with his andune. I looked away at the first sight of blood splattering across the sand, trying to ignore his strangled screaming as two other Duskans ran to his aid.

"This way!" Kieran was beside us again, somehow having obtained a cut along his cheek. It bled openly down the side of his face, dripping off his chin and staining his shirt, but he didn't seem to notice, running towards the shattered gate and waving his hand for us to follow him.

Stumbling through the sand, I followed, trying to track the three sandcats as I went. The two that came from the south had reached Casper. I felt my heart pinch with pity and sorrow as I heard the camel bellowing, high-pitched and terrified. The first sandcat had leapt up, raking its claws into the camel's chest and dragging them down through his flesh as it fell back to the ground. The second cat latched onto his leg, and even though its jaws didn't even fit around it entirely, I heard the crack of Casper's bones as it forced its jaws together.

I tried not to think of the brief moments when I had connected with Mulligan through my bering, feeling what he felt, sensing what he sensed. The exhilaration and the magic that had coursed through me was like nothing I'd ever experienced before. I couldn't imagine what it would feel like to share such an animal's pain.

We charged past the ruins of the gate, turning back only briefly to assess the damage. My heart leapt into my throat when I saw it.

Three of the Duskans lay dead on the ground, one of them missing an arm and another marred beyond recognition. Two others were bleeding profusely from wounds across their chests and backs, and the last five were staggering in an uneasy dance around just one of the sandcats. The other two were occupied with Casper, who was trying desperately to get away, but without the help of one of his legs, and with the added weight of the sand-sled, it was hopeless. I felt my whole body ache with sadness as I looked at the pulsing green glow of life slowly fading around him, little pieces of him being torn away from the places the sandcats had attacked.

"Come on," I was still holding Sakura's hand, although mine had gone limp. She gave my hand a squeeze and tugged, encouraging me to follow her, Alchemy, and Kieran farther into the Oasis.

With a shaky breath, I trailed after them. I was breathless enough from the fear that chased my pulse into a thundering rhythm, but at the sight of the Oasis, I found myself gasping for even a single breath.

The body of water before us stretched like a great river through the dense, jungle-like foliage around it, glittering in the dying light of day and revealing colorful corals and bright fish through its crystal clear water.

I could have stood there admiring the view for hours, but the snarling and screaming and baying behind me was enough to keep my legs pumping, and we raced past the shores of the lake into the thick of the palm tree forest, dodging around thick bushes and kicking past the vibrant flowers that hung low beside our heads.

"Where's the well?" Sakura panted, yelping as she tripped over a root. Alchemy, on her other side, gripped her arm and hefted her back to her feet. Behind us, I heard something tearing through the Oasis, growling and roaring.

"I don't know-" I gasped, looking around. What sort of a well was it? One made of stones? One in the ground? I didn't even know what I was looking for. "Chem, can you back up a little? You're *right* in my ear, and it's not helping." I shut my eyes for a moment, trying to blot out the buzzing in my head.

"Are you kidding? I'm nowhere near you," Alchemy's gravelly voice came from somewhere ahead of me, and when I snapped my eyes open, I saw that he was up beside Kieran, and the nearest person to me was Sakura, who was still holding my hand.

"Then what-" I shook my head, running out of breath and energy. My leg was throbbing, every inch of me was covered in sweat, and that blasted *buzzing* would not go away.

I tossed my gaze around, searching the Oasis, but there was no sign of any other animal. Could the sandcat chasing us be Cursed? Had I just tuned the irritating sound back into my mind? No, this was different. Now that I focused on it, I could only hear it clearly with my head titled one way. Alchemy's hum was there, too, always in the background, but it was different, much darker and fuzzier. This one was lighter, higher in pitch. It was some other magic.

"This way!" I yelled, pulling Sakura sharply to the left. Alchemy swerved after us without question. I heard Kieran protesting, but I didn't have time to see if he would follow. The sound of the sandcat pounding after us was heavy in my ears, almost drowning out the buzzing. It was all making my head spin.

"Ksega, you'd better know what you're doing," Sakura wheezed as I yanked her along behind me, leaping over exposed roots and ducking under the drooping branches of tall green plants.

"Just stick close," I rasped, slowing my pace. I heard her intake of breath, prepared to argue, but I held up my free hand, closing my eyes and focusing on that distant, lighter buzz. "This way." It was harder to focus when my eyes were open, but there were too many obstacles blocking the path that made it dangerous to keep them closed.

"Hurry, boy," Alchemy, who was made solely of bones and therefore probably couldn't feel any physical pain, sounded worried. And that terrified me.

"I'm trying," I ground my teeth together, stumbling around the trunk of a palm tree. My heart pummeled into my gut as I heard a crash from up ahead. Another one of the sandcats was tracking us. If we didn't find the well soon, we were as good as dead.

Veering to the right, I guided Sakura through the bushes and over another tangle of roots. The buzz was getting louder now, pulsing in my ear with a regular beat, like that of a heart. It pounded in my head, matching the beat of my own heart, the pump of my arms, the throb in my leg.

The sound hit me in waves, weak at first, but then stronger. Stronger and stronger and stronger until it became so unbearable it was enough to cause a searing pain to rip through my head. I cried out and snatched my hand away from Sakura's, stumbling to the ground. My knees stung as the fabric of my pants tore, and the skin scraped along the sandy ground. I heard a hoarse scream echoing around us, and it took me a moment to realize it was tearing itself from my own throat.

"Ksega-" Sakura's voice was hardly audible above the other sounds warring in my mind.

"Keep going. It must be close. Go!" I felt myself being scooped up into someone's arms and held tight against a thin figure. Alchemy. I tried to thank him, but I couldn't even look him in the face.

My eyes weren't open, and try as I might, I couldn't lift my eyelids. My mouth was sealed closed. Breathing was a struggle. The only things open were my ears. Open, and listening. I heard the invigorated roars of the sandcats, the thundering of Alchemy's feet in the sand, the dark buzz and the light buzz, the rustling of the plant life around us, all of it swirling and swelling and shrinking and spinning until it was nothing but chaos.

All I wanted was for it to stop. I felt like my skull was being cleaved in two by a red-hot rod of iron. I could feel the beads of sweat rolling on my skin, soaking my clothes and dampening my hair. Everything was so *hot*. I was thirsty. I was on fire.

Quiet. I pleaded, trying to force the sounds away. *Give me quiet*

Someone shouted something. Was the voice desperate? Triumphant? Panicked? All three? It didn't matter. So long as something brought about the end of all this noise, I would be satisfied.

I was jerked forward suddenly, out of Alchemy's arms, and I felt myself falling. Down, down, down, with nothing around me. I tried to reach out, tried to open my eyes, but it was no use.

And then I hit the water, and everything went silent.

28
SAKURA

*T*he water was freezing.

When my body first smacked into the surface, it was nothing but relief. The burning heat from the desert was gone. The dry itch in my throat was erased. The sand vanished from my eyes and my nose and every little crevice of my boots and shirt.

And then the chill seeped in. Icy fingers clutched at my shirt and my hair, tracing patterns along my skin and freezing me to the bone. Thin layers of ice spread across the surface of my flesh, locking me in a position of terror. I couldn't breathe, I couldn't move, I couldn't even see.

The ice swept up my body, encasing me entirely. I was stuck, blind and helpless, sucked down deeper and deeper into the depths of the well. I felt my eirioth writhing uneasily beneath the surface of my skin. I implored it to set itself free, to break through the wall of ice and restore warmth to my body. But whatever magic this was, my eirioth was powerless against it, and I felt it dwindling into a small flame in the pit of my stomach, able to do little more than keep me alive.

And what about Ksega? He had no eirioth to keep him warm. He wasn't even conscious. He'd been whimpering and sweating and twitching when Alchemy had thrown him into the well, and as far as I could tell, the water hadn't revived him.

What sort of sick magic had this well been created with?

I tried to blink, and was mildly surprised when a film of the ice gave way, leaving me with a thin, blurry screen to look through. Water whirled past me, all different colors. It glowed brightly, flashing and twisting with a life of its own. It was like fire, mesmerizing and dangerous.

I couldn't see Ksega, but I could just make out Alchemy out of the corner of my eye, his billowing clothes frozen in warped walls around him, skull eerily glowing beyond the ice.

It felt like ages that we were trapped like this, yet it couldn't have been more than a few minutes. I'd never been able to hold my breath for very long.

A bright flash of light told me something was about to change, and before I had the chance to prepare myself for whatever may have come next, I felt myself falling. It was only for a moment, and seconds later my body landed on hard stone, my head knocking against it and setting my vision awhirl, bringing everything in and out of focus. I heard the impacts of two more bodies beside me, and while my vision was still swimming, I knew who it was.

"Ksega?" I asked, surprised at how clear my voice was, now that the sand and desert heat had been taken away. There was no response.

"He's still unconscious," came Alchemy's voice, very close by. "How are you?"

"I'm okay," I grunted as I forced myself to sit up, feeling the chill slowly receding from my body. Blinking a few times brought my vision back to normal, and I cast my gaze around to see that we were in some sort of round cave room with one long tunnel as the only exit. Bizarre floating crystals provided a dim violet light.

"You hit your head pretty hard, there. You're sure you're alright?" he placed a gloved hand on my shoulder, and to my amazement, all our clothes were completely dry.

"Yes, I'm sure." I nodded, brushing his hand aside before turning to face Ksega. He was lying on his side, longbow pulled awkwardly across his back, eyes closed, and to my dismay, still sweating heavily. His damp hair was plastered to his forehead, and his eyebrows were low and scrunched together.

"He looks pretty miserable, doesn't he?" Alchemy commented as I rolled him onto his back. His breathing was hoarse, and his shoulders twitched as I moved him. I undid the top few buttons of his shirt, hoping to cool him down, but the fabric was already soaking up the sweat that slicked his chest.

"He needs a doctor." I looked up towards the tunnel. "Are we in Old Nightfall, then?"

"Must be." Alchemy mused, pulling the hood of his cloak down and crouching on Ksega's other side. "I've never seen this happen before. There's something different about his bering. I'm not sure if all bering-mages have the abilities he does, but he's a special one." He lifted one of Ksega's limp wrists, then let it fall to the ground, pushing at the boy's mop of hair. I shoved his hand away, scowling.

"Stop prodding him like a piece of meat. Stay here while I go find him some help." I rose to my feet, checked for my flame-sword, and started off down the tunnel before he could argue.

The tunnel was long and narrow, and I couldn't see the end of it, although it was straight. The rock around me was smooth, arching evenly over my head and dotted by more of those glowing crystals. While they provided soft light, I still felt my stomach turn with uncertainty at the shadows that lurked in the edges of the path.

There was no way to tell what time it was, or where we were. A part of me was terrified that the well hadn't taken us into Old Nightfall at all, and that this may have been a place Duskans tricked people into venturing towards when they spoke of things they didn't believe in, like dark magic. Maybe the Duskans didn't actually know what the well did. Maybe Irina had told us of the well as a way to silence us. She was a witch, after all. What if it had been her that had created the Curse in the first place?

Don't be stupid. I shook my head, keeping my eyes sharply ahead of me. *She isn't old enough to have made the Curse. No one is.*

But the source of it must have been alive somewhere, lurking and waiting. It controlled the Curse, tried to control Alchemy, and kept itself hidden all the while. I intended to find it, and if that meant exploring this strange place the well had brought me to, so be it.

"Hello?" the voice that came from ahead nearly made me jump out of my own skin.

Within seconds, my flame-sword was in my hand, and a blade of fire had sparked through it, casting flaring twirls of light along the tunnel walls as a figure walked seemingly out of thin air before me. Whoever he was, he gasped and stepped away from the flames.

"Hey, easy, I wasn't going to attack." The man squinted past the light, trying to get a look at me. I angled it to block most of my face, only leaving enough space to look him up and down.

He was tall, but not as tall as Ksega, with light skin and very dark hair. He wore clothes like none I'd ever seen, almost like the traditional robes Carlorians wore, but . . . different. Sharper. Sleeker.

"Who are you?" I demanded, flicking my gaze nervously behind me. When I looked back, the light from my flame-sword flared brightly, and I squinted as I saw some sort of dark marking on his neck. Who was this man, and where had he come from?

"I could ask the same of you." He replied dully, his dark brows lowering. "What are you doing here? How did you find the portal?"

"Why is it important?" I challenged, trying to swallow down the anger in my voice. I had to remind myself that I was only stressed out. This man could help me. He could help Ksega.

"Are you here alone?" he asked, ignoring my question. While his face displayed his obvious dismay, the rest of his body was casual. He assumed a friendly stance, and while his arms were crossed, it was a position of laze, not authority.

"No. One of my friends is sick. He needs a doctor." I looked over my shoulder, but I couldn't hear anything. My heart skipped a beat as I realized I could no longer see Alchemy and Ksega, only the long, dimly lit tunnel stretching on and on into nothing.

"Don't worry. Follow me. They aren't far." The man stepped forward, about to step around me, but I tightened my grip on the flame-sword, causing it to jerk to the left. He froze, holding his hands up. "I'm okay. I'm going to help you. Show me where they are."

I stared at him for a long moment, contemplating. Ksega needed a doctor. I couldn't move him on my own, but if I brought this man to him and he saw Alchemy, there was no telling what sort of reaction that would warrant.

If the people of Old Nightfall were as aloof as everyone on Horcath was led to believe, they could very well think of themselves as the highest race of them all. It had been a long time since any of the kingdoms had had disputes over where a person came from, or the color of their skin. The Curse had united the kingdoms more than anything, elevating the need for survival over that of whatever twisted standards people held each other to.

But did the Curse reach Old Nightfall? Said to be a kingdom so high in the sky that not even birds could reach it, there was nothing there for the Curse to corrupt. Maybe the Nightfallers knew that. Maybe they were done waiting to see what the other races would do. Maybe they had created the Curse to wipe everyone else out so they could claim Horcath as their own.

It was a weak argument, but it made sense. Man's greed was unmatched by any power but magic, and the Curse was greed, if nothing else.

But it was only one man. If it came down to it, he wouldn't be much trouble for Alchemy and I to handle. Besides, Ksega needed help, and this may have been our only way to find it.

"Fine." I lowered the flame-sword, but kept it burning. I could feel it draining me of my energy, but I wouldn't let it show. It wasn't just my strongest weapon, but my only one. None of us had had time to grab our packs when the sandcats had attacked, and I didn't have Ksega or Alchemy by my side. Even as it ate away at my strength, I would keep the flame-sword alive until I was with them again.

The man in front of me breathed a sigh of relief, stepping warily past me and into the tunnel. I walked beside him, but kept the flame-sword ready between us. When we'd walked a little way down the tunnel, I blinked, and suddenly Alchemy and Ksega were there. The former stood with arms crossed, looking down at Ksega, who was still lying on his back, struggling to breathe.

When we stepped into the little dome-shaped room, Alchemy looked sharply from me to the newcomer. I could see the confusion in the way he stood, but I ignored it. As far as I could tell, the man hadn't noticed his skull yet, having crouched beside Ksega to examine him. I let my flame-sword curl into wisps of smoke, but I kept the handle tight in my hand, and was sure to stand close behind the Nightfaller, watching closely as he pressed the back of his hand to Ksega's forehead.

"He's burning up. How long has he been like this?" he looked up at me, then let his gaze flicker briefly to Alchemy, and he gasped, jumping to his feet. His hand disappeared inside his pale robes, and when he pulled it back out, revealed a long, thin knife trapped in his fingers.

"He won't hurt you." I said quickly, then paused, looking up into Alchemy's empty eye sockets. "Well, not unless you try to hurt us." I looked down at Ksega. "He hasn't been like this for very long. It started when we found the well."

The man before us didn't move, his green eyes flitting between the three of us, trembling hand still brandishing the knife. I could have reached out and smacked it out of his grasp, if I had felt like taking away any scrap of control he thought he had, but I ignored it. He couldn't do very much with an oversized needle, anyway.

"I-" he shook his head, moving his lips as if he was going to say more, then closed his mouth, dumbfounded.

"Well? Can you help him?" I prompted, gesturing at Ksega as my impatience grew. He looked at me, eyebrows raising. I nodded at him and said, "I'm talking to you. Can you do anything for him? It's obvious he's sick."

"Yes, that much is clear." He looked nervously at Alchemy again. "Can I help him? No. But . . . well, maybe the doctors can. If we can get him there." He looked down at Ksega once more, worrying his lower lip between his teeth.

"Chem can carry him." I said simply, and Alchemy stepped forward without a word. The Nightfaller flinched and backed into the wall of the room as the skeleton stooped over and lifted Ksega's limp body back against his chest. Ksega groaned, and one of his hands clenched into a fist as his face contorted in pain. I felt a pinch of desperation bite at my chest, and I glared at the Nightfaller. He cleared his throat and, tucking the little knife back into his robe, led the way down the tunnel.

We followed him, and I made sure to walk directly behind him, almost aggravatingly so, hoping it would encourage him to pick up his pace. It didn't really work, but he did speed up a little every time he looked back at Alchemy. His light skin seemed to pale another shade whenever his eyes looked over the black bones.

"So," I said as we walked, trying to ignore the way my skin itched at the shadows behind us. The farther we walked, the darker it seemed to become. "What's your name?" I was hoping the conversation would not only help settle his nerves, but mine as well.

"Gian." He answered crisply, glancing over his shoulder at me. His expression was one of indifference, but I could still see the glint of sweat on his brow and the wariness dancing in his eyes.

"I'm Sakura. This is Chem, and Ksega." I tried not to let myself be bothered by how unnatural it felt to introduce Ksega. He was supposed to say his own name. I cleared my throat, brushing the feeling aside, and asked, "Are we in Old Nightfall?"

"Where else?" Gian scoffed, giving me a troubled look.

I would have said something — I wasn't sure what — but at that very moment we were no longer in the tunnel. We had taken steps seemingly like any other, but now we were out in . . . well, I wasn't sure *where* we were.

The ground around us was soft and white, swirling like a mist. It didn't feel quite solid beneath my feet, but as I took another step, it supported me. It rose in great white plumes all around us, doing little to conceal the pale, shining buildings before us.

There were houses in neat rows, and stacked one on top of the other so high you couldn't see the tops. There was a great blue building to our right, long and wide, with gorgeous birds — owls, by the looks of them, but in the most magical and bizarre colors and patterns I'd ever seen — flitting and perching around it.

And there, in the distance, rose the spires of a glorious castle, thinner and taller than any building I'd ever seen before. It rose high above the other buildings, winking in the bright sunlight.

"Welcome to the Glass City." Gian deadpanned, waving a hand boredly at the splendid structures.

"It's incredible," I marveled, my eyes wide as I drank it all in. We were standing on *clouds*. The buildings were made of *glass*. And the *people* we saw . . .

All of them were tall and lithe and pale and dark-haired and perfect. Every one of them wore robes of silver and ivory and gold, like Gian, although some in different styles than others. The women had their hair in dramatic updos, pinned in place with lavish gold and copper clips. The men wore their hair down, and while most of them had shaggy hair that curled around their ears, some of them had it grown closer to their shoulders, like Gian did.

"Incredible? The most incredible secret, maybe. The home of the most incredible slave owners, perhaps." Gian growled under his breath, marching us past the first rows of houses. There were gasps from around us as people saw Alchemy, the hood of his cloak down around his shoulders, but none of them moved to stop us. Were there no soldiers? Was Gian a soldier? Why had he been in the tunnel?

"I'm sorry?" I frowned sidelong at him, trying not to get too distracted by the sparkling glass houses beside us. You couldn't see inside, but there were designs etched into the glass, great swoops of wind or streaks of rain, and even the jags of flashing lightning.

"Nothing." He waved a hand in dismissal, but his jaw was still clenched. I decided to drop the topic. All I cared about right now was getting Ksega some help.

I almost tripped over my own feet at the thought. Hadn't it been only a couple days ago when thoughts of nothing but finding the Curse had consumed my mind entirely? Wasn't that what I should have been looking for here? A reason for these people to have created the Curse would be all I needed to prove it was them, and all that was left after that was finding the source hidden somewhere in this magnificent kingdom. And yet I found myself shoving those thoughts aside for now. They would come back once Ksega was out of danger.

Gian led us through a maze of stacked glass homes, buildings for who knew what purposes, and growing crowds of curious people. They all gawked and stared at us, eyes roving over my grubby, stained clothes, the whimpering, sweating form of Ksega, and most of all, Alchemy. Even without the fact that he was a living skeleton, his height alone was enough to draw attention. The people here were tall, but while some of them may have beat Ksega, they hardly came to Alchemy's shoulders.

"Where are we going?" I asked finally, stepping closer to Alchemy to press my hand against the side of Ksega's face. He was burning up. "He can't stay like this much longer. He's going to have a stroke or something."

"The only doctors are in the palace," at least at this, Gian's expression broke into something akin to sympathy as he looked back at me. "I'm trying to get us there as fast as possible. But someone like me might not be able to get you in to them. I'll do my best." His gaze rested for a moment on Ksega's flushed face. "They should take him in either way, though, looking like that."

I felt my heart sink at those words. The *only* doctors were in the palace? I had been a little surprised at how small Old Nightfall was — the entire kingdom was roughly the size of the City of Bones — but how could the kingdom's only doctors live in the palace? Surely the people had other ways of treating their illnesses.

"Why are the doctors only at the palace? What if someone gets hurt?" I asked, less because I was curious and more because I needed something to focus on. My worries were eating away at my mind faster than I could handle.

"Does it look like we get hurt much around here?" Gian replied. "We don't even get sick. There's no real reason for us to have any doctors. The royal family only employs them in case one of *them* gets sick." He looked again at Ksega. "I suppose we're lucky they do, otherwise it looks like your friend would be in a bit of trouble."

"Just hurry and get us to them." I snapped, feeling my teeth grind together in irritation. I tucked my flame-sword back into my belt, deeming the people around us safe enough. None of them spoke a word as we passed, and none moved towards us.

My thumbs trailed over my knuckles anxiously, leaving my hands itching for something to do. Something to fight, something to eat, something to hold, anything, so long as it didn't leave me feeling so alone, floating in an abyss of my own thoughts like the very clouds we walked upon.

Thankfully, as I'd noticed before, the kingdom was small. It was wider than it was long, and we reached the palace within an hour. It had no extravagant gates or walls or defenses. Nothing barred our path until we walked right up the sleek glass steps to the tall, broad double doors, where four men in robes like Gian's, only with glinting gold shoulder plates, stepped forward to stop us.

"This boy is sick." Gian said without preamble. "He needs the physicians."

One of the robed men frowned and peered at Gian, and it took me a moment to realize he was looking at his neck. I followed his gaze, my eyes resting on the black mark I'd seen before. It was odd: a single triangle with a rose above it. It was hardly any bigger than my thumb.

"They may enter." The man said, then gestured to one of the others. "Escort them to the physicians' quarters." His eyes narrowed at Gian. "But you may not."

I looked in confusion between the two of them, but the other guard was already motioning for us to follow him, stepping toward the great glass doors as they swung open inward, revealing the most gorgeous room I had ever seen. I looked questioningly back at Gian, but he only nodded once in encouragement, then turned to go back down the stairs.

"Please, miss," said one of the guards, and I looked back at him. He was eyeing Alchemy, but didn't comment on his appearance. "Follow me." He said, leading me inside.

With only one more look at Gian's retreating back, we followed the guard into the splendor of the Glass Palace.

I woke up swaddled in the softest blankets I'd ever felt, cocooned so snugly in the fabrics that I never wanted to leave them. My head felt light and empty, more so than it had in days, and my whole body was relaxed. I could feel the distant bruises littering my flesh, but they seemed far away and unproblematic at the moment. Here, trapped in the lush cotton of this bed, I was able to let go of every dark thought, and just give in to the pleasure around me. And then I came to my senses.

Sitting upright in the bed, I gasped, looking around me. I was laid in the center of a lustrous four-poster bed, constructed entirely from glass. Around me was a room of glass, all of it tinted a soothing blue but the windows, which gave me a clear view of nothing but miles and miles of clouds and endless sky. In the room itself, there was a bedside table, a small washroom, a larger table with chairs, an unlit hearth, and other unnamable furnishings, all of them carved elegantly from glass. There were beautiful designs etched throughout the room: long dragons winding around the pillars that supported the ceiling, or snowflakes blooming like great skeletal flowers across the floor. I spotted clouds and a sun and moon carved into the ceiling above my head, dotted with large-eyed owls with intricate swirls coating their feathers.

The room was stunning and magical, so much so that I was almost certain I was dreaming. No place could be so sunny and beautiful with winter so near, and there was certainly no type of glass strong enough to build castles out of. Except I knew I wasn't dreaming, because I remembered things. I remembered falling through the well, and I remembered meeting Gian and walking through the Glass City. I remembered Ksega pouring sweat and struggling to breathe, and Alchemy carrying him into the palace and all the way to the physicians' quarters, where he was laid on a literal bed of clouds and tended to by the doctors. I had been allowed to watch, but was instructed to stay out of the way, given a plush glass seat upholstered with a soft white animal fur to sit in. I remembered falling asleep in that chair, *not* a luxurious four-poster bed.

I was just about to swing my legs out of the bed when I looked down and realized I was no longer wearing the clothes I had been wearing in Old Duskfall. Instead, I was in a nightdress made from the softest silk imaginable, and that was it. The silk was so light I felt naked.

"Ah, you're awake!" a voice startled me into dragging the thick blankets up, instinctively covering my body. I hadn't even heard the crystalline glass doors open.

"Sorry! We didn't mean to startle you." Two women had entered the room, one of them perhaps a few years older than me, and the other much older than both of us. The physical attributes they shared, such as the long, straight raven-black hair and the hawk-like noses told me they were mother and daughter. They even had the same jutting chin and hollowed cheeks. I also noticed that they had the same rose and triangle tattoo on their necks that Gian had.

"It's alright. I just . . . wasn't expecting to wake up in this." I lowered the blanket, looking down at my nightdress again. It shone almost silver in the light, which I noticed was coming from strange floating orbs above sconces in the walls.

"We saw you had fallen asleep, and decided you needed a better place to stay," the younger woman said, offering me a kind smile. The two of them held bundles of clothing, and one had a tray of food balanced in one hand.

"We changed you into the nightdress and disposed of your clothes. We hope you don't mind. They were just a bit too . . . *tattered* for further use." The other woman said, smiling and revealing thin wrinkle lines near her eyes.

"Oh. Yeah, that's fine, I guess. What about my sword?" I pulled my legs up into a criss-cross beneath me, eyeing the platter of food as the older woman set it down on my nightstand. It had a small cup of berries I'd never seen before in all shapes and colors, and some sort of muffin set on a plate beside it and a glass of what smelled promisingly like mulberry wine.

"They were left with your companions. Eat quickly. We'll need to decide on an outfit for you to wear before you come before the king and queen." The younger of the two said, and I looked up from the platter of food.

"The king and queen?" I echoed, feeling my heartbeat accelerate. I'd never had any dealings with nobles aside from Duke Ferin and his wife. I didn't know how to conduct myself in front of *royalty.*

"Of course. It isn't every day we get two strangers and a . . ." the older woman trailed off, and I nodded in understanding.

"Right. I suppose we are a bit of an odd group, aren't we?" I sighed and scooted to the edge of the bed, popping a few of the strange berries in my mouth. I chewed them contentedly, relishing their sweetness, when a thought struck me. I sat up straighter and turned to the women, mouth open, but the younger of them cut me off.

"Yes, your friends are fine. Or at least, the tall one is. He hasn't left the boy's side. As for the boy himself . . . he still hasn't woken up." My heart sank. "But the doctors say he's doing much better. His fever is almost entirely gone, and he's breathing normally again. He should wake up by the end of the day."

The end of the day. What time was it?

Looking out the window, I guessed it couldn't have been more than just a couple hours past dawn. I had fallen asleep sometime late the night before. Were nights any different here than they were in Horcath? Where *was* the kingdom of Old Nightfall?

"I'm Cicily, by the way," the young woman said, smiling as she organized what I now assumed to be clothes on the long glass table. "This is my mother, Raegan. You can feel free to call on us should you need anything." She smiled brightly at me, and though I was tired, I returned it.

"Thank you, Cicily. I'll be sure to do that. I'm Sakura."

"Lovely to meet you. Now hurry up and finish your breakfast," Raegan instructed, tapping me on the shoulder and waving a hand at the platter. "We need to get you into one of these dresses as soon as we possibly can."

Unwilling to argue with the stern-faced woman, I wolfed down the remainder of the food. The berries were sweet, and the muffin just the slightest bit bitter. Washed down with the wonderful tang of mulberry wine, it was the best meal I'd had in days, with the possible exception of Jhapato's excellent pancakes.

When I'd finished, Raegan took the platter and left the room while I slipped out of bed and made my way over to Cicily's side to view the dresses she had laid out on the table.

"This one," she began, pointing to the one at the very end. "Is Mum's favorite. I wouldn't have picked it — I didn't think it would look the best with your eyes — but she insisted, so I brought it along."

I nodded mutely. It was a thin dress of purple velvet, with a dipping neckline laced in gold. Definitely not something I would wear.

"This one is one I thought you might look good in," she went down the line of dresses. "This one matched your eyes best, and *this* one is my personal favorite." She finished with a small clap of her hands and an excited squeak.

The second dress was a pale red, with a fuller skirt and no sleeves. The third was a rich green, meant to match the tone of my eyes, but the fourth dress was what really caught my attention. I'd never been one for fancy clothes, much less dresses. Back in Carlore, it was customary for most people to wear robes and pants, all of which had a very flowy, airy nature, perfect for running or climbing or dragon riding. Dresses had never been ideal for any of those activities, all of which I found great pleasure in.

But I couldn't deny that I thought dresses were beautiful, and this one was easily one of the prettiest I'd seen. Made from a light ivory fabric, it was simple and elegant, with only one strap sleeve and a line of gold thread tracing along the neckline. What really made it stand out, though, were the gold-beaded feathers of gray, white, and silver that hemmed the bottom of the skirt.

My heart swelled with love at the sight of them, reminded painfully of Sycamore. They looked so similar to her pristine white feathers, and her ashy gray beak. What I wouldn't have given in that moment, just to throw my arms around her neck and plant a kiss on her head.

"This one." I said softly, letting my fingers run gently over the feathers. "Definitely this one."

Cicily looked at me for a long moment, as if trying to gauge my emotions, but I offered no explanation, keeping my eyes locked on the dress.

"This one it is, then. Go on behind that curtain and slip it on, and then I'll help you fasten the back." She handed me the dress and gestured to the little curtain in one corner, one of the few things not made entirely of glass. I accepted it and went where she had instructed as she gathered the other dresses up into her arms.

When I put the dress on, I tried not to think of Sycamore or of home. It was difficult, but not impossible. I had other things to distract me.

"Cicily?" I asked as I came back out from behind the curtain, turning to let her do up the back.

"Yes?"

"Are you a slave?" the silence that followed that question was enough to answer it. She finished tying up the back, and I turned to face her. She wouldn't meet my gaze, but said, in a low voice,

"It isn't as bad as you make it sound."

"Slavery is illegal." I reached out to grab her arm, hoping she would look me in the eye, but she wouldn't, staring down until she found her voice again.

"The laws of your land aren't the same as the laws up here, remember that." She looked up at me now, her eyes wise beyond her years. "This is our way of life, Sakura. We all know what it's like to live like this, and not only do we accept it, but we enjoy it. Slaves here are like servants in your lands." She smiled wistfully. "I promise. It isn't bad."

"I don't understand," I shook my head, brows furrowing. "Why?"

"We're underlings." She shrugged, and I felt my eyebrows raising. Even people without magic didn't deserve to be treated lower than others. She laughed at my expression. "Like I said, it's different for us. Not having magic . . . it's the same as being born without a limb. You're automatically below everyone else. But it's alright." She gripped my shoulder and turned me towards a chair and vanity. "Trust me, we're all okay. Don't worry about us. Now sit down, and let me do your hair."

Cicily did a remarkable job with my hair, twisting it into a beautiful braided crown and decorated with gold beads and silver feathers, to match my dress. I tried not to let the sadness show in my eyes as I thought of Sycamore and Honeysuckle.

After I was all ready, she let me look at myself in the mirror. I hardly recognized the way I looked, so elegant and regal. My dark skin contrasted stunningly with the pale colors of the dress, and I had to admit it looked *right*, me surrounded by the silver feathers.

"You look amazing," Cicily said proudly as she led me out of the bedroom.

She guided me down long corridors of glass, all of them coated in elaborate carvings of various types of weather. Snow and sleet and rain and storm, all of them portrayed together in great canvases of sheer glass. It was dazzling.

It wasn't a long walk to the throne room, and I felt a little dismayed by that fact. My nerves were jumping and jittering all over the place, and I tried to regain my composure as the wide doors opened to let us inside.

The throne room was magnificent, with tall arching beams of glass criss-crossing over each other along the ceiling, and, slightly to my surprise, an entire map of Horcath etched in uncanny detail across the smooth floors.

I was relieved to see Alchemy, no longer in his tunic and cloak, but a long white and gold tailcoat, leaving his ribcage and legs exposed in the front as he stood off to one side, close to the raised dais upon which sat three glass thrones. He held the silver handle of my flame-sword tightly in his ungloved hand, and when I moved up beside him, he offered it to me. Even though I had no place to sheath it at my side, I accepted it, taking comfort in the familiar heft of the metal.

In the largest throne, the one in the middle, sat a man perhaps close to Gamma's age, with salt-and-pepper hair and fading blue eyes. He wore white and gold robes like the other men, but had an extravagant golden cape draped across his shoulders, lined in a sleek white wool, and a thin band of gold sitting atop his head. His hair was long and sheer, longer than the hair of any other Nightfaller man I had seen thus far, and I guessed that if he had been standing, the ends of his hair would go almost all the way to his heels.

In the second largest throne, to his right, was a woman with white hair and a lined face, and deep-set green eyes. She was dressed like many of the other women I had seen, such as Cicily, and the only embellishments her outfit had were the gold and silver rings on her fingers, and the twisted wire of gold that curved across her head.

The third throne sat empty.

"Your Majesty," Cicily led me to Alchemy's side, then bowed to the king and the queen. "Your Highness."

"Where is the third one?" the king demanded, and I felt a chill run down my spine at the authority that rang in his voice.

"Still bedridden, Your Majesty. He should be well by tonight." She replied, keeping her low bow. The king only grunted in response and said,

"Leave us."

Cicily and the few guards that had stood in the room departed, and when the doors closed, the air suddenly felt suffocating. The reality of where I was and what I was doing had almost entirely been lost, and now it slammed back into me with such a force my legs nearly gave out.

"Who are you?" the king asked, and for a long moment, I didn't answer, secretly hoping Alchemy would. But he remained silent, so I swallowed my terror and said, in the strongest voice I could muster,

"I am Sakura Ironlan. My companions are Ksega Copper and . . . Chem." I looked briefly at the skeleton, but there was no way to tell who he may have been looking at. He was eerily still, as he often was, and I wanted nothing more than for him to say something so I knew I wasn't entirely alone.

"And why are you here?" the queen asked, her voice shrill and sharp. I took a deep breath. This was it. This was what we had been building up to.

"I'm here about the Curse." I said simply. "I'm here to put a stop to it."

The king and queen were quiet for a very long moment, staring at me so intently I was sure they could see the fear that pulsed through every fiber of my body. I tried to keep my breathing steady, tried not to let my gaze drop from their steely ones.

I was almost to the point of losing my nerve when the queen spoke, her voice softer now.

"You've come to the wrong place, my child." She shook her head slowly, eyes moving to Alchemy. "We are so far above the Curse, we do not know of its effects. We have heard the tales, but few of us have ever seen it in person. The extent of its power has never fully been known to us. We do not concern ourselves with the troubles of the world below. We are happy up above, and we are unaffected by its destruction." Her eyes narrowed as she stared at the skeleton. "Have you brought this wretched creature here to spread it to our own people?"

For a painfully long moment, I didn't answer, only stared dumbly at her. They didn't know about the Curse? But *everyone* knew about the Curse.

"I- no, I would never," I stammered, blinking in surprise. "I thought . . . I mean . . . you really don't know about it?"

"Child, don't waste our time. What is this about?" the king ordered, and I shook my head, at a loss for words. Finally, Alchemy pitched in.

"The Curse is growing stronger. It takes bigger animals, it kills more people. It's ripping Horcath apart piece by piece, and we are looking for a way to stop it." His voice echoed creepily around the throne room, low and grating, and it sent a shiver down my back.

"You are looking in the wrong place." The king shook his head. "You will stay until your friend is healed and then leave, and never tell anyone about how to find our kingdom again. Am I clear?"

I stared at him, still not believing that this had all been for nothing. Was he lying? Did I dare challenge the king to his face when he had told me *I* was the wrong one? Did I dare risk the hospitality and kindness he had shown us?

"Thank you." I said thickly, bowing low, just as Cicily had done. "Your Majesty. Your Highness."

Then Alchemy and I turned and walked to the doors, which opened for us, and let us out into the corridors.

Once we had walked a short way, I stopped, and he followed suit beside me. A silence stretched between us, and while I wanted to speak, to thank him for everything he'd done but tell him we had nothing else to chase, I couldn't find the words.

"I'm going to go check on our little archer friend." He said finally, then placed a hand on my shoulder. I didn't look at him. "Go and try to get some more rest."

He walked away, towards the physicians' wing, and I towards my quarters, trying to remember which way it was. But he and I both knew rest was something far from my mind.

29
KSEGA

Water swarmed around me, pulling me, pommeling me, dragging me all around.

I couldn't see. I couldn't breathe. I was drowning.

Panic squirmed through me, and I tried to move, tried to swim, to get to the surface, but my body didn't listen. I couldn't move. Everything felt dead and heavy but me, trapped inside my own motionless body.

I couldn't even open my mouth to scream.

Distantly, I heard a yell. I tried to flex toward it, to bring myself closer to the voice as it came again, and again, and again. Soon, I could make out what it was saying.

Ksega.

That's me! I tried to shout back. *I'm Ksega! Help me! Save me!*

"Ksega."

Help me.

"Ksega, *wake up.*"

My eyes opened.

I gasped, sitting up, the world spinning around me. Air. I was breathing air. There was no water, no icy cold. I was sitting . . . on a cloud?

"Ksega?" the familiar voice came from my left, and I looked to see Alchemy seated beside me, wearing an odd white and gold coat. Looking down at my own body, I saw my shirt was gone, and my torn pants had been replaced with a sleek black pair.

"Where are we?" I asked, eyes wide as I looked at the skeleton again, then all around me.

The room was wide and pale, made from what appeared to be glass. Or maybe ice. It was empty but for the cloud and Alchemy's chair, but the glass had dramatic carvings of mountains and birds all across it.

"Am I dead?" I looked down at my hands, turning them over. I didn't feel any different, but I remembered when I had passed out. I remembered pouring sweat, and I remembered the cacophonous buzzing and scraping and crashing echoing around in my head. All of that was gone now. I felt fine.

"You're not dead, you idiot. You're in the Glass Palace of Old Nightfall. How do you feel?" Alchemy leaned forward, tilting his head at me. I shrugged.

"Great. Refreshed. A bit of a headache, and maybe a little warm, but," I shook my head, smiling at him. "Better than I've felt in days."

"Good. Those doctors must have worked wonders on you. You were really sick. You were sweating so much you were like a slippery fish; I nearly dropped you a few times." That warranted a snort from me, and he huffed as I slid out of the bed.

"Where's my shirt?" I asked.

"Gone. They took our clothes, and gave us some new ones." He replied.

"And my bow?" I felt strangely naked without my longbow nearby, and the weight of my quiver at my hip.

"They gave me your weapons. I'll go get everything. Stay put." Alchemy stood up and left the room, the *tick tick tick* of the bones of his feet hitting the glass echoing strangely around the chamber.

I stood there for a long moment, looking at the room around me, then poked experimentally at the cloud bed I had been lying on. It wasn't solid, but my hand didn't pass through it. It was like the most wonderful pillow in existence.

I heard the door click open again behind me, and I turned and said, "That was quick- oh." I snapped my jaw shut as I saw who had entered. It definitely wasn't Alchemy.

A girl who couldn't have been much older than I walked across the room, a pleasant smile on her face. She was about as tall as Sakura, but that was where their similarities ended. Her skin was smooth and pale, and her eyes wide and blue. Her long black hair had been put up into an intricate series of braids and buns, and accented with ribbons of silver and gold.

I didn't take much notice of her hair, though, or the long white and gold robes she wore, because the thing my eyes were instantly drawn to was her face. It was long and narrow, and easily the most beautiful face I'd ever seen.

"You must be . . . Saga?" the girl asked, smiling politely at me. Her voice was like liquid honey.

"I- um," I blinked, clearing my throat. "Ksega. I'm Ksega. And you are . . . ?"

"Lilyan." Her smile broadened just a bit. "It's nice to see you've woken up. I heard you were quite sick."

"Yeah, I guess I was." I looked up over her shoulder as the door opened again to reveal Alchemy, entering with a pile of white and gold clothes topped with my longbow, belt, and quiver of arrows in his bone hands. He crossed the room quickly, set the clothes and weapons on the cloud bed, nodded to Lilyan, and left again without a word.

"I've met the skeleton briefly," she said once he'd gone, watching the closed door for a long moment before looking back at me. "He seems very fond of you. I've heard he hardly left your side."

"That's Chem," I said, feeling my chest warm at her words. "Ever the loyal friend."

"You must be very grateful to him, for carrying you here all the way from the entry place." Lilyan remarked, and I shrugged awkwardly.

"I guess so. I was unconscious the whole time." I turned and lifted the clothes from the cloud bed.

It was a long white shirt, laced with gold thread that created a vest pattern within the fabric. I slid my arms through the sleeves and was surprised at how soft it was, instantly molding to my body and keeping me just the right temperature.

"Would you like a tour of the palace?" Lilyan asked, I looked at her in mild surprise. I had originally assumed she was in a position of power or high status, based on the way she was dressed, but Alchemy and I were also dressed in fine clothing, and wouldn't it be a servant's job to give someone a tour of the palace? Still, I would think a face this pretty would be more at home in a diplomatic setting than one of service.

"Sure." I said, and her eyes brightened excitedly.

"You can leave your bow here. We can come back for it after the tour." Her grin was contagious as she backed toward the door. It made my skin warm as I followed her out of the room, and I was pleased to find that no traces of my limp were left.

There wasn't much to say about the first half of the tour. She showed me around the lower levels of the palace, which included the servants quarters, kitchens, and the ballroom. The middle floors had most of the bedrooms and the throne room. It wasn't until we went up to the top floor that she slowed down, just before we reached the top of the stairs.

"This is one of the greatest rooms in the entire palace." She grinned, and I couldn't help but return it. She reached toward me and grabbed my hand, pulling me up the last few steps and into a great circular room, dragging me into the middle of the giant snowflake carved into the floor.

"Woah," I breathed, looking up at the crystal chandeliers above, and the great arching windows on all sides. There was a set of doors in the far wall, with rearing reindeer etched into the surface of the glass.

"Isn't it beautiful?" Lilyan squealed, lifting our hands up and twirling beneath my arm with a giggle. "I love to come up here when I need to think. Hardly anyone else comes up here. It's used for the most formal events, like weddings or coronations, so it's empty most of the time."

"It's wonderful." I said, smiling down at her. She laughed again, the sound like a melody that bounced off the glass walls around us, and leaned closer to me, taking my other hand.

"Do you want to see my favorite part of the entire kingdom?" she asked quietly, her eyebrows inching toward her hairline in a question.

"I would love to." I replied, and with another excited squeal and a squeeze of my hands, she was leading me toward the tall doors.

"Okay, close your eyes," she said when we reached the doors, releasing my hands to reach for the door handles. I closed my eyes.

I heard the doors click open, and felt a soft wind blow against us. Her hands closed around mine again, and she guided me gently forward several paces before we stopped. I heard the excited little laugh she let out, then her saying,

"Open them."

I did, and instantly I felt the breath leave my body. We were on a wide, curving balcony, without any rails, and surrounded by slowly swirling clouds of blue and pink and gold. Below us, the glass was clear. But not only was it clear, it was allowing me a view directly through the clouds, and I could see all of Horcath beneath.

I crouched down to my knees to look through the glass, and Lilyan did the same beside me. I was mesmerized, gawking down at the kingdoms. There was no way it was a painting. The details were too real, too perfect.

"Where are you from?" she asked, and I automatically looked towards Wisesol. I could see the Port, and even the little town of Rulak, way over in the northeastern corner. My heart squeezed with warmth as I thought of Gamma and Jessie down there, making perfumes and driving caravans around.

"There," I said quietly, pointing toward it. I could just make out the thin line of the roads linking the main towns together, and I wondered if Jessie was down there now, with Tooth and Dagger dragging her caravan along as she transported goods and people between the towns.

"I've heard of that kingdom! It's one of my favorites. I've always been fascinated with bering." She looked up with a gasp, eyes widening as she looked at me. "Are *you* a bering-mage?"

"I am," I said, and her eyes sparkled with wonder. I couldn't help but grin at her as I felt heat creep into my cheeks. No one had ever looked at me like that before. "I'd show you, if there were any plants around here."

"That's okay." She bit the inside of her cheek and shrugged, leaning back to sit on her legs. "I'm a whorle-mage!" she held a hand out toward the clouds, and thin strands of cotton-like cloud stretched out to wind between her fingers, curling around her arm and sending small gusts of wind through her hair.

It sort of reminded me of the way Sakura controlled her eirioth. I paused at the thought of Sakura. I hadn't seen her since I'd woken up, and neither Alchemy nor Lilyan had mentioned her. Was she here? I would have asked, except at that moment, Lilyan released her hold on the wind and clouds and gasped in excitement, looking at me with another bright smile.

"I should show you the Owl Barn! Come with me," she scrambled to her feet in a most un-lady-like fashion, taking my hand again and dragging me back towards the stairs.

"The what?" I chuckled as I came up alongside her, having to shorten my strides to let her keep up.

"The Owl Barn! It's where we train all of our owls. Let's go," she took the stairs two at a time and, with no other option than to follow, so did I.

"Why do you have owls up here?" I asked as we walked briskly through the corridors. I tried to drink in all the artistic carvings in the walls, but she was walking too fast for me to dwell on the designs for more than a couple seconds.

"Oh, they're special owls! It's said that they were the first inhabitants of Old Nightfall. They're *stunning*, not like the boring brown and gray owls I've heard you have down in your world." She spoke as if Horcath was a completely different universe, even though we had just seen it from the great balcony. "Most people here have one. I actually have seven. They all live in the Barn except when delivering letters or working on official business." I was tempted to ask what official business a creature such as an owl might have in a kingdom like Old Nightfall, but before I got the chance, a man with a bushy black mustache and thinning hair appeared around a corner in front of us. He started at the sight of Lilyan, immediately folding into a bow.

"Your Highness! Your presence was requested in the throne room earlier, but-" the man stood up, his eyes briefly hovering on our clasped hands. "-you didn't show. I've been looking for you all over." His eyes lifted to mine, narrowing slightly, and I cleared my throat and lowered my gaze, catching sight of an odd black triangle on his neck. Something else sat above it, but I couldn't see it clearly.

"My apologies, Norman." Lilyan said smoothly. "I was taking a bath. Did I miss anything vitally important?" the man, Norman, shook his head and opened his mouth to speak, but she cut him off. "Then nevermind. If anyone asks where we are, we'll be at the Owl Barn. We'll be back in time for lunch." Then she tugged my hand and started down the corridor again. When I looked behind us, Norman was gone.

"Hang on," I said, looking down at her as my pulse quickened. "You're a princess?"

"Not *a* princess, silly. *The* princess. The only child my parents had. The sole heir to the throne." She stood up a little straighter as she spoke, then pressed her lips together thinly and looked sideways at me. "I was scared to tell you, since I didn't know how you would react. Most people don't like that I'm the princess."

"Why is that?" I frowned. "It doesn't change anything to me."

"I think you would have treated our friendship differently if you had known from the start," she admitted, and while I wouldn't say it out loud, I knew she was right. But was she? Were we really friends? I had to remind myself I'd only just met this girl. And yet here we were, walking hand in hand, laughing and exploring, and it all felt *right*.

We walked together out of the palace, passing a few other people as we went, several of them with the same odd black markings on their necks that I had seen on Norman, and stepped out into the broad cloud streets of Old Nightfall.

The kingdom was somewhat smaller than I'd expected, but no less grand than the rest of the palace. The buildings were in rows and in stacks, all of them clean and precise and beautiful, sparkling in the light of the sun and shining blue reflections onto the clouds we walked on.

According to Lilyan, the Owl Barn was all the way on the other side of the kingdom, which, although she made it seem like a great journey, wasn't very far. But I humored her dramatic complaints of exertion with light laughs all the while, glad to finally have a chance to walk somewhere without a stressful goal in mind.

At the back of my thoughts, I knew we were here for a purpose, and I had no doubts Alchemy and Sakura had already addressed the problem of the Curse. Considering Alchemy was sauntering around the palace unattended, I could only assume some sort of progress had been made. The question was whether it was positive or negative progress.

But I could find the answer to that question later. For now, it was enough to just walk and laugh.

The Owl Barn was massive, ridiculously tall and very long, with giant patterned owls carved into the walls and doors and even the roof. There were pillars of glass in the shapes of trees and branches, and on them perched any number of owls.

Lilyan had been telling the truth. They were more beautiful than any bird I'd ever seen. There was a bright green owl with a large, fanning white tail, and golden feathers dotted throughout its swirly wings. There was a dark blue owl with vibrant pink eyes and broad silver talons, and there were hundreds more when we stepped inside the barn.

It was neat and clean, but filled with birds. They perched on the shoulders of their caretakers, on the glass trees, on the floor, in the glass rafters. They flew around or walked along the ground, dragging whip-thin or foot-long tails, carrying heads of all shapes and sizes and boasting beaks and feathers and talons of all colors imaginable.

"This is one of mine!" Lilyan pushed past some of the other Nightfallers standing around and lifting a violet owl into her arms. It had eyebrows as wide as my palm, and big teal eyes. "Her name is Giselle."

"She seems very tame," I noted, hesitantly reaching out to pat the owl on the head. I caught a movement out of the corner of my eye, and looked up to see a man watching me.

He was almost as tall as me, with a stubbly black beard and hair that came almost to his shoulders. His green eyes were almost challenging, like those of the purple owl he had perched on his arm. When our gazes met, he nodded at me. I didn't recognize him, but I nodded back anyway before looking back to Lilyan, who had somehow managed to obtain three more owls, all of them various shades of vibrant pink.

"This is Gregory, Gabe, and Gwenny." She held her arms wide to make room for all of them. I nodded, smiling at her joy. It reminded me of how Jessie reacted whenever she saw her horses.

I followed Lilyan through the Owl Barn, marveling at the beauty of the owls, and listening to her happily explaining each of their names and personalities. As much as I loved to listen to her, there was something missing. While she was capable of keeping herself entertained perfectly fine, and she was stunning to look at no matter what she was doing, I found myself struggling to find anything to say to her. Small talk was never this difficult when I was trying to talk to Sakura. With her, we were always nit-picking and insulting each other. With Lilyan, it was all sweet words and even sweeter glances.

"As much fun as this is," I said when Lilyan had finally set all her owls down. She looked up at me curiously. "I'm a bit hungry, and I'd like to check in with my friends, if that's alright." She smiled and nodded.

"Absolutely! We can head back to the palace, and I'll have someone prepare you and your friends some lunch." She took my hand again and led me out of the Owl Barn and back into the sunlit roads of cloud.

We reached the doors of the Glass Palace and stepped inside shortly past midday, and by then I was starving.

Lilyan led me back through the corridors, past the room where I had woken up, and explained she was taking me to the chambers my friend had been given. We passed a servant on our way, and she ordered her to go and bring us some food. The mention of it made my stomach growl, and I tried not to let my mouth water.

It didn't take long for us to reach Sakura's chambers after that, and when Lilyan opened the door, we stepped inside to see her and Alchemy standing near one of the tall windows on the other side of a long glass table. When we entered, both of them turned around to face us, and Sakura's eyes immediately went down to our intertwined fingers. I wasn't sure why, but as soon as I noticed, I tugged my hand free of the princess'. She looked up at me curiously, but only said,

"The food should be here soon. I'll find you later. Bye."

Before she left, she brushed her fingers against mine, so soft I almost didn't feel it. Then the door clicked shut, and it was just the three of us.

We were all quiet for a long moment, and it gave me a chance to look at the room. It was wide and blue, and no different from any of the other rooms in the palace: immaculate and beautiful. As my eyes trailed along the edges of the windows, they fell on Sakura, and I raised an eyebrow.

She was wearing an ivory dress with silver feathers on the bottom, and golden detailing. It looked extraordinary against her dark skin, and the gold and feathers in her hair. Even if her beauty didn't begin to compare to Lilyan's, I felt heat crawling up my neck as I met her gaze.

"Getting friendly with the ladies, are we, Ka-sega?" she huffed, crossing her arms and rolling her eyes. I blinked, swallowing down the fuzzy feeling that had blossomed in my belly, and stepped farther into the room, a frown twitching across my face at the name.

"She was just giving me a tour of the palace." I looked up at Alchemy, then back at Sakura. "Did we learn anything about the Curse?"

"No." Sakura spat, her expression souring further. "Turns out the people of Old Nightfall know less about it than anyone else in the world. They thought we'd brought Chem to infect them with it, or something like that. Either way, we aren't going to find any answers here." She sank into one of the glass chairs around the table, setting her elbows on the tabletop and resting her face in her hands. "Erabeth was right. This is stupid. There's nothing left to chase. No one found anything before, and we aren't going to find anything either." She let her hands fall and sighed, looking up at me. "I'm sorry I dragged both of you into this. It doesn't look like it's going to lead us anywhere."

"There's nowhere else I'd rather be than here, Ironling," Alchemy said softly, reclining against the side of the table. "I haven't exactly got anyone to go home to. I think it was a worthwhile effort. And who's to say this is the end? We can still find something, surely, if we-"

"No." She shook her head, cutting him off. "We have nothing to go on. I don't even know where to begin. I just want to go home."

I stepped forward and took the seat across from her. At that moment, the doors opened and two servants, women who appeared to be mother and daughter, entered and set several trays of food down before us. My heart leapt when I saw a number of sweet desserts among them. Sakura thanked them as they left, and I eagerly began to fill a plate for myself.

"There's nothing wrong with going home," I said as I scooped some sort of dark cherry cobbler onto my plate. Sakura half-heartedly dished herself a bowl of some type of meaty soup. "But do you really want to go home when we haven't changed anything?" she looked up, scowling at me, and I shrugged. "Chem's right. We can still find something new."

"Why don't you ask your new lady friend?" she said with a roll of her eyes.

"Maybe I will." I said, cracking open a freshly baked loaf of bread that appeared to have swirls of cinnamon in it. A plume of steam rose up in front of my face, and I tore a hunk off the loaf. "You know what, I think you're jealous." I said, stuffing a portion of the bread into my mouth. Sakura scoffed and rolled her eyes.

"What, that she probably gets the attention of every boy that lays eyes on her and I don't?" she snapped.

"No, that she gets *my* attention." I spooned myself a bowl of a different type of pudding, one that looked to be flavored like some sort of red berry. When I took a bite, I wasn't disappointed as an explosion of sweet and sugary goodness coated my mouth. I took a piece of the cinnamon bread and scooped it through the pudding, greedily devouring it. Sakura snorted and didn't say anything else.

"I think Ksega has a point." Alchemy said, poking curiously at a bowl of berries shaped like little stars. "We shouldn't give up just because a king said we were wrong. There are other places to look. Maybe someone from Freetalon. The Curse sort of acts like a poison, I suppose. Maybe one of them created it."

"If it were made as a poison, then other Talons would be able to heal it, too." Sakura sighed and slurped at her soup. "We don't have any leads."

"Then we'll find one." I insisted, taking a bite of a brightly colored cobbler. This time it was an explosion of sweet and salty flavors that filled my mouth. "Give us the rest of the day. If none of us can come up with something, we all go home, but we're not quitting this easy. Deal?" I looked up at her hopefully. I knew she wanted to go home. I wanted to go home, too. But I knew that if I went home now, I would regret not pushing her to keep chasing this. I wanted to see this through to the end, and I knew, deep down, so did she.

She held my gaze steadily for a long moment, her eyes narrowed in doubt. I could see her turning the idea over in her mind. She stayed like that for a long moment, which I used to take another bite of bread, then a few more bites of some sort of roasted bird. I wondered where they got all this food from.

"Alright. We'll do that." She said finally, pushing her plate away without eating another bite and standing up. "We all do our best to find something new, and if we don't have anything by dinnertime, we go home."

"Deal." I grabbed the last of the cinnamon bread and stood up as well.

"Meet back here when night falls, then." Alchemy said, sliding off the edge of the table. "Good luck to you both." He stalked around the table and left the room. I munched on another bite of bread, shrugging at Sakura. She pressed her lips into a thin line.

"See you later, I guess," I said, reaching forward to take a swig of the drink that had been set before my plate. It was sweet and sour, but the latter was a bit overpowering. I scrunched my nose at it and set it back down. Sakura frowned at me, but only sighed and waved a hand at me as she said,

"Go on, then. Go talk to your hussy."

"She isn't a hussy," I rolled my eyes and walked up to the door. I opened it, but flashed her a grin before I left and said, "You look *great*, by the way."

Then I shut the door and went searching for the princess.

I wasn't very surprised to find Lilyan on the glass balcony with the view of all of Horcath. Something had told me she would be up there. I didn't blame her for using it as a place to escape. Ever since she'd first shown it to me, I'd felt myself being drawn back to it in my mind, and I had to consciously force my feet not to take me there.

She was sitting on the glass, sewing something. Her hair was no longer put up in its detailed braids, and now sat in two neat plaits on her shoulders. She didn't see me approaching until my boots thumped on the clear glass of the balcony, and she looked up. Her face lit in a smile when she recognized me.

"You found me!" she moved to stand up, but I stopped her with a press of my hand on her shoulder, and I lowered myself to the floor beside her. I had taken a detour to retrieve my bow and my quiver of arrows, and I set them on the glass beside us now. "I guess it wasn't very hard though, was it?" she laughed softly, adjusting the fabric that sat in her lap.

"Not terribly." I admitted, cocking my head to examine what she held. "What are you sewing?"

"A scarf." She held the silk up to show me a complete silver scarf. She was sewing flowers and vines in bright gold thread along the edges. "It's a gift for my mother, for her birthday." She bit the edge of her lip as she carefully pushed the needle through the silk and pulled the thread through.

"It's very nice. I'm sure she'll love it." She hummed happily at the compliment, and I took a slow breath, trying to find the right way to ask what I needed to. "What do you know about the Curse?"

She looked up, and I saw the surprise flash in her eyes. "Uh," she shrugged, shaking her head. "Not much. Isn't it like a disease or something?" I sighed.

"Right. So you don't really know. Well, we're trying to find the source of it. We think someone with powerful magic may have tried to create it to use against their enemies, but . . ." I trailed off, pursing my lips and shaking my head slowly. What was the point in trying to make her understand, if she didn't know what the Curse was to begin with?

"Maybe it was one of the kings," she suggested, and I raised an eyebrow at her. She went on, "You know, the kings of the kingdoms? Aren't they all enemies or something?"

"No." I shook my head, drumming my fingers against the glass. "They haven't fought since before the Curse. Now, everyone is allies in the war against it." I dragged a hand down my face with another sigh.

"Isn't that exactly what you're looking for, though?" I dropped my hand to give her a questioning look. "Have you never read the history books? We have so many of them in our library in the palace."

"I'm not a big reader. What do you mean?" I leaned closer, curiosity piqued.

"There were all kinds of wars before the Curse, right?" I nodded. Everyone knew about the Havoc Ages. "What about the most recent ones? I remember reading about one between Coldmon and Brigthlock. It ended in a bloody mess, and the king of Coldmon died because of the king of Brightlock's hunger for power." She paused in her sewing, tapping the needle thoughtfully against her thumb. "Maybe it was him. That would make sense. Brightlock has always been obsessed with growing and expanding. They took the Shattered Mountains from Old Duskfall, and they took the Evershifting Forest from Calore."

"They didn't take *all* of the Evershifting Forest," I said, frowning at the map beneath us. I was looking at Brightlock, and I could see how much it had expanded across the eastern side of Horcath. "But you do have a point." I looked up at her, a smile pulling across my face. "You're a genius, Lilyan." I looked up at the sky around us. I had at least another five hours before it was dinnertime. "How would you like to go back to the Owl Barn for a little while?"

30
SAKURA

*B*y the time I wandered back into my chambers shortly before it was time for dinner, I was tired of wearing the silver dress. Beautiful as it was, it restricted my movement too much, and the amount of times I had been forced to shorten my stride to keep from stepping on the skirt was getting on my nerves.

I was glad to see a fresh change of clothes had been left on the end of my bed, along with a very nice pack and a bedroll, with a satchel full of provisions beside them. I knew we had worn out our welcome, and we would be leaving instead of staying the night, but I wished we wouldn't be leaving with such a grim result to our quest.

I had found Cicily and Raegan in the palace, and had asked them about the Curse, but neither of them had been very helpful. I had asked others, too, but most of them seemed less inclined to talk to an outsider. I doubted Alchemy had any better luck. As for Ksega, I was sure he was capable of wooing any girls into sharing whatever information he wanted.

I wasn't sure why it bugged me so much, seeing him flirt and spend time with other girls. It wasn't like he was *mine*, and I definitely didn't like him. So why was I so irked whenever I thought of him holding that other girl's hand? He'd held my hand before, too, just not like that. There was no reason for him to spend so much time around someone he'd only just met, unless he liked them. And there was no problem with him liking people.

So *why* did I care?

Fidgeting with the back of my dress, I let it slide off my body, and I shrugged into the new clothes I'd been given. They were much simpler, a baggy shirt and a pair of snug pants. Once I was in them, I felt much more at ease than I had at any other point in the day thus far.

The door swung open as I set the beautiful dress down on the bed, and I looked up to see Alchemy stepping inside, his shoulder blades sagging. I knew from the way he flopped into one of the glass chairs alone that he'd had no more luck than I had.

"You think Ksega's come up with anything?" I asked, trying not to let my disappointment show.

"I guarantee it." Alchemy replied, although there was little conviction behind the words, and he was looking out the window, where the sky had turned a deep shade of orange as the sun sank lower and lower into the distance.

I was about to ask him if he truly thought this had all been worth it, because it really did seem like a waste of time and energy to me. It seemed like we had gotten hurt and worn out and risked our lives for nothing. It seemed like Erabeth had been exactly right, and maybe I should have stayed home after all. But before I got the chance, the doors opened again and Ksega sauntered in, kicking the door closed behind him and going to lounge smugly in the fur-lined chair beside the bed. I rolled my eyes at his self-satisfied smirk, trying to ignore how fluttery it made me feel.

"Let me guess. She knew something?" I asked.

"Yup. She proved us all to be idiots." He kicked his legs up over one of the armrests, leaning back on his arm on the other. "We've been looking in the wrong place the whole time. We were looking for *where* the Curse might have originated, and *what* kingdom may have the power to create it. But we didn't look at *who* had the motive to do it. Do you remember the last war before the Curse? Obviously we weren't around, but surely you've learned about it?" he prompted, and I nodded.

"Of course. My people were involved in that war for a short bit. Carlore and Coldmon allied together against Brightlock, but when Brightlock moved to claim more of the Evershifting Forest, Carlore wanted out. We knew we couldn't fight them, so Coldmon was left to fight alone. I think it ended in the death of one of the kings."

"It did," Ksega confirmed, raking his free hand through his hair. "The king of Coldmon. And it turns out, that wasn't the only royal the king of Brightlock had killed. He had murdered two of the heirs to the throne of Duskfall when fighting for the Shattered Mountains, and he killed several nobles of Carlore when taking sections of the Evershifting Forest. He was completely power-hungry, and even now, you can see how controlling the king of Brightlock is. He's still trying to expand his kingdom. Maybe the Calderons control the Curse."

I looked over at Alchemy, who had sat up straighter in his chair, curiosity aroused. It was an interesting theory, and made more sense than some of the other ideas we'd chased.

"But the Curse affects Brightlock, too," I reminded him, remembering the runeboars that had attacked the town around Oracle Lake. "Why would he attack his own people if he's trying to grow his land?"

"Maybe it isn't intentional," Alchemy pitched in, and both Ksega and I turned our attention to him. "When the Curse is being summoned by whatever source it has, I can feel it. It tries to control us then, urging us towards one specific target. If a king had such power, I have no doubts he would use it on his enemies. Can you imagine the sort of destruction that could be caused if a hundred Cursed animals converged on a single spot?" he shook his head for a moment, then continued, "The problem is that the source never tries to control us for longer than a few hours. Whatever power it has over us, it's limited, and that makes it unpredictable. When it isn't being controlled by the source, the Curse has a will of its own, and the only thing it knows is ruination, so that is what it seeks. It doesn't know its target, it only knows it has to destroy." Alchemy stood up and adjusted the way his jacket sat across his shoulder blades. "Only because I was human am I able to resist it." A low rattle rushed out of him, something akin to a sigh. "I never should have been taken by it, but . . ." he shook his head. "I was weak. I was already corrupted in my own way, and it took advantage of that. Now the best I can do is help to find a way to stop it. I think this is a good lead. I think we should follow it."

"I agree." I said, sitting down on the end of my bed beside the packs that had been set there. "But we need a plan. Walking into that throne room without one was one of the most terrifying things I've ever done. The king of Brightlock is someone we know is powerful, and we won't be invited into his throne room like we were here. There are systems and rules, and Chem won't be accepted as well in Brightlock." I folded my hands together, clenching my jaw as I tried to think.

"We can work the details out later," Ksega said patiently, and I glanced at him, irritated at his nonchalant posture. "For now, it's time to leave the Glass City. We can go back to Erabeth's home and stay with her while we figure this out. Who knows, maybe we'll manage to get her to join us." He grinned. "Wouldn't it be nice to have another girl on the team?"

Normally, I would have answered no, but Erabeth was different. She was hardened, she was a warrior. She was respectable, and she would be a worthy companion to travel with, and now that Ksega had suggested it, I knew I didn't mind the idea.

"Fine. We'll go back to Erabeth's home and work things out from there. Now," I stood up and rolled my shoulders, my fingers tingling with the excitement of another journey about to begin. "Let's go get some dinner, grab our packs, and get back on solid ground."

We didn't receive an escort back to the cave where the entrance was, but it wasn't until we'd reached the front of the cave, staring down into the dimly lit tunnel, that I realized I didn't know how to get back through the well.

Luckily, we had been tailed to the cave.

"I wanted to make sure you got back okay." Gian appeared seemingly out of the clouds themselves, a bright-eyed purple owl perched on his shoulder. He nodded once at Ksega. "Good to see you up on your feet."

Ksega only grunted and nodded, a confused expression plastered on his face.

"We could use a little help getting back, actually, if it's not too much trouble," I told him.

"Of course. This way." He and his owl led the way into the tunnel, disappearing into it after only a few strides. When we followed, he re-materialized ahead of us. "You need the assistance of someone on this side to get through." He glanced over his free shoulder at us, scanning the group. "Did they not send anyone with you?"

"We didn't exactly make our departure a well-known affair." I admitted, and he shrugged, causing the owl to ruffle his violet feathers.

"To each their own. Everything is done with fanfare in this kingdom, most of all the public punishments." Gian's voice was harsh and spiteful, and I could see how rigid his back was as he walked. I couldn't help but frown as I thought of everything he had said since I'd met him.

"Why do you talk about them like that?" I asked, and he snorted.

"Like what? Like they deserve to die? Like I want to see their heads rolling across their fancy glass floors?" he chuckled darkly. "It's because I do. All they ever do is look down on people like me, making our lives miserable, making us cook their food and make their beds and wash their clothes and clean their rooms and care for them and their owls and *everything*, and what thanks do we get? *None.*" His fists clenched at his sides, and I shared a startled look with Ksega.

"So why do you stay?" I asked, trying to keep my voice as low as I could. There was another scoff.

"Because I have to. You see this?" he turned to walk backwards, pulling the neckline of his robes back and arching his neck so we could see the tattoo inked into his skin. "It means they own me. Others will tell you it isn't like that. They'll say we're happy, and we do this because it's our way of life, but they're all lying." He sneered at us before turning to walk forward again. "We're *slaves*, and we will never be anything more."

We were all silent for a long moment, lost in our thoughts. I could hardly believe what I was hearing. I'd call it treason, but I would also call it truth. In many ways, I found myself agreeing with his anger. Cicily and Raegen had accepted the way they were treated, and they were happy because of that. But just because they accepted it didn't make it right. Gian looked at the facts. He looked at the heart of the problem, and he defied it, fearless of the consequences it might bestow upon him.

"So you *can't* leave? Even though you already slander the name of your king?" I asked, and Gian looked back at me again, his brows lowered.

"Why do you care so much? But yes, I have to stay here. The only act of defiance I can show is with my tongue." He spat bitterly, glaring.

"You're lucky they haven't cut it out, with the way you speak," Ksega commented, and Gian laughed, the sound bouncing off the walls around us.

"Maybe so. But they aren't like that. If they inflict punishment, it is swift and sure. And it can only be inflicted once." He didn't have to say the word for us to know he meant death. But it wasn't just death. It was murder. Gian had every right to fight back when he was a slave. It was illegal, and it alone was punishable by life in a prison. But not here. Here, it was the way they lived, despite how wrong it was.

The dome-shaped room appeared before us, seemingly out of nowhere, and we stopped. I looked up at Alchemy, over at Ksega, and finally across at Gian.

"Thank you. You've been one of the chilliest people up here, but you're by far the most honest." I said, giving him a single, firm nod to show my respect. I saw surprise register briefly in his eyes, then he returned the nod and held his hand out to the center of the cave, beneath one of the floating crystals.

"Don't move. You'll be back where the well was before you know it." He curled his fingers slowly into a fist as the three of us stilled in our small huddle in the middle of the room.

A gust of wind whirled through the tunnel, wrapping around us. It grew thicker and stronger and faster, whipping up our hair and into our eyes. I squinted through it, realizing Gian had become a blurry outline beyond the twists of the wind, his arm still outstretched.

Something shifted beneath our feet, and suddenly the stone was gone, and we were floating, swirling through a portal of air and wind. Warmth bloomed outward from my chest, enveloping me entirely as the wind swirled about me and I was lifted higher off the ground. Alchemy and Ksega hovered beside me, and I could see Ksega's marveling expression as the cave warped and shifted around us, bending into unreal shapes as it faded away.

I looked at Gian's silhouette, wishing I'd had some way of helping him more, but knowing that it was likely I would never return to Old Nightfall, and he would probably remain a slave to the royal family for the rest of his days. Then I saw a thin black ribbon snaking through the wind, laced with green, and my heart skipped a beat. The frail line reached Gian's closed fist, and then everything shattered.

The world flipped upside down, the wind curled in on itself and punched into my chest, sending me flying backward, but there were no walls for me to hit. I was simply lost in space, wrapped in warmth and wind and falling down, down, down from the kingdom in the sky.

I fell into the sand with a grunt that knocked the wind from my lungs, and before I got the chance to recover it, someone else fell beside me, his elbow digging painfully into my ribs. With a screeching gasp, I rolled away from him, just in time to avoid another figure slamming into the sand. I sucked in a breath, trying to still the trembling of my arms, and yelped when a *fourth* body fell to the ground around us, landing awkwardly on a tree root and rolling into the base of a bush with a grunt.

I pushed myself up, staring wide-eyed at the three of them. Ksega was scrambling up as well, his own expression similar to my own, and breathing heavily, looking wildly around him. Alchemy stood and dusted off his jacket, and Gian . . . looked like he was about to scream.

"It's okay!" I said quickly, reaching forward to steady him as he sat up.

"Where- I don't-" he looked around with wide eyes and a shaky voice. A fluttering sound above caused all of us to look up and see his purple owl tumbling through the air, not-so-gracefully swooping up at the last second to perch on the floppy branch of a bush, flapping his wings frantically in his panic.

"This is where the well was," I explained, looking up through the canopy of the palm trees around us. The sky was darkening fast, and I could just make out the speckle of stars through the leaves. "We're in the Oasis."

"So you mean . . . I'm not- you took me-" he shook his head, jumping to his feet. He swayed unsteadily, looking at the trees around him. There was awe and fear in his eyes as he backed away from the tall trunks, inching into the only place free of plants, where the well had sat before.

"We're in Old Duskfall. You aren't in the Glass City anymore." Ksega clarified, glaring over at Alchemy. "Chem, you dolt, why would you do that?"

"You couldn't have expected me to leave him like that." Alchemy crossed his arms over his chest. "I have spent years trapped in this life I cannot escape, and I am constantly having to fight and rebel and resist the Curse's power. Nobody deserves that sort of fate, and if I can help someone else avoid it, then by all the stars, I *will*."

I gawked at him, shaking my head slowly. Ksega and Gian and I were all breathing heavily, winded and bruised from the fall, our packs and weapons set askew across our bodies. I huffed a humorless laugh.

"And you think this is better? He knows *nothing* of the kingdoms down here! Look at him! He's scared of the *trees*, Chem-" I began scolding.

"I am not *scared*." Gian interrupted, although his voice trembled.

"-and now he can't get back up there. You think you solved the problem?" I finished, ignoring Gian.

"You were tempted to do the same thing, don't deny it. Yes, I do think this is better for him. He can learn and he can adapt and he can be *free*. He's his own man now, Ironling. Let him be one." I would have argued with him further, except at that moment, there was a rustling from the bushes behind me.

I whirled around, flame-sword already in hand, and heard Ksega unslinging his bow. There was the familiar hiss of leather as Alchemy drew his smith tooth daggers, and I heard Gian and his owl shifting uncomfortably.

Out of the bushes stepped a familiar figure. Dark skin, dark eyes, and dark hair put into a braided bun.

"Spirits and saints!" Erabeth recoiled at the sight of us, her sword in hand, instinctively flinching away from the fire that had sputtered to life from my flame-sword. As soon as I recognized her, I dropped the flame, feeling relief sprout in my gut. "You three!" she gasped. "We've been looking everywhere for you!" she sheathed her sword, her gaze falling on Gian and narrowing at him and his owl. I noticed Taro was perched on her shoulder, and he was inspecting them as well.

"You have?" Ksega asked, slinging his bow back over his shoulder. I could hear the same relief I felt reflected in his voice, and could see it in the way his shoulders sagged from their tense position. Alchemy, too, sheathed his bone daggers into the leather pouches strapped to the bones of his arms.

"Of course we have! We heard there was a massive sandcat attack here, and we had to hurry to get over. I knew you were here, so I came along. There were six people and one Horcathian camel dead when we got here. Two of the soldiers survived, but you were nowhere to be found." She shook her head wonderingly at us, but I hardly noticed it. Six people found dead? If only soldiers had survived, did that mean Kieran's body had been found, too? I felt a spark of pity for the light-hearted man. He didn't deserve a death like that.

"*You* looked for us?" I furrowed my brow at her, and she shrugged, saying, "Yeah, sure."

"Thank you, Erabeth." I said, feeling even more relief course through me. If it hadn't been her who found us, we would have been in heaps of trouble.

"That's Beth to you. Did you find it, then? The well?" Erabeth's eyes went to Gian and his owl again. "You went to Old Nightfall?"

"We did." I confirmed, then continued before she could say anything more. "How long have you been looking for us?" she shrugged.

"Maybe the better half of a day." She looked up at the sky. "It's late. We should head back to the camp. All but Bones, that is," she waved a hand at Alchemy. "But first, who is this?"

"Later," I grimaced as I tucked my flame-sword back into my belt, a twinge of pain blooming in my shoulder. "Chem was being stupid and gave us all some bruises."

"I've got sand in my mouth," Ksega complained, curling his nose. "Do you have any tea?"

"You're unbelievable." Erabeth rolled her eyes. "You better have found something good, if you went through all this trouble, you know," she said, and I raised an eyebrow at her.

"I thought you said it was stupid. Suicidal."

"Maybe it is. But you went for it anyway." She puckered her lip at me, brow furrowing as if she were trying to solve a mystery about me. I tried not to squirm under her scrutiny. "I respect that." She said finally, and I raised my eyebrows in surprise, feeling pride swell within me. Then she nodded and turned to walk back into the dense foliage of the Oasis, calling over her shoulder, "Now come on, there's plenty of tea and bread to go around. You have an adventure to tell me about. And then, maybe," she quirked an eyebrow back at us as she vanished into the shadows. "You have an adventure to bring me along on."

Character Guide

A guide to the main characters within the story (alphabetized), with pronunciation guide

Please remember that these guides contain spoilers for the contents of The Cursed Mage.

ALCHEMY

"alchemy"

Description: *A Cursed seven foot tall black skeleton; brightly glowing green cracks run through many of his bones — these are the result of the bones being broken and damaged over time*

Age: *Unknown*

Mage Type: *Underling*

Home: *A cave deep within the Evershifting Forest; previously Talon, the capital of Freetalon*

Specialties: *Fighting, with or without his twin smith tooth daggers*

ERABETH CAWSON

"air • uh • beth, caw • son"

Description: *A five foot tall Duskan woman with bronzed skin, long black hair, and dark brown eyes, often accompanied by her red-brown hawk, Taro*

Age: *Twenty-four years old*

Mage Type: *Andune-mage*

Home: *City of Bones, the capital of Old Duskfall*

Specialties: *Fighting with her curved saber and driving a sand-sled*

GIAN PAWN

"gee • an, pawn"

Description: *A six foot tall Nightfaller man with pale skin, thick black hair that comes to his shoulders, light stubble on his chin, and olive green eyes, often accompanied by his purple and black owl, Light Ray*

Age: *Twenty-six years old*

Mage Type: *Underling*

Home: *Glass City of Old Nightfall*

Specialties: *Making smart remarks*

KSEGA COPPER

"say • guh, copper"

Description: *A six foot, three inch tall Solian boy with light skin, shaggy blond hair, and bright blue eyes*

Age: *Sixteen years old*

Mage Type: *Bering-mage*

Home: *Rulak, a town in northern Wisesol*

Specialties: *Archery, sneaking around, and stealing things*

SAKURA IRONLAN

"sakura, iron • len"

Description: *A five foot, four inch tall Carlorian girl with dark skin, long, dark brown hair, and dark green eyes*

Age: *Sixteen years old*

Mage Type: *Eirioth-mage*

Home: *Hazelnut, a town in Carlore*

Specialties: *Fighting with a sword or with her flame-sword*

Creature Guide

A guide to the creatures within the story (alphabetized), with pronunciation guide

Please remember that these guides contain spoilers for the contents of The Cursed Mage.

EIRIOTH DRAGONS

"air • ee • oth, dragons"

Description: *Large dragons, typically ranging between eight and ten feet tall at the shoulder; broad wings; covered in colorful feathers; sharp beaks, and long scaled feet with sharp claws*

Breeds/Variations: *All eirioth dragons are the same breed, but their feathers can be a mix of any and all colors; their beaks and claws can range from yellow-gold to black, or even mottled; their tails can be long and whip-like or broad and fanning*

Where They Can be Found: *Eirioth dragons no longer exist in the wild, but are bred and raised in Carlore, and often make life-long bonds with one human*

Temperament: *If raised properly, an eirioth dragon is undyingly loyal and loving; the tempers of eirioth dragons strongly resemble those of pet dogs*

HORCATHIAN CAMELS

"hor • kay • thian, camels"

Description: *Giant camels, typically ranging between nine and twelve feet tall at the shoulder; big chests and long, thick legs; thick, sand-colored fur to keep them safe from sandcats; flat backs, lacking any humps; broad, flat heads with tusks, horns, or both*

Breeds/Variations: *The only variations in Horcathian camels are height and whether they have tusks, horns, or both*

Where They Can be Found: *Horcathian camels are only able to survive in the Duskfall Desert*

Temperament: *Horcathian camels are very calm and gentle*

RAPTORS

"raptors"

Description: *Winged reptiles that are typically the size of large dogs or wolves; some are able to breathe fire, others able to breathe ice, and some have no special abilities*

Breeds/Variations: *There are many types of raptors that have adapted to various parts of Horcath, such as water raptors, which are various shades of blue with webbing in their wings and feet; there are forest raptors, which are various shades of green with branches for horns and moss growing on their scales; there are mountain raptors, which have pale scales and icy claws and horns; there are fire raptors, which are various shades of red and orange*

Where They Can be Found: *All across Horcath*

Temperament: *Very violent and aggressive, to be avoided at all costs*

RUNEBOARS

"rune • boars"

Description: *Giant wild boars with tens of tusks and horns curling from their heads and mouths*

Breeds/Variations: *The only variations are the unique numbers of tusks and horns*

Where They Can be Found: *In the Evershifting Forest and the Veiled Woods*

Temperament: *Very aggressive and unpredictable, to be avoided at all costs*

SANDCATS

"sand • cats"

Description: *Giant cats with coarse, sand-colored fur, tall ridges of fur along their spines, long, thin tails, and jagged black stripes on their sides*

Breeds/Variations: *Some sandcats have longer manes than others, and none has the same striping as another, but aside from that they are almost identical*

Where They Can be Found: *Sandcats are only able to survive in the Duskfall Desert*

Temperament: *Very wild and aggressive, to be avoided at all costs*

SEA WRAITHS

"sea, wraiths"

Description: *Giant sea serpents that lurk in the Great Lakes and it is speculated, though not confirmed, the Endless Sea; they can range from only five feet to almost fifteen feet in diameter, and can be up to nine or ten miles long; most sea wraiths have spines or fins on the ridge of their backs, and their tails thin into whips*

Breeds/Variations: *There are only four documented types of sea wraiths; they can be various shades of blue, silver, and green, with highlights of pink and purple on their spines or scales; the four types of sea wraiths are not named officially, but have been given nicknames by sailors; the first type is commonly referred to as the "drowning rain" wraith, which is able to store large amounts of water in its mouth and spew it out with enough force to break bones; the second is known as the "screaming lady" wraith, which lets out a terrible sound much like that of a screaming woman as it wraps itself around its victims, crushing them in its vice-like grip; the third is known as the "viper" wraith, which has long, venom-filled fangs that contain enough toxins to kill a full-grown Horcathian camel within minutes; the fourth and final type is called the "leech" wraith, which has thousands of razor-sharp teeth coating its throat to shred its victims to bits when swallowed*

Where They Can be Found: *The Great Lakes*

Temperament: *Extremely aggressive, to be avoided at all costs*

SLATE-WOLVES
"slate, wolves"

Description: *Large wolves covered in long, silky silver fur that is highly coveted across all of Horcath; long, bare tails that resemble those of a rat; ugly, narrow faces with a strong nose and broad ears; all slate-wolves are completely blind, but have the benefit of heightened hearing and smell; long, thin legs that end in bare claws, somewhat resembling a bird's*

Breeds/Variations: *Aside from size, one slate-wolf cannot be told from the next*

Where They Can be Found: *The Slated Mountains*

Temperament: *Very wild and aggressive, to be avoided if not trained to encounter them*

SMITHS
"smiths"

Description: *Giant beasts that resemble wolves and bears; thick, matted fur that is difficult to penetrate; aside from great size and strength, smiths vary greatly, with some possessing more wolf-like traits, while others are more similar to bears*

Breeds/Variations: *No smith is the same as the next; they can be any number of shades in the black and brown color range, sizes can differ, and physical abilities can differ; some smiths that are more bear-like can stand on their hind legs and swipe with their front paws, while some that are more wolf-like are swift and agile*

Where They Can be Found: *The Evershifting Forest and occasionally, though it is exceedingly rare, the Veiled Woods*

Temperament: *Unpredictable and aggressive, to be avoided at all costs*

Acknowledgements

I don't know where to begin with this, so I'll start by thanking me. Specifically, little me, who once upon a time decided to start writing and resolved to never give up on the dream of being one of the cool, published authors. Well, here we are. I finally made it – little me would be in utter shock.

I also have to thank my parents. They put up with me sharing the first little stories I made, and always encouraged me to keep writing. I still remember the day I sprinted through my parents' room and told my mom that I'd done it, I'd actually *finished* writing a whole entire book. She and my dad have always said that I would get to this point one day, and I would be lying if I said I'd always believed them, but as usual, I'm now forced to say they were right. So thanks, Mom and Dad, for not letting me give up.

And thanks to my brother, Isaac, as well. He never really did anything remotely related to this book, but there were other books he did play a part in. He had a character named after him in an old trilogy of mine, and I distinctly remember playing ping-pong in my grandmother's dimly lit basement as I told him all about it. After that, he became so invested in the character that we spent over an hour talking about his role in the story. Isaac may not show as much enthusiasm for being a part of my works anymore, but the knowledge that he once did is enough to earn him some recognition.

I guess since everyone else in the family got a mention, Indiana, my younger sister, should as well. She annoys me to no end, and I'll never stop making snappy remarks in her general direction, but I have to admit that on the rare occasions when she's a somewhat decent human being, she isn't all that awful to be around, and she has some pretty good ideas. She helped me with several scenes in an old project, and still brings up whatever I'm currently working on whenever she knows I'm in a bad mood. Never underestimate the intuition of a younger sibling.

There are others who believed in me from the very beginning, and one of special note is Natalie Allen. From the first day I told her about the book I was writing, she had sworn to buy a copy as soon as it came out. That project has long since been set aside, but her words of encouragement and excitement have not been forgotten. She's a big part of why I'm still writing, and I'll always be grateful for that.

Thanks to my proof-readers, Mom and Cass, and for all the feedback you gave me to make The Cursed Mage the best it could possibly be. I'm so excited for you both to read The Cursed King, and to hear whatever feedback you have for it.

Thanks to my aunt, Alicia, for taking my author photos and putting up with my awkwardness.

And thanks to all of The Book Nook's members, and your feedback and advice. I don't think my writing would be half of what it is now without input from Olli and tips and tricks from Faith and unnecessarily-in-depth-but-helpful-nonetheless rambles from Necro, and encouragement from all the others.

Even those who are newer to the support gang, like Monkster High and Murray (never question the nicknames). Every person who's said a kind word or made a comment on Alchemy's nakedness or even acknowledged the fact that I write at all had a part in shaping all the stories I write, so my thanks goes out to all of them, and yours should too.